Asper tried to ignore the screams. She tried to ignore the blood in her eyes as she struggled to crawl out from under the chaos.

She tried to ignore how her heart stopped beating for a moment as she felt a scraw's beak reach down and narrowly snap shut just short of her neck as it rushed over her.

She would be scared later, in the safety of a temple where no one could see her but her god and no one would care if she fell down and started weeping. These fears were for her alone.

Right now everyone else needed her to survive.

She clambered to her feet once she was free of the carnage. The scraws' charge had slowed and the creatures waded amidst the melee, clawing and snapping at Karnerians struggling to drop spears and pull out swords. One of the beasts went down beneath a throng of black-clad soldiers, even as one more creature pulled something red and glistening out from the melee and tossed its head back, swallowing it whole.

For a moment, Asper could not help but marvel at it, even as Dransun rushed out of the alley mouth to drag her into the shadows. She had seen violence before, she had fought monsters and demons, she had faced horrors from beyond any world or god she had ever known.

Somehow, none of it seemed to compare to the crimson splendor of mankind.

THE MORTAL TALLY

**BRING DOWN HEAVEN
BOOK TWO**

SAM SYKES

orbit

www.orbitbooks.net

Copyright © 2016 by Sam Sykes
Excerpt from *God's Last Breath* copyright © 2016 by Sam Sykes
Excerpt from *A Crown for Cold Silver* copyright © 2015 by Alex Marshall

Cover design by Lauren Panepinto
Cover photos by Arcangel-Images
Cover copyright © 2016 by Hachette Book Group, Inc.

Orbit
Hachette Book Group
1290 Avenue of the Americas
New York, NY 10104
orbitbooks.net

First Edition: March 2016

Orbit is an imprint of Hachette Book Group.
The Orbit name and logo are trademarks of Little, Brown Book Group Limited.

The publisher is not responsible for websites (or their content) that are not owned by the publisher.

The Hachette Speakers Bureau provides a wide range of authors for speaking events. To find out more, go to www.hachettespeakersbureau.com or call (866) 376-6591.

Map by Lee Moyer

Library of Congress Cataloging-in-Publication Data

Names: Sykes, Sam, 1984- author.
Title: The mortal tally / Sam Sykes.
Description: First U.S. edition. | New York, New York : Orbit, 2016. | ?2015
   | Series: Bring down heaven ; book 2
Identifiers: LCCN 2015043163| ISBN 9780316374897 (softcover) | ISBN
   9781478931232 (audio book downloadable) | ISBN 9780316374903 (ebook)
Subjects: | BISAC: FICTION / Fantasy / Epic. | FICTION / Action & Adventure.
   | FICTION / Fantasy / Historical. | GSAFD: Fantasy fiction.
Classification: LCC PS3619.Y545 M67 2016 | DDC 813/.6—dc23 LC record available at
http://lccn.loc.gov/2015043163

ISBNs: 978-0-316-37489-7 (trade paperback), 978-0-316-37490-3 (ebook)

Printed in the United States of America

RRD-C

10 9 8 7 6 5 4 3 2 1

For Dad, who thinks this is noble.

THE MORTAL TALLY

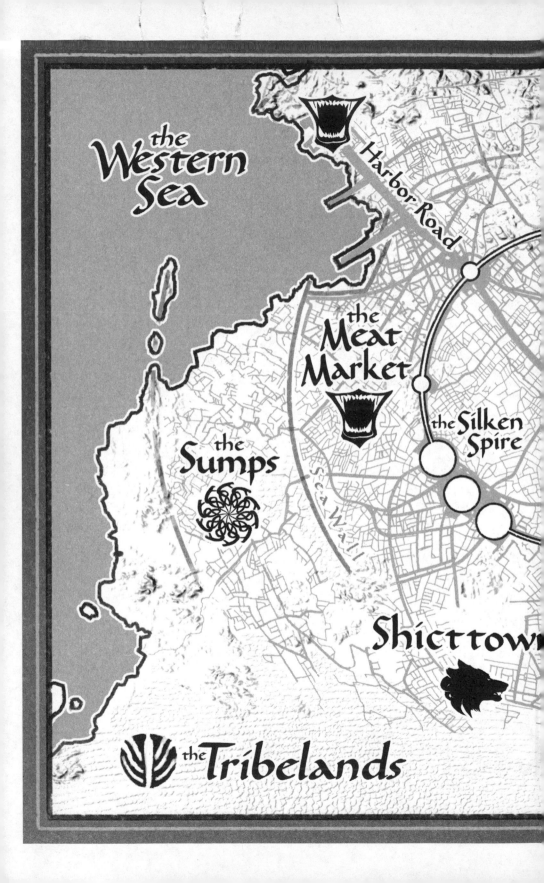

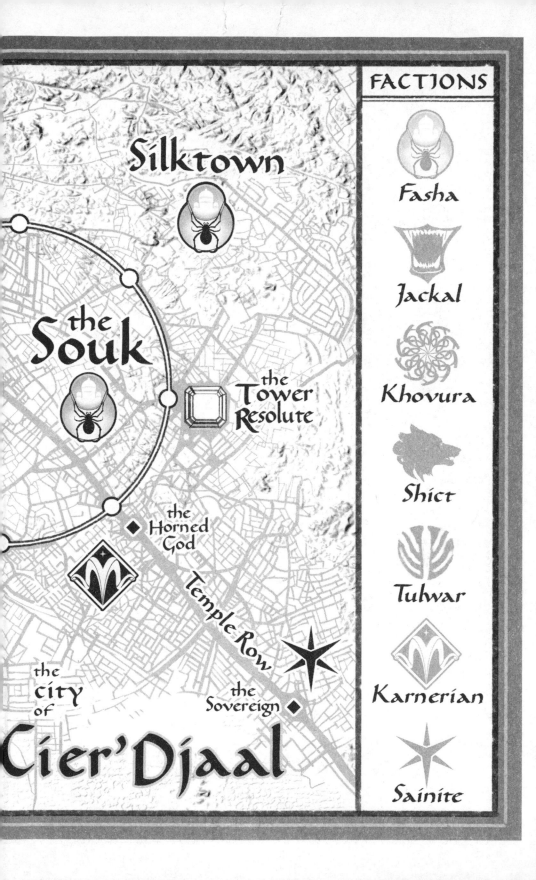

WHERE DEAD MEN TREAD

PROLOGUE

The Seventy-Eighth Year
Rhuul Khaas

*M*an believes in nothing until he destroys it.

Among my colleagues and those alike in thought and prestige, during the conversation about the flaws of mortality—it is a lengthy conversation and the flaws are many—the subject of their seemingly inherent ingratitude continues to vex.

Show a man a book and teach him to read, he will continue to express himself by painting on the walls with feces. Show a man how to till his soil that he might grow more abundant crops, he will eat dirt to spite you. Show a man the face of heaven, he will pick up a sword and attempt to cut its eyes out.

Coarse, I know, but strive to understand our frustration.

We have danced around this subject in countless conversations across countless hours within countless days. So much that even our own very long lives seem wasted from all the time we've spent in deliberation. Yet it continues to plague us precisely because, with all the knowledge we have uncovered in those very long lives, the answer to mortality's mistrust of us continues to elude.

Until now.

As with so many problems, speech proved inadequate for solving it. Only when I put ink to paper, as I do now, does it become clear. Nothing is truly real until it is written down.

Thus do I realize why it is mortality fears us.

A man—

Pardon. That must sound dreadfully narrow. It could easily be a woman, or a shict, or any of these creatures.

A mortal does not necessarily fear what he does not understand. Rather, a mortal fears that he is understood.

In his primitive mind, a darkness ahead is not an opportunity to learn, beckoning him to enter. When he gazes upon it, he does not see the unknowable. He sees—or thinks he sees—something within, staring out at him, understanding him, learning about him.

This thought, understandably, frightens him.

It is difficult for us to understand—or rather, for the others to understand, at least—for the collection and dispersal of knowledge remains our primary function. To understand and be understood, in our eyes, is the natural way of things. To the mortal, however, it is his greatest vulnerability, his greatest anxiety.

Yet also his greatest ecstasy.

For it is within this unknowing that he feels most comfortable with his gods. They remain so far away that he is insignificant to them and he takes solace in this, knowing that they understand him and, having not killed him yet, must love him. It is the vast gulf between his world and theirs that he creates a meaning to fill. It is in this great silence between them that he finds them comforting.

And there exists no doubt in my mind that, were the gods to open heaven and step down to stand before him, his first act would be to pick up a sword and try to kill them.

And that is why he resents us. We are too close for him to be unknown to us, yet too far to be able to be struck down. We are messengers, and our voices make his ears hurt. We are shepherds, and he has no wish to be herded. We are here and he cannot deny our existence, yet he cannot kill us and thus we are unreal.

Perhaps it sounds mad, but I find a certain strength in that philosophy.

The others, perhaps, view the mortals' defiance as blasphemy. But I? I confess to a fascination with their logic. And the more I study it, the more I realize the wisdom in it.

In destroying, in hurting, in slaying, he understands. What takes us ages of deliberation to know, he knows in the instant he puts metal to it. He knows if it can be destroyed and what it will take to destroy it. He uses every part of his intellect in figuring out how to destroy it that it might not harm him, and, in doing so, he understands it. All of it.

Whatever it is. Be it construct or living matter, be it written word or speech, be it law or love or truth or...or...

I get ahead of myself. Oerboros and Kyrael often chastise me for this.

In my writing this down, it all seems so clear. Yet I know I could not show the others. They would think it madness, naturally. Or worse, seek to inform higher powers—distant though they may be. Yet someday I hope to refer to these notes and use them as the foundation for something greater. In this I hope to understand the mortal. In this I hope he understands me.

Perhaps it will hurt. But that may very well be the price of this knowledge.

Accept no truth that comes bloodlessly.

Adhere to no law that is not earned.

Trust no creation that you cannot destroy.

> *From the annals of His Word,*
> *The First and Final Testament of He Who Held the Light,*
> *Khoth-Kapira*

ONE

PAPER MEN, FOLDED

When the pale light of dawn finally found Lenk, he was staring into the eyes of a dead man.

It was not a killer that he had studied for the past evening. The angles of the dead man's brow, chin, and jaw were sharp, but they lacked the tension that belonged to men who killed for any other reason than a very good one. Or what they thought was a very good one.

Rather, in the scars on his face and the coldness of his eyes, Lenk saw a hard man. Not a desperate criminal; here was a man who had drawn steel enough times that he had simply forgotten why he'd started. Or even when he had ever begun.

Granted, it had been days since Lenk had seen a bath—or a stream or a mirror—but he had to admire the detail of the man. It was a rather good likeness of himself, he thought.

The words *dead or alive* framing his face, however, were new.

The sound of sloshing water caught his ear. He crawled quietly to the slatted window of his room and peered out. Farmers, their Djaalic skin made darker by years of honest labor, were just now emerging from their huts. They rolled up their breeches, picked up their tools, and waded into the murk of their rice paddies.

The Green Belt, as it was known, was home to such people. So named for its position beneath the city, the narrow valley had proven the only place in the region capable of sustaining agriculture. In years past, it had fed Cier'Djaal. Now it made rice to sell. But year in and year out, the farmers had remained the same. Good folk, honest and hard.

How many of them had seen a wanted poster like the one in his hands? How many of them knew his face belonged to the dead man called "the assassin of Cier'Djaal"?

How many of them, he wondered, had relatives back in a city in which he had left behind so many corpses?

Pain shot through his stiff muscles. These weren't the thoughts of an innocent man, he knew. But even the most devout priest, after six days in a tiny room with no contact from anyone, would start to wonder what he'd done to deserve such isolation.

Lenk felt tempted to go out there, into the mucky fields, and talk to the first farmer he saw. He'd tell them who he was, what he had done, all the people he had killed—or supposedly killed—and simply wait for their response. Whatever happened next would have to be better than the isolated waiting, the paranoia, the wondering.

He told himself this.

Yet when one of the farmers glanced his way, toward his tiny room, he ducked away from the window and let the slats fall shut, plunging the room back into darkness.

He took a deep breath, rose to his feet. He walked to the single door and stared, for the fiftieth time that morning, at its handle. He hesitated to call his quarters a cell—he could leave anytime he wanted, assuming he was willing to face the consequences alone.

And for a man, even an innocent one, who had been in the wrong place at the wrong time, there were many.

True, he had been there when the riot had been touched off. True, he had climbed over the dead bodies to escape the carnage. True, he had fled the city just as riot became war and war became massacre. True, the circumstances under which this had all happened, it could be said, did not make him seem innocent.

But he was.

He told himself this.

And, for the fiftieth time that morning, he laid a hand on the door's handle.

"I wouldn't."

A shudder ran down his spine at the sound of the voice. Lenk expected he should have been used to it by now, considering how often he heard it.

Yet when he turned around and saw Mocca standing there, he forgave himself for his alarm.

He merely resigned himself to the ire he felt at the sudden appearance of the man in white—for it was still less disturbing to think of him as a man.

"Six days," Lenk said. The sound of his own voice was a rasping, grating thing to his ears. "Six days I've watched fires burn over the city walls. Six days I've watched people carrying bodies out on the road. Six days of waiting with stale bread and drifting cinders and distant screams. Six days..." His eyes drifted back to the door. "And I have heard *nothing* from Kataria."

And there, leaning against the wall as though it had been waiting all this time for him to arrive at this conclusion, was the sword.

"I'm not going to survive a seventh," he said, reaching for the weapon.

"What, pray, do you expect to do?"

Lenk was so accustomed to Mocca's voice that he didn't even need to turn around to know he was wearing that half-delighted, half-arrogant quirked eyebrow. As though he knew something Lenk didn't and was just waiting for the young man to stumble around long enough to be amusing before telling him. Lenk resolved not to give him the satisfaction.

"There's a lot you can do with a sword, even without knowing what you're doing," Lenk replied. "That's how I got here."

"A point," Mocca replied. "Rather, what do you expect has happened to her?"

At this, Lenk cast a glare over his shoulder. "Maybe she was captured. Killed. Trampled to death, speared, gored, branded, whipped, burned, I don't fucking know. There's a *war* going on not five miles away from here. If I went through every possibility I'd be here all fucking day."

"Possibilities are easy to live with," Mocca replied. "They're distant things, cold breezes on warm days. Certainties are harder." Beneath shadows cast by his white hood, his smile looked sinister. "Certainties crush people."

"Look, I know being able to appear wherever and whenever you want permits you a certain degree of crypticism, but if you could kindly get to the point."

"It's possible she has been captured. It's possible she has been killed." Mocca shrugged. "There are a lot of people out there living with the possibility they might die and the certainty that *you*"—he pointed a finger at Lenk—"are to blame for it. Thus I can say with certainty that they will flay you alive for the possibility that they might not have to live with that fear."

If there was anything more aggravating than a bastard who could appear out of thin air, it was a bastard who could appear out of thin air and who insisted on always being right.

And because Mocca was that kind of bastard, Lenk took a moment to draw in a deep breath before letting the blade slide out of his hand and clatter to the floor.

Mocca was right.

That thought settled upon Lenk's shoulders, bore him to the ground as he pressed his back against the door and slid down to the floor. A shot of pain flared up in his side in protest. His fingers brushed against his tunic; beneath the cloth and the dressing beneath it, the wound felt tender.

Six days.

That number seemed real only when he felt the pain. Because only when he felt the pain could he remember how it had all happened.

Two powers had sat down in Cier'Djaal with the intention of making peace. It didn't matter that both had brought their armies with them: the black-armored, fanatic legions of the Karnerian Empire and the reckless, beast-riding louts of the Kingdom of Saine. The people of Cier'Djaal naïvely believed that the negotiations would prevent their homes from becoming battlefronts.

And they just might have, had he not been there.

Lenk wanted to say it was just bad luck that had brought him to the window overlooking that meeting. He wanted to say that it was an elaborate series of circumstances that had made it look as if he had shot the bolt that had killed the negotiator and caused the two armies to accuse each other of having him do it. He wanted to rail against the gods who had put him there, bleeding from a wound as the city and his life fell apart around him.

But six days was a long time. Long enough for him to realize that there was no such thing as luck, nor circumstance, nor even gods so petty. There were only moments in which men like him had a choice to put down the blade and walk away or not.

He glanced sidelong at his sword.

Sometimes those moments lasted longer than six days.

"If you're bored," Mocca suggested with a tone that might have sounded sympathetic coming from someone less horrifyingly arrogant, "we could always return to our last discussion. I hope you've been giving some thought to my proposal."

"I'm not *bored*." Lenk leapt to his feet, ignored the pain, and strode toward Mocca. "I'm *impotent*."

Without even looking up, he walked straight into Mocca. And without even blinking, he walked straight through Mocca. The man's entire body shimmered, his white robes quavering like water that had been struck by a stone. When it resettled and he was whole again, his dark brows knitted in disapproval.

"You *know* I hate it when you do that," Mocca said.

"I don't know anything." Lenk whirled on him, deliberately walking through him once more. "I don't know how this all happened. I don't know what to do. I don't know where Kataria is. I don't know if she's coming back."

He turned to walk back through Mocca, but halted. He regarded the man—even though he knew Mocca was definitely *not* a man—through narrowed eyes.

"And I don't know why you're still here or even what kind of crime against heaven you *are*."

Any man would be angry at those words, and Lenk desperately hoped that Mocca would be furious. He searched the man's face for it: a scowl, a baring of teeth, a curse boiling behind his mouth. Anger would be something human, something understandable.

But it was a calm face that stared back at Lenk, a smile tugging at the corners of slender lips.

Mocca was not angry.

Mocca was never angry.

And Lenk suddenly found himself staring at the door again. But even if he could escape Mocca's stare, he could not escape his voice. It was calm. It was confident. It was so very cold.

"You know who I am," Mocca said. "You know my name."

"Names," Lenk replied without looking up. "*Names*. You have so gods-damned many." He threw his hands up, tossing each one into the air. "God-King, Flesh-Shaper, Heretic, Murderer, Slaver." He paused before spitting the last one: "*Demon*."

He turned to face Mocca. And he saw it. One last ripple across the water, one more twitch of the lip, one final flash of light behind eyes that became all the darker for its absence.

"One more," Mocca said softly.

Lenk opened his mouth. Silence.

"Say it."

"Khoth-Kapira."

The name fell from Lenk's mouth. And in the deafening silence that followed in its wake, Mocca changed. His body was firmer, his phantom flesh was more solid, and his smile was something altogether more sinister.

"Before I was sent to hell," he whispered, "that name burst from every mortal mouth from where we stand to where the sun rises. God-King, Flesh-Shaper, all those other titles were merely words. My name...was heavy with meaning. My name built cities. My name united people. My name"—his smile grew broader—"was *everything*."

Demons, unfathomable though legends portrayed them as being, were not horrifyingly complex. Possessed though they once had been of heavenly grace, they were creatures of straightforwardly mortal ambition. They plotted, true. They schemed, yes. But above all else, they wanted. They craved.

And Mocca's craving was etched across his face in his smile.

"No," Lenk said.

"Just listen."

"No."

"What have you got to lose?"

"To a demon?" Lenk laughed, a shrieking, breathless sound. "Every—"

"No," Mocca interjected. "Do not finish that word. Do not finish that *thought* if you can help it." He pointed to the slatted window and the world beyond it. "That city, and any life you hoped to find in it, is dead. You stand in this room, alone, pining after a woman who may not even be alive. You have had six days to come to this fact, but out of respect for you, I shall make it perfectly clear."

Lenk blinked. When he opened his eyes, Mocca stood but a hairbreadth away. And with a breathless voice, he spoke.

"You do not stand to lose everything. You had precious little on this miserable little stain of creation to take and it has *all* gone. All you are left with is ash and darkness and thousands of people who want you dead if it'll distract them from the truth."

"Demons don't know truth. Demons lie."

"No one *but* a demon would know what it is to look upon creation and see nothing but flaws. When I gazed upon mortalkind, I saw suffering, disease, war, hatred." He vanished, reappeared at the window. "Heaven charged me to watch creation." He raised a hand to the slats, watched it disappear, immaterial, through the wood. "And I watched it wither.

"The view from on high is absolute. The sound of a spider's legs skittering toward a squirming fly is deafening up there. I saw everything. Every rape, every murder, every fire, every gorged cannibal, every orphaned child, every starving creature straining to remember it was once a man even as it pawed through offal for scraps."

Something within the man—if he could still be thought of as that—changed in the moment he turned to face Lenk. His eyes drank the darkness of the room and became black as night, and his words took the weight of his name.

"Demon," he said. "The swine that rutted in the muck I beheld called me that. I heard their words clear as any. But to my people..." He threw his hands out wide. "I was *KING*."

And that weight, that terrible weight, struck Lenk like a hammer. The air rippled, a gale from nowhere howling out from behind Mocca, sending his robes whipping about and casting Lenk to the floor with its force.

The walls of the room fell away. The floor split apart. From somewhere deep in the earth, pillars began to rise: great columns of golden stone, each one carved in the image of a robed man with a short beard and a halo of serpents, granite eyes staring down upon Lenk. From between them, banners of white and red and gold flew, depicting encircled bands of snakes. And behind Mocca, the last wall of the room was swallowed by a great golden light.

Lenk shielded his eyes. He heard footsteps. He felt a shadow upon him. When he looked up, it was not Mocca who stared down at him. It was not the man he knew. This man stood taller, prouder, wrapped in a robe of the most pristine white and crowned with a halo of golden snakes that writhed and twisted and held themselves aloft with regal bearing, with ruby eyes glistening with an intensity reflected in the man's own gaze.

"And I was," the king that Mocca had been said. "I called the water that cleansed the filth and blood from the earth. I wrote the laws that made the animals civil. I abolished war. I cast out sickness. I healed the wounded and fed the hungry." His smile was broad, triumphant. "Demon, they call me? I wear the title with pride. If it was a demon's hubris that made beast into man, then it was a god's vision that made it possible. I built heaven on earth, Lenk. And I can do it again."

He held his hands out in benevolence, his skin painted gold by the light flowing from behind him.

"All you need to do . . . is . . ."

"Is what?" Lenk didn't even hear himself, so weak and small his voice was against the splendor before him. "Is what?"

"Stand aside."

"What?"

A small word. Fraught with confusion. The barest exhalation to summate the profoundest ignorance.

Yet it was enough to banish everything. Lenk's eyes fluttered, and when he saw clearly once again, Mocca was gone. The golden light, the pillars, the banners, and the warm wind had all followed, leaving four lightless walls and a solid floor upon which Lenk sat.

Alone.

But not for long. The door shuddered on its hinges with a pounding whose urgency suggested that it had been going on for an appreciably annoying time. Lenk glanced at the window, saw the silver dawn light turning to golden day through the slats.

How long had it taken for what had just happened?

What *had* just happened?

Questions concerning demons, though pressing, were hard to focus on when the sound of wood rattling filled one's skull. Lenk clambered to his feet and reached for the lock, then paused and recalled something that had been established when he had first arrived here.

The password.

"Ah." He paused, trying to remember it as he spoke through the door. "Is it raining outside today?"

"It's going to be raining red after I stab you and throw you off the fucking roof if you don't open this door."

That was not the password.

And considering the fury with which the threat had been delivered, it was a little alarming how quickly Lenk undid the lock and threw open the door. He could scarcely help it, though. No more than he could help the wild-eyed look of need that crossed his face when he stared at his visitor.

Bright-green eyes framed by dirty golden hair. Long pointed ears poking out between braids, flattening against her skull in a show of aggression. Lips curled up in a sneer, overlarge canines left threateningly bare.

It was decidedly more alarming that this sight should relieve him so much.

"Where the hell have you been?" he asked.

Kataria held up a dirty burlap sack with a moist brown stain.

"Getting breakfast," she grunted.

"For six days?"

"For a few hours," she replied, shoving him out of the way with her free hand and stalking into the room. "The other six days were spent taking care of some things."

"And you didn't send word? Didn't stop in?" Lenk shut the door behind her, followed her to the center of the room. "You couldn't be bothered to stop by and relieve me from wondering if you had been captured, executed, or—"

He caught her movement only in glimpses. First the whirl of her hair, then the thrust of her gloved hand as it shot out to grab him by the collar of his tunic. Finally he saw her teeth flashing bright white as she drew him in and pressed her lips to his, pushing past his teeth with her tongue.

After a few breathless moments, they parted with heated exhalations. She sighed, pressed her forehead against his as she ran a hand up behind his head, fingers coiling through his silver hair.

"There's got to be an easier way to make you shut up," she said.

"You punched me the last time," he said.

"And what did you learn?"

He laughed. It wasn't funny, of course; few of her jokes, which mostly revolved around violence and flatulence, were. And this wasn't the sort of situation that lent itself well to humor.

But he couldn't help it. It had been so long since he had spoken to anyone who wasn't Mocca, so long since he had felt his hands touch warm skin that wasn't his. He breathed her in, the scent of dust and leather, and felt the sweat of her brow kiss his flesh.

But she did not return his laugh. When she pulled away from him, her eyes were hard and her mouth tight. And he felt his own lips pull into a frown in response.

"What's wrong?" he asked.

She opened her mouth as if to say something. Then sighed and shoved the burlap sack into his arms.

"Eat first," she said. "If we're lucky, you might choke and you won't have to worry about it."

For close to an hour, they sat on the floor and ate in silence.

Or at least they ate without words. The food Kataria had brought was a chunk of unseasoned and mostly cooked ox—it was the only edible animal this side of the Green Belt—and crunchy black bread. And they were people used to eating quickly and without utensils.

Some of us more than others, Lenk noted as he watched Kataria rip off a string of ox flesh with her teeth. The half-cooked blood dribbled down her chin and onto the lean muscle of an abdomen left exposed by her half shirt.

His eyes lingered there, upon her pale flesh and the blood staining it, stark against the absence of other grime. He squinted hard as he bit off more bread and chewed it.

Six days, he noted. And yet she wore no dust, no mud, no stains of travel upon her skin. Her shirt was dirty, as always. Her doeskin leggings were caked in dust, her boots likewise muddied. But her skin was clean, pristine.

She had washed recently.

A hand went to her belly, wiped the blood off with her glove. He looked up and caught her fixing him with a hard stare. She swallowed her food, took another bite, and only then started to speak.

"The bad news," she said through a mouthful, "is that the wanted posters are everywhere. Every village and farmhouse out here knows what happened in Cier'Djaal. And they all know that they have you to thank for all the refugees, vagrants, and bandits that have started crawling along the Green Belt."

He nodded, only half-listening. His thoughts were otherwise occupied. Had it really taken her six days to find that out?

"The good news is that the posters aren't too accurate," she continued, swallowing. "I've listened to some conversations, asked those who didn't mind these." Her pointed ears twitched in demonstration. "No one's *quite* sure what you look like beyond the obvious: male, human... short."

At this he finally looked up. "Short? How short?"

"Doesn't matter."

"Like, shorter than average or short like a child or—"

"The one thing *everyone* knows about you, though," she interrupted, "is the *very* obvious." She pointed to the top of his head. "Namely, the fact that you've got a pelt like an old man."

"It's hair," he muttered, touching his silver locks. "Not a pelt."

"I've talked to Sheffu about it."

"What the hell would Sheffu know?"

"Considering he's paying to save you from whoever might want to take advantage of whatever reward is offered by those posters?" Kataria asked. "Anyway, he says we can still proceed with the plan, just so long as we do something about it."

"Something," Lenk repeated, echoing her ominous tone.

"Yeah." She rose to her feet, pulled a slim-bladed hunting knife from her belt. "Something."

With the shearing of a blade the only sound to disturb his thoughts, Lenk watched another lock of hair fall to the floor before him. He reached down, took it between his fingers, and held it up. There, shorn from his head, dull and gray, he supposed it didn't look so unlike a pelt.

Just a piece of fur that could have come from an animal.

Any animal, really, so long as it had fangs and claws.

For what else was he?

Certainly not a man. Men were creatures of desire, of reason, and, most importantly, of choice.

Two weeks ago he might have called himself a man. He had wanted a new life, free from the bloodshed that had followed him ever since he had picked up his blade and called himself an adventurer. He had sought it in Cier'Djaal's walls, looking for the perfect place to lay his sword to rest; maybe in the corner of a dusty little shop, or over a mantel, where he would one day point it out to grandchildren when they asked for stories.

Desire and reason he understood.

It was that last part, choice, that he always had trouble with.

Everything he had found in Cier'Djaal, he'd found with the blade. He'd found war between the gangs of the Jackals and Khovura. He'd found war between the Karnerians and Sainites. He'd found war between rich and poor, shicts and humans, tulwar and humans, all with the blade.

And with the blade he'd found himself in the middle of it, unable to put it down and walk away.

What could one call a man who couldn't let go, even for the sake of his own life, but an animal? What could one call a man who was turned loose at the whim of another but an animal?

That was what Sheffu wanted. An animal. Any animal, really, so long as it had claws and fangs. Lenk just happened to be the one that needed something from him.

Of course Sheffu didn't see it that way. He used big words like *righteousness, savior, necessity* to describe what he called a "duty that must be served to preserve mortalkind's right to sovereignty."

And he'd used these words to convince himself—if not Lenk—of the necessity of going to the Forbidden East, to the last known holdings of the demon known as Khoth-Kapira, to find any and all information that could be used to stop the demon's return to the mortal world.

Lenk glanced at the spot where Mocca had stood.

If only he knew.

But for all that he didn't know, Sheffu knew enough about men and animals alike to know what they'd do when cornered. He had promised Lenk that, if he would do but this one task, Sheffu would clear his name. He was a member of the aristocratic fashas of Cier'Djaal, and such a thing wasn't *entirely* outside his power.

What could Lenk do, he asked himself, but hold on to the sword?

What choice did he have?

Another shearing sound filled his ears. Another lock of hair fell into his lap.

"What if we ran?" he asked.

"Ran?" Kataria seemed nonplussed by the suggestion, taking another clump of hair and lightly cutting it away. "Where to?"

"I don't know," he said. "Back north, maybe. Or further south. Somewhere where I'm not wanted for the murder of hundreds."

"That would be nice, wouldn't it?"

"We could move back with your parents, maybe."

"My parents." Her voice was flat. "My tribe, as well?"

"Yeah. Sure."

"My tribe that's warred with human scum for centuries?"

"There'll be tensions at first," he replied, a grin touching his face. "But I'm likable scum. They'll come to love me."

"Firing their homes? Eating their livers? Hanging them up by their feet in trees and cutting their throats so that they might water the—"

"You could have just said no," Lenk said.

"I didn't want to sound pessimistic," she chuckled. "Past the Green Belt, it's nothing but desert. To get out of here, we'd have to have help. To get help, we'd have to talk to people. To talk to people, we'd have to—"

"Let them kill me for the reward money, right." He sighed, leaning forward and burying his face in his hands. "We're stuck here, aren't we?"

"Well, *you* are, yeah." She cut another thick strand. "I could leave anytime I wanted."

He didn't know why his hands shot up at that. Not until they curled tightly around her wrist.

"Don't," he whispered, his voice soft and desperate.

Only in that whisper, the breathless hush of his voice, was it clear. Not all these days, when he had been without her voice, her warmth.

Only in that long moment, that long hesitation before she placed her hand upon his, did he know why he clung to her.

"I won't."

That moment of hesitation stretched out, long after her words had failed to soothe him. He lived in it, that moment, dwelling on why it had taken so long for her to touch him, so long for her to say those words. Why was she clean? Where had she been for six days? Why did it hurt so much to think?

He lost himself in that moment, as she sheared the last lock, turned the blade, and scraped his head raw. And he didn't look up until she dipped a cloth in a basin and drew cold water across a suddenly naked scalp.

"Think it'll work?" Kataria asked.

Lenk stared at his pelt lying on the floor before sliding over to stare into the washbasin. When the water settled enough that he could see himself, he wasn't sure what he was looking at. This hairless man had his scars, his angles, his jaw, but there was something in his cold blue eyes that hadn't been there before. A deep weariness that he hadn't had two weeks ago.

The eyes of a dead man.

"Yeah," Lenk replied. "It'll work."

How could it not?

Even Lenk didn't recognize whom he was staring at.

And as he rose to his feet, trudged to the door, and plucked up his sword, he wasn't sure if that was such a bad thing.

TWO

FRAYED

*T*he *important thing here,* Asper told herself, *is not to breathe too deeply.*

That seemed logical to her. Breathing deeply had a calming effect, steadied the nerves. For this next part, she had to be nervous.

She leaned out of the alley mouth, peered into the square. Signs with phrases like *Fine Tailors, Excellent Curry,* and *Reasonable Solicitors* greeted her, their hinges creaking in a stale breeze as they swung like men from nooses.

She wondered if this place had been busy before the war. She wondered if this place had seen a lot of people: harried men darting between businesses, frazzled mothers trying to ignore children pulling at their skirts as they passed the sweetshop.

Her eyes drifted down to the cobblestones of the square, to the corpses splayed upon the streets, cooling in the morning air.

Yeah, she thought to herself. *This place was probably really busy.*

She took a deep breath, then reminded herself not to do that. She glanced over her shoulder at the five or so men and women behind her, their faces alternately resigned and terrified. Only the man at their front, wearing a guardsman's armor still immaculately polished, had an expression that looked anything like that of someone ready to do what they were about to.

"Clear?" Dransun asked.

She leaned out, listened. On the wind were no sounds of stomping boots, clashing steel, or war horns. She looked back to him and nodded.

"Whenever you're ready, then," he said, returning the gesture.

After another breath she waved a hand and slipped out of the alley into the square. The five or so volunteers shuffled out softly behind her.

She could feel their nervous stares on her back. Understandable. This was a war zone, after all; nervous stares were warranted, but they should be on alleys and entrances, not on her.

They looked to her because they were scared. And because they looked to her, she spoke to guide them.

"Remember, we prioritize the wounded," she said. "Stop the bleeding, apply tourniquets if you need to. If no wounded, then we look to the dead. Children first, no matter what. Leave the soldiers." She glanced over her shoulder, saw them still looking at her. "*Now.*"

Fear had its advantages. So long as they were at least a little afraid of this northern woman, they could be counted on to do as they did: scatter about with makeshift medical bags filled with whatever supplies they had been able to find, kneel over bodies, check for pulses and wounds, ask where it hurt. She was gratified to hear a few groans rise from the bodies, to see a few people being helped to their feet.

Gratification later, she reminded herself. *Work now.*

She scanned the square, careful not to let the fact that this was becoming routine keep her from noticing something subtle, like a chest rising and falling. She crept over to a man, glanced over his body.

Dark-skinned Djaalic, civilian clothes, no beard; young man, probably a merchant's apprentice, strong and able-bodied. He stared up at the sky with a concussed look, bleeding from a gash in his temple. Shallow wound, she noted, not threatening.

"Can you hear me?" she asked, leaning over and looking into his eyes. Glazed, but they swiveled to stare into hers: conscious, awake, coherent.

"I...I think I got hit," he said, breathlessly. "I didn't want to come to work today. But Master Hassun said we had to go to Silktown. I told him the fashas weren't letting anyone in but..." His voice drifted off. He swallowed hard. "We were going and the foreigners came out and everything just kind of went—"

"Stop," she interrupted. There would be time for this later. "Your wound isn't serious. Looks like you just got clipped."

The glaze slid from his eyes, and the face softened in recognition. "You're the northerner," he said. "The one who works with Aturach over at the temple. They say you—"

She interrupted again. "Can you walk?" There would be time for *this* never.

He struggled to his elbows, looked at her. "Yeah. Yeah, I can walk."

"Great," she replied, grabbing him by the arm and hoisting him ungently to his feet. "Then you can help carry people." She pointed to her volunteers. "Go tell them you're here to help and do what they say."

"What?" He looked at her, astonished. "I just watched my master and all my friends get killed. They said you were merciful, that you'd—"

"I *am* merciful." Her voice was cold and straight as a scalpel. "That's why I'm offering you a choice of helping or waiting for death instead of hurrying you along myself." She sneered. "There are only two kinds of people in this square: corpses or help. If you're not one, then I can damn well leave you here until you turn into the other."

His mouth hung open at that and she held her breath.

You've done it this time, she thought. *Pushed him too far. He's going to lock up, freeze, sit here and wait to die like you told him. Or worse, he'll go and tell the others what you said and no one will trust you. Damn it. How the hell am I supposed to know how far to push?*

Lenk would have known. Kataria, too. Gariath would have had people marching in lockstep with just a look.

But none of them were here right now. It was only Asper, staring the man down, holding her breath. And a little thought, so soft and silent that it might not have even been hers, speaking from a very quiet, very dark place in the back of her mind.

Strike this one. The rest will follow.

She clenched her teeth to keep the horror from showing on her face.

"Northern bitch," the man finally muttered before turning and shuffling toward one of the volunteers, leaning over to help her with a wounded man.

Yeah, she thought. *He'll be fine. Send him to the Temple of Ancaa, though.*

She would have taken him along anyway, even if he had refused. Just as she would have taken along anyone she had threatened. Thus far, though, no one had been able or willing to call her bluff. Hence her productive volunteer force.

"Come on, come on," Dransun barked from the alley mouth. "Get them out of sight. We'll take the backstreets back to Temple Row." He looked to Asper. "You almost done?"

"Almost," she called back.

He nodded, shepherding the volunteers and their wounded and dead back into the alley. More walking than not, she noted, only two dead and only one of them a child.

A good day, she thought.

And something inside her cracked, just a little.

No, not a good day. How could a day with just *one* dead child be considered good? How could this day be better than any of the others, all of them riddled with corpses and bloodstained streets and glassy eyes staring up at the cinders drifting over the breeze?

I can't do this. From that tiny crack inside her, the thoughts came leaking out. *I'm not made for this. I'm not a warrior, I shouldn't be here. This shouldn't be happening.* She looked skyward, as though if she screamed loud enough, someone in heaven might hear her. *THIS SHOULDN'T BE HAPPENING!*

A sharp, warbling wail cut her thoughts in twain. Somewhere in the distance, a war horn sounded. The crack inside her fused itself shut as her pulse quickened and her breath returned to fevered rapidity.

Fear had its uses.

"Priestess!" Dransun called out. He gesticulated wildly to the alley mouth. "We have to go *now*."

She nodded, moved to join him. She took care not to hop over the bodies left behind; it seemed somehow more respectful to step around them. And yet the moment she felt a hand reach out and wrap around her ankle, she realized that practicality, too, had its uses.

"Please." A pained groan rose from the cobblestones. "Please... help..."

She saw bloodied hands grasping the hem of her robe. But past that she saw a blue coat, a pale-skinned northern face, a tricornered hat on a mop of unruly flaxen hair. And emblazoning every part of that coat in which one could conceivably put it was the Six-Pointed Star of Saine.

A Sainite.

A soldier.

Bleeding profusely from his belly, if the long red smear on the cobblestones showing where he had pulled himself to get to her was any indication. He looked at her with a blank expression, in too much pain to show any fear or desperation.

"Help...," he groaned. "Please."

"We're Talanites," she replied, as coldly as she could manage. "Neutral. We can't take any soldiers."

"Hurts. Hurts so bad, please."

"I can't." She could feel herself forcing the words through clenched teeth. "I *can't*."

"Please...please..."

He wasn't hearing her. Of course, why would he? She could barely hear herself. She glanced over to the alley mouth, saw that Dransun was wildly shaking his head and gesticulating *no, no*, and *fuck no* in profoundly fearsome gesture. And yet, past him, she saw that her volunteers and the wounded had all disappeared. No one had seen him. No one had to know. She could take the man's coat, burn it, pretend he was—

Dransun caught her eye again. His gesticulation became wild flailing. What was he trying to say? He hadn't taught her those hand signals he was using. She squinted, made the signal for *repeat*. Dransun pointed to his lips, mouthed the words carefully. And on the third try, she finally understood what he was saying.

Behind you.

Too late.

"Priestess." A heavy voice, heavier even than the sound of iron soles stepping over cobblestones, reached her. "You should not be here."

His black plate armor rattled with every step, the sound of a miniature thunderclap. He carried himself with a proud bearing, straight and unyielding as the long sword at his hip. In the smooth darkness of his face, shorn of every bit of hair on cheek or scalp, the wrinkles of a man approaching middle age were beginning to form. Yet these were mere lines in a face unmarred by emotion, whether pity or anger.

Speaker Careus, Most Honored Envoy of the Holy Empire of Karneria and Voice of Daeon the Conqueror, was used to such sights as the carnage that surrounded him.

"Speaker Careus," she replied. She caught the quaver in her voice, quashed it immediately. She might not be a warrior, but she knew how to speak with them. "You know why I'm here. You agreed to honor the terms of our mission." She narrowed her eyes. "Are you here to renegotiate?"

And normally, she knew how to speak to priests. To challenge Careus's honor would be to invite him to prove he was honorable, as any priest would do. And as any warrior would do, Careus would usually prove his honor by the biggest, most obnoxious show of force he could possibly think of.

Daeonists, Asper thought, resignedly.

"Sweeps for Sainite forces are currently under way," Careus replied. "We mean no harm."

"We," Asper noted. *Of course, with Karnerians, there's always a "we."*

And "we" made themselves known in quick time. From the opposite end of the square, they filed in: sandaled feet in perfect lockstep, spears high and proud over helmeted heads, black tower shields drinking in what light remained of the morning. A Karnerian regiment, every piece of metal polished to obsidian, came to a harmonious halt at a single wave from Careus.

"Given the corpses around here," Asper replied, "I'd say whatever you *mean* seems to have little bearing on what you *do*."

"Instructions were handed to civilians to evacuate areas of conflict," the speaker replied. "The gluttonous and greedy that lingered in hopes of profiteering have wrought their own fate."

"You've made their entire *homes* into areas of—"

"Our holy charge remains the same as it ever was." Careus spoke over her, eyes drifting down to the Sainite clutching at her leg. "Preserve the city and its people. And to do so, we must cleanse it of interloping pagans." His sword came out of its scabbard in a long, ringing note. "If our purpose is doubted, then let action clarify."

She cried out something between a curse and a plea. The sound of the Sainite's scream was thick and wet, something that filled the spaces between flesh separating and ribs cracking beneath steel. He spasmed as Careus withdrew the blade, lying still only when the life leaked out of him to stain her boots black.

Karnerian culture was something she understood only slightly better than the Sainite, if only because Karneria bowed to a god rather than a monarch. But she knew enough of speakers to know that they were the word of their god, and thus she had always assumed them to be creatures of stoic dignity and contemplation.

"You unspeakable *ass*!"

Careus's frown suggested that speakers were certainly not used to being called that.

"He was *wounded*!" she snarled. "He was begging for aid!"

"Aid you are not legally permitted to offer by the terms of our agreement," Careus replied coolly, stepping aside as the Sainite's blood oozed toward his plated boot.

"You could have let him go! You could have taken him prisoner! You could have done *anything* but that!"

"That is where you are incorrect, priestess," he said, voice cold. "In service to Daeon, the Empire of Karneria can do only as the Conqueror wills. And the Conqueror wills that this city be—"

The air screamed. Careus made a sudden sound. And whether it was a curse or a prayer he shrieked, she wasn't quite sure. As it turned out, it was rather hard to make sense when one had a crossbow bolt lodged in one's shoulder.

"Like that, you Karnie fuck?" a shrill voice cried from somewhere on high. *"Hold still, I got another one for you."*

Careus tore the bolt free with his left hand; no blood followed, Asper noted, meaning it had failed to pierce the armor. His right shot up, clenching into a fist. The Karnerian soldiers responded to the silent command, their leader barking a swift order.

They surged in good order, engulfing both Careus and Asper before she could get away. Their shields formed a solid square, held over their heads to protect from the few stray bolts that followed.

Through the cracks in the defense, Asper looked to the roofs of the square. Blue coats fluttered in the breeze, tricornered hats stark and black atop fair-haired heads. A small squadron of Sainites crouched upon a roof, and standing brazenly at their forefront was a wiry woman with a snarl that could be seen even from so far down.

"Blacksbarrow," Careus muttered from beside Asper. He glowered at one of the nearby soldiers. "How far away are our archers?"

"Two squares away, Speaker," the soldier replied. "Do we send a runner?"

"He'd be shot down before he even left the phalanx. That pagan harpy has us pinned down tighter than—"

Before he could finish, one of the shields rattled as another crossbow bolt ricocheted off it.

"C'mon out of there, Careus!" the woman called Blacksbarrow shouted. *"We got business to settle, you and I! That was my cousin you just gutted like a dog!"*

"Another one?" Careus shouted back. "How many more of your inbred relatives must I slay before I finally dislodge you from this wound of a city, pagan?"

"Every man here is my brother! Every woman my sister! Saine is family, you Karnie fuck! And every gods-damned one of us looks out for each other. Now are you going to come out and die like a man or am I going to have to come down there and knock?"

Careus held his breath, spoke an order to the unit. "Stay in fist formation. Protect the priestess at all costs."

"I'm neutral, Speaker," Asper said. "If you let me speak to her, I can—"

"You cannot trust a pagan's word, priestess. Their vile cliff god will hold them to no account." He shouted through a crack in the shields, "Accustom yourself to this chill, Blacksbarrow! You will miss it when you burn!"

"Yeah, that's what I was hopin' you'd say."

Her laughter was coarse and nasty, the sort one heard only in the seediest of taverns at the dirtiest of jokes. The warbling bugle call that followed was shrill and tinny, a jagged piece of metal ripping a wound in the sky.

And still, neither sound was quite so spine-clenchingly horrible as the ones that followed.

A shrill avian cry. The beat of great feathery wings.

And the panic of men.

"BIRDS INCOMING!" one of the Karnerian soldiers screamed. "SCRAWS, SPEAKER! THEY BROUGHT SCRAWS!"

"Vile pagans," Careus snarled. His voice rose to a commanding bellow. "Re-form! Wheeling phalanx! Assemble!"

Whatever fear might have been in the quavering of their voices as they acknowledged the command, it was not enough to keep the Karnerians from reassembling into a wedge formation, the broad end aimed at the rooftops and Asper held tightly in the middle.

But whatever courage might have been in the raising of their shields, it was not enough to keep her confidence against what came rising over the rooftops.

They came like storm clouds upon the sky, long goatlike bodies ending in jagged hooves and beginning in sharp raptor talons. Their eyes, bright and unblinking with animal ferocity, shone as sharp as their spear-like beaks and jagged horns. But it was their wings, black as night and filling the sky with the sound of thunder, that made Asper gape.

Scraws.

So that's what they looked like up close.

The Sainites on the rooftop scrambled into saddles behind the pilots seated on the avian creatures' necks. As soon as they were settled, the snap of reins sent the beasts aloft, flying into the sky and wheeling in a great circle around the Karnerian formation.

"*Rain steel, boys!*" Blacksbarrow called from the back of the lead beast, a magnificent creature whose ebon feathers were crowned with gold.

Asper had only a moment to admire the scraw before her head was forced down. Crossbows hummed in off-key melodies, sending bolts flying down to meet the Karnerian shields.

While some found cracks in the defense or soft patches of metal to punch through, most found only unyielding iron as the formation marched to match the scraws flying circles around them, turning like a spoke of a great wheel, shields always held before them. Those who fell from stray bolts were offered the elegy of a command from Careus, another man stepping up to take his brother's position.

The whole thing was really quite orderly, Asper noted. Truly humans had come far enough that their killing each other could be as efficient as possible. And she would have taken the time to appreciate it more if she hadn't glanced up at the alley mouth and seen Dransun still there, watching helplessly.

Her status as a priestess and a foreigner might afford her protection from Careus and Blacksbarrow—at least in theory—but the common people of Cier'Djaal, "protected" though they also were, could ill afford for her to be here when the smoke cleared and questions were levied.

"Careus!" Asper cried to be heard over the shrieking of scraws and the stomping of boots. "You need to let me out! I can't stay here and—"

The tinny shriek of a bugle sang a terrible war song that was echoed in a quintet of avian screams, far closer, far angrier than the ones circling them. Against that sound the soldiers' cries of alarm almost seemed an insignificant thing.

"*Jousters! Right behind us!*"

Almost.

Helmets craned up and over armored shoulders to look at the roof-tops behind them, just in time to see the shadows of dark wings and the glitter of armored barding as more scraws came sweeping over. These bore but single riders, armored just as their steeds were, each one bearing a barbed lance set against the saddle. Plumed helmets flapped wildly in the wind as they swept down from the rooftops in a wedge formation and landed upon the cobblestones. They lost not a bit of momentum as hooves and claws thundered across the stone and bore them down upon the exposed rear of the phalanx.

"Blacksbarrow, you clever shrew," Careus snarled. "Reverse formation! *REVERSE!*"

In an instant the great weakness of the Karnerian phalanx became known. Even the most well-oiled machine has to come to a dead halt before it can change direction. Soldiers scrambled to bring their spears about to meet the charge, but their timing was too slow and their weapons were too short.

This didn't become completely clear until the bodies started flying.

The shrieks of the scraws carried even over the screams of the soldiers as the beasts tore into their ranks. Their wings were folded, their heads were lowered, and their eyes remained unblinking even as they crushed Karnerians under hoof and rent them under claw, the jousters' lances ripping through shield and spear alike.

Asper tried to ignore the screams. She tried to ignore the blood in her eyes as she struggled to crawl out from under the chaos. She tried to ignore how her heart stopped beating for a moment as she felt a scraw's beak reach down and narrowly snap shut just short of her neck as it rushed over her.

She would be scared later, in the safety of a temple where no one could see her but her god and no one would care if she fell down and started weeping. These fears were for her alone.

Right now everyone else needed her to survive.

She clambered to her feet once she was free of the carnage. The scraws' charge had slowed and the creatures waded amid the melee, clawing and snapping at Karnerians struggling to drop spears and pull out swords. One of the beasts went down beneath a throng of black-clad soldiers, even as one more creature pulled something red and glistening out from the melee and tossed its head back, swallowing it whole.

For a moment Asper could not help but marvel at it, even as Dran-sun rushed out of the alley mouth to drag her into the shadows. She had seen violence before, she had fought monsters and demons, she had faced horrors from beyond any world or god she had ever known.

Somehow, none of it seemed to compare to the crimson splendor of mankind.

※

"I'm just saying that, in the grand scheme of things, this wasn't the worst way this could have come out."

"I'm sure that'll be a comfort to the widows and orphans I have to tell that to tonight. 'Sorry, darling, but the grand scheme ordered your husband to be trampled to death in a melee between foreigners.'"

The men were fighting again.

"You don't have to tell them that."

"You're right. *You* do. This is *your* temple, holy man. *You're* in charge. *You* should be the one to tell them why we aren't out there doing more."

As they always were, lately.

"The Jhouche were disbanded, *Captain*. Don't presume to command me and *don't* presume that filling these people's heads with hopelessness will amount to anything. The only way we succeed is if they help and the only way they help is if we convince them it's worth hanging on."

Aturach would always speak in such a way: lots of hollow promises, lots of bids for optimism, lots of nothing getting done.

"I could do more with a pack of harsh truths and six men with swords than your entire volunteer service, holy man. If you want to convince these people that it's worth hanging on, you need to show them we aren't going to be pushed around by foreigner scum."

And Dransun would always respond just like that: calls to action, brave speeches, a lot of colorful words to justify getting a lot of people killed.

This would go on for a little while longer, at least. Soon enough their arguments would become less coherent, more heated. Rationality would be exchanged for insults, insults for posturing, and posturing for sulk-ing. Meanwhile, on the floor below them in the temple proper, more people would be dying. And in the streets outside, where the war raged, more people would be dying. And no matter how few hours in the day, there seemed always to be time enough for men to sit around making asses of themselves.

She took a sip of her coffee.

Not that anyone asked my opinion.

The steaming hot liquid bit her with a force that tea had failed to match after the third day of… this, whatever it was she was doing.

Coffee made more sense, in any event. It was easier to brew, kept her more alert. There were downsides: It was harder to ignore the squabbling when she was sharp. But coffee had one trait that made it absolutely necessary.

When she looked down into the black liquid, she couldn't see anyone staring back at her.

"It's not like I don't admire the hell out of what you're doing here," Dransun said with a sigh. "It's just…"

And this was it, the moment when the match was decided. When Dransun fell back into his chair to sit beside her, when the strong soldier disappeared and all the gray hairs, old scars, and armor settled down on the slouching softness of a weary man. This was when Dransun relented.

One more aged, creaking relic to add to the pile, Asper thought, casting a glance around the area that had become their farce of a war room. *This seems to be the place for it.*

The attic of the Temple of Talanas seemed more a graveyard than a place venerating the Healer ought to tolerate. Here ancient medical supplies rusted on shelves and wooden idols of the winged God of Healing gathered dust in corners. When Dransun finally cracked, they'd leave him up here, she thought. She would follow. Aturach probably wouldn't last long enough to crack.

"When I first joined up with you, this was a mission of maintaining," the guardsman continued. "Try to minimize the damage the *shkainai* could do, save who we could. And when we thought this was going to be a brief thing that would see one side dead within a few weeks, that was going to work."

The implication, the hanging dread in Dransun's voice, finally caused Asper to look up. Beneath the weariness on his face, fear was beginning to show through. And it was reflected on the thin, boyish features of Aturach as Dransun removed a pair of parchments and set them down upon the table.

Aturach merely stared at them, as though Dransun had just put a human head on his table. After a moment Asper shot him a glare as she reached out and took them. She unfurled them, gave them a quick glance over.

"These are letters," she said.

"From one of my old subordinates in the Jhouche," Dransun said. "He fled to one of the outskirt towns outside the Green Belt on horseback, sent word to me as soon as he heard." The guardsman leaned forward, settling his elbows upon the table. "The situation has changed."

"What?" Aturach looked to Asper with alarm. "What do they say?"

Aturach had a soft face, too soft to keep the panic off his high cheeks and thin eyebrows. He wasn't ready for this news. Not that Asper could blame him; the rest of his fellow priests had been killed and he, at the ripe age of twenty-four, had found himself in the position of Cier'Djaal's high priest of Talanas. She almost didn't want to tell him.

But there was precious little use for a soft man these days.

"The Sainites and Karnerians both have supply convoys coming through the desert," Asper sighed.

She threw the papers onto the table. Aturach moved to snatch them up and pore over them in the desperate hope that she had misread. She leaned back in her chair and draped an arm over her face. Not that she *thought* she would scream, but if she did, better she smother the sound.

"This says they're a month out from the city," Aturach muttered.

"I got those letters yesterday," Dransun replied. "My contact is close to the border. The convoys will be here in two weeks." He leaned forward, forced Aturach to meet the severity of his stare. "That means more troops and more food and weapons to supply them. This city won't even be standing after they're done with it."

"So...so what do we do?" Aturach's gaze swiveled to Asper. "What should we do?"

"What we should have been doing in the first place," Dransun snarled. "We stand up to those dogs. We fight. We outnumber them twenty to one!"

"A regular army we've got here." Aturach gestured to the attic's door. "You figure I should go down there and start rallying the forces? Have the widows and cripples make up the vanguard? Orphans on the right flank, beggars on the left?"

"You've fed them, sheltered them, tended their wounds." Dransun stomped the floor. "Below us they're all crowded together like puppies mating. You've given them *everything*. They *owe* you."

"The gods of the Karnerians and Sainites make demands," Aturach hissed. "The Healer gives. If we start telling them that mercy has a price, they'll stop helping us altogether." He rubbed his eyes. "It's bad enough that the Temple of Ancaa is taking in refugees on the promise of conversion only."

"If the Ancaarans are willing to get things done," Dransun growled, "then maybe conversion isn't too much to ask."

"You understand nothing of—"

"Don't presume to lecture *me*, you—"

"This is about faith! This is about—"

"Survival trumps faith. No one will pray if no one—"

And on, and on, and on.

Asper's eyes drifted to one of the idols in the corner. It seemed not so long ago that she and Aturach had prayed before it together in the temple's main hall. Once the refugees started coming, of course, they had moved it up here to make room for another cot for another body from another fight.

She had thought, at the time, the Healer would approve.

Perhaps you've been going about this the wrong way, Asper thought to herself. *Maybe the Temple of Ancaa has it right. Take in the refugees who swear to serve Ancaa. Ancaa smiles on that. Ancaa protects them. Maybe gods don't give a shit what you do so long as you say their name with a smile on your face.*

A fleeting thought. One of many.

Yet it was this one that caused that dark, quiet corner of her mind to stir, as a voice hissed in agreement.

They should bow to you, not a god.

She shook her head, as if she could force it out through her ears. Just a thought, she told herself. Just a fleeting thought. One of many.

When she looked back to the table, she saw that the argument had stopped. Both men were staring expectantly at her, and for a moment her blood froze. They hadn't heard that, had they? They didn't know. They couldn't know.

Right?

"Well?" Dransun asked.

"Well what?" she replied.

"What do you think we should do?" Aturach asked.

"Why do I have to decide?"

"Because this simpering pup will do whatever you tell him," Dransun growled.

"And this old goat only ever seems to move when you push him." Aturach shot a glare to the guardsman before his expression softened. "More than that, though, it's you the people respect. You're the one out on the streets, bringing them back here."

"You're the one stitching their wounds," Dransun agreed, nodding. "Northern or not, they'll listen to you and abide by what you have to say."

"So should we," Aturach said.

Asper took in their expectant stares for a moment.

"I'm flattered," she said. "Speechless, even." She eased back in her chair, took a very long sip of her coffee. She smacked her lips, calmly regarded the two men, and spoke softly. "Now kindly get the fuck out."

Dransun merely looked annoyed. Aturach, though, looked as though she had just slapped him with a dead puppy.

"That's no way to talk to people who are—"

"People who are many things," Asper interrupted. "Fearless, compassionate, and incredibly annoying. None of those are useful for this decision." She rose from her chair, knuckled the small of her back, and found that woefully inadequate for easing the ache from her bones. "If you're handing me this decision, then it'll be made when I say it is."

She walked to the attic door, opened it, and made an inviting gesture. "Until then, gentlemen, it's not like we don't have enough to do."

They grumbled their assent, exchanging curt glances with each other and her as they slowly shuffled out of the room. Aturach turned, an apology playing on his lips before she held up a hand to silence him, shutting the door shortly after.

She half-regretted that. Not out of any concern for Aturach's feelings, but because, in the silence that ensued, there was nothing to deafen her to the symphony of little pains that followed.

She could almost plan her day around them by now. Her back was stiff from sunup to sundown. Her feet ached from running from soldiers and her fingers hurt from either tending to wounds or keeping would-be thieves from the temple.

But it wasn't until she was alone, when all was silent and even the distant sounds of carnage were muted, that she felt the worst pain. There, beneath the skin of her left arm, she could feel it. Something writhing. Something gnawing. Something watching as she pressed a hand to it.

And felt that dark corner of her mind stir in anticipation.

It will not end happily, you know.

She shook her head to silence it, made a move to turn back to the letters. If it would not be still in idleness, then that was a good enough reason to start getting something done. Perhaps there was something else that Dransun's source had mentioned regarding—

She froze.

There, upon the floor, a shadow stood dark enough to drown the scant light afforded by the tiny attic window. She followed its sprawl for what seemed an impossibly long time to a pair of dark feet.

And there, at the center of the room, back turned to her, he stood. As though he had been standing there all this time.

He had been standing there all this time, for he had intended to be seen there at precisely this moment. She knew this because he was not a man of possibilities. He was a man of certainties.

And she knew this because she knew him. This man. This darkness of a man.

"Do you suspect them of lying to you?"

His voice was as deep and vast as his shadow. And yet she could sense no malice in either. His was not a predatory darkness, something that sought to snuff light. His was an ancient darkness, something so deep and impenetrable as to be beyond such concepts.

"They say the people trust you, that they look up to you," the man of certainties continued. "You, pale and northern. Far from your home, farther from theirs. Does it not seem odd that they should look to you for solace?"

"They don't see me." Her voice crept timidly from her throat. "Not as a person. They see me in the middle of the war, they see me carrying bodies or barking orders. I'm an action, not a person."

He did not face her as he spoke. "Can an action die?"

At this her left arm twitched. "What are you doing here?"

And finally did he turn to face her with eyes that looked as though they had simply forgotten how to blink. Dark circles rimmed a darker stare, and the face and scalp were shorn clean of hair. His body was thin, sinew wrapped in dark flesh wrapped in a threadbare robe. Not sickly, but far from well, he looked like a man whose concerns no longer included things like sleep or food.

"Hearing the other side of the debate," he replied.

No cryptic allusion in his voice. No riddle in his words. He was a man of certainties. And what he was certain of, she was certain she did not want to know.

"More soldiers are coming?" he asked.

"In two weeks," she replied.

"Two weeks." The man looked to the window. "I wonder if there will be anything left to fight for."

"There will be." The answer sprang to her lips. "We're going to do something."

He looked back at her, away from her gaze and to her left arm. She knew he was not looking at mere flesh. His eyes slid past that, past sinew and blood, past bone and marrow. He knew what lurked beneath her skin.

"Amoch-Tethr."

He knew its name. The name of the curse in her flesh, the thing that spoke to her in darkness and ate her fears.

"Soldiers, weapons, humans . . . ," he whispered. "You need none of them. Everything that you could ever need for change lies within you."

She could feel it: him, her, whatever horror it was. Amoch-Tethr, the thing inside her left arm, squirmed and writhed in joy at being recognized. Inside her head its voice was a noise of excitement, a wet purring that raked across Asper's skull. She drew the sleeve of her robe over her arm, clutched it protectively.

And inside her, Amoch-Tethr snarled.

"No," she said, to both the man and the thing.

"Why?"

"Because I know what this thing does to people."

"And you know what people do to people."

"*No.*"

What was that reflected in his face, she wondered? Acceptance of her choice? Contempt at her outburst? His eyes, for the moment, chose not to speak.

And so she felt compelled to ask. "What have you come to tell me?"

At this the faintest smile crept across his features. "That more eyes than you know are watching you." He glanced to her arm. "Both of you." He turned, walked to the window. "And I wonder if they will like what they see."

She resisted the urge to ask for names, numbers, intentions. He had said precisely as much as he meant to and not a word more. She knew him only from meetings like this, in brief moments and shadows. But in those moments, she had known everything about him, through his eyes, through his shadow, through his certainty.

Such was the man called Mundas.

He came to a stop before the tiny attic window. His eyes drifted to a wooden idol of Talanas.

"A thought," he said. "Have you tried asking the gods?"

She said nothing. He didn't need to hear anything. The smile returned, a ghost on his lips.

"Before it all comes to an end," he said, "promise me you will try." He looked to the window. "I want to know how long it takes them to answer."

She couldn't say when he had left. How he had left. He was simply gone, as though he had never been there.

THREE

A Veil So Thick

He did not dream often.

But when he did, he dreamed of her.

The stages were always different. Sometimes they were the grand halls of a palace, statues marching the length of a golden hall to hail him, the returning emperor. Occasionally they were musty theaters that smelled of old wood and cracked paint, motes of dust dancing in shafts of light that opened upon him and presented him to a hundred empty seats.

But she was always the same.

She would appear in the distance, and always in golden light— walking down a shimmering path through the pillars, emerging from a halo from the back of the theater. At first he would see her only in the curves of her hips, the easy stride of her long legs. Then in finer details: the flutter of dark hair, the tilt of a proud chin, the dark eyes beneath heavy lids.

And it always ended the same way. She would come to him, kneel beside him, trace delicate fingers down his cheek, and whisper in his ear.

"Dreadaeleon."

It came from far away, to brush his ear so tenderly close that every-thing else seemed so very cold in the silence that followed. And so he reached for her, to hold on to her and keep himself warm.

"No," he whispered back. "Call me 'northern boy.'"

"I can't today."

"Of course you can," he murmured. "This is a dream. We can do anything."

"I wish it were, Dreadaeleon."

A long sigh. Warm, humid, ugly. And her voice was suddenly too real.

"But I need you to get up now."

Dreadaeleon blinked and suddenly realized that his eyes hadn't been closed. He hadn't been asleep. That became abundantly obvious once he tried to rise and felt his body protest. Muscles stiffened, skin tingled as he hauled himself out of the comforting numbness of the silken sheets.

Around him, at the corners of his eyes, the golden pillars and empty seats faded from view as wispy tendrils of broodvine smoke sighed out of his nostrils.

He couldn't remember when he had even lit up a seed, much less when he had succumbed to the dream the broodvine created. The Venarium had warnings about this: Broodvine addiction had sent enough wizards into hallucinatory madness to warrant the extreme cost and difficulty of acquiring the seed in the first place.

Mind-altering substances were particularly dangerous to altered minds, after all.

Dangerous for lesser wizards, anyway, Dreadaeleon thought.

For they *were* lesser, the ones who had disappeared into their own dreams and become gibbering lunatics. He was stronger. He controlled the substance. And he knew this anytime he looked into her eyes and whispered her name.

"Liaja."

Because anytime he did, he saw in her eyes, felt in her fingers, a great need. A hunger, a desperation only he could satisfy. A lesser wizard could not.

And just as he knew her hungers, he knew her despairs. And when he looked into her frown, those honest lips unable to hide her fear, he knew why she had stirred him.

"They're back, I assume?" he asked, voice croaking.

She nodded. He sighed, leaned forward, and clutched the back of his pounding head. His hair felt greasy; when had he washed last? He could have sworn he had just emerged from a splendid tub of marble and brass moments ago.

"Which?" he groaned.

"The Karnerians this time," Liaja replied.

"How many?"

"Three."

"Three?" His eyes flashed. A burst of crimson light swallowed iris, pupil, and white. "You woke me up for *three*?"

Her lips pursed. "You promised."

You did, old man, he reminded himself. *Stupid to do it in the first place, but there it is.*

And so he sighed, ignoring the groan of his body as he disentangled himself from the sheets and scavenged up his discarded trousers. He hauled them up over his legs, secured them lazily, and walked to the jug of water on the nearby nightstand.

"Shouldn't you hurry?" Liaja asked, watching him all but ooze across the elegant room. "Or at least dress more?"

"We've been through this at least a dozen times already," Dreadae-leon replied, pouring himself a cup. "They know I'm here and they know what I can do to them." He guzzled the water, tossed the cup on the floor. "If they want to continue throwing their lives away, they can damn well do it at my leisure."

Liaja looked away, pulled her robe a little tighter about her body. "I wish you could find another way to deal with them."

"As do I, I swear," he replied. "But they're idiot barknecks who bark at an invisible man in the sky. Who could reason with that?"

At this she fixed him with a glare. "I also wish you wouldn't talk that way about the gods. It's not right to go blaspheming so freely." She shuddered, looked out the window. "Especially when it comes to Karnerians."

He walked to her side and took her gently by the chin. "Karnerian, Sainite, Khovura, or Jackal. So long as I'm here, you'll never have to worry about them again."

And the look she offered in return made him realize just how cold the morning was.

"Worry is in abundance lately," she replied. "How could I, in good conscience, keep it all for myself?"

He rolled his eyes.

Poets.

Without saying anything further, he slid the paper-and-wood door to their room open and stalked out into the hall of the bathhouse. Once this hall had been filled with steam, giggles from the girls mingling with the breathy slavering of their wealthy clients. Today, though, the only things emerging from the doors were the girls' unpainted scowls.

As though it were somehow *his* fault that business had dried up.

They did not debate this, of course. They slid back behind their paper doors as he walked past. And the opinions of prostitutes were low on the list of trifles that plagued him. More pressing ones awaited him as he emerged from the bathhouse into the bright light of the city square.

This had once been a charming little area catering to those nobles and merchants too wealthy for street prostitutes but too poor to have their own personal ones. Once. Its neatly trimmed hedges and fig trees had been stripped bare, and small shanties dotted the square.

Dirty, tired faces peered out from those shanties: refugees who wore fear and reverence plain in their eyes, at once terrified of and grateful for his presence.

And who could blame them? In a city as war-torn as Cier'Djaal, the only places where soldiers feared to tread were the places where wizards slept.

"Dreadaeleon Arethenes!"

Most soldiers, anyway.

Dreadaeleon stepped forward, shielding his eyes against the glare of the morning as he did. Soon enough, their uniforms pristine against the grime and dust of the shanties, the Karnerians came into focus.

Three of them, as Liaja had said, standing well away from him and armed with nothing but a scroll. That was new. But thus far, all the spears and shields they had brought against him had produced nothing more than corpses and molten metal.

He slowly raised his arms, spreading them half in invitation, half in challenge. His ribs showed through his skin. He couldn't remember the last time he had eaten.

"Sirs," he said flatly, "you have business with me?"

They exchanged nervous looks before the one in the lead approached. He removed his helmet, revealing a youthful, narrow face.

"Dreadaeleon Arethenes," he repeated in a quavering voice. "Your crimes, too numerous to commit to paper, have forced this meeting. By order of the High Command of the Karnerian Occupying Force, you are hereby commanded to surrender to atone for your crimes."

Atone, he reflected bitterly. As though the people huddled around here, the people *he* had saved, were not just an inconvenience to brutes trying to kill each other, but some sin that he should answer to an imaginary god for.

"I see," he said. He looked at the scroll in the Karnerian's hands. "That is a hefty piece of parchment, sir. Does it perhaps list how many of your compatriots I have killed for threatening this bathhouse?"

The Karnerian stared at him flatly a moment. "It does."

"And how many is that?" Dreadaeleon asked.

Another moment of hesitation. "Eight."

"Eight," he repeated. "And is that list big enough to note how many Sainites I have killed, as well?" His smile was bleak and humorless. "Just so I'm not accused of favoritism."

"Seven," the Karnerian growled.

The smile faded and Dreadaeleon's voice went hard. "And is there any room left on that scroll to tell you how I killed them?"

The Karnerian did not answer. Dreadaeleon felt his eyes flash, spoke his next words through clenched teeth.

"Say it."

"Electrocution," the Karnerian replied, slowly at first, "incineration, decapitation, freezing, shattering...and crushing."

Dreadaeleon was silent for a moment. He let those impressive words hang in the air. For the soldiers threatening him, for the refugees cowering behind him, for the girls who scorned him.

Half-naked, unwashed, underfed, and alone, Dreadaeleon stood still and silent, the most dangerous man in Cier'Djaal that morning.

"Then tell me, with all that death, what made you think you could get the drop on me with the pathetic disguises you're wearing"—he spit the next word—"*concomitant?*"

All three recoiled as if struck. The lead one stepped up to answer, but Dreadaeleon's eyes were on the two at his sides. Just beneath their helmets, he could make out lips twitching, eyes flashing red.

"The fuck do you mean?" the lead Karnerian demanded.

"Please," Dreadaeleon said with a sneer. "Vulgarity sounds as natural coming from a wizard's mouth as poetry does coming from a pig's. Have some dignity and drop this charade."

"What evidence do you have to—"

"Plenty," Dreadaeleon interrupted. "For one, the Karnerians don't have a High Command of Occupiers, they have a Holy Order of Libera-tors." He pointed to the two other Karnerians. "For two, your two silent companions have been casting the spell to uphold this pathetic glamer the whole time. And finally, your face looks remarkably like that of the soldier who came to make these very same demands to me two days ago."

He narrowed his eyes to thin, burning slits.

"Right before I performed items one through three on that list."

The Karnerian cringed and exchanged brief glances with his com-panions before his eyes began to glow an eerie crimson.

Suddenly his body shimmered and became transparent as light bent around him. The dark-skinned features of a Karnerian soldier faded, replaced by the dark skin of a Djaalic. The black armor twisted and dis-sipated, revealing a slender body in a clean brown coat.

A glamer. A simple bending of light and shadow to make something appear that wasn't there. Even without the idiotic oversights of their disguises, such a feat of magic gave off so much energy he would have sensed it a mile away.

His fellows followed suit, shedding their disguises like shadows in sunlight. They slowly pulled their coats aside to reveal tomes attached to their hips by thin bronze chains.

Spellbooks, Dreadaeleon noted. Thin, with only a hundred pages or so, their bindings without creases and their chains clean and shining. So unlike his own book back in Liaja's room, beaten and dust-covered and—

His eyes snapped wide at the realization.

"Apprentices?" he spit. "They sent *apprentices* for me?"

"You refused to answer the Venarium's summons," said the lead man—more a boy, really, trying to summon up a reasonable facsimile of authority. "This was the only way."

"I have nothing to answer for." Dreadaeleon sneered, sweeping his gaze across the three, each one as young and callow as the last. "Not to apprentices, at least."

"Apprentice or Librarian, concomitant or Lector," another of them said, stepping forward, "we all swore the same oaths to the same laws. The Venarium's authority over magic is absolute."

"Not over me."

"*No one* is exempt," the third apprentice snarled. "You violated our most sacred law. You turned Venarie upon foreign powers." He gestured to the shanties and the beggars therein. "*This* is not what it means to be a wizard. You involved yourself with this war and so involved us all. The Lectors demand answers."

"Then give them this one." Dreadaeleon drew in a deep breath, closed his eyes. When they opened again, his power flooded out in bright-crimson rivulets. "If the Venarium has words to trade with me, they can do so without petty disguises and they had *damn* well better bring more than three."

He breathed out. Within him something welled up, some terrible fever-heat that he clenched within his throat and loosed from between his teeth. The barest hint of his power, of what boiled within him, and he saw the apprentices shrink away.

He thought that would end it. He saw the calculations working upon their faces as they mentally compared their own strength to his. He saw the despair tug at their lips as they found themselves lacking.

What he did not see was their retreat. Just as he did not see why they had bothered putting up such a flimsy illusion to disguise themselves.

Not until the lead one spoke.

"We did."

He caught it then, subtle as a breeze on a summer's day: a slight change of temperature, a gentle pressure upon his temple. His left temple.

He whirled, saw the flash of crimson eyes, the crackle of electricity upon outthrust fingers as a fourth apprentice standing high atop a nearby roof shouted a word that was painful to hear and split the sky apart.

It took only a moment for the bolt of electricity to reach him. But Dreadaeleon needed only a moment to recognize the weakness in the spell and to step exactly half a pace to the right and let the wild electricity go flying past him to strike the cobblestones and sputter out.

Undisciplined stance, Dreadaeleon noted, glancing up at the apprentice. *Hasty chant.* He reached a hand up. *Unsteady fingers.* He felt the air ripple between his fingers. *No control.*

"And this is what they sent against me?" Dreadaeleon thrust his hand out and watched the sky tremble, an unseen force snaking up to the rooftop. "Who the *hell* do you think you're dealing with?"

He snapped his hand shut and saw the apprentice buckle as an invisible vise closed around him.

He snapped his arm back and the apprentice came with it, hauled off his feet, off the roof, onto the ground, and across the cobblestones. The unseen force tore the boy across the cobblestones, screaming to his companions for aid and leaving bloodied smears where he struck.

To their credit, the noise that came out of their mouths *might* have been a cry of concern. Dreadaeleon couldn't tell: It was hard to hear over the sound of a frail, coat-clad body caroming off a lamppost and skidding to a halt upon the cobblestones.

The pressure left him in a long, slow breath and he knew the flicker of Venarie within the apprentice had gone out.

Stupid, he cursed himself. *If you had any control, you wouldn't have killed him.* He shook his head. *No. NO. It's their fault. The Venarium sent children to fight me. Weak children. Stupid children!*

And children who, apparently, could not take a hint when it lay broken and bloodied on the stones before them.

He felt the spell forming before a word had left their lips. He whirled on them, saw the lead one whispering a chant behind his fellows, who stood before him with their hands outstretched and eyes alight with expelled Venarie.

Dreadaeleon's snarl twisted on his lips and became a word of power. He thrust his hands out, heat boiling behind his palms.

And then he showed them why the Venarium was right to fear him.

In a great, cackling torrent, the fire came. It sprang from his hands like a living thing, reaching across the square to grasp at the apprentices with red-hot fingers. It found instead the shimmering air of an invisible barrier as the two boys spoke louder, intensifying their wards against the flames.

They were disciplined, Dreadaeleon recognized: studied all the right books on wards, listened to their masters' lectures on defensive magic, knew how to hold back flame for a time. He almost hated to teach them that discipline could take one only so far.

But harsh lessons taught best.

He spoke his word louder and the flame responded with a peal of crackling laughter. A torrent became a pillar, a great serpent of flame that drove against the apprentices' wards, forcing them back a step, then another. Their faces contorted with the effort of holding back the flame. Then there was that fleeting moment of recognition, that single horrified breath when they opened their eyes and knew they had nothing left to give.

Then there was only the flame sweeping over them.

He wasn't sure what they felt at the end. The air being burned from their lungs, perhaps, or maybe the reek of their own fat popping and sizzling. Or maybe they just went from boys to the blackened chunks smoldering on the ground too quickly to feel anything.

Stupid, stupid, stupid, he cursed them, the Venarium, and himself.

And when it came to the final apprentice, standing over the bodies of his companions and trying desperately not to look, he had no more curses left to give.

A final word escaped the boy's lips. His hands thrust skyward. The light bent between his hands, forming a bright column of red that shot into the sky. Dreadaeleon prepared himself, awaiting the fire that would inevitably follow. Yet only after a few moments of nothing happening did he realize what had just occurred.

"A signal?" Dreadaeleon asked. "Why? Why the hell would you call *more* of your fellows here?" He gestured to the corpses staining the cobblestones. "Why do you let the Venarium *use* you like this?"

"We all knew the risks when we volunteered," the apprentice replied. His duty fulfilled, his spell cast, he allowed the pain to show in the clenching of his teeth and the tears in his eyes.

"Volunteered?" Dreadaeleon's face screwed up in a failure to comprehend. "Why?"

"We are the Venarium, heretic," the apprentice replied with a coldness that belonged to a much older man. "We all have our duties."

Dreadaeleon had no response to that. A response would have required a presence of mind that was suddenly robbed from him as he felt the distinct sensation of his head cracking open.

Pressure, viselike and unrelenting, bore down on him, felt in his very bones. He felt feverish, then frigid, fluctuating back and forth. He felt it first from behind, then from above, then all around.

And then he saw them.

On the rooftops, in the mouths of alleys, at the gate leading to the square they appeared. Tall, stately, clad in long brown coats, cleaned and buttoned all the way up. Their collars were drawn up around their faces, obscuring everything but the cool, passionless eyes through which they surveyed him.

Librarians. The special agents through which the Venarium's will was done. At least a dozen of them, all watching him, unmoving, unblinking.

He suddenly felt aware of the chill across his naked torso, of the tremble in his knees, of the quaking in his hand as he swung two outthrust fingers from person to person, electricity dancing upon their tips. They did not so much as blink at his threat, nor did they make so much as a move to intercept him.

"Do not think such a thuggish display will move us."

A voice, every word precisely pronounced and piercingly clear, came with the sound of boot steps upon cobblestones. Flanked by a pair of Librarians, a man emerged from the square's gate. Beneath his clean black robes, not a hairbreadth of flesh was visible but a face, harshly angular, hard-eyed, and painfully familiar.

"The Venarium frowns on such coarse displays of power," Lector Annis said, folding his hands behind his back and regarding Dreadaeleon coldly. "But we are far too old and far too wise to be intimidated by mere fire."

"Perhaps if your masters taught the value of intimidation, you would not be down three apprentices," Dreadaeleon replied.

"Do not attempt to assign blame to me for your crimes, concomitant," he said. "Though perhaps it was my mistake to assume you would respect the authority of the Venarium, considering your conduct."

"I have done nothing but—"

"Violation of the Sovereign Tower Treaty," Annis interrupted sharply. "Invocation of Venarium Law under False Pretenses, Involvement with Foreign Powers of a Military Nature, Unregulated Use of Venarie within a City." He glanced down at the smoldering corpses of the apprentices. "Murder."

"They didn't have to fight," Dreadaeleon replied, voice cracking.

"Their duty was to assess your power that we might better understand how to deal with a renegade of your particular status." Annis sneered, glancing Dreadaeleon over disdainfully. "And we witnessed nothing more than a display of savagery. How you have not burned this city to the ground in your recklessness is nothing short of astonishing."

"Fine, then!" Dreadaeleon forced his voice into a cackle, threw his hands out wide. Flames leapt to his hands, pyres forming upon his palms. "If your assessment is complete, then come and test it! Let's add a few more verses to my litany of charges!"

He saw the twitch on Annis's face, a crack in the perfect porcelain of his composure that indicated he was sorely tempted to do just that. The Lector raised a single gloved hand to shoulder level.

"That," he said softly, "will not be necessary."

He snapped his fingers. From behind him another Librarian came out. Or rather another Librarian was pulled out, hauled by the chain leash wrapped around his hands and the horrible thing that was attached to it.

Dreadaeleon thought of it as a thing for, try as he might, he could not rack his brain for a word that would do such an aberration justice.

To look at it, one would think it a dog of some kind: four legs, a thin torso, a square head, and something resembling a snout. But as it drew out into the square, he could see that it was without fur, its body instead wrapped in thick ribbons of parchment with arcane sigils inscribed upon them. But only when it came into the daylight did all descriptions fail.

Between the sheaves of parchment was moist, quivering flesh. Flesh that was not its own. Rather, it seemed composed of many different kinds of flesh in many different pieces. Dreadaeleon saw tongues lolling, livers squirming, genitalia flopping; all long dismembered from whatever poor fools they had come from, all glistening like new in a shifting, heaving, twitching mockery of a living thing.

It came to a halt beside Annis, sat obediently like a hound as the Lector leaned down and placed a hand upon its head. His eyes flashed open, bright crimson, as he whispered a single word.

"Go."

And it obeyed.

Its voice was something between a warble and a thick sucking sound, its appendages flabby and slapping as it bounded across the cobblestones toward Dreadaeleon. It had no eyes that he could see. Yet he knew it was looking at him, just as he knew that its eerie cry was for him and him alone.

Without thinking he thrust his hands out. The flames upon his fingers became sheets of red, fanning out over the thing and engulfing it.

For all of two breaths.

It came leaping out of the fire, unscathed, unburned, glistening and wet as a newborn. It picked up speed, continuing its rush, its eerie cry reaching a crescendo as it closed the distance.

And Dreadaeleon was running.

What few refugees had dared stay when the magic had started flying now turned and fled screaming, trying to get out of the way as Dreadaeleon charged down an alley, and then another, and another, trying to lose the thing.

Not fair, he thought with what mental capacity was not currently overwhelmed by fear. *Not fair, not fair, not fair, NOT FAIR.*

That thing was immune! To fire? To magic? It didn't matter, *nothing* should be immune.

He could still feel the pressure on his temples, even as he twisted down each alley. He could still sense magic, even far away from the Librarians. That thing had its own Venarie, its own power, wild and twisting and clashing off it and barely held together with its parchment wrappings.

The sound of its call grew loud in his ears and what energy he had left for thought was quickly subsumed by terror as he rounded another alley and came to a dead end. The wall of a house with a tall window loomed up before him. He whirled and saw the thing bounding toward him, warbling and wailing.

Two fingers up, unsteady and trembling. A word on his lips, weak and stuttering. A bolt of lightning sprang forth, jagged and shrieking toward its target. It struck the thing as it leapt into the air. Electricity crackled off its flesh-and-paper body, leaving it unscathed and hurtling toward Dreadaeleon.

It struck him in the chest, bearing him backward and through the window. Glass shattered and tore at his bare flesh as it bore him to the floor. Someone was screaming, running from whatever room he had ended up in. He didn't know which. He didn't know who that was. He didn't know what was happening.

Not until much later, when he felt the weight of the manacles around his wrists, the stifling heat of the gag across his mouth, the chill of the cobblestones as a pair of Librarians dropped him at a pair of well-polished boots.

"Dreadaeleon Arethenes," Lector Annis said softly, "by order of the Venarium, you are under arrest."

FOUR

LEARNING TO DROWN

It was a peculiar feeling to be walking among people who would eagerly plant a piece of steel in one's neck for a few pieces of gold.

Not that Lenk had never walked among people who wanted to kill him, but their motives tended to be a little more financially independent. Of course, he supposed, any one of the people walking along the docks might have reason to kill him besides the bounty—vengeance for the many, *many* people whose deaths he had likely caused when the war in Cier'Djaal erupted, for example.

But if no one was stepping forward to demand that, he wasn't about to compel them.

For as detailed as the wanted posters had been, they hadn't been detailed enough to account for what he might look like with no hair. And when he walked among them, bald and dressed in the shabby clothes of a merchant, his sword bundled up and hidden in a basket full of branches on his back, the people of the tiny village of Gurau seemed to pay no more attention to him than they would to any other pale, dirty fellow with too little hair.

But even as much as his northern skin made him stand out, far more attention was offered to the woman walking beside him.

Her notched ears were hidden beneath the dirty hat on her head, but her pale flesh—and so much of it on display from her hunter's leathers—drew more than a few stares.

Yet somehow, for all the fishermen and washerwomen who stared, she only ever got irritated when she sensed his eyes upon her.

"The hell are you looking at?" Kataria growled.

The first words she had said to him since they had left the safe house, and they came out on flecks of spittle. Angry as they were, they were better than silence.

But he was content to shake his head, look away, and let the silence return. Because even that was better than telling her that he was looking at her clean skin and dirty leathers and wondering where she had gone and why he had spent six days without a word from her.

She had her reasons, he was sure.

He wasn't about to compel them.

The farmers of Gurau had risen with the dawn and been long in the fields. Those who remained behind were the fishermen. Both had been prosperous enough for the village to thrive as a trading hub and expand over the shores and onto the Lyre River to better accommodate the traders who plied up and down the clear blue waters.

A place like this was where he would have liked to settle down, before everything had happened: idyllic, peaceful, full of hardworking people who hadn't seen a sword in their lives. It was some cruel god—or one with a solid sense of irony—who would show him such a place only in passing as he walked down the docks to the man at the end, the man who would put him back on the path to bloodshed.

At the edge of the docks sprawling over the Lyre, Sheffu stood beneath a canopy tent set up for the comfort of traders. Yet only a few people milled around, fussing over various wares. Amid the fisherfolk in their shabby garb, Sheffu fit right in.

Which, Lenk thought, must be a little insulting. After all, even if he was a saccarii, Sheffu was also one of the ruling fashas of Cier'Djaal.

His threadbare robe was a match for the tattered silk veil he wore around his face, a garment that would have looked shabby even on one of the people of Gurau, let alone compared to the opulent robes and jewels normally worn by fashas. But Sheffu spent his fortunes on other pursuits.

Pursuits, Lenk knew as he caught the fasha's gaze, that he was about to become a part of.

"You are late." Sheffu cast a wary gaze around the docks as Lenk and Kataria approached. "I instructed you to arrive before dawn. The fishermen have already risen and I have no desire to draw the attention of strangers."

"Anyone who shows you attention will quickly realize the same thing

I did," Kataria muttered. "You're a lunatic saccarii with paranoid delusions of demons."

Sheffu shot a glare at her, then looked to Lenk as if he would reprimand her. He merely shrugged.

She was right, after all: Nothing about clandestine meetings between a fasha and a pair of northerners in a fishing village over the possibility of demons returning to the world sounded particularly sane.

But then again, Lenk had met those demons.

"I did not smuggle you out of Cier'Djaal in exchange for sarcasm," Sheffu hissed. "I did not expend the last of my fortune to be branded a lunatic. You wish to see proof of demons?" He gestured in the general direction of Cier'Djaal. "Look at the hell I have plucked you from. Look at the ruin this city has become. Khoth-Kapira's hand is in it. I know this."

Lenk heard a bemused chuckle in his ear. He saw Mocca at the corner of his eye, but he did not look. No one else could see him and it wouldn't do for him to go staring at the empty air. After all, *he* wasn't the crazy one here.

"So you say," Lenk said, rubbing his eyes. "And you say that you need me to help you prove it. Both of those statements sound insane to me, but you're the one paying, so let's just get on with it."

Sheffu regarded him coldly, clearly not pleased with his lack of enthusiasm. Yet he seemed to consider this enough, anyway. He beckoned the two of them beneath the tent to a nearby crate. He produced a scroll from the sleeve of his robe, unfurled it atop the crate, and hunched conspiratorially over it, gesturing for Lenk to join him.

A map of the region, he saw: the blue scars of the Lyre's tributaries twisting through the sands of the Vhehanna Desert. Yet there were no indications of cities or settlements. Even Cier'Djaal was not on it.

"An old map, charted long before mortals raised their first houses. We are here," Sheffu said, gesturing vaguely to a patch around the desert. "In ancient times this was nothing but dust. There was no need for the people to seek the bounty of the river. They had everything they needed *here*."

He slid his hand across the map, tracing the length of the Lyre to a drawing of enormous spires reaching out of what looked like a thick forest. Each one was carved into the image of a rearing serpent, eyes ablaze and fanged mouth gaping.

"Rhuul Khaas, the Serpent Throne," Sheffu whispered. "The first and last bastion of Khoth-Kapira. Its many subjects sweat and bled to erect statues of their God-King. Its countless cities were erected in glory to a crazed tyrant. Many things wrought by his hand were lost there." He tapped the parchment. "This map was one of the few things that was not.

"I spent no inconsiderable fortune to acquire it," Sheffu continued. "And it will be what will lead us to the ruin of Khoth-Kapira's ambition, that we might learn what brought him low and how to prevent his return." He circled a finger around the spires. "And whatever secrets he had, we will find them here, in the Forbidden East."

Lenk heard a chuckle in his ear. Mocca's voice was as airy and passing as a breeze. "We actually called it something else back then. Not so many people would be tempted to settle in a place called 'the Forbidden East.'"

"But it *did* exist?" Lenk muttered to his unseen companion.

"It did," Sheffu said, thinking the words had been meant for him, "it does. And that is where you must go."

"Right." Lenk nodded. "And what, exactly, do you think we'll find there?"

"A demon's work is never exact," Sheffu replied. "They are shaped by sins we have yet to name. To know one's secrets is to know one's mind, to know one's mind—"

"So you don't know?"

Sheffu remained silent for a moment. "The legends are...muddled."

A long, weary sigh escaped Lenk. "Of course they are. If they were useful, we'd call them something else, wouldn't we?"

Sheffu glared at him for a moment. "Only fragments of tales survived the fall of Rhuul Khaas. But they all spoke of Khoth-Kapira's hubris, his need for control...his pride."

Kataria's ears twitched. "Sorry, do I hear a point to this or was that just you breathing hard?"

"Of all his creations, his artifices, his slaves, he valued one thing above all else," Sheffu continued, ignoring her. "Books. Nothing endured longer than the written word. You have seen one of his works, the book called His Word."

Lenk nodded, recalling an immense, pristine tome he had seen back in Cier'Djaal. A tome said to contain the last words of Khoth-Kapira. Or so Sheffu claimed.

"Books." Kataria all but collapsed with the force of her groan. "Why is it always books with demons?"

"They understand what mortals always failed to," Sheffu replied. "Nothing in this world is real until it is written down. And all that he wrote, he entombed in Rhuul Khaas, in a place he called *Thafun Mokai*. The Library of the Learned."

"That's what you want me to find?" Lenk asked. "A library?"

"Anything that we can use against him, we will find there."

"What, are you expecting me to find his diary so you can embarrass him to death?"

Sheffu remained silent for a moment. "Tell me, Lenk, what harms a demon?"

The fasha turned his stare to the young man. And the young man simply stared back before speaking a single word. "Memory."

"Indeed. The only pain they feel is the knowledge that they were once not so twisted with sin." Sheffu rolled up the map, thrust it toward Lenk. "The Library of the Learned contains all of Khoth-Kapira's memory. If we hope to stop him, we must find it."

"Stop me from what, exactly?" Mocca's voice spoke beside Lenk's ear, before making a tsking sound. "Ah, yes, I forgot. My work is never exact. Convenient, that."

"What makes you so sure?" Lenk asked, doing his best to ignore the phantom voice. "Not to second-guess this"—Lenk pointedly omitted the word *insane*—"plan, but going to a mythical place to find something that might not exist doesn't sound easy."

"No?" Sheffu's laugh was black beneath his veil. "Well, perhaps if it is too hard, you can go back to Cier'Djaal, yes? Find a nice little home, tend to the hearth, and wait for someone to gut you and drag you through the streets by your innards?" He glanced at Kataria. "Bring her along, maybe. Hell, perhaps I'll come, too. Everyone you ever spoke to can die along with you by the sin of association."

"Dramatic, isn't he?" Mocca hummed.

Sheffu apparently saw the ire spark across the northerners' faces, for he held up a hand for peace.

"If I speak harshly it is because our circumstances are harsh," the fasha said. "And if my aim seems like it is to terrify, be assured, I merely speak the truth. Whatever hell our city might be in now has Khoth-Kapira's hand in it, and whatever he has planned will make this war seem like afternoon tea."

"You expect me to do it for Cier'Djaal, then?" Lenk asked.

"No," Sheffu said. "I expect you to do it for Farlan Sandish."

"Far…" Lenk blinked. "Who?"

Another scroll slid out of Sheffu's sleeve. With a snap of his wrist, he unfurled it and handed it to Lenk. "An immigrant from Nivoire. Arrived in Cier'Djaal two years ago, owns a little rice paddy at the very edge of the Green Belt. Here's a copy of his deed, his writ of immigrant citizenship, and his license to sell rice. Take it. I have more."

"And he fits into this because…"

"Because he's you," Sheffu said. "Or who you will be, once you complete this deed." Beneath the veil, the barest ghost of a smile could be seen. "This is your new life."

Just like that. A few words and this no longer seemed so insane, so futile. The thought of chasing down a library, a book, whatever Sheffu wanted, that seemed no more real. But the words on this paper, the name on this deed, that seemed real.

Farlan Sandish.

His new life.

"Your journey will not be easy," Sheffu said. "The Forbidden East cuts through the tribelands. Many clans of tulwar and war parties of shicts stand between you and Rhuul Khaas. It will take many days of travel and much…"

Sheffu was still talking. Lenk knew this, but he didn't see a need to listen much. He knew this monologue. It had come out of a hundred mouths of a hundred men who had offered him the same thing a hundred times.

If only he would pick up his sword one more time. If only he would go on this one last adventure. If only he would kill just this one more time.

Somehow it always came down to that. The names changed, the foes changed, the promises changed. But the request was always the same, the way was always the same.

Always blood. Always the sword.

"Fascinating, isn't it?"

Mocca's voice—uncomfortably close—cut Lenk like a blade. For the first time, he dared look at the man in white. Funny; he knew that Mocca was nothing more than air and light, yet in that moment, he looked so very burdened.

"Listen to him talk." Mocca gestured to Sheffu, who was now going over some route on the map that Kataria seemed to be paying cursory attention to. "He invents all these vague reasons: instincts, theories, a hand he senses. And he thinks these reasons fit to make a man to throw his life away."

He turned to Lenk and, at that moment, his stare was something hard and sharp.

"Are his promises enough for you?" he asked. "Are you willing to throw your life away for a name?"

"I have no choice," Lenk whispered, so softly as to not be heard by anyone else but the man meant to hear him.

"Then," Mocca replied, "what life do you have to offer?"

The wind picked up, carrying the reek of the river that stung Lenk's eyes. He blinked. When he opened them, Mocca was gone, and he was aware of two pairs of eyes on him, neither of them happy. Though, as usual, Kataria's glare mustered just a bit more fury.

"Sorry, what?" he asked.

"Are you listening to this…this…" Kataria turned her scowl on Sheffu and snorted. "How the hell is anyone supposed to insult you if you won't show your ugly face, you fucking reptile?"

"What's going on?"

"You weren't listening." Kataria flung the accusation as she whirled on him. "You weren't even fucking listening. He's bringing in a fucking bug and you just sat there and you weren't even listening."

"He is not a bug," Sheffu protested. "The tribelands between here and the Rhuul Khaas are treacherous, fraught with creatures that have no love for humans. A guide was required to bring you through the shicts and—"

"*I'm* a shict," Kataria snarled. "Am I not good enough to get us through it? Am *I* a 'creature'?"

"Shicts *and* tulwar," Sheffu continued over her. "The guide I hired has a solid reputation for successful negotiations with *every* tribe east of here."

"You hired a fucking *bug*," Kataria snarled. "You'd take a *bug* over me."

"Who?" Lenk shook his head. "What *bug*?"

"A customary pardon is requested." A voice, a monotone so flat it could have been an iron struck over Lenk's head, spoke up. "This one is under the impression that the term *bug* is a slur intended to be derogatory in nature for the race of couthi."

The newcomer stood so still, one might have thought him a bunch of laundry strung over a pole, if his robes hadn't been far too fine. He stood a full head and a half taller than any of those assembled, his black garb falling around him like an inky waterfall. Four sleeves accommodated an equal number of limbs: two with large clawed hands, two smaller ones with finer fingers, all of them folded in a polite pose.

As strange as that all was, though, it was the couthi's face—or lack thereof—that drew Lenk's attention. A hood was drawn up over his head and resting across his face was a portrait of lush, rolling landscapes set in a gold frame. The creature inclined this in greeting.

"This one offers the requisite overture of pleasure to introduce himself as Man-Khoo Yun," he said in that unerring monotone. He turned his gaze—if he could, indeed, see from behind that portrait—to Kataria. "Though this one procures adequate offense to risk alienation of a client by noting that he was not informed that a shict would be party to the proceedings."

Lenk's eyes widened in surprise. He looked to Kataria's hat, covering her ears. "How'd you know she was a shict?"

"This one notes the unfortunate by-products of a lifetime of war," Man-Khoo Yun replied, irately as his monotone would allow. "Among them, an instantaneous recognition of one's traditional foe."

"You got something to say, bug," Kataria snarled, "you say it to me and you use less words."

"Forgive me, Man-Khoo Yun," Sheffu said, stepping forward even as Lenk moved to hold Kataria back. "Your reputation as a negotiator with the shictish tribes is well known. I thought you were acclimated to their presence."

"This one notes that *negotiation* is specifically and definitively dissimilar to *association*, esteemed client," Man-Khoo Yun said. "This one would be more inclined toward forgiveness if aforementioned client acknowledged that no acclimation is possible with a race born of perfidy."

"What'd I just say, *bug*?" Kataria growled. "You like big words so much, I've got a few for you, you spider-sucking, goat-fucking—"

"Calm down," Lenk interrupted.

"I'll be plenty calm once I cut him. Shicts and bugs, they—"

"We don't have time for this right now," Lenk hissed, clapping a hand on her shoulder. "And you cutting him isn't going to make anything easier."

She turned on him and the anger ebbed from her eyes. Her mouth hung open wordlessly and something brimmed in her eyes, something wet and glistening with hurt. She snarled, shoved his hand off, pushed past him, and stalked away.

"This one musters adequate humility to annotate this moment as evidence of shictish instability," Man-Khoo Yun spoke. "If so desired, this one volunteers a wealth of subsequent anecdotal evidence as to the accusation."

"If you would be willing," Sheffu spoke to the couthi, though glancing at Lenk, "we may be able to renegotiate our contract as to—"

"She's coming," Lenk said.

Sheffu nodded briefly to Man-Khoo Yun before turning back to Lenk. "Understand," he whispered, "that this is not a mission that can afford complications. If you desire me to fulfill my end of the bargain and give you a new life…"

"Any life I have includes her," Lenk replied simply.

He turned to go to Kataria, only to feel a hand clamp down on his wrist. He looked down, saw Sheffu's sleeve peel back to reveal a thin, flexible wrist, as though no bones were beneath the flesh that shimmered with a scalelike texture.

"There is more to this than just *your* life," Sheffu said, his voice punctuated by a serpentine hiss. "So much more."

Lenk pulled away, feeling a clammy wetness where the saccarii had clutched him.

Of course there was more to this than his life. As though he needed reminding, between the war raging to the west and whatever lay to the east.

Granted, there was something wrong with Sheffu, as there was something wrong with all the race of saccarii. Something that made their bones flexible and turned their tongues pointed and made their limbs shrink back into their bodies. Something that made this quest, however mad, of the utmost importance to them.

Everyone had problems.

Lenk's, at that moment, stood at the edge of the dock.

Kataria was shivering. Or perhaps just trembling with contained fury. Her eyes were cast down at the river, her hat hung low over her head.

He took a step toward her. An airy voice brushed against his ear.

"I wouldn't, if I were you."

An irritating twinge at the back of his neck told him Mocca was right behind him, just as it told him the man—hallucination, whatever—was probably right. But he couldn't take another six days of this. He couldn't take another six breaths.

He had to know.

"Hey," he said, approaching her.

She did not reply. She did not even look up. Her eyes were locked upon the river flowing beneath them. He cleared his throat, rubbed the back of his neck.

"Sorry about that, back there," he said. Her ears pricked up. Encouraged, he continued. "For not listening to you about the couthi."

"Yeah, well," she sighed, rubbing her eyes. "I guess it's my fault."

Relief fluttered across his face like a moth. And as with a moth, it didn't take much for her to reach out and crush it between her fingers.

"My fault for thinking you might be paying attention to something other than yourself."

She finally deigned to look at him, and her eyes shook in their sockets. There was wetness there, nearly boiling over with the heat of her scowl. He found himself matching it, his jaw clenching without his even noticing.

"I said I was sorry," he said forcefully. "You either take that or you don't."

"What am I going to take, Lenk?" she asked. "All you're giving me is empty words."

"Just what the hell am I supposed to do, then? What the hell *did* I do? You've been bristling since dawn and I haven't seen you—or anyone—in six days, so forgive me if I'm a little slow but if I fucked up, I'm going to need you to tell me."

Something changed in her eyes. A little more wetness. A little less fury. She turned away and he felt a stab in his chest. Something told him it would be a mistake to reach out and touch her.

It was that pain in his chest that made him do it anyway.

"Kataria," he said softly, "what happened?"

"How long have I been with you?"

The question came swift as a blow. And as from a blow, he staggered.

"What?" he asked.

"How long?"

"Two years," he said. "Longer."

"Two years." She stared at him now with eyes hard as stone, bereft of tears. "Two years and you're still every bit the stupid, round-eared human I threw away everything for. My people, my tribe, my ways... all for two years. And you."

Her eyes narrowed to thin slits. Fire burned behind them. Her words came like poison.

"Six fucking days go by and you suddenly forget who I am?" She approached him, so close he could feel the heat of her breath. "You want me here, I'm here. You need me here, I'm here. But after two years, don't you ever ask me about something as meager as six days, *Farlan*."

She seemed such a nebulous thing as she turned to stalk away at that moment: a thing of fire and boiling water, shifting and twitching with contained fury. She was hard to hold as he reached out to seize her by the shoulder, hard to even look at.

So hard, in fact, that he didn't even notice her elbow. Not until it smashed upward and into his nose.

The blood flowing from his nose was decidedly less nebulous.

He watched her stalk away from the docks, villagers scurrying out of her way. His nose ached admirably, trying to distract him from the deeper pain welling up in his chest.

And failing.

Still, however numb he was, he was not so desensitized that he couldn't feel the presence of someone behind him.

"Don't," he said, with a quavering voice. "Don't fucking say it, all right?"

"What do you think I'm going to say?"

That was not Mocca's voice. He turned around to see a woman standing before him.

As he was rather embarrassingly used to finding himself the same height as most women, her height struck him. Short, angular, hard: She was like a blade in a black sheath. He would have guessed her to be a warrior of some sort, had it not been for the fine cut of her loose-fitting garb that suggested merchant work.

Her hair was bundled beneath a broad-brimmed hat, beneath which blue eyes glimmered with a genuine—if stiff—smile.

"Because if it's that you shouldn't have tried to grab her, I think you already got that." She held out a white cloth to him. "But I'm not going to apologize for thinking you should clean yourself up."

He took it without a word and began sopping up the blood. The white cloth quickly turned a dark red, and he absently returned it to the woman. She cringed, took it demurely between two fingers, and promptly dropped it over the edge of the docks.

"That's quite a bit," she said. "She must have been pissed."

"Annoyed, maybe, but not pissed," Lenk replied. "When she's pissed, she uses teeth." He coughed. "Sorry."

"About the handkerchief? I can afford more."

"About you having to see..." He made a vague gesture off in Kataria's direction. "That."

The woman followed his gesture, frowning. "Will she be back?"

"Eventually." That word tasted sick with doubt in his mouth. "Before we have to leave, anyway."

"And you're certain being stuck on the river with her will be a good idea?"

He managed a weak smile—or a strong sneer, it was hard to tell. "Is unwanted advice the price of the handkerchief I ruined? I think I'd rather pay in coin."

"You only have to listen to it," she replied with a smirk. "If you don't care for it, you can throw it into the river with the handkerchief. But..."

At her hesitation, he waved her forward. "Go on."

"You're trying to appeal to something that isn't there. She's too used to conflict. And you're too unused to peace." He must have worn his confusion plainly, for she gestured to his shoulder. "If the way you wear that sword is any indication, anyway."

"My sword?" Lenk glanced at the burden on his back, only then remembering he wasn't supposed to have one. "Oh, no. This isn't a sword. This is . . . this . . ." He cleared his throat. "This is the bundle of sticks I carry around. For reasons."

She met his smile with a flat expression. He sighed, adjusted the basket on his back.

"Look, so long as you're doing me favors, maybe you can keep that to yourself. I don't need people knowing about this."

"Why? Are you ashamed of it?"

That question surprised him. Though not quite as much as the answer that tumbled out of his mouth.

"Yes."

"Why?"

"It's not what I want to be comfortable wearing, let alone using. The world's got enough killers without me adding to the pile."

"Are you a killer?"

"I carry a sword, don't I?"

"That's not enough to make you a killer. A sword is merely an extension of a will, not a curse that dictates what you do."

"Sure, everyone thinks that at some point," Lenk replied, suddenly feeling quite tired. "But you carry one of these long enough, you start thinking of it less as a tool or an extension or whatever and more as an answer. And the more you use it, the easier it is to start using that answer for every problem." He glanced over her clothes. "Look, you look more like you could afford to pay someone to hold this iron for you than use it yourself, so I don't blame you, but this thing's a burden."

Whatever mirth had creased her face up to that moment was drained in a breath. Her face fell flat, whatever energy it had held now flooding her eyes. Her stare became a blade unto itself, pinning Lenk where he stood.

"I have seen many swords," she said softly. "And I have seen too many bodies fall beneath them to believe that they were all equal."

Hers was not a harsh voice. Hers was not an imposing figure. Yet there was something in her tone that made Lenk feel a bit colder.

"What kind of merchant did you say you were?" he asked.

"I didn't," she replied. "But as it happens, I'm taking some rice down the river, past Jalaang and into the east." She extended a hand to him. "Shuro."

He took it; her grip was firm, her palm cold. He cleared his throat.

"Sandish. Farlan Sandish," he said. "How far are you taking it?"

"However far they'll pay for sixty pounds. They can't grow anything out past Jalaang."

"Sixty pounds? Won't that take up too much room on the boat?"

"Boat?" Her lips curled up in a bemused smile. "You don't come to the Lyre much, do you, Farlan?"

He thought to ask, but before he could, the dock started to tremble with hundreds of feet. The children came first, a tide of hip-high squealing waifs charging down the docks to the edge. Laborers followed: fishermen with fish on the line, washerwomen with repaired silks, spice merchants, silk dealers, more than a few people taking care to hide whatever it was they planned to hawk. And at the end came the elders, in no particular rush as they ambled after the crowd and left Lenk, befuddled, behind them all.

Before he could ask, Shuro took his hand and smiled. "Come on. It's something of an event here."

"What is?"

She didn't answer as they found their way to the crowd gathered about the edge of the docks, fighting not to fall in as they leaned over and looked downriver. She glanced around, found a stack of crates suitable for climbing, and led him up it. He tried to follow the excited gaze of the crowd, squinting as the sun rose to cast a glare off the river. But even from here, he could see a distant shadow growing steadily larger as it loomed closer.

And within the span of ten breaths, he realized that the vantage point wasn't at all necessary.

It moved slowly on four legs the size of tree trunks, yet with each titanic stride it took, it cleared ten feet through the water. Its hide was a thick shade of green, glittering as the sunlight danced off the water to kiss its colossal body. A broad head bearing night-deep eyes swung precariously with each step.

At a glance—and a glance was not nearly enough to take in the vastness of the thing—Lenk would have sworn it was a moving statue hewn of jade and adorned with obsidian eyes. Yet only as it drew ponderously up beside the docks did he realize that there was not enough stone in the world to compose a beast this vast.

It towered above the dockhouses, tall as three of them stacked atop each other, its massive back adorned with what appeared to be a platform topped by a wooden canopy. From its head, where a mouth should be, eight long green tendrils hung precariously, dipping into the water. It came to a halt, the waves it kicked up sending the docks rattling, and settled on its tremendous limbs with a slow groan.

Almost immediately rope ladders descended from the platform atop its back. People began to disembark, crates and sacks were lowered from great ropes. And the crowd below swarmed up to meet those coming down—hawking wares, asking for news from downriver—until the arrivals and merchants became a continuous swarm off the back of the thing, which seemed quite unperturbed by the commotion.

Of all of its qualities—Lenk called it an it, for he knew not what else to call it—that was what unnerved him: the utter indifference to everything smaller than itself. Did it even notice them, he wondered? It must, to have halted as it had.

"This, for the record, is why it's an event." He suddenly became aware of Shuro at his side, who looked up with a grin. "Even if he didn't bring goods and news, the arrival of the Old Man would be enough to wake the town."

"The Old Man?" He turned to her, agog. "It has a *name*?"

"Well, it seems something that big ought to, right? But this is just one of a few. The river gets a bit too choppy east of Jalaang to accommodate boats, so the Old Men are around to help."

"Where did they come from?" Lenk asked, staring up and forever up.

"No one's quite sure," Shuro said, hopping off the crates. "The Old Man certainly won't tell you, so we all assume it's best to just not ask." She gestured for him to follow as she turned to leave. "They'll want us to load soon."

She had already disappeared into the crowd by the time Lenk made it down. But before he could do the same, he felt a voice brush past his ear.

"Curious, isn't she?"

Mocca's voice slipped past as easy as a breeze. And without thinking, he replied.

"She's pleasant," Lenk said. "And not a hallucination. That's more than I can say for my company of late."

"People come either pleasant or honest. Never both."

"She only just met me. What could she possibly have to lie to me about?"

"You only just met her. How many lies have you told her, Farlan?"

The breeze died along with Mocca's voice. The humid reek of the river seeped into Lenk's clothes, made him roll his shoulder. The sword rolled once and settled back.

Heavy as ever.

FIVE

TIMING

When the seventh day finally came and its pale-blue dawn had turned to a remorseless golden afternoon, Gariath decided that this would be the day that he died.

Not that any god had decreed it; gods were for humans and thus useless. Nor did any fate demand it; fate was how idiots explained their idiocy. Gariath did not believe in gods or fate. He believed in things he could touch.

Such as the empty waterskin he dropped from his hand, watching the very last drop of liquid fall from its lip to be swallowed by hungry sand.

Thirst was a long and painful way to die. Fortunately he had quicker options.

He looked long to the horizon, over the cresting dunes to the sandy ridge. There they stood painted as shadows upon the morning. A little closer today, as they had been creeping closer each day since he had spotted them.

Timid guests. Too shy to come share his company.

He could not see them from so far away. And whenever he came closer to them, they scurried away and hid. But they never bothered to hide their scent. And now, as the breeze changed, he could smell their caution turn to certainty, as if they agreed that this was a good day to kill him.

He turned and stalked back down the dune, to the shallow valley that had served as his camp the night before. No fire had burned; there wasn't enough scrub in the desert for that. No food remained; they had eaten it all two days ago. And now there was no more water.

He could tell it was his campsite only by his companion slumbering upon the ground. And even *he* was difficult to differentiate from a giant rock.

In fairness, Gariath admitted, it was hard to tell the difference between a boulder and a vulgore even when the latter was alert and ambulatory. Two tons and ten feet of red flesh and bone that resembled nothing so much as the fruit of a night of tender and terrifying love-making between a gorilla and a rhinoceros, few people would dare rouse a giant such as this from his slumber.

Few humans, anyway.

Gariath, though, was *Rhega*. Dragonman. Gariath was out of both water and patience, thanks to this creature. And thus it came all too easily that he should raise his broad foot and kick his companion squarely in the back of his head.

"Uh?" Kudj rumbled from his slumber, turning to regard Gariath through squinty eyes. His brow hung heavy, weighed down by the thick horn jutting from his forehead, making it hard to tell if his eyes were open. "Kudj uncertain if squib know this, but society consider it rude to roust by kicking."

"We're out of water," Gariath replied.

Kudj sighed, a great heaving noise, as he clambered to his feet, looming over Gariath and leaning forward to rest tremendous arms on tremendous knuckles. It was little surprise that they should be out by now, Gariath thought. He was far from small himself, and between their combined seventeen feet of girth, they had consumed what little they had brought fairly handily.

"Our guests?" Kudj asked.

"Close today," Gariath said. "Closer than before."

Kudj nodded as though this, too, were inevitable. "Squib see them?"

"Smelled them. They'll attack today."

"Naw." Kudj waved a massive paw of a hand. "Shicts not prefer straightforward confrontations."

"They fear us," Gariath muttered.

Kudj's laughter was decidedly bleak for how loud it was. "Shicts not scared, just efficient. Don't fight unless they have no chance of losing. If squib see them, it because they let squib see them." He looked up at the sweltering sun, squinting. "Maybe wait another day before attacking. But..."

Six days of travel together had been enough to teach Gariath when the vulgore was about to say something stupid. And he knew Kudj was about to say something stupid when he looked over his shoulder, back in the direction they had been walking from all this time.

Back toward Cier'Djaal.

"Oasis town not far from here," Kudj grunted. "Two days. We move fast, make it in one. Shicts not come too close to human towns. We leave now, we maybe even make it by..."

Kudj's voice withered as he turned and met the scowl scarred across his companion's face.

It took quite a bit to make something as big as a vulgore sigh with the kind of defeat that made Kudj's gigantic shoulders slump. But Gariath was nothing if not dedicated.

Four days ago Kudj had proposed turning back. Three days ago Kudj had argued about turning back. Two days ago Kudj had made several bodily threats about what would happen if they didn't turn back. Today Kudj didn't even bother asking.

Just as well; Gariath never felt like explaining.

To him it was simple. Cier'Djaal was a wicked place. Its people consumed each other for gold, stepped over corpses in the street on their way to jobs that made them labor for coppers, ate rotten meat and moldy bread and congratulated themselves on how much better they were for it.

Cier'Djaal was not a city. Cier'Djaal was a disease, an infected wound upon the land whence the human infection spread.

And they—all of them, Lenk and the others—had chosen it over *him*.

He would not go back. He would not even look in the direction for fear that the scent of cowardice and greed would overwhelm him. He never bothered to explain this, either.

How it wasn't obvious to everyone was beyond him.

So he turned away from Kudj and he walked away from him and he did not look back.

"Kudj initially drawn to squib's fearless willingness to leave all comfort behind," the vulgore rumbled. "But Kudj ponders what point is made by wandering out to die in desert."

Gariath's sole reply was a glare cast over his shoulder. Kudj knew the answer, as did anyone with passing knowledge of humans. Though the Karnerians and Sainites might fight each other in Cier'Djaal, it was no place for nonhumans. Kudj sighed, holding up a hand in acknowledgment.

"Kudj flee because Kudj afraid," he said. "Squib not afraid. Why squib go?" He looked out over Gariath's head to the dunes beyond. "Nothing out there. What squib want to find?"

And Gariath stopped. In six days Kudj had never asked that. In six days Gariath had never thought to come up with an answer.

His concerns had always been for what had been behind him: the city and its stench, the humans and their weakness, his companions...

Former companions, he corrected himself, *as weak, as cowardly, as stupid as any other humans.*

He wasn't sure what he had hoped to find out here in the desert. Not gods. Not fate. Nothing but sand stretched before him, rising in great dunes. And somewhere beyond them, someone waited to kill him. Death was all he would find out here.

And behind him there was life. There was water. There was food. There were things to touch, there were people he had once called by name. They all waited back there, in that city.

That city they had chosen over him.

And with that, Gariath knew he could only go forward.

"Squib?" Kudj called after him as he trudged forward. "*Squib!* What Kudj supposed to do now?"

And Gariath had no answer.

Everyone had to choose their own way to die.

⊷ ⸱━━◆━━⸱ ⊶

After it had taken everything else from him, the sun finally took time.

How long, he wondered, had he been trekking through the desert? How long had it been since he left Kudj staring absently at him? An hour? Maybe even another day? Had night passed without his noticing?

Under his own sun, the one in the north that bashfully peeked out from behind storm clouds on occasion, he would have called that impossible. But here, in the desert, the sun was a different creature.

The heat cooked his skull, sent his vision swimming and darkening at the edges. His limbs creaked beneath him as he trudged over dunes and into valleys, muscles burning without water to soothe them. His tongue lolled from his jaws, head swaying precariously on his neck.

The sun here was something constant and avaricious, reaching down to pluck the water from his mouth, the strength from his limbs, leaving him barely enough strength to go on. Yet he did go on, and as if in punishment, the sun left him enough thought to realize that he was alone.

Again.

He had abandoned Kudj.

No. He had enough sense left to deny, at least. *No, Kudj is weak. He would go crawling back to the humans and beg for their scraps.*

The humans.

The anger that suddenly boiled through him made the sun feel chilly in comparison.

He could still see them now, their faces etched in his mind as clearly as they had been when they had rejected him. Their mouths had been flapping, as usual, as the city burned down around their ears. They spoke of retreat, of skulking and hiding and waiting until the war between the humans had passed and they could come out and collect the remains.

He could remember them clearly: the tall one with his scheming eyes, the other tall one with her useless worry, the pointy-eared one with her feckless stupidity, and Lenk...

Lenk, who had met him so long ago, coaxed him away from the graves of his sons to go out and try his hand at living again.

Lenk, who had been the only human to stand against him and had thus earned the right to be called by a name.

Lenk, who had spoken of trying to find a home in that city, that city full of strife and greed where he was not Gariath, not *Rhega*, not even a dragonman. In that city he was an "oid," just one of thousands to have been branded that for the crime of not being human.

And Lenk had chosen that city over him. They all had. They had chosen sickness over strength, cowardice over courage, they had chosen to stay in a world where he had no name. Just a slur.

They had rejected him.

No, no, NO. He roared inside his skull. *They didn't reject you. You rejected them. They were weak, cowards. They would eat the broken meat of that city and drown you in their vomit. They're useless. They always were.*

Better, then, to die out here, under merciless sun, where his bones would be bleached and his skin would melt away to nothing. His death would be clean. Theirs would be rotten and vile.

They will die without you, he told himself.

He told himself this many times as he trekked over the dunes. He told himself this as the sun cooked his thoughts inside his skull. He told himself this as his legs slowly gave out, as the air burned in his lungs, as he swallowed a breath and tasted only sand.

When he finally collapsed to his knees, he could think of nothing else. And so he rode that thought, facedown into the sand and into darkness.

His ear-frill twitched. Someone was speaking.

He knew this and only this. Not what time of day it was, not how long his eyes had been shut, not even if he was still alive.

Someone was speaking. Someone was close. Someone was drawing closer.

Theirs were voices he didn't recognize, full of words that were full of hard edges. But he understood the language, even if he didn't understand the words. He had spilled too much blood not to know the language of killing.

His nostrils quivered. He could smell them: the threat on their breath, the excitement in their sweat, the malice in their steel as knives were drawn. The shadow that fell over him was cold, cold enough to let him know what was going to happen.

He would die here, bleed out on the sand and watch the sun take everything that was left.

That's fine.

He had no delusions about what would have happened out here, no great dreams of finding meaning in the sands. He'd had no intention of doing anything but walking out somewhere quiet and dying alone, even if he hadn't known that when he set out.

He heard a knife being drawn from a sheath, smelled the oil of the leather.

This is where you end.

He felt a hand reach down and take his horns, raising his head to expose his throat.

It was always better this way. They were always cowards. They never deserved you.

He felt his last hot breath leave his mouth as his jaw gaped open. He felt steel brush against the red flesh of his throat.

And they will never know how you died.

And then he felt flesh in his hands.

His claws wrapped around a thin neck before he was even aware of the blood thundering in his veins. A roar tore from his throat before he even knew he had one left. His eyes snapped open before he even remembered he was supposed to be dead.

It appeared, then, that there was something the heat could not take.

It took him only a moment to recognize the creature squirming in his grasp as a shict. Or what he thought was a shict, anyway; this one was dark of skin and hair, unlike the pink one he had left behind. Though this one was growing pinker with each moment Gariath's claw tightened around his throat, it was the shict's bulging eyes that drew his attention.

For in them he saw his onyx scowl, his reptilian snarl, his many, many teeth. He saw himself.

Still alive.

He snarled, hoisting the writhing shict into the air as he clambered to his feet. The effort was monumental, his body begging him to lie down and see if he couldn't convince the shict to have another go at it. But he found it, somewhere within the burning muscle, the will to smash his captive back to the ground, half burying him into the earth with an eruption of sand.

His foot came up and then down like a headsman's ax, finding the shict's spine and near folding him in half with the force. His foe's head jerked sharply upward, eyes still wide, as though he was wondering just how the hell this had happened.

Gariath admitted to some curiosity himself. But no answer was forthcoming from within. His body slumped, muscles failing him, and every breath was agony, but he was still standing, still breathing.

He was alive. Somehow.

And perhaps not for much longer. His ear-frills twitched at the sound of bowstrings creaking. His nostrils flared at the scent of fear and anger. He looked up and beheld shadows painted across the sand.

Shicts. Desert shicts. Ten? Twenty? It was hard to tell their number; his eyes felt as though they were melting out of their sockets. Yet even through darkening vision he could see their eyes, wide and terrified at what he had just done to their companion. And even through swimming head he could hear the sound of their bowstrings being drawn.

An arrow shrieked, bit into his shoulder. He fell to the ground as two more screamed over his head. He found the shict's broken corpse through blurred vision, hauled it out of the sand, and held it up before him. It shook with the impact of two more arrows. Though shicts were meager and he was large: another arrow found his side, another his knee.

Pain racked him anew. A body that had been fitfully slumbering now screamed at being awoken so harshly. He felt each blow shake him, his body begging him to drop the corpse and let the rest of the arrows come.

Not now. His head, baked and broiled as it was, would not listen to his body. *Not this way.* He gritted his teeth, striving to bite back the pain, failing. *I'm not ready.* Another arrow shrieked past, grazed his neck. His blood cooked on his flesh as he screamed out in pain.

"Please!"

Gariath did not believe in gods; none would answer him. Gariath did not believe in fate; whether he lived or died was in no one else's hands. Gariath believed in simple things, things he could touch.

"RUA TONG!"

Though sometimes things he could hear would do just as well.

They came flooding over the dune in a wave, war cries tearing from their lips even as long, killing blades flashed in their hands. Their garb was scant: half robes of orange and red that left the gray muscled flesh and fur bare. Their bodies were lean and fierce. Their faces, simian and wild, were flooded with yellows, reds, and blues bright as any war paint.

They were howling.

They were fearless.

They, Gariath realized, were tulwar.

The line of shicts whirled about to bring their bows against this new-found foe, launching arrow after arrow into the onslaught. Some fell, arrows taken to the throat or heart. Others merely staggered as broadheads found shoulders or knees. None stopped.

They crashed into the shicts with blades flashing, hacking through the hafts of bows, cleaving arms from shoulders, cutting gashes in chests. Blood spattered them, adding to the wild colors that painted their faces. The shicts let out cries of alarm, turning to flee even as the tulwar rushed to chase them and cut them down upon the dunes.

Gariath wanted to laugh. It was all quite funny to him, after all. To have come this far, to have faced the shicts, and still to be alive and alone.

Sometimes life was simply unfair.

But he found he had no breath for laughter. He had no breath left to even stand upright anymore. That brief rush of life that had refused to let him die ebbed away, sending him to his knees and crashing face first into the earth.

He didn't feel the hands around him, turning him onto his back. Nor did he even feel the arm that wrapped around him, propping him up. All he knew was the sensation of cool water dripping down his throat as a skin was forced between his jaws and emptied.

He did not open his eyes until there was no more left to drink. And when he did, he beheld a face riotous with color.

The tulwar's peculiar coloration was no war paint, he knew. The vivid red, blue, and yellow across their faces was in their blood, lighting up in the thick gray knots of flesh of their faces when their fury was up. And this one that loomed over him was vivid indeed, the colors of his face burning brightly through the blood that washed his muzzle.

But it wasn't until he saw the tulwar's eyes, bright yellow and hard with concern, that he knew the name that came to him.

"Daaru," he said.

"The *Rhega* lives, then?" The tulwar's face was split with a broad white smile, fangs glistening. "Good. I would have hated to have wasted an entire skin of water on a corpse."

In another moment Gariath became aware of his position: cradled like an infant by the tulwar. A massive red hand shot up, shoved Daaru away.

"Get off me, you monkey," he snarled as he tried to rise to his feet.

"The *Rhega* lives," Daaru laughed. He made a move to help the dragon-man rise, only to be warned off by a snarl. "If the desert cannot kill you and the shicts cannot kill you, I am starting to wonder what could."

Gariath did not answer that. To speak would be to let Daaru hear the weakness in his voice, to let him know just how close both the desert and the shicts had come. More than that, though, Gariath did not trust his own voice.

Had it really been his that had cried out like a coward's? Had it really been his that had sounded so weak, so terrified, so frail? Was he so afraid that he had screamed out for help rather than die with dignity?

He did not know. And he sure as hell wasn't going to let Daaru be the judge.

"You can walk?" Daaru asked. At Gariath's pointedly firm nod, he grunted. "Our camp is far from here. We had to come a long way to find you."

"Find me?" Gariath asked. That would mean they'd known he was out here. And that could only mean...

"*Squib!*" Like an overlarge puppy, Kudj came loping over the hill on his knuckles, tumbling down the dune to arrive in a spray of sand before Gariath. His grin was broad and toothy. "Kudj feels vindicated in seeking help of traditionally problematic element to see squib alive."

"We came across the vulgore on our way to Shaab Sahaar," the tulwar said. "He pointed us in the direction you went. I'd like to say that it was fate that led us to you." Daaru chuckled. "But you don't really bother covering your tracks."

They were laughing. As if this were a happy occasion. As if he *hadn't* just disgraced himself by crying out for help.

"Shengo!" Daaru cried out to a nearby tulwar. "Grab your pack. We have wounded to tend to before we leave. Tell Haangu to bring up the beasts. We have a ways to go before..."

Daaru's barked orders, the grunted acknowledgments that followed, Kudj's various expressions of joy, went unheard by Gariath. His wounds were tended to, the arrows plucked out and the cuts treated. He was given more water, and food, as well.

And yet he felt no pain, no hunger, no thirst. An uncomfortable numbness had set in, an emptiness that had previously been filled with agony and fear. In its place uncomfortable questions had settled.

Why? Why had he called out? Why had he been afraid to die?

He had no answer.

Soon he was fit enough to walk. Soon they took off toward wherever it was that Daaru wanted them to go. Soon Gariath went with them.

Shamefully still alive.

SIX

RIVERS AND SHADOWS

Salaried contract compels this one to advise you to engage all aural sensibilities for what this one is about to tell you, *shkainai*. There is only one way into the Forbidden East and there are many ways to die in getting there."

Shortly before midnight the members of Sheffu's expedition gathered to speak. In hushed whispers at the edge of the deck, far away from the other passengers, they huddled. Most of them, anyway.

She had not been asked to attend the meeting.

"The city of Jalaang shall be within proximity within one hour. This one has been contracted to acquire additional supplies. Past the city, the Lyre suffers an infestation of river bulls and sailbacks, necessitating transport unorthodox, such as the one we stand upon."

She could hear them, of course. Over the conversations of the other passengers clustered upon the deck, over the murmur of water rippling from a colossal stride. The low rumbling noises of the Old Man beneath her feet couldn't drown them out. Even with her ears tucked beneath her hat, the couthi's jarring monotone rang in her ears like a cracked bell.

And still, his was not the voice that set Kataria's teeth on edge.

"Okay," Lenk said, "that's two. There are more ways to die, I take it?"

She had spent all day avoiding him, lingering at the opposite side of the vast platform upon the Old Man's back. She had tried conversing with other passengers—albeit only a little. She had tried meditation, staring out over the riverbank, even singing at one point.

Somehow she always heard him as clearly as if he were standing right beside her.

"The potential for fatality experiences exponential growth as eastward projection grows." There was the rustle of parchment as Man-Khoo Yun's fine-boned finger prodded at a map. "Desert becomes forest, in which the desired destination resides, the sole passage to which remains a tiny gap in the surrounding mountains. A sufficient amount have died there to earn it the dubious human honor of affixing a foreboding moniker."

"That being?"

"The Gullet."

Lenk sighed. "Of course."

Kataria found herself echoing that sigh. Not for the same reason, of course. Inappropriate sarcasm in response to legitimate danger was fairly expected at this point, but there was only so much of it she could take.

This, she told herself, was why she was avoiding him.

Yeah, she told herself. *That's it*. She closed her eyes. *Coward*.

"The mountains are situated to form a border between breeds of less civil natures than your most humble self, *shkainai*. The deserts to the west are claimed by tulwar clans, while the forests hold qithbands of reprehensible shict tribes. Both claim the Gullet as their own, finding it prosperous hunting ground."

"For game?" Lenk asked.

There was a deliberate pause before Man-Khoo Yun spoke. "Amongst other things." Paper rustled as he rolled up the map. "Research suggests that the uncivil breeds favor conflict with each other before engaging with foreign interference. It remains doubtful that their base natures will suspend in order for them to pursue hostilities with us."

"If we're lucky."

"Fortune, luck, invocations of faith, and fate are irrelevant, *shkainai*," the couthi replied. "Tulwar can be trusted to be hapless and naïve. Shicts can be assured to be vile and perfidious in their pursuit of hostilities."

"You have a problem with shicts."

A statement, rather than a question. A challenge meant to be answered. She found her ears quivering beneath her hat, attentively listening to what the couthi had to say next.

"Disclosure of opinions political and economical violate all non-judgment clauses included in standard guide contracts, *shkainai*. Do not let it trouble you."

"Considering the fact that I travel with a shict, it troubles me. Speak plainly."

Silence followed. In its wake Kataria heard her teeth grinding.

"This one was selected to deal with the shicts," the couthi spoke softly, "because this one gave them everything. Homeland, mate, children, house . . . everything this one had, they took, and left only ash and blood in their wake. This one was selected for this contract because this one knows the shicts. And you do not know a shict, *shkainai*, until you have witnessed their cruelty firsthand."

A pause. Then the couthi spoke.

"But you should know that, should you not, *shkainai*?"

And she felt him. As clearly as she would if he were right next to her.

She felt his eyes drift to her, picking her out of the crowd. She heard his lips part to say something, heard his hot wordless breath. She felt him, heard him, could almost smell sweat forming upon his brow.

Now, she thought. *Do it now. Turn around. Face him.*

Her legs didn't move. Her fingers tightened on the deck's railing. She closed her eyes, pressed her lips tight, did not look at him.

Not as she felt his eyes leave her. Not as she heard his mouth shut without a word. Not as he turned and walked away, until she could hear him no longer.

Not a word.

Not one word had he spoken in her defense. Not so much as a vulgarity thrown at the couthi. He had left without a word and had left her with a silence so deep and so cruel that she could not escape the thought that came next.

What did you expect?

It didn't come from her head. That thought struck her hard in the chest, knocking the wind from her lungs.

You haven't spoken to him since this morning, she told herself. *You haven't seen him in six days. You haven't told him what you've been doing.*

She choked on that last thought.

You haven't told him.

There were a number of reasons why, of course. It would hurt him when he needed her, now wasn't the right time, they were about to head off into certain danger.

And so on.

But these were not thoughts, not words. They were whispers and smoke and lies that left her with every shuddering breath she took. They weren't solid, like the pain in her chest. They weren't warm, like the wetness at the corners of her eyes. They weren't words.

Like the ones she hadn't said.

"Can you hear me, shict?"

Her ears twitched. An unfamiliar voice; not hers, not his.

"Did you hear everything?"

This voice was low, guttural, possessed of a quivering reverberation, each word rattled out of a choked gullet. Each syllable was drawn out, and in the spaces between, there was a dry clicking sound.

"Of course you did. Your misbegotten breed knows how to listen," the voice rasped. "You never rise above your base nature. You cannot suppress your savagery." A black, oily chuckle. "I meant every word."

She turned and saw, at the opposite edge of the deck, Man-Khoo Yun. The couthi stood tall and rigid as a tree, his larger set of hands folded behind him, his smaller set folded in front. She could feel his scowl keenly as any blade and knew that, behind the tastefully framed painting of rolling hills and blue skies he wore over his face, he seethed.

This was his voice. His real voice. Free from its chilling monotone and filled with hate.

"Whatever you've done to fool this human," he hissed in a low voice meant only for her, "I do not believe it. I do not trust you, I do not trust your breed, and I do not have any intention of allowing you to violate the contract."

He made a soft, wet, chittering sound. Her ears folded back on themselves at it.

"We arrive in Jalaang in less than an hour, shict," he hissed. "We depart in another eight. Our contract guarantees that I will see this expedition to its destination. *I* guarantee that if you are there tomorrow, you will regret it."

Regret?

Shicts didn't have a word for regret. She hadn't learned it until she met Lenk. Humans had so many nuances to attach to it—when it was necessary, when it was undesirable, which gods approved and which gods didn't.

She hadn't come to understand all the complexities of regret quite yet. But she knew eight hours was a long time to wait for it.

So, she thought as she strode toward the couthi, reaching for the hilt of the long knife at her belt, she might as well get a head start.

Maybe the couthi saw it. Maybe he didn't. Maybe he would see it only when it was naked in her hand, cutting through that fucking landscape, his fucking head to follow.

She didn't care about humans, couthi, or anything; her sole concern was for the blade in its sheath, soon to be in her hand and soon—*very soon*—to be in someone's face.

Or it would have been her sole concern, if not for the hand that shot out and suddenly clamped upon her wrist.

"Don't do it."

A woman. One she had seen before: that strange, short, slender little thing wrapped in nice black clothes and with cold blue eyes under a broad-brimmed hat. She had scarcely looked as if she could carry a walking stick back on the docks that morning. Yet the force with which she held Kataria's wrist suggested she could do much more than just keep the blade in its sheath.

What had she called herself?

Shuro.

"This doesn't concern you. *Yet*," Kataria snarled through bared teeth. "Though if you don't take your hand off me, I can make time for you."

If the threat affected her, it didn't show in Shuro's impassive blue stare. All the same, she eased her hand off Kataria's wrist. But when the shict moved to pass her, she stepped in front of her, eyes still on her knife.

"You show steel here, you're going to draw eyes," Shuro said.

"No, that won't happen until I start eating his face after I cut it off," Kataria growled.

"And what do you think they'll see?"

"I don't care what—"

"They'll see a couthi—weird, unusual, but *valuable*—being assaulted by a shict—dirty, treacherous, and savage. What do you think they'll do then?"

"I'm *not* dirty!" She winced after saying it, finding her hand drifting to her hat. "You're not supposed to know I'm a shict. That's what the disguise is for."

"A hat is not a disguise." Her eyes drifted down to Kataria's exposed middle. "Particularly when you're wearing shictish clothing. And *particularly* when you go showing shictish fangs whenever you get angry."

Kataria took a step backward. Her face twitched, canines bare. "You think I didn't notice? You think I don't see the way they stare, hear what they say?" She jabbed a thumb to her chest. "I'm not going to change who I am for them. Let them know. Let them see. I don't care."

"You should," Shuro shot back.

"Why should I?" She narrowed her eyes upon Shuro. "Why should you?"

The woman remained silent for the moment, lowering her face and regarding Kataria out of the corners of her eyes. "Would you like me to ask why it matters what they say? Why you're so eager to spill blood?"

Kataria did not reply.

Some part of her very much did want to be asked that. Some part of her very much did want to say what made it seem as if getting into a fight would be infinitely preferable to spending another moment here. Some part of her...

But that part wanted to be asked by him. Not this woman.

Shuro nodded, taking her silence as statement enough. "I respect that. I ask that you respect that I need to get to the same place as you."

"You don't know where I'm going."

"I do. And I don't want anything jeopardizing me getting there."

Kataria's nostrils flared as she let out a breath of hot air. "Or else?"

At this, Shuro stepped away. The look she spared Kataria was as brief and cold as the breath that blows out the last candle in a dark room.

"Or else," she replied curtly.

Her eyes lingered long enough for Kataria to appreciate the intent behind them before she turned and stepped away, disappearing into the crowd of passengers and leaving Kataria alone on the deck with no sound but that of the river churning beneath her.

⊹ ⋯ ≍✦≍ ⋯ ⊹

While the passengers hadn't been forthcoming with information, it didn't take Kataria long to figure out what the Lyre meant to Cier'Djaal.

So named for its many tributary "strings" that ran across the desert, the Lyre was used to bring in grain from outlying farmlands and take silks and spices to the borders of northern Muraska and the eastern realms controlled by the Karnerians after successive conquests. While the city's wealth came from the silk, its life came from the river, and to control it was to control everything.

Thus the walled fortress of Jalaang.

It had originally been built to deter tulwar uprisings, she pieced together. But whatever had broken the will of the tulwar so long ago had apparently done so permanently. Now any of those apelike creatures who came to Jalaang did so to trade. And thus the garrison had slowly turned into a trading outpost.

From the deck of the Old Man, Kataria could see the city's lights burning brightly as the colossus rolled to a slow halt among the fishing boats and river barges at the docks. Even in the dead of night, it was easy to see where the city had struggled to make good return on the coin pumped into it.

Buildings that had been erected as armories now stood as warehouses stacked with sacks of rice and crates of grain. Barracks had been emptied and repurposed as bathhouses, the silhouettes of prostitutes visible in their lighted windows. Training fields had been turned into makeshift bazaars rife with stalls, catapults were still and dusty in the streets, the gates at the western and eastern ends of the city stood wide open.

While not nearly as dizzyingly huge as Cier'Djaal, Jalaang was nonetheless a worthy monument to the fashas who had built it: rife with coin, goods, and humans.

Even after she'd hung back at the edge of the deck to let all the other passengers off first, even after she'd let them unload their goods and depart, even after she had climbed down the rope ladder leading off the deck and stood alone on the docks, she could feel their presence.

It was difficult to say exactly what she felt. *Smothered* might have been a good word. *Exposed*, painfully aware of being in a land that she did not belong in, would have been better. But more than either of those, she could feel *humans*.

In the alleys between the repurposed barracks, in the windows peering down at her, in the streets, sparing glances as they collected filth from the buildings...

"Hey."

Right behind her.

"So the Old Man apparently knows the route enough to go to Jalaang by itself," Lenk said, "but not any further than that. The couthi went into town to meet up with a guide. He said there's an inn that can put us—"

A screech. The air shuddered. Her heart stopped beating. Something very far away shouted something very loud in her ear in the span of a single breath.

"—somewhere down toward the end of the street," Lenk finished.

Her ears stumbled over his voice. She blinked, suddenly feeling very light-headed. His voice was muted, as if he were speaking with dust in his mouth. He hadn't heard it.

"Not too much time to rest here," he said, "maybe six hours of sleep and enough time to get breakfast. The couthi was pretty certain about being here at—"

The noise came again. This time as a long sound that rang in her ear like a wailing wind, something that had come from a long way away just to find her. A name she had never been called by, a song whose every verse was an arrow in a throat and a cry in the night.

"—I know things didn't go so well back there, but if you just—"
A howl.
"—I don't know what I did to—"
A howl no one could hear but her.
"—please, Kataria, just—"
The Howling.
"Fuck, would you just *look at me*?"

She didn't remember turning around. She could barely remember him, truthfully, until she felt his hands on her shoulders, his eyes boring into hers.

"Whatever's happening, whatever you're thinking, whatever I did, I can't do anything unless you *tell me*." His voice shook in his throat. "I don't know if I'm supposed to know what's going on or what, but I am in some deep shit here. People are talking about all the killing I've done and all I've got to do and..."

He looked down, drew in a breath. His hands tightened upon her shoulders. When his eyes met hers again, they weren't his. They were too wild, too desperate, too wet to be his. They belonged on someone weaker, someone more scared.

Or, somewhere in the past six days, had he just turned into that person?

"I need to know," he said, "if you're here with me."

But she knew he hadn't. There was something behind those wet, quivering eyes, something solid and cold that had never really cracked.

Weak people had it easier, she thought. They broke, they gathered themselves, they rose again, so many times that it became their personality. Strong people, they just broke.

As he would break if she left him now.

And so she took his face in her hand, felt the calluses of her fingers across the scar on his jaw. She leaned forward, felt the shudder of his breath upon her lips. She pressed her head to his, closed her eyes, and whispered.

"I'm here," she said.

She could hear the long, slow exhalation of his breath. She could hear the sound of the howl in her ears. She could hear the lap of the waves as the Old Man settled slowly upon the bank and loosed a long, low groan.

And none of them were loud enough to drown out the sound of her thoughts.

Coward.

⸻ ⋈ ⸻

It took just an hour: half to find the inn that the couthi had told them to find, another for him to fall asleep. By the time the moon had just started to decline past its apex, the sound of his breath was no longer in her ears and the dust of the streets was in her nose.

She had left her bow behind to avoid the kind of attention a weapon like that would attract, going out with only her hunting knife. Not the wisest idea. This was a city that slept with one eye open: Even after midnight she could hear feet scuffling in alleyways, voices emerging from shadows, the word *shict* being repeated with various degrees of contempt and appraisal.

Shuro's words kept creeping to mind, unbidden. About how easy she was to spot, about how little her life meant to the people of this city. There was wisdom in that, at least, and she would be wise to heed it.

But that would imply she had a choice.

For an hour that had felt like a year, the howl had been growing inside her. It was no longer inside her ears. It was in her skull now, her heart, her blood, and her skin. It was fear in her step, hunger on her breath, something that burned in a way that demanded it be answered.

And she had set out after it, following that sound through the dusty streets, down the darkened alleys, to where the stone houses of Jalaang became wooden warehouses and the shadow of the city's wall grew deep.

But as consuming as the howl was, it could not completely shut out instinct. And as hungry as she was to sate it, she could not ignore the twitch of movement at the corner of her eye.

She did not slow her pace, lest she give away that she had noticed. She fought down the hunger, the howl, to let her ears open to the sound of footsteps, to her left and far above. Someone on the rooftops was following her, slowing when she slowed, quickening when she quickened.

Cover. The thought came unbidden. *They've got a clean shot at you.* The movement followed, carrying her to the mouth of a nearby alley.

As soon as she was hidden between two rising wooden walls, she whirled and scanned the rooftops. She spotted her pursuer almost immediately: a thick-bodied shadow, black against the night sky, crouching at the edge and peering down at her.

No weapon that she could see. That made sense. Surely a shot would have been fired by now. A stalker, then: someone watching, someone waiting.

But for what purpose?

Her ears pricked up. A foot scraped behind her. Before she could even think to turn around, a hand shot out of the darkness, clamped around her mouth, and drew her back into the shadows. She raised a hand to lash out behind her, another hand seized her by the wrist, held it fast.

She heard the voice before it spoke, in the hot breath upon her ear and the tongue sliding across teeth. And when it finally took sound, she could barely hear it for the howl that echoed through her ears.

"What kept you?" it asked.

She could give no answer, not as the hand tightened over her mouth and dragged her into darkness.

⁑

She resisted, of course, as much as could be expected.

She raised a hand, only to have taut fingers wrap about her wrist and bear it down above her head to join the other. Her body jerked in an attempt to rise, only to find a weight bearing down upon her hips, pinning her to the straw. She struggled in a manner more feral than valiant, a beast trapped but unbroken.

But to no avail. However much the hunger pained her, hers was not the greatest in the room.

She bared teeth in a snarl and was met with one in kind: just as feral, just as toothy, broad canines flashing above her in a grin full of savage glee. Whatever else lurked in the shadows painting her captor's face, she could not tear her eyes away from that grin, those teeth, as they descended and brushed against the tender flesh of her throat.

There they hovered. Hot breath passed between them, upon the sweat-slickness of her skin. The growl that came from them was something low and hungry that Kataria felt in the pit of her stomach. They brushed against her throat for a moment before they gave way to tenderness, a kiss placed gently just above her collarbone; a hand released her wrist, came down to trace gentle fingers across the length of her jaw.

Freed, Kataria's hand snaked across her captor's back, felt muscle quiver beneath skin. It found the back of a neck, entangled itself in a dozen black braids. And, seizing it tightly, pulled sharply down toward her throat.

Her captor indulged her. Lips became teeth, biting down upon her throat, tender and furious in equal measure. The howl that had been in her ears tore itself from her mouth, the sound of hunger receiving the barest satiety.

She let the teeth linger until she could stand no more. She pulled her captor's hair once more, bringing a face upward.

Above those large canines, Kwar's dark eyes glittered. Beside Kataria's fingers tangled in her braids, her long ears, four notches to a length, quivered. Sweat glistened upon the dark skin of her brow as she leaned forward, pressed her lips against Kataria's, the muscle of her belly pressing down on her own as she lay across her.

It lasted for an eternity before she released Kataria. Breathless, she smiled at Kwar, moved to brush a single braid out of her eyes.

"You scared the shit out of me," she said. "Why can't you ever just say hello?"

"Because I'm not boring." Kwar licked her lips. "Your fault, anyway. You should have been paying closer attention."

Kwar reached out, gently taking Kataria by the cheek. She could feel the tremble in her fingers as they guided her chin upward, exposing her throat. Everything about the woman wanted to explode, to burst out in snarling fury, to claw and bite and take. It took everything within her to have the patience to be gentle.

But she was gentle. In the touch of her fingers upon Kataria's cheek, in the kiss of her lips upon Kataria's neck, in the warmth of her breath as she whispered softly.

"I missed you."

"I was delayed," Kataria replied, leaning back upon the bed of straw.

"By what?"

"Doesn't matter."

Not a lie, she told herself. Or at least it didn't feel like one.

"I expected you hours ago." Kwar spoke between kisses as her lips traveled over Kataria's collarbone, over the skin of her breast, down to her belly. "I was worried you had forgotten."

"Never," Kataria replied, breathless.

Again, not a lie. She had never stopped thinking about this moment. Except for all those moments when she was thinking about Lenk. Or all those moments when she was cursing herself for not telling Lenk about Kwar, or Kwar about Lenk, or anyone about anything.

There should have been more curses just then, she thought, savage words to turn upon herself for her cowardice. And maybe there were. She couldn't hear them, though, not over the howling in her skull, the hunger in her stomach that rose as Kwar's lips slipped lower, teasing lightly the tender skin just beneath her navel as her hands went for the buckle of her belt.

Her leggings were around her calves in a bunch before Kwar finally lost patience and let her lips travel south one more time and find their way between her thighs. Kataria's fingers tightened their grip on her hair, her teeth clenched in an attempt to stem the sound that came from her lips.

For the first time since that morning, the Howling quieted. For the first time, the hunger felt sated. The pain abated, the fear subsided, sound and hate and shame and fear were silent.

And she was left with only the sound of sweat dripping from her skin, the sound of Kwar's tongue speaking to her, the sound of herself, her scream and her sigh, as she lay upon the straw and released herself.

Sense came back to her slowly, crawling back from wherever she had sent it. Eyes fluttered back open, beheld the shadows painted by the lanterns hanging from the warehouse's roof. The scents of wood and earth were there, an afterthought past the heady rush of Kwar's sweat filling her nostrils. And soon thereafter she felt the arm around her back, the breast she laid her head against, the fingers that smoothed a lock of hair over her ear.

The feel of Kwar's warmth beneath her, the sound of Kwar's breath in her ear, the way everything was so quiet and perfect.

It was nice to pretend that this was how it could be. For a moment.

This isn't right, something inside her said. *You can't do this to her. Tell her now. Or don't. Just leave and don't tell her. Never see her again. Don't do this to her.*

Her brow furrowed, a frown creased her face. And she said nothing, letting the world stay silent for just a few moments longer.

"You flinched."

She opened her eyes, looked up to see Kwar looking down at her.

"Dreaming," Kataria muttered, eyes closing again. "How long have I been asleep?"

"Not even an hour," Kwar said. She leaned back against a box, drew Kataria closer to her. "You can sleep more, if you want. I can stay up for a while longer."

"And you think I can't?" Kataria shot a single-eyed glare at her.

"Not as long as I can." Kwar met her with a grin. "Someone's got to. This is a human city. Not friendly to us."

"How'd you get in, then?"

"Because humans can't do anything right."

It would be just as easy to stay here, she thought. Just as easy to lie here and watch the dawn rise. She saw it so clearly in her mind: the same dawn that a young man with a sword on the docks would see as he desperately scanned the morning crowds for her until, prodded by the urging of his guide, he dejectedly climbed aboard the Old Man and left her here with a new life.

It would be just that easy.

But when she closed her eyes and held her breath, she saw something else. She saw that same young man tearing through the city, sword in hand, searching for her. She saw a warehouse door flung open, daylight glinting off the silver of his blade. She saw Kwar leaping to her feet, a roar on her lips and a dagger in her hand.

She saw blood on the straw.

Something inside her chest started to hurt. It was hard to breathe all of a sudden. She swallowed and it tasted sour in her mouth.

"I need to go." She clambered to her feet, drew her leggings up.

"But..." Kwar bit back the rest of that thought. She rose to her feet, brushed herself off. "Right, yes. I should be escaping soon, too."

That wasn't what she wanted to say, Kataria knew.

Every time Kwar tried, her lips trembled, her gaze wavered, and she changed the subject. But there was a moment when the fear shone plain on her face and Kataria could sense she was about to ask where her lover disappeared to so suddenly and mysteriously.

Frankly, Kataria wondered why she hadn't already. Maybe she was scared of the answer.

Kataria certainly was.

"You have the map I gave you?" Kataria asked. "The one that tells you where we're going?"

"I do," Kwar said. "I wish you weren't going there, though. The Gullet's not safe."

Kataria cast a look over her shoulder. "When have you ever cared about safety?"

"When the world started being more dangerous than I am."

"What do you mean?"

"It's not just the Gullet," Kwar said. "Word of what's happened in Cier'Djaal has reached the tribes." She tapped her ears, indicating the notches. "The Seventh Tribe has a new leader and she wants to strike at the city while they're weak. She's hungry." She hissed the name: "Shekune."

"All shicts want to strike at human cities. Most shicts haven't."

"Most shicts," Kwar said, "don't wear flayed human scalps on their masks. She's burned a dozen human outposts and twice that many tulwar villages. She is dangerous, Kataria."

Kataria cringed. "I can take care of myself."

"And if you can't?"

"Then I've got you, don't I?" she replied with a grin.

For once Kwar did not return the grin. The glitter of her eyes was gone, leaving only two dark orbs that stared at Kataria intently. When she spoke, it was in a choked, wet whisper.

"I hate you, you know."

"You have a strange way of showing it," Kataria replied, looking deliberately down to fasten her belt.

"I'm not being funny. I mean it. Ever since..." Kwar looked away. "Ever since my mother died and my father turned Thua into a coward, I haven't felt... I mean, I knew I'd never feel that scared again. I *knew* I wouldn't."

Kataria didn't look up, even as Kwar stepped closer toward her. She couldn't bear the thought of what she might see in the khoshict's eyes if she did.

"And I shouldn't. When I'm with you, most of all, I shouldn't."

She made a point of fiddling with her belt buckle, anything to avoid looking. But when a dark hand wrapped gently about her own, she couldn't help it. She looked up. Kwar's eyes were wet.

"But I do," she said.

Kataria clenched her teeth, trying to hold back a question to which she already knew the answer. It did not help.

"Why?"

"I don't know. I'm scared you'll leave. I'm scared you'll die. I'm scared you'll wake up and think you're not supposed to be with me. I'm scared. And I hate you for doing that to me. I *hate* you."

She took Kataria by the shoulders suddenly, drew her in, wrapped arms about her and held her tightly. Her voice was a sharp, desperate whisper.

"Don't go."

No more words came, from her or Kwar. No more sounds at all. No more Howling to hear, hunger to sate, pain to ease. In that warehouse, there was no space left for anything but them.

And the vastness with which Kataria wished she could say something.

＋－＊＜≣＞＋－

How did Denaos do it so easily, she wondered?

Long after she had made her excuses and departed, with the agreement to meet again farther up the river, a different pain came. This one gnawed at the back of her neck, a pair of jaws that clamped down every time she thought of Kwar, or of Lenk, or of the lies she had told them both.

Denaos glided between lies like a falling leaf, never losing track of any of them, never bothered by any of them. Could he have done this more easily? Was it *supposed* to be easy?

She didn't know why she was asking. She already knew the answers, and they weighed heavily on her shoulders. Each step down Jalaang's dusty roads felt as if it would be the one to drag her down to the earth.

Yet heavy as her head was, it was not so clouded that she could not hear the sound of a pair of feet landing on the street behind her.

Her knife flashed into her hand as she whirled about and beheld a pair of eyes glittering with familiar darkness. A fearful thought struck her as she wondered if Kwar had followed her. But there was nothing of Kwar in the face that looked at her, except for the eyes.

She never had looked much like her brother.

"Easy," Thua said, raising his hands. "I'm not here to fight."

She knew this to be true. Despite the thick brawn of his muscle—left bare by the kilt and sandals he wore—Thua was never much for combat. His face was softer than Kwar's, a deep frown where her smile was. Kataria snorted, sheathed her blade.

"Doesn't anyone in your family introduce themselves without leaping out of the shadows?" she asked.

"I thought you would have heard me coming."

Thua's ears, notched the same as Kwar's, twitched. True, the Howling that bound all shicts together should have tipped her off to his presence. Had she not been consumed with varying degrees of guilt and terror over what she was doing to his sister, it certainly would have.

Of course, she opted not to tell him that.

"I've been distracted," she said.

"Understandable," Thua said. "You must have a lot on your mind, what with your trip to the Forbidden East and all."

"You heard." A statement. Not a question.

"Everything," he replied, his ears twitching again. "I was on the roof of a warehouse. Your human friend is loud." His face was cold as stone as he regarded her. "Is he your friend, sister?"

She forced her face still. She couldn't let him know how close the implication had struck her. "You shouldn't be here, Thua."

"Kwar thought so, too. She asked me not to come."

"Asked?"

Thua sneered. "Told. I came with her anyway. This city is full of humans. It's not safe for us here." He narrowed his eyes on her. "Least of all her."

Kataria had never liked pacifists. And while Thua was not, strictly speaking, a pacifist, he still had that same air of insufferable moral superiority that made his every word cut as keenly as any blade. She would, she decided, be perfectly justified in responding with a more straightforward blade, or at least in punching him in the face a couple of times.

Maybe it was respect for Kwar that made her turn away. Maybe it was respect for another shict that made her start walking. Or maybe she knew she couldn't attack him without proving him right.

Pacifists were annoying like that.

"She loves you."

It was only when the words were spoken aloud that the pain in her chest became unbearable. Only then did she feel as if she might actually fall down and not get up again. Instead she settled for simply whispering in reply.

"I know."

"Do you? Because you don't act like it," he snarled. "I'm not going to say I know exactly what's going on with you and that human, but I know enough. I know that I'd take out my blade right now"—he paused—"if I didn't think it would make my sister cry.

"She never cried when we were little. It was always me. Me who had the skinned knees, me who got picked on. She was always the one to protect me. I've only ever seen her cry once." He fell silent. When he spoke again, his voice was weak and choked. "She can call me a coward all she wants. I do what I must to protect her."

He drew in a sharp breath, took a step closer.

"And that's why I'm asking you, Kataria, to go. Go on the Old Man with your human. Never come back for her, never visit her, never think about her, if you can help it. You know what she feels for you, you know this won't end well. So if you feel at all the same way, please...just leave her behind."

The dirt shifted. He took another step closer.

"Do you love her?" he asked.

"I don't know," she said.

Another step.

"Do you love *him*?"

"I don't know."

A hand was on her shoulder.

"Why can't you just choose—"

And suddenly her ears were full of sounds: of the Howling rising up inside her, of her fist cracking against his jaw as she whirled around, of his body striking the dirt.

"*I don't know!*" She was on top of him, her fist slamming against his jaw. "I don't know, I don't know, I don't know! Don't you think I would have done something by now if I did, you little shit? Don't you think I fucking know how this ends? That's what's so hard. No matter what I do, someone is going to hurt, and I don't fucking know how to *not* hurt people."

By the time she realized her hands were around his throat, he was gasping for breath and his blood was trickling onto her fingers from a gash in his jaw. Her ears were still ringing, alive with the Howling. It took every breath inside her to release him, to get up and turn away from him.

"I'm sorry," she said. "I wish I knew. I wish I hadn't done that. But I don't and I did and I'll figure something out. So until then, just leave me the fuck alone, all right?"

She stalked off before he could say anything. She couldn't take another word. Blood was on her hands, dust was on her skin, the Howling was in her ears. The moon was disappearing beyond one wall, dawn would soon peer over the other. The night was over.

And all was silent.

SEVEN

LADIES-IN-WAITING

Silf had many sons, it was said, but only seven daughters.

Denaos knew this—as any friend of the Patron did—for they had all visited him at least once in his life: Ambition and Poise to get him into places he should not be, Skulk and Whimsy to get him away from places other people thought he ought to be, and Savvy to get everywhere else.

But it was Silf's first two daughters that everyone—the friends of the Patron and strangers alike—knew. And it was with those two daughters laid out, brightly polished and sharpened on an oil-kissed cloth before him, that his concerns lay tonight.

For tonight was a very important function and tonight demanded just the right lady.

Silence: scalpel-thin, a point as delicate as a fasha's finger. Bravado: long and serrated on one side viciously hooked at her tip. He plucked up both daggers, weighed them in either hand, let out a thoughtful hum.

Someone screamed from the other room; this was nothing special, someone had been screaming for hours now. But this time it was loud enough to be heard through the thick wood of the door.

That was the scream of someone ready to talk.

Silence it was, then.

Likely the poor fool in that room had already been introduced to Bravado. Just as well. Silence wasn't as messy as her sister. He slipped the blade back into her sheath, took her in hand, and opened the door.

A blast of fetid warmth struck him. The air was thick with the scent of suffering, the sound of agony. He couldn't really be repulsed; he'd known what to expect. There were little rooms like this all over the city. The Jackals called them "antique shops," places the guild took someone with the intent that they be forgotten. They were cramped, musty little rooms buried under the streets, tombs for the living that they might choke on their own agony while the simple folk above went by without a care for what happened beneath.

For a long time, Denaos had tried his hardest to be one of those simple folk, going so far as to leave the city, the Jackals, all of it.

But he was back now. This was where he belonged. In an antique shop, with a relic made of flesh, and in the company of a dark-tressed woman in dark leathers.

"I didn't think you were going to come." Anielle regarded him coolly as he entered the room, eased the door shut behind him. "This sort of thing never was your style."

Didn't used to be yours, either, Denaos thought, but did not say. Times were hard for the Jackals, so the Jackals demanded hardness. While she might not be hard, Anielle *was* a Jackal, through and through.

But this . . .

The room was narrow, barely twelve feet by twelve feet, and most of that space dominated by the long table upon which their captive was strapped.

What he had been before he got here was irrelevant—a merchant, a thief, a father, a brother. What he had been before he decided to throw his lot in with the Khovura and take up arms against the Jackals was irrelevant. Because as of this moment, he was no longer a man, he was just one of the Jackals' many antiques to be locked away and forgotten.

But not before they made him talk.

Judging from the mess, Denaos saw, Anielle had been hard at work; and with Bravado, as he'd suspected. Yet for all the blood spilled and flesh hewn, there seemed to have been no progress. In one corner the bucketman, with his chemicals and mop, twitched in anticipation of the blood he would have to clean up. In another corner the scribe tapped quill to empty parchment, waiting for a confession he could take down.

Scribes, cleaners; everything was so organized with the Jackals since they'd become the only game in town. Time was, they'd have done something like this under a dock with a hammer and nail. Bureaucracy, it seemed, was the natural evolution of any organization, even a thieves' guild.

Even the stench of torture—the dried blood and sweat-slick suffering—was absent here. The air was permeated with the scent of packed herbs, stale incense, things they used to mask the odor of things dying. It wasn't even as though the stink could reach so far above as to let anyone know what went on below. They just did this to further the illusion that they were civil people practicing civil business.

As opposed to criminals torturing people to death.

Denaos clutched his fingers around Silence, took a step forward. Anielle placed a hand upon his arm, drew his eyes to a meaningful stare.

"If you don't want to do this . . . ," she said.

He said nothing, gingerly pulling away from her. The offer wasn't for his sake, he knew, but for hers. She wanted to see if he would take it or if he was the hard kind of man the Jackals demanded. He knew he was, just as he'd known he was so many years ago when they had him kill for them.

No matter how hard he had pretended he wasn't.

He lingered at the side of the table, appraised Anielle's work. That it should be a saccarii they'd captured was not surprising: The Khovura's ranks were heavily composed of Cier'Djaal's misbegotten natives. That Denaos could recognize him as one after so much torture, though, was slightly more noteworthy.

Anielle had worked with no restraint, carving great chunks out of the man's scale-riddled flesh, cutting lines over thin, shriveled lips, gouging out one yellow, thin-slit eye and leaving a bloody mess in its wake. Denaos had only rarely seen a saccarii outside of his tattered veil.

Damn thing was probably uglier before Anielle, he thought. He slid Silence out of her sheath with an oiled hiss. *Still, one works with the tools one is given.*

He leaned close, let the saccarii's remaining eye snap open, search the room frantically before settling on Denaos.

"Good morning," the rogue said, a smile spreading across his face. "Or is it evening? Was it morning when they dragged you down here? I suppose you must be hungry by now."

The saccarii said nothing, jaw fused tight with agony, single eye wide and unblinking. Denaos chuckled, looked away politely.

"Sorry, that must seem terribly rude." He looked back at the saccarii. "I didn't mean to insult your intelligence. I'm not going to offer you food. I'm not going to tell you there's a way out of here." He leaned closer. "If you were stupid enough to go against the Jackals, you're smart enough to know you're going to die here. You know how this works."

He brought Silence up, held her delicately by the pommel with two fingers of his left hand, twisted the tip gently against the tip of one finger of his right.

"And I'm betting you know how it ends, too," he said. "I bet you've been around long enough to see how it all ends. Someone sees the way we're running things, figures they can do it better, we bloody some noses, and so forth. The names change, but it always ends the same.

"We find whatever dark hole they lurk in. We shine our torches down it. And we burn. We burn as far back as we possibly can, until children can't see through the smoke and wives smell their husbands' cooking flesh. Sometimes people escape. Sometimes we let them. But these are the Jackals we're talking about, you know. Respectable organization. Image means a lot."

He let the tip of Silence graze against the saccarii's arm and watched as it tensed up, thick veins popping out of underfed, scaly flesh.

Funny thing, violence: It was just like telling a story. Show a man enough blood and bruises, he yearns to catch his breath. Threaten to take that away and one has his attention.

"A few days of fighting, a few dead bodies, that's nothing," he said. "We do a little symbolic cutting and we call it a day. But this..." He drew Silence across the man's arm, painting a thin red line parallel to a vein. "This has gone on for months. People are dead. Important people. We've got a lot of burning to do.

"I don't want to say you can save them," he said. "Your family, your friends, whoever you're trying to protect. I don't want to insult you." He slid his finger down the cut, gingerly hooked a nail under a flap of skin. "But I want you to think about it, how much smoke there's going to be when we get to burning."

He saw the man's eye water. The smile faded.

"And who is going to choke on it."

He hooked his finger under the strip of flesh, dug his finger into the wound he had just cut. He could feel tendons separate and clench as he probed the wound. He could feel the saccarii's scream, torn from somewhere deep, somewhere a blade like Bravado couldn't touch. It was Silence that heard the secrets, Silence that knew what part of a man she could find them in.

He twisted his finger just enough to touch it, that part of a man he didn't know he had. Not enough to cause serious damage, nor even enough to prolong pain, just enough to let him know that Denaos knew things about people.

And how to break them.

He slid his finger out just as suddenly, left the saccarii panting on the table, his lanky, naked, bleeding, broken body fluttering like a moth under a pin. They waited in silence, Denaos giving him a chance to come to the reasonable conclusion.

"We know someone's feeding you information, we know we have a traitor," Denaos said. "Tell us who the informant is and we'll make the rest of this clean."

The saccarii's breathing slowed. His struggles stopped. The bucket-man reached for his mop. The scribe looked up, placed quill to paper. For a long moment, the only sound was the flabby patter of a blood drop upon the tile.

When the saccarii's eye finally opened, it was calm. And it stared at Denaos with such lucidity as to suggest there were parts of a man that he, too, knew very well.

"My grandfather was given fifty coppers for land he stood on for fifty years because a fasha wanted to build a house on it." The saccarii's voice was racked, a quavering thing forced out of a broken throat. "My father broke his back working for the man who lived in it. My wife died in the riots so the Jackals might keep that man in his house. My child became a prostitute so that he could choose a nicer home to die in than the shack built over his family's graves."

And those shriveled lips peeled back into a smile. It did not brim with false confidence, nor even with snide mockery, as Denaos had seen all men try to affect. This was a smile he had rarely seen before, belonging only to grandfathers who died surrounded by family, and grandmothers who saw lights grow brighter even as theirs died out.

"What more can you do to me, Jackal?" he asked. "I am already in hell."

Other gods would have judged him more kindly: as a father, as a husband, as a son pushed too far. They would overlook his sins: the blade he had carried, the blood he had shed, the cause he had sworn himself to. Perhaps, they would say, he didn't deserve a swift line painted across his throat with a keen blade.

But he got it anyway.

For down here, far below the busy people with their coins and their families and their kinder, gentler gods, Silf reigned supreme. Far down here with the antiques, his judgment was absolute. Far down here, with his daughters to watch, his sentence was carried out.

And the only sound that followed the hush of flesh being opened was Silence, clattering to the floor as Denaos let her drop and walked out, an empty eye staring after him as he did.

"The *fuck* did you do that for?" To the credit of Anielle's professionalism, she at least waited until the door to the antique room was closed before spitting at his feet. "He was ready to break!"

"He wasn't," Denaos replied, taking a moment to scrape the spittle off on the doorframe.

"Hours," Anielle said. At his confusion, she sneered. "In case you were wondering how long I had worked on him. Seven hours of cutting." She gestured back to the door. "A few breaths in there and you decide he doesn't know anything?"

Denaos hadn't said the man hadn't known anything.

It was almost certain that the saccarii had known something. The Khovura seemed in the business of knowing everything.

It had been mere days since the footwar between the Jackals and the Khovura had gone underground. It had seemed like a sound strategy at the time: If the Jackals couldn't win a straight footwar, they'd use the warring Karnerians and Sainites as a smoke screen to regroup.

Yet going underground had merely left them cornered. The Khovura had found every cell, every rat's nest, every warren that held a Jackal. In mere days, two hundred-sixty-seven had been killed.

They were sure of the exact number because the Khovura took immense pains to have every mutilated corpse strung up, sent back, or otherwise delivered to the Jackals.

Treason was the only answer. For the Khovura to have known the location of each den and the movement of every Jackal foot soldier, someone had to have been feeding them information. Denaos had no doubt that the saccarii strapped to the table could have given them the informant's name, appearance, and favorite fucking color, if he had wanted to.

But Denaos had said he hadn't been ready to break.

Silence had not been the first lady to caress Denaos's palm, her blade not the first he had shown a man's throat. Numbers, he found, he could forget when he closed his eyes and saw them flash before him. He couldn't remember how many men he had taken from the shadows, how many bright-red ribbons he had painted across flesh, how many had lain twitching before him as he slunk away.

The eyes, though, he could never forget.

He knew what a man ready to die looked like.

No need to tell her that, of course. No need to dwell on those eyes. He would see them again, as soon as he went to sleep. He stepped past Anielle, moved toward the dimly lit staircase at the end of the narrow hall. But as soon as he did, he felt her hand clamp upon his arm.

"I didn't bring you down here just to be nice," she said. Her dark-eyed gaze was hard and even. "We're losing this war to rats and you're the last man we brought in. People are talking, Ramaniel."

He paused. For a moment he had forgotten that was his real name. Or one of them, anyway.

"Yeah?" he asked. "Think they might let me go home early, then?"

She wasn't smiling. He couldn't help it. The joke was too funny.

No one left the Jackals. No one but him, anyway. And what were the chances of that happening twice?

Anielle offered no resistance as he pulled away from her and trudged wearily up the cramped spiral staircase and into the dark corridor above. Sightless, he counted his steps: five paces forward, left turn, three paces forward, right turn. He spotted the thinnest halo of light, an orange ring as tall as a man, at the edge of the darkness. He approached it, knelt down, and groped blindly, the reek of cheap, ancient wine filling his nostrils.

His fingers found a handle, jerked it sharply to the right, and then pushed. The door creaked open, the wine cellar's dim lantern light greeting him as he crawled out of an immense wine cask, muttering curses.

As far as hidden entrances went, this had been one of the Jackals' better ideas, but it wasn't without its downsides. The stink, he thought, would never get out of his clothes.

Yet in an instant, the reek of cheap wine was overwhelmed by the reek of cheap tobacco, and Denaos knew that he had bigger problems.

Yerk, tall and thin as a knife, stood at the cellar's door. His hood was pulled up over his face, every feature shrouded in darkness but for the glow of his burning cigarillo. Yet Denaos had known this rogue long enough to know when he was staring, just as he knew that Yerk's stare was never, ever a good thing.

"Rezca has requested our presence in the usual place." Yerk's fondness for cigarillos did not make for a melodious voice in the best of times. Of late the stress of war had made him about as pleasant to listen to as a rusty nail being hammered into a cat's paw. "We have a visitor."

All the same, Denaos did not miss the change in Yerk's tone. He canted his head to the side, curious.

"We have a visitor?" he asked. "Or we have a problem?"

Yerk took a long drag, exhaled a cloud of smoke.

"Yes."

⸺ ⸺◆⸻ ⸺

Problem, Denaos decided, was a word Yerk understood poorly.

A problem was another den struck by the Khovura. A problem was another gang of Jackals executed by a Karnerian priest or Sainite military court. A problem was another merchant getting brave and refusing to pay protection money.

Denaos had dealt with problems before. Denaos could deal with problems.

The woman sitting at the table at the center of the room was not a problem. She was punishment sent by a vengeful god for one of the numerous sins he had committed.

Someday he hoped to figure out which one.

"Asper." He greeted her with a curt nod as he strode into the room; no use trying to hide, she already had that steely gaze locked upon him.

"Denaos," she replied, gesturing to the only empty chair at the table. "Join us."

It was decidedly audacious for any outsider to speak with such authority at a meeting of the Jackals' heads, let alone a priestess. The offense did not go unnoticed. Anielle made no effort to disguise her scowl, Yerk passively blew a cloud of cigarillo smoke in her direction.

Only Rezca, his eyes hidden behind the glare the lantern cast on his spectacles, said nothing. He merely ran a hand over the hairless flesh of his scalp, steepled his fingers before him, and mimicked her gesture.

Denaos picked his way through the empty tables of the bar. The windows had long ago been boarded up, the doors nailed shut. The sole light was from the lantern hanging over the lone occupied table, where the last leaders of the Jackals currently sat with a decidedly enterprising interloper.

"So I assume you're going to tell me what we're doing here." Denaos eyed Asper as he sat down. "I trust you have a dramatic monologue prepared?"

"Start with how you found us," Anielle snapped before Asper could say a word. "Who squealed?"

"No one squealed," Asper replied tersely. "The Temple of Talanas takes in all the wounded we can, including former members of your..." She paused, likely searching for a word better than *gang of murderous thugs*. "Organization. One of them told me where to find you."

"It is common practice to take the tongue, eyes, and ears of those who involve outsiders in the game," Yerk muttered, putting out his cigarillo and drawing a fresh one. "They are left only with their nose, that they might smell the shit they're in."

"You'd not find a hairbreadth of flesh on the man that wasn't cut, burned, or torn off," Asper said. "We found him in an alley after the Khovura were through with him."

"Then he should have been ours to pick up," Anielle said.

"Should have." Asper turned her gaze upon Anielle. "But wasn't."

Among Asper's many gifts as a priestess was a tone that could convey an overwhelming sense of moral superiority with even a few words. And among Anielle's many talents as a rogue was the ability to slip a knife into someone's kidneys with the barest of movements. That being the case, Denaos slid a hand under the table to place it over Anielle's just as her blade had come free of its sheath.

"Whatever you did for him was obviously enough to get him to tell you where to find us," he said. "So I'm assuming whatever you need must be immense for you to seek us out."

At this she flinched—or perhaps cringed—as though it had just now dawned on her what manner of people she had sought out. She stared down at her hands, perfectly flat upon the table.

"Like I said, we took in a lot of people," she said. "Beggars, soldiers, guardsmen, other priests...there's no end to the names because there's no end to the victims. Every day the Karnerians and Sainites find a new place to fight and we come through and pick up the pieces. And..." A sigh that contained all the exhaustion of a hundred years came free. "It's not working.

"The Temple of Ancaa is taking some of our overflow, but they're making demands. They want supplies, food, wine. We've taken every spare building we can muster, rallied every gutter-priest we can find, and it's still not enough. So long as the Karnerians and Sainites keep fighting, we'll eventually be overwhelmed."

She rested her head in her hands, drew in a shuddering breath.

"Something has to change," she said, "and soon."

Ah, there's the monologue. Nice lead-in, too.

Certainly this would have worked on the kind of broken-down, bent-backed rabble she was used to ministering to at her temple. But even by the standards of thieves, the Jackals were a practical sort. No one who knew them asked them for a favor, no one who knew them appealed to their sense of mercy, and no one, *no one* conned them.

And even the best religions had all the makings of a very good con.

Asper's suffering, so thick as to suffocate, was met with unimpressed stares across the table.

Sensing this, she moved her eyes quickly to Denaos, who offered a pointed glare. It had been days since they had seen each other, but years since they had been apart. One didn't go through what they had gone through without learning how to convey oneself through eyes alone.

And Denaos's eyes intended to remind her keenly that she was speaking to thieves.

"The fashas have more coin," Yerk muttered.

"Silktown is locked *down*." Asper slammed her hands onto the table. "With Ghoukha dead, some upstart—Mejina, I think his name is—is trying to step into his shoes. He's keeping everyone out of the district and killing anyone who tries. There's no way you didn't know that."

"And so you came to us?" Anielle chuckled darkly.

"Look, I wouldn't have come to you if I didn't think you'd benefit from this." Asper turned her attentions back to the other rogues. "And you wouldn't have met with me if you weren't desperate." The table tensed collectively. She leaned forward. "The Khovura are winning this footwar."

"You are not a Jackal. You're not even Djaalic, *shkainai*." Anielle sneered at the woman. "What would a foreigner know of the footwar? Or was the pig you rescued free with his squealing?"

"I've been here almost a month, and in that time I have spoken to damn near every man, woman, and child that hasn't been killed," Asper snapped in response. "But I could have had a day and talked to a drunk baby and still figured out what's going on. The Khovura are smoking out your rat's nests and stomping on whatever comes scurrying out."

"The traitor is of no concern to you, *shkainai*," Yerk said.

"Yerk, you dumbshit," Anielle growled.

"If she's here, she knows already." The hooded man waved a hand. "She merely does not know it's none of her business."

"I'm not asking to make it my business," Asper said. "My concern is for the people and they should be yours, as well." She swept a glare around the table. "Or hadn't you noticed they're not on your side?"

"That the common man resents the rules of the game is not what one calls a revelation," Yerk said. He was already on his third cigarillo, betraying the stress his voice strove to hide. "We are, after all, in the business of thievery and murder."

"And yet," Denaos muttered, "that wasn't always the case."

Asper looked at him intently. Yerk's cigarillo burned bright as he drew in a sudden breath. Anielle shot him a glare that she'd likely shown the saccarii they had left bleeding out. And Rezca...

Rezca merely sat in silence.

"This is Cier'Djaal, after all," he continued, clearing his throat. "Thievery and murder were the stones they built this city on. The people have been used to it since long before the Jackals wiped out the other guilds. And the reason we were able to do that is because we had the people cooperating."

"I recall breaking hands, burning houses, and writing ransom notes," Anielle said coldly. "Not cooperation."

"One hand broken meant a hundred others were throwing coins to us," Denaos replied. "It wasn't fear that kept them paying. It was the trust that we could keep things in the city under control."

"The commoners view you as the boots on the fashas' feet," Asper said. "The Khovura are offering them a way out from under the heel, even if it's through massacre. You *need* to show them that it's you who runs this city. Not the men with all the coin or the men with none of the coin, but the men who can take it at will."

"You have a suggestion, then."

Rezca's voice, when he finally spoke, was not loud. Yet every gaze immediately went toward him as he looked over the rims of his spectacles at Asper.

"I do," Asper said. "Thieves are no longer the city's concern. The Karnerians and Sainites are ripping every neighborhood apart. The approval of the people will go to whoever can drive them out."

"We're Jackals, not soldiers," Anielle said. "Even if we *weren't* reeling, we're not cut out to fight a conventional war."

"The war has long since become unconventional," Asper said. "The Karnerians took the Sainites' garrison when the fighting broke out. The Sainites have been launching sneak attacks from bases hidden around the city. You can sniff them out, sabotage them, break weapons, and poison supplies. Convince them that this war will cost them too much to make it worthwhile."

"And then, when the dust clears, let it be known that the Jackals were the ones to do it." Denaos sniffed, glanced to Rezca. "The merchants start showing their gratitude. We get more supplies. We turn the tide of this war. It's not a bad idea."

"It's suicide," Anielle piped up. "We're down leaders, weapons, and men and you want to spend the rest of our energy on fighting a war? A *real* war? The Khovura will overrun us while our backs are turned."

"They're doing that already," Denaos replied, voice harsh. "Do *you* have a better idea?"

If Anielle's glare had been sharp before, now it was keen enough to decapitate him where he sat. Understandable, he thought: She hadn't clawed her way through the ranks of the Jackals just to be second-guessed in front of a *shkainai*.

"This plan, of course, neglects that it takes two to fight a war," Yerk muttered.

"I've got a plan to handle the Karnerians," Asper said. "Trust me on that."

"Trust a foreigner." Anielle's voice dragged out like a blade. "A foreigner who doesn't know the Jackals, doesn't know the game, doesn't know the *city*. She's an outsider's outsider. What right does she have to speak for the people?"

"No more than we do," Yerk muttered, puffing contemplatively. "How long has it been since a Jackal was seen on the streets? How long has it been since we showed our faces to the sun?"

"Oh, don't tell me you're buying into this shit." Anielle gestured to Asper. "Two weeks cleaning puke and she thinks she's not pale as snow? She's not a Djaalic, she doesn't speak for them, she never will."

"I'm not Djaalic, either." Denaos gestured to his own face. "Yet you trust me to sit at this table."

"That's different, *Ramaniel*"—she spit his true name—"and you know it."

"It is," Denaos replied. "Because we're *thieves*, not a bunch of pious morons tonguing a god's feathered ass." He caught Asper's glare, made an apologetic nod. "No offense. But this isn't about the people's hearts, it's about their money."

"The fuck is wrong with you?" Anielle shot to her feet, her chair clattering to the floor behind her. "Both of you? After all the shit we've seen, you're so scared that you'll let a *shkainai* order you around?"

"This isn't about orders, it's—"

"No, it's about pride. It's about having—"

"No other way, of course. If there were—"

"Vote."

This time Rezca did speak loudly. His voice was echoed by the thump of the wooden idol he slammed down upon the table and pushed toward the center. The two-faced image of Silf, carved from ebonwood and holding out a bowl, leered at everyone at once.

"This isn't how it's done. There are rules," Anielle growled. "Not all the heads are present."

"We are the last," Rezca said. "We vote now."

He reached into his vest, produced a gold coin, and tossed it into the idol's bowl. A vote in favor of Asper's plan, Denaos noted with some surprise. Usually Rezca was keenest to observe protocol, something that listening to an outsider certainly didn't fall under.

What's changed, then, old man?

Anielle spit curses as she fished out a coin from her pocket and threw it into the bowl. A copper coin lay flat and dull, a firm vote against. Unsurprising.

Less surprising was Yerk's toss of a silver coin, indicating a vote abstained or withheld. Much, much less surprising was the firmness with which every set of eyes settled upon Denaos. Being unable to see either Yerk's or Rezca's, Denaos was intent on the two women, both rapt in him, anticipating his next move with an almost predatory tension.

He had had a dream like this once.

Of course, he'd been naked in that one and there had been a goat in it somewhere.

He reached into his pocket, felt the cold metal of coin as keenly as he felt the heat of Anielle's stare.

She wasn't wrong, of course; trusting a priestess to understand the politics of thieves wasn't the best idea even in the best of situations. And she was far from wrong in stating that the Jackals could hardly spare dwindling resources and men to fight an enemy that didn't refer to war as a game.

Denaos couldn't fault her practicality, instinct, or coldness—one didn't become a head of the Jackals without ample amounts of all three. And Asper's plan was lacking in all of those.

And even when he tossed a gold coin into the bowl, he still wasn't quite sure why he had done it.

Desperate circumstances, he told himself. Desperate circumstances called for desperate measures and desperate hope alike. Or perhaps he couldn't think of a better plan himself.

Yeah, sure, he chuckled inwardly. *That's it.*

"You're fucking joking." It was a cold contempt that slid out on Anielle's voice, mirrored in the scowl she swept across the table before settling upon Denaos. "We used to run this town and now we're so scared that we're taking orders from *shkainai* heretics?" She shoved the table as she rose, tipping Silf's idol and spilling the coins. "We deserve to burn."

No words were exchanged as she stalked out of the room. Nothing more than a pointed glance was offered from Rezca to Yerk, Yerk to Denaos. The vote had been cast, the decision made. Whatever plan they came up with from this point, Anielle would endure.

Or cut their throats in the night. Desperate circumstances, after all.

Yerk followed, the glow of his cigarillo heralding his passage as he slipped into the shadows. Rezca rose last, turning to likewise vanish, and instead hesitating at the edge of the lantern's glow.

"You've become accustomed to the city, priestess," he said without looking back. "I assume you're aware of its history? With the riots?"

She nodded. "I am."

"Then you are no doubt aware of how many died in a single night, how many more in the city suffered in the months that followed."

Her voice quavered a little when she spoke again. "I am."

Rezca let out a low hum. "Understand, priestess, that we long ago ceased to be a gang. Today we are a business, like any fasha, and we are expedient. They rule by suggesting what terrible things might happen if they did not, we rule by showing. This plan of yours falls...outside of our nature."

"I'm sure you can do it."

"As am I." His words came out on a sigh that belonged to a far older man than he. He raised a hand as he walked out of the light. "Remove her."

The two Jackals behind her moved forward, one of them withdrawing a black cloth. Asper stiffened as he draped it over her eyes, but did not resist beyond offering a pointed glance to Denaos before he tied the blindfold tight. A pointed glance that did not go unnoticed.

"I'll take it from here, boys," he said, holding up a hand.

The two Jackals exchanged looks before glancing back at him. "Rezca said that the wartime protocol—"

"If this were a war, Rezca wouldn't be agreeing to this plan," Denaos said. "He's not a general, this isn't a fortress, and you still do what I say, understand?"

"Yeah," the Jackal said, stepping away from Asper. "Sure, Ramaniel. Whatever you say."

He waited until they had left before reaching down to take Asper's hand. Hers shot out first, finding his grip despite her blindfold. Her fingers eased neatly into his, he noted; hands like hers shouldn't be so familiar with hands like his. Hers sutured wounds shut, applied balms, set broken bones. And his...

His polished antiques and left them in dark rooms.

They walked in silence.

She never asked him about the name Ramaniel. She never asked him who that man was, whom that man had killed. She never asked him why Anielle had spoken that name as if it should be whispered in the dark. She never asked him who Denaos was, whether he was a man or a lie, which one of those names had more blood on it.

She never asked him, because she knew he wouldn't tell her, not unless she needed to know.

She trusted him.

And that she did made him want to vomit.

It was only when he guided her to the door, only when her words disappeared between the creaks of the hinges, that she spoke.

"He called it 'the city.'"

He paused, glanced at her. "What?"

"Rezca. He called it 'the city,' not 'my city' or 'our city.' He's been living here longer than you, hasn't he?"

"Yeah, well..." Denaos guided her out into a cramped alley between two looming houses. "Neither of us belong here. And if you hadn't noticed his skin, we've got more than just that in common."

"He's northern. I get that," she said. "But the others talk about him like he's in charge. Surely he's got some connection to Cier'Djaal."

That wasn't a question, Denaos noted. Fortunate, since he didn't feel like answering. She was searching for justification, a reason why it was necessary that she had reached out to a gang of murderers for help. He wasn't about to tell her.

That would be a conversation for a god with keener ears than Silf.

Summer had been waning for the last week, yet as he guided her out from the alley and into the run-down neighborhood of the old city, the air was stifling. Somewhere far away, homes were on fire. Somewhere too far to hear, the Karnerians and Sainites were clashing again. And between here and there lay a string of corpses.

"How many?"

The question came suddenly. He didn't even know it was his mouth speaking it when he heard it. Yet when Asper paused and tilted her head toward him, the rest came easily.

"How many people have you taken in?"

She didn't answer. Not until he had taken in a breath of warm air, tasted a tinge of smoke.

"Injured," she asked, "or dead?"

"Yes."

She turned away from him. "The two hundred twenty-seventh person injured was brought in just before I left to see you here. By the time

I was out the door, he was the four hundred eighty-ninth we sent to be cremated."

Silence descended over them like a cloud. Denaos held the smoke in his mouth, his breath caught in his throat. In the absence of sound, he thought he could hear, somewhere far away, the sound of war.

Asper moved to remove the blindfold.

"Not yet," he said suddenly. "There are a pair of crossbows trained on you right now. Turn a quarter to the right." She did so and he nodded. "Count fifty paces, then take it off. Take the first left you see and it'll take you back to the Souk. You can find your way from there?"

She nodded. Her face looked toward him, as though she wanted to tell him something, as though she could see him through the blindfold. But she said nothing, instead marching off as directed.

Of course, she couldn't see through that blindfold.

Of course.

And had she seen that his knees had shaken so badly that he'd had to lean against the wall to keep from buckling over and vomiting out on the streets?

Of course not, he told himself. *If she had, she'd realize what a fucking mistake she'd made. If she had, she'd realize the idiocy of asking us to clean up this war when we were the ones who started it. If she had, she'd realize just how fucking stupid it is to think that the Jackals can stop people from dying.*

Something rose in his gullet. He held it down under his tongue until he felt it might just burst out his throat. Slowly it subsided. He swallowed bile, tasted acid in his nostrils. His breath came in slow and sweltering.

Ah, well, he said to himself. *Cut her some slack. Yourself, too.* He closed his eyes. *No need to worry too much. Four hundred eighty-nine dead. Last time this happened, you killed at least twice that.*

EIGHT

A Matter of Grit

Now, I know you shaved your head and all, but I feel like I'd be poor company if I didn't point out that the wanted posters were not wholly artistically inaccurate. The person that notices your scars or that brutish slope of your jaw is bound to recognize you. I trust you realize that this is not a wise idea?"

"Yep."

"I trust, then, that you also realize that your flimsy excuse of going out for supplies is pure rot. Even if it weren't midnight, the couthi has already taken care of all that you'll need on the journey to the Gullet."

"Yep."

There was a long sigh.

"I trust, then, that I'm wasting my breath?"

Lenk didn't bother answering that. Mocca had known him long enough now to know when his silence was final. Or perhaps he just peered into Lenk's mind and saw that he wouldn't answer.

Whichever, if it meant he could move through the dusty streets of Jalaang in silence, so much the better.

In his defense, the idea of going out to search for supplies at midnight was only mostly rot. This was a city born of the same loins that had birthed Cier'Djaal, after all. The streets of Jalaang weren't quite asleep, with a few hardworking—or particularly desperate—merchants manning a few stalls or storefronts here and there in the shadow of guard barracks. And those souls currently trudged through the streets, necks bent as though the sun were still beating down on them.

Though it was hard to deny Mocca's point.

Even now he saw a few posters bearing his visage on the walls. The hair was still the most striking thing about it, but anyone who looked closely enough would be able to figure out his identity.

It would have been much safer to sit in the middle of the modest room the couthi had rented him, completely alone in a perfectly silent room with nothing to keep him company but his thoughts.

Which made the possibility of being recognized as a murderer infinitely preferable.

Men like him were ill suited to thinking. Men who carried swords looked no farther than the tips of them. Men like him were better suited to living hilt to blade, cut to cut, body to body.

For when things grew silent enough to think, those bodies would be his sole company.

Here, at least, he was moving. Here every eye cast his way held suspicion. Here he was surrounded by enemies he had yet to make, blades that had yet to be drawn.

Who could possibly think about Kataria in a place like this?

Ah, shit.

The memory of her gnawed at the back of his skull, a wound yet to heal. Every time his thoughts drifted from the weight of his sword on his back, his mind filled with the memory of the last stare she had given him.

Surely, if the slow-moving gentleman in front of him had known this, he would have understood why Lenk coarsely shoved him out of the way.

"I can understand that you care little enough for yourself," Mocca said, glancing over his shoulder as the man stumbled and cursed, "but that's hardly reason to violate the social contract."

"Shut up," Lenk snapped in answer to both Mocca and the aggrieved man as he stalked into darker streets.

"My, but we get snippy when we're in emotional turmoil, don't we?" In the blink of an eye, Mocca was suddenly beside Lenk, keeping pace with him despite a leisurely stride.

"If you were more than a ghost," Lenk muttered, "I'd show you more steel than snip."

"I'm a mental vision sent far from hell and thrust directly into your head to be made manifest through your thoughts," Mocca replied. "Not a ghost. Don't be absurd."

"There are other words for you, you know. Shorter, less kind words."

"Vulgarity remains the fool's imitation of conversation," Mocca said. "Sheffu's relative education affords him no more distinction than that of your average rube." He cast a sidelong grin at Lenk. "What's he told you about me, anyway?"

"That you were a tyrant and a murderer before you were sent to hell," he replied. "That you reigned over mortals as a god and made them thralls to your will, that you treated them as so much chattel and swine and, before you were cast down into hell, you were—"

"*Point being*," Mocca interjected, "amongst the insipid drama, any actual knowledge might very well be lost. The tales know me as God-King, but make no mention as to how I came to carry the title."

"What? You were *elected* God-King?" Lenk asked, eyeing him warily.

"Divinity is democracy, Lenk," he replied. "No god can rule a man without his express consent. I offered mortalkind nothing that any other god would not. I offered them cures to their diseases. I brought order to end their violence. They lived in fear of the night and its many horrors, I promised them light."

"Then why were you cast down?" Lenk asked. "Why did the gods throw you into hell?"

"Because," Mocca said, "I did what they could not. I kept my promises."

Lenk forced his eyes ahead as he turned down an alley. "I've fought demons before, you know. Everything that crawls out of hell tells the same story: They're the victims of petty gods and the world's unfair."

"Would that not suggest we have a point?" Mocca asked.

"Or that lying is common to all of you," Lenk snapped. "And even if you were victims, I've never met a demon that spared much thought for a mortal life. It's your Khovura that are running rampant in Cier'Djaal, killing people."

"The Khovura are not mine. They are the destitute and desperate, the impoverished and in pain, those who were so betrayed by fashas, betrayed by gods, betrayed by their own city that they would turn to *demons* for salvation."

"But you—"

"Look at yourself, Lenk." Mocca's voice was cold as a wind blowing over a corpse. "You're running. You're terrified. You have every right to be. Cier'Djaal burns now, but it was dying long before the Karneri-ans and Sainites came. The fashas have heaped so much filth upon the people that they choke on it. Shicts fight tulwar, tulwar kill couthi, *everyone* hates humans. This world screams out in pain and no one in heaven is listening."

He held his arms out wide in helpless demonstration.

"What could I possibly do to it that it hasn't done to itself?"

There was a dearth of arrogance in Mocca's voice. In its wake a sad-ness rimmed his eyes, something soft and dark as nightfall. His frown was deep, his shoulders slumped under the weight of a helplessness unbecoming of a god-king.

Lenk resented that. The arrogance of the demons was legendary. Arro-gance he had been prepared for. But no legend spoke of empathy in demons. No legend told him what to do if one of them actually had a valid point.

But they were still just words. And Mocca was still just a demon. And there was no shortage of demons among the carcasses Lenk had left behind him. A demon was a creature of lies, of empty promises, of a thousand names. And Lenk had mind for only one name.

Farlan Sandish. Immigrant from Nivoire. Owned a small rice paddy on the very edge of the Green Belt.

It was for Farlan that Lenk didn't answer. It was for Farlan that Lenk turned away from Mocca and began to walk down a dirty alley.

He had scarcely taken ten steps when he saw what he thought was a heap of rags and garbage stir beside him. Garbage, though, rarely car-ried bowls and spoke.

"Alms, sir?" The beggar extended a skinny, pale arm without looking up. Thin fingers clutched a wooden pendant carved to resemble a holy phoenix, along with his bowl. "Talanas smiles on those who exemplify his mercy."

Perhaps it was that the man's voice sounded so familiar that caused Lenk not to answer. And perhaps it was Lenk's lack of an answer that made the man finally look up. His skin, though covered in grime, dis-tinctly had the pale tinge of a northerner's. His hair, though slathered in dust, was fair and coarse. This was no Djaalic.

And instantly Lenk recognized him. He had met this man, so long ago it could have been a dream. But he remembered this man, back in the Souk, back before any of this had happened.

This man had said he was from Steadbrook, a village that had been turned to a pile of ash that Lenk had crawled out of. And once he realized that Lenk had come from the same place, he had screamed with a horror in his eyes.

The same kind of horror that was now dawning upon him as he recognized who was talking to him.

"Demon!" he screamed now, as he had screamed then, leaping to his feet. "*DEMON!*"

He whirled to run. Lenk's hand shot out, seized him by the back of his collar, and jerked him back. The man had a bit of height on him, but his body was frail and filthy, and when Lenk slammed him against the wall of the building, he heard something crack.

"I told you," Mocca said with a sigh. "Did I not tell you?"

"Shut up," Lenk snarled over his shoulder.

"Ah, I must have done something so gloriously amazing to have pissed off the gods like this," the beggar chuckled. "Fled the north to escape you and found Cier'Djaal, fled Cier'Djaal to escape the war and found you."

"*You* don't say a fucking word." Lenk pressed his forearm against his throat. "If I get any hint of you going to any guard, any shopkeep, even *thinking* about telling someone who I am, I'll gut you where you stand."

The beggar's eyes were cold, appraising. He stared Lenk down with a hard glance and spoke with a harder voice. "Aye," he muttered, breathing shallowly. "And you would, wouldn't you? A killer of your renown wouldn't bat an eye over another corpse in his wake, let alone a dead beggar."

"I didn't do this," Lenk said. "I didn't start this war."

"An entire city says otherwise. You expect me to believe you over them?"

Lenk spared a glance for his filthy clothing. "Looks like they didn't give much of a shit about you."

"There I was just scum," the beggar replied. "No one bothers scum. No one minds when scum goes fleeing because no one minded that scum was there in the first place. But here I'm just someone waiting to die, like all the others who fled." He sniffed. "I preferred being scum."

"I don't give a shit what you want to be or what you are once I leave," Lenk said, "so long as you're quiet about it. You never breathe a word of this and whoever kills you won't be me."

"You expect me to believe that?" The beggar laughed bitterly. "Scum doesn't look down on much, but everyone spits on the word of a murderer."

"I told you I didn't—"

"I'm not speaking of Cier'Djaal," the beggar snapped back. "I'm not speaking of everyone who's died in there or all the people who will. I'm speaking of your first handiwork. I'm speaking of Steadbrook."

Steadbrook.

The village he'd been born in that had played host to a life he couldn't remember, full of parents without faces, friends without names, and loves and lives that he had spent a very long time trying to not think about.

Somehow it had never seemed real until he heard the name spoken aloud.

He knew all the things he *should* think when he heard it: toil in the fields, the scent of manure, awkward fumbling beneath a girl's skirt at a harvest festival, the scent of tobacco that clung to him whenever he sat down in his grandfather's chair.

But when he heard the name, when he closed his eyes, all he saw was shadow and flame and all the smoke and screams that had come with it.

"Don't remember me?" The beggar laughed again. "Aye, that's probably all that saved me. I kept to myself, didn't go to any festivals, didn't attend any gatherings. I was fleeing shit back east, didn't want a life there. But I got one."

The beggar's voice quavered. His eyes glistened.

"I had a life. I had a wife. She had a name and so did I." He spoke through clenched teeth, the words trembling. "Gathwer. That was mine. You took hers."

"I don't remember." Lenk's voice sounded distant in his ears, like someone else's.

"Her? I'm not surprised."

"Any of it. I remember shadows, fire, people dying." He shook his head. "Bandits."

"Bandits?"

"Or shicts. Or tulwar. Or a Karnerian raiding party looking to expand eastward. A barn fire that got out of control, something, I don't know. It's happened before."

Gathwer's mouth hung open. "You murdered the lot of them and you have the blasphemy to say you don't remember—"

"Do *you*?" Lenk seized him by his dirty clothes, slammed him against the wall of the building. "Do you remember seeing me kill them?"

Gathwer held firm, as firm as a man like him could, before answering. "No. But I remember you. I remember the sullen, brown-haired kid with the dark eyes and smelly grandfather. I thought you just another farmer's runt until the night it happened. You disappeared in the fire..."

He raised a trembling finger and thrust it at Lenk.

"And *you* came out of the ashes," he hissed. "At first I thought it was someone else. He had your features, your build, but his hair was gray as a mule and his eyes were cold. But it was you. Gods help me, I know it was you."

"Horseshit." The word came too late, too quavering to sound convincing to either of them. "*Horseshit.*"

"Wizardry, a god's curse, demons," Gathwer said. "I don't know what caused it and I don't care. I don't care what made you do it there or in Cier'Djaal. I don't care where you're going so long as you stay the hell away from *me*."

His arms were skinny from years of hunger, his muscles shot with weakness. Yet when he shoved out, Lenk felt his legs go out from under him, suddenly bloodless. He fell to the ground as Gathwer took off running, disappearing down another alley.

He should pursue, he knew, lest the beggar go and report him to some guard.

Failing that, he should begin counting off the reasons why the beggar had to have been lying, why that story was insane.

Failing *that*, he should run and find a dark place to hide until things started making sense again.

But men like Lenk were ill suited to thinking. He lived body to body, cut to cut. And perhaps the only way out of this was more cutting.

He could only hope Farlan Sandish would be a different man than he was.

"This isn't any wiser than before," Mocca protested.

Lenk, of course, was not listening. His legs had found their blood and his ears had found the sound of dirt crunching under his feet.

"Really, have you not learned that yours is not a life that begs haste?" Mocca's voice was shrill as he hurried to catch up.

Lenk, of course, did not answer. He could not afford to. He had to keep moving.

"Will you at least stop long enough to tell me where you're going?"

"Back to my room, then to the docks," Lenk said, turning down another alley. "There were some boats there. I can cobble enough money to hire someone to take me upriver."

"Unnecessary," Mocca said. "Guards must be inundated with false reports about the assassin of Cier'Djaal. I highly doubt that anyone will take the word of a filthy northerner."

"I don't care about that," Lenk said. "I have to get out of here."

"What? And go where?"

"Anywhere, I don't know. Away from here. Away from all of this."

"All because of the ravings of a madman?"

"He wasn't mad." Lenk turned a glare upon Mocca. "I looked into his eyes. He believed what he was saying."

"No one ever accused the insane of insincerity. It's highly possible he was terrified to the point of lying. Or perhaps he misremembers."

"That would make two of us, then," Lenk snapped, the ire rising in his voice. "I certainly don't know what happened that night. Or the night before. Or any other night. When I think of Steadbrook it only comes in flashes, snippets like stories I've overheard. I can't remember the first girl I ever kissed or my mother's face or what I did on that farm. I can't remember how anyone died or what I was doing before I picked up this."

His hand went to the bundle of sticks on his back, found the hilt of his blade as though it had reached out for him. He pulled it free, the sword shining bright against the waning moon, eager to be out and unhidden.

"Maybe he was lying," Lenk said, looking over the naked blade, "maybe he was scared. But I can't say he's wrong."

"What does it matter?" Mocca held his hands out. "Lies or truth, it's in the past. We've come this far for the future, to find a new life, to—"

"*We* have done nothing!" Lenk all but roared. "*I* came this far for a life. *My* life. Because *I* wanted something good." He held the blade up, looked at himself in its reflection. "But how the fuck would I know what that even looks like?"

"You're overreacting." Mocca's voice came out on an exasperated sigh. "Though I suppose I should hardly be surprised. Your desperation to find any excuse to flee from responsibility is growing a tad predictable."

"Responsibility? For all this shit that fell on me?"

"Despite what poets and priests might say, fecal matter does not fall from the sky. One has to step in and then decide whether or not he wishes to clean it off."

"I'm not going to listen to a demon about matters of cleanliness."

"As I said, whatever stories you've heard are—"

"*DEMON*." Lenk spit the word, let it sizzle on the air. "Whatever the stories, whoever the storyteller, *that's* the word they use for you. And whatever you did to earn it, you still earned it. Tell me whatever you wish, but don't expect me to listen to any lectures on responsibility."

Mocca's face grew hard, his eyes narrowing to thin slits. "The world is not so vast as mortals pretend it is, Lenk. Trust someone who has had eternity to watch it rot."

The stare Lenk returned was as hard, as dark, and much, much colder.

"The list of things I trust is growing shorter every breath," he said simply. "And on it, you are at the very bottom."

There was, Lenk decided as he turned away and stalked out of the alley and into the streets, very little satisfaction in arguing with a demon.

Granted, he hadn't been certain what he was expecting. Demons—insofar as he had experienced—were prone to dramatic speeches and senseless gibbering in equal measures. But then again, most of those demons had been in the process of trying to kill him. He could have tolerated a declaration of doom laced over fiery rhetoric. He could have suffered a howling, shapeless shriek hurled at his back.

But the funerary silence that fell between them as Mocca watched Lenk depart without a word was something altogether too chilling.

He slid his sword back into the makeshift sheath on his back. In the echo of his words, he was given time to think. Gathwer's words still hung about his neck like a yoke, dragging his head down as he made his way through the streets.

He tried to ease his thoughts with bigger concerns, such as how to get back to the inn. He glanced up and saw that he was at the center of a dusty square between a cluster of merchant stands and the looming wall of a barracks. He looked down the street he thought led to it, then let his eyes settle upon the shadows.

And the man who crouched within them.

His gaze lingered too long, he stiffened too noticeably; either way the man came creeping out of the shadows, eyes wide and bright as the naked sword in his hand. Lenk heard footsteps on dust behind him, cast a glance over his shoulder, and saw three more men emerging from the alley and street mouths. Two held shorter blades, the third a spear, each one made of new steel, untested and shiny.

Djaalics, though not from Cier'Djaal, if the cut of their shabby clothes was any indication. Their eyes were big, but the fear within them was not so thick that it could hide the intent echoed in their weapons. Lenk made a show of sliding his sword out from behind him, shrugging off the bundle of sticks and raising the blade.

"It's not worth it, boys," he said. "I don't have any money and you're not going to like how this ends."

The first man, the one with the biggest sword, seemed to register the words, but merely looked over Lenk's head to the three behind him.

"You're sure that's him?" he asked.

One of them held up a wanted poster bearing his image. The man looked it over, then looked back to Lenk and nodded.

"Yeah, it's him."

"But he's got no hair," the man with the spear said.

"I'm not him," Lenk said. But he could see in their eyes that they were not listening, or at least not convinced.

"It doesn't have to be hard," the lead one whispered, stepping closer to Lenk. "It doesn't have to be messy. We don't even have to kill you, if you just cooperate. The fashas, they'll..."

Apparently he could think of no reassuring way to end that sentence. Lenk held up his blade, edged his way toward a wall to take all of them in his view. They made no move to stay out of his line of sight, clustering together. Inexperienced, Lenk recognized, standing too close together, probably thought it'd keep them safer.

"He's not going to listen," one of the men with the short blades hissed. "We've got to do this. We've got no choice."

"You've always got a choice," Lenk replied, coldly. "Yours are to see this end cleanly or in a mess on the dust."

"He can't take all of us." One of them went into a twitching stance of readiness, holding his blade out as if it were a lance. "Come on."

"But—"

"I SAID GO!"

He loosed a shriek as he charged toward Lenk. The one with the spear shakily echoed him, following. But once they drew closer and the one with the blade made a lunge, the spear-carrier faltered, perhaps out of fear of accidentally striking his friend. Or out of fear of being killed.

Lenk wasn't about to stop to ask.

He let the one with the blade make his move, lowering his sword as he stepped deftly past a clumsy thrust. His blade came up in an instant, finding reflexes sluggish and flesh unguarded. Blood spilled on the ground, spattering in a bed upon which the man fell, unmoving.

The one with the spear faltered further, stepping back as he jabbed his spear, as though Lenk were a dog who could be held at bay with a stick. When he pressed forward, undeterred, the man turned the spear sideways and held it up before him as a makeshift shield.

Perhaps he was inexperienced with the weapon, or perhaps he just underestimated Lenk's strength. He certainly looked surprised enough when Lenk leapt forward, bringing his blade down in an arc upon the center of the spear, behind the weight of the head, to cleave first through wood and then through sinew.

Splinters flew amid drops of scarlet as Lenk planted a boot in the man's stomach and jerked his blade free in a wet burst. He leapt over the man's body and rushed toward the other one with the short blade.

This one leapt back as Lenk swung, narrowly avoiding a cut across the chest. Immediately he tried to get back in with a low thrust, attempting to use the short blade to get inside Lenk's swing. A sound plan with a clumsy execution; he stumbled on his own feet and Lenk darted back, bringing his blade up to hack at the man's wrist and send the blade flying from his hand.

He screamed, clutching at his wounded arm with his good one and then holding both up as a flimsy shield as Lenk's downswing came upon him. Bone snapped, dust crunched beneath a body, and Lenk turned and saw, through the red that dotted his face, the last one.

The man with the big sword stood now, as he had stood the whole fight, with eyes wild with amazement. He held the weapon in front of him, hands wrapped one over the other on the hilt, as though it were a ward that would keep Lenk at bay.

It did not. And as Lenk advanced, he took a step backward. His lips quavered, trying to form words that wouldn't come. A plea? A threat? Lenk didn't know, Lenk didn't care. He couldn't afford to.

He sensed the man's uncertainty, rushed to capitalize upon it. The man brought the blade down in an awkward swing. Lenk met him in a lock of blades, twisted his own grip so that the man's weapon pointed down and hammered a fist against the man's now unguarded jaw.

He staggered backward, dizzy from the blow. When he recovered, the fear was gone from his stare. Now his eyes were simply bright with surprise.

Perhaps he hadn't even noticed it when Lenk had driven his sword through his belly.

He stared down at the weapon dumbly. Again his lips twitched. The words came on a slurry of blood and tumbled upon the dust. He followed them as Lenk pulled his weapon free and stepped backward.

Through the sound of his own heart beating, he almost missed the sound of footsteps approaching behind him. And when he turned into a swing, he almost tore off the head from which two blue eyes stared at him.

"Easy." Two hands caught his wrist, held the blade quivering a finger's length from the soft flesh of a neck. "Easy." And though his flesh and his steel were both painted red, her voice was calm. "It's over."

That woman, the one in black. What was her name?

"Shuro," he whispered.

"Farlan Sandish," she replied.

It took him a moment to remember that name. And in that time, she eased his sword down and away from her. Suddenly aware of what he had almost done, as well as what he just had done, he stepped away. She raised the brim of her black hat, observed the bodies, and knelt down beside them.

"They came after me," he said. "I didn't—"

"I know," she said. "I saw. They attacked first."

He paused. "What else did you see?"

She looked up at him meaningfully. "Nothing else."

True or not, he chose not to challenge her statement. "What are you doing out here?"

"Same as you, I'm sure," she said. "Jalaang's best prices come after midnight. I was closing a deal when I heard the commotion." She pried open one of the dead men's hands, observed his palms. "Soft hands." She glanced at the weapons lying scattered and unbloodied. "Too soft of this kind of steel. These weren't warriors."

"Then they—"

"They had no business drawing them on someone who was," Shuro said. "Don't explain yourself to me." She glanced up at the sky. The moon was gone entirely, indigo night having given way to pale dawn. "In fact, you'd do well to not mention this to anyone. The Old Man is leaving in a little over an hour. The guards here don't get paid enough to find bodies in that time, let alone find who made them."

She looked at him. Her eyes seemed different from when he had seen them in Gurau. Brighter, more alert, maybe.

"Head back to the inn. Take the back alleys. I'll tell the innkeeper there's a problem with my room. Check to make sure he's gone, then go up to yours and wash quickly. Be at the docks when the time comes."

He furrowed his brows at her. "But how can I—"

"And don't. Ask. Questions." She rose up, carefully checking her clothing for any traces of blood. "You don't need me to tell you that, do you?" At his shake of the head, she nodded. "Be quick, Farlan Sandish."

That was good advice, Lenk knew. She was clearly a woman who knew more than she was letting on. It would be smart to listen to her.

But then again, just about anything would have been smarter than what he'd done.

He knelt beside one of the dead men, looked over his face. Plump cheeks, clean-shaven, not a single blemish beyond wrinkles of middle age, let alone a scar. He wasn't just not a warrior, he was someone who shouldn't even have heard of battle outside of what stories he told his children.

Did he have children?

"Merchants."

Lenk did not start at Mocca's voice. Nor was he surprised to see the man standing amid the slaughter, white robes unsullied and expression unflinching. His hands were folded behind his back as he surveyed the dead men.

"The one with the big sword was, at least," he continued. "His business in Cier'Djaal did poorly. A fasha came to collect on his debts. He took all he had left to buy that sword, hoping to collect on your bounty. This one"—he glanced at the one with the spear—"was his brother-in-law and partner. The others were his cousins, in similar straits."

"How do you know?" Lenk asked.

"I try not to pry, where possible, but the thoughts of dying men are difficult to ignore. Their final wishes, their hopes and prayers, go out for miles in all directions. Mostly, though, they think of their families."

"And did they?"

"They did," Mocca said. "From the moment they saw your face on the poster to the moment they saw your face painted with their own lives."

Mocca, in cruelty infinite, said nothing for a moment, that his words might hang in the silence like a man from the gallows. And when he spoke, his words were a macabre mercy.

"It won't stop." He looked at Lenk, unblinking. "There will be more to come. Men, women, old, and young. Some greedy, some wicked, but most of them desperate. For them to live, you must die. No matter what life you crave, what life you had, all you will have is more of this."

He gestured over the dead men. And in the spaces of dry dust among the pooling blood, his point lay.

"What do I have to do?" Lenk asked, so weak he barely recognized his own voice.

"Do as the woman instructs. Go to the Forbidden East."

"And then?"

"Then," Mocca said, "stand aside."

Lenk glanced up and he was gone. And despite the rising light of dawn, the world seemed a darker place.

NINE

VIPERS FOR BEDFELLOWS

Wizardry was, above all else, an art of preservation.

Common barknecks failed to appreciate this about wizards—unsurprising, as they tended to care only about the parts that involved making things explode—but then, the process of Harvesting was not something typically shared with people outside the Venarium.

Those with but meager flesh and bone to lose could be content to bury or burn their dead. A wizard was made of sterner stuff that just couldn't be wasted when he died.

His hair was woven into coats that could become wings in an instant. His skin would be taken to be made parchment for spellbooks. His bones would be wands, his teeth charms, his blood ink.

A wizard's body was not a perfect society, though; not all body parts were equal. There were often leftovers: livers, tongues, genitalia, other body parts that did not possess enough of a magical charge to be used in much.

But wizardry was, above all else, an art of preservation.

Hence the Charnel Hound.

"If I look up," Dreadaeleon spoke, voice echoing into the emptiness of his cell, "and you're still looking at me, I'm going to be upset."

From the stone bench upon which he lay, he looked up. And, true to his word, he was upset.

Few would blame him, he suspected. Who would *not* be upset by the amalgamation of flesh and paper sitting at the doorway of his cell? Up close, while the beast was still, he could make out the individual parts of the people's anatomy that made up its own: here a severed scrotum, there a knot of tongues, a few grafts of hairy flesh unsuitable for parchment. And all of it was wrapped up neatly, held together by paper inscribed with magical writ.

It had four legs and a snout, and though it had no eyes—at least in the traditional sense—he was certain it was looking at him.

He didn't blame it. That was its job, after all.

"I should *think*," Dreadaeleon insisted, "that something like your-self"—he made a vague gesture at the creature—"what with all the exposed cocks, would appreciate the concept of privacy."

He looked meaningfully at the chamber pot in the corner—the chamber pot that had yet to be emptied since his incarceration—and back to the Hound. And while it had no face—though it did have bits of people's faces—Dreadaeleon strongly suspected that Admiral Tibbles was not sympathetic.

He'd named it Admiral Tibbles.

Admiral Tibbles was poor company.

It wasn't that he was mad, goodness no. Three days of isolation was not enough to afford him the luxury of insanity. But three days of iso-lation, three days of no books to read, three days of meals delivered through a slot in an iron door without a sound, three days of no one to talk to but Admiral Tibbles...

Or...or had it been three days?

It was hard to tell down here—they *had* taken him down, hadn't they? Or had it been up? There were no windows, the sole source of light being a single glass globe dangling from the ceiling from which a static glow beamed incessantly, moment to moment.

What were they doing up there—or down there, depending? Mak-ing funeral arrangements pending his execution? Arranging another trial? Or were they just going to leave him down here with Admiral Tibbles as punishment?

Punishment. He sneered at the word. *Punishment for what? For using your power for purposes other than hiding in a tower and doing paperwork? For making a difference out there in the world where things matter? What could they possibly have to punish you for?*

He paused.

Well, aside *from the fact that you violated your chief oath as a member of the Venarium by using your powers on fellow concomitants. But aside from treason and murder, they've got nothing.*

He got up from his bench, started pacing. Admiral Tibbles's sightless gaze followed him as he moved from one end of the room to the other. As it sensed no magic from his franticness, the creature's directive to intervene was not activated.

That was fine; Dreadaeleon had no more thought to spare for the Hound or even his own life. His waking moments were devoted to Liaja.

What had they done to her? She had been accomplice to his crimes— no, not crimes, he corrected himself; activism—and the Venarium typically were not inclined to treat accomplices any better than the accused. But she had done nothing wrong! They couldn't just punish her, could they? She was a citizen of Cier'Djaal and was not subject to Venarium law. Doing so would violate the Sovereignty Pact.

Just as you did? he asked himself.

No, it was different when I did it, he replied. *I was trying to protect people. I protected them from the Karnerians and Sainites.*

The law's the law, old man, he told himself. *If you get excuses as to when it is and is not applicable, it kind of defeats the purpose, doesn't it?*

Yes, but a law that applies rigidly would assume that all people, places and circumstances are exactly the same, at all times, and—He paused, embarked on a brief flailing fit. *Whose side are you on, anyway?*

He looked down at his hands, saw them thick with sweat. His clothes—the threadbare tunic and breeches they had given him when he arrived—clung to his body with perspiration. His body was too thin, the suggestion of his ribs visible even through the damp cloth as it clung to him. They weren't feeding him enough. He was wasting away.

"See?" He turned to Admiral Tibbles and held out his arm. "Look. Thin as a bone, thin as a—"

He fell silent. The skin of his arm began to bubble and twitch. Something long and thin began to move beneath the flesh, pressing up against it and drawing thick, tuberous veins across his arm. He watched on in horror as the skin began to split, warm blood trickling down his arm and pattering on the floor. Worms, great purple things the size of fingers, began to snake out, gnashing little tooth-ringed circles for mouths as they writhed and coiled across his arm.

He didn't scream. Not anymore.

He closed his eyes, counted to ten. When he opened them again, his arm was once more whole. He could still feel the warmth of the blood, the pain of his flesh splitting apart, the scent of his own meat exposed to air, but there was no evidence of its having ever happened.

Broodvine hallucinations were even more powerful when they were involuntary.

It was too hard to think without the seed. Any amount of time longer than a few breaths spent in his own head invited the walls to start moving and the air to start whispering to him.

He glanced over to the door. Admiral Tibbles stood tense, eyeless gaze directed intently at Dreadaeleon. It could sense the magical nature of his hallucinations, but not the source. They had done this a thousand times in the hours he'd been here. In a few more moments, it would sense no more threat and return to its sitting position.

That's what it *usually* did, anyway.

This time, though, the Hound gingerly turned and stepped away from the door, settling down by its side.

"Well, well," Dreadaeleon muttered. "Seems I'm feeling important today."

There was only one reason the Hound ever did that.

And an instant later, it came through the door.

Or rather, *they* did.

Four of them: two women, two men, each one clad in a concomitant's brown coat and wearing a spellbook at their hip. They filed into his cell carefully, never fewer than six eyes on him at any time as they moved to form a semicircle around him. Admiral Tibbles watched from the edge, impassive.

"Concomitant Dreadaeleon Arethenes," one of the women suddenly spoke, stepping forward, "Member in Poor Standing, you are—"

"Member?" he interrupted her. "I've not been disbarred yet? Are we that desperate for fees?"

She flinched. "You are hereby commanded to attend a council regarding probationary release."

That caused him some pause. "Release?"

"*Probationary* release," the woman replied. "A council has been called by Lector Shinka and tentatively approved by all *remaining*"—she spoke the word with a sneer—"Lectors regarding outside developments involving your case. Your attendance is mandatory."

"Shinka?" he chuckled. "Well, it would have to be her, wouldn't it?

Lector Annis and I aren't on the best of terms and Lector Palanis must still be dreadfully cross at me." He smirked. "Assuming he's been able to emerge from his rooms in the past week?"

The woman's hands coiled into fists. "Lector Palanis is indisposed," she said. Her poise broke for just a moment, enough to let a scowl form on her face. "As you damn well know, you heretic fuck. You did it to him."

"Did what to him?" Dreadaeleon's laugh was short, bitter, and mean. "I heard only rumors as I was dragged down here. Some say he hasn't eaten in days, some say he never leaves his rooms, and some say the concomitants who don't do their chores get the privilege of cleaning up after him when he shits the bed. Which is it? The first? The second?" At her trembling rage, his grin grew broader. "All three?"

It was poor form to boast about one's own victory, even in the Venarium. It was decidedly cruel to revel in the outcome that had left Lector Palanis an emotional wreck. And taunting men and women who had the power to kill on the spot, at their discretion? That was downright foolish.

Perhaps he was just feeling frisky.

The woman seethed visibly, the dim light of Venarie roiling to life behind her eyes as she summoned countless spells to kill him in countless ways. He stood at the center of the room, hands folded behind him, smile unflinching.

One of her compatriots moved beside her, laid a hand on her shoulder. She drew in a breath, held it. The light faded from her eyes and she regarded him once more through frigid poise.

"Come with us, concomitant," she said. "The council awaits at the forty-second floor."

"The top? Excellent." He stepped past her, noting with some satisfaction how the remaining concomitants tensed. "There's a window on the thirty-third floor I should like to go by on our way. It has a lovely view of the courtyard grounds and I've not seen daylight in some time."

"That is not our approved route," the woman said.

"We can afford to take the time," Dreadaeleon replied. "The council is about my release, isn't it? It's not like they'll do much without me. Now, let's step lively, dear."

"And just what the fuck makes you think you can speak to me that way?" she growled after him.

He paused in the doorway, cast a cold smile over his shoulder. "The fact that they sent four of you."

It was a valuable skill for a man to know, upon entering a room, how many people wanted him dead.

While it was by no means an exact science, upon entering the vast circle that made up the main room of the forty-second floor of Tower Resolute, Dreadaeleon had at least a pretty good idea.

The concomitants who had escorted him immediately filed away to join the twenty or so others of their rank at the far wall. Stationed before them in another circle stood five Librarians, the Venarium's elite, with their black mantles, and Lector Annis was at the very center.

It was likely that they all wanted him dead, with two or three wanting him dead, burnt to ashes, the ashes fed to sharks, and then the sharks also dead.

At a guess, anyway.

Lector Annis looked up through rigid visage, made a gesture. The door closed at his bidding behind Dreadaeleon. Two concomitants stepped before it.

Dreadfully poor taste, he thought to himself as he glanced over the thirty or so wizards with murder in their eyes. *It's not as though he needs to demonstrate his power here.*

He glanced down at his side. Admiral Tibbles looked up over a snout made of various chunks.

"Shall we?" he muttered.

It was easier to keep his head high and his stride bold than he'd thought it would be, considering company and circumstance.

And he considered both. Very carefully.

No matter how much they hid it behind protocol and law, power was still everything to wizards. To them he was still dangerous enough to warrant four concomitants and a Charnel Hound. To them he was powerful enough to warrant five Librarians. To them he was strong.

And he was well on his way to demonstrating that.

Right up until Lector Annis stepped aside and revealed an unexpected attendant.

It had been days—weeks, maybe—since he had seen her. She looked more tired, less well fed, but no less strong now than she had looked when she had straddled him and smashed her fists into his face, again and again. And her smile was no less sincere now than it had been.

But he did not return it.

He never would.

Not after what Asper had done to him.

"I'm finished." Dreadaeleon spun on his heel.

"Dread, wait," Asper began, reaching out for him.

"I have no desire to be here," Dreadaeleon said to the nearest concomitant. "Take me back to my cell. Apologies for the inconvenience."

"Concomitant Arethenes."

Annis's words speared through the air to land directly between Dreadaeleon's shoulder blades and pin him where he stood. Every concomitant and Librarian leveled their gaze at him, their eyes suddenly alight with the red flame of Venarie.

"Every member in good standing in this tower is fully authorized to use lethal force to detain you." His body trembled with the ire his voice sought to contain. "And if there were a record of this meeting being kept, I would demand it be noted that I consider that authorization a gross underestimation of the sort of prejudice with which a criminal like you should be treated."

It felt almost disrespectful, out of that admittedly very verbose and eloquent threat, to pick out just a few words.

"There's no record of this meeting?" Dreadaeleon asked, turning around.

"Lector Annis was, regrettably, not informed of this meeting until quite recently."

The voice was crystalline to Annis's metallic. It sounded right, coming as it did from a soft smile set within a pretty face framed by elegant curls. A woman, dressed in a Lector's robes, emerged from the ring of concomitants, neatly closing a book in her hands.

"As indicated in the bylaws regarding External Non-Sovereign Affairs, we are permitted limited session without adhering to normal council law," Lector Shinka said, smiling. She gestured to Asper. "Affairs such as the one proposed by this young lady."

Asper smiled meekly, offered a wave. "Hi." She awkwardly turned to take in the unresponsive circle around her. "Hello. Asper. Is my name."

"Such a bylaw can only be invoked if the external party is deemed to have merit enough to stand in Venarium council." Lector Annis cast a sneer over Asper's dirty robes, settling on the phoenix pendant around her neck. "A priestess? What is your relation to the criminal?"

"Dreadaeleon and I were colleagues," Asper said. "Adventurers in each other's company."

"Were," Annis noted coolly.

"There were some...disagreements."

"Disagreements?" Dreadaeleon snarled and stormed forward, kept in check only by Admiral Tibbles's moving in front of him. "You leapt atop me, called me a worthless boy, and damn near broke my nose!"

Asper's face twisted in anger, but she said nothing. Annis's eyebrows rose appreciatively at her.

"This is true?" he asked.

"There's more to it than that," Asper replied through a heated breath. "But it's true."

Annis nodded slowly, turned, and made a gesture. "Merit of the external party has been approved by the Primary Lector."

"Oh, you smug son of a—" Dreadaeleon began to spit.

"The Secondary Lector concurs." Shinka flashed a warning glare at Dreadaeleon before her expression softened to a smile once more. "I trust we may proceed informally now? The external party—"

"My name is Asper," the priestess interrupted.

"Of course it is." Shinka's laughter was more than a little condescending. "Asper approached the doors to Tower Resolute late last night. Despite the unorthodoxy of her arrival, I agreed to see her. We spoke at length regarding the circumstances surrounding Cier'Djaal's recent..." She waved a hand, searching for a word. "Upheaval."

Asper flinched at the word, doubtlessly forming a lengthy rant on the inhumanity of deeming Cier'Djaal's hundreds dead a mere "upheaval."

Always like that, Dreadaeleon hissed inwardly. *Always thinking of the poor and the persecuted, yet all too glad to tread on those closest to her.* He narrowed his eyes. *"Boy," she called you. "Useless, worthless, selfish, cruel, little." We won't be playing her game, old man, will we?*

"None of which is our concern," Annis replied. His hands folded behind him, he strode to the center of the circle. "The disagreement between the Karnerians and the Sainites is a military matter, intervention on our part would be explicitly prohibited by the Sovereignty Pact. Two gangs of rock-headed thugs killing each other are not our concern."

"Normally I'd agree," Shinka offered, following him into the middle of the circle. "But the priestess makes a logical case for our intervention."

"The words *priestess* and *logical* do not belong in the same train of thought, let alone in the same sentence as an idea like that. However persuasive you might find her, we are expressly forbidden from—"

"You don't get to sit out a war like this."

Annis fixed Asper with a glower that suggested he was very surprised that she had spoken at all, let alone interrupted him. The sentiment was echoed through the circle of concomitants, a collective tension settling over the room. Asper, though, remained insufferably steely as she approached the Lector.

"With all respect, sir," she continued, "if you were to look outside your tower, you'd see people suffering. They are trampled underfoot, burned from their houses, caught in the midst of melees and made prey by the scavengers that follow. They had every intention of remaining neutral, as well."

She swept her gaze outward, to the concomitants and Librarians surrounding her.

"They, of course, did not have the advantage of a tower."

Typical, Dreadaeleon thought. *Always orating, always posturing. One wonders how well her resolve fares without an audience.* He sneered. *These are Venarium, not peasants. They can't be swayed without ten forms of written approval from a Lector.*

"This war may be between two outside forces, but they are not rocks," Asper said. "They are whirlwinds. They suck in everything around them—weapons, gold, people—batter them about and hurl them at each other and leave the shattered remains in their wake before they move on." She leveled a pointed gaze at the assembly. "They've not yet moved to your tower, it's true, but—"

"And they will not." Annis stepped toward her, looking down a pointed nose. "One could hardly blame you for not knowing the intricacies of the Sovereignty Pact, but I trust you grasp the meaning of the latter word." He brought his hands together before him. "It is an agreement between the Venarium and all civilized nations of the world. They observe our right to self-govern in exchange for our staying removed from their conflicts."

"Yet for all that we have stood by the Pact, foreign powers have not always responded in kind," Shinka interjected. "A host of offenses

against the Venarium by Karneria and Saine alike have been committed in the past." Her smile dropped to something cold. "Lest we forget
Tower Prime."

A collective cringe swept through the chamber at the mention of
Tower Prime. Even Dreadaeleon was not immune to the memory: It
was one of the first lessons taught to any wizard.

Venarium historians had yet to discern exactly which religious
order—Daeonists, Talanites, Gevrauchians—had led the charge that
killed a hundred wizards and burned a thousand years of knowledge.
But they agreed on a conclusion, if not a culprit. And thus a staunch dis-
regard for the affairs of the religious had been at the core of Venarium
teachings since.

"We forget Tower Prime because we are in no position to challenge an
army," Annis snapped back. "For every wizard in the world, there are a
hundred barknecked imbeciles with sharp sticks. Our powers are limited
and their ignorance is not. It was not so long ago that we were hated,
feared, and hunted the same as any shict or tulwar. The Venarium was
created to see an end to that and I will not be the one to initiate a return."

"That only proves my point," Asper said. "Their ignorance has not
changed, Lector. As soon as they think it's prudent to do so, they will
find a new reason to come after you."

At this Annis stood still, his eyes focused intently on her. The air of dismissive contempt eased a little as he waited patiently for her to continue.

At which point Dreadaeleon could no longer keep silent.

"You can't possibly be listening to—" he began to say, but was suddenly cut off by a lifting of Annis's hand.

As well as the magical gesture that accompanied it and smashed him
to the ground beneath an invisible force.

"Proceed," Annis said.

Asper's face twisted into a concerned frown as Dreadaeleon squirmed
beneath the rippling force of Annis's spell. "Is he going to, uh..."

He most certainly was *not* going to, uh.

At a glimpse, no one in the room—even those trained to see such
things—would think of Annis's magic as anything more than a simple
demonstration of force designed to shove Dreadaeleon humiliatingly to
the ground. But here, beneath the rippling wave of force, Dreadaeleon
had more than a glimpse.

He could feel the intricacies of the spell, whereby the force reached past his skin to press down on his bones, to squeeze his lungs and crush his throat. His body writhed like a wineskin with a hole in it as the air was slowly, subtly, methodically forced out of him.

And she's *just staring like an idiot*, he thought, finding it funny that, through all the breathless agony racking him, he had enough left in him to glare at Asper still.

Well, perhaps not so much funny as infuriating. Also painful.

"Lector Annis is well aware of the limitations of his own power." Shinka laid a hand upon her associate's arm, offering him a pointed glare. "As aware as he is that protocol forbids unsanctioned execution, even at an informal meeting."

Annis's lips perked into a small smirk. His hand lowered. Dreadaeleon felt a great weight lifted from him, leaving him gasping on the floor. Asper cringed, pried her eyes away from him.

"Uh, right," she said. "Look, businesses have been looted by Karnerians and burned by Sainites, houses have been pillaged by Sainites and destroyed by Karnerians. They've found plenty of reason to drag everyone else in their war and only one reason to avoid involving you."

Realization dawned upon Annis's features with a concerned knitting of his brows. "They lack the power to challenge us."

"But not for long." Asper moved to a window, pointed out toward the desert. "Soon—sooner than you'd think—convoys bearing more supplies, more troops, and more weapons will arrive in the city. Cier'Djaal will be overrun with proper armies, instead of mere garrisons. And sooner or later, they'll turn their sights on you."

Annis said nothing. He folded his hands behind his back and strode to the same window, staring out over the city as though he could see it unfurling before him: rivers of soldiers moving through streets flanked by burning houses, all converging on his tower.

"They already do not trust us, Primary Lector," Shinka said, moving beside him. "The Karnerians consider us godless heathens. The Sainites view us as potential rivals for power. Their pretense is the same as it was when Tower Prime was destroyed. They await only the resources to carry it out."

A long moment of silence passed before Annis spoke again. "What do you propose?"

"Armies are businesses," Asper said. "If they can't justify the occupation of the city, they can't bring more troops in. If we can inflict enough losses on their garrisons to make the city seem inhospitable, the convoys will become rescue missions instead of reinforcements."

"Direct action against a foreign power?" Annis shook his head. "Impossible. We answer to a higher council. They would never permit members in good standing to violate the Sovereignty Pact."

Asper's eyes drifted over to Dreadaeleon. "How about a member in poor standing, then?"

Annis's face did not so much fall as plummet and crash upon the floor. Whatever vestiges of indulgent humor might have played upon his features were instantly replaced by a frigid, unblinking harshness. He drew his hands up behind him, strode to the center of the room, and spoke with a voice that could cut stone.

"Every member in good standing present is hereby ordered to return to their duties," he said clearly.

At this the concomitants exchanged nervous glances and the Librarians shifted uneasily, as though they were wondering if he had simply misspoken. The scowl with which he whirled on them was decidedly edifying.

"*Leave*," he snarled.

With not quite enough haste to upset good order, they filed out of the room. Concomitants left first, whispering nervously as soon as they mistakenly thought they were out of earshot. Librarians followed, falling in a perfect line before exiting the room, the last one sparing a cautious glance over his shoulder before shutting the doors.

Dreadaeleon finally had enough feeling in his legs to rise back to his feet. And no sooner had he done so than he saw Annis swoop over to Asper and drink her in his shadow.

"Contrary to what impressions our isolationism might give, I do have an idea of who you are, priestess," the Lector growled. "And it is only out of concern for our reputation that I do not hurl you out of this tower for suggesting the kind of heresy you have just done."

Funny, Dreadaeleon thought, but seeing Asper cringe the way she did at his threat did not bring him the joy he'd thought it might. Rather he took a tentative step forward, only to be met with the fleshy figure of Admiral Tibbles situating itself before him.

Really? he thought. *Is the dog not a member or is he just in poor standing?*

"I have humored this suggestion all I am willing to," Annis continued. "To violate protocol by admitting you was amusing. To skirt treason by hearing you suggest we violate the Sovereignty Pact was daring. But to hear you recommend we release this... this..."

The stare he turned upon Dreadaeleon was not hateful. Hate was something far too tame and altogether too insignificant to adequately describe the sort of coldness that radiated from Annis's stare and froze Dreadaeleon's blood in his veins.

What was in Annis's eyes, at that moment, was knowledge. His was a promise that he would see Dreadaeleon die and there was nothing the boy could do about it. Not a threat, not a posture. Just a fact.

And one that made Dreadaeleon feel that he might have been spared the worst of it if he had just been crushed to death a moment ago.

"Lector," Asper said, "I am aware of Dread's issues, but—"

"You are not." Annis whirled that frigid stare upon Asper, honed it to a jagged icicle and thrust it straight between her eyes. "Whatever pithy hymns you have to quote, whatever false sense of hope you swallow when you look up at the sky and pretend to hear a god, you are not aware. You do not know what he has done. You do not know what he will do. You do not know what you are asking of me."

And Asper said nothing.

She did not flinch.

She did not blink.

She did not back away.

"I am asking nothing of you, wizard," she said, crushing whatever fear might have lurked in her voice beneath an iron certainty. "I wouldn't presume to think for a moment you could give a shit about anything beyond your tower, and I wouldn't ever make the mistake of thinking you'd ever think a human life is worth more than your own.

"I am telling you, right here, right now, what is going to happen. This war will eat you. I have seen it happen. I will see it happen a hundred more times this week. I am telling you that you have a way out. You have a renegade wizard who has already been seen fighting the Karnerians and Sainites. All you need to do is find a way to lose him for a few days, let him go out and wreak some havoc and then collect him.

"I'm not asking you to do a gods-damned thing. I'm telling you this is the best thing you can possibly do for yourself, and if you don't like that, then I'm telling you the next-best thing you can do is stuff your head deep inside your own ass, pretend that you came up with this idea instead of me, and then do it anyway."

And Dreadaeleon suddenly knew why he hated her so much.

Not for the years he had craved her affections and been left wanting. Not for the humiliations she had heaped upon him when she had called him useless, selfish, and small. Not even for the bruises and blood she had left on his face.

She stood now before a man who could incinerate her with a thought. She faced a man barely in control of himself, who belonged to an order for whom a lack of control was a death sentence.

And she would not back down.

When faced with this kind of conflict, he had crawled into a hole with a whore and filled it with smoke. And she...she stared at Annis as if he were a naughty boy who wouldn't go to bed.

He hated her for that.

And he hated her more for the fact that it seemed to be working.

Lector Annis's words were breathless as he spoke. "There will be considerations. Precautions, pretenses..."

"Claim he's ill," Asper said. "Have him sent to the Temple of Talanas. Even wizards need healers. We'll say he escaped on his way there. After he's adequately hindered the armies..."

"And what makes you think I'd do this?" Dreadaeleon spoke up. "You intend to use me as meat for your hounds and then put the bones on trial."

"I would promise leniency in your sentence, concomitant, but considerations for heretics are strictly prohibited by protocol," Shinka replied. She cast a thoughtful look to Annis. "But, as today seems to be the day for violating such..."

Annis's mouth twitched, as though the idea he was trying so hard to swallow might come back up any moment. "He shall be under guard. The Charnel Hound will follow him."

"Discreetly," Asper pressed.

Finally he drew in a long breath and held it. "Under such consideration, the Primary Lector proposes acceptance to the external party's proposal. With reservations." He affixed a glare upon Dreadaeleon. "*Severe* reservations."

"The Secondary Lector," Lector Shinka spoke softly from behind, "concurs."

Lector Annis stood frozen for a moment, eyes locked onto Asper, perhaps considering whether he ought to revoke his agreement immediately and incinerate her for tempting him so. If she could see the same frigid anger on his face that Dreadaeleon saw, though, she did not blink at it. Nor did she scramble to get out of his way as he turned and stormed out of the room.

But in Dreadaeleon's defense, he at least didn't stumble when he did.

"He seemed unenthused with the idea," Asper noted after the doors had slammed shut.

"Do give him a bit of slack, child," Shinka said, laying a hand upon her shoulder. "He is so rarely asked to compromise everything he swore to uphold."

"And yet you seemed convinced he would agree to it," Asper noted.

"He has every reason to believe in the power of human ignorance, and every moment to consider how many lives hinge upon his ability to protect them." Shinka cast a glance to Dreadaeleon. "I expect, had you proposed something twice as daring involving someone else, he'd have accepted willingly." She approached Dreadaeleon, making a beckoning gesture. "Speaking of which, if you'll accompany me, young criminal, we'll be on our way to making arrangements."

"Wait!" Asper reached out, stopping just shy of touching the Lector. "I'd like to have a moment alone with Dreadaeleon, if possible."

"Possible, yes." She cast a raised brow toward the boy. "But desired?"

Dreadaeleon sneered, folding his arms and looking away pointedly. "Fine."

"Ah, why not? This seems to be the night we forsake all propriety, after all." She strode past Dreadaeleon, offering a smirk as she waved a hand. The doors flew open. "Don't take too long."

"Could you maybe take"—Asper gestured at the Charnel Hound and blanched—"*that* with you?"

"Unfortunately, the processes of binding a Hound to its quarry are slightly less complex than those of reversing it. Worry not. It won't judge you."

Shinka passed through the doors, made another gesture to beckon them shut with a quiet *click*. Even a sound as soft as that seemed to echo, though.

But then, that might just have been a by-product of the horrifyingly awkward silence that hung between them.

Dreadaeleon had no particular motivation to break it. There was at least some small satisfaction in watching Asper search for a conversational topic by staring at her feet. Eventually the priestess's eyes drifted to Admiral Tibbles. She cringed.

"His eyes…are…are those someone's *balls*?"

"Charnel Hounds are the result of combining several fleshy 'waste' articles from Harvesting," Dreadaeleon replied. "The resulting flux of latent Venarie renders them immune to magical interference."

"I see. And they're made out of…cocks."

"Amongst other things."

She flashed a grin. "So, what, when you pet them, do they turn into draft horses?"

"No."

"Oh. Because, see, it's—"

"The Charnel Hounds, as the name implies, are composed primarily of flesh and sinew. For them to grow in the manner of an erection, as you implied, would require an active blood flow, which they lack. Yes, I understand this is an attempt to use humor to ease tension. No, it didn't work. Yes, you can kindly fuck off now."

She sighed, rubbed her eyes. "Look, Dread, I'm sorry for—"

"For what?" he interrupted, fury flashing in his stare. "For which part? For involving me in your machinations without ever consulting me, even as I was present in the room? For pummeling me like a savage? For calling me…me…"

He didn't dare say them, the names she had called him. To do so would be to acknowledge them, to relive the humiliation, to feel just how keenly they had stung.

"All of it? I don't know." Asper shook her head. "I didn't mean for things to happen as they did, or at all. I'm at the temple now, we've got more and more injured in every day, I couldn't think of any way to make it stop other than this."

"Of course you couldn't, you fool female," Dreadaeleon snapped. "The thinking is what *I* did." He jabbed a thumb to his chest. "*I* am the wizard, *I* am the brains, and if you had just let me do my job, we'd not be in this situation. But *no*, you had to go and—"

She slapped him. Hard enough to let him know that she had to actively resist the urge to do much worse than that. And still, the gaze she thrust upon him was much harder.

"I'm willing to apologize for how things turned out," she said, "but not for what I did. I don't give a shit if I hurt your pride or your face. You. Killed. *People.*"

She thrust a finger in his face with each word forced through gritted teeth. "You. Your magic. Your carelessness. Your arrogance. *You* killed people. That's why I beat the shit out of you, *that's* why you're here. There's no grand conspiracy to stifle you, you dumbshit, you're in this situation because of *you*."

She stormed past him, shoving him aside as she did. Admiral Tibbles watched, impassive as something without eyes could possibly be, as she swept toward the door.

He hardly felt the shove, nor even the slap anymore. A numbness overtook him, emptying him of rage, of shame, of every thought and feeling, so that her words might echo through him as keenly as they did through the chamber.

"If this plan is such a gods-damned offense to you," she said, "then feel free to opt out. Kick and scream, refuse to do it, I don't care. I'll find another way. But if you have any desire to make things right and maybe save your own skin, you'll at least consider it."

He heard her footsteps thunder in the chamber. He heard the fury with which she slammed the door open. And before he knew it, he heard his own voice, soft and barely there as he called after her.

"There's a woman," he said.

Her footsteps stopped. The door's creak went silent. Without looking up, he continued.

"She works in a bathhouse called the Sleeping Cat, near Silktown." He swallowed hard. "Whatever happens to me, I'd like to know she was safe."

A moment of silence passed.

"What's her name?" Asper asked, as soft.

"Liaja," he said. "She calls me 'northern boy.'"

A sigh. Warm and tired and resigned. The door eased shut, leaving him alone in the chamber.

Almost.

"Well, then," he sighed, looking down at the horror of flesh and sinew at his side. Admiral Tibbles looked back up at him, indifferent to the satisfied smirk he shot. "I told you I was feeling important today."

TEN

An Iron Wheel Turns

Gariath's time in Cier'Djaal had been brief, but it had taught him a valuable lesson.

A city could be gilded in coin and swaddled in silks on the outside and be a festering, diseased shithole on the inside.

Gariath's time in Shaab Sahaar had yet to begin, but it had already taught him another valuable lesson.

Sometimes a city could be a festering, diseased shithole on the outside, too.

Granted, he was a mile outside its borders, but he couldn't imagine the collection of towering wooden spires and domed huts of baked clay looked better up close. The buildings rose like pimples upon the landscape, surrounding a vast lake of an oasis and drowning the blue water in their mud and wood.

Any trees that had once grown on the lake's banks had been chopped down to make those towering spires. Any greenery that had once crawled from its shores had been smothered by clay huts. For miles around it was surrounded by flat, barren desert and it somehow *still* managed to be the ugliest thing he could see.

His days-long journey there had given Gariath plenty of time to hear about the city's history—how it had begun as a holy place, evolved into a marketplace, become a home for thousands—but it had taken him just one look to decide he hated it.

To him it was a place of weakness, like any other city. The desert was here to breed hardness, strength. The beasts that roamed it were fierce and gave good meat. The water that dotted it in oases was sweet and worth coveting. The desert had made the tulwar strong.

They deserved that strength, Gariath felt.

"The first thing I do is get so drunk I will vomit."

If only the tulwar felt the same way.

"Then so much *more* drunk that the vomit looks appetizing." A long-fingered hand clapped Gariath on the back. He looked down to see the broad, simian smile turned up at him. "But this time, I will only *think* about eating it."

Haangu. Daaru's stupid cousin.

"You'd have to be able to think first." Another pair of hands appeared behind Haangu, jerked up the back of his half robe, and pulled it over his head. "And if you could do that, you'd remember being thrown out of every drinking house in Shaab Sahaar like the ape you are!"

Shengo. Daaru's ugly cousin.

"I remember kicking your hairy ass clearly enough!" Haangu roared as he fought to escape his tangled garment.

Finding no apparent egress from his garb, Haangu settled for seizing it in his hands and tearing it from his torso, exposing a broad gray chest spattered with silver fur. His face was livid with a riot of yellows, reds, and blues. With a howl he charged after his brother, who met him with a snarl.

Their scuffle began with fists. Then escalated to teeth. Then finally became a brief tumble across the sand, before they finally scrambled to their feet and ran off, hooting with laughter, toward the distant city.

Not a city, he reminded himself. *A wound. A wound that makes maggots out of people.*

"Idiots."

"Young," came a voice from behind.

Perhaps Gariath's mistake had been to think all tulwar were like Daaru. Tall and proud as he approached, hand resting on the hilts of the swords tucked into the sash of his half robe.

His eyes were bright and clear, his jaw strong, as his lips curled into a smile, as he watched his cousins tumble across the road of pounded dust that led up to the city. He winced as one of them pushed the other and the fight began anew.

"Specifically," he said, "they are *duwun*."

"*Du*-what?" Gariath snorted.

"Young souls," Daaru replied. "Their Tul forgets each life the moment it's over, remembers nothing but the moment where meat is good and blood runs hot. And when they die, their Tul finds a new body and begins again."

That seemed like a lot of words to say *idiots*, but Gariath didn't protest.

"Ah, but there will be time to tell you all about this later," Daaru laughed. "And so much more." His eyes drifted down to the scabs forming on Gariath's flesh. "Two days ago you had arrows jutting from those wounds. Now you're already healing."

"I do that sometimes," Gariath grunted.

"I wouldn't believe it if I wasn't looking at it. You shouldn't be alive, but somehow—"

"I am." Gariath did not so much end Daaru's thought as dismember it with a gnashing of his teeth. "I always am."

He had no desire to remember that day when Daaru had found him. Even less desire to remember what he had cried out.

"No matter." Daaru waved a hand. "My children will not want to know why, just how you did it."

"Children?"

"Two of them. We think the boy's *duwun*, but the girl's *saan* for sure. But you'll see." He smiled. "You'll stay with me, of course. The least I can do for the story you'll tell my children is offer you food and shelter."

"Fine, whatever." Gariath snorted. "I don't care."

"Good. *Good.*" Daaru thumped his chest. "Be gruff. Scare them a little. The boy could use more nightmares." He glanced back up the road, where the brawl between Haangu and Shengo had somehow necessitated the drawing of swords. "I should settle this. I promised my aunt I wouldn't bring them back bleeding."

Gariath watched Daaru sprint over, drawing his own sword as he did. Steel was common in tulwar disputes, Gariath noted. Swords were drawn for everything from matters of honor to deciding who got the biggest piece of meat at dinner. There seemed to be absolutely nothing a tulwar was not willing to settle with mindless, abject violence.

So Gariath was forced to admit there were some points about them he liked.

He turned and made his way down the road to the rest of the caravan. Daaru's hunting band wasn't much: a pair of carts to hold the prizes of their hunts, a pair of oxen to pull them, the few male and female tulwar who had come—sans the two who had been killed in the strife with the shicts. And at the rear, lumbering on his knuckles, Kudj observed distant Shaab Sahaar and all its spires.

"Kudj regard architectural decisions with trepidation," the vulgore rumbled as Gariath came walking up. "But Cier'Djaal only comparison. Kudj perhaps limited in cultural appreciation."

"They're the same," Gariath growled in response. "Cier'Djaal, Shaab Whatever. Every city is a hunting ground where people make meat out of each other."

"Discussion with squibs leads Kudj to believe Shaab Sahaar product of necessity to defend against shict raids." Kudj sniffed. "But Kudj not mean to diminish squib's metaphor."

"I can still smell the reek of Cier'Djaal days away," Gariath said. "And they choose to imitate the humans."

"Where squibs supposed to live?"

"Out there."

Kudj followed Gariath's gesture out to the desert. The vulgore scratched his chin thoughtfully.

"Avoid plentiful water of oasis in favor of trackless wastes." He hummed deeply. "Kudj confess to difficulty in following squib's logic."

"So they stay here?" Gariath snorted. "Grow weak? Sick?" He snarled. "Daaru was strong in the desert. He fought. He bled. There was honesty in that. Now he talks about his children, telling stories..."

"Squib has multiple interests? Fighting and bleeding limited conversation."

"I thought he was strong." Gariath fixed his glare on the distant city. "I thought they were all strong. But they're no different than humans. They would sit in their homes and grow weak while the humans eat each other. They would have me sit with them and wait to die."

"Why that squib's concern?"

"Well, it's—" Gariath paused, turned his scowl toward Kudj. "Do you mean they're the squibs or I am?"

Kudj reared up on his hind legs, rolled a massive shoulder. "Kudj find it matter little. Squibs all the same."

"They can't see it," Gariath snarled after him as he trudged away. "I can. They act like their city is different than any other festering wound. Diseased, reeking..."

"Mm." The rumble of Kudj's voice joined the rumble of his knuckle-dragging stride. "Squibs never like wounds unless they ones to cause them. Squib humor."

There was a good retort for that, Gariath thought. As the caravan rolled away, he looked to his left and right for one. But, finding no sharp rocks with which to deliver his retort to the back of the vulgore's skull, he resigned himself to stalking after.

Perhaps Kudj had a point. Just because the tulwar had a city didn't necessarily mean they were weak, stupid, and ugly.

There could be all sorts of reasons they were weak, stupid, and ugly. It wouldn't be fair to deny them the chance to prove it.

——— ✦※✦ ———

As it turned out, the tulwar met Gariath's unspoken challenge with the same vigor with which they met any other challenge.

The stench of anger hit him first.

Hot and dry like a parched throat. It dripped from the eaves of the sloping roofs of the spires. It seethed out of the vents of clay houses. It paved the dirt roads and snaked out of alleys.

Other typical stenches—fear, hunger, despair, desperation—were present, too. Shaab Sahaar's aromas were many, but they all carried a heated edge of rage.

And nothing reeked stronger than its people.

They milled in teeming numbers. Beating rugs out of windows, selling meat from street-side grills, sitting in porches and in doorways, passing cups back and forth.

Most were warriors, tall and muscular. Many were elders, shorter, with rounded bellies and sagging breasts. Gray flesh and gray fur were left mostly bare by their half robes of many different colors—*chota*, they called the garment. And more than a few carried swords hanging from their sashes.

Though their anger was quickly being replaced by a different odor, one that grew stronger with every step Gariath took deeper into the city. And while a sentiment such as "What the fuck is that?" couldn't quite be put into an aroma, the tulwar's alarm at his presence was evident enough in their wide-eyed stares.

But then, he admitted, those might have been more for Kudj.

The tulwar thronging the streets backed away from Gariath as he made his way down its central street, regarding him and his hulking companion with little more than startled mutters. Daaru's influence, he supposed. Or maybe the fact that he was a seven-foot-tall, toothy creature in the company of another, much bigger creature.

Whatever. It made for an easier trip down the street.

"Squib see Daaru?" Kudj asked, looming over Gariath.

"Maybe," Gariath grunted. "They all look the same to me."

"Ah, squib not perceptive." The vulgore gestured to his own face. "Faces different."

Gariath squinted to see, but the vulgore was correct. In the tulwar's faces, the thick folds of flesh varied. Some sloped a little deeper, some twisted a little higher; when their tempers flared and their colors showed, Gariath imagined they would be a sight bordering on fearsome.

The few whose colors flowed into their faces at his presence let their colors die when he glared at them.

"You're taller," Gariath grunted. "What do you see?"

"Many squibs." Kudj's thick eye ridges rose. "*Many* squibs. Too many for so few squibhouses."

It was, Gariath thought, difficult to notice these things when he didn't care about them, but once again Kudj was right. The tulwar choked streets too small for them, peered out of the doors and windows of houses too small for the numbers in them; the crowds were thick enough to make the berth they gave him insultingly small.

They were too close. They teemed. Their scent was overpowering. Their reek was everywhere.

Except for...

His nostrils quivered. A new scent. Something stale, pungent; he had smelled it before, but so long ago that he could barely remember it. Despair? Arousal? Hunger?

He received his answer as soon as he saw the coiling smoke.

Tobacco. Ordinary, average tobacco from a wooden pipe.

He would never have noticed the source out of such a crowd without the odor. But he followed the smoke to the eaves of an overcrowded wooden house, to a column running down from the roof to the dirt, to the old tulwar sitting cross-legged on the earth.

His gray mane was streaked with white, the flesh pattern of his face sagged, his belly was round beneath the faded orange of his *chota*, and a string of wooden beads hung from a neck thick with loose flesh. Yet behind the veil of pipe smoke, his eyes were yellow, keen, and staring.

Yet all this was not as noticeable as his lack of scent.

There was the pungency of tobacco, but that wasn't a true scent. There was nothing to this old tulwar. No anger, no despair, no greed, lust, or hunger. He sat there, scentless, silent, staring.

As if he knew.

Knew everything.

It struck Gariath as ironic that this should irritate him, this creature and his lack of smell. He couldn't explain it. Something about the satisfaction, the confidence with which the tulwar carried himself even as he sat in dirt.

Before he could make a move to share this particular thought, his nostrils flared, invaded with a sudden riot of aromas.

Excitement. Anger. And…feces?

A high-pitched shriek pealed through the crowds. Gariath's attentions were turned from scent to sound to sight as he looked high to the eaves of a towering wooden spire and the dark shape hanging from it.

He had never seen a baboon, but he had heard stories of them from the humans. This thing—this beast—had the same hard-packed muscle covered in dense black fur, the long snout of naked red flesh, the long arms with which it hung from the spire's sloping eaves, the dangling tail.

He hadn't *heard* anything about their being the size of horses, but then, he hadn't been listening very closely.

The beast released its grip, falling to the second story of the house and landing upon its sloping roof. It shattered shingles beneath its feet as it loped across and leapt. The crowd parted with a collective cry as it struck the road in a cloud of dust.

It looked up, peeled back lips the color of blood to reveal yellow fangs the length of daggers. But the crimson of its flesh paled against the bright red of its eyes, focused right on Gariath.

The crowd continued to part as it came charging toward the dragon-man on all fours. Its mouth gaped with a shriek, spittle flying from fangs as it barreled toward him.

Before he could act, the beast screeched to a halt just before him. It snorted, blasting him with hot air, as it rose onto short legs and pounded its fists against a barrel chest. Its shriek was ear-piercing this close, its breath hot and reeking.

"Hey, *shkainai*!"

At the edge of the crowd, a female tulwar wearing an earth-brown *chota* and carrying a stick with a hook at the end called out to him.

"You speak human?" she called. At Gariath's nod she grunted. "He's just showing his dominance. He doesn't have your scent, so he's trying to figure out where you stand."

As if to emphasize this, the beast growled and lunged forward, forcing Gariath back a step.

"Whatever you do," the female called, "don't show fear. Don't take another step back. Don't look away from him. And don't—"

If she was about to say "don't punch him in the face," she was going to be disappointed. As the beast shrieked and lunged forward again, Gariath's fist shot out and met its jaw with a resounding crack.

It fell to the ground in a cloud of dust. It lay prone for only a moment before leaping back up to its feet. Its shriek became a squeal as it scurried and cowered behind the female, who regarded Gariath with a deep frown.

"Or just hit him like a savage." She leveled her crook at Gariath. "This was a breeder, *shkainai*. If you damaged him, you better have money to pay for a new one."

Gariath narrowed his eyes at her. This was where the tulwar came to escape the humans? To build houses and grub for coin like them?

"He will pay for *nothing*." The deep voice of Daaru preceded his stride as he swept past Gariath from behind and thrust a finger at the female. "Ululang, you have been warned. Gaambols are supposed to be kept at the *edge* of the city."

"They need to drink, don't they?" the female named Ululang growled back. "The quickest way to the oasis is through the streets."

"The streets are crowded enough without you bringing beasts into them!"

"Yeah?" She cast a glare toward Gariath, then over his head to Kudj, looming nearby. "You don't hear me complaining about the beasts *you* bring here. The streets are too crowded for vulgores and..." She squinted at Gariath. "I don't even *know* what that thing is."

"They are both guests of Shaab Sahaar," Daaru said. "No different than your clan. We are stretched thin right now. Further than anyone can remember, but Shaab Sahaar has turned no one away before."

The female snorted, slung her hook over her shoulder, and cast a fleeting glance to Gariath. "No tulwar."

She bared sharp teeth and loosed a shrill whistle. From nearby roofs more of the giant simians came leaping down to fall neatly in line behind her as she led them through the streets, their tails raised and bright-red buttocks flaring.

The crowd resumed its normal shuffle. Daaru sighed and returned to Gariath.

"Yengu Thuun clan," he snorted. "Nice people, if you meet them out where their beasts have room to roam. Not fit for the city."

"And who is?" Gariath grunted. "Besides humans."

"It's no secret that the humans control the desert," Daaru interjected. "We build because we defend ourselves. We seek coin because we must trade. And you..." He gestured to Gariath. "They have never seen anything like you, except..." He glanced around warily. "It's not important. We have to survive. Now more than ever."

Something in the tulwar's voice dropped from a growl into a sigh beyond weariness.

"Come," Daaru said, heading into the crowd. "My wife will be waiting."

Gariath followed, swaying slightly as he did. The anger was dizzying, boiling behind calm faces and squinting eyes. It peeled off every tulwar here. This city was a pot of oil, waiting for a torch, and the scent was everywhere.

Save for one spot where there hung only the reek of tobacco.

But when Gariath turned to look, the old tulwar was already gone.

—— ❈ ——

True, his experience with tulwar had been limited, but Gariath felt comfortable enough to draw a few conclusions about them.

The differences between males and females were limited to such things as a few subtle curves on the latter and slightly bigger fangs on the former, for one. They had absolutely no idea how to contain their emotions, by either scent or sight.

And, if Daaru's daughter was any indication, they were born obnoxious and grew only more obnoxious as time went on.

She, a four-foot-tall runt with barely any fur on her and wrapped in a red-and-yellow *chota*, sat beside him at the edge of the fire pit at the center of the house's central room. In the four hours during which Gariath had been subjected to her father's hospitality, she had taken three bites of her dinner and spent the rest of the time sitting.

And staring.

Meat sputtered on a metal grill above a smoldering flame. The tulwar insisted on barbecuing it with thick, spicy pastes instead of letting the meat speak for itself, but Gariath didn't mind. It was passable and plentiful.

And yet it was not the meat they had brought back to the city. That had been sold to someone else. This meat had been bought from someone else, which had in turn been bought from shictish traders, he had been told, rather than coming from an honest kill.

That bothered Gariath, but so did a lot of things in this house. Such as the little tulwar girl. So he shoveled a piece of meat in his mouth so that he would not feel tempted to curse at her.

After all, it wasn't her fault her father had raised her stupid.

"I bet you killed a hundred of them!"

And it wasn't as if she were the worst of his litter, either.

"Wow! Shicts! And only two days away? They're so close! I bet they're right outside the city now, lurking in the filth and eating rotten meat!"

That particular line of excited blather belonged to a three-foot-tall blur that was currently running circles around the fire pit. Gariath caught glimpses of it whenever it stopped long enough to grab another piece of meat. Enough, at least, to know that it was a boy with even less fur than his sister, with a head too big for his body and eyes too big for his head.

"Is it true that their arrows are poisoned? I heard their arrows are poisoned. Auntie Hamaa says that the shicts smear their weapons with shit and—"

A loud crack pierced the air. The boy came to a sudden halt, rubbing his head where a wooden skewer had struck him.

"Do I raise gaambols or tulwar?" a woman clad in a purple *chota* growled at the boy, color flaring into her face. "A tulwar wouldn't run as you do, but a gaambol wouldn't say such things in my house."

"But Mama," the boy whined, "that's what *Auntie* says, not me!"

"Then you can act like a beast in *her* house. Shicts speak filth, not you."

You all speak the human tongue. What sense does it make to choose words to qualify as filth?

Gariath kept that thought in his head, instead biting down on another piece of meat. When the food ran out, he noted, the conversation would get very colorful.

The boy's face brimmed with color for a moment, though it was in pale, immature hues. He looked across the fire pit pleadingly. "Father, I—"

"You disrespect your mother, Duja." Daaru's lips perked up into a smirk at his son. "You should be grateful she didn't have anything heavier to hit you with." He cast eyes across the fire pit toward Gariath. "You don't want to disrespect our guest, too, do you?"

"No!" Duja roared emphatically. He ran to Gariath's side, took the small wooden plate from him, and heaped it with more meat before setting it back down before Gariath with a stiff bow. "Forgive me, honored guest."

"It's fine," Gariath replied, taking another piece.

"It is *not* fine," the boy snapped back. "I have shamed my mother and father. I have shamed my ancestors. I have shamed my Tul." Instantly his eyes brightened, his previous injury forgotten. "Do you also have a Tul, *shkainai*? Are you *duwun*? I bet you are. I bet—"

"Duja!" his mother barked from across the fire pit. "Remember our deal. Honor both guests before you pester them."

The boy blinked and then, remembering the massive vulgore that had been too huge to enter their home, quickly heaped meat upon another plate and ran it outside. His mother watched him with a growing frown.

"And be careful!" she called after him, then looked to Daaru. "I don't want him spending too much time around the vulgore. It's liable to crush him by accident."

"Him, Thamla," Daaru corrected. "Not 'it.' *His* name is Kudj." He waved a hand. "And he is *duwun*. He was bound to die sooner or later."

Thamla sighed and nodded, with an alarming amount of casualness, considering what her husband had just said. She leaned over, took another skewer of meat, and laid it on the grill. She glanced up at Gariath with a deeper worry in her eyes, but said nothing.

Presumably there were only so many its she could be concerned about at one time.

"Still, I am in no hurry to have another one," she said. "Even if he is *duwun*, you must watch over him."

Gariath's eye ridges furrowed at that word. They kept saying it like it meant something, but it sounded like babble to him. Perhaps that showed too plainly on his face, for he was surprised to hear a soft voice speak up beside him.

"*Duwun* means his Tul is young."

He glanced down at Daaru's daughter. She loosed a gasp and immediately looked down at the floor, regarding him through the corner of her eye.

"If you wanted to know," she offered meekly.

Before Gariath could affirm that he hadn't, Daaru spoke up.

"The tulwar do not teem like humans and shicts," he said. "There are only ever an exact number of us at any one time. Our bodies die, but our Tul"—he tapped his chest—"is reborn elsewhere as another tulwar. The *duwun* have forgotten so many lives that they have not much care for this one."

"I'm *saan*, though." His daughter spoke up once more, careful not to look at Gariath. "My Tul is older."

"Like her father and mother," Daaru said, smiling. "Whoever she was before she was born as Deji, though, she must have been very rude." He grunted at his daughter. "Your fathers and mothers were all warriors. Why do you not look our guest in the eye as they would?"

Color flooded Deji's face. She stared intently at the ground, as though she were selecting a spot she might dig up and bury herself in.

"It's fine," Gariath grunted again, turning his face to his meal.

It wasn't that he intended to be ungracious—he might have spent much of his life in a cave, but even the *Rhega* had laws of hospitality—but everything about him itched.

That might just have been the woven rug upon which he sat. Or it might have been the air, stifling in this big baked-clay house. Or perhaps it was some allergy from the tulwar's beds, made from timber they bought from humans and covered with hides they bought from shicts.

Of this entire house, all that he knew for certain belonged to the tulwar was the swords on the wall. Everything else here reeked of human, of shict.

Of *them.*

He could smell the tall ones in the sheets, the short one in the rugs, the pointy-eared one in the meat. He could smell Lenk in the steel. And each time he thought of them, he could not help but feel a pain in his chest for the humans who had left him.

No, he told himself. *You left* them. *They wanted to sit in the reek and grub through the filth for coin. They chose streets full of shit and humans choking on gold over you. You don't need them. They'll die without you.*

And yet their stink would linger. In the air, he would smell them.

Human weakness. Human filth. Shaab Sahaar reeked of it as surely as Cier'Djaal did. If it were up to him, they would burn in the same fire.

Gariath chose not to say this.

So, by his estimate, he was a good dinner guest.

The rest of the meal passed mostly in silence. The boy would occasionally come barreling in to collect more food for Kudj outside. The girl would offer a few more shy words before quietly slinking off to her side of the house. The husband and wife would share a few quiet words of concern whenever they thought he wasn't listening.

He wasn't. They weren't saying anything interesting. So he felt justified in setting aside his empty plate and rising up to walk out into the warm night.

The houses on the banks of the oasis fed by the Lyre River were all clay, older ones from the clans that had initially settled this area—Daaru's own Rua Tong included, he had been told. But even here, amid the old houses, he saw human chairs on porches and shictish hides over doorways.

A rumble caught his attention. Beside the house Kudj was a dark round shape against the night sky as he lay on his back and slumbered noisily. Sprawled out on the peak of the vulgore's rounded belly, Daaru's son strained to snore as loud.

"We think, in a past life, he was one of my fathers."

Daaru emerged from the house behind him, his grin broad and white in the dark. He looked over Duja as the boy squirmed and rolled over on Kudj's ample girth.

"He does nothing but eat, sleep, and make messes," Daaru said as he packed a long-stemmed pipe. "Just like my grandfather. That would explain it, wouldn't it?"

"Or he's stupid, lazy, and dirty," Gariath grunted.

Daaru laughed, lighting his tobacco and taking a few puffs. "As is any child. But that, I think, does not make sense."

Gariath stared blankly at him for a moment. "But him being his own grandfather does?"

"I don't know what gods you have, dragonman, but ours is dead." He gestured overhead, to a sky alive with stars. "When he lived, his stride spanned kingdoms and his brow scraped the sky. And when he died, every drop of blood he shed became a tulwar."

"So you worship a dead god," Gariath snorted.

"We do not worship Tul." Daaru's eyes were bright as flame as he turned them to the dragonman. "We *are* Tul. As he is eternal, so are we. We are born, we die, we come back again. Life means little, death even less."

The *Rhega* had no gods. The idea of being terrified of something dwelling in the sky was absurd. The idea of being terrified of something dwelling in the sky that was dead, even more so.

He liked that last bit about death, though. Pithy.

"That's lucky." Gariath watched as Kudj stretched. "If the vulgore decides to roll over, he might come back as his own brother next time."

"He'll be fine," Daaru said, taking a long inhalation on his pipe.

"His mother seemed to disagree."

"His mother worries too much." Daaru loosed an ashen sigh into the night. "But I welcome it. If she is worried about the boy, she has less time to complain to me about leaving the city."

"To hunt?" Gariath asked.

"Something like that," Daaru chuckled. He shot a meaningful look at Gariath. "Do you have children?"

Gariath, in turn, cast a meaningful look away from Daaru. "Yes."

"Then you understand. It's for them that I do this." He sighed, folding his arms and leaning against his house. "Those are my father's swords that hang on my wall. Once they were used for better things: fighting shicts, fighting humans." He drew in a deep breath. "Fighting..."

Gariath said nothing.

"What I do now is not fighting." Daaru slumped to his rear, rested his arms on his knees. "What I do now is kill. I kill for coin. I kill for food. I sell honor and I am not the one to decide the price." An iron pause followed, something heavy and full of crude edges. "For this my family eats. It is what I must do."

Gariath said nothing.

"Perhaps if I were *duwun*, it would not matter as much. But I am *saan*, as my fathers were. My burden is memory." He rubbed his neck. "Here, at least, I have my family. Here, at least, I am tulwar."

He looked up to the sky with a weary smile.

"What more can I do?"

Gariath said nothing.

"You could try not being such a coward."

Or at least Gariath had *intended* to say nothing.

He was a little surprised to hear the words come from his own mouth. Though if the tulwar's wide eyes were any indication, not as surprised as Daaru.

"What is a tulwar?" Gariath gestured out over Shaab Sahaar. "I met one out in the desert, watched him fight with the fury of a hundred. I lost him somewhere in the streets, and who are you? A creature that lives in human houses, sleeps on shict hides, speaks the human tongue?"

"There are many clans in the city—Rua Tong, Yengu Thuun, Tho Thu Bhu—and they all have their own dialects," Daaru replied, his voice a low growl. "A common language makes it easier for life to—"

"Easy." Gariath barked a gruff laugh. "Life is not supposed to be easy. It's something big and ferocious that bites and claws and only respects you when you fight back. Those that hold their own know what it means to grow strong."

"Do not speak to me of strength, dragonman." Daaru rose to his feet. Even in the dark of the night, the colors blossoming beneath his face were bright as firelight. "I carry more than swords on my shoulders. I carry lives. I carry people."

"Your family, yes," Gariath snarled. "Your wife, who takes the coin the humans give you and buys the meat the humans sell her. Your daughter, who speaks the tongue of people who would buy and sell her like meat herself. Your son, who watches you leave to scrounge at their feet for—"

"*YOU ARE A GUEST.*" Daaru's roar shook the curtains in the window. "I did not bring you to my home to mock me."

"Then why did you bring me here?" Gariath met his voice with a growl, something low from a low place. "To see your city? To see your family? So you could show me what kind of life you lead?"

"And what if I did?" Daaru drew in a breath, struggling to control the anger painting his face. "What home do you have that I am keeping you from? Or were you merely wandering the desert for fun? The other clans will know you, in time, and your bravery. You could have a *life* here."

"What life?" Gariath growled. "There aren't enough lives to go around for all the bodies flooding the streets."

"It's the shicts. They attack our villages, send more and more refugees to the city, and—"

"And you buy their hides and you buy their meat and you buy human wood and you buy human steel." Gariath threw his hands out in a sweeping gesture to the city. "How long before all this is gone? How long before I look at tulwar and human and can't even tell the difference?"

"And what would you have us do? Starve?"

"Die today, you die as a commodity, something traded between humans like coins. Cast this off, die as a tulwar, die proud and free."

Daaru's face now was a flurry of color. The reds, yellows, and blues shifted with every breath, growing brighter and dimmer like the beating of a heart. Yet even that furious color paled in comparison to the anger burning in his eyes as he locked a scowl upon Gariath.

"You are not the first to speak of that," Daaru all but spit. "Years ago someone else said the same thing. It was repeated over and over until it was in the mouth of every tulwar in the tribelands. And do you know what happened then?"

Gariath said nothing. He did not back away as Daaru stalked toward him. He did not look away as Daaru scowled up at him.

"The Uprising happened," the tulwar growled. "Three months of slaughter. Collapsing of thirst in the desert, dying under arrows when we stormed Cier'Djaal, cut down by the fashas' dragonmen mercenaries in the streets. And for what? The freedom we wanted belonged only to the dead we picked up when we limped back to the only things we had left."

He looked long to the side of the house. Even through all the uproar, Duja had not stirred from his slumber. Kudj yawned in his sleep, reaching up to scratch an errant itch on his belly. The tulwar boy instinctively reached out, seizing one of the behemoth's tremendous fingers and holding it close.

"Family," Daaru said. "I was too young to join the Uprising. I was too young to burn my father's body when they dumped him at my mother's door." He turned his eyes, the anger even and steady in them, back to Gariath. "I am *saan*, not afraid to die, dragonman. But my son is still too young to burn my body. It is not my time."

Gariath merely leaned down so that he was face-to-face with the tulwar. His words were pushed between teeth on a soft growl.

"Then I guess Tul isn't so eternal after all."

There were many ways to win a fight.

Some ended in a single blow, some ended in so much blood a man could choke on it. But the real victories, the ones that counted the most, did not end in death.

The real victories left scars.

Daaru, in that moment, was alive with fury. His body shook beneath the fur, his lips were peeled back in a baring of simian fangs, and his face exploded with colors. And yet his hands hung at his sides, his feet stayed where they were, and he took not another step toward Gariath.

He held the dragonman's gaze for another moment before storming over to where Kudj slept. He reached up to the vulgore's prodigious gut and snatched his son up in both arms.

"*Pada?*" Duja muttered groggily. "What are we—"

"You come inside," Daaru snarled. "Your mother is worried."

"But *Pada*, my friend, he—"

"He's not your friend. He's *gaacha*."

"Stranger?"

"*Gaacha*." Daaru pushed open the curtain to his house and hesitated, casting one final scowl over his shoulder at Gariath. "We speak Tong in this house."

His voice trailed off into murmurs as he disappeared into his house, words that died quietly in the night and left behind a cold quiet. A breeze lazily wended its way through the choked streets, eventually finding its way to Gariath.

And its reek was overpowering.

ELEVEN

THE THRILL OF PAIN

Well, that ain't good," the woman beside her said.

Kataria considered those words and found them an adequate description for what she saw.

It had once been a village: a collection of small huts built upon the banks of the Lyre, a couple of boats and roughhewn docks leading over the water. The people here had likely been simple folk, hard workers who drew their lifeblood from the river and its many fish. They would have been rugged to have lived this far out, coming in from the day's fishing, bone-tired but not so much that they couldn't cook what they'd caught for their families.

So she assumed, anyway.

Whatever they had been, they were dead now.

A single dead tree grew from the center of the village and they decorated it. Tulwar men and women, their fur spattered with blood and their clothing torn, hung by their ankles from the branches. Their throats had been slit, their blood left to stain the earth around the tree's roots. They swayed stiffly in the breeze, tongues lolling from open mouths, forever choking on their last cries.

Their huts were piles of ash and rubble, smoldering carcasses that exhausted their last sighs of smoke into the wind. Their boats were splintered bones in the water. The ground was painted with the inky shadows of vultures that had yet to descend.

"You seen this before?"

Kataria glanced to the saccarii to her right, a woman named Chemoi: a scrawny creature, scaly flesh mostly bare in her half shirt and breeches, ochre eyes peering out from a head wrap.

"Yeah," the shict replied. "We call them *white trees*."

"That ain't make much sense," the saccarii said.

"Not yet," Kataria said. "After a few days, once all the blood's drained out, the corpses go pallid and pale. Then they get picked at by scavengers until only bones remain." She sniffed. "White tree."

"Huh." The saccarii looked out from the deck atop the Old Man. "That's fucked up."

Kataria was careful to conceal her grin. She couldn't help it; she had described white trees to companions before. After being met so many times with vomit, it was kind of refreshing to see a reaction so mild.

"Always wondered why they did that," Chemoi said. "To be honest, I was hoping we wouldn't see something like that."

"Why? You got a weak stomach?"

"I've seen too many dead tulwar on this river to be much afraid of them," Chemoi grunted. "But if the shicts are up in Chee Chree territory, that's bad news."

"Chee Chree?"

"Tulwar clan. The poor bastards bleeding out there. When times are bad for the shicts, the shicts come out here to trade. When times are good, they feel like flexing a bit and come out here to raid. Usually just steal stuff and kill a few tulwar."

Kataria stared over the ruined village as the Old Man's lumbering stride carried them past it.

"Looks like they did a lot more than that," she said.

"Right," Chemoi said. "Which means they must be feeling fucking *great*. Bad news for us." She glanced sidelong at Kataria. "If it comes down to it, you think you could shake the shicts off for us?"

"Maybe," Kataria replied, shrugging. "I could try, anyway."

"Ain't like that answer," Chemoi grunted. "But I like it better than your bald friend's. He just shrugs. He any handy with that sword?"

"He does his best."

Chemoi shook her head. She stalked off, muttering. "Bad, bad news..."

Kataria couldn't help but give the saccarii credit; not many people got right back to work after witnessing a white tree. But Chemoi immediately started barking orders to the several other saccarii scrambling across the deck of the Old Man.

They called themselves its crew, though she wasn't quite sure what they did. They didn't seem to have any control over the colossal creature. Most of their duties seemed to involve picking things off its hide, speaking soft words to it, and making sure cargo was distributed evenly across its back. They seemed to concern themselves mostly with its comfort, which, she supposed, was what a crew did.

And she couldn't imagine war-hungry shicts would be good for the Old Man.

She turned and leaned on the railing, staring at the scorched village as it faded from view. Ordinarily she might have taken umbrage at a saccarii presuming to lecture her on shictish ways, but Chemoi had been dead-on.

To a shict, trade was an insult, dealing with a diseased people—it didn't matter whether tulwar or human, they were all diseased. Tribes did it as a last resort when game was scarce.

War, though? War meant times were good. Warriors were strong, hunters were keen, arrows were plenty, and grudges could be settled. Shict tribes would happily wait through lean years, gorging themselves on dreams of fights to come in lieu of meat.

But even in good times, shicts didn't kill everyone. Even in good times, shicts left houses standing. They stole instead of broke, tore instead of burned, left villages intact so that their foes might come back and repopulate for the next raid in time of plenty or trade in the next lean year.

Chemoi understood enough to know that shicts who burned were ready for war. But what she didn't understand—and what Kataria could not bring herself to tell her—was that shicts who burned a village to the ground did so because they could not see a need for those people to exist any longer.

The tribes out here did not intend to make war. They intended to eradicate.

She thought back to her night in Jalaang, the time she had spent with Kwar, the last few words they had exchanged. She had spoken of a new leader of the tribes out here, a name that was still lodged in Kataria's skull like an arrow.

Shekune.

What had Kwar said about her? She tried to remember Kwar's words,

Kwar's voice, the heat of Kwar's breath, the feel of Kwar's hands upon Kataria's sides as they slid down to her hips and coaxed her breeches down, the sensation of Kwar's lips as they—

Oh, come on.

Kataria thumped her skull with the heel of her hand, bit her lower lip, came up with a thousand curses in her head for her thoughts.

Just as she did every time she thought of Kwar. Because every time she thought of Kwar, her thoughts inevitably slid to those moments.

And her heart tightened inside her chest. Her thoughts became a river as sure-flowing as the Lyre beneath her. As they flowed to Kwar, soon after they flowed to shame. And shortly after shame, they inevitably floated to him.

She turned and saw him as he stared out over the other side of the river, to the north. The distant peaks of the Akavali Mountains, the barrier between Cier'Djaal's and Muraska's countries, loomed large and silent against the blue backdrop. It was a vast, unchanging range, the same snow-covered peaks rising and falling, over and over and over.

It probably said something dire that Lenk preferred to look at this rather than talk to her.

Or perhaps it was just him.

The couthi, Man-Khoo Yun, leaned over him, whispering something from behind his portrait. Lenk, however, simply waved off whatever it was. And though it was impossible to tell what a couthi's emotions might be, Kataria guessed by the way Man-Khoo Yun stiffened and stalked away that his couldn't be great.

And Kataria leaned on her elbows against the railing and stared at Lenk. Him, leaning forward, back bent from the weight of the sword on it. Him, scratching at the gray stubble growing in on his shorn pate.

Go to him. Talk to him.

The thoughts, whether born of guilt or of frustration, always came unbidden when she looked at him for more than a few moments. And, whether from fear or from sadness, she had done her best to avoid them, ignore them, bite them down between her canines and grind them to gristle and swallow them until they rested as iron weights in her belly.

But she started walking toward him anyway. Mouth dry, chest hurting, ears trembling, she came to stand beside him. She leaned on the railing next to him, her arm brushed against his. He felt warm.

She remembered a time when that feeling had not pained her.

"Hey," she said.

He glanced at her. "Hey."

No other words. He continued staring out over the mountains. She followed his stare to those distant peaks. Together they stood in silence.

She remembered a time when they had done this and it had not hurt to do so.

"What'd the bug want?" she asked, at last.

"Same shit." Lenk waved a hand. "Warning me about shicts, tulwar, gaambols."

"What's a gaambol?"

"I don't know." He sighed, clutched his head. "I don't know anything anymore, and the fact that I don't is all that's keeping me from realizing how fucked everything is."

He had never been a big man, or a powerful man. When she had first met him, he looked small, runty. Had she not seen the battles he'd walked away from, she would have thought he might break if she touched him. But she knew him. And so she smiled and laid a hand on his shoulder.

And remembered a time when she'd done this and it hadn't felt as if she were stabbing him in the back.

"The couthi says there are no other human villages," Lenk said. "From here it's all tulwar clans. But there are a few small spits of beaches between here and there that can be landed upon. The saccarii say the Old Man sometimes stops there to pick up crates left behind by smugglers." He stared out over the mountains. "It's the last possible chance to get off before we enter the Gullet."

She regarded him for a moment. "You're thinking of leaving?"

"No." His answer came swiftly, accompanied by a morbid chuckle. "Lenk might. But Farlan Sandish has a library of the damned to find. He can't leave that behind."

And he turned. And he looked to her. And it hurt to meet his eyes.

"But you could," he said.

He said it so simply. Almost as if he expected her to go leaping over the railing right then and there. And in his eyes she could see the fear that she would. In his eyes she knew they thought the same things. She was here for him, to protect him, to see him to the end of this.

But he couldn't ask that of her, couldn't ask her to go with him into the unknown like this. They had done that together a hundred times before, but this time they both knew it was different, even if they didn't know why.

Or at least *he* didn't know why.

And just like that, he had given her a way out.

Could it really be that easy, she wondered?

If it wouldn't doubtless have drawn attention to her, she would have burst out laughing right there.

No, of course not. She couldn't leave him. Not like that. Nor could she stay with him. Not like this. Leave him to die, hurt herself to stay, it was all so wonderfully, painfully, horribly hard.

And that was funny.

"Nah." She shook her head. "I'm here. You're helpless enough getting breakfast on your own, let alone finding a Library of the Lurid."

"Learned," he corrected.

"Whatever." She shrugged. "Besides, how would they even stop this thing? They don't seem to have a means of controlling it."

"You noticed that, too, huh?" Lenk glanced at a nearby saccarii. "I don't get it. I mean, I don't get how something this big even *exists*, let alone exists the way it does. I haven't seen it eat or stop moving."

"Barely two weeks ago, you were fighting and killing some kind of horrific snake-demon-old-man-thing," Kataria replied. "Seems a little late to start getting fussy about the weird things you see."

"That was a demon, though. Unnatural. This thing is…" He leaned over the railing, looked down at the great green hide of its flank. "It's big and scary, but it doesn't *feel* scary, you know?"

"How should I know?" she asked.

Lenk continued staring for a moment, brow furrowed in thought. After a moment he leaned back. He looked around cautiously for a moment. Then he reached down and took her hand, so swiftly it didn't even hurt.

"Come over here for a moment."

He led her to the rear of the deck, behind a few stacks of crates. His hand darted to her waist, removed her dagger. Weeks ago that might have felt easy. But as his hand brushed the skin of her midriff, she felt a flush rise to her cheeks.

"Keep an eye out, will you?" he whispered as he ducked behind some crates.

"The hell are you doing?" she asked, though she kept a lookout for anyone who might approach.

"It's too far up to see from the railing." Lenk wedged her knife into a space between the planks of the deck, pried up the old wood with a bit of difficulty. "I want a closer look."

"Why?"

He looked up at her. "Well, fuck, if I'm going to trust this thing to carry me to the Forbidden East, I'd at least like to know what it is."

He set the plank aside. Beneath it the Old Man's green hide pulsated and flexed with every colossal stride it took. Kataria knelt down beside the hole in the deck, peering at the creature's flesh. Or *was* it flesh? It looked like it, certainly, but the muscles underneath bunched up and stretched in a way she had never seen before.

"Look at that," she muttered. She reached down, fingers brushing against a large cyst upon its skin. "What the hell do you think that—"

She didn't finish that thought. As soon as her fingers touched the cyst, it suddenly twitched like a living thing. It split apart, tiny fronds unfurling from it and stretching out. Within, glistening petals of many different colors suddenly blossomed and rose up. It bloomed, like a flower.

It *was* a flower.

"Shit." Lenk's voice was thin with astonishment. "It's a *plant*. That's why it doesn't need to eat or stop." He let out a short laugh. "It's just one giant walking plant."

Whether from stress or wonder, that short laugh grew longer. And whether it was because he was *that* stressed or just a gods-damned idiot, that long laugh took a hysterical edge. And despite how strange he looked, Kataria couldn't help but smile at him.

Somehow it was easier when things were like this. When there were unknown places to go, when there were horrific monsters to slay, when there were giant walking plants to ride. When they were adventurers, no longer pretending to be normal, when their eyes were on each other's backs and their hands were on their weapons, things made sense.

He wanted to leave it all behind, of course—all the fighting, all the bloodshed. Yet here he was. Ready to do it again. And here she was, right beside him and ready to help.

But perhaps this was just the kind of people they were. Dreams of springtime weddings, litters of children, growing old in front of a fireplace, hand in hand: These were poison to them, slow-acting venoms that killed them. Their comforts were simpler things: blades in hand, horizons before them, miles behind them.

And all the world to discover.

It didn't entirely make sense, the way she smiled. But the desert was scant of a lot of things besides just water. Whatever hope she found out here, she seized and grabbed and strangled until it stopped trying to get away.

And looking at him, laughing as he did. And the way he looked at her, the fears chased away from his eyes for the moment. It almost made her believe things could, somehow, be all right.

"All right," Lenk said, wiping a tear from his eye. "Keep a lookout. I'll replace the plank. I don't feel like explaining this to the saccarii."

"Right," she said.

She sprang to her feet and returned to the railing. It was odd to feel so light after that, as if feeling comfortable were some kind of disease. But after so long without it, she wasn't ready to give it up, no matter how little sense it made.

His eyes, wide and free of fear, lingered with her. And the sensation of freedom they had brought her walked with her to the railing. She felt whole again. Just like that.

Could it really be that easy?

Her eyes caught a shudder of movement in the distance. On the crest of a tall dune on the south side of the river, she saw a lone figure mounted upon the back of a yiji. And though there were miles between them, Kataria knew the rider. Because the rider knew her. And across those miles, Kwar reached out with her Howling.

And instantly Kataria slumped against the railing.

No, of course it's not that easy. The thought carried her chin down to the railing, where she buried her head in her hands. *It never was.*

TWELVE

Rats in the Basement

Darkness wasn't so bad.

People feared it for the same reason Denaos thrived in it: One never knew what lurked inside it. But where the common man feared thieves and murderers, he saw possibilities. One could pretend to be anything one wished in the dark.

Sometimes, in darkness like this, he liked to imagine that he was somewhere else. Somewhere other than Cier'Djaal. He liked to imagine that he didn't owe this city anything, that he wasn't the man who had nearly killed it, that he hadn't had a conversation about this with Anielle this morning.

But even in darkness, he couldn't pretend it hadn't happened. He couldn't pretend it had even been a conversation.

He could still hear her voice in his ears, demanding to know who this priestess was who presumed to command the Jackals, why he had agreed to her plan. He could still hear himself arguing back, telling her that her idea was a good one, that it might be the only thing that could save Cier'Djaal.

He could still hear her black, unpleasant laughter as she looked at him and spoke.

"Given all the 'help' you've given it, perhaps the kindest thing you could do for Cier'Djaal is leave, Ramaniel."

Denaos opened his eyes. He looked from his left to his right. He looked above him.

That *had* been this morning, hadn't it?

It was hard to tell down here. The darkness was no longer darkness, it hadn't been for at least two hours. This far in, it was something alive, something that expanded with every breath and pressed up against him.

He knew the ground beneath his feet and the walls around his head only as a theory, things he suspected might be there but couldn't know about for sure. The darkness's breath robbed all the air down here, made his head feel light and his legs feel bloodless.

He felt a hand press just between his shoulder blades. His hand had already been around his knife, but he held it, and his breath. He counted the fingers on his back: big finger, little finger. As they had discussed.

"Junction's two hundred paces behind you," a voice whispered in his ear. "Three-way intersection. We've got knives in the east and west tunnels, we're taking the south."

He nodded.

Of course she wouldn't be able to see that, so he shuffled awkwardly around to where he thought she was standing and muttered back, "Got it."

It was dark. The smell of stagnant water and weeks-old shit cloyed his nostrils. He could barely hear for the blood pounding in his ears. Yet somehow he still had sense enough to know she was smiling at him with that shit-eating grin.

"'S dark," she said. "You wanna hold my hand?"

"Just move," he said. "I'll follow by scent."

"Smells like shit down here."

"Don't make me say it, Scarecrow."

She chortled blackly. She would. She had always been comfortable with this sort of thing, all the way back to when they were both pulling low-man work.

But him? He had taken the task of shaking down orphans just so he could avoid sewer jobs.

It had been worse back then, of course.

Back then the guards had given more of a shit and the fashas had promised the people that they'd clean up crime. Back then the Jackals had been just one gang of criminals among a hundred, and they'd all had need of the tunnels for the same reasons. Back then footwars were done dirty and in the dark.

The actual use of the tunnels—the smuggling, the transport, and the healthy payoffs that came with those things—was reserved for the heads and higher-ups in the gang. The job of going down there and cleaning out the tunnels of other gangs was given to the low-men, along with a dagger and a scented mask.

No lantern, of course. That'd give away their position. So every low-man who managed to pull sewer duty would wander around in the lightless labyrinth, going off of feel and memory, to clean the path for the smugglers, hoping they would bump into someone with their pointy bits before someone else did it to them first.

Scarecrow, back before they had started calling her that, had been one of the few who had earned their rank down here in the dark, hearing others' gurgling cries as she jammed her blade into them.

But she had never seen them.

While those experiences had made her one of the most uncomfortable people to share a drink with, he could think of worse people to take down into the sewers.

The sewers under the newer parts of the city were elegant, streamlined affairs full of right angles and walkways. It didn't take too many turns for them to start hearing the sound of voices thick with Sainite accent echoing off the walls. A distant light grew brighter at the end of the tunnel, illuminating Scarecrow's slender form and the giant crossbow strapped to her back. They slowed their pace, careful to move quietly as they made their way to the corner.

Sandal was hunched there. His short, stocky frame was swaddled in leather and his head was wrapped in a thick cloth, the sole gap being where a wooden visor with a thin slit for his eyes peered out. Clad as he was, he might have looked comical, even with the bandolier of fireflasks strapped across his chest. Denaos didn't dare make fun of him, though.

Sandal the Candle had done even worse than sewer work to earn his rank.

Denaos crouched down beside him, muttered lowly, "How's it look?"

Sandal glanced over his head, replied through the muffle of his head wrap, "*Wfll, thfrf's mhtbf tfn hr sf. Bffn khhpfng fn fyffhr mhrh, bht's hll clhfr nfw.*"

Denaos met the man's gaze, consideration etched across his face. He scratched his chin, gave a thoughtful hum, and nodded slowly.

"Sandal," he said, "I hate you so fucking much."

He edged past the stocky man and peered around the corner.

The tunnel opened up after about another twenty feet into a large chamber that formed the nexus of three tunnels. Originally built large enough for work crews to get their equipment into, this one had apparently found a new purpose and a new crew.

One with far more sinister equipment.

Ten of them, maybe twelve; it was hard to tell. Some men, some women, all in the blue coats and tricornered hats of Saine. By the light of several lanterns, some stacked crates of supplies, some unpacked weapons, some made the barest effort to stand guard, lounging on stacks with crossbows in their laps as they traded bawdy jokes. Makeshift barricades had been erected at the mouths of the tunnels, with more Sainites guarding the ones that reached east and west.

Denaos had to give the Sainites credit: Moving supplies down into the sewers was not a terrible idea. The Karnerians had the advantage on the ground, making it impossible to hold a conventional base. But then, one never accused the scraw-riding Sainites of being conventional.

No room for the beasts down here, though. Had scraws been part of the deal, Denaos never would have come down here. While he'd never seen a scraw, he'd seen the aftermath of the Karnerians who had fought them.

Accessing secret caches of weapons and supplies across the city, such as this one, would be trivial for an army so mobile.

Likewise, eliminating a few gangs of paltry thieves would be as petty a task for those birds as plucking worms from the earth. Should the Sainites decide to turn their full might against the Jackals…

He closed his eyes, drew in a breath.

Easy there, he cautioned himself. *Now's not the time to go listening to reason.*

He eased back behind the corner. Scarecrow looked at him expectantly. He just had to trust that Sandal did, too.

"I count twelve," he muttered. "There's a lot of cover for them, though, so there might have been more." He glanced to Scarecrow. "Who do we have in the other tunnels?"

"Lowbrow and his boys're in the east," Scarecrow grunted. "The Cado twins and their sister are taking the west." She grinned as she pulled her crossbow off her back. "Just waitin' for us to start the music."

"They know this isn't a shakedown, right? No eyes left open. If this gets back to the Sainite command—"

"Ain't gonna," Scarecrow said as she loaded a bolt and cranked her weapon back.

Sandal offered a gesture that *might* have been meant to be reassuring. "*Yff lfhvf thfs th fs. Gfnnh bf fnf hfll ff h shftshfw.*"

"All right, then." The dagger slid into his palm. "We do this dirty."

They filed out around the corner, as smoothly now as all those years ago when they had first started doing this. Noses to the ground, eyes on the target, hands on their steel.

Scarecrow took point, sliding down to one knee and aiming her crossbow down the hall. Without a moment's hesitation, Sandal broke into a run. He tore a pair of fireflasks from his bandolier, snapped his index and ring fingers. The flint and steel bands around the digits sent sparks kissing the oil-soaked fuses of the flasks. They burst into flame, tiny pyres blossoming in his hands as he charged down the tunnel, silent but for the crackle of his fire.

"Oi! *OI!*" one of the Sainites called out, leaping off a crate and aiming his crossbow. "Foreigners have breached the—"

Denaos felt the wind cut past his cheek. He saw Scarecrow's bolt jutting from the Sainite's throat an instant later. The soldier groped at it feebly, trying to gasp out a last word.

If they hadn't heard his cries of alarm, though, his compatriots certainly noticed him slumping to the ground. They scrambled for weapons, some grabbing swords and shields, other seizing crossbows to be loaded.

But it was all too little. In just one more moment, as he came within spitting distance of the barricades, Sandal the Candle showed them how he'd gotten his name.

They flew from his hands, the fires from their fuses painting red serpents in the darkness. They struck a shield, a crate; targets didn't matter. The fireflasks exploded in a spray of black glass and black oil. Flaming globs sizzled upon coats, upon hats, upon wood and stone and hair and skin.

And then, with a hundred red mouths, they began to chew.

Whatever facade of a defense the Sainites had been forming dissolved into a dozen screams straining to be heard over the roar of flame. They fought to tear off flaming coats, to pull the oil from their hair, to throw blankets over their comrades who'd gotten the worst of it.

It was for those gentle and compassionate souls that Denaos drew his blade.

He let Sandal hurl another flask over the barricade to explode in a cloud of flame before he followed it. He vaulted over the barricade and launched headlong into a tackle toward one of the Sainites who had been busy trying to extinguish a comrade. The man looked up, reached for the sword at his hip, but found Denaos's forearm pressed against his chest, pinning his arm and driving him back into the wall.

His knife worked a quick, messy romance upon the soldier: three steel kisses to the belly, one to the throat. He let the man drop, whirled about to see another one rushing at him with blade and buckler. The blade lashed out, a thrust made desperate by the surrounding flame and screams, easy enough to avoid. The shield that caught him in the back, less so.

The shock of a steel rim smashing between his shoulder blades sent him to the ground. He rolled with the blow, tumbling out of the way before an arcing sword could find him. Without looking he swept out a long leg and found an ankle. One of the soldiers fell to the stones before a comrade, tangling them up and giving Denaos a chance to leap to his feet.

How the fuck are there two of them still standing? he asked himself. *Who the fuck was supposed to take care of them?*

He stared down the east tunnel. Neither Lowbrow nor a single Jackal hood could be seen through the darkness. Either they were taking their sweet time or—

Sword. SWORD.

The one still on his feet leapt over his prone comrade, pulling a blade out and taking a wild swing at Denaos. He darted back, but the Sainite refused to give him an opening. Each stroke was followed by another and another, driving Denaos back a step each time, until he felt his foot catch on something.

He glanced down and saw a smoldering corpse of one of the less lucky Sainites, skin red and clothes black. He glanced back up, but the delay had cost him. He narrowly caught the soldier's arm as he came in for another swing. The Sainite lashed out with his shield, catching him on the chin and sending his head swimming.

But he didn't need to think for this next part. Now that he'd done it for as long as he had, murder had become just another reflex.

In and out, six times each, as quick as an eye could blink. Past the coat, past the leather beneath, past the flesh and into the belly. His dagger left dark-red smears upon the soldier's clothing, and the glassy-eyed, wide-mouthed look of a dead fish on the soldier's face.

Before the body could go totally limp, Denaos spun it about and shoved it toward his companion struggling to his feet. The other Sainite caught the weight of his dead comrade full-on and staggered back with the corpse, struggling between holding it and holding his weapon.

Denaos capitalized on that before he could make up his mind, rushing up and reaching around the body to deliver four quick stabs to the soldier's side. He let out a shriek, slumped to the ground with his dead companion bearing down upon him. Whatever strength he might have had to push the corpse off was ebbing with every breath out of the many wounds in his flank.

It would have been kinder to lean down and finish it, Denaos knew. But it was more practical to let the man bleed out and avoid the possibility of a stray blow's catching him.

To watch him, though, as his life wept out . . .

That was neither kind nor practical.

Yet Denaos did it, all the same.

The fires died alongside the soldiers, chewing through the crates and cloth and settling to smoldering cinders in a matter of moments. Denaos crouched low to the ground as the smoky belches of their feast wafted overhead and spread throughout the tunnels. When the air tasted a little less foul, he rose to survey the damage.

Or the mess, at any rate.

What supplies could be consumed by flame had been rent to cinders and ash. The weapons had been blackened and stained by fire. The Sainites themselves lay prone upon the ground. A fortunate few had bled out from Denaos's handiwork or Scarecrow's bolts lodged in chests and throats.

The unlucky ones bore Sandal's signature, their sloughed skin left in tarry black-and-red patches upon the stones.

Denaos let loose two short whistles, the agreed-upon signal.

Sandal came shuffling up in response. He carried a short blade wet with blood, though that was nothing compared to the blood seeping between his fingers as he clutched a wound in his side.

"Ouch." Denaos winced. "Got careless, did we?"

"*Nf mhrf thhn yff,*" Sandal mumbled. "*Hfs fnyhnf fvfr nhtfcf thht yfh hnlf hvfr sffm tf shfffr glfncfng blhws whflf lhss fmphrtfnt pffplh ght mhthlftfd?*"

Denaos narrowed his eyes at Sandal before glancing over his head. "Did I need to know any of that?"

"Specifics, nah," Scarecrow grunted as she came shambling up a tunnel to join them. "He ain't pleased, though."

"He can add his name to the fucking list." Denaos wiped his blade clean, replaced it in its sheath. "Where the hell were the others? Drunk or just stupid?"

"Wouldn't-a grabbed the stupid ones for this one," Scarecrow grunted. "And the one's that I chose wouldn't-a disappointed me by showin' up drunk."

Sandal sighed from behind his head wrap. *"Fsn't ft hbvfhfs?"*

"The Candle's right," Scarecrow grunted. "Smells like a rat."

"That can't be the case," Denaos replied. "Only the heads even know about this idea. And none of them knew who I was choosing for this job." He eyed Scarecrow. "You, on the other hand?"

"Ain't got rats." Scarecrow stroked the butt of her crossbow with the sort of intensity that suggested she thought it might just reach out and stroke her right back. "I run clean."

"You run with people named Lowbrow."

"Ain't. Got. Rats," she grunted emphatically.

Denaos's ire slipped through clenched teeth. "Well, how else do you explain it?"

Scarecrow's lips stiffened as she looked down her nose at Denaos. Sandal stared at him intently, the glistening of his eyes visible beneath the slits of his visor. He felt himself take a step back.

Accusations—like courtrooms and lawyers—were luxuries for common men who never found their way into the dark places under Cier'Djaal. Those people could afford to throw them around like seed to birds, content that gods or laws would protect them.

But among proper folk, like the Jackals, whose gods were silent and whose laws carried only one sentence, accusations were sharp and weighty as any dagger. And, as with a dagger, one threw them only if one was damn sure one wanted someone to bleed.

They said nothing. They made no accusation. The only thing Scarecrow and Sandal showed, in the tension of their stances and the rigidity of their postures, was a suggestion.

But one did not just suggest that one of the heads of the Jackals might be a traitor.

Not unless one was comfortable with the possibility of hanging from the Harbor Gate by one's throat.

Scarecrow and Sandal were veterans. They did their duties, followed their orders, earned their ranks like good soldiers. They knew the rules. They knew the sentences. They knew he could gut them then and there and not a soul would say a word against him for doing so.

And he might have on principle—or from paranoia—had a sound not caught his ear.

"*Hurts...*"

A whisper. No, something softer than that. Something wet and weak that had crawled out of a dead mother lying in the gutter. A whimper, oozing through the eastern tunnel toward them.

The woman arrived a moment later.

He had only a feeling that the figure at the mouth of the tunnel was a woman, just as he had only a feeling that it was a human. The figure, slight and wispy as a shadow in the orange-red glow of the smoldering fires, stood with a bowed head and arms hanging limp from stooped shoulders. She would have looked like any of Cier'Djaal's destitute and pathetic.

If she hadn't been wearing Khovura black.

"*In my body,*" she whispered. Her voice slid out of her throat on a thin trail of drool. "*It hurts.*"

Denaos signaled to Scarecrow. Her crossbow was up and loaded in an instant, fired an instant later. Weak and waif-like the woman might have been, but that was no cause for pause.

The fact that she didn't so much as shudder when the bolt struck her square in the belly? That was cause for pause.

"*The Disciples said I was chosen,*" she said. She didn't even seem to notice the three feet of wood and steel jutting from her abdomen. "*They said the seed had taken root. They said we would change things.*"

She took two slow, lurching steps forward into the firelight. And in the light, Denaos could see that she was not alone.

"*But where are they now?*"

He hadn't known Lowbrow well—only as a promising thug with a mean streak a mile wide—but he knew the man's features well enough from their passing encounters. Strong jaw, thick muscle, the sloping forehead that had given him his name; nice guy, strong-looking.

Though he looked a lot less strong as his limp corpse was dragged by the ankle by a woman half his size.

"The Disciples left. The visions won't come. Khoth-Kapira won't answer me and… and…"

She looked up. From under a mess of sweat-streaked black hair, eyes completely white and unblinking stared up. Her mouth opened too wide for her head, her lips stretching from ear to ear, and she croaked.

"It HURTS."

Her mouth craned open. Her head swung like the rusted hinge of a splintering door. From somewhere deep inside her, her croak became a scream and her scream became something else entirely.

Something that erupted from her throat in a spray of red.

It began as a column of flesh that rose out of her throat, born from somewhere deep within her body. It writhed, her flaccid body swaying with the motion as it twisted this way and that, as if searching for something. Eventually it angled itself toward Denaos and, with a sudden ripple of flesh, became more.

A dozen eyes opened. A dozen fangs glittered. A dozen forked tongues flicked out, spewing feral hisses into the darkness. The pillar of flesh blossomed into six serpents, bursting out of the woman's gaping craw like the lashes of a scourge, their yellow eyes glittering in the gloom.

"Run." The word sounded distant and dim in Denaos's ears, even as it tumbled from his lips. *"RUN."*

He couldn't tell if he had said that or just imagined that he had. He couldn't tell if Scarecrow and Sandal had heard him or if they were moving. His feet would not move. His eyes would not blink. And he could not tear them away from the sight of the woman.

As she took a step forward and rushed toward him.

Arms flopping bloodlessly at her sides, the serpents writhing from what had been her head, she charged toward him inhumanly fast. She collided with him, knocking the breath from him before he even remembered how to breathe. They struck the stones in a tangled mass of flesh and fangs.

His knife was up, slashing wildly as a matter of instinct, the flailing of a beast caught in a trap even as the snare tightened around its ankle. He was cutting, slicing, hacking; blood flew through the air. But was it his? For every time his blade found flesh, he felt a dozen pinpricks as fangs bit through his leathers.

He screamed. Without knowing what good it would do, he screamed. The fangs tore his voice from his throat as easily as they tore his blood from his skin. Through the gnashing of teeth and the glittering of eyes, he saw one head rise up above all others, its serpentine mouth split as its eyes locked upon Denaos's.

His voice went raw with his scream. So loud that he only barely heard the shattering of glass and the crackling of flames.

Fire blossomed on the creature's back, spreading over it in a single smoke-choked breath. The heads jerked away from Denaos, exploding in spasms of shrieking fear as each tried to pull away from the fire rising upon it. Denaos in turn jerked away from them, kicking the limp body off himself and scampering away.

He glanced at the mouth of the west tunnel. Sandal stood for as long at it took to raise a hand with a single finger. One favor, one courtesy, one that Denaos would have to pay back one day. And then he was gone, disappearing down the tunnels.

His breath returned to him, and with it merciless sensibility: eyes to see the darkness closing in around him as the flames of Sandal's fireflask spread, ears to hear the shrieking of the serpents as they were eaten by the flames.

And dread inching up his spine as he heard the sound of more footsteps echoing down the tunnel from which he had just come.

His feet found the sense to move before his brain found the time to think, sending him flying off down the eastern tunnel. Perhaps it was instinct or perhaps he still had enough sense to know that Jackals never all escaped down the same route.

He flew, stale air rushing past him. But no matter how quickly he ran, he could not escape the thoughts that came to him.

The heads. One of the heads is the traitor. No one else knew. No one else could have known. We only told Scarecrow and Sandal. They chose the people. Lowbrow, the Cado twins, they're all dead. It had to be one of them. Rezca, Yerk...

Anielle...

No! That thought punched through the fear racking his skull. *Not her. Never her. It could have been a coincidence. Maybe the Khovura just stumbled upon you.*

But the farther he went into darkness, the more he realized that was impossible.

He could hear them. Dozens of them. Their feet were in the tunnels, scraping across the stone walkways and sloshing through the waterways. Their arms were on the walls, nails dragging across the stones. Their eyes were on the darkness, their bodies were hidden in the gloom.

And every one of them was screaming.

"*—lies. They lied to us. They said we'd be strong. They promised. They—*"

"*—where are the Disciples? Why did they abandon us? Did I do it wrong? Did we not do what you asked? Come back. Please, come—*"

"*—it hurts it hurts it hurts it hurts it hurts it hurts oh gods oh gods oh gods oh gods—*"

"*—make it stop. Please. I'm sorry. I'm so—*"

Men. Women. Khovura, all of them. In such numbers that it could be no coincidence. Someone had sent them down here.

"Hello?" a dull voice called out in the darkness.

A man's voice. Slow. Slurring. Heavy.

"Is someone there?"

And terribly, terribly close.

"Please, come out. I don't want to be here."

"*Hush. Hush now.*" Another voice. This one rasping, harsh, a rusted knife sharpening itself on a dull stone. "*No fear, no voice.*"

"The others, though," the man said, "they all say it hurts."

"*It does, at first. You must kill them to make it stop.*"

"How?" the man moaned. "It's so dark down here."

"*Back. We go back to where we came from.*"

The sound of heavy feet plodding. The sound of a heavy weight being dragged. The man began to move in the darkness, away from Denaos.

He held his breath, waited a few moments, and began to follow. This man—or at least the thing he carried with him—sounded as if he knew the way. The sound of shrieking grew dimmer as he went, distant echoes in the darkness.

Whatever fear he might have felt, Denaos shut it out. He shut out fear for himself, fear for Sandal and Scarecrow, fear for what he might be following and fear for who had betrayed him to put him here.

One foot after the other. Each one soft, each one soundless. That was all he could do for himself now.

In the distance a pinprick of light appeared. It grew with each step until he could make out the unmistakable whiteness of daylight seeping from an access grate overhead.

And, just as quickly, he saw the silhouette of his quarry. A big man, but not so huge as to make the heavy sounds of movement he had heard in the darkness. His body sagged to his left, his foot dragging behind him. What, Denaos wondered, had he been doing to make that noise?

The answer came a moment later, as the man stepped into the ring of daylight and Denaos choked on his scream.

It sprouted from the man's left shoulder, a tuberous, flaccid stalk of sagging, wrinkled flesh that dragged on the floor behind him, threatening to topple him with every step. It resembled nothing so much as a limp phallus, twitching and pulsating on the floor. That was not quite the most horrifying thing about it, though.

"Here?" said the man.

The fact that it spoke was.

"Here."

It shuddered to life, rising of its own accord. The puckered flesh of its tip peeled back to expose a hairless, wrinkled face that looked like that of an old man gone unkindly in the night. Its eyes pinched shut by red cheeks, it cast a sightless gaze about and spoke through puckered lips.

"Can't hear them."

"Then we can go, right?" the man moaned. "Say we can go."

"Finish what we started. Khoth-Kapira chose us."

The man could but moan as the grotesquery that was his arm snaked forward, dragging him deeper into the darkness of the sewers.

When he could no longer hear the man's shuffling steps, Denaos crept into the light. Overhead, daylight shafted through a metal grate. A retractable ladder hung at the lip, half drawn up. The grate looked heavy, but Denaos suspected that with a bit of finesse he could—

"There. THERE. I see one now!"

Or fear. Fear was also handy.

"Wicked meat! Hold still!"

Denaos leapt up and seized the ladder, hauling himself up. His ears filled with the sound of pounding footsteps, the man screaming, the creature hissing. He reached up, shoved the grate. After a grunt of effort and a groan of metal, it gave, flying backward and clattering.

"No! NO! COME BACK!"

He scrambled out of the portal just in time to see the phallic stalk of flesh come slithering into the light. It looked up at him through its pinched eyes, its toothless mouth open in a wail as it snaked up toward him. He kicked the grate down, it struck the hairless face, sent it shrieking back to the depths.

He tore off running out of the alley, into the sprawling daylight. His eyes, familiar with the dark, seared in their sockets as he was suddenly assaulted with daylight.

It reflected off the white walls of sprawling manses, off the brilliant windows of towering shops, off the polished brass of countless statues and fountains. Lush green lawns rolled like hills in the distance. Elegant fences rose up around him. People in fine silks and finer jewelry surrounded him.

And, after a moment of appalled stares, the nobles of Cier'Djaal politely turned their noses up and resumed ignoring him.

He was in Silktown.

"Hey! You!"

And he really ought not to be.

He looked up, saw a small gang of men in the armor of a fasha's house guard staring accusingly at him. He took off before they could draw their swords, sprinting away and twisting down a corner. He found another alley soon enough, pressed himself inside, and disappeared into the shadows.

The guards rattled past, too slow to catch him and too inattentive to notice him. He waited until they rounded a corner and disappeared. Then he waited until the rumble of their armored pursuit faded from earshot.

Then he fell to his rear end, and began to laugh.

It was a loud, black, and wholly inappropriate sound, doubly so considering the dead comrades he had left behind in the tunnels. But he couldn't help it. It was either laugh or start screaming.

"Back the way we came," he thought. *That's what that thing said down there. They got in through Silktown. Even the house guards wouldn't have missed those things. Not unless they were ordered to.*

He leaned back, closed his eyes, felt his grin stretch so vast it might well have split his face apart.

All this fucking time, he thought, *they really did have a fasha working for them.*

THIRTEEN

In Heaven We Are Queens

If one didn't look closely, one would think it was just some kind of hideous growth.

It sat between the shoulder blades of a man facedown in the water, tiny pincers at the ends of its spindly legs clinging to his moist flesh, a long proboscis spearing down into the back of his neck. Its wings were folded against a translucent abdomen that had grown bloated with blood. Its compound eyes stared blankly out into nothing. If it weren't for the occasional twitch of its abdomen expanding, one wouldn't even know it was alive.

This, Asper had learned in her short time mucking through the shit of the Sumps, was the best time to grab them.

Hecatines fed on human blood to feed to their young, storing it in their abdomens until they could return to their nests. But the act of feeding rendered them insensate, numb to anything around them and easy to manipulate.

If not to dislodge, Asper thought as she leaned over the corpse.

A few quick tugs found the creature locked firmly on to the corpse. She pulled a scalpel from her belt, using it to gently cut the flesh from the insect's pincers and proboscis. Dead though the man might have been, there was no need to go mutilating him. Yet the creature's needle-like nose tore the flesh all the same, coming free with a ripping sound.

She cut it free, pulled the immobile, bloated insect off, and placed it in the satchel at her hip. Left behind was a gaping, bloodless wound where the creature had clung.

This sort of butchery had bothered her, at first.

But it was worth it. When they awoke from their comas, the

hecatines would instinctively latch on to the closest thing and disgorge their meals—now purified by whatever it was that lurked inside their abdomens—by thrusting out their proboscises. If the closest thing happened to be a victim of blood loss, they proved invaluable in saving lives.

Surely, she reasoned, any decent human being who had passed would forgive the indecency shown their carcass.

And if they don't, she thought as she shut her satchel tight, *fuck 'em*.

That thought echoed bitterly inside her, bouncing off some emptiness where vigor and patience had been drained dry by all the days of endless wars and endless victims. It fell down into the very pit of her stomach, where it sat like a lead weight.

And in response, something inside her yawned a gaping mouth to consume it.

It made its presence known almost immediately. Her left arm began to burn. She felt her knees buckle suddenly, the aches of her body suddenly overwhelmed by a deeper pain. Something living, old, and wicked stirred inside her flesh.

And spoke in an eloquent, dulcet voice.

Ah, Amoch-Tethr said, sliding into her thoughts, *have I arrived at a bad time?*

She did not speak to it. She tried not to think about it. But she could not help but feel it. His twitching, breathing, grinning presence.

No, she told herself. *Not "his." It's an it. A wickedness.*

I resent that, he replied.

Her mouth fell open. She stared down at her left arm. "You said you wouldn't listen to my thoughts."

It struck her only a moment later that she should be more offended by that than by any other part of this unholiness.

I can't very well help it when you start screaming them, Amoch-Tethr replied. *Do be careful, though. You'd not want to be seen talking to yourself.* It paused. She could feel his gaze shifting through her. *Though I suppose there's precious little chance of that occurring all the way out here.*

The Sumps carried a multitude of reputations: as a dangerous slum filled with those criminals too vile to be accepted into the Jackals, as a breeding ground for disease bred in the stagnant water that had come when the old seawall collapsed, as the very last hope of the very poorest to make a living in Cier'Djaal.

It was only after the war between the Karnerians and Sainites broke out that the Sumps had started being thought of mostly as a graveyard.

The waters that seeped through the shattered streets and crumbling buildings had rendered the place unfit for battle by any self-respecting army. Thus, many people had come here to escape the violence. It hadn't taken long at all for them to find another kind of violence here.

They ceased to be people once they entered the Sumps. Here they became prey for the murderers, the thieves, the rapists and the disease and the stray beasts. The luckiest ones died quickly.

Today the Sumps stood placid. The waters of the drowned district were still as glass, burbling contentedly when she waded through them. Its violent citizens ejected, it had found new occupants to better fit the tranquil surroundings. They drifted lazily through the drowned streets, bloated and pale and peppered with hecatine bites, staring up at the sun through eyes as glassy as the water.

And every time she came here, there were more bodies.

They didn't blame you.

In the silence, Amoch-Tethr's voice rang out in her head.

When they died, they did not scream how you could not save them. They did not curse your name. Their last words were not for you.

In the silence, Asper could feel him stare at her.

Would you like to know what they said?

She looked down at her arm. Without quite knowing why, she whispered, "Yes."

And in her flesh, she could hear him answer.

The children cried out for their parents. The parents cried out for their children. The childless cried out for the ones they never had. The orphans simply cried out.

And in her flesh, she could feel him smile.

And there will be so much more.

"I'm trying." She did not know why she said this. She did not know what justification she owed him. She did not know why she was weeping. "I'm *trying*. But there are so many people and there are so few of us that I can't—"

Oh, but you can. How long have I lingered in your flesh? How long have you kept me a secret? How many countless lectures did we sit through from healers and priests? What did they say?

He twisted inside her. His smile became a spasm of pain shooting through her arm.

Treat the disease. Not the symptom.

"People aren't symptoms," she shot back.

But they can be diseases, Amoch-Tethr replied. *You know their names. Blacksbarrow. Careus. Fasha Mejina.*

"What are you saying?"

A thin red line appeared in her left arm. With a sticky popping sound, the flesh split apart, curling over itself to expose the red sinew beneath. The muscle pried itself open, and in the folds of meat, a smile brimming with sharp, gnarled teeth grew wide. A long black tongue flicked out and its voice spoke from a black place ten thousand years away, with brimstone on its breath.

"*Treat them,*" Amoch-Tethr said.

She felt it all at once, a pain so fierce that it caused her to double over, threatening to send her toppling headlong into the water. She opened her mouth, a groan tumbled out. But it was not her voice. This was not her pain.

But it consumed her. It filled her head with images—Blacksbarrow, Careus, countless others. It filled her body with the need to consume them—every drop of blood, every sliver of bone, every scrap of flesh—until the pain went away.

Treat them save them kill them eat them burn them protect them kill them kill them KILL THEM.

His thoughts. Her thoughts?

Hard to tell. Hard to think. Hard to breathe. She couldn't. She had to. She needed to—

"Asper."

A hand fell upon her shoulder. She let out a snarl, whirling about with her left hand. It struck hot flesh, sent her assailant falling back with a cry of alarm.

Only when she saw Aturach's face, wide with shock and pain, did she realize what she had done. She tried to hide her arm, but when she looked at it, her skin was once again whole. The pain she had felt so keenly was gone, released upon the air.

"Aturach," she gasped. She moved forward to treat him. "I'm sorry."

"My fault," he said, holding up a hand. "I shouldn't have sneaked up on you, here of all places." He cringed. "Though, here of all places, neither of us should be, you know."

"We're low on hecatines and high on victims," she replied, sighing. "It had to be done."

"By you, though? The Sumps aren't safe. What would happen if you got knifed here? Where would we be?"

"I can take care of myself."

"If you're going to tell me *that* lie, you should at least look at yourself in the mirror."

She didn't need to look at herself to know what he spoke of. She could feel the dark circles under her eyes, the frown weighing down her mouth, the grease in her hair and on her skin. She could feel the bend in her neck and the crick in her back.

It would be accurate to say she looked like hell.

"Anything you want to fucking say on that matter, Aturach?"

Accurate, but not wise.

He touched his cheek where she had struck him. "You aren't going to help anyone if you work yourself to death, Asper."

"Well, I don't have a lot of choice, do I? The people who volunteer either die in the city or flee once we've patched them up. You, me, and Dransun are the only ones around who will help."

"There's the Temple of Ancaa, still," Aturach said.

"They're only taking the overflow," Asper replied. "They don't know how to treat the wounded. It's down to just us three."

A dark-green shape fell out of the sky, the buzzing of wings filled her ears as it flew past. The hecatine settled on the corpse its comrade had just been feeding upon and began searching for a vein.

"And these things," Asper sighed.

She leaned forward and began to turn the corpse over. The hecatine buzzed, making way for it.

"What are you doing?" Aturach asked, a tinge of disgust in his voice.

"It needs a fresh vein for more blood," she replied. "And this guy's not going to miss—"

She fell silent as she looked upon the corpse's face.

Dark-skinned Djaalic, civilian clothes, no beard; young man, probably a merchant's apprentice, strong and able-bodied. He stared up at the sky with a glassy look, bled out from a wound in his chest. He still had a scar upon his temple where he had been struck.

Back in the city, where she had first met him.

Back when she had saved him.

"Asper?" Aturach said, looking over her shoulder.

"This man," she said, "I saved him. Days ago. He was complaining and being an asshole, so I..." She looked up, eyes wide. "I sent him to the Temple of Ancaa with the other overflow."

"Huh," Aturach grunted. "He probably ran away, then, after he— wait, where are you going?"

Asper didn't answer him. She pushed past him, waded through the water to another drifting corpse. She seized him by the shoulders, drew him close. A well-fed man, nicer clothes, elegant beard; older, a merchant, lost his business in the war. Dead from a gash across his neck.

She had saved this one four days ago. She had treated a shallow wound and sent him to the Temple of Ancaa.

"No," she whispered.

She splashed through the waters again to a woman, rolled her over. This one had been savaged thoroughly before she died. Middle-aged, shabby clothes, stretch marks on her flesh; mother of three, she had told Asper about them when Asper had pulled her out from under some rubble six days ago.

And sent her to the Temple of Ancaa.

"*No.*"

"Asper, wait!" Aturach cried out, trying to follow.

She tore through the waters, found them all. More corpses: a young man who had been a baker's apprentice, a young woman who had worked at an inn to help her younger sister, a grandmother who had lost her home to Sainite commandeering. Their injuries had been minor. She had sent them all to the same place.

How had they all ended up in a graveyard?

"Those fucking heathens," Asper muttered under her breath. When that was not good enough, she screamed to the sky. "*Those fucking pagan PUKES!*"

"What is it?" Aturach finally caught up to her, breathing heavily.

"We trusted them," Asper snarled at him. "We *trusted* them and they just sent everyone out here to *die!*"

"Who?"

"The Ancaarans!" She swept her hands over the floating graveyard. "Don't you see? Everyone we sent to them, they sent *here*!"

Aturach's despair deepened on his face with each dead face he saw. "Look, there must be—"

"What? An explanation? Did they *all* feel better?" She pointed to the dead grandmother. "Did *she*? I had to carry her up the stairs to their temple, Aturach!"

"That doesn't—"

"It fucking *does*, you spineless piece of—"

"*DON'T FUCKING SAY THAT!*" Aturach roared. "Don't... just..." He gritted his teeth, his hands clenched into trembling fists. "I see it, Asper. Same as you. But the Ancaarans are wealthy. They have the room to help these people. We need to tread carefully here."

He sighed, reached out, and touched her shoulder. "Ancaa is a new religion, even in the south. There's precious little experience to be had with them, but I've got it. Let's think this over."

She drew in a deep breath, reached up, and laid her hand on his. "You've always been more diplomatic than me, Aturach."

"We work well together that way," he said.

She nodded. Then she seized his fingers, tore his hand off her, and stormed off toward the gates of the Sumps.

"Think just how much more diplomatic you'll seem when you're apologizing for me after I've caved their gods-damned *faces* in."

***

"Heathen though you may be, priestess, I am making every attempt to understand your anger."

The voice of the pudgy priest of Ancaa was dim and droning, accompanied by the rattle of his emerald headdress as he settled back in a finely carved chair behind a finely hewn altar atop a finely woven carpet. His manicured fingers played with a necklace of jade that hung heavy around his throat, as he pouted at the dark stain on his carpet.

"Though I have no desire to understand your odor."

Asper, for her part, had no desire to justify it. The water of the Sumps hadn't dried from her run to Temple Row and still dripped from her clothes onto the carpet.

As she saw it, the Temple of Ancaa, with all its polished stone and marching pillars and stained glass windows, could do with a bit of grime.

Maybe a bloodstain or two, as well.

"Don't change the subject," she snarled. "We've been sending victims with minor wounds to you on the basis that you had the room to hold them." She thrust an accusing finger at them. "You *said* you could."

"And we could," the priest said, "and we can. There is more than enough room here." He gestured to the stained glass skylight depicting a tide of humanity joined in a twisting ring. It shone down on him as if to suggest a massive halo for a very small man. "For the faithful of Ancaa."

Asper's finger fell, her hand curling into a fist. At a loss for words, she stormed forward to deliver a more direct objection. Angry as she was, though, Aturach was quicker and scurried in front of her.

"We had an agreement," he protested. "We would take *everyone*, regardless of faith."

"The agreement has changed." The priest's reply lilted out of his pouting lips. "It was deemed no longer beneficial to Ancaa."

"What was unbeneficial?" Aturach demanded. "The part about helping people or housing people? I've read through your scriptures. Ancaa helps the poor and the destitute."

"Ancaa does," the priest said. "And our temple is full of those who are poor and destitute *and* adhere to the proper values."

"Proper? *Proper?*" Diplomacy, apparently, had a limit. And it ended in a sputtering rage that sent Aturach at the priest with a raised fist. "What's proper about tossing people into the *Sumps*, you bloated—"

"Aturach." Asper laid a hand on his shoulder, drew him back. "Be at ease."

He trembled beneath her touch, but slowly lowered his fist. "I suppose that wouldn't have helped anything at all."

"Of course not," she said, pushing past him and raising her own fist. "You have no upper body strength. You wouldn't even leave a bruise."

"Don't think to bring violence in here, you ruffian," the priest said, backing up into his throne as she approached. "Ancaa protects—"

His voice leapt into a frightened squeal as she leaned forward. She met his eyes, found them quavering as she leaned closer. She glanced up at the glimmering emeralds set in his headdress. A dozen weary women looked back at her, reflected in the jewels.

"Nice jewels," she said. "A mark of your station?"

"W-when I was chosen," the priest said, "they were bestowed upon—"

"I know. I remember how they looked on the last guy that wore them." Her scowl swept down to meet his gaze again. "They looked nice then, even as he choked on his own blood."

"If you are trying to threaten me..."

"I don't make threats," Asper said. "I'm not a soldier. I'm not a thug. I'm a healer. I'm trying to keep people from dying and there is no *end* to people who want to keep me from doing that. Or you."

"We are of different faiths," the priest said, trying to force some spine into his words. "Do not pretend we are alike."

"I haven't read your scripture or heard your sermons and I don't care. But when your predecessor was shot down like a pig, we became alike. We became targets for the Karnerians, for the Sainites, for the Jackals and the Khovura. Because *we* are the ones that do what they can't. *We* are the ones that can mend what they destroy. *We* can keep this city, these people, standing."

There was no mercy in her voice. She did not plead. She did not threaten. She merely stated.

"And the only way we don't all end up bleeding out in an alley is if we stand together."

In any holy woman's life, if she was lucky enough, there would come a time when she would gaze upon someone's face and see it. The moment when color came back to cheeks, when darkness fled from eyes, when a mouth was held just slightly open, speechless. It was a moment when she, charged with explaining how such a world could possibly make any sense, finally made someone understand.

The moment came as it would: through compassion, through patience, through example.

The Ancaaran twitched away from her, swallowing hard.

Or fear, she thought. *Fear's fine, too.*

The priest's eyes darted to the shadows. And as though she were some evil presence simply waiting to be acknowledged, a low voice hissed from near a pillar.

" 'Obey me or face apocalypse.' "

No one had noticed her there until she came walking out of the gloom. She stood so short and so thin that no one would have.

" 'Heed me or suffer.' "

But her yellow eyes burned above her veil with an anger that belonged on someone large, someone vast, someone imposing. And her stride was that of a warlord through a field of ruin.

" 'Do as I say or you will die.' "

Fasha Teneir, in an unassuming silk robe, wearing a chain of silver hands joined together around her neck, stepped into the ring of light cast by the stained glass.

"The same words regurgitated by the same gods of the same people since time began," Teneir hissed. "Typical."

Asper felt the anger roiling through her take a step back, becoming something wary. Muscles tightened in anticipation, rather than fury.

No doubt Teneir was an anomaly among the ostentatious fashas, with her humble wardrobe and modest jewelry. But even with that, there was something in the rigid way the saccarii woman held herself that made her look as hard as any thug or soldier. That something sensed the violence that lurked beneath Asper and dared her to come try to unleash it.

"Fasha Teneir." If Aturach saw the same thing, he at least held down the recognition as he addressed the saccarii. "I would have thought you to be in Silktown with the other nobles. Are you not hoping to ride out the violence there?"

"Your assumptions betray your snideness, Talanite," she said. "Fasha Mejina and the others may cower behind their dragonmen and pristine walls. My place has always been here, with the people." She swept her scowl to Asper. "The *true* people of Cier'Djaal."

"Surely the Djaalics are one people, Fasha," Aturach said.

"To the blind, perhaps. To the ignorant, the weak"—another pointed glare to Asper—"the *foreign*."

She whirled about and swept a hand about the great temple hall, its marching pillars and its bronze braziers and its stained glass.

"But I have lived a life above the filthy streets and I have seen Cier'Djaal from on high. I have watched the merchants eat the people, the thieves eat the merchants, the fashas feed the thieves. I have seen this city as it was truly built, with one man standing upon the broken backs of a hundred."

Her voice sank low beneath her veil. "This is a city of many people, Talanite. And each one is defined by the size of his coin purse. We are divided, priest. And the *shkainai* would divide us further."

"She has done *nothing* but aid us—"

"In what?" Teneir cut Aturach off. "What happens when these people are healed? How long until the next holy war? The only way to stand against foreigners, against thieves, against corrupt fashas is *united*. And because we stand divided, we are meat for the *shkainai*." She turned her glare back upon them. "Ancaa will save this city. And when she does, she will reign as one god over one people."

Aturach's mouth hung open, lips still groping for words to match the shock painted on his face. Asper, by contrast, knew exactly what to say.

"So, what?" she growled as she stormed toward the fasha. "You're sending people out to die to set an example? To intimidate them into belief?"

"I am letting them know the price of heathenry," Teneir replied sharply. "I am forging a new world with one less war to fight. My vision for Cier'Djaal—"

"Is *bullshit*," Asper interrupted. "You think you're the first asshole to think it was a great idea to kill people to prove a point?" She shoved the fasha, sent her staggering backward. "You're not even the first person this *week* to give me a lengthy speech about why *their* murder was justified."

Teneir brushed her robe, as though Asper's touch were unclean. "I do what I must for Cier'Djaal."

"And I do whatever I can," Asper snarled, "for its people. All of them."

"You think yourself some great *shkainai* savior? Some northern deliverer of the poor?"

"I took an oath to heal the wounded, to tend to the sick, to comfort the dying, no matter the cost. Skin doesn't matter. Location doesn't matter. Faith doesn't matter."

And then, in the span of a single breath, all the heat fled Teneir's eyes. What remained behind was something cold and appraising, something that belonged in the eyes of a merchant and not a visionary. And with that look, she spoke very softly and very slowly.

"Then convert."

Asper had been expecting a number of different responses from the fasha—and a number of those she had been hoping would warrant fisticuffs. But this statement, delivered as plainly as the letters on a contract, stunned her.

"What?" she asked.

"Convert," Teneir repeated. "If faith does not matter, then it should be a small matter to agree to kneel before Ancaa and swear a new oath."

"It's not just that, it's…it's…"

"A matter of sums?" Teneir turned her back to the woman, made a fleeting gesture. "The temple shall be reopened to all who require it, regardless of faith. I will dedicate my fortunes to their aid. I will refurbish and restock the Temple of Talanas, if you wish. I will even throw open my own estates to them and every comfort therein. All this shall be done…"

Teneir turned that appraising look over one shoulder.

"Assuming you were not lying."

Every curse seemed too tame. Every retort seemed too feeble. Every word she had felt as though it would simply tumble out into a formless, astonished plea. And yet she knew any plea would be met with silence. From fasha, from Aturach, from heaven.

And so she stood there, without a single word.

Kill her.

But not everyone was at the loss she was.

Maim her.

Beneath the flesh of her left arm, Amoch-Tethr twitched. His teeth bared themselves in a smile. His eye rolled about, trying to see. His voice was a brimstone-tinted cackle in her skull.

She is eager to trade one life for so many. Let us comply. Let us treat her to smoke and flame, seize this temple, and use it to help the many.

"I can't…," she whispered.

Then don't. Let me do it for you. You may be the savior and I shall be your humble aide. I will make it quick. Do not worry. She will feel nothing.

She felt her arm tremble, begin to rise.

All you need to do is close your eyes…

She felt her eyelids grow heavy and fall shut.

All you need to do is close your ears…

Aturach was saying something. Teneir was saying something. She could hear neither.

And let…me…OUT.

Crimson flashed behind her eyes. For but the briefest of moments, she saw it. Him. Towering, terrible, black as pitch upon a field of flame and blood, his mouth craned open in shrieking laughter and with blood staining his teeth. His terrible feast, endlessly feasting on corpses, forever choking on ash, perpetually glutted, and always, *always* starving.

Her eyes snapped open. She seized her left arm. Something inside her screamed. The world looked alien around her, fragile and delicate and fit to be consumed. She tried to speak, but her words were breathless, her mouth was dry.

Asper turned. Away from their curious stares, away from their inquiring voices. She ran from the Temple of Ancaa without a scream.

Without a word.

FOURTEEN

THE GULLET

This can't be right."

It felt good for Lenk to say it aloud, after he had been thinking it for the past half an hour.

But it was a small comfort. And that comfort only grew smaller as it was pressed between the tremendous cliff walls that rose out of the river on either side.

The dry desert air that had scraped at his throat for so long was gone in an instant, drowned beneath a humidity that became oppressive in the span of a few breaths. Walls that had been sheer blasted rock suddenly blossomed into vivid green life.

Trees rose out of the crowns of the cliffs, their leafy canopies drooping into the chasm as if bowing in greeting to the newcomers. Vines crawled across the rock, into every crack and out of every crevice. And everywhere flowers bloomed, a riot of colors that sent spirals of shed petals twisting with every stray breeze that blew down the chasm.

The Old Man took another shuddering step into the chasm. Waves kicked up by its massive stride rolled up against the bases of the rock walls. A low-hanging tree branch shook as its green hide brushed against it. The sky erupted with color as a flock of birds, each one bright and dazzling as a gem, took wing and flew overhead, complaining noisily to the impassive creature that disturbed their roost.

Lenk watched them as they wheeled overhead, swooped past the Old Man's head, and went flying off down the chasm until they disappeared.

Into the Gullet.

He wasn't sure what he had been expecting. Forbidding gates with ominous warnings carved in them, perhaps. Or maybe an arch from which hung the skulls of those foolish enough to enter before him. He had expected more *death*, as clichéd as it was.

Not that there wasn't plenty of that here, he thought as he glanced over the railing of the deck.

Upon the small beaches formed in coves at the bases of the cliffs, they gathered. Through the blue waters of the Lyre, they waded. Two-ton hunks of smooth gray blubber upon squat little hooved legs.

River bulls.

Their snouts, broad and flat and brimming with curving tusks, each bore a long, sharp horn that thrust into the air like a scimitar. The rotting wooden hulls of vessels that had borne treasure-seekers this far littered the river, each one bearing neat puncture marks, the work of the bulls' horns and testament to their legendary territorialism.

Yet big as they were, their bulk was tiny against the colossal stride of the Old Man's legs, and their bellows were squeaks lost in the titan's great groans. When it was clear that their posturing would do nothing, they quickly swam out of the Old Man's path.

I suppose that explains why we couldn't come here by boat, Lenk thought.

Yet even the thought of being spun around like a child's doll upon a river bull's horn wasn't enough to diminish his awe of the ever-thickening jungle around him.

"This was desert just a few miles—no, just a few *feet* back," he muttered. He felt a prick at his arm, looked down to see an insect crawling across his skin. "I can still feel the sand in my shirt. But now..." He held up his arm, stared at the insect—some winged orange-and-green thing. "I've never seen flowers or bugs like these before."

He flinched as a scaly hand clamped down on his arm suddenly. It drew back, a greasy red smear where the bug had been.

"If ya had," a voice grunted, "ya'd know that the ones in the Gullet ain't the sort ya let sit on yer skin."

Chemoi glared at him. Her fellow saccarii busied themselves in the background. Some scuttled across the deck and rappelled down the Old Man's flanks to dislodge parasites. Others lingered at its head, whispering soothing words that apparently helped it continue.

Lenk supposed he should be flattered that she had taken time out from that to tend to him.

"West Lyre's gentle, pinky. She coddles merchants 'n' other soft-skinned shits with sunshine 'n' beaches." Chemoi wiped her hand on her baggy trousers, heedless of the nasty stain it left. "This far east she's a lone mother with three kids, two jobs, and a big fat boil on her ass. Nasty, nasty bitch." Her hand slid into a pocket of her trousers, produced a small clay pot, and thrust it into Lenk's hands. "Watch that ya don't give her reason to turn on ya."

Lenk removed the pot's lid and sniffed at the mixture, instantly recoiling. Bugreek, it was called: a mixture of animal fat and oils that was said to be offensive enough to keep insects from landing on any flesh anointed with it. Chemoi's own flesh, left generously bared by the cloth wrapped about her chest, glistened with a liberal application of the stuff.

Curiously, the saccarii tending to the Old Man seemed far less concerned with clothing than their city-dwelling kin. They walked about in various states of undress, exposing skin flecked with patches of scaly, toughened flesh. This condition—and the reactions they drew from Cier'Djaal's citizens—was why most saccarii went around clad head to toe. Out here, Lenk supposed, there was no one to be shocked.

Yet here, as in the city, the saccarii still wore wraps about their heads that left only the ochre of their eyes revealed. And Chemoi fixed hers on Lenk in an impatient glower.

"Thanks," he said, scooping out the mixture and applying the reeking stuff to his arms and neck.

Chemoi nodded her approval before turning to join her companions in attending to their living vessel. They busily hurried about the deck, darting around the other passengers, whom they outright ignored.

Fitting, Lenk thought, since the passengers seemed to be doing their best to ignore each other.

At the stern of the deck, Shuro sat atop a few crates of cargo, poring over a trade manifest. Sensing his eyes upon her, she glanced up just long enough to shoot him a warning look. They had taken care not to be seen together too much since the incident at Jalaang. That might have led to some uncomfortable questions.

Though no one seemed interested in asking them.

Man-Khoo Yun stood, four arms folded in four sleeves, staring out over the edge of the railing from behind the portrait over his face. He had said not a word since they had entered the Gullet, and he had deigned to move only to cast looks to the bow of the deck.

Kataria lingered there, perched expertly upon the deck's railing, one hand gripping a support beam holding the deck's wooden canopy up. Her bow and quiver hung loosely around her shoulder, arrows rattling with each stride of the Old Man. She leaned out, staring over the Old Man's head and into the reaches of the winding Gullet ahead, with such ease that he might have called it reckless if he had not known her better.

But he knew her well.

Talk to her.

So well that he knew that sounded like a bad idea.

And yet he had to. Too many fitful nights, sleep filled with the faces of dead men. Too many silent days, not so much as a breath shared with her.

And so he took a step toward her. He had to talk to someone. Anyone.

"Your priorities fascinate me."

Well, almost anyone.

He would have liked to ignore Mocca. He would have liked to even pretend that he could. But even that small comfort was impossible when the man in white suddenly appeared at the periphery of his vision.

"You are surrounded by a miracle of life blooming in one massive, sandy graveyard." Mocca stood at the edge of the deck, hands folded behind his back, staring out over the greenery of the Gullet. "You are assaulted by a verdant sprawl of life while, not two miles away in the desert, a young woman spends her dying breath pleading for water she will never find."

He cast the barest of smirks over his shoulder.

"You bear witness to the impossible, and your sole thoughts are for a woman who is not thinking of you. There's a poem here, had I but pen for it."

There were moments when Lenk almost forgot that no one else could see Mocca. Just as there were moments when he almost forgot he shouldn't be seen talking to the wind. He sauntered up to the railing, dropped his voice low.

"This is not a good time for you to be here."

"No? When would you like me to come back? Shall I wait for you to approach her and her to rebuff you? Should I come later tonight, when you're sleeping two feet away from her and wondering how it feels as though it's two hundred miles?" His smile grew softer, a sadness curling the corners of his mouth. "Or shall I come again tomorrow, when you're alone but for the wind carrying away the last traces of her scent?"

"Did you have a point?" Lenk asked, pointedly not looking at the man. "Or did you come here because you couldn't keep these dramatic gems to yourself?"

Mocca pursed his lips. "Admittedly, I was rather proud of them. But regardless of whether you believe it or not, I actually don't have a vested interest in seeing you make a fool of yourself."

Lenk looked over his shoulder to Kataria. A breeze caught her, sending her hair whipping about her face. Her face cracked with a grin, broad canines bared as she laughed at the sensation. And he instantly looked down to his hands, trembling upon the railing.

"They weren't clean kills," he said. "They weren't warriors. They were merchants."

"They weren't your fault," Mocca replied. "They were trying to kill you."

"I know that, but..."

He inhaled. He released his breath slowly, placing one hand on the other to keep it from shaking. The breeze wended its way past his nostrils, carrying the scent of her sweat.

"I need her." Even saying it made him ache. "I need her to feel normal. I need her to make me believe this, the dead men, all of this, is all worth it. But every time I close my eyes, I can see their faces, I can see my sword bloody in my hand, but I can't see her."

The silence hung unmercifully short, Mocca's voice cut unmercifully deep.

"Perhaps there's a reason for that."

Something about it—the words, the way he said them, they way they sounded so right—made Lenk want to strangle him. And if he had been less focused on not looking crazy, he might have tried.

"You live your life in waking nightmare," Mocca said, looking out over the river. "Your dreams are empty but for songs made of a dying man's last breath. Tell me, when you envision your new life, what else is there beyond her?"

Lenk's mouth hung open as he tried to formulate an answer, but none would come. Any ideas of what he might do, the shitty shops and farms he might run in Cier'Djaal, were hazy in his head. Whenever he envisioned his new life, only one thing about it was solid.

And she was not speaking to him.

"If so much could be placed upon just one person, no one would have need of gods," Mocca said. "Perhaps she feels the stress of this burden and your insistence on putting it upon her." He rolled his shoulders. "Or perhaps she's simply drifting elsewhere. I lived a thousand lifetimes, you know. I can say without uncertainty that no love is eternal."

"Then what am I supposed to do?" Lenk's voice rose enough to draw some curious stares from the saccarii crew. "Be a weapon? A tool for Sheffu? For you? Just pick up my sword, close my eyes, and think happy thoughts as I start hacking?"

"Sheffu is a man of fears. He asks you to close your eyes that you might not see the terrible things surrounding you. I am a being of reality. All I ask is that you open your eyes and take it in." He gestured grandly to the greenery blooming out before them, the forest that should not be. "And all its horrible beauty."

Lenk glared at the man. "So, about that point you supposedly had . . ."

"Is there no pride taken in interpretation anymore?" Mocca's sigh was exaggerated and dramatic. "It's a wise man who stops and considers his surroundings. Fail to do that and you will one day open your eyes, look around, and wonder how it is you came so far and have nothing to show for it but the sand beneath your feet." He glanced over Lenk's head. "Much as you'll wonder how it is that everyone on board here has stopped moving and you haven't even noticed."

"What?"

Lenk looked over his shoulder and got his answer. Everyone on deck had gathered at the railing, standing there in stunned silence, all of their eyes drawn up to the cliffs of the Gullet's northern side.

When he turned back, Mocca had disappeared. He cursed under his breath, then turned and walked to the edge of the railing, stopping beside Kataria. Her bow was in one hand, the other resting upon an arrow in her quiver.

"What is it?" he asked. "What's going on?"

She did not answer. She did not have to.

As soon as he looked up, he saw them. Dark shapes huddled at the edge of the cliff, stark against the greenery and black as though they drank the sunlight. The only flash of color among them was the glint of silver, as they carried steel swords and spears naked in long, simian hands.

Tulwar.

He had seen them before, back in Cier'Djaal. But those had been different: silver-furred, eyes bright yellow and faces alive with color. These, thicker and taller than their cousins, were the color of pitch. Their eyes were dark and their faces were painted bone-white.

And while the boisterous, violent nature of tulwar was legendary, these merely stood silent, watching the Old Man's progress with marked interest.

And unsettling as they were, the beasts they rode were infinitely stranger.

Great simian creatures, taller than a horse at their shoulders, leaned forward on their knuckles. Black fur covered their bodies but for their red faces, which were left bare. In contrast to the tulwar riding upon their shoulders, the beasts seemed restless, shuffling on their feet, offering occasional hoots and baring fangs at the passersby.

"All apologies are offered if this one presumes ignorance on the part of passengers," Man-Khoo Yun said, a strain at the edge of his monotone. "But if there exists any biped present that is not currently teeming with concern, this one suggests immediate amendment."

"It's all right," Lenk said. "We knew there'd be tulwar out here. We've prepared for this."

"We're prepared for tulwar," Shuro said. "*Not* Mak Lak Kai."

"I'm guessing there's something I should know about why that's bad."

"It'd take too long to tell you every reason why," she said. "Suffice to say the tulwar—violent, barbaric, and murderous as they are—consider the Mak Lak Kai clan to be a bit unhinged." She looked to Man-Khoo Yun. "They usually stick to the forests. What are they doing out here?"

"And why are they not attacking?" Lenk added.

"Theories within probability would likely suggest a cursory cost-benefit analysis on their part to be unfavorable. This one humbly professes minimal knowledge as to the behavioral patterns of the unwashed." He angled his portrait to regard Kataria. "Perhaps savagery in residence can shed light upon the subject."

Lenk wasn't quite sure what he expected Kataria's retort to be—something involving violent ejection of bodily fluid, probably—but the shict said nothing. She didn't even seem to notice the couthi, let alone his insult. Her eyes were hard as they stared out over the tulwar, her ears erect and quivering.

She knows something.

Lenk looked back up to the cliffs, made a quick count. "About fifteen of them. Each one riding some kind of..."

"Gaambol," Shuro said.

"Sure. Gaambol...ape...thing. Way too many for us to fight, no matter what you call them. If they wanted a fight, they would have done it by now." He looked to Man-Khoo Yun. "We'll go ahead with the plan."

The couthi regarded him for a moment before bowing his painting in acknowledgment. One of his smaller hands rose and made a gesture at Chemoi. Orders were barked, feet scurried across the deck, weapons were drawn.

They had gone over this a dozen times since leaving Jalaang, enough that Lenk was starting to feel like an expert on tulwar behavior—as it pertained to avoiding getting savagely beaten by them, at least.

The saccarii reached for fishing harpoons, cutlasses, anything they could seize to make it clear that they would not be cowed. Yet anything that lived in the desert was still hard up for supplies even in the best of times. And so three saccarii walked to the railing with crates clutched in their arms and tossed them overboard.

Each one tumbled off the flank of the Old Man and splashed into the river below. Cork panels had been secured to them to keep them from sinking, and each one was filled with food, wine, and a little bit of coin. Not enough to really count as a "tribute," but enough to make tulwar consider taking the easier bargain.

The tulwar watched the crates as they struck the water, but made no move to go down and retrieve them. Their attentions almost immediately turned back to the Old Man as the behemoth slowly made its sauntering way past them. One of their gaambols let out a shriek, slapping the ground, as though insulted by the offering.

"They ain't movin'," Chemoi hissed, worried. "They ain't takin' it."

"They're Mak Lak Kai," Shuro said. "Very proud. If they're going to take it, they'll wait until we're gone." She swept her stare out over the assembled. "That's a big if, though."

Lenk wondered why it had not occurred to him how unlike a merchant Shuro was. Perhaps Mocca was right about his inattentiveness.

"Best thing to do now is just return to our business," she said. "If we keep staring, they'll take it as an insult."

With wary glances they sheathed their weapons, slowly dispersed, and went about their business. Shuro purposefully walked away before Lenk could inquire about her expertise. With a sigh he turned and began to walk back to the bow with Kataria.

The shict hadn't shouldered her weapon like everyone else.

"Something wrong?" Somewhere behind, one of the gaambols let out a warbling hoot. "I mean, aside from the obvious?"

"They aren't attacking," she said, as though that answered it all.

"And?"

"And they aren't going to attack." She looked at him with the same intensity with which she had scrutinized the tulwar. "I saw wounds on some of them: cuts, puncture marks from arrows. They had just come from a fight."

The observation struck Lenk, but he merely nodded. That Kataria should notice more than he did at such a distance was not surprising.

"I guess that explains what they're doing out here," Lenk muttered. He looked over his shoulder. A few of the bolder tulwar had begun following the Old Man's course on their gaambols; leisurely, as though just to suggest they *could* attack, if they wanted to. "But who were they fighting?"

She merely fixed him with a look.

"Didn't see the arrow wounds?" she asked. "Who else would they fight in the middle of a forest?"

"Shicts?" he whispered. "Out here?"

"I..." The hardness in her eyes faltered for a moment before she looked away. "Maybe. I couldn't say for certain." And yet something in the way she paused suggested it was more that she *wouldn't* say for certain. "At any rate, I don't think it'll be an issue."

"You're sure?" Lenk asked. "If they saw we were giving tulwar supplies to leave us alone, they might start getting ideas."

"Don't be stupid," she snorted. "Shicts don't posture like those apes.

They hunt. They follow, they observe, they wait, and then they strike when you least expect it."

Somewhere to the south a faint whistle cut the air. It grew louder in a heartbeat, ending in a crunch of wood and a spray of splinters. Lenk blinked, and when his eyes opened, an arrow quivered in the wood of one of the deck's support beams, two fingers away from his head.

"Yeah," Kataria said, "like that."

"Shicts! SHICTS!"

The cry, and dozens more like it, was taken up by the saccarii as they were sent scrambling across the deck. Lenk didn't need to hear it, for once he looked upon the southern cliffs of the Gullet, he could see them.

Everywhere.

Perched on the bluffs. Emerging from viny undergrowth. Crouched atop the bending branches of bowing trees, their hair as thick and tangled as the forest and their faces hidden behind the empty grins of wooden masks. The khoshicts, dark-skinned and dark-haired, appeared on the cliffs like a bad dream.

And their arrows sang a dozen harmonious dirges.

Lenk's boots thundered across the deck as he ran. His heart pounded in his ears. The Old Man groaned, the river shifted around its colossal ankles.

The sky was swallowed by the sound of arrows: their shrieking flight, their heads crunching into wood, their soft-as-rainfall whisper as they found a saccarii who was too slow and sent him squealing to the deck.

"Farlan!"

A cry. It took him a moment to remember that was his name. The name he had given Shuro.

The woman in black crouched behind a nearby crate. She grunted, shoving forward to send it sliding down the deck toward him. He crouched low, stopping it with his shoulder and whirling to take cover behind it. It shuddered as two arrows struck the wood. He drew his sword instinctively, then stared at it in his hand, quite unsure what good it would do against an enemy with twenty yards of water between him and it.

Then again, how *did* one fight an enemy that appeared out of nowhere?

The cliffs had been bare just a few moments ago, and suddenly they were swarming. They might as well have been shadows, dark shapes gliding effortlessly from branch to branch, their only sound the hum of bowstrings and the whistle of arrows. Where had they come from? What did they want?

And why—the thought crept unbidden to the fore of his mind—*didn't Kataria notice them?*

Eyes following thought, he sought her out across the deck. But through the chaos of the six remaining saccarii trying to find cover and the falling arrows, he couldn't find her. The saccarii cried out, but they were not panicking. They found cover behind crates, crouched low behind railings. They had made this run before, they were no strangers to calamity such as this. Shuro, too, seemed safe enough, crouched behind her own crate. She hardly even looked concerned, her face tense but unpainted by fear.

The Old Man's clip through the river was quick, and it hardly seemed bothered by the tiny arrows that found its hide. Perhaps they could just wait until the shicts ran out of arrows or the Old Man outran them.

Perhaps they could survive this.

"MAK LAK KAI!"

It had been a nice thought, anyway.

But any hope of waiting it out went dashing away as soon as he looked to the northern cliffs. The tulwar, blades bared and faces awash with white, appeared upon the ridge, carried by the swift lope of their gaambols. Their simian mounts shrieked and hooted, their frenzy propelling them to ever greater speeds as they pursued the Old Man. Above the wail of arrows, above the roar of the river, the howls of the beasts and the war cries of their riders cut across the sky, clean as any blade.

And they cried as one.

The gaambol in the lead, a burly red-faced brute carrying an equally fierce-looking rider, suddenly wheeled to the right. Its pace didn't so much as falter as it took a flying leap off the cliff's edge, colliding with the Old Man's flank. Its clawed fingers scrambled for purchase as it pulled itself up.

Lenk braced himself, holding his sword as menacingly as a man on his rear end could against one ton of fur and fangs. Yet the gaambol cast him nothing more than a blank-eyed stare. Its rider barked something guttural, kicked its neck with his heels. The gaambol growled in reply and hauled itself up to the top of the deck's canopy. The wood overhead groaned with the weight as the beast took off running. Lenk saw it a moment later, flying over the river and striking the cliff wall.

The shicts, for the first time, made a noise: a cry of alarm as the gaambol effortlessly scaled the cliff, taking arrows without complaint as it made a leap and seized one of the shicts.

Shrieking, it picked the frail creature up in two hands and smashed him—once, twice, again and again—against the rocks until there was nothing left but a red smear upon the stone and a battered carcass that the gaambol tossed carelessly into the river below, like a worn-out toy discarded by a child with a short attention span.

Okay, then, Lenk thought, releasing a breath he hadn't noticed he was holding. *They're using us as a bridge to get to the shicts. So long as they see us only as that, we'll be—*

"*MAK LAK KAI!*" Another gaambol, another rider pulled itself up over the railing. This one, though, came leaping onto the deck. This, apparently, was enough to startle the saccarii and they immediately broke cover to get away. The gaambol swept its red simian snout from side to side, beady eyes taking in the chaos, suddenly over-stimulated.

A long black limb shot out, snatched up a screaming saccarii. Its nostrils twitched as it sniffed at the creature squirming in its grasp. Then, as if finding no other use for him, it opened its jaws lazily and brought the shrieking man toward it.

"*NO!*"

Lenk would have been surprised by his own voice if he hadn't been so busy rushing headlong toward the giant beast. He would have been surprised by that, too, if he hadn't been so consumed with fear.

The Old Man needed its crew and, between the shicts and the tulwar, it was fast running out of them.

Lenk closed the distance in a leap. His blade flashed, bit deeply of fur and flesh. An animal shriek cut the air. A spurt of crimson spattered the deck, the saccarii following. The man went scampering away, but the gaambol hardly seemed to notice. It clutched at its wounded arm, gaped at Lenk like a child scolded as he held his bloodied blade out before him.

That astonishment lasted all of two breaths.

Its rider bellowed a command, kicked at the brute's neck. The gaambol needed no encouragement to launch itself at Lenk, swiping a clawed hand out. He darted back, dancing out of range. The beast snarled, brought that same hand down in a vicious slap. He slipped away once more. The gaambol drew back a hand bristling with splinters, bared yellow fangs in a shriek.

The sound cut through his ears and into his skin, sending the hairs on the back of his neck rising. But he kept his distance, his blade up. He had fought beasts before. One blow of those giant hands would mean death. And there was nowhere to run.

Stand your ground, he reminded himself. *Don't drop your guard. Wait for the opportunity to—*

It howled, leaping toward him, long arms outstretched, long fangs bared.

He darted forward into the beast's charge, ducked low beneath its arms, took his sword in both hands, and jammed up. Flesh, then tongue, then bone, and then the spatter of blood that came washing over him as his blade punched up under the gaambol's jaw and into its skull.

It fell without another sound, bearing him to the deck beneath its weight. Its paw groped blindly for a target its glassy eyes could no longer see, a growl choked on steel escaping from its throat, before it finally went still.

He took a breath.

And then held it as the beast's rider loomed over him, a short, thick blade in her hand. Her snarl was every bit as feral as her mount's as she bared teeth and brought the blade down. He caught her wrist with one hand, the other trapped beneath the creature's bulk.

But her arm was longer, her muscle brimming beneath black fur while his own quivered beneath flesh that suddenly seemed so frail. He saw his own terror reflected in the blade as it slowly came down toward his throat.

He cried out a name.

Between heartbeats, a bowstring answered. The female tulwar jerked, blinked as though puzzled by the arrow that stood quivering in her bicep. The next found her throat, appearing there with nothing more than a whisper. Brow knitted in consternation rather than anguish, she grunted once and toppled over.

He felt hands slide under his arms, help haul him out from beneath the dead gaambol. He felt them wrap defensively around him as they hurried him behind the beast's carcass. Arrows continued to fall around him like rain, thudding into the corpse. The canopy shook overhead as more riders spurred their beasts to leap to the other side of the river.

When he turned to see his Kataria kneeling beside him, he felt none of the reassurance he felt he ought to. Rather his voice was breathless, crawled out of his lips.

"Did you know?" he asked.

"What?" she replied.

"Did you know? Did you know they were here?"

"I..." She shook her head. "No. I didn't. How could I?"

"How could you pick out wounds on a tulwar but not see shicts in the cliffs?" He seized her by the arm. "*How?*"

"Get the fuck off me," she snarled, shoving him off. "I just saved your life."

"And how many of us have you killed, *shkainai*?"

A voice he hadn't heard before. Thick and creeping and guttural, a glistening insect crawling out of a rigid shed carapace. He would never have known who it was if Man-Khoo Yun had not risen up as a black shadow over him.

"You waste words on trying to reason with them, human," the couthi gurgled. "They have no remorse. They have no souls. They care for nothing but violence and treachery."

"This *isn't* the time," Lenk hissed, gripping his sword.

"No. It is far too late for that." He stood, heedless of the arrows flying past, heedless of the shrieks of the tulwar. "I was hired to protect Sheffu's interests from shictish interference." All four arms extended, began to gingerly undo the clasps of his black robe. "From any shict."

Kataria snarled. "So, that's it? Sheffu didn't trust *me*?"

"He was right to do so. He, as well as I, knew of the Howling."

Lenk blinked, looked to Kataria for explanation. Her mouth merely hung open, astonishment plain on her face.

"What is he talking about?" Lenk demanded, rather than asked.

"She has been in contact with her twisted kin the entire time, human. She has been lying to you. But do not fear."

His robes slipped off. What lurked beneath was a body long and lean with muscle, skin the color of bone drawn tight and peppered with scars. Man-Khoo Yun's larger hands flexed, the long fingers cracking as the smaller ones withdrew two wickedly curved daggers from his belt.

"I am more than capable of handling this."

His hands went up, undid the clasps holding his painting against his face. It fell to the ground in a clatter.

"After all…"

From beneath a nightmare of scars that crisscrossed his white face, from beneath the eyes that shone glistening black like perfect obsidian orbs, from behind the pair of mandibles that clicked with every word he spoke, Man-Khoo Yun offered a fanged smile.

"I have experience with them."

FIFTEEN

Liquor, Heaven-Sent

It was Arexes, the Architect, who first invented beer.

Or so the tale went.

After he had erected the sky to hold up heaven over earth, but before he went on to create the Thousand Marvels in a Single Day, the God of Craftsmen was said to have discovered the liquid by accident after discovering that he had dammed up a river and that barley was fermenting in the puddles left behind.

He refined it, placed it in his tankard, and, for a single moment in his eternal life, let himself relax before he went on figuring out how the rest of the world worked.

The tale had always fascinated Asper, if only because it seemed to be one item on a very short list of things the various faiths of the world would not fight over.

No one agreed on how the world had been made—Daeonists said the Conqueror had found it and made it his own, Zamanthrans said it had been formed when the Sea Mother grew lonely and sought to make a companion out of earth. No one agreed on who had created mankind—Sainites said that they were the seventh finger of Galatrine, Khetasheans said that they had grown in the footsteps of the Wanderer.

But everyone seemed content to let Arexes have the credit for beer.

Asper's own theory was that this was because the various brewers' guilds—all ardent worshippers—might be less inclined to share their craft if their scriptures were disputed. But her private hope was simply that beer had been the first thing that religions could agree on and would eventually unite the world in a frothy, drunken orgy of friendship.

Starting with her.

That, she reasoned, was a pretty good justification for the fourth tan-kard that was set down before her. She reached an unsteady hand into the small purse on the table, produced a few coppers, and handed them to the serving girl.

The lass—maybe a little over seventeen, wearing a dress that had been patched many times—accepted them with a nod and took off, deftly skirting the only other tables in the bar: the ones laden with Sainite sol-diers, each one laden in turn with leering eyes and groping hands.

Not that her attempted avoidance stopped the soldiers, loud and rowdy and deep in their cups, from trying to reach out for her.

Asper knew she should feel angrier about that than she did. But the only way an establishment like the Glutted Cat could keep open was by catering to soldiers. Sainite presence kept looters and thieves away, and while it might eventually invite Karnerian aggression, that would at least be only one army to worry about instead of both.

That, too, should have made her angry.

That should have made her seize the tankard, empty it out upon the floor, and smash it over the head of the nearest Sainite. Then smash it in the face of the next one, and the next one…

And so on, she told herself, *and then on to the Karnerians until every last one of them lies bleeding on the floor. It's the only way anyone's ever going to be safe again.*

But you can't stop there.

No, I can't. There are more Sainites. More Karnerians. More soldiers, more thieves, more assassins, more monsters pretending to be men.

Even as they feast upon the flesh of the weak. They shall never be glutted.

Never, she told herself. The Sainite table let out a raucous laugh at some bawdy joke. *Never.*

You must purge them.

I have to stop them.

You must kill them.

I need to protect them.

You can end it.

I can save them.

You can save them all.

I can—

She was distracted by a sudden cramp in her hand. She looked down and saw her left hand trembling about the tankard, fingertips pressing indentations into the copper. Beneath the flesh something twitched. She felt a prick against her scalp, the sensation of a spider's spindly limbs skittering across her brain. And her breath left her at the realization.

Those weren't her thoughts.

That wasn't her voice in her head.

And just like that, Amoch-Tethr was there.

Not in her head, not in her thoughts, *there*. Seated at the table beside her, in the periphery of her vision, he stared at her. She did not acknowledge him. She never stopped hoping he was just a bad dream, a hallucination.

She had not drunk nearly enough to believe that.

But she could see his shadow in the corner of her eye. She could feel the excited shudder of his breath. She could hear his voice, as dark and cold as the wavering of doubt at the end of every prayer.

"*They will never stop,*" he whispered through a mouth made just for her. "*The city will drown in rivers of blood.*"

She dared not look at him. To look at him would be to acknowledge him, that he was real. No one else could see him, she knew. He was her demon, her burden, her nightmare.

She stared straight ahead, forcing herself to watch the Sainites as they peered up. The serving girl was making another round.

"*The children will reach for the hands of their parents,*" Amoch-Tethr said, "*and brush the fingertips once before they disappear beneath the tide.*"

She clenched her jaw. She watched one of the soldiers reach out and seize the girl by her arm, draw her in tight. She watched the fear behind her smile, growing plainer as she was drawn closer to his unshaven leer.

"*The heathens and sinners will crack open the bones left behind,*" he continued, his voice rising in ecstasy, "*they will suck on the marrow and choke on their laughter.*"

She felt her heart beat between every word he spoke, and every word was a cold clear sound in her ear. She watched as the Sainite drew a hand up to the serving girl's dress, intimately fingered a tear there. He tugged sharply, tearing a little more. The dark circle of a nipple was bared. The girl let out a squeal.

Asper felt her hand tremble, grow warm, burn as bright as the anger growing behind her eyes.

"And you," Amoch-Tethr said softly, *"can stop it all."*

The tankard broke in her hand, the copper folding like paper beneath a grip suddenly red-hot. A whiff of acrid smoke hit her nostrils, but she did not care.

She had but one thought. And it was revenge. On every soldier, every fasha, every thief who ate these people.

Starting, she thought as she eyed the soldier's leer, *with this one.*

All she needed was one more word.

"AND WHAT THE FUCK ARE YOU DICKHEADS DOING?"

That was not it. Nor was it just one word.

And yet it was enough to get her to look up—enough to get everyone in the bar to look up—at the woman who stood in the doorway, eyes ablaze beneath her tricornered hat, gloved hands on hips and dangerously close to the saber she wore at her belt.

"Did I fuckin' miss a gods-damned order from High Command that told us all to gather round in a circle jerk?"

Wing-Sergeant Blacksbarrow stormed into the bar. A Sainite leapt to attention with every step she took. All but the one burdened by the girl on his lap, who merely met Blacksbarrow's fury with a quiver-eyed gape.

"You," she growled, leveling a finger at him. "I don't remember you havin' shit for brains when I sent you out here, so maybe you can remember what your orders were."

"T-to secure the district," the soldier replied. "The first twenty buildings."

Blacksbarrow cast a slow look around the bar. "Looks like you got to the first, at least. How about…"

The fury ebbed from her voice as she suddenly laid eyes upon the serving girl. And in one steady stare, she seemed to take in everything: the tears in her dress, the tension in her body, the fear in her eyes as she quickly averted them from the wing-sergeant's gaze.

When she spoke again, her voice was cold iron. "How much do they owe you, girl?"

"Thirty," the girl replied. As if only now aware of her position, she stood from the man's lap. "Thirty zan." She caught herself. "C-coppers, I mean."

The wing-sergeant stared her down before slowly reaching to her belt and removing a pouch. She tossed it to the girl, who caught it with a jingle of coins.

"More there than thirty," she said. "The rest is for you to get into the back room and not come out for the next half hour."

"Y-yes, madam. Thank you, madam."

The serving girl made a hasty bow and scurried to the back room, the barkeep cautiously following her. The soldier she had been sitting upon cast a forlorn glance after her, as though he hoped he could likewise disappear. But as Blacksbarrow's shadow loomed over him, he gave up, rising from his chair and facing her.

"Refresh my memory," she said coldly. "What's your rank?"

"Crossbowman, first class, Sarge."

There was a tremor in his voice. Despite the fact that he stood a good half head taller and likely thirty pounds heavier, the soldier's posture trembled ever so slightly under Blacksbarrow's gaze. If Blacksbarrow was aware of the difference in their stature, she didn't show it.

"First class?" Blacksbarrow took her hat off, whistled appreciatively. "Must have earned yourself a medal somewhere."

"For valor at Temple Row, the W.S.—" He caught himself. "The *old* W.S. awarded it to me before he died."

"Must have thought you deserved it, then. A lot comes with that rank: first-access privileges to chow and beds. That'll come in handy."

"For what, Sarge?"

"Recovery."

The confusion addling the soldier's face was knocked clean off by the hilt of a saber smashing against the side of his head. The sole sound in the tavern was that of his body hitting the floor. Not a single protest from his fellow soldiers was raised as Blacksbarrow swept a hard stare across them.

Asper herself was dead quiet, but for a breathless curse.

"Karnies," she said. "We're fighting Karnies. Fucking, ass-tonguing, masturbating-over-their-own-piety Karnies. We're not drinking on duty. We're not making trouble for the locals. And we're sure as shit not grabbing girls like we're fucking degenerates."

She brought one foot up. Then down again, on top of the fallen soldier's ribs. There was a crunch. He groaned as she pointed the tip of her blade at him.

"This is a good blade, boys and girls. If I have to sully it by knocking some sense into any more of you, I'm going to be very displeased. Even more than when I have to sully my boot by jamming it up your rectums.

"You two." She pointed her blade to a pair of soldiers—a man and woman who crisply stood at attention. "Pick up your friend. Take him back to temporary barracks. Everyone else gets half an hour to sober up and then rally at the northeastern square. Scalps are moving out on patrol at sunset and I won't have it said Wing-Sergeant Blacksbarrow let 'em walk around like they own the place."

"*Sergeant!*" they bellowed in collective acknowledgment.

In another moment they began bustling about: securing gear and weapons while their comrades picked up their unconscious friend. Blacksbarrow observed them with a firm nod before she sheathed her saber and turned to depart. She only just caught sight of Asper as she did, and their eyes met.

What was that behind Blacksbarrow's iron gaze? Asper wondered. Was it concern for the serving girl? Compassion for the weak and the terrified? Or was it simply concern for her mission and the discipline of her army?

"Priestess," Blacksbarrow said. As if suddenly aware of whom she was talking to, she cleared her throat. "Apologies. I hadn't expected to have to do that today."

"*Lying,*" Amoch-Tethr purred in her ear.

"Morale's under strain. The scalps just won't let up." Blacksbarrow's voice contained an edge of unnerving sympathy, as though she genuinely blamed this whole thing on the Karnerians. "But we've got the people and the right on our side."

"*Lying,*" Amoch-Tethr giggled, leaning closer.

"But there's something coming soon that'll change things, priestess," Blacksbarrow said, obviously speaking of the convoy that Asper was not supposed to know about. The wing-sergeant offered her a wink as she replaced her hat. "Then, gods willing, the nightmare will be over."

Lying.

That hadn't been Amoch-Tethr.

Blacksbarrow muttered a farewell, barked an order, and led the rest of the Sainites out. The bar was left empty, bereft of any sound but the noise of her own breath.

She looked to the chair beside her. Amoch-Tethr was gone, as though he had just been waiting for her to admit it to herself. As though his entire purpose was to make her realize the futility of it all.

The war would never stop.

Dreadaeleon could carve open heaven and rain fire down upon the Karnerians, Denaos could cut every Sainite throat in every Sainite bunk of every Sainite barrack. They would find more soldiers, more weapons, more bodies.

How is it, Asper wondered, *that they can always find more warriors and I can't find a single person willing to do something good?*

Teneir's voice came slithering back into her head, coiling around her brain, hissing into her ears.

"Assuming you were not lying."

Lying. How could she be lying? How could she have poured so much blood into the streets, spoken so many words to freshly orphaned sons and freshly widowed women, gone so many sleepless nights tending to wounds she knew would never heal right, and be *lying*?

And how was it, she wondered, that Teneir could have done none of that and still be so much more valuable than Asper?

How could it be that money was more important than faith?

"Ah, there you are."

She looked up. Dransun came stalking into the inn. He was moving a little more stiffly lately as his new injuries argued with his old injuries over which of them hurt worse. And when he eased himself down into the chair beside her, his groan was louder than the rattle of his armor.

"I figured I'd find you here," he said.

"There are a hundred taverns in Cier'Djaal," she replied, taking a swig out of her dented tankard. "It's just dumb luck that you found me here."

"A hundred twenty-six," Dransun said. "I know them all. The Glutted Cat's right between the Meat Market and the Souk: nice enough for a soldier, not bad enough to get your throat cut in. Perfect place when you want to drink until you disappear." He glanced around the tavern. "Speaking of, do they have anyone working today or . . ."

"War's on, Captain," she replied, taking another sip. "People take cover."

"No matter. Now's not a good time for drinking, priestess. We've got plans to make."

"We tried plans," Asper said. "Plans don't work. Drinking works."

"I can see how that might be tempting." He winced. "Aturach told me what happened."

She merely hummed at that, not bothering to look up from her tankard.

"But there's a way around it," Dransun said. "See, fashas might be removed from the people, but they still need their trust. Way I see it, we've got a golden opportunity to convince them that now's a good opportunity to show some generosity."

He leaned forward on the table, began sketching out a plan with his hands in the air. She wasn't looking. And by the time she reached the bottom of this tankard, she wouldn't be listening, either.

"Right now, Fasha Mejina's got Silktown on lockdown," Dransun said. "He's trying to make a show of force to take up the leadership that Ghoukha held. Some might not be willing to let that happen. If we can convince them that they can earn the respect of the people and show up Mejina by—"

"I'm converting."

The words spilled out of Asper's mouth. The captain reeled, as if they had struck him. She didn't mind that; she'd felt the same way when she first came to this conclusion, one day and several pints ago.

"Teneir's right." She held up a hand to silence protest. "She's a conniving, villainous bitch, but she's right about one thing. It's not about faith, it's not about gods, we're here to help people. She's got money, she can buy all the room, food, and medical supplies we need."

She leaned back in her chair, breathed out an ale-soaked sigh.

"The original plan was a good one," she said. "But we can't inflict enough losses on the Karnerians and Sainites to discourage them fast enough. We can keep the people safe with Teneir's money. We can wait out the whole war, if we have to.

"You just said you knew this city, right? How many people do you think that is? How many hundreds? How many *thousands* could be saved with just a few words?" The breath that came out next took something with it, something from a part of her that had been soft and tender for far too long. "How could I not?"

She had expected the words to take longer to come out. She had expected speaking them would be painful. Yet when she heard them, it all sounded so logical, so simple.

Funny, she had expected the weighty weariness that had been hanging off her for the past few days would simply fall away once she came out and admitted her plan. And yet, as she sat there, it all just seemed to settle down upon her like a blanket tucked up beneath her chin that would smother her and carry her off to somewhere warm and dark.

Still, she thought, that was all right.

"I don't know... maybe if you had some fucking principles."

She looked to Dransun. He had recovered his sensibilities quickly enough, his face now knitted in jaw-clenched anger. His voice came out hot and angry.

"The fuck are you talking about converting. You're a fucking *Talanite.*"

"Yeah? And I've heard you swear to Ancaa before. I thought you'd be—"

"Sister, I'm a *guard*, I pray to whoever the fuck will keep me from getting carved up in an alley. But *you're* a priestess. You're supposed to stand for sterner shit than I do."

She drained the rest of her tankard, slammed it on the table, and rose to her feet. She affixed a scowl upon him. "I told you, this isn't about gods."

"You're right. It's not." He pointed out the door. "It's about *them.* It's about the people. It's about this city. It's about the fucking fashas who can't be bothered to keep people from dying unless it profits them in some way. It's about telling them—fashas, Jackals, foreigners, whoever—that this is *our* city.

"What do you tell the fashas when you convert, then? They control *everything* already and now you want them to tell us who we can pray to?"

"If you felt so strongly about this, why the fuck did you become a guard here?"

"Same reason I'm trying to keep this city from falling apart while Mejina and his cronies are sipping wine behind gates in Silktown," Dransun snarled. "This is *my* home. I don't give a shit who owns it, it's *mine.*" He pursed his lips, stared at her intently. "I wanted it to be yours, too."

She held up a pale hand. "I'm not Djaalic."

"No, you're not. But I am. All the people you're helping are. You're the only foreigner in the city that *isn't* killing people. That counts for something."

"It does. It's going to count for a lot more once I convert." She slammed her fist on the table. "You think it didn't bother the shit out of me, too? I didn't just decide to do this without thinking maybe I'd be better off just killing myself and letting everything else work out without me. But saving people is more important than saving face."

"You can't save people's lives by putting them in the hands of a woman who doesn't give a shit about them."

"I took an oath to help people."

"Yeah? Why not break that, too?" Dransun spit. "Seems oaths mean about as much to you as faith does."

Her entire body seized up, trembling with contained fury. She wanted to hit him. She wanted to strangle him. She wanted to pick up the tankard and smash it against his head until he couldn't speak for the blood pouring from his mouth.

No, she realized as she felt her left arm burning beneath her sleeve. She wanted to do worse.

But she restrained herself. From acting, from speaking, from doing anything except turning around and stalking out.

Tomorrow she would go to Teneir. She would say some words that meant nothing to a deity that meant nothing. What kind of loving god would object to her helping people? What kind of loving god would have let it get this far?

What gods couldn't do, she would.

She would convert. She would save them all. And everything would be better.

And at that thought, something in that soft and tender part of her chuckled blackly. She felt Amoch-Tethr grinning from within her as his voice slid through her body on wisps of black smoke.

"Lying."

SIXTEEN

The Harmony of Slaughter

Admittedly, it looked bad.

Arrows flew from the southern cliffs, falling in sheaves to impale themselves in saccarii too slow to find cover and tulwar too eager to join the fray. They found wood and flesh alike—suspiciously never finding their way even close to her—and the wail of their flight consumed the screams of their victims.

And that was bad.

The wood of the deck shuddered. The Old Man groaned in protest as it was turned into a mobile battlefield. The canopy trembled as gaambols hurled themselves, hooting and shrieking, over the river and clambered over the colossus to take the fight to the shicts, heedless of anyone who got between them and their prey.

And that was worse.

But despite the arrows falling and the beasts snarling and the bodies bleeding out around her, Kataria could see but one moment. A moment when Lenk looked over his shoulder and, in his eyes, she saw the accusations that Man-Khoo Yun had hurled at her, of her treachery and her collaboration with the shicts.

A moment when she saw that he believed them.

That moment. That was the worst.

"Your treason was not unforeseen, savage. Sheffu anticipated this."

But it wasn't the worst for long.

Man-Khoo Yun approached her, stepping over a moaning saccarii, ducking beneath a shrieking arrow. The short, curved blades he wielded in his smaller hands glistened in the dying light of the sun and she could see her own fear reflected in them. His eyes, black and polished, drank in that fear just as the mandibles serving as his mouth devoured it hungrily.

"Wait!" Lenk imposed himself between the couthi and her, holding up a hand. "Just wait. We have more important—"

"He anticipated this, as well."

Man-Khoo Yun's arm—one of the big ones—lashed out and caught Lenk in the side, batting the young man away as though he were a mere insect. Within the robes, the couthi had looked so rigid that he might break if he bent. Now, as Lenk went crashing to the deck, the four-armed creature brimmed with taut, twitching muscle. And his eyes were alive with fury.

His smaller hands lashed out, steel flashing through the air. He was quick, impossibly quick for such a towering creature. She sprang backward, but the tip of a blade caught her by the narrowest margin, painting a red line across her belly.

The wound was shallow, but the pain spawned panic. The couthi continued advancing even as she darted ever backward, his blades flashing, the scars wrought in his face making his smile something horrifying. There was nowhere to run. There was no escape.

Her ears trembled instinctively, crying out in a language with no words. Her Howling echoed inside her own skull, screaming out to someone, to anyone.

Someone heard. Someone answered.

The wind cried out. As did Man-Khoo Yun, a breath later. An arrow quivered in his foot, pinning him to the deck.

Kataria looked out to the southern cliffs. Among the foliage, among the shadows of her kinsmen, she could see one body standing clear of cover, one face staring out without a mask to cover it. From so far away, a pair of long brown ears trembled and a pair of broad canines flashed in a smile as a single woman raised a hand in greeting.

Kwar.

And Kataria's heart quickened a beat.

She was halfway tempted to wave back before she saw a black shape descending from the cliffs. Kataria's ears trembled again, the warning unspoken but not unheard. Kwar looked up, saw the gaambol loping down the cliffs, teeth bared and arms outstretched.

Kataria hoped her Howling had reached Kwar in time. She hoped the khoshict would react in time. She hoped that Lenk hadn't just seen the smile, anxious and relieved at once, that had flashed across her face.

But hope had little use on a battlefield, especially one as cramped as this.

She heard mandibles clacking in a snarl. Man-Khoo Yun devoted all four of his arms to pulling his leg free, flesh popping as he did. But by the time he looked up, she was already running.

Distance, she told herself through the sound of her feet pounding on the deck. *Get some room to shoot.* The bow of the deck loomed before her, the green brow of the Old Man bobbing up and down. *Remember how tall he is. Turn around, draw, put an arrow between his...*

No more words. No more thoughts. No more noise. Nothing but an arrow's feathers between her fingers and a bowstring creaking. Nothing but instinct, the Howling in her ears and the prey in her eyes.

Man-Khoo Yun's mandibles spread, teeth bared in a snarl as he leveled his scowl at her. She held her breath, loosed her arrow.

It went sailing through the space the couthi had just occupied. The creature sprang to the side, clung to a support beam. She drew another arrow, fired, only to see it strike the beam as Man-Khoo Yun swung on one long limb up to the canopy's ceiling. He clung there by his talons, a spider of bone-white skin and seething fury.

Too fast, she thought. *How is he so fast?*

She forced herself not to think. Not of the rattle of his claws as he skittered, upside-down, toward her. Not of the clattering of his mandibles or the shine of his eyes. There was nothing but the arrow in her fingers, on her bowstring, at her earlobe, flying through the air.

Quivering in the wood of the canopy.

She cursed, looked to her quiver, found an arrow, looked back up. She caught only a glimpse of bone-white palm before it wrapped around her throat and jerked her off her feet. Talons pricked her neck, blood dripped down her body. She thought nothing of that, of anything but the flash of steel.

He clung to the canopy with one arm, his smaller arms free to slash their cruel blades at her. She brought her bow up in a desperate attempt to fend them off. But every chip and splinter the blades took off was by chance; her bow was unwieldy and eventually he'd find an opening to—

A screech.

There was an arc of silver. A spatter of warm life coated her face. She shut her eyes instinctively.

When she opened them, a long thin blade was lodged in the couthi's arm. Kataria took it in with one swift glance: the blood that ran down the sword to stain a hand as slender as the blade it gripped, the black sleeve that concealed the tremble of muscle, and the thin, angular woman who stood beneath the couthi.

For one breath she met Shuro's cold blue stare.

And saw nothing in there.

Shuro's hand twitched. She twisted the sword's hilt. Another spurt of blood burst from the couthi's arm and he released his captive. Kataria fell to the deck amid the broken hafts of arrows. The couthi retreated from the blade, leveling black eyes upon the woman.

"This was," Man-Khoo Yun clacked through his mandibles, "unforeseen."

"Apologies," Shuro said, flicking blood from her weapon. "But I have a duty to fulfill."

"Of course."

These were the last words the couthi spoke. The next sound out of his mouth was something shrill, clicking, and guttural. He swept across the ceiling, a blur of pale flesh and silver steel, toward Shuro. Even as his larger hands kept him to the canopy, his smaller hands and their wicked blades lashed out. There was a desperate need behind each blow, a spider's fangs seeking prey.

And yet each slash was met with the thin, delicate-looking blade dancing in the hand of this thin, delicate-looking woman. Shuro parried each slash, turned each blade, ducked low beneath each furious swipe of claw, and met each snarling curse with stony silence.

For one more breath, Shuro met Kataria's eyes. And in that moment, they spoke a single, silent command.

Kataria took up her bow, nocked an arrow, and loosed. It found its mark this time, sinking into the couthi's back, just a finger's length left of his spine. He let out a shrill, screeching wail, falling to the deck in a jumble of spasming limbs. But before either woman could move to finish him, he swept his arms out and sprang to his feet.

He swung his glare from side to side, snarling once before skittering on all sixes to the edge of the railing and disappearing over it. To where, she had no idea. Nor did she have time to wonder, for she instantly felt a cold stare upon her and a cold hand to accompany it.

Shuro's face was spattered with blood, marred by dirt, graced by a single cut across her cheek. And yet, behind all the grime, she looked unnervingly pristine. Her breathing was calm and even, her brow was bereft of any sweat beneath her hat, and her eyes.

Deep and blue and cold as snow, despite all the carnage around them...

"Who are—" Kataria began to ask.

"No," Shuro interrupted. "Wrong question."

The statement, and the chill with which it was delivered, struck her silent. But only for a moment.

"Where's Lenk?"

"Better."

Shuro bade her follow and led her in a crawl across the deck. Blood smeared the timbers. Bodies crowded her: the tulwar who had been too reckless to avoid the arrows, the saccarii who had been too slow. Kataria tried not to look, tried to keep her thoughts on finding Lenk, on getting out—

"Please."

A voice croaked at her. A clammy hand wrapped about her wrist. She looked down and saw one of the saccarii, arrows jutting from his leg and back, eyes wide and weary above his veil.

"Please, you're a shict," he rasped. "They're not shooting at you. Tell them we're not enemies. Tell them to stop this—"

His words, along with the rest of him, were cut dead by a sudden flash of metal. A great iron mass of metal, hammered to resemble a crude, twisted star, had come whirling through the sky, striking the saccarii with one of its jagged blades and splitting him in twain. Kataria felt his life spatter against her skin, watched his eyes freeze in uncomprehending fear, saw his grip go limp on her wrist.

She looked up to the northern cliffs, where the blade had come from, and saw another just like it. Atop the shoulders of a gaambol, a tulwar rider pried one of the massive blades from a sheath on his back and tossed it down. The giant simian he rode caught it, took it up in both hands, drew it all the way back over its head and—

"Get down!"

Shuro seized Kataria and dragged her to the deck. With a shriek the gaambol hurled the giant blade. It went sailing overhead, tumbling in a flurry of metal to bite through the railing and continue. Somewhere on the southern cliffs, the sound of metal splitting flesh filled the air, and a shictish death cry rattled through Kataria's skull.

"*Bokka* knives," Shuro said. "Those apes of theirs can throw them as far as any bow can fire."

They continued crawling across the deck until they reached the bled-out corpse of the gaambol from earlier. The beast had proven remarkable cover, its hide peppered with arrows. They found Lenk there, huddled beneath its bulk. Strange that he should look so weary and harried, Kataria thought; the couthi hadn't hit him *that* hard, had he?

He looked up, eyes wild. "Man-Khoo Yun, is he—"

"Fled," Shuro answered.

"Shuro drove him off," Kataria added.

"Shuro, you…" Lenk looked at the black-clad woman, to the bloodied sword in her hand, then clutched his head. "No, fuck, how'd this happen?"

"It's called the Gullet, Lenk," Kataria muttered. "You didn't think it was going to be easy, did you?"

"*No jokes.*" He whirled on her, teeth set and eyes narrowed. "You don't get to fucking joke right now. The couthi said, he said…"

"The couthi was a traitor. Sheffu didn't trust us," Kataria said. "The couthi was *lying*, Lenk."

The fear drained from his eyes, and the look he fixed upon her was something cold and hard as rock. "Then why haven't you shot a single arrow at them?"

Lying had never been her talent. She could stalk prey for miles without being seen, fire a dozen arrows before anyone even thought to look in her direction, but the subterfuge of civilized races was beyond her. She didn't understand the rules to their games, couldn't speak the language of their lies.

So when she looked at him, when she saw the set of his mouth and the pain seeping into the corners of his eyes, she knew the truth shone through the blood on her face.

And when his hand shot out and snatched her bow, she shouldn't have been surprised.

And yet...

"What are you doing?"

"This fucking plant-thing won't move any faster," Lenk snarled as he stood up, pulled an arrow out of the gaambol's corpse. "The only way we make it out is if one of us fights back."

He swept to the bow of the deck. Arrows whizzed past him. *Bokka* knives tumbled over the canopy, sometimes under it. He nocked the arrow, took aim at a shict on the southern cliffs.

The Howling filled the air, an unspoken warning buzzing through the ears of every shict within a mile. In a single breath, every shict knew that someone was about to fire back. And in that same breath, every shict knew exactly who he was aiming for.

Kataria could see her unmasked grin and her wild eyes, just as plainly as if she were standing before her. Kataria could feel Kwar's heart tighten as she saw the arrow leveled at her. Kataria could hear Kwar's lips part as she spoke a single word meant for just one person.

And Kataria was on her feet.

Lenk was handy with a bow. Not good, not shict good. But good enough that she couldn't let him.

"No!"

She wasn't quite sure what was happening until she collided with him, bringing him down to the deck. Only when she knelt over him, stared into his wounded eyes, did she realize what she had done. Only when she felt her chest tighten and tears form in her eyes did she realize whom they were for.

"You..." he whispered, unable to finish it. "You *did*—"

"Lenk, I'm sorry," she said. "I'm so sorry, I—"

"Trouble."

Shuro's voice was sharp as her blade as she joined them at the bow. She pointed to the southern cliffs. There, perched upon a jutting branch, stood a single shict. His mask was carved with an eerie grin, and he raised his bow and drew back an arrow, its head wrapped in cloth and set ablaze.

"They're going to torch us," Shuro said. Even with this grim knowledge, her voice did not hasten. "Someone needs to do something."

Someone did.

The Howling coursed through her. Kataria could feel feet pounding on stone, wind in hair, cold steel in hand. But it was only in that last moment that she actually saw Kwar, the khoshict leaping out of the underbrush toward the archer with the flaming arrow.

Kwar's arm snapped forward. A dagger flew from her hand. It tumbled through the air and struck the archer's arm at the precise moment his fingers loosed the arrow.

The shot went wide, its fire trailing across the sky. It went clear of the deck's bow, narrowly missing it to sink into the head of the Old Man. It lodged just behind the colossus's right eye, smoldering there.

And just like that, everything else that had happened didn't seem so bad by comparison.

The Old Man let out a bellow. Unlike its impassive groans, this noise was shrill and full of fear. The creature began staggering one way and then the other, its tentacles clawing at its face in an effort to dislodge the projectile.

It swung its massive body, smashed against the cliff walls. The agile or lucky shicts and tulwar went screaming, fleeing from its bulk as each impact shook the cliff walls. The clumsy and unfortunate ones went tumbling into the river, the sound of their terror lost in the sound of the Old Man's wailing pain.

The deck fragmented; support beams split, railings shattered. The Old Man's trumpeting wails filled the sky and sent the stones themselves shuddering.

The creature reared up on its hind legs, sending the river below teeming with waves. The deck gave out beneath Kataria's feet. Lenk and Shuro were lost in a moment, scattered along with everything else. She could but clutch her bow in a desperate bid to hold on to at least something as the deck became vertical.

She skidded down it amid a shower of broken arrow shafts, *bokka* knives, and flaccid, tumbling corpses. Instinct seized her, bit back panic. She had no thought for Kwar, for Lenk, for anything but a drawn breath as she went flying off the Old Man's back.

And the river rose up to meet her.

⊷⊷⊱⊰⊶

First bright light.

And then darkness.

Lenk's lungs realized what was happening far before his brain caught up. He kicked his legs, flailed his way to the surface of the river, where he burst in a spray of froth and a gasp of air. The water churned around him, waves kicked up by the maddened Old Man as the colossus thrashed about in the river.

Each wave sent bodies roiling, chunks of meat in a great stew. Shicts struggled to get untangled from their quivers. Tulwar fought to get away from their thrashing, panicked gaambols. And everywhere they were disappearing beneath the water.

Lenk never saw the river bulls. Not wholly, anyway. He saw the blurred outlines of their gray bulks beneath the water, eerily elegant for creatures so massive. But wherever he saw their horns, parting the waves like the bows of ships, another body vanished beneath the water with a drowned cry. It didn't matter who. Dead or alive, tulwar, saccarii, shict, or...

He saw a horn burst out of the water, begin sweeping toward him.

And he was already thrashing for the shore.

His clothes were sodden, weighed him down. The sword on his back caught the waves, held him back. The shore seemed so distant and every time a wave crested before him, it looked farther and farther away. But fear was stronger than despair. He could feel the river bull behind him, the great emptiness beneath him being filled as the beast drew closer.

His feet kicked beneath him, found sand. He slipped, tripped, stumbled his way up the shore and onto a small cove that lay in a gap within the southern cliffs. He took a moment to catch his breath, coughing up water as he did. The sound of carnage behind him was distant, smothered by the crash of waves and the anguish of the Old Man. Yet even that was a distant echo, fading.

In the silence he could afford to hear himself breathe and, shortly thereafter, hear himself think.

Kataria, Shuro, Man-Khoo Yun: Had any of them survived? No way to tell from down here. He glanced up, saw the Gullet's overgrowth oozing from the cliff face. The cliffs were sheerer here than elsewhere, with precious few handholds in sight. But the vines and branches growing from it looked sturdy enough. A few more moments to breathe and he might have the strength to scale it.

Or maybe he'd just have enough time to shit his pants at the sound of water erupting behind him.

The river bull came bursting out of the waves, its broad maw agape in a bellow, tusks glistening like sabers. On legs that looked almost comically small for its bulk, it rushed toward Lenk.

Lenk's stomach dropped into his boots, gave his feet new weight as he turned and ran down the cove. The stretch of sand, he saw, ended at a cliff face in another hundred paces, leaving him nowhere to go but back in the water. The river bull, if its snorting anger was any indication, seemed to have no problem with that idea.

Sweat poured down his brow, stung his eyes. When he wiped them clear, he saw a figure, white robes clean and unsullied, standing on the shore sixty paces ahead.

Mocca did nothing more than raise a hand and point a finger at the cliff face. Lenk strained to see—and he would have missed it had he not—but there, little more than a surreptitious crack in the cliff face, was an opening just big enough for a man.

He pushed the last of his strength into one more sprint, twisted and turned into the opening. A meaty thud followed as the river bull tried to wedge its bulbous body in after him and found barely enough room for its massive head. The beast snorted, thrust its horn at Lenk as he stepped away. When it found it could not follow, it pulled back and shot Lenk a look with its beady eyes, as if to accuse him of cheating, before it waddled back into the river to join its brethren before all the good corpses were taken.

The hole where his stomach had been was filled with dread.

Suppose Kataria knocked her head before she fell, he thought. *Suppose she's unconscious, with those things in the water.* And just as easily, something small and spiteful slid into that thought's place. *Suppose she deserves it. She didn't fire back. She stopped you from firing on them. She betrayed you. She—*

No.

He bit his thoughts down as he bit back the pain in his body.

Get to high ground. Take stock. See what you can do.

He was about to head back out to the beach when he noticed a glimmer of light behind him. He turned and saw daylight spilling through a gap in the cliff, up and beyond. It shed light into the passage and there, carved into the cliff, he beheld a small staircase leading up, big enough only for one man to climb.

His mind too full of fear to ask questions about how or why, he shook as much water as he could from his clothing and started to climb.

Simpler men, he supposed—men less accustomed to looking over their shoulders—might have simply counted their blessings when stairs such as these appeared. Lenk, though, could only wonder at who had built them.

And he could but ponder, with mounting discomfort, what Mocca intended him to find by being shown them.

The air grew warmer as he ascended the stairs. The sunlight grew brighter. Flecks of sand covered the topmost stairs as he emerged into a blast of searing air. Yet just as quickly, a warm blanket of humidity settled over him.

He emerged somewhere caught in a battle between worlds. To the west the land sloped downward in dunes leading back toward the desert. The east, however, saw a march of forest, the same vivid flowers and greenery as had grown out of the cliffs.

The cliffs.

The thought sent him running to the edge, looking out over the river.

How high had he climbed? he wondered. It hadn't seemed such a trek, yet from up here the Old Man's wail sounded so distant. The colossus's pain had dimmed to a dull discomfort. It shook its massive back, shedding the last remnants of its deck and canopy to send them sprawling into the water. Now that it was free from its burden, Lenk could see a mass of bright-yellow, -red, and -blue pinpricks, unfurling and blossoming into stars upon the greenery of its hide.

Flowers, he noted. *The damn thing's blooming.*

The Old Man let loose one final trumpet. Apparently calmed of its fear and rid of its pain, it groaned and resumed its march down the river toward the east, as though nothing had changed and its passengers didn't lie dead in its wake.

The Lyre, once pristine and blue, now bore an ugly wound. Amid shattered timbers, bobbing crates, and scraps of leather, Lenk could see stains of red upon the water, bits of bodies that the river bulls had not yet gotten to. The beasts themselves now basked upon the beaches, apparently sated by the feast of carnage that even the Lyre seemed to choke on.

I guess, Lenk thought, *that's why they call it the Gullet.*

On the northern cliffs, the remnants of the tulwar war band looked over the devastation with passing disinterest before spurring their gaambols about and departing. In the foliage upon the southern cliffs, there was no sign of the shicts. In the waters... the waters...

There was no sign of golden hair. No flash of pale skin. Nothing.

She was not down there.

She was not—

Wait. He caught a stir of movement, there upon the southern cliff face. Like a beetle, he saw a black-clad figure making its way up the vines.

Shuro. She survived. And if she did, then—

Then what?

Then had none of it happened? Then was all of what Man-Khoo Yun had said not true? Had she had a single arrow fired at her? Had she *not* tackled him when he tried to fire back?

He shut his eyes. He clutched his head. They hurt. Everything hurt. Worse than his aching body, than the scratches and cuts, the thinking hurt. He couldn't do it anymore. He couldn't think. He couldn't breathe. He couldn't—

"Lenk."

His eyes snapped open. Mocca stood before him and forced his voice through gritted teeth.

"Behind you."

Sand shifting, steel on leather, a breath held. He heard them. He whirled.

He saw the dagger before he saw anything else, a long blade clenched in a dark hand as it came down toward his head. His hand snapped up and caught a wrist, felt the tremble of muscle, the fury behind the blow as he struggled to keep the blade aloft. A sharp pain exploded inside him as a knee found his side and dug in. With a snarl he lashed out a fist. Only through blind luck did it catch a jaw, send his foe reeling back.

He tore his sword free from its sheath, brought it up before him. His opponent responded in kind, pulling a short-handled hatchet from her belt with her left hand to join the knife in her right.

A khoshict, only a hair shorter than he. The rigid muscle of her body was left recklessly exposed by her half shirt and kilt, and all of it trembled with restrained anger. Yet her eyes, wild and dark and framed by a riot of black braids, bore no such discipline. The murder in her scowl was reflected in the sharpness of her canines, the twitching of her ears.

The steel of her blades as she came at him.

She made as though to stab with the knife, turned suddenly to bring the hatchet down in a vicious chop. He caught it on his blade, twisted to avoid her knife as it lashed out at him. His boot shot up, caught her in the belly, knocking her back.

Despair was forgotten. Anger was shed, pain left behind, all that remained was an emptiness too small for thought to enter, a quiet where instinct spoke in between echoes of clashing metal.

She came at him again and again, from the front, the sides, leaping and lunging and seeking. Her hatchet hacked, sought to tangle up his blade to give her blade an opening. His sword found each blow, his eyes never far from that wicked steel, never letting it get close enough to cut. No thought to it, nothing but recognition of where the blows would land and where the blade would seek.

And when he recognized his opening, he took it without thinking. Her hatchet came up low, angling for his kidney. He caught it on its sword, stepped into the blow before her knife could lash out, and brought his forehead against the bridge of her nose. He hoped to hear a snapping sound, but was forced to settle for a pop and the trickle of blood down his brow.

The khoshict sprang back. Blood from her nose spattered her face like war paint, exaggerating the mounting fury in her snarl. The blow stalled her for only a moment, though; she leapt forward, hatchet drawn and hungry.

Lenk fell back, ready to meet her, only to realize his mistake once she drew up short. Quick as a breath, she flipped the dagger in her hand, caught it by the blade, and hucked it overhand. He blinked; the blade disappeared from her hand and found itself in his thigh in a burst of pain.

No room for thought, for protest, even for instinct. His leg was working one moment, and then it was not.

He fell to a knee, felt the heat of the sand on his wound. His blade came up just in time to catch the hatchet coming down. But he couldn't find another hand to keep her fist from smashing against his jaw.

He took the blow, took her wrist, jerked her forward. His blade might have still been tangled with her hatchet, but there was length enough to deliver a sharp cut across her exposed abdomen. Not enough to do the right kind of damage—she was too slippery for that, jamming her foot into his chest and kicking off him before he could do more than cut a red line across her dark skin.

His grip on the sword tightened, tearing the hatchet away from her as she retreated. He staggered to his feet, biting back the pain as he tore the knife from his leg and tossed it aside. Weaponless, painted scarlet, she showed no fear in her stance as she spread her arms out wide and spit red at his feet.

"The fuck are you waiting for, *kou'ru?*" she grunted.

Pain gave him pause, instinct made him listen to it. Out of the corner of his eye, he caught another shape approaching. Another khoshict: male, thick with muscle, and bearing a hatchet in each hand.

"*Kwar!*" he cried out.

She whirled and, with only the slightest of glances, caught the hatchet he tossed her way. Side by side, they began to advance toward him. Slowly; they had both seen too much of him to think they could do this quickly. Yet he saw the anger in the female's stare, felt her desire to rip him apart as she bore her scowl down upon him, never taking her eyes off him.

Pity. If she had, she might have noticed the black-clad woman rushing toward her from behind.

The male must have caught wind of Shuro. He whirled just in time to avoid being cut in twain as she rushed between the two shicts, silver and red flashing as her blade bit at his flesh.

She spun, narrowly ducked beneath the female's hatchet. The blade caught the brim of her hat, tore it free from her head. And from her scalp poured a mane the color of an old man's. Short, dull, silver.

Like mine, Lenk thought. *Eyes, too.*

She shot him an urgent look. They spoke to each other in the same language. He saw her plan in the tension of her body and the poise of her blade.

They launched together, Shuro rushing at the male and driving him back in a flurry of blows from her thin-bladed sword.

But Lenk's wound aggravated his stride, slowed him. It was the female khoshict who rushed faster, harder, lunging at him and getting inside the reach of his sword before he could even take a swing. The weapon fell from his grasp as she tackled him and bore him to the sand. He could barely find the purchase to grab the hatchet in her wrist and pull it away.

If she noticed, she didn't care. If she heard her male companion crying out for help, she didn't react. If she thought of anything but the human under her and her hands wrapped around his throat, she sure as shit didn't show it.

Air left him as she tightened her grip. Instinct gave way to blind animal panic. His hands shot out, trying to catch her with a fist, trying to dislodge her. Futile. Even as his vision darkened, her eyes burned bright with hatred.

She was like him. There was no room in her for mercy, no room for anything but the desperate need to kill.

"Your fault," she said, through clenched teeth. "Your fault she's gone."

Her grip tightened, crushing his throat.

"She's gone."

Tears brimmed at the corners of her eyes.

"I'll kill you."

Her voice was as short and hard as her knife, words that were meant to be uttered to someone moments before all lights went out.

"I loved her."

He struck her. Again. Bruised her cheek. She wouldn't relent. He could fight no more. No more air. No more thought. No more light.

And he still felt it.

The rush of air. The shriek of metal. The feeling of something striking the earth just a hair away from his ear.

There was a moment of darkness, and suddenly breath returned to him. The khoshict was gone, the bruise from her fingers on his throat still felt. Vision returned. He saw first the khoshict, stepping away from him, her eyes turned south. He saw next the arrow, quivering in the sand.

And then he saw her.

Kataria stood upon a dune, the sun at her back. Her bow was drawn, an arrow nocked and leveled in his direction. And he could not tell whom she intended to hit.

"This goes in the eye of the next one to move."

The battle fell still as she came down the dune. Shuro edged away from the male, just as he did from her. All eyes were upon Kataria and almost none more intently than the female khoshict's.

"You're alive," she gasped. Her smile was tremendous; it was almost impossible to believe her face had just been contorted in such hatred. "Kataria, you...I was going to..."

"You were going to kill him, Kwar," she said. "I can't let you."

The female, Kwar, looked from her to Lenk, mouth dropping open, eyes going wide. He saw the fury drain from her face, and in the emptiness left behind, a warm, ugly realization dawned.

"No," Kwar said. "No, no, no, *no*." Her head fell into her hands, and she was shaking. "No, you can't...we were so..." When she looked up, her face was wild and pale. Tears poured down her cheeks. "You can't *do* this to me. You can't!" She thrust a finger at Lenk. "He's *human*. He's one of *them*! And I..."

Words left her. She hurled herself at Kataria, as if to strike her. She was stopped as the male khoshict rushed forward and caught her. Kwar snarled, beating on him with her fists.

"Let me go, Thua! Let *go*!"

Thua would not let go. He took each blow without a word. Flinching, wincing, but never protesting. Only after cuts started to form on his face did he release her. She stalked back and forth, but made no further advance.

She merely looked at Kataria, eyes glistening, ears drooping, face trembling as she tried to hold something tender between her teeth.

"I hate you," she said, "you know."

And she was running. The woman who had just nearly killed Lenk, so soundly thrashed him, was off running and crying into the dunes like a little girl. And he was left dumbfounded, staring at Kataria and asking for an answer to a question he didn't have the breath to speak.

Thua cast a baleful look at Kataria. "I asked you to leave her," he said. "Should I have begged?"

And he, too, went into the sands.

Lenk lay there for a long moment, trying to find the breath to ask what had just happened. But it was unnecessary.

When Kataria turned to him and he looked into her eyes, he realized he already knew.

SEVENTEEN

SERMONS TO THE DIRT

One wouldn't guess it by their name, but being a gutter-priest was a respectable calling.

Or at least it had been.

Relatively.

In some instances, anyway.

Everyone in Cier'Djaal had an agenda that began and ended with a payout, including the healers. They just happened to be more careful about concealing it, owing to the various oaths of selflessness and charitableness they had taken. Talanas might frown on a greedy man, but there was no scripture that said the Healer ever had to know how much of a tithe he left.

No sensible thug trusted a healer. Presenting oneself in a state of wounded vulnerability gave a healer power. They could call the guards or a rival gang, gouge one for money, whatever they thought wouldn't violate their oaths. It offended a rogue's sensibilities, however hypocritical they might be.

Gutter-priests, by contrast, were honest. They charged a single fee for a single commodity: silence. The fee might not cover knowledgeable procedures, sanitized equipment, or treatment that precluded messy scars and infections, but anyone who had reason to know a gutter-priest would risk malpractice over trusting a holy man.

Once the Jackals carved up their rivals and assumed control of Cier'Djaal, things had changed. They had healers on the payroll now. With no rival gangs to sell to and the promise of a slow death for traitors, the healers' loyalties could be guaranteed, within reason.

But Cier'Djaal hadn't been a reasonable place for a while now. And whoever the healers were loyal to were the kind of people Denaos didn't want knowing where he was.

You can't trust their gods, but you can trust a gutter-priest.

It was a truth Denaos had learned long ago in Cier'Djaal, a truth he couldn't afford to deny right now. The same truth that had driven him to find a half-rotted, run-down apartment and rent it with no one else to know. Trust was something rare and exotic in Cier'Djaal at the best of times.

"Here, drink this."

And these were not the best of times.

He looked down at the cup presented to him. The mixture inside could, if he was feeling particularly kind, be described as sludge. It was thick, gray, almost like porridge in its consistency. Only the way it rippled as he took it suggested it was a liquid instead of, say, a boiled-down rat.

"What does it do?" he asked.

"It fixes things, probably."

"Probably?" Denaos cringed at the mixture. "That's not reassuring."

"You didn't pay me for 'reassuring.' My mother treated snakebites with this tea for years."

"*Tea*? This is tea?"

"What the fuck did you think it was?"

"A war crime?"

"Look, you came to *me*."

"Yeah, yeah. Hold on."

It always struck Denaos as somewhat rude to pray to another god when in the presence of a priest. But gutter-priests being what they were, he suspected the one he'd hired didn't take too much offense when he muttered a few words to Silf before tilting the cup back and downing the mixture.

It didn't so much slide down his throat as crawl down it like a living thing. It settled in his belly like a hard lump and, for a moment, he felt a clammy sensation come over him. It was instantly burned out of him as his sinuses went ablaze and his skin began to tingle wildly. The tea churned in his gut for a moment, but he bit back the nausea long enough to reach for another cup—this one filled with a stiff whiskey—and down it.

"Huh. You're not dead."

"I paid you specifically to *avoid* that," Denaos muttered. "So if I do die, I expect to be buried with my refund."

He looked up at the man standing before him. A little paler than the average Djaalic, Heverish Slythe could only claim half blood, likely one of the many circumstances that had led to his becoming a gutter-priest to begin with. His clothes were clean, but hung well-worn upon a skinny frame. The polished Phoenix of Talanas that hung around his neck looked awkward on his shabby self, as if he had stolen it from a more respectable priest.

Slythe's thin face crinkled as he smiled a smile that Denaos hadn't seen in years. The kind of thin, vaguely creepy smile that confirmed this man was not the sort of person anyone decent would trust.

Which is likely why he had trusted Slythe for years, ever since he had first come to Cier'Djaal so long ago.

"Silf would frown on you going back on a deal," Slythe chided.

"You're a Talanite."

"Just saying." Slythe glanced over the fang marks peppering Denaos's shirtless body with a practiced eye. "Anyway, if there's any poison in you, it's probably mild enough to just piss out. Drink water. Light some incense, it'll keep the toxins from reaching your brain."

"I traveled with a healer for a while. She never said anything about incense."

"How much did you pay her?"

"Nothing."

"Well, there you go." Slythe walked to the table beside the door of the tiny room they lurked in and began to replace jars and vials into a healer's bag. "Water and incense should do you fine. If you start to feel numb or nauseous come to me." He paused, looked thoughtful. "But if you're feeling numb or nauseous, you've probably got an hour until death, so maybe you should just go to the nearest whorehouse and go crazy."

"Wait, what?" Denaos stood up, rising off the cot rather shakily. But he supposed that might be from the whiskey. "What did I drink that tea for, then?"

"Well, there's not a lot of cures for snakebites," Slythe said, slinging his medicine bag around his shoulder. "So mama made a tea that would react with the poison to give someone a quick death and spare them the indignity of shitting out their own innards."

Denaos rubbed his face. Sweat dampened his brow, made his hair stick to him. "Why the fuck do I keep giving you money, Slythe?"

"Maybe you love me." Slythe chuckled. "Good to see you again, though, Ramaniel. Wish you'd found me sooner."

"Why? You going somewhere?"

Slythe didn't answer. Not with his voice, anyway. But the pained expression on his face spoke enough. Denaos slumped with his sigh.

"Ah, fuck, Slythe."

"Everyone with any sense is leaving, Ramaniel," Slythe said. "The *couthi* are starting to leave."

"You were here through the riots, through the gang wars, through everything." Denaos cast a perplexed look at the Talanite. "Fuck, I remember we drank wine the night the Jackals hung the Morose Family on the harbor walls. This city's been in shit so deep it covered the Silken Spire and you never moved."

"It's different this time." A wince flashed across Slythe's face. "Rumors are spreading, Ramaniel. Word is that the Jackals can't fight the Khovura. Word is the Khovura are hunting them in their own dens. The Jackals can't keep control of the city anymore."

"You don't believe that shit, do you?"

"I do," Slythe said. "Because I remember a time when rumors like that wouldn't have gone further than twenty ears before all of them were hacked off by Jackal knives, along with the tongues that spread them. If the Jackals can't control rumors, how can they control a city?"

"We've had some bad luck."

"Bad luck? The Khovura aren't bad luck. They're a curse from an angry god." Desperation creeped into Slythe's voice, painted his face with fear. "The Khovura aren't the Morose Family, or the Isstaacca, or any other gang we've ever seen. Some dealers have reached out to them, went down to their part of town to do some business. Never heard from them again until I saw them running around with the other Khovura, screaming...what's that word they always say?"

"*Kapira,*" Denaos muttered, looking down at his feet. "*Khoth-Kapira.*"

"What kind of fucked-up gang does shit like that? The Khovura aren't a gang, not a guild, not anything we know. They don't bargain, they don't threaten, they don't play by the rules. They appear anywhere you think about them, like ghosts."

"They aren't ghosts." *Demons, more like*, he thought. He neglected to say this, of course. It certainly wouldn't do anything to convince Slythe to stay. But then, what would?

Slythe was too polite to press the issue, but he was dead right: Silence was the first line of defense on any thief's battleground. A gang that couldn't keep people from talking was a gang that couldn't very well keep hold of a city. This was Cier'Djaal, after all, people had expectations. And if even Slythe knew about the Jackals' weakening position, then so did others.

And if others knew, then . . .

Denaos shook his head. These weren't thoughts he wanted to have at the best of times, let alone while he was standing in a shitty apartment, half-naked and covered in snakebites with the knowledge that his friends were being hunted by demons in the sewers below. There was a time for thoughts like these.

But he didn't have nearly enough whiskey for it.

"Listen," Slythe began, "if you need me, I could maybe stick around. We've been solid for a few years and—"

"Don't bother," Denaos replied. He reached into his pocket, pulled out a pouch that weighed heavy with coin. "I've always thought you an intelligent man, Slythe." He tossed the pouch to the gutter-priest, who snatched it out of the air with a falcon's precision. "Don't go disabusing me of that now."

"Yeah, sure." Slythe pocketed the pouch as he walked to the door. He paused, glancing over his shoulder. "Good to see you again, Ramaniel."

He heard the door shut behind Slythe, heard him go down the creaky stairs to the room below, heard him open and shut the door and disappear into the streets. He heard the cot groan under his own weight as he settled down upon it. He heard the sound of an insect buzzing, seeking egress from a windowless wooden box masquerading as a bedroom.

And he heard the thought echo through his skull.

My name is Denaos.

That was his name, wasn't it? Denaos, a rogue out of Redgate who had hooked up with a silver-haired kid and his band of miscreant adventurers. Denaos, a lech and a liar and a thief. Denaos, by all accounts a selfish man who ought not to be affected by such a thing as a city he no longer called home tearing its own guts out through its seedy underbelly, let alone affected by a man he hadn't seen in years suddenly up and leaving like it was nothing worth noting.

Denaos shouldn't care, shouldn't give a shit, shouldn't feel nearly so heavy as he did now.

These worries that hung over him like a funeral shroud belonged to another man. These belonged to Ramaniel. Ramaniel, the urchin who had grown up on the harbor road and become Ramaniel the Jackal. Ramaniel, the man who had cut the throat of the Houndmistress and plunged Cier'Djaal into riots that had given the city the scars it still picked at today.

But Ramaniel was dead.

He had died the day Denaos had walked out of Cier'Djaal and headed north. And he was never supposed to live again. Unfair, Denaos thought, that he should be here, concerned over something like friends leaving. After all, he hadn't been this concerned when Lenk had left, had he?

But that's different, isn't it? Lenk's an adventurer. He's got a sword. He can take care of himself. When the Jackals fall and the Khovura spill out onto the street, this city's going to drown. Merchants' daughters and bakers' boys and little squalling brats ogling toy store windows. They'll all be fucking dead, just like they died in the riots.

He blinked. A thought struck his head numb.

How many people have the distinction of having killed Cier'Djaal twice?

The thought was an iron weight, settling heavy on his head and carrying him down to the cot. His head hit a straw pillow and just kept going, as though it wanted desperately to detach from his neck and crash through the floor. Maybe the tea Slythe had given him *was* going to kill him.

That would be fine. After all, he had died once before, hadn't he?

Ramaniel is dead, he thought as he closed his eyes. *No reason Denaos has to go on living.* He yawned. *You can just wake up as someone else tomorrow.*

＋＋ ≡◈≡ ＋＋

Denaos awoke suddenly, sweat pouring down skin that felt as if it were on fire. His skull pounded, his guts churned, his breath tasted foul. Agonized, but alive; Slythe's tea had failed to kill him.

Maybe it would have been kinder if it hadn't.

Denaos half-stumbled out of the cot, walked across a creaky floor to the chamber pot—or chamber bucket, really; the place had come cheap. He dropped his trousers, turned and squatted, and waited for the music.

Instead of the sound of bowels evacuating, he heard something crashing downstairs.

Denaos clenched, froze, stopped breathing as he ran down a list of possibilities between the poundings in his head.

Had the Khovura found him? No. They'd have made a much louder noise and he'd be dead already.

The Jackals, then? Come looking for him for answers about what had gone down in the tunnels? No. They wouldn't come this near the Sumps when Rezca had given the order to stay low.

Sainites looking for revenge? Karnerians looking for an ally? Venarium? Shicts? Tulwar?

By the time he had run down several more possibilities of decreasing likelihood, several moments had passed and no one had burst through his door and made him shit himself yet. Yet the sounds of movement from below persisted as someone maneuvered through the tiny box masquerading as the apartment's dining room.

Denaos hiked his garments back up, pulled a dagger out from his belt, and crept out of the room.

The first thing he had done when he rented this shithole was test where the creaks were. And while the answer to that was mostly "Everywhere," he managed to pick his way around enough to descend the staircase in relative silence. He drew in a breath and held it as he slipped down the last step, blade in hand and ready to gut.

But when he saw the intruder, he found words came easier than a blade.

"What the fuck are you doing here?"

At one wall, standing before an open cupboard, Dreadaeleon glanced up at Denaos with a decidedly bored expression. A shattered plate lay on the floor beside him, the rest of the cupboard's contents—an empty whiskey bottle, two more plates, and one knife—laid out on the tilted table at the center of the room. The wizard sniffed, then returned to sifting through the cupboard.

"Was the whiskey for disinfecting those wounds covering you?" he asked. "Or do you reek for reasons a decent mind should not inquire after?"

"That's what you've got to say to me?" Denaos asked. "You disappeared days ago while the city went to hell and no one had any idea where you were. Should I tell Asper you just strolled in here like you owned it?" At that a thought occurred. "How the fuck did you even *find* me?"

"My presence or lack thereof would have made no impact on the city's current circumstances," Dreadaeleon replied. "My whereabouts, as it happened, were in a Venarium tower after I was arrested by a Charnel Hound. Our erstwhile female companion already knows that, as she was the one who arranged my release. As for how I found you, given that I can make a man explode with a thought, I should think I could find a barkneck thug easily enough." He patted the bare cupboard, searching. "Have you got any money?"

If a man had led a life so exceptionally fraught with ill deeds that the gods could curse him, he might very well hear something quite as insane as what had just come out of Dreadaeleon's mouth. And as Denaos had committed more than his fair share of sins, he simply stared at the knife in his hand, wondering if it might just be easier to plunge it into his own throat and avoid this whole conversation.

"I'm sorry, what?" he settled on asking, instead.

"Gold," Dreadaeleon said. "Silver, if you've got it. Coins. Currency. Something I can buy things with. Have you got any?"

"No, no, the other part," Denaos said.

"Which other part?"

"The one with Asper. She contacted you?"

"She did. She persuaded the Venarium to release me in hopes that I would cause enough damage to the occupying Karnerians to convince them to leave." Dreadaeleon patted down the cupboard, frowning at the hollow sound that followed. "Seriously, is there a hidden panel here? Some kind of secret knock or something?"

"Why would I have a hidden panel in a cupboard?" He held up a hand to prevent any response. "How is gold going to help you kill Karnerians, anyway?"

"It won't. I have no intention of killing Karnerians."

"Then why—"

Dreadaeleon held up a single finger. "Permit me to expedite this: Yes, Asper did a service to me. A service that scarcely makes up for the way she..." He paused, his face grew hard. "I consider us even, at any rate. That being the case, it's my intent to depart Cier'Djaal as soon as I can, leaving as few carcasses in my wake as possible."

"So what, you're just going to betray Asper?"

Dreadaeleon shot a sneer at Denaos and the aloofness slid off his face, revealing cold contempt beneath. "Oh, yes, I would so *love* to hear a murderer lecture me on morality. Perhaps from this unlikely source of compassion, I'll have a change of heart and you, Asper, and myself will all save Cier'Djaal together? Frolic off into the sunset, hand in hand, as the grateful denizens of the city wave tearstained handkerchiefs at us?"

"Would you even recognize gratitude if you saw it? She got you out of prison, didn't she?"

"Prison?" Dreadaeleon's laugh was bitter as stale water. "The Venarium is as much like a prison as a grave is like a nice place to rest your head. She did not 'get me out' of anything. She merely delayed my execution. The Venarium does not release heretics. She and they merely want to use me until they can quietly dispose of me. I don't intend to let them."

"How do you know?"

"Because I..." Dreadaeleon turned away. He breathed a long, cold breath. "They know what I've done, Denaos. I wouldn't release me, either." He stalked to a nearby bookcase with criminally few books and began to search it. "What's it matter to you, anyway?"

"Asper gave me the same deal. It sounded pretty good to me," Denaos said, following him. "And it would have worked. It still could, if you live up to your end of the bargain. We can hit the Sainites in the tunnels while you hit the Karnerians from above. We can help this city. We can—"

"No, wait, I think I wasn't clear. What's it matter at all?" Dreadaeleon looked over his shoulder. "Suppose we evict the Karnerians and the Sainites. What do we do about the Khovura? Or the shicts? The tulwar? How can you cure a city dying of countless diseases?"

"How can you not *try*?" Denaos swept up to the boy. "With everything she's seen, every problem she's come back from, how can you think that Cier'Djaal can't fend this off?"

"Because I don't care," Dreadaeleon sneered, returning to his search. "If you do, then count me as surprised but still not interested. Frankly, I would have thought you'd have left by now."

Denaos stared at him, stone-faced for a moment. "Maybe sometimes there are things you can't run from." He snorted. "And maybe someday, when you're an adult, you'll understand that."

And Dreadaeleon went stock-still at that. His arms fell to his sides. He stared blankly at the bookcase. His body went stiff as a corpse and his breath was the last exhalation of the dead.

"An adult," he repeated flatly.

And then he whirled upon Denaos.

He had only a moment to glimpse the burning crimson filling Dreadaeleon's eyes before everything around Denaos became a blur. He felt his feet torn out from under him, he felt himself sail through the air, he felt his back collide with the wall in a spray of splinters. A great pressure pinned him against it, a tremendous unseen hand that tore him two feet from the floor and slammed him once more against the wood.

"Don't you ever presume to lecture me, asshole." Dreadaeleon advanced upon him, hand outstretched, the air shimmering around his fingers as the magic blazed within his scowl. "Don't you ever presume to think that you're *anything* more than an insect compared to me."

His hand tightened and Denaos felt the pressure increase, choking the air out of his lungs.

"You, Asper, *everyone* seems to think they can talk down to me. They all seem to think *I'm* the one that doesn't get it." Dreadaeleon forced each word through clenched teeth. "Look at me now, you fucking barkneck. Can *you* comprehend how I'm doing this?"

Denaos opened his mouth, but only a thick gurgling sound came out.

"Then under what circumstance would you presume to know more than I do, hm? Answer me." His eyes burst into tiny infernos. *"ANSWER ME."*

Denaos could do nothing more than kick his legs, slam his fist impotently against the wall, as though that would do anything. Dreadaeleon seemed unmoved by the gesture, advancing upon Denaos, hand slowly tightening into a fist.

"It's *you* that doesn't understand," Dreadaeleon said. "None of you do. You, Lenk, Asper, you're all content to let yourselves be used like tools. They tell you it's for the good of the city, of people who don't respect you or care about you at all, as though *they're* entitled to your efforts just by their own miserable existence.

"Do whatever you like. Do it for gratitude or gold or for gods, like Asper, but leave me out of it. I am not a tool that people can use as they wish. I am *not* a fool they can betray. And I am *NOT A BOY!*"

Dreadaeleon snapped his hand over his shoulder. Air returned to Denaos as the invisible grip released him. Air welcomed him as he hurtled across the room and struck the wall. He tumbled to the floor, the pains he had felt earlier forgotten as so many more-pronounced agonies took their place. He coughed, gasping air into burning lungs, and clambered unsteadily to his feet, dagger out and held shakily before him.

But Dreadaeleon did not seem to notice. He walked to the door and waved his hand, bidding it open by means of an unseen force. He stalked out of the apartment into the night, not bothering to close the door behind him.

Denaos fell to one knee and collapsed onto the floor.

"Yeah," he coughed, "you better run."

The only response was the distant barking of a dog as he fell to the floor and went dark.

—— ——

Had he the consciousness to do it, Denaos might have reflected on how unfair it was that he dreamed this time.

He dreamed of fires and houses burning beneath a night sky and of serpents coiling around cold bodies and craning jaws to swallow them whole. He saw women slitting their throats to water gardens of ash and watched snakes grow out of the dust like trees.

Silf was not an enigmatic god, despite his dominion over thieves. He was the Patron, a businessman: Give him a favor, he'll give his blessing, and what you do with it is up to you. He didn't send visions, riddles, signs; that was the province of frivolous, flighty deities.

Which made Denaos wonder, then, if perhaps some other god was looking out for him at that moment.

He had, at least, consciousness enough to wonder that as he groaned to wakefulness.

Before he saw anything, he felt the scratchy sheets of his cot and the pillow underneath his head. The humidity of the Sumps seeped in through an open window, bathing him in sweat. His previous aches had coalesced with the fresh agonies inflicted upon him by the wizard to conspire to make it painful even to open his eyes.

And when he did, he saw her.

The desperate concern painting Anielle's face didn't fit her. Hers was a face made for cooler emotions. The lips parted in murmured prayer, the mussed strands of dark hair hanging in front of her eyes, the frown scarring her face: These were features she wore poorly. They made her look unkempt.

Vulnerable.

Upon her recognizing his wakefulness, her face slid into a more familiar contempt. "Moron," she muttered as she pressed a damp cloth against his head. "The point of being a thief is to *avoid* danger."

"How'd you find me?" he asked, voice creaky in his throat.

"Followed your connections," she said. "Found out who owns these apartments and pressed them." She glanced at him. "Another part of being a thief is to leave a not-quite-so-painfully-obvious trail."

"Yeah, well," he said, "maybe you're a better thief than a healer." He grabbed the cloth off his head. "What the hell was this supposed to do?"

"I don't know!" she protested. "I've seen healers do it before. I thought that's what they all did!"

"For fevers," Denaos replied. "Not for getting the shit kicked out of you by a wizard."

"Is *that* what happened? There's wizards involved now? What grudge do they have against the Jackals?"

"Not the Jackals, just me." Denaos sat up in his cot, rested his head against the wall.

"Wouldn't surprise me if there were. Everything else about this is fucked up enough for it to happen." Anielle leaned back in the chair she had pulled up next to him. "Scarecrow came out of the tunnels, told me what happened."

Denaos looked at her. "And?"

"And... it gets worse." Anielle shook her head. "The knives we sent out to mess up the Sainites all had the same thing happen: They got the job done and got ambushed immediately afterward. Like someone had told them to wait for the Sainites to soften them up first."

"Shit." Denaos rubbed his face, found his hands greasy with sweat.

"Rezca's been in a fit, tightening down security, recalling everyone from everything. He's been decrying this whole operation as fucked." Anielle looked at him meaningfully. "It is, you know."

"It wouldn't be if someone weren't ratting us out," Denaos said. "Only the heads knew about this. It had to be one of us. And now they've got a fasha supporting them, so—"

"They what? How do you know?"

"They came into the tunnels through Silktown." Denaos looked back at her. "Makes sense, doesn't it? A fasha sees the other team is getting the upper hand, reaches out to someone in the Jackals to rig the game."

"You've thought this before, remember?" She leaned forward again, her intentness turning to warning. "Ghoukha's whole house went up in fire because of it."

"How else would they be in Silktown? Mejina's dragonmen have been keeping that place locked down. *Someone* had to let them in. Now would be the ideal time, wouldn't it? Ghoukha was the most powerful man in this city and now he's gone. Anyone would be reluctant to go after another fasha now."

Anielle blanched, looking down at the floor. "Still."

"I can't think of another fucking idea," Denaos said, rising up and swinging his legs over the cot. "I've tried, but I just can't. This fits, Anielle. Fits like a gods-damned boot." He rose up, stalked to where he had left his tunic and spare daggers in a crumpled heap. "Find the fasha, find the rat. Find the rat, kill the Khovura's advantage. Take back the underground, take back the city, take back the—"

"*No.*"

Anielle hurled the word, rather than spoke it. It struck Denaos against the back of his head, made him almost dizzy as he turned around.

When he had first seen her so many years ago, it had been only a few days after he had sneaked off the boat from Muraska he had stowed away on. She had been a boyish-looking girl: too skinny and too tough, like an overcooked chicken. But he had taken one look at her and hadn't dared make fun of her.

She had stood strong then, feet planted firmly on the ground and arms folded across her chest, chin upright and daring the world to take a swing at her. No matter what about her changed—when she grew from a girl into a woman, when she grew from a gutter-runner into a

Jackal—she had always stood firm. Whether she was seducing a mark, acting the hapless damsel to fool a guard, cutting a purse or a profit or a throat, she had always stood firm.

Until now.

Now, painted dark by the dim, flickering light of the candle on the bedside table, she shook. Now her hands were clenched at her sides in a way that looked almost petulant. Now she was the scared little girl she had never been.

And Denaos found that frightened him more than anything else.

"No?" he asked.

"No, Ramaniel. Just..." She shook her head. "Fucking no. No more." She approached him. "No more gang wars. No more fasha conspiracies. No more fucking Khovura turning into demons. No more... *no more of this.*" She gestured to his open window. "We always knew this was going to happen someday. We cut down the gangs that came before us knowing that we'd be cut down ourselves, eventually."

"I don't remember having that discussion," Denaos said, "or that thought."

"Then you're a fucking idiot. We played a good game. We cut them up bad. But they're not playing by the rules and we don't have the time or the men to learn the new ones." She drew close to him. Close enough that her breath felt hot on his skin. "We've lost. *I've* lost friends, money, almost everything."

She reached up. She laid her hands upon his shoulders, shaking so badly he thought they might throttle him. But in another moment they calmed, sliding down and settling upon his chest so that he could feel his heartbeat press against her palms. She looked up at him, the desperation in her eyes clouded by tears.

"I'm not going to lose the rest."

Anielle's hands ran across his chest, up his neck, cradled his jaw. There was no tenderness in her touch, no delicacy in fingers fit for cracking locks as easily as they braided hair. Her fingers betrayed only tension and desperation, a need to hold him, a need to remind herself that he was still there.

He knew the sensation keenly. He could feel it in his own hands as they slid down and settled upon her hips.

Maybe that was why he didn't resist as she drew his face close to hers. Maybe that was why he closed his eyes and let his aches and pains fade away as she pressed her lips against his. Maybe that was why he found his fingers curling under the hem of her shirt.

He tore the garment free from her as she raised her hands over her head. Her tight-fitting undershirt came after, both garments pooling upon the floor in a heap.

Beneath the leather and cloth, he scarcely recognized her body. Her breasts were full now and her hips sloped away from her waist in a womanly curve. Yet in the core of her body and the way her ribs showed as her arms stretched overhead, she was still the skinny little girl he had known so long ago.

And he was still the same scared little pale boy. The remainder of his clothes came off with their own desperation, eager to do this, lest she slip away while his hands were off her and disappear into the night and leave him alone. He tossed his breeches aside, slipped out of his drawers, and took her by the shoulders.

In kinder times, in nicer rooms, in better days, he would have guided her down gently like the man he had once been. But these were not those days. These were the bad days, when shadows were for blades, not lovers, and things were done harshly.

He threw her down upon the cot, heard her gasp as he hooked his fingers into the waist of her breeches and pulled them free, tossing them aside. Her hand was up in an instant, seizing him by the hair and drawing a pained snarl from him as she pulled him down on top of her.

No room for words between them. No room to ponder what a bad idea this might be, why they'd stopped doing it in the first place. No room for the doubts and fears and sorrows of these past weeks. They pressed themselves so tightly, feeling their skin slick with each other's sweat, that there was no room for anything but each other.

Only her fingers in his hair, his lips at her throat, and the sound of her breath escaping her in a moan as her legs coiled around him and he entered her.

There was nothing kind about it. There was nothing soft about his hips pressing against hers as he entered her, about her arms looping around his neck and pulling him close, about his fingers twisting in her hair. There was no tenderness, no romance, no easy sighs of satisfaction.

They were not that kind of people. And no matter how many names they had taken over the years, they could never pretend to be.

They were Ramaniel and Anielle, two young punks out of the gutters of Harbor Road. They were wild youths who had smashed wine bottles against walls and fallen into drunken embraces in back alleys. They were cutthroats who had made love on rooftops as rival gangs' hideouts burned in the streets below. They were Jackals who wore identities easily and tossed them aside just as easily.

Whatever was left beneath those identities was what they clung to now.

No names. No words. No lies.

Just each other.

And when she craned her head back and let out a scream, and when his grunt came with an agony all its own, and when they fell limp and breathless into each other, whatever they had left was something they dared not let go of.

And when they lay still, when a passing breeze blew through the window and brought brief relief from the humidity, there was still no gentleness. They clung to each other, reluctant to let go and return to a world where shadows brought no comfort.

Denaos stared a long time at the wood of the ceiling. And when she spoke first, he only barely heard her.

"Let's run."

"What?"

"I want to leave." Anielle spoke into the night, not looking at him. "Tomorrow, maybe. Tonight if possible. Head to Jalaang, take a boat upriver, and cross the mountains into Muraska. I want you to come with me."

He didn't respond, perhaps wondering whether, if he remained silent enough, she would simply not speak of it again.

"Ramaniel?"

No such luck.

"I can't," he said, and it hurt.

"Why not? Don't you want to go with me?"

"I do," he said, and meant it.

"Then why? We don't owe the Jackals shit."

"Not them, no."

"Then what? Your friends?"

He didn't answer but for a look. She knew full well what he was going to say. He could see it in her eyes just before she buried her face in his chest.

"Fucking moron," she whispered. "This city's always been rancid, Ramaniel. The riots were going to happen sooner or later. You don't owe Cier'Djaal any more than the Jackals."

"I killed it," Denaos said. "I caused the riots."

"You didn't. We all did. I was part of the Kissing Game, too, remember? I killed three fashas and seven nobles. I pretended to be their slaves, their friends, their lovers. I don't feel guilty at all. The Houndmistress had the poor eating out of her hand, but she was just one woman. You killed just one woman and you'd let it ruin everything you had?"

"She wasn't just a woman," Denaos said. He pulled away from her, sat on the edge of the cot. "She was...someone great. Someone that said all this shit about changing the city and if you could have heard it, you'd believe it." He buried his face in his hands. "And we fucked that up."

He could feel the woundedness in Anielle's stare. "You loved her."

"I did," he said. "I loved what she was going to do and I wish to any god out there that I hadn't been such a fucking coward, that I could have told the Jackals to fuck off and let her fix this city."

"She would have killed all the Jackals, Ramaniel. She would have killed *me*. Doesn't that mean anything to you?"

He looked over his shoulder at her. She looked so small, smaller than she had been even when she was that skinny little girl, as she pressed against the wall. He couldn't help but smile.

"We could have had new lives," he said. "We could have forgotten the shithole we came out of. We could have disappeared, Anielle. Like ghosts."

"It's not that easy."

"Yeah." He looked away from her. "Anytime something big happens and shit's about to change, everyone says, 'It's not that easy,' like that's reason enough to not try. Maybe that's why Imone—"

"Who?"

"The Houndmistress. That's why she was so great. She knew it wasn't easy and wouldn't stop trying." He bit his lip. "Fuck me, Anielle, but I've got to try. I've got to at least fucking try to fix this."

"For her?"

"Not for her."

"For Cier'Djaal."

"For *us*." He stood up, faced her. She looked as vulnerable as he felt. "For kids who won't be taken in by gangs and wind up like we did. I started this. I can't not at least try."

"And if you fail?"

"Then...I'll go away with you. Wherever you want. But before that, we do one last thing together. We find the fasha who's supporting the Khovura, pass that on to Rezca, and hope everything turns out all right."

"And then we leave?"

He nodded. "Then we leave."

She stared at him. He had known Anielle long enough to know when she thought an idea was stupid. And it didn't sound that right to him, either. It sounded like something Asper would say, that stupid woman, in a fit of pious righteousness. He wasn't a priest. He wasn't a selfless Talanite. He worshiped the Patron, who asked only that he look out for himself.

But if there was a chance...

Anielle closed her eyes, nodded briefly. He returned to bed with her, held her in his arms. But it was for nothing.

Whatever they had been clinging to was gone, carried out the window on a stale breeze and leaving them alone with the stink of their own sweat.

EIGHTEEN

Ten Fingers Pointed Skyward

The *Rhega* had no elders.

They grew old. They died. Like anyone else. But there was no reverence for age or the wisdom that came with it. A *Rhega*, if he was canny enough to live so long, simply told his offspring what they needed to know and then left.

After all, Gariath thought, what else would one do with old age?

Apparently, waste everyone's time by making it some giant, masturbatory spectacle.

That wasn't what the tulwar called it, of course.

They called it *Humn Tul Naa*. Many Old Souls Meeting.

Gariath thought a better name would be A Lot of Gassy Old People Pretending to Be Important, but he wasn't sure how to say that in the tulwar tongue.

Nor was he sure that any of the tulwar would approve, considering the significant effort they had put into preparing for it.

They had begun that afternoon, taking brooms and rakes to the center of Shaab Sahaar and clearing the city's square of gaambol shit and other refuse. They had worked well into the evening, until now, in the dead of night, when they gathered around a large circle reserved for an entirely different kind of refuse.

One by one they made their way to the circle, ringed by salt and dotted with cushions for sitting. From every corner of the city, with bent backs and gnarled canes and potbellies, they came. Grandmothers. Grandfathers. The colors in their faces long since faded, their fur fallen out in patches to reveal sagging skin.

The *Humn*. The Very Long Lives. Spiritual leaders of the tulwar.

Old, decrepit pieces of shit to whom the proud, the brave, and the ferocious unquestioningly bowed.

Only *saan* tulwar—those men and women who earned for their families by the edges of their swords—were allowed to witness. In clothes of many colors, arms crossed and blades sheathed, they clustered around the circle in which the *Humn* sat, observing in utter silence.

As though any of this mattered.

Gariath was allowed—or at least convinced—to observe the proceedings from the outskirts of the circle.

He glanced across the circle, to the red-and-orange-clad cluster of tulwar. The Rua Tong clan. Daaru's clan. Daaru glared back at the dragonman. Things had been cooler between them since the evening Gariath had berated him; the tulwar had invited him, but made a point of not standing beside him.

He suspected Daaru thought to impress his guest with this ceremony, to show him that tulwar roots ran deep enough not to be severed by human influence.

"Did no one remember to bring drink?"

That, of course, remained to be seen.

"We are intended to be fasting," one of the *Humn*—a thick-bodied tulwar with a long beard and wearing Rua Tong's colors—muttered from the circle. "It is custom before *Humn Tul Naa*."

"I have obeyed the custom," the voice that had spoken earlier protested. This one belonged to a particularly large elder, potbelly poking out from beneath a purple-and-black *chota*. "It is not breaking a fast to drink."

"Water, Gowaa," an old woman tulwar with a wizened face said, her breasts heavy with age and her gray hair done up in a braid. "It is not breaking a fast to drink *water*. You Tho Thu Bhu would drink the Lyre dry if it were made of wine."

The other tulwar behind the heavy one called Gowaa, also clad in purple and black, let out a rumble of discontent. He held up a hand to silence them.

"We Tho Thu Bhu Clan take great pride in our craftsmanship," Gowaa replied. "Food and wine, as much as any blade or bow. It would insult us to reject our skill."

"Enough." A bitter hiss came from the fourth and final member of the circle. This one looked lean and haggard, hair in sparse patches, eyes sharp, body wiry beneath a green-and-brown *chota*. "If I died and came back in my next life, you still wouldn't have begun without me to cajole you."

"Very well." The powerful-looking Rua Tong tulwar raised his head and his voice. "*Humn Tul Naa* is called. The *saan* and *Humn* are gathered here today to speak of the clans, on behalf of the clans, for the clans. Let the clans be recognized." He raised his right hand, drew a circle in the air with his finger. "Dugu Humn Rua Tong."

The orange-and-red-clad tulwar who stood in a cluster behind the one called Dugu echoed his gesture, Daaru included. There were nearly twice as many here as in any other clan present, Gariath observed. Perhaps that was why they took the lead in speaking.

"Gowaa Humn Tho Thu Bhu," the fat tulwar said, making the same gesture. His clan mimicked it.

"Sagar Humn Yengu Thuun," the woman said. Her clan, dressed in brown and white, made the same gesture with her.

"Dekuu Humn Chee Chree," the lean one muttered. His clan was the smallest, but all held the same wary liveliness in their eyes as their chieftain.

All eyes drifted to one side of the circle, where two empty cushions sat. Behind one of them were a pair of tulwar dressed in simple gray robes. They made the gesture, all the same.

"So noted is the absence of Mototaru Humn Muusa Gon," Dugu said. He looked to the other cushion, behind which there was a very noticeable gap that the other tulwar seemed reluctant to fill. "So noted, with gratitude to Tul, is the absence of Chakaa Humn Mak Lak Kai."

"*Much* gratitude," Gowaa added.

The other tulwar muttered agreement. The gesture was repeated once more, a complete circle drawn with the right hand from the right to the left. The Chee Chree clan and their patron, though, remained still and silent.

"Shall I come back once the ceremonies are completed?" Dekuu grunted, folding his long arms over his chest. "The Mak Lak Kai are a problem which the Chee Chree have no interest in discussing."

"Nor the Yengu Thuun," Sagar added. She scratched a stray itch beneath her chins. "My clan asks me to come before you today to speak of the situation of living space."

"Again," Gowaa added, rolling his eyes.

"Yes, again," Sagar snapped back. "We have no room for our gaambols. The other clans crowd us when it is our turn to get drinking water, which always comes *last*, I note."

"It is true," Dugu said, scratching his beard. "But your gaambols require quite a bit of water, no? Is it not fair that they drink after families and children have drunk first?"

"At the very least," Gowaa muttered, "it is just as unfair as the other clans being forced to endure their smell."

"Families and children are one thing," Sagar replied sharply. "But Tho Thu Bhu take more and more water each day for their metals."

"We need weapons and tools," Gowaa replied. "We need to cool the metal. What would you have us do?"

Murmurs of discontent rose from the assembled clans, a canvas upon which accusations were painted and condemnations spattered. Every now and then, one of the *Humn* would say something to cause one clan or another to raise its voices in agreement or outrage. And every now and then, another would retort with an equally outrageous word.

They all spoke the human tongue, but it all sounded like so much gibberish to Gariath. The scene would have reminded him of vultures squabbling over a corpse, save that he had seen enough of that to know that carrion-gobbling squabs had a touch more diplomacy.

Gariath flashed a decidedly unimpressed sneer across the circle at Daaru.

"*Enough.*" Dekuu spoke through bared teeth, worn and dull and yellow. "The Chee Chree did not come to your city to hear you bicker like children over the biggest piece of meat." He narrowed his eyes. "Yet only the Chee Chree seem to have noticed that we are *dying*."

"I see plenty of you standing here now," Gowaa replied, eyeing the assembled tulwar behind Dekuu. "Many *saan*, hale and hardy. Certainly enough to take up space in Shaab Sahaar."

"There were more," Dekuu growled. "So many more. More *saan*, more *duwun*, more *tulwar*. Our villages sprawled to the edges of the forests of the Forbidden East." He thrust a finger at Gowaa. "You know this, Tho Thu Bhu, for it was our lumber you used to make your bows, your houses, your boats."

"Which we shared—which we *still* share—with the Chee Chree."

"You give us bows long after our enemies are gone, you open your houses long after ours are burned." Dekuu swept his gaze about the assembled clans. "You speak of cramped quarters, scarce water, sharing food when there is too little. Let us speak of the cause."

A collective tension coursed through the assembled clans, as though they knew what he was going to say next. Even Dekuu seemed to speak with some reluctance, and when the words came, they came heavy.

"Let us speak of the *shicts*."

The murmurs died down. Glances were exchanged, as though they spoke of ghosts instead of pointy-eared vermin.

"Even the Chee Chree have heard of the strife in Cier'Djaal," Dekuu continued. "And the humans' problems have made the shicts bolder. They're beginning their raids well ahead of the season. We were not prepared for them."

"Nor were the Yengu Thuun," Sagar said. "The Chee Chree share a border with them. Raids are inevitable. But for them to range so far south, into *our* lands, is unheard of." She narrowed her eyes. "There is talk that this is not just raiding. There is talk that this is—"

"I have heard," Dugu said, rubbing his eyes. "I have heard of their new leader, this...Shekune. I have heard how many tulwar she has killed." He looked to his fellow elders. "What would you have us do, then? There is room for the Chee Chree in Shaab Sahaar. Here we are safe."

"Here is not home," Dekuu said. "And without the Chee Chree in the forests, we will not have the lumber to keep your wooden houses up and your tools crafted. The shicts are animals. If they sense weakness, they will attack."

"If they are animals, let them root around in the trash," Gowaa said. "We have seen this before. They will glut themselves, vomit, and move on."

"This is not like before," Sagar said, shaking her head. "Not at all."

"Perhaps they are out of season, perhaps this is not like before." Dugu made a sound low in his chest, scratched his chin. "But I do not think the shicts have changed their tactics." He eyed Dekuu. "Have they?"

The Chee Chree's lips stiffened before he shook his head. Dugu sighed wearily and nodded.

"We have fought the shicts before," he said. "Always it is the same. They watch from the shadows and wait until the strong leave to hunt, then come in and attack the weak. They shoot at our backs and then run away when we turn around. They are always there, and never there. To fight a shict is to fight a bad dream. It cannot be done."

Dekuu narrowed his eyes. "Mak Lak Kai fights."

"Mak Lak Kai belongs in the trash with the shicts," Gowaa growled. "Chakaa and her clan are walking disasters. *Malaa*, all of them. Better they die out there than be trapped in here with us."

"They are tulwar," Dekuu snarled. "They are clan. And they *fight* for their homes."

"Without restraint, sense, or regard for anything beyond their own bloodlust," Sagar said. "They are *malaa*, outside the Tul. Gowaa is right."

"Then perhaps he was also right about everything else!" Dekuu snapped. "Maybe we don't need to worry about Chee Chree being slaughtered like animals by shicts! Maybe Yengu Thuun's reek *is* our biggest problem!"

"We have all lost to the shicts, Dekuu," Sagar growled. "Do not presume that you speak to a coward."

"I do not presume I speak to a coward." He leapt to his feet. Color flooded his face. "I presume I speak to *three* cowards!"

And then things got a little interesting, at least.

The Chee Chree clan surged forward in a shouting mass, their faces bright with red, yellow, and blue. The Yengu Thuun replied in shrieks not so unlike those of the gaambols they rode. The Tho Thu Bhu beat their chests and howled as the Rua Tong raised their fists and roared to be heard over everyone else.

Eventually their rage overtook their senses. Their speech slid into different tongues and the gibberish of their argument was compounded. Perhaps this, as Daaru said, was why they spoke the human tongue. It was simply more efficient.

Why they chose to also bicker and squabble like humans, Gariath already knew. One could not be surrounded by human amenities, human goods, human tongue, and not pick up their weakness, their greed, their *disease*.

As he watched the tulwar continue to bicker and spit, he saw them transform in his mind. He saw pointy ears, lips spewing sanctimony, a gangly stoop, lips curled upward in arrogance, a mop of silver hair. He saw them, all of the humans. *His* humans. And the memory of them became real, felt real in the clenching of his fists and the flaring of his nostrils.

Them, with their greed and lust for gold. Them, with their selfishness and cowardice. How they'd always hid behind him when it came time to kill. How they'd run screaming from the messes he would clean up. How they'd needed him.

Right up until they had left him.

"What of the human city?"

Perhaps that memory was what caused him to speak up.

"What of Cier'Djaal?"

Or perhaps he just had grown tired of the tulwar prattle.

Either way, his voice boomed over theirs. Slowly they fell silent. Slowly they turned their eyes to him. Some with shock, surprised that he had spoken. Others with horror, having not even seen him before. Daaru, though, shot him a look rife with concern.

A gracious guest probably would have respected his host enough to retract his query.

"You sit and whine like children while they feast on flesh and spit the bones at you."

Or at least have been less of an asshole about it.

"You need more space?" He pointed westward. "It's there. You need more water? They sit on a river and pull water from the earth. You need steel? Wood? Stone? They have *everything*." He looked down his snout at them. "And you have a square full of shit."

The assembled *Humn* exchanged glances. Dugu was the first to speak. "You, dragonman, are a guest of Daaru, yes? Of Rua Tong?" He held up a hand. "It is forgivable, then, that you do not know the ways of the tulwar. *Humn Tul Naa* is where the *Humn* speak for their clans."

"Until they start speaking for themselves," Gariath replied. "Or did I see some *other* group of tulwar just screaming at each other like infants?"

"If they do not have *Humn* where you are from, do they not at least have manners?" Dekuu snarled. "Who are you to speak to us?"

"I have heard tales," Gowaa hummed, eyeing Gariath carefully. "There are tulwar who have journeyed to Cier'Djaal and returned with stories of you, creature. Tell me . . . is it true that you defeated the fasha's pets? The dragonmen?"

"His name was Kharga," Gariath said sternly. "He was *Drokha*, not 'dragonman,' and nobody's pet." He snorted. "And I beat the shit out of him."

He knew the silence that fell over the tulwar.

It was the silence in the hesitation of a prayer. It was the silence that hung in the air for a breath before a sword left sheath and entered flesh. It was the silence that came before the last words a dead man spoke.

It was the silence of change.

And he had not felt it for a very long time.

When it was broken, it was by Dugu's low rumble, somewhere between the growl of a great warrior and the weariness of an old man.

"You have been among us for some time," he said, "and as Daaru is *saan*, you are welcome. If you know of the... *Drokha*, did you call them?" He nodded, scratched his beard. "If you know of them, do you also know of the Uprising?"

"I have heard the word," Gariath said.

"Mm. The word. Sometimes it feels like just that. A word." Dugu leaned back, settled on his cushion, closed his eyes. "But when it was first spoken, it was more. It was starving children, forgotten honor, and hungry blades. It took us across the desert, through the armies of Cier'Djaal, all the way to the very heart of their city.

"Then Uprising was the stone under our feet, the silk over our heads, the blood on our hands, and the humans cowering in their houses. Then Uprising was Tul and the two were the same."

He opened his eyes. His face was grim and gray.

"That was a moment. Then the dragonmen came."

"A sea of them, from wall to wall," Gowaa said, "they came pouring from every crack and gap in the house."

"You exaggerate," Sagar said. "There were maybe only a thousand."

"Fifty." Dekuu's face was twisted into a frown. "There were fifty. And they slaughtered over a thousand tulwar. Chee Chree arrows could not pierce their hides."

"Yengu Thuun beasts could not climb high enough," Sagar added.

"Tho Thu Bhu shields shattered under their axes," Gowaa sighed.

"Rua Tong corpses choked the streets. And Muusa Gon..." Dugu looked to the two gray-clad tulwar, who observed the retelling stoically. He shook his head. "Many tulwar died that day. Many more died in the days that followed as we marched back to Shaab Sahaar. And here we stayed."

"Here we built," Gowaa said.

"Here we live," Sagar said.

"Here we die," Dekuu muttered.

"Why?" Gariath growled. "I have been to Cier'Djaal. It is in *chaos*. It is ready to be destroyed. It *begs* for it. A thousand warriors—"

"Would be a thousand fewer fathers and mothers," Dugu said. "Perhaps you have heard the wrong things of our people, dragonman. We are tulwar. We are of the Tul. Our god is dead, and so we are eternal. This life is fleeting, and so is its suffering. We will die, we will return, and the problems of this life will be forgotten to all but the oldest of *Humn*.

"Cities of men will fall, shicts will come and go. But Tul is eternal."

He raised his right hand, drew a circle in the air from right to left. The gesture was taken up, first by *Humn*, then by *saan*, until all did it. All but Gariath, who merely stood there, scowling across the circle as Daaru looked back and smiled.

———————

The streets of Shaab Sahaar were empty of bodies that night. But as Gariath stalked down its dusty streets in the shadows cast by its towering spires, he noted that did not mean it was rid of stench.

Yet the reek that tormented him that night was not the same as the one that had greeted him when he arrived. Now his nostrils quivered and took in scents he had not noticed before: hides that smelled of shicts, bottles that smelled of couthi, and everywhere, in the wood and steel and dirt, the smell of human.

This city reeked of them. Their greed. Their weakness.

How could it have come to this? In Cier'Djaal, Daaru had been rife with anger. In the desert he had faced down the shicts with no fear on his face at all. He was bold, fearless—annoying, also, but no more than the average human. Gariath had hoped all tulwar were like that, so full of fire and fury.

But now?

Now he didn't even know what the tulwar were. Their voices sounded so whiny in his memory now, so full of weakness and excuses to avoid what needed to be done. They were no warriors. They were fathers to mewling whelps, old men sitting on cushions and waiting to die, women cleaning up after gaambols.

He couldn't even smell the gaambol shit anymore, so strong was the reek of—

He paused. His nostrils twitched. A familiar scent tinged the air. Pipe smoke?

"How are you finding the city, *shkainai*?"

Gariath forgave himself for not having noticed the tulwar until he spoke. He had, at a glance, thought the creature to be another pile of refuse. But now he saw the plume of smoke, the gray flesh, the round body.

He recognized this tulwar from only a few days ago. The old one who smelled of nothing but smoke. The tulwar was dirty, sitting beside a wall in unwashed and tattered robes. His lips and teeth were stained from years of puffing on the pipe that hung from the corner of his mouth.

Yet through the veil of smoke, Gariath could see that the tulwar's eyes were keen, bright, and full of something that had been dead in the stares of the tulwar at the *Humn Tul Naa*.

"I liked it better when I first got here," Gariath finally answered.

"Time with the *Humn* will do that." The old tulwar chuckled. "With so many garbage-heaped alleys and filthy streets to behold, who has time to spend discussing the intricacies of the Tul?"

"I have heard of heaven from humans," Gariath grunted. "Their living gods are stupid enough. A dead one seems less than useless."

"It's too easy to call the Tul a dead god. But the Rua Tong could be forgiven, seeing as they have never been interested in thinking about things they can't hit with big metal sticks."

The old tulwar rose with a groan and the pop of vertebrae. He walked stooped, a muscular body now paying the price for all its weight, as he approached Gariath.

"There are only so many tulwar in the world at any one time," he said. "No one is quite sure of the number, but there are never more nor less than this number. When an old man in the Rua Tong dies, a breath later, a baby girl in the Chee Chree is born. Different bodies, same Tul. Tul is the individual and the collective. This, they say, is what makes the tulwar eternal. What is not finished in this life will be finished in the next."

He looked up at Gariath. Those keen eyes lingered on him for a long moment. Then he puffed a cloud of smoke and turned to walk away.

"Or it could all be oxshit, who knows."

He began to shamble away. And Gariath would have been glad to let him do so, one more insipid old fool among many, if not for one thing. In the moments when the old tulwar sucked on his pipe, the lapses in smoke revealed a peculiar scent. Not anger, not fear, not anything pleasant.

And he had smelled nothing like it before.

"But that's insane," Gariath suddenly called out.

The old tulwar stopped, but did not look back.

"The world is not kind. It's full of weaklings, cowards, morons, all of whom would eagerly kill you to feast upon your carcass." He narrowed his eyes, loosed a low growl. "People betray you. People lie to you. You can trust no one and blood is all that you're guaranteed. If the Tul continues to return you to such a shitty world, then it's no blessing. It only gets worse."

At this the old tulwar looked over his shoulder. He grinned, his yellow teeth showing. "That was precisely the line of thinking that led to the Uprising."

"You know of it, then."

"Every tulwar does."

"Then tell me of it. Or enough of it that I understand how it turned them all into weaklings."

The old tulwar turned to face him. He knuckled his lower back, straightening up with a pop. This was a creature who had been powerful in his prime, someone strong and tall.

"Understand that fate has not been kind to the tulwar of the desert," the old tulwar said. "At all times are we pushed. North is the Lyre, south is endless desert. Shicts to the east, humans to the west, sun from above and no water below. The humans had just swept into our lands to take what we had to farm their rice. A bold move, but our trade with them brought us blankets, steel, things we couldn't get on our own.

"We thought it fair enough. We lend our service to the humans, they give us what we need to fight the shicts. But while we were watching the forests to the east, the humans took more from us. Still, we thought nothing of it. Whatever they grew on that land they would sell to us. Rice was cheap."

The old tulwar's smile grew grim, the kind one wore after a joke told at a funeral.

"But if you've been among humans, as you say, you know what happened next. They raised the price on rice, meat, silk, everything. We could not pay and they had no more work that needed doing. What could we do but starve?"

"You could fight," Gariath growled.

"Some said that."

"The Rua Tong?"

"You would think so, wouldn't you? The Rua Tong are brave warriors. Heroes, even." The old tulwar plucked his pipe from his lips. "Heroes, though, are made for stories. They have people to rescue, golden ages of peace to usher in, dragons to slay." He eyed Gariath sidelong as he emptied the ashes onto the floor. "No offense."

Gariath merely snorted in reply.

"But once the dragons are dead and people are safe, no one has use for a hero. They have fields to till, children to raise, swine to herd. Heroes can pick up a sword and slay anything of flesh and blood. How do you ask them to kill coin and contracts?

"Trade disputes don't make for good stories," the old tulwar said. "So the clans turned to the thinkers, the intelligent among themselves."

"I saw little of that," Gariath replied.

"You wouldn't have. They were absent from tonight's meeting."

"These . . . Mak Lak Kai?"

The old tulwar stifled a chuckle. "One turns to the Mak Lak Kai when one has a death wish."

Gariath narrowed his eyes, racking his mind for the name of the other clan. It came to him in a whisper. "The Muusa Gon clan."

The old tulwar nodded slowly. "They called themselves the philosophers, the great thinkers. It was they and their *Humn* that said Tul meant something different."

He raised his right hand, held up a finger and drew a circle from right to left.

"Not serenity."

He raised his left hand, reversed the gesture and drew a circle from left to right.

"But suffering. The other clans agreed. And thus . . ."

"The Uprising," Gariath finished.

"You stand here in the monument to our decay, so I trust you know how it ended." He plucked a pouch from a fold in his robes, emptied a few pinches of tobacco into his palm. "And you seem smart enough to understand why the clans would be reluctant to walk that path again."

"Almost," Gariath replied. "From what I heard, the Uprising went to the very heart of the city. I have seen it. I know how vulnerable it is. Victory was within their grasp. Why did they relent?"

The old tulwar paused. For a long moment, he did not say anything, merely staring at the tobacco in his palm. Slowly he packed it into his pipe, struck a match produced from his pouch, and lit it. He took several long puffs.

"It was the *Humn* of the Muusa Gon who led the Uprising," he said, at last. "Mototaru, they called him. First inside the city. First to gaze upon it. First to climb the Silken Spire and stare out over it. His was the hand that clutched the torch ready to set the city ablaze."

"And?"

"And he did not. He climbed down, put the torch out, turned around, and left without a word."

Gariath loosed a low growl.

If the old tulwar spoke the truth, if the leader of the Uprising had left his following without a leader or a plan, its pitiful showing against the *Drokha* made more sense. Stupid sense, but sense.

And yet something nagged at him enough to demand that he speak again.

"He stared out across the city. What did he see?"

The old tulwar offered a thoughtful look. "You have been there. What did *you* see?"

"Wealth. Greed. Gluttony. Fear."

"Perhaps he saw something different." The old tulwar took a long drag on his pipe, then turned around. "Or perhaps something that you did not. Either way, it does not matter."

He began to walk away. His back bent with each step, his feet dragged, he became someone very old, very weak, a shadow that diminished with each step as he walked off into the night.

"What happened to the leader?" Gariath called after him. "What happened to Mototaru?"

"Dead," the old tulwar replied. "Like so many."

"Will he return?" Gariath asked before the idiocy of the question struck him. "Under this Tul?"

"Not if he had a choice," the old tulwar said. "After all, he agreed with you." He raised his left hand, drew a circle in the air. "It only gets worse."

NINETEEN

A Breath Withheld

The fire burned.

Lenk knew this. He had gathered the wood from the cliffs. He had struck the blaze with the tinder he had salvaged. He had cleared the sand from the rock he sat upon. Yet he knew all this only because he remembered doing these things.

He could not smell the smoke. He could not feel the warmth. His entire body felt numb, bloodless.

Kataria was not there. Not at the fire. She sat upon the crest of a dune nearby, a shadow painted black against the light of the moon. Here the landscape was dotted with scrubgrass and thorny brambles, forest and desert forever battling. She looked like just one more prickly shrub among them all. Her ears were aloft, erect, listening.

Just twenty paces away. He could have called out to her, walked to her, yet the very thought made him weary.

His head still reeled from what she had told him. Her disappearances, the Howling, the betrayal, the name Kwar; he knew things only in fragments, jagged shards that lay upon the ground and that he couldn't even pick up, let alone piece together. Yet he knew, all the same.

She had betrayed him.

In ways he couldn't even count.

She had departed shortly thereafter, ostensibly to scrounge up food. She hadn't made it far. Nor did it matter. His body was weak from hunger, yet the very thought of eating left him nauseous. What would it have changed?

And so he sat there, with the fire he could not feel and the smoke he could not smell, staring into its blazing embers and wondering if it would hurt if he thrust himself headfirst into the flames.

Something happened. The wind shifted, maybe. Or the sand stirred. Or a cloud raced briefly across the moon or some shit. Lenk didn't know. Lenk didn't know when Mocca had shown up to sit beside him. Hell, he hadn't even known Mocca could show up without making some smart-ass comment.

Yet there the man—or the demon, or the God-King, whatever he was—sat, silent and staring into the fire without a word. A long moment of one-sided conversation between them and the fire passed, the flames sputtering in indignation at their silence.

When the quiet broke, it was Lenk who broke it. And his voice cut itself on the shards left behind.

"Salvaged a map from the riverbank," he said. He made a show of jabbing the fire with a stick. "The Forbidden East is within a day's walk. It's all jungle from there on in, so we'll need—" He caught himself swallowing hard. "Some supplies and ... and shit."

Mocca merely nodded.

"Figure we can just follow the river." He pointed with the stick to the east. The dark shapes of trees loomed in the distance. "Should be safe this far up, I think. I figure if the shicts or tulwar were going to come back, they'd have done so by now. There are only four..." He caught himself, coughed. "Three, sorry. Three of us left. We should be okay, right?"

Again Mocca nodded.

"Right," Lenk confirmed to himself. "Shuro said she could probably find some more food. A lot of the supplies washed up on the banks. If we spend a little time looking for it and find enough, we can fuck, fuck, fucking fuck it all. Gods fucking *DAMN IT.*"

With each roar he struck the stick against the ground, until it shattered in his hand and left splinters in his flesh. When it was nothing but a nub, he still waved it, his rage not yet spent. And so his anger leaked out of his eyes in tears.

"She made a fool out of me," he said, sucking air through clenched teeth. "She betrayed me. She killed gods know how many and I should have fucking seen it and I didn't and she was fucking a ... a *woman* the whole fucking time and ... and ..."

He hurled the nub into the fire. His hand trembled, as though he instantly regretted it, before it clutched at his scalp. His head sank with such force it might well have snapped right off his neck.

"First the Khovura," he said. "Then Cier'Djaal goes to war. Then the Forbidden East. Now this. What did I do wrong? Which god did I piss off so bad?" He shook his head. "Even when we left, I didn't care so much. I didn't mind holding the sword again, because I thought that's not what made me a man. I thought I could have the sword, live with what it did, so long as I had her.

"She was what made me a man. Maybe the only thing." His sigh came out wet and shuddering. "When did I fuck it all up?"

Silence was his answer. The fire crackled, the night settled silently over him.

For only a moment more.

"When you bound your life to hers."

He had almost forgotten Mocca was there. When he looked up, the man in white was staring into the fire, but his eyes did not reflect its glow.

"All your myths and legends about how mortal races were born," he mused, "and all of them celebrate your weakness. The gods gave you strength you didn't have, life you didn't deserve, they say. But I saw the first mortals crawl out of the mud. And when you stood up, you were whole. You were complete. Like any other animal."

There was an immense age in Mocca's voice, and it settled like the heel of a well-worn boot on a broken neck.

"It is not other people that make you complete, no more than it is other dogs that make a dog complete. They may assist in the hunt, join you in scavenging in trash, but no matter how many you surround yourself with, you will always just be one." He looked at Lenk. His eyes drank the light of the flames. "And if you are only a human conditionally, then you never were one."

Only then did Lenk remember that Mocca was not a man.

Not a human, not a hallucination, not even a nightmare. He was something more, something old and terrible, something that had watched stars die and heard the cries of mountains being born. He had heard the death rattles of mortals immeasurable and had eternities to do so.

And he was here right now. And listening.

"What do I do?" Lenk asked.

"That is the wrong question." Mocca turned back to the fire. "If you do not exist without her, then any choice you make is irrelevant. You will either die or you will not, depending on what she does."

Lenk followed his gaze to the flames. "What's the right question?"

"What do you want?"

Lenk considered this. He stared into the fire until his eyes hurt. After a very long time, he spoke.

"I want," he said, "for it not to hurt anymore."

"You want life."

"I do."

"Then you must let go."

"Of what?"

"Of everything. Life in thralldom—be it to god, blade, or another person—is not a life. It is a comfort, something to numb you so long as you can cling to it. It is safety, but it is fragile and weak, something you crush and watch fall limp on the ground. Freedom, true freedom, is terrifying.

"I have read your poems and heard your songs. Mortals always speak of freedom as the feeling of wind in their hair or arms wrapped around someone warm and soft. But I have felt imprisonment and I have felt freedom. And I can tell you this."

He turned his stare to Lenk and the young man could feel himself slipping into the emptiness of Mocca's stare, like the last drops of water past the lips of a man long dying of thirst.

"When you are free, Lenk, all you will feel is the last sour breath as you look over a yawning nothingness where the world used to be."

Lenk felt his breath grow heavier. "Then what?"

A smile, soft and sad, tugged at the edges of Mocca's mouth. "Then you jump."

The fire sputtered. The shadows shifted. And Mocca shifted with them, growing hazy and insubstantial. Clouds of smoke wafted through his body, taking pieces of him with them as they disappeared into the night sky, until there was nothing left of him.

A log crumbled and the fire, an old man roused from a nap, roared back to life. Lenk looked up and saw her.

Skin cast red by the flame, eyes golden with its light, Kataria stood at the edge of the shadows. How long she had been there, what she might have heard, he did not know. Her face betrayed nothing, numb and painted with flickering shadows.

"Hey," he said, after a long moment.

"Hey," she replied.

He looked at her collarbone, her hip, her left ankle, anywhere that was not her eyes or her long, twitching ears. When he finally ran out of places to look, he turned his attentions back to the fire.

"Find anything?" he asked.

"Yeah, uh," she began, awkwardly taking a seat opposite the fire, "there's some fruit that grows in some of the trees here. She said"—she caught herself—"I hear they're safe to eat." She blinked. "I forgot to bring them."

"Ah."

He said nothing. For a very long time, he said nothing. And only when a very long time became an hour or more did he realize that he was afraid to speak.

But why? he wondered. What could possibly happen? Was he simply going to look up and see her there, giggling, before she jumped up and said, "Surprise, you dumb fucker! I never did any of that!"

He closed his eyes. He swallowed something cold and heavy. His mind racked itself for something to say to her, but he couldn't think of anything but a singular word, repeated over and over and over.

Why?

In a dozen ways, he asked it.

What did I do wrong? What's wrong with me? How could you do this? What happened over those six days?

And each time his mind wandered to an answer, he shivered. And each time he shivered, he felt the empty space beside him. Mocca would have known what to ask. Mocca would have known the answers. Wispy and insubstantial as he was, he would have known.

Mocca's not here, he told himself. *This isn't something Mocca can solve. This isn't something that anyone can solve but you. Just say something. Say something now, you dumb fuck. Say something. Say something. Say—*

"It wasn't you."

She spoke first. Her voice was flat, but not hard. Not a knife cutting a wound, just a stone. An immutable fact of life.

Why did it hurt, then?

"I mean, it was," Kataria continued, fingers brushing one of the feathers in her hair. "You wanted a new life in Cier'Djaal and I couldn't go with you and I thought..." She shook her head. "But it wasn't. I didn't mean for it to..."

She buried her face in her hands, let loose a long breath.

"But it did."

"How?" The word stumbled out of his mouth before he was even aware of his lips parting. "How did it happen?"

"I don't fucking know." She looked up at him. Her eyes glistened. Her mouth trembled. She held her hands out helplessly. "It just...did."

"Oxshit." He rose to his feet. "*Ox. Shit.* That doesn't just happen. There had to have been something." He paced back and forth, searching for an answer in the dirt. "There was a...a problem somewhere. I didn't pay close enough attention, we didn't do—"

"Don't you think I already went through this?" she interrupted, voice straining. "Don't you think I sat there, wondering whose fault this was? Don't you think it *killed* me when I realized it wasn't anyone's?"

"But..." He clutched his head, as if there were something there that would answer all of this if he could just wrench it out. "With a *woman*? Another woman? How is that even—"

"Lenk," she said, "don't. Please."

It was not her voice that did it. There was no threat there, no hardness. What was in her words, just those three words, was something soft, something tender, something so fragile and vulnerable that he could have simply reached out and crushed it in one hand.

And that part of her belonged to someone else now.

He looked at her. Tears fell from her eyes. She trembled, refusing to acknowledge them. And he did the same, turning his eyes up to the sky. The moon was beginning its descent now.

"Four hours until dawn. I'm going to bed," he said, pointing to somewhere away from the fire. "Over there. I'm going to close my eyes for three and a half." He looked back to her just one more time. "When I open them, you'll either be here or you won't."

She opened her mouth, as if she wanted to say something else, but looked down at her feet as he turned and walked away.

Perhaps there was more he could have said. Perhaps there was more he could have done. Perhaps there was something so perfect, so elegant, so painfully and poetically true that he could have simply spoken it and all of this would have been fixed.

Perhaps Mocca would have known.

But Mocca was not here. There was no answer. There was nothing more to say. And when he opened his mouth to speak, all he tasted was a single sour breath.

ACT TWO

A ROAD OF COLD WATER

TWENTY

Kings and Pilgrims

The Five Hundredth Year
Majeno Daro

I lost her today.

This, in itself, should not be so remarkable. I have seen thousands die. Occasionally in a single day. Thousands were dead before I set foot upon this dark earth and thousands more die in the dominions I cannot control, in the bleak realms of Ulbecetonth and Raskansha. Those do not bother me.

Why should they? The mortal frame, after all, is exactly what it sounds like. It is a fragile, breakable, corruptible thing made of tender meats and porcelain bones. They came to peace with this early in their years and it seems to trouble them not at all, given the rate at which they kill each other. This does not bother me, either.

Indeed, none of this should bother me.

And yet . . .

I lost her today.

A child. Not especially more fragile than her friends. Not prone to illness, despite what befell her. From what I knew of her, she was exceedingly aver-age: obeyed her mother and father, skinned her knee frequently, burned her hand in the fire once when she was too young to know better.

The disease that claimed her, too, was nothing I had not seen before. The cough was more persistent in her than it was in most children her age, but it seemed to be nothing overtly alarming. The medicine I prepared to counter this was slightly stronger than the average dose, but nothing particularly dangerous. I anticipated a positive response and a quick recovery.

I did everything right.

And I still lost her.

Just like that. I attended her house to check in on her and found her mother and father on their knees on the stone, wailing and screaming and looking at me as if I could have done something. As if I had done nothing.

And... I couldn't tell them anything. Nothing beyond what I already knew.

The dose was correct for the illness, I am certain. I am absolutely *certain. The medicine has worked a hundred thousand times on a hundred thousand different mortals. Everything about it should have worked. It was* supposed *to work.*

Yet there she was, in her bed, not breathing or moving. And her parents were on the floor, beseeching me, begging me to return her. And I, whom they had called God-King, could but stare down at them, my hands empty and my mouth empty.

And through all this, the girl's grandmother was tranquil. She merely sat in her chair and stared out the window. Was she unaware that she had just lost a granddaughter? Had she simply not cared for the child? Why was she not beseeching me? Cursing me? Looking to me?

I stepped over the girl's parents to ask the grandmother. And she merely smiled at me and spoke to me in this calm, gentle manner. Her words still ring in my ears.

"I loved her dearly," she said. "I am sad to see her go," she said. "But if she had to go, then she had to go," she said. "It is simply how things are."

She said.

With such insufferable serenity as to suggest she knew something I didn't. With such infuriating ignorance as to suggest that this was the right answer. With such... such arrogance *that I felt myself shaking just to look at her.*

Her, so fragile, so weak, with age bending her back and skin drawn tight. Her, who would have died at the hands of rapists or worked herself in the field, had it not been for me. Without my city, my law, my labor, *she would be dead, and she presumed to speak to me as though she knew something I didn't.*

But it is not her fault.

We were sent to assure their faith, to make their grievances known. But in doing so, we have merely reinforced their ignorance. We have emboldened them to look at death and shrug their shoulders. We have taught them to take comfort in the inevitable. We have taught them to believe in a flawed design.

It is not their fault.

It is the fault of those above, who look away when they speak their prayers. Those above, who do not so much as hear them. And this grandmother, this frail, insignificant insect of a woman, presumes to speak to them? I cannot help her. Her ignorance is too deep. She will only hinder me.

It is her parents I must aid. Those who scream and wail and bleed for me, who hold out their hands and pray to me, who clutch the hem of my robe and weep and beg me to change things.

I cannot fail them.

I have grown too idle, too lax. I was content to look at them all as one monolithic entity, mortalkind. I did not look at the intricacies of their systems, their bodies, their organs.

Corpses can no longer be trusted to yield anything of value. I will ask Oerboros to speak to the slaves, select from them one weak, one ill, one healthy, one strong—from each race: tulwar, human, shict. I will ask Kyrael to speak to the Disciples, bring me more subjects. Their bodies will tell me where I failed, tell me how to improve, how to prevent this from happening again.

Their families will be compensated for their suffering. One way or another.

> *From the annals of His Word,*
> *First and Final Testament of He Who Cured the Ill,*
> *God-King Khoth-Kapira*

TWENTY-ONE

THE ORACLE

So," Liaja said after a moment's study, "it's a dog?"

Dreadaeleon cracked open an eye. Sunlight seeping through the shutters made his vision hazy, but he could see the silk of her robe clinging to her back as she leaned over the abomination in the corner.

Admiral Tibbles, despite being at least partly made of male genitalia, appeared unfazed by the attentions of a beautiful woman.

"Yes," he said. "It's a dog. In the same way a nebulous fluctuation of unstable energies stitched together by flesh and sinew might be called a cat."

Liaja looked over her shoulder, a playful smile across her face. "No need to get snippy. I was curious." She turned her attentions back to Admiral Tibbles. "You can hardly blame me. They call it a Charnel Hound, after all. And it *acts* like a dog."

What dogs she had seen that Admiral Tibbles would remind her of them, he dreaded even thinking about.

Admiral Tibbles, for its part, didn't seem to mind Liaja's attentions. It sat on its haunches, staring eyelessly forward, watching Dreadaeleon whenever he rose out of bed, following him when he went to use the privy, staring at him whenever Liaja turned her affections to him.

It didn't *really* get weird until that last part.

The thing didn't even have eyes, but Dreadaeleon had the distinct impression that it watched him more intently when he was intimate with Liaja.

Not that she seemed to mind any more than Admiral Tibbles did. She had reacted with fear, at first, then revulsion. Now she was curiously patting its head, scratching what she thought was its belly, frowning with disappointment all the while.

"It doesn't seem like a very friendly dog, though," she mused. "Can it do tricks?"

"It can," Dreadaeleon replied, reclining on the bed's mess of silk sheets. "It can track a wizard for a hundred leagues, emerge from the most brutal spells unscathed, and snap bone and rend flesh as though they were paper."

"Yes, but can it fetch?"

He blinked. "Yes. Yes, it fetches heretics and other violators of law every day, have you not been listening?"

"But what makes it do that and not, say, roll over?" Liaja inquired, turning back to Admiral Tibbles. "What controls it?"

"Its command scroll." At her curious look, he gestured to the creature. "Somewhere within its innards—the innards that its outsides *aren't* made of—is a scroll upon which its commands are written."

"A scroll?"

"Yes. Made from wizard skin, the scroll determines how far it can range, who it follows, what actions it will permit its charge to take, and so forth. For example..."

He flicked his fingers. His eyes glowed red with a hint of power. Stray sparks danced across his fingertips.

And instantly Admiral Tibbles rose to its feet. The Charnel Hound turned its sightless gaze upon Dreadaeleon and visibly tensed. Liaja gasped and took a step backward. Dreadaeleon released the spell, letting the energy fade away. Slowly Admiral Tibbles resumed its sitting position.

"The scroll instructs it to monitor expulsions of energy from me under certain circumstances," Dreadaeleon said. "Had I unleashed anything, it'd have torn me to pieces."

"But how does it know?" Liaja inched closer to the creature. "Can it read the scroll? Who writes it? Do they know what you just did?"

"The scroll is integrated with the Charnel Hound's innards, communicating with it the same way a body communicates with everything else," Dreadaeleon continued, "and there are a class of specialist flesh-crafters who..."

His voice trailed off as he became aware of a distant sound. A faint ringing in his ears that grew annoyingly louder set his teeth on edge. He growled, shook his head to dismiss it.

"Who do what?" Liaja asked.

"Since when did you become interested in this, anyway?" Dreadaeleon replied, more snappishly than he had intended.

"It's magic. Should I not be?" Liaja rolled her eyes as she rose and approached him. "What a charmed life you must lead that a dog made of cocks can seem mundane."

"Need I remind you this thing is little more than a living shackle designed to hobble me? I imagine the bars of any prison seem exotic to someone seeing them for the first time."

Liaja looked toward the window, the sunlight streaming in. "Yes, I imagine they might."

A fleeting look. One she attempted to obscure by discreetly turning her face. But he caught it.

They came more frequently now, these looks. Sorrow and fear and worry where once she had worn gentle smiles only for him. In the days before this—the Venarium, the war, everything—she had never worn such looks.

Or had he simply never noticed?

"Speaking of," she said before he could voice such a thought, "does the Venarium approve of you being here?"

He hesitated. Just long enough for suspicion to cross her features.

"Of course," he said. "Why wouldn't they?"

"I witnessed your battle in the square," she replied, "as much as I could bear to." She tugged at her sleeve. "It was vicious. Some of the girls, they huddled in their rooms at the sound, so frightened were they."

"It was a misunderstanding."

"It didn't look like a mis—"

"Oh, for *fuck's sake*, Liaja." He groaned, sitting up in the bed and rubbing his face. "I have had few enough hours free of imbeciles and authoritarians in the past week that I could count them on one hand. If you can't quell your insipid curiosity for at least one more, could you at least trust me when I say you have nothing to worry about?"

And the look was there again.

No longer fleeting, nor discreet. Her eyes went wide, her mouth hung open. She turned away, her gaze directed to the floor, as though she had just been struck.

He winced. He hadn't meant to do that.

But what choice did he have? The more she knew about the Venarium, the more danger for her. The Venarium intended to turn on him—he knew they would—and he wanted her to be of no use to them, to give them no reason to seek her out and turn her against him.

Of course, if you had really thought that, you wouldn't have sought her out in the first place, would you?

The ringing in his ears returned. It grew louder with each thought.

Had you really cared for her, you would have just let her be. But no, you had to see her. You had to show her that the Venarium couldn't hold you, didn't you?

The noise sprawled like a serpent in his head. He could feel it tighten in his skull, suffocate his thoughts in heated coils.

And why shouldn't you? Why should you apologize for being able to do what others cannot? The Venarium think you're a criminal, Asper thinks you're a pawn. But they need you. Their plans hinge on you. You're the one who will save everyone. She should know that. She should be on her fucking knees and—

He shook his head, trying to shake free whatever had nestled inside his thoughts. The ringing dissipated only after severe shaking.

Too hard to think. His mind was full of fog, bats, and whatever else the broodvine had left in there.

The broodvine.

How long had it been since he'd had it? Days? Weeks? How long had he been free from the Venarium's cell? He needed it. Needed it to think. Just a few seeds. He needed the clarity of fantasy, the freedom that came from knowing that nothing was real.

"Your body may have a few hours to spend with me, but your mind is clearly elsewhere, *northern boy*."

Those last words, always uttered so affectionately before, carried scorn when Liaja spoke them. And when he looked up, the look she shot him was not quite so fleeting, not quite so hidden, and filled with not merely dread.

"And from the look in your eyes," she said softly, "I have much to worry about."

He turned from her. "Exhaustion," he said. "Mere exhaustion."

"It is not mere exhaustion," she replied sharply. "I am not a mere woman." She gestured to their surroundings. "*This* is not a mere home

I am tending while the man of the house is away on business. This is a bathhouse, Dreadaeleon. And I have seen your eyes on the faces of any number of hungry, empty men who come here to sate themselves."

And at that he erupted from the bed. Exhaustion fled him, his naked body trembling with the force that crackled up through his being and into his eyes. Power, crimson and ethereal, wafted from his eyes.

Admiral Tibbles was on its feet, staring at him intently, waiting for him to move. He did not care about that. Liaja stepped away from him. And he cared nothing for the fear in her eyes, the way she tried to close herself off with her arms.

She's afraid of you, old man.

The coils around his skull tightened.

She should *be afraid of you.*

"Do *not* presume to speak to me of meres, woman." He advanced. She trembled. "Do not presume that I am anything like any number of any snatch-sucking, barknecked swine that have come in here rutting for whores."

He reached out for her. His hands shook around her skin, sensing the tension therein before he ever touched them.

"Can't you see?" he asked, voice hoary and desperate. "Can't you see what I am? They're afraid of me. The Venarium. They turned me out because they thought I'd die out here. But if they fear me, I can escape them. I can leave this whole city behind. I can take you *with* me, Liaja."

"I..." The fear fled her eyes, and left behind was something colder and appraising. "It's not that simple, Dread—northern boy." She shook her head. "It's not. I was bought by this bathhouse. I have a debt."

"I can pay it off," he said. "There are ways. I can find them. I can find money, I can turn lead into gold. Fuck, I could just fly out of here with you, anytime I wanted."

"It's...no." She turned away from him. "It can't be like that."

"Why not?" His voice rose into a whine. He seized her by the shoulders, whirled her around to face him. "Why *not*?"

Her skin was cold under his touch. She turned about without a hint of resistance, a cold dead fish that flopped limply in his hands. As though she were trying to play dead.

"Because," she replied, eyes brimming with tears, "you scare the shit out of me."

His breath left him. All earthly sensation followed. What remained in him was something crackling, bristling, and stoked to a raging fury within him.

The power. The Venarie. The magic. It flowed through him—fire in his breath, lightning at his fingertips, ice in his stare. It fought to tear itself out of his hand as he pressed it to her face.

Her face.

Like porcelain.

Like glass.

Too fragile to hold back the fear coursing through her. Too stiff to turn away from him. Too weak, too strong; he needed her, he hated her, he couldn't live without her, he couldn't stand to be with her another moment.

The ringing in his ears grew loud.

Her lips moved, but he couldn't hear her. He shut his eyes, shut his ears. And then...

She was gone.

Where was she? Where had she gone? He had held her, a thing of trembling glass, and now...

The ringing in his ears faded.

He opened his eyes.

In his hands was a man.

A man whose dark Karnerian skin was pale with fright, whose eyes were staring up at him with a fear he wouldn't have shown his god. This man was kneeling before him. Dreadaeleon's hands were around his throat. His hands were slick with blood.

He tasted air stale with ash on his breath. He smelled fire and electricity. The sun was bright, too bright for morning. The air was cold and the bodies...

The bodies were everywhere.

Karnerians. Their black armor was curled and smoking from flame, split apart by lightning, impaled by icicles still lodged in their chests. They littered the cobblestones of the small square, tangled amid shattered shields and splintered spears.

But that was impossible. He had just been in the bathhouse. He had just been with Liaja. He had heard her, felt her, smelled her.

The broodvine. The hallucinations.

Had it all been a dream? Or...was this the dream? No. He could hear the crackle of fires smoldering, feel the chill and the electricity, smell the char.

At least fifty. All dead. And at the center of the destruction, staring eyeless and impassive, was Admiral Tibbles. The Charnel Hound did not so much as move. It had watched, it knew just as he knew that he had killed these men.

Despite having no memory of it.

"Mad." The man was talking. Dreadaeleon had almost forgotten about him. "You're a madman!"

Given the circumstances, Dreadaeleon found himself hard-pressed to deny that.

"There are treaties! Laws! You can't just...just..."

Oh. He was talking about something else.

"My brothers." The Karnerian's voice was choked, thick with sobbing. "They were my *brothers*. And you...you did..."

Words failed him, so he tore a dagger free from his belt. Unfortunately, the dagger, too, would fail him.

Jolts of electricity leapt from Dreadaeleon's fingertips and into the man's scalp. The Karnerian twitched, as though whatever candle burned within his head had suddenly been snuffed out, and simply slumped over, coils of steam rising from his body and carrying the smell of burnt hair.

He glanced to Admiral Tibbles. The Charnel Hound's command scroll had been made by an art unknown to Dreadaeleon, but it doubtless permitted slaughter like this, as per the terms of his release.

But that didn't make the dead man in Dreadaeleon's hands any less offensive.

Gruesome, Dreadaeleon noted, glancing around. *Not half as gruesome as what you've done here, though.* He winced at the scattered corpses. *You did do this, didn't you, old man?*

Perhaps he had. But why couldn't he remember it?

It had to be the broodvine.

But how? The hallucinations, he had been controlling them—or so he thought. He had been days without the seed. He couldn't have smoked so much that it had affected him so deeply, could he?

And yet he couldn't recall how he had gotten here. Or even why he would be here. Much less how he had killed fifty men.

It would seem to make sense. The Venarium *had* released him for precisely this purpose, hadn't they?

But he couldn't trust them. Because he knew they didn't trust him.

Of course, he thought. *Why would they trust you and your judgment when they could simply control you through some magic? Who knows how many wizards they have at their disposal to do just that?* He gritted his teeth. *Dominating another person is not an easy task, but it can be done... can't it? It must be. How else could they—*

He forced his thoughts quiet. He forced his breath to slow. He closed his eyes, let his arms hang limp at his sides. When his head stopped pounding and his mind ceased to throb, he let his senses extend and began to search.

Magic had to come from somewhere. Its presence left changes upon the world. Introducing more fire raised temperatures, altering the pressures of the air induced headaches, and so forth. Dreadaeleon merely had to reach out and see what he could sense.

There.

Sixty degrees to the west. One hundred and twenty-three feet ahead, twenty-six feet up. And close. So very close. Fluctuations of hot and cold washed over him in violent tides. Power was being spent without a single care for who knew.

A sound caught his attention. He glanced to the center of the square. Admiral Tibbles was on its feet, its eyeless gaze turned to the edge of the square.

One hundred and twenty-three feet away and twenty-six feet up.

The hairs of the back of his neck stood on end. He felt a tingle at his fingertips. He leapt to the side.

An arc of lightning lashed from the sky, striking the cobblestones where he had stood and leaving behind a black smear.

He looked up and saw his assailant. Upon the roof of a nearby building stood a thin body wrapped in a black cloak, a hood pulled over its features. It looked like something out of the stories that barknecks told each other about wizards.

A posturing amateur, he thought. He pulled back his sleeve, leveled two fingers up at the roof. *Let's show him how it's done, old man.* He called the lightning to his fingertips, felt the energy seep through his stare. *Let's show him—*

He never finished that thought.

As it happened, it was hard to think when a hundred pounds of embalmed organs smashed into one.

"Get off me!" Dreadaeleon snarled, beating at the flesh of Admiral Tibbles. "Get the fuck *off* me!"

The Charnel Hound seemed in no mood to indulge his plea, bearing down upon him with all its weight. That was obnoxious, but really it was the pedantry that annoyed Dreadaeleon.

"You're fine with me killing fifty men but not shooting one wizard?"

Admiral Tibbles had no means of retorting and Dreadaeleon's wriggling over onto his stomach seemed a poor counter. He felt Tibbles seize the tails of his coat, as if attempting to drag him elsewhere. With a little effort, he shrugged free of the garment. With a little magic expended, he pushed the air behind him, launching himself off the stones and away from the Hound.

And with fury and power burning in his eyes, he whirled on the creature.

Admiral Tibbles was already rushing toward him, loping along the stones and leaping over bodies.

No sense in wasting anything on a direct attack. His eyes desperately searched the square for anything of use. All around him, all he could see were shattered armaments and mangled bodies.

He called the power to his hand, reached out with a grasp that extended beyond mere flesh. The air rippled around one of the Karnerian carcasses as an invisible grip seized the body. He flung his arm forward and the magic followed, hurling the limp body across the square at the Charnel Hound.

The creature nimbly darted beneath it, picking up speed. Dreadaeleon reached out again, seized and hurled a fallen shield. It struck the beast, staggering it for but a moment before it continued its rush. Dreadaeleon gritted his teeth.

Think, old man, think.

He looked around the field, spotted a shattered spear. He reached out, seized it, pulled it toward him. Admiral Tibbles burst into a frenzied charge. Dreadaeleon waited until the Charnel Hound had drawn close enough, waited until it leapt to tackle him to the ground, and…

Now.

He made a gesture, brought the spear up before him, leveled the head upward and the butt toward the earth. Admiral Tibbles struck the weapon chest-first, sliding soundlessly down its shaft and bearing the weapon to the ground. Dreadaeleon acted quickly, seizing another spear with magical grip and jamming it through the creature's flank.

Impaled crosswise, Admiral Tibbles flopped haplessly upon the ground, struggling to gain footing against its clumsy position. Dreadaeleon allowed himself a brief, black chuckle.

His mind soon turned to other problems and his eyes followed, looking to the rooftops to search for the hooded wizard and finding only shingles and empty air.

Think you can run from me, you little shit?

He didn't even need to close his eyes to sense the wizard. He was expelling magic at a rapid pace, probably in an attempt to put as much distance between himself and Dreadaeleon as possible.

He'd be easy to track and weak when Dreadaeleon finally caught up to him.

He set off. Despite the unfamiliarity of this district of the city, the reek of expended magic all but dragged him through the winding alleys and streets, unerringly toward his quarry.

And through each pulse of pressure, each fluctuation of temperature, his fury grew. Caution fled him. In its wake power grew: thunder at his hands and fire on his tongue.

Just when his body felt fit to explode, he found his target. Trapped between two tall buildings, the hooded wizard hopped up and down, groping feebly for the top of a wall separating this district from the next. Dreadaeleon smiled cruelly, striding into the alley after him.

"Can't lift yourself, can you?" he spoke loudly, his voice reverberating with power waiting to be unleashed.

The hooded wizard whirled at the sound, pressed himself against the wall. He thrust his fingers out threateningly. But Dreadaeleon could see the tremble in his arms, the buckling of his knees. This boy was drained.

"Too much energy spent fleeing," he said, continuing forward. "And how much did you spend controlling me in the first place? Couldn't have been easy."

"Stay back, murderer," the wizard proclaimed.

The quaver in his voice was followed by a word of power. It was uttered feebly and accompanied by shaky posture, and the lightning bolt that flew from his fingers went wide, flying well over Dreadaeleon's head without his even ducking.

"Murderer?" Dreadaeleon asked. "Is that what this is?" He let out a thoughtful hum. "Are you here on a mission of vengeance?"

"You…you betrayed the Venarium," the wizard said. "Fuck protocol. You *killed* our own and somehow you're still free."

"You're pissing words instead of soil, but it reeks all the same," Dreadaeleon interrupted. "Spare me your packaged rhetoric and tell me who sent you. Annis? Palanis?"

The wizard shook for a moment before responding by opening his mouth and breathing out a cone of white mist. An icicle the size of a dagger coalesced, flew at Dreadaeleon with a wave of the wizard's hand.

Dreadaeleon merely extended his own limbs, spreading his hands out. The air rippled and the icicle struck a wall of force, shattering into shards that melted as he passed.

"I hadn't expected better, but I had expected something more clever. Assassination is so…straightforward." He chuckled. "I'd be less insulted had they sent someone slightly less inept."

Dreadaeleon held his palm out. Fire blossomed upon his skin, stoking itself to a great, crackling flame. The hooded wizard's hands were up, not in magical gesture but in plaintive pleading. He was speaking something that went unheard over the roar of flames.

"I had hoped to send a message with your failure," Dreadaeleon said. "Perhaps I'll spell it out with whatever ashes remain."

He felt the heat of the flames crackling against his skin. He felt the smoke choking his nostrils. He heard the roar of flames.

And a ringing in his ears grew louder.

He thrust his hand out and promptly felt warm flesh encircling it.

"Thank you, *shkainai*. Thank you."

The flames were gone. A pair of dark hands covered his own. A man knelt before him, head bowed in gratitude.

"No," Dreadaeleon whispered.

The man muttered praises over and over. The air was warm, with candles burning from chandeliers hanging overhead. Carpet was beneath his bare feet. Walls of polished stone adorned with paintings and expensive art rose up around him. A long silken robe covered his body.

"*No,*" he whispered again.

This was his robe. This was his carpet. This was his home. This man was thanking *him*. He knew this. He felt it.

And he fought to deny it.

"Not now," he whispered, shaking his head. "Not now, I was doing something. I was ... I was ..."

"There, you've seen him and thanked him. Be on your way now, sir. We've matters to attend to."

He looked behind him to the end of the grand room he stood in. In the mouth of a hallway rimmed with curtains, Liaja stood, the silk of her robe mingling with the curtains to make her appear something ethereal. Yet the command in her stare was clear, and the man, after one more bow, headed toward the doors leading out of the room. Two servants stood on hand to open them and see him out.

His servants.

"This one threatened to cut his head on the stones unless he was permitted to see you," Liaja said, chuckling as she came up behind him. Her hands slid around him, drew him close. "I wonder if you'll ever get tired of them coming to spill gratitude at your feet."

Her hands were warm upon his chest. Her lips were soft upon his neck. And he could feel her every breath through the swell of her breasts as she held him closer. It felt familiar, this closeness, as though he had shared it with her a hundred nights before in a place not her bathhouse. The hands around his, the gratitude of the old man: These, too, felt familiar. As if he had known them since ...

Since he had saved Cier'Djaal.

Of course. How long had it been? Days? Weeks, at least. Yet he remembered casting the rivers of flame and scars of lightning that had swallowed the Karnerians and cleaved in twain the Sainites. He could remember the scent of ice in his nostrils from when he had painted the dens of the Khovura and the Jackals in frost, curing Cier'Djaal's undercity of its criminal plague.

The chill of gold as the fashas heaped it at his feet, the slither of silk across his body after the merchants offered him theirs, the women who had clamored for his bed and the men who had looked upon him with envy.

He remembered them all.

No, that didn't happen... His head hurt. *Did it?*

"You are coming to finish supper, aren't you?" Liaja asked, sliding away from him and slinking back down the hall. "I fear the chefs will be insulted if you miss another meal."

"Hardly my concern," he replied without realizing it. "There's yet more to do in the city: stragglers to mop up, thieves to rout, and so forth."

She hummed. "Not all ills can be cured by force, northern boy, no matter how powerful the magic."

"No, they..." He furrowed his brow. "They can't."

But they were. They had been. Magic—his magic—had driven the scum from the city and propped him up on a pedestal. It had called the city to his feet and the city had fallen there, eagerly, chanting his name.

He was the hero.

You are, his mind told him. *You're the hero, old man.* You *saved the city. Not Lenk or Denaos or...*

"Asper."

"Hm?" Liaja turned to look at him.

"Asper, the priestess," he said. "What happened to..."

"Please," Liaja groaned, cringing. "Let's not bring that up again before we're about to eat."

But he knew. From the cold lump that slid down his throat to settle in his stomach, he knew.

He remembered it, everything. Asper—the fear in her eyes, her blood on his hands, the screams torn from her throat as he laughed and asked her who was so weak and helpless and—

"NO!"

He screamed. He turned. He ran.

From his home and from her.

The scenes of wealth became a blur around him as Liaja called after him. But all he could see was the life draining from Asper's body. All he could hear was her screaming, begging, weeping.

Perhaps that was a dream. Perhaps *this* was a dream. Perhaps they were both real. But he would not accept it. Not so easily. He could still hear her screaming.

When a ringing in his ears grew louder.

He struck the doors of his home and tumbled through, headfirst.

His head hurt. The ground beneath him was cold. He was content to live with these two facts alone, his eyes shut and body curled into a little ball. He did not dare open them for fear that he would awake to something worse.

But a slow chill crept into him. Screams faded from his mind, leaving behind only heavy silence that settled down upon him like a stone.

He came to remember the feel of his dirty clothes, his ragged boots, the tangle of his hair. He shivered. His coat was gone. He had left it with Admiral Tibbles, he remembered, when he escaped.

This, then, was reality. Or, at least, something close enough that he could open his eyes.

A house. A wealthy man's house. Carpets marched the length of a polished wood floor. Tapestries of spider's silk adorned every wall and each of them bore the sigil of a thin hand holding a single coin between two fingers. He had seen this sigil before, on the wealthy men who came to Liaja's bathhouse. He recalled the name of the fasha who owned those men.

Mejina.

Dreadaeleon crawled to his hands and knees. Something crunched under him. He looked down and saw glass embedded in the carpet. The shattered window looming over him left little doubt as to where it had come from.

It must have made a hellish racket as he came in. And yet the only noise he heard was the sound of birds chirping in a garden outside. No feet coming up the stairs, no servants raising alarms. The hall was the picture of serenity.

He got to his feet, staggered down the hallway. His head felt too heavy, his neck too thin, as though the former might simply snap off the latter and roll down the hall. And yet the aches in his skull were a clear, coherent pain. The pain, at least, was real.

He forced himself to think of simple things: of one foot in front of the other, of the door at the end of the hall, of turning the knob and opening it and entering the small study within.

So much was dedicated to keeping himself from thought that when he saw the dead body lying cold and drained upon the floor, he couldn't muster more than a blank stare for it.

A wealthy man, if the cut of his clothes and the oil in his hair were any indication.

"Fasha Mejina," he muttered. "You're looking well."

The dead fasha *did* look almost peaceful, the blow that had choked the life from him having come so cleanly and quickly that he'd had no time to do more than open his eyes in surprise, as though he had just received a bill rather than been killed.

Not killed, Dreadaeleon corrected himself. Murdered. He had been strangled.

And Dreadaeleon had probably done it.

Dreams or no, broodvine hallucinations or reality, all these fleeting images and experiences had one thing in common: violence. In each and every one of them, he was hurting or scaring or killing someone or many someones. If even half of what he had seen was true, if even a *third* of these waking nightmares had been real, he had killed many.

So many.

And, for a reason even he didn't understand, all he could do was laugh.

Too perfect, isn't it? he asked himself. *The Venarium will be after you now. You've killed so many. Everything's gone to shit in a single day. It can't just be coincidence, can it?* He looked up to the ceiling. A skylight beamed in the outside world, still blue and bright. *Maybe you'd better start believing in gods, old man.*

That was not the right reaction, he knew. He should be planning his next move, or his escape, or, barring either of those, running around in circles and screaming.

But there was nothing left in him for schemes and panic. All that remained inside him was in his feet, forcing him to trudge wearily out of the room, down the stairs, and out the door of Mejina's household.

A ringing in his ears grew louder.

But he was used to it by now.

He was greeted by a red sky and the scent of rot. The people lay in rivers of flesh and bone, of blood and vomit, their bodies intertwined in knots of limbs and their eyes bulging from their sockets and staring glassily at the sky overhead. Buzzards and seagulls and birds of all kinds, shrieking with delight at the abundance, feasted on their carcasses, glaring up at Dreadaeleon with indignation, as though he were intruding on their meal.

Puddles of red-tinged vomit squished beneath his shoes.

His head swam on the aroma of death.

The dead reached out in final spasms before the meat was wrenched from their bones by beaks.

And Dreadaeleon, for his part, simply kept walking.

TWENTY-TWO

AN EMPTY SKY, SPRAWLING WIDE

Like many adventurers, Lenk worshipped Khetashe, the Wanderer.

Known derisively to some faiths as the God without Altars, Khetashe was popular primarily with vagabonds, vagrants, and other misplaced. Khetashean doctrine, sparse as it was, suggested that the god had abandoned his place in heaven to go searching for something greater on earth. Because of this, he was a deity understandably scorned by the followers of more rooted faiths.

How, they asked, could a god who had removed himself from heaven possibly look over his flock? How, they asked, could any sane individual follow a deity who wasn't looking out for them?

Reasonable questions.

But there were aspects of the faith that Lenk found soothing. The idea of a god who had his own agenda was one he found more digestible than most faiths. Other gods had lengthy diatribes justifying their authority. Khetashe got right to the point.

And so, when other gods sent their omens in vague, easily misinterpreted gestures, Khetashe more or less smacked his followers right upside their fucking heads.

And that, Lenk knew, was why he was staring at an empty patch of sand where Kataria had once lain.

"Not much more to say beyond that, is there?"

Mocca, apparently, agreed with Khetashe's omen.

The man in white stood beside Lenk, his figure hazy and insubstantial like the smoke from the dying campfire in the morning light. His hands were folded behind his back as he stared down at that same spot of earth.

"The appeal of mortality has long been perception," Mocca sighed. "Those possessed of ages infinite speak haughtily of seeing the greater scheme in these things. But there is something beautiful in the primitive, animal whimsy of a mortal's desires, don't you think?"

He looked to Lenk, who did not look back.

"For what it's worth, though, I am sorry."

Lenk said nothing. Not that there weren't things he wanted to say. He wanted to curse, to scream, to ask why, to call her a vile name just on the off chance it might make him feel a little bit better. But at that moment, breath seemed a precious thing he could not waste.

Kataria was gone.

And he was alone.

The dawn felt cold. And he needed to move. He spun on his heels, stalked toward the pile in which he had left his sword and what meager supplies he had scavenged, and began to shove the latter into a dirty satchel.

"You've not even had breakfast," Mocca said, following. "Are we leaving so soon?"

"We are," Lenk replied. He counted his rations: just a few stale chunks of bread and a couple of strips of dried meat that had survived in a crate. It'd have to last.

"I suppose I can understand the desire to get as far away from this spot as possible," Mocca said. "But take care. The Forbidden East lies before you and the way forward is—"

"Not going to the Forbidden East."

"What?" A note of irritation, singular and iron, crept into Mocca's voice.

"Nothing left for me out here," Lenk replied. He plucked up the satchel, secured it to his belt. "Mission failure. Quest abandoned. Whatever the fuck you want to call it. Time to get out."

He started stalking off, following westward the ridge overlooking the Gullet. The river wended back to civilization. He could follow it. Food would be more plentiful around water, he reasoned.

Mocca suddenly appeared at the corner of his right eye. "Do you not owe a service to the fasha who aided you?"

"You yourself said he was crazy." Lenk swatted at Mocca, as though he were another puff of smoke he could brush away.

The man in white merely appeared at Lenk's left, quicker than he could blink. "I never questioned his source, merely his interpretation. There are answers that lie in the Forbidden East."

"Why do you care?" Lenk demanded, glaring at him. "You know why I was sent here, right?"

"To find the Library of the Learned," Mocca said.

"To destroy *you*," Lenk shot back. "To find something to kill *you*. The fact that you're pushing me toward it regardless suggests to me that either you think there's nothing out there that *can* kill you or that something there can help you. Either way, going would be a fucking waste of time."

"Sheffu, dramatic as he was, sent you here for answers," Mocca replied. "And in the Library of the Learned, there are answers to questions that I need answered, as well."

"Answers to questions I never asked," Lenk said, shrugging him off. "Answers that don't concern me."

He continued stalking on and, in the moments when he heard nothing but sand crunching beneath his feet, he expected that Mocca had abandoned him. That impression lasted only another three paces.

When he looked up, the man in white stood before him, the haziness of his figure banished and replaced by something that looked all too real. Mocca's eyes burned, alive with something terribly old that had seen things not intended for eyes mortal or otherwise. And when he spoke, the man's voice was a pit that swallowed the sound of wind and earth.

"Understand that, while my affections for mortal shortsightedness were genuine, I remain unconvinced of the depth of their wisdom." His hands fell at his sides. "There is more at stake here than you realize, Lenk, and the thread of your life crosses those of others in ways that would make your head hurt to know."

Lenk met Mocca's glare with one of his own, yet even in his skull it felt impotent and weak in comparison. The man was spewing cryptic gibberish, he told himself, in a bid to stall him.

He's a vision, he told himself. *A ghost. Nothing more. Just walk through him.*

His body did not seem to believe him. His legs felt numb, his blood ran cold beneath Mocca's gaze.

The man in white opened his mouth and breathed out darkness. The world around Lenk grew dark and large. Shadows stretched from every corner of the earth to consume the sun and wind. Even the smallest scrub bush seemed to loom over him. The empty desert became a yawning void, a blackness that stretched for eternity and left no room in the world for anything but him, a frail mortal, and the God-King looming before him.

"You cling to life with such ferocity as to strangle it, marveling with dread at the rotting corpses of your fathers for fear that it will one day be you. You cannot see beyond the blood painting your own hands, even as you bleed out upon the cold ground."

Mocca's voice grew. Into something old. Into something deep. A stale wind coursing through the deeps of a cavern long quiet, with only dust and bone to bear witness.

"You have not seen what I have seen, the dreams that haunt me in the dark place I am shackled in, the torments of a world that could be if I could but raise a single finger."

He spread his arms out wide, as if to embrace all of creation. And beneath him the earth rumbled as if it would rise so he could do just that.

"Let me show you, Lenk."

The earth erupted as a great spire burst from the sand, an obelisk carved of pure obsidian thrusting high into a sunless sky. Lenk fell to the ground as the earth split and cracked and more rose. Buildings of obsidian and marble, homes carved from perfect faces of stone, aqueducts running a spider's web over a skyline, domed libraries with banners flowing and torches lit, temples crowned with the statues of learned men and women.

In the span of an ancient breath, a city of white and black, of day and night, had grown around him.

Where there had been only coarse sand beneath his feet, a polished street now loomed. He leaned down, stared into the stone, and saw his reflection. But before he could even state breathlessly his astonishment, he saw another reflection, and another, and another.

He looked up and saw them. Tulwar and humans, shicts and couthi, some races he had never even seen before, all walking alongside each other. Some shoulder to shoulder, some hand in hand, some haggling, some embracing, some laughing and some arguing. People. Everywhere. This was their city.

This was their home.

"What is this?" he whispered. "A vision?"

A woman passed him by, toting a burden of baskets filled with vegetables. She stumbled upon a ledge, dropped her load. Instinctively he moved to help her pick it up, but found his hands passed through it entirely.

"A dream," a voice replied. Mocca stood at the center of the road, eyes again bright, voice again clear. "Or a memory. Old as I am, it's sometimes hard to tell the difference."

"A memory of what?"

"What I beheld, what I wrought," Mocca said. He reached out, touched a passing tulwar on the shoulder. The tulwar acknowledged his touch, met it with a smile. "What is known as the Forbidden East today, Rhuul Khaas on the lips of the fearful and ignorant, was once my home. And I shared it willingly."

"These people, they all lived here?"

"Lived, worked, died. All under my eyes."

Lenk looked to the man in white, who stood stark and pristine even among the shadows of this memory. "For your glory?"

Mocca met his stare evenly. "For their safety. They required my guidance, my knowledge, my wisdom. What they asked for, I gave. What they needed, I had."

"For what? What did you gain?"

"Do you not believe that I would do it simply because it was the right thing to do?"

"I believe you are in hell for a reason."

Mocca frowned at this before looking back over the city—his city. "It was the edict of the gods that we Aeons, their servants and messengers, be cast into that dark place for our hubris in daring to assert control over the mortal realms. And it was mortals who struck us down. Perhaps rightly so. We craved to control them."

"To know their fear."

"To know their love." Mocca sighed, turned back to Lenk. "We, the

Aeons, were always cursed to live between heaven and earth. Too godly to live alongside mortality, yet forever wishing we could be as they and share our own fears, our own loves. To a mortal the two are so very close. And the Aeons could not tell the difference, either.

"Perhaps the other Aeons saw it differently—Avictus, Ulbecetonth, Oerboros—but to me, worship was as close as I would ever get to that need. There is a...a certain hollowness that is made full from being needed, wanted. To be the only one who could offer comfort, solace, judgment, was a sensation I craved. Perhaps to the point where I simply could not bear to let it go."

Mocca's sigh was immense, a wind that spread through the city and carried the people with it. They vanished into dust, their smiles and tears turned to tiny motes that disappeared into the endless shadow. Lenk watched them disappear, heard his own voice echo through the streets.

"And why do you tell me this?" Lenk asked. "For pity?"

"Would that be so bad?" Mocca asked, offering a weak smile. "Would you yourself turn down a bit of pity right now, empty and alone as we both are?" He waved a hand. "I merely mean to remind you, Lenk, of what is at stake. Not a girl, no matter how much you love her, but the future.

"Sheffu spoke rightly. I was called God-King, Shaper of Flesh, all those titles. I ruled an empire vast as the sun could stretch. But empire itself is a force of creation and it was my creation that brought people together. Tulwar and shicts, humans and couthi, all mortal races together."

"And you expect me to help you?"

"I expect you to do what you will regardless," Mocca said. "But you will see so much in the Library of the Learned. And so much of it, I want you to see. You are the one who hears me, Lenk. You are the one I speak to. You are the one I wish to see enter my world.

"I implore you to think beyond your heartache and your agony. Think of the city you left behind, the streets soaked in blood as men kneel in gore and praise gods above for giving them this hell." He looked intently at Lenk. "And think of what good I could do."

Lenk met his gaze for a long time and slowly let out a breath. And with it, the city vanished. Its bricks became dust, its spires became shadows, its streets became sand. The sun emerged and chased the phantoms of civilization away like a bad dream.

But it had not been a dream.

Despite the sweat dripping down his temples, he could feel the chill of the sunless world. Despite the roar of the Lyre River from the canyon beyond, he could hear the laughter of the people. Despite there being nothing but scrubgrass and sand for miles around, he could remember temples and towers. It had not been a dream. It had not been a memory.

Just as Mocca said.

The man in white, too, was gone. Left behind was nothing more than an empty patch of sand and a few words that had never been spoken, left scrawled on Lenk's memory.

"All you need to do," they whispered, "is stand aside."

Lenk stood for a moment, staring at that empty patch of sand, letting those words echo through his mind. Before he drew in a long, slow breath and started walking.

East.

A man wiser than he could have said why. Perhaps he realized, in that vision, that it would be impossible to head back downriver given how far they had come. Perhaps he felt the need to keep going, to no longer look over his shoulder for a place where comforts like Kataria were.

But in some part of him, somewhere dark and deep, he could still feel the phantom city around him. He could feel the streets, the spires, the people and their laughter and their lives.

And perhaps he just wanted to feel that. One more time.

When they had first set out, Lenk had wondered why this part of the Vhehanna region was termed "the Forbidden East."

Four hours of walking into it, the closest he had come to figuring that out was that it sounded better than "the Distinctly Humid and Slightly Inexplicable but Otherwise Just Like Any Other Forest East."

The rise of the Gullet had marked the beginning of a sloping incline in the landscape. The desert of the Vhehanna lay in the valley below, scrubgrass and trees sprouting up upon the slopes and finally giving way to a verdant forest once it plateaued.

It was even greener and more alive here than it had been in the Gullet. The trees grew vast and twisted with age, coated in vines and wearing crowns of colorful flowers. The underbrush's leaves bristled, reaching out for him as he walked past. In his ears the songs of life: birdsong, insect buzzing, the distant call of other beasts he couldn't identify.

Yet even the smother of trees and the symphony of the forest couldn't hope to drown out the roar of the Lyre River. Here the smooth walls of the Gullet had given way to a wider chasm, the current broken by innumerable waterfalls and rapids. He had ventured away from the ridge ages ago, yet the sound of the river never seemed to change, no matter how near or close he got.

It would have been crazy to suggest that it seemed as if the river were following him. Or perhaps not nearly crazy enough, given that he frequently spoke to a hallucination.

Mocca had been absent for much of this journey, though. Since his persuasive case back at the scrubland, the man in white hadn't spoken another word. Lenk occasionally thought he saw him in a flash: standing at the ridge overlooking the Lyre, admiring a flower formation hanging from a particular tree. But once Lenk looked in his direction, the man in white vanished before he could utter a word.

Well, he thought. *Why the fuck do I keep a hallucinatory spirit guide around if he's never here when I want to talk to him?*

Lenk's thoughts were full to bursting with the images he had been shown. The memory of the city and its sprawl never seemed to fade. If anything, he began recalling details he had missed before: the smooth steps leading up to a library, the clean burnt-incense smell of a healer's house, the smile on a tulwar's apelike face as he waved to a passing shict.

Could it have all been real?

Careful, he cautioned himself with a voice that seemed to be growing dimmer each time the thought came back. *He's not Mocca, he's Khoth-Kapira. God-King. Cast into hell as a demon after oppressing mortalkind. No one would fault you for suspecting a demon of deceit.*

That was all true, of course.

And yet, if his intent *was* to deceive, wouldn't Khoth-Kapira deny his wrongdoing instead of owning up to it? Could a demon not feel remorse, even after centuries in hell? Could a demon not reflect, given eternity to do so?

Could a demon not find a new life?

As Lenk so desperately wanted to do?

Doubtless there was more at work here than Mocca was letting on. And yet, all the same, there was no way back. Wherever this road ended, it lay east.

He stumbled suddenly as his toe struck a rock jutting up from the ground.

The graphic cursing he threw at the rock did not seem to faze it much. Nor did the baleful scowl he turned on it. In fact the rock merely stared back, a distinct lack of awe at his fury reflected in its eyes.

Eyes?

He leaned down, cleared away some of the underbrush surrounding the stone. A pair of stone lips were revealed to him beneath the brush, followed by an ear, and then a broken nose. From a shallow grave within the sodden earth, a face stared back at him. He wedged his fingers into the soil, pulled it up, and inspected it. A man's head, he wagered, possessed of angular features and serene expression. There were fragments of broken stone beneath a crumbling chin, as though this particular head had had an elaborate beard at some point.

And, presumably, a body.

He looked around, spied something leaning out of a nearby tree. A pair of granite hands he had mistaken for branches, so covered with vines and dead foliage they were, were raised in a gesture of benediction. He approached the tree, hopped up onto its roots, and brushed away more of the foliage. Its foundation was tilted by roots growing up under it, its body cracked by the trunk growing around it, but it was whole, hale, and standing a head taller than he.

He spied a narrow crevice at the top of the statue's broken neck, a gap the tree had not yet filled. He raised the head, set it upon the statue, and stepped back. A man in robes stared back at him with a blank expression.

He glanced around. Surely, no one built a single statue out in the middle of nowhere for no particular reason, did they? But nothing else was out here but the trees, marching in orderly fashion along a twisting trail of soil and leaves.

Wait.

He walked forward carefully, feeling the earth beneath his feet. The soil was wet but firm, with barely any give to it. He knelt down and dug at the earth with his hands, tossed soil and dead vines aside until his fingers struck something hard.

Bricks. Bricks upon bricks, laid with expert precision, their surfaces polished so smooth he could almost see himself in them. He dug more, found more: stretching out for who knew how long.

There was a road here. Out in the middle of a forest.

"No," he muttered. "The trees are too close together for that to be the case. The road came first." He looked back at the statue, bent low by the tree growing around it. "And the forest grew up around it. How long did that take?"

He rose up, surveyed the trees, hummed in thought.

"They're too haphazard to have been planted by someone, so it happened naturally," he said, scratching his neck. "With a desert nearby. Someone had to have built this before the forest began. How long ago? And who?"

It was only when he received none that he realized he had been talking aloud and expecting an answer. It was only when he noticed that he was completely alone that he realized he had been expecting Mocca to be there.

The man in white was always around to answer questions like this. Every time he was uncertain, every time he was afraid, every time he despaired, Mocca had always been right there, like a thought, to reassure him.

And the fact that he was not made something lurch up Lenk's spine.

The sound of brush snapping and leaves scraping caught his ears.

And when he turned around, he did so with a hand on the hilt of his sword.

At the edge of the underbrush, a tremendous black shape paused, as if suddenly embarrassed that Lenk had noticed it. A gaambol, the massive apelike creature walking on its knuckles, stood between two twisted trees.

Up close and without the heat of battle tingeing his senses, Lenk found the thing looked markedly different from the ones he had seen in the Gullet. This creature's back was arched and unbroken by riders, its black fur was thick and lustrous, its muzzle had the color of long-dried blood.

But it was the beast's eyes, so large did they loom as they studied Lenk intently, that made him pause. The creature looked almost intelligent. Intelligent enough to maybe realize Lenk did not want a fight. Or so Lenk hoped as he backed away slowly.

And hope he did.

Until the gaambol's lips peeled back, baring fangs in a terrifying roar.

His sword was out, quick as a breath. But the beast was faster than breath, faster than even blinking. It hauled itself with long arms, launching itself at Lenk with claws outstretched and fangs bared. Lenk's blade lashed out, catching it across the arm and drawing a deep red gash. The creature hardly seemed to notice, its tremendous hand snapping and batting at the sword with such ferocity as to tear it from Lenk's grasp.

He had scarcely enough time to notice it was gone before the other hand shot out and caught him square in the ribs. Air exploded from his mouth as he was sent flying, striking the sodden earth in a spray of dead leaves.

It was only by instinct that he managed to scramble to his hands and knees. There was not enough breath left in him to go any farther. His head lolled on his neck, felt as if that blow might have knocked it clean off if his neck were any less thick. Breathless, his vision darkening from the impact, he looked up. He couldn't see his sword anywhere, could barely see the beast. The gaambol looked like one shadow among many as it came loping toward him.

The yellow of its fangs, broad and glistening with spittle, was bright as day.

But the flash of silver that parted them was all but blinding.

He wasn't sure when it had happened, but suddenly the shadows had been joined by another. Something small, agile, the flickering of darkness at the edges of a candle's light, appeared before him. He could make out the broad sweeps of the beast's arms, the shrill hoots of its rage as this new shadow danced beneath its grasp and met it with a flashing silver strike.

And before he could even see her, he knew her name.

"Shuro," he gasped.

His vision cleared slowly. She came to him in fragments: the lithe twisting of her black-clad body, the bobbing of her silver hair, the shine of her sword as it flashed out, again and again, leaving bright-red letters painted upon the gaambol's flesh.

The creature shrieked with every swing of its arm, its entire body bristling in a futile attempt to catch her. But she was as the light reflecting off her thin blade: flashing, elusive, and painful.

Lenk caught a glimpse of her eyes. There was no fear in them. No pity. No recognition that she was even in a battle. This fight, like every other fight, was simply reflex to her.

The gaambol reared up on its hind legs, brought both its hands up over its head, and slammed them down in an attempt to crush her beneath its palms. And she merely stepped forward, into the beast's arms, and thrust her blade up.

The gaambol did the rest of the work.

Its downward motion carried its chin onto the tip of her sword, its ferocity brought the blade bursting all the way out of its mouth. And Lenk could see in its eyes, so bright and intelligent, that it had but a moment to comprehend what had just happened before the light left them.

Shuro jerked her sword free in a spray of blood as the beast slumped, motionless, to the ground. Her expression registered no joy or relief at its death. She barely seemed to notice, staring at it as though she expected it to get back up at any moment.

She did not so much as blink. Not as blood trickled down her face, not as Lenk got to his feet and approached her, not as she whirled around and aimed her red-slick sword at his throat.

"Easy," he said, holding his hands up. "Easy."

But there was nothing hard about that face. Her blade wasn't driven by fear, merely instinct. The tension in her body contrasted sharply with the ease in her deep-blue stare.

"You could have been killed," she said, without lowering her weapon.

He said nothing to that, merely stared down the length of her blade and into her eyes.

"Had your sword been out sooner, you could have gotten inside the reach of its arms and killed it as I did." She finally lowered her blade. "Were you trying to reason with it?"

He lowered his arms, but still said nothing. She turned away, glancing to the underbrush.

"Your weapon is there," she said, pointing. "You should collect it. There are a number of other things you should do. Or should have done, at any rate. It was foolish of you to leave without telling me. I was—"

"What are you?"

She turned around suddenly and, for the first time, her face grew harder. But he only barely noticed that. His eyes were on her hair, the color of an old man's, and her form, unmarred by a single cut despite the beast she had just struck, and her eyes.

So cold and blue like his own.

"You're not a merchant," he said.

"And your name isn't Farlan," Shuro replied.

Her lips curled at the corners, a smile sad and nervous. She sighed and dropped her blade, smoothed her hair out behind her ear, and, for a moment, looked like a very normal woman.

"We should talk," she said softly.

TWENTY-THREE

SHE WHO STOOD UNBLINKING

The Temple of Talanas was quiet, clean, and idyllic.

The pews were empty. Supplies had dwindled to the point that those in need had to venture back out into the war-torn streets to find sustenance. Those who could walk had carried those who could not back to destroyed businesses or meager shanties or wherever food might still be found.

The cries of wounded men bleeding out and the children who wept over them were fled from the walls. They had left to seek out a place with more open air and more sky. For Temple Row was a noisy place of late, and no god seemed able to hear those within.

The floors had been scrubbed. Those who had lingered, in a final show of gratitude, had mopped the grime from the hardwood, then scrubbed the stains of blood clean, then bent their backs to pluck the bits of bandage and bone out from the cracks between planks.

Asper sat at the front of the temple, staring at the wooden idol of Talanas, his hands outstretched in benediction and his smile serene above his long beard. She had been staring at him for the greater part of four hours now. After the second hour, when it was clear that he was not going to emerge and offer advice, she had made coffee.

So now she sat, and she sipped cold coffee, and continued to wait.

For what, she did not exactly know. An answer would have been nice. Teneir's ultimatum, in her lithe and hissing voice, still rang out in her head, every word a sizzling drop of venom on her brain.

"If faith does not matter, then it should be a small matter to agree to kneel before Ancaa and swear a new oath."

And just so, her reply, the one she had rehearsed, rang out in thoughtful reply.

"I accept. I recognize Ancaa as my god."

Eight words. For a thousand lives. They sounded so simple, even in her head. Hollow, empty, just a few things she would babble on her knees in a new temple as she casually wondered what she'd have for dinner that night.

And she would be fed, along with the countless people that could be saved with Teneir's limitless resources. Just for eight words. Simple economics. A bargain, really.

Why did it hurt her head, then, whenever she thought about it?

It was this place, she told herself. Too quiet, too clean. She thought best in carnage, with the stink of blood in her nostrils and the sound of suffering in her ears.

But she knew she was lying, merely avoiding the answer she knew she had to confront. She was denying the truth: that they weren't mere words, that it wasn't just a temple, that the idol before her was not mere wood.

This was her faith. This was her god. This was all the blood and sweat she had poured into this city and all the hymns and prayers and ideas that had made her able to do it.

In chaos or quiet, this would be no less difficult. In suffering or in serenity, the problem would be no less painful.

And in faith or faithlessness, the answer would be no less clear.

Talanas would understand.

"The appeal is not lost on me."

It was not the suddenness of his words that made Asper's blood run cold. Nor even was it the fact that he suddenly appeared beside her, seated on the pew as though he had been there the whole time. Rather it was the dread certainty in his voice, the knowledge that whatever he spoke he knew would come true.

Such was the power of Mundas.

"Beyond war, the collectors of mortality are frequent and varied," the dark man with the wide eyes said as he looked at the idol of Talanas. "Disease, predators, heartbreak; there are any number of things that could simply appear one day and make a person cease to exist. To that end, the idea of a deity—an immovable, unchanging pillar of creation that stands firm in the world—must be comforting."

He turned to her and she shuddered beneath his gaze. The world seemed to go dark around him, every ounce of light swallowed within his eyes.

"The flaw with this problem, of course, is that the idea of an unchanging creator looming over a forever-changing creation is incongruent. Can a deity create something so different from himself? Can something so far removed from his creation possibly care for its fate?"

She did not bother asking how he had gotten in here, where he had come from. She could but look back to Talanas.

"One presumes that they have had much longer to learn things than you have," she said. "If they don't know everything, then they probably know more than you do."

"A god can learn."

"They can."

"Then they can change."

"I suppose so."

"Then their power must be limited."

Asper did not so much lean forward as fall, caught only by the burying of her face in her hands. Her coffee spilled out onto the freshly scrubbed floor, a poor substitute for a bloodstain.

"Did you come here just to be pedantic?" she groaned.

Mundas did not answer. After a moment she looked up through her fingers at him, as though she were a child who had just dared to speak back to a parent. But the stare he cast her way, so vast and consuming, was too dark to be like a parent's.

So slowly as to make the pop of each vertebra heard, he turned his head back to the idol of Talanas. "You are frightened."

She regarded him carefully. "What would you know of it?"

"Everything. The troubles of Cier'Djaal are numerous, yet yours are complex enough to stand out."

"How could I not be frightened?" she said, her voice soft and trembling. "It's funny. When I was young in the temple, my mentors always preached faith in Talanas, that he would do what was right. Yet the moment blood is shed, all I can think is, 'What did I do?' Faith suddenly seems like such a foreign concept. All I want is something to blame. Something I did or something he didn't do. Some failure that would explain it.

"All this time, all these deaths, the thought that Talanas might have turned on me, on all of us, must have crossed my mind a thousand times." She sighed and felt her body grow weak. "Never once did I think I might turn my back on him."

Mundas did not reply. Or blink. He did not even breathe, so far as she could tell. But to watch him was to see something that she should not, and she kept her eyes upon the idol.

"But to forsake so many lives that could be saved. Wouldn't that be the same thing? Teneir's rich. Rich enough to feed, shelter, and protect everyone in this city, if she wanted to. If I were to turn that away, all because I felt..."

She left that thought hanging, not certain what it was she *did* feel. Unlike with so many other gods, there was little said in scriptures about Talanas's vastness. Where Daeon was ever-present and Gevrauch was eternal, the hymns always emphasized how very close Talanas was to mortalkind, how his powers and concerns lay within them. Somehow the idea of a god had never seemed big until this moment.

"You speak only in two terms." Mundas did not look at her, but his voice had a gaze all its own: one that locked upon her and stared right through her. "Either you forsake your god and save thousands or you kill them all for the right to worship as you see fit. Do you see it so simply?"

"Is it not?"

"Should anything involving a deity be simple?"

She blinked. He was gone from his seat, suddenly standing before the wooden idol and scrutinizing it carefully.

"Your conflict holds weight only if all of what you assume to be true actually is. You assume forsaking your faith would lead to something wicked."

"It would," she said.

"How do you know?"

"I...I just do." She rose from her seat, stalked toward him. "All the years I've put into a god, a faith, will mean nothing if I can just throw them away so easily."

"Easier than throwing all the lives away?" Mundas asked.

She blinked again and he was gone. And he was everywhere. She turned and he stood, staring out over pews that were suddenly filled with dozens of him. All of them stared forward, their unnerving stares focused on him as he spoke back to them.

"Do you suppose they pray that you will do it?" he asked his congregation of copies. "Do they lie awake praying for their god to save them? Or for you to?"

"What does it matter, so long as they're saved?"

"What, indeed? It would make more sense, then, to pray to Teneir, would it not? She has the means to save them. They are hers to take, if she chooses." He looked at her. "*If.*"

Asper stared back, agog. "You think she wouldn't save them?"

"She turned them out. She treats lives as currencies, something to barter with, as common as coin. What are a few dozen, hundred, thousand coins to a woman as rich as she?"

"So she's lying?"

"She might be." The congregation answered in dozens of unified voices. "She might not be."

The rightmost pews spoke up. "You can be forgiven for searching for certainty in heaven."

The leftmost pews followed. "So many people do."

And slowly Mundas—the first Mundas—regarded her himself. "But gods have yet to deliver them, haven't they?"

"Then what can be done?" she all but demanded, sweeping up to him. Perhaps it was the desperation of her situation—or just her frustration with his obtuseness—that made her speak to him thus. "Tell me what to do."

"I cannot. Any more than Talanas could." He looked to the idol, a hint of longing in his face, as though he sought the same answer she did. "But..." He glanced back to her. "If faith has failed, can flesh deliver?"

His eyes slid down, past her shoulder and to the skin of her arm. Beneath the skin, within the folds of sinew and the marrow of her bones, she could feel something react.

She could feel the curl of a smile, the eager glitter of eyes. Amoch-Tethr peered out of her flesh with eyes unseen, beheld Mundas with delight, and spoke on a voice of smoke and char.

My goodness, he said. *Am I being flattered?*

"NO!"

She clapped a hand over her arm, as though that would do any good. She pulled it away from Mundas, as though that would keep him from staring through her. She loosed a loud snarl, as though that could drown out the sound of Amoch-Tethr's laughter in her head.

As though anything could.

"You would view the violation of your oath as an acceptable tool to save the hapless lambs," Mundas said. "But not Amoch-Tethr?"

"He's not a tool," she hissed. "Before I had a name for him, I thought he was a curse. But he's not that, either. He's not a monster, a demon, or anything I have a name for."

She held her arm up to the light seeping in from the windows. But only for a moment before she turned away for fear that she might actually see what lurked within, staring back at her.

"At the Temple of Ancaa, I saw something," she whispered. "A vision of a black mouth, open forever, choking on flame and skin and grinding bodies between teeth. It said nothing, didn't speak a word, but I knew a name, all the same."

And Amoch-Tethr looked at her, through the sinew and flesh of her arm. And Amoch-Tethr smiled, with black teeth and breath of smoke, and spoke in a voice that rang out through her skull so clear it sounded like her own voice.

Say it.

"The Maw Eternal." Three words. Yet spoken in such a way, about such a creature, they tasted foul in her mouth. "I don't know what he is, but he is no tool. And whoever will die because of Teneir would be a pittance compared to what he can do."

She looked up. Mundas, singular and whole, stood at the idol, staring at her.

"What," she asked, "can he do?"

Mundas did not answer. He turned on his heel, looked toward the door. He vanished, appearing again at the rear of the pews, his back turned to her and Talanas alike.

"Only what he is allowed," he said.

She took a breath and he vanished again, reappearing upon a pew, head bowed in thought.

"And everything he can," he added.

She held that breath as he appeared at the doors, moving to disappear through them. When she spoke, her voice was an airless scream.

"You *owe* me!"

He paused. She licked her lips.

"You've come to me so many times now with questions and I've answered you," she said. "Tell me this one thing, at least. What is he? What are *you*?" She held her left hand up. "What's inside of me?"

Mundas folded his hands behind his back. His body grew still. His voice sounded soft, fragile; human, for the first time since she had met him.

"The word they used was *Aeon*," he said. "You know it."

"What the demons once were."

"What they still are. *Aeon* meant the same thing, be it for heaven-sent or hell-bound. 'Outsider.' Amoch-Tethr..." He let the name linger, an iron axhead hanging over a soft neck. "Like all us Renouncers, he was something more. Not unlike yourself. Perhaps that is why he opted to remain with you, even now."

"How do I get rid of him?"

"Does he cause you agony?"

She paused before speaking. "Yes."

"Within you he is a curse borne only by one poor soul, as he has been for centuries. Outside you he would wreak more devastation than you could possibly know."

He looked over his shoulder at her. His smile was something sad, the kind a grandfather spared for an ill child just before he told her one last bedtime story.

"And still," he whispered, "that may have been kinder than what is to come."

She opened her mouth to respond, but heard only the wail of hinges and the slam of wood. Mundas disappeared in a bright flash of sunlight, insubstantial as a shadow and distant as a nightmare. In his place, as the doors swung open, was a skinny youth, sweating through his robes and looking at Asper with wild eyes.

"Aturach?" she asked.

When his only response was a breathless wheezing, she seized a nearby jug of water and thrust it into his hands.

"Easy," she cautioned as he guzzled it down. "Drink slowly. Breathe deeply."

"No time." The look in his eyes, terrified and desperate, made her believe what he said. "Came from Silktown. Dransun. He gathered the refugees, led them to the gates."

"What? What for?"

"Said it wasn't right," he gasped, pausing to drink more water. "Said

Teneir was corrupt and if she had all that money..." He shook his head. "Said someone had to do something. I tried to talk him out of it, but—"

"But what?" Asper took him by the shoulders, looked him evenly in the eye. "Aturach...what did he do?"

"He's there now," Aturach said, "with all of them. The refugees."

"In Silktown?"

Aturach paled. "He didn't get any further than the gates. Fasha Mejina found out and met him there." His lips trembled; he was afraid to speak the next words. "With his dragonmen."

"You're part of this city, fashas! Why aren't you protecting us? Open up your gates and let us in!"

Shouting. Screaming. Weeping. Cursing.

"Fuck the fashas! Fuck your houses and fuck your dragonmen!"

Glass whiffling through the air and shattering. Stone grinding as bricks were torn up. Wood cracking, sticks smashing on the street. Grunting, bodies shoving.

"My sons are dead! My daughter is all I have left! The foreigners won't come to Silktown. Please, let us in!"

And so much pleading.

How many were there? Two hundred? Five hundred?

Asper couldn't tell. It had been impossible for her to tell how many were assembled when she arrived at the gates of Silktown. And in the thick of the mob, all the men and women and children seemed to blend together into one sweating, heaving, shouting mass of flesh and hair.

She could barely see over their heads when she stood on her toes. And when she did, she saw what they held. Some raised sticks, threw stones in defiance. Others shook effigies of well-dressed fops in dirty silks. A few held up wailing babies in plaintive pleas.

And towering over them, deaf to their pleas, stood the dragonmen.

Three of them, the shortest one at least ten feet tall, stood before the gates of Silktown, Cier'Djaal's wealthiest district. Each one thick as a mountain, bodies covered in scales the color of stone, they barely seemed to notice the crowd beneath them. Lazily they leaned on massive weapons, looking in a bored way down long snouts topped with rhinoceros-like horns. Stones and bottles flew, shattered against them, and they did not so much as flinch.

"Death to the fashas! Death to their pet lizards!"

To them this was just another job.

"People of Cier'Djaal! I implore you to listen!"

And for some this was an opportunity.

"Your cries do not fall upon deaf ears!" a shrill voice shouted out over the crowd. "We are doing all that we can to negotiate an end to hostilities! Please, I beg you, return to your homes that we may—"

"My home is burned to the ground, you son of a bitch! Fuck your negotiations, Mejina!"

Another stone flew out, aimed lower. A dragonman casually lowered his hand, let it bounce off his wrist. When he drew it back, he revealed a quivering slip of a man.

Atop a small, hastily erected stage, Fasha Mejina addressed the crowd. A thin man, he was wearing silk robes that were too big for him. His gold chains and rings looked too heavy for his wrists and neck. And the elaborate red and gold face paint he wore was not thick enough to conceal the sweat pouring off him.

This was the man, Asper realized. This tiny little man was trying to control Silktown. She had only heard his name up to this point. She had expected someone bigger.

But the fasha, cowering behind a wall of house guards impotently holding shields and spears against the crowd, looked positively pitiful.

"Citizens, please," the fasha called out, a distinctly obnoxious haughtiness in his voice. "We can come to an understanding. Silktown is the last bastion of Cier'Djaal untouched by violence."

He had once been a fasha of minor wealth. Just a few spiders to assure him a healthy silk trade, with modest investments in spices and wine. But with Fasha Ghoukha dead and Fasha Teneir concerned elsewhere, he'd tried to make a larger name for himself.

"Surely," Mejina continued, "you wouldn't want to despoil the last vestige of our city's serenity with aggression. Surely you are interested in peace." He gestured to the dragonmen behind him. "Behind these gates, Cier'Djaal's finest minds are hard at work." Mejina spread his hands out over the crowd. "For you, dear people. Every day we agonize over how to stop the violence. Every night we lie sleepless over concern for your safety. Every—"

"Every word that comes out of your mouth is shit!"

"Our money paid for those walls you hide behind! Let us in!"

"Please! The foreigners killed my husband! I have nothing!"

The words were followed by howls. The howls were followed by bricks. The bricks were followed by a sudden roar and a press of humanity as the crowd surged forward.

Mejina cowered back. The house guards rattled their shields as they gave way before the crowds. The crowd continued to push forward. Until one of the dragonmen leaned forward and let out a bellowing roar that sent them reeling back.

They recoiled, Asper noted. But they did not flee. She could feel the tension roiling off the crowd, smell the violence they barely controlled. She had seen this before: people ready to burst, bodies ready to snap. All it would take was one word from one person with nothing to lose.

And everything would go to hell.

She had to stop it. She had to stop them. She had to find Dransun.

"Please, let me through."

"Priestess, the fashas, they've got so much and they won't let us in! Talk to them, please!"

All Asper saw was their hands.

"I'll do everything I can, but I need to find Dransun. Where is he?"

"Enough of this oxshit! I say we climb the walls, remind these fuckers who they serve!"

Some were reaching for her as she pushed her way through the mob. Many hands were upraised in fists of anger. More still clenched makeshift weapons and hurled debris at the blockade before the Silktown gates.

"Dransun! Where is he? Have you seen him?"

"Fuck off, northern! We're busy here! Death to the fashas! They drain us dry and toss our corpses to the foreigners!"

She made herself see only the hands.

Because she knew what she would see if she looked at their faces.

Fear and desperation were painted in the streaks of their tears and the open wailing of their lips. But where despair failed, anger grew in dark scowls and eyes filled with fury. They gnashed and screamed and hurled curses and bricks.

They were ready for blood. But it wouldn't be their blood that was spilled.

Because no matter how aware she was of the righteousness behind their anger, she was more aware of the three great shapes towering over the crowd.

So tall that their horns brushed the arch of the gates of Silktown, the three dragonmen looked too gigantic to be real as she got closer. But so close, she could see the annoyance flashing in their eyes, hear the great breaths taken with each twitch of their nostrils, see their weapons...

A hammer. An ax. A blade. Each dragonman carried a weapon as big as a human and clenched in hands big enough to swing them. She had seen firsthand the destruction they could wreak on stone and wood. She thought what they might do to flesh, to bone, to—

No, she commanded herself. *Don't think about that. Dransun first. Dransun can help you disperse the mob. We'll solve the rest later. No one has to die here.*

"No one has to die here," she whispered, as if doing so would make it more real.

No more than necessary.

Amid the oppressive heat of the crowd, Amoch-Tethr's voice was an icy serpent coiling around her spine.

You can solve it all here, he whispered to her, *all with just one life.*

Almost against her own volition, she found her gaze drawn to the gates. Through the forest of limbs and screams before her, over the heads of the house guards cowering behind their shields, beneath the shadow of the dragonmen, the world parted so that she could lay eyes upon a singular man.

"Fasha Mejina," she whispered.

Kill him, Amoch-Tethr said. *I can make it quick. He will not feel a thing.*

"No."

The dragonmen will flee, having no reason to remain. The people will see you as a savior. The fashas will learn to fear you.

"*No,*" she insisted, clutching at her arm.

The foreigners would obey you, Amoch-Tethr all but purred. *One life for a thousand. Ten thousand, maybe? How many must die before you're willing to kill?*

And that thought lodged itself in her head, an iron sliver sinking into her scalp.

Gods help her, he was starting to make sense.

Could she live with one more death? She had seen the fashas' homes, their sprawling manses on the hill. She had seen Cier'Djaal's slums, where the poorest drowned in filth. Could the death of one of the former for the lives of a thousand of the latter be such a bad idea?

Even if it came from Amoch-Tethr?

She forced herself not to look down at her arm, even as she felt Amoch-Tethr staring at her. She looked away and spotted her quarry in the crowd. His polished armor and gleaming badge spoke of Jhouche authority, but his howl of anger and upraised fist painted him as just one more face in the mob, no different from any other.

"Dransun!" she shouted to be heard over the furor of the crowd. "*Dransun!*"

And when he did not look up, she started shoving her way through until she could seize him by the shoulders and forcibly turn him around. He bristled under her grasp, his face contorted in outrage that only barely softened at the recognition of her.

"Priestess," he said, "you shouldn't be out here."

"No? Were you just going to lead everyone to their deaths without me, then?" She tightened her grip on his shoulders, her hands trembling with restrained fury. "After all we've done for them, Dransun, you would just—"

"*They can't keep doing this!*"

His bellow carried over the din of the crowd. He tore free of her grip, raised fists as though he might strike her. She braced herself, watched his hands tremble in the air, the metal of his gauntlets rattling. His fingers shot up to his temples, clutched his hair in great fistfuls as he let out a wordless scream.

"For so long, they've dictated everything in this city," Dransun snarled. "Our homes, our freedoms, they've bought *everything*. We can't let them dictate who we worship. We can't let them take that from us, priestess." He swept his shout over the crowd. "*SOMEONE HAS TO DO SOMETHING!*"

His fury was taken in by the crowd, compounded into a formless bellow, and thrown out at the gates of Silktown. The people began to roil, stew boiling in a cauldron over an open flame. Their shouts seethed like steam, they surged and lapped at the wall of guards, they spat and bubbled with bricks and bottles.

"Not like this, Dransun!" Asper shrieked, straining to be heard. "You can't give them a reason to kill you!"

"I already know what I can't do, priestess," Dransun replied sharply. "I can't sit idle and wait for gods to save us. I can't let the city I raised my children in rot. I can't..." His fury wilted on his face, something soft and wet with tears blooming in its wake. "I can't let them do this to you, Asper. Not after everything you've done."

Despite his tears, she wanted to strike him. Despite the fear in his voice, she wanted to strangle him. Despite all of that, she kept her hands at her sides.

"That was my decision," she said sternly. "Not yours. Not theirs. Not anyone's."

"You're wrong, *shkai*—" He caught himself. "Priestess." He shook his head. "We are men and women, fully grown. You can't carry us on your back. You need to let us stand up with you."

She wanted to scream at him for that. For a lot of things, really. For leading this mob, for forcing this conflict, for doing it all for her, for showing her a kind of tenderness she hadn't even seen in her companions before.

Or had she? How many lives had been taken to preserve hers?

Perhaps, she thought, it never could end without death.

But perhaps it need not end with more than one.

And she wanted to scream at that, too. But instead she slid her hand around Dransun's neck, pulled him closer, pressed her forehead against his.

"You led them here," she hissed. "You brought them here. Can you lead them out?"

"What?"

"Can you get them out? Can you get everyone out?"

"I... I might be—"

"Yes or no, Dransun."

He stiffened beneath her grip. "Yes, I can." His breath was hot, his voice hard. "What are you going to do?"

"If you have any mercy for me, Dransun, you won't ask me that. Just be ready."

This is necessary.

She told herself this as she pushed her way through the crowd, ignoring the elbows thrown her way as she did. Through the roars of anger and wails of fear, she made her way to the front of the crowd and looked to the man in soft silks. Fasha Mejina.

This is glorious.

Amoch-Tethr told her this as he received her answer. He burned beneath her sleeve, beneath her flesh. She could feel the curse inside her arm, the hungry devourer stirring with the promise of another meal. With one touch she would end this. With one life she would save thousands.

This is right.

She wasn't sure which one of them said that.

The tower shields of the house guards trembled, barely able to hold back the mob as they surged forward. Through their cracks she could see their bearers' fear; these were no Jhouche, these were nothing but pampered trophies for fashas to flaunt. The real power loomed overhead, the dragonmen not seeming to notice her as she made her way toward the front.

With the next surge, she told herself. She peeled back the sleeve of her left arm. *Run with the crowd, break through the shields. Grab Mejina before anyone can think otherwise. End him before anyone can stop you.* She took a deep breath. *You can do this. The guards haven't noticed you, the dragonmen haven't noticed you, Mejina hasn't—*

She looked up. Through the shields of the guards and the shadows of the dragonmen, a pair of glittering eyes set in a painted face looked straight at her.

Mejina had.

She halted, staring back at him, into the eyes of the man she would kill. The man who would feed Amoch-Tethr. The man whose death would save Cier'Djaal.

That man stared at her, and she felt uneasy beneath his eyes. As though, just by looking at her, he knew what she was planning. As though he could look straight past her, past her flesh, into what lay beneath.

Stop it, she told herself, shutting her eyes. *STOP IT. You're being paranoid. He can't tell—*

"Amoch-Tethr."

She froze. A voice, a whisper, a sound so far away and so close it felt like a knife blade scratching at her throat. She opened her eyes, saw Mejina's lips curl into a smile, twitch ever so slightly.

"I hadn't been told you'd be here." Mejina was whispering to her, his voice terribly soft and terribly close. "This must look terribly clumsy to you."

"How?" Asper mouthed. She looked down at her arm, to Amoch-Tethr. *"How?"*

"Still, I'm sure you'll find something to appreciate in this."

She looked back up at Mejina. But Mejina was not there. His clothes were, his skin was, but the creature that stood there was not Mejina. This creature's eyes quickly flooded with darkness, turning pitch-black. This creature's smile split its face apart, baring knife-long teeth in a twisted grin for but an instant.

"That's not Mejina," Asper said. Her voice rose up. "That's not Mejina! That's a—"

"I have tried to be merciful, Cier'Djaal!" Mejina's face had returned, a mask once again donned by this creature as he extended his hands wide in benediction. "Let no one say it was Mejina who forced this to happen!"

"Everyone!" Asper cried out, whirling to look over the crowd. "Everyone, get out of here! This isn't—"

A wordless shriek of terror rose up through the mob, devouring her voice in a wave of noise. They did not even look at her, their eyes turned up to heaven, their fingers pointing to the sky, their bodies swallowed by the shadows falling over them.

"Please, for the love of gods, run! *Get out*—"

Her voice was knocked from her as she felt the earth move beneath her feet, sending her to her knees. When she next drew breath, it tasted coppery in her mouth.

And when she held it, she felt the warm blood painting her body.

She knew what happened next only in fragments. In screams and wails and pleas for mercy, in arms and legs and torsos hacked apart and flying through the air, in a sky painted scarlet and man-size blades flashing silver.

And then, and only then, did she know fear.

They moved through the mob like farmers through wheat, their faces expressionless and reptilian features unreadable, as though this was but one more chore to do before knocking off. And like farmers through wheat, they threshed.

The dragonmen threshed a bloody harvest.

Their blades and hammers moved with heavy method, each swing sending bodies flying and gouts of gore spraying. Their feet ground the dismembered and the hapless beneath heavy soles, leaving patches of thick paste in their wake. Without mercy, without blinking, without a word, the dragonmen waded into the crowd with resigned machination.

Gods raining fire upon a living hell.

"—*mad! They're fucking mad! Run! RUN FOR YOUR—*"

They fled every which way, knocking each other over and trampling those left behind.

"—*please, wait! I can't keep up! Don't leave me—*"

They screamed until their voices ran dry, they choked on the blood that painted their faces.

"—*Mama? Mama! GET UP! I CAN'T—*"

The people broke, the people wailed, the people died. And Asper, struck paralyzed by the scene before her, could but stare, seeing it all, hearing it all. And yet the carnage was not so merciful as to be loud enough to drown out the sound of their voices.

"Ugh. I think I got one in my eye," a great voice bellowed.

"So close them. Not like you'll miss any," another replied.

"Or just keep walking. They're like roaches. Bound to step on one of them."

The dragonmen, talking casually among themselves. Cracking jokes and chuckling. Sighing in boredom and resignation. As if this was just another job. As if all these dead people were just more chores to deal with.

"Boring," one of them complained. "How long until we get a real fight?"

"Remember the Uprising?" another said. "Seas of tulwar. Feisty ones at that. Now *that* was a fight. Send them back, I say."

"Kill what they pay you for," the third growled. "And be thankful it's easy work."

Screaming. Bellowing. Shrieking. Sighing. Bleeding. Wailing. Pleading. All the sounds, all the voices, they blended together in her head until all she could hear was a singular sound.

Amoch-Tethr.

Laughing.

No more. That was her thought, short and loud in her head. *No more.* Those were her legs, moving beneath her. *No more.* That was her left arm, burning bright and hungry as she tore off toward the dragonmen, toward the house guards, toward Mejina and whatever beast wore his suit.

It was by luck that she met the dragonman first, his foot coming down in front of her, kicking up a cloud of red-tinged dust. It was by instinct that she darted away as his ax swung at her, his black eyes narrowing on her with a familiar contempt.

"You."

She knew him. The scars on his snout had been carved by hands she was familiar with. The glare he leveled at her was one she recognized. This was the dragonman Gariath had fought, so long ago. Ghoukha's former bodyguard.

The one called Kharga.

"Lost your way, pinky?" he snarled, hefting his tremendous ax. "Or have you just lost the *Rhega* who was with you?" His nostrils quivered. "I still smell his self-righteous stink all over you."

"P-please," she whispered, too soft. "Please, stop this—"

"Now, if he were here, that'd be something, wouldn't it?" He chuckled as he raised his man-size ax over his head. "Must be my bad luck that made me stuck with you, instead. Oh, well."

It was by instinct that she rushed forward.

It was through cruelty that she made him suffer.

Her left hand lashed out. A hellish red light engulfed her flesh, painted her bones black as Amoch-Tethr roared to life inside her. She touched the dragonman's knee, no more than four fragile fingers pressed upon iron scales.

It was enough for Amoch-Tethr to feed.

The dragonman's howl of pain cut through the crowd like a blade itself. Steam burst from beneath Asper's palm in great reeking gouts. She knew what was happening: scales peeling back and blackening, blood bubbling and bursting, muscle strands shriveling into gray ash. But she could not feel it. What she felt was something altogether different.

Cold water forced down a throat after six months in a desert. The sputter and crackle of a fire after a live hound is thrown into it. A belly full to bursting, a mouth stained with blood, and a desperate need to keep eating.

These were not hers to feel, but she felt them all the same. She felt the gnawing need and the ecstasy of the consumption. She felt Amoch-Tethr's voice, wild and hot inside her.

Yes, yes, YES! More, more! There must be more! It's so exquisite! Ah, but if you could see it! I need you to see it! I need you to—

"KHARGA!"

Another roar. The earth shook. Asper looked up to see one of the dragonmen rampaging toward her, giant hammer in hand and coming down to crush her like an insect.

She leapt away, tearing her hand free in a burst of steam and a peeling of flesh. The hammer came down with a crash, shattering the cobble-stones and sending them flying through the air on a cloud of dust. Asper reeled, coughed, tried to find the wind that the impact had knocked out of her. And through it all, Amoch-Tethr would not stop screaming.

No, no, NO! I need more! Please, give me more! I beg you, let me taste it! Our work is not done. We have not saved everyone! Get back there!

She rose up, tensed her arm. The light dimmed with every breath, even as Amoch-Tethr's moans rose to a climax.

We can do it. You and I! We can save them all! All you need to do is—

She felt something catch her. Pick her up off the ground, drag her away.

"Let me go!" she screamed. "Let me go! They have to pay! They have to suffer!"

Whoever they were, they didn't hear her. But she heard them.

"Get the priestess out of here! Hurry now!"

"We can't lose her here! Back to Temple Row!"

"Find Dransun! Tell him we'll get as many of them out as we can, after her!"

And as she squirmed in their grip, she could see them. The merchant the temple had taken in and fed after he lost everything. The young man she'd kept from bleeding out after he lost his arm. The mother whose child's dislocated shoulder she had set.

They came back. The people. All she had done.

She watched the scene of carnage shrink as she was dragged farther away from it. The bodies of the dead shrank and dried up like rain puddles in the sun. The flashing blades of the dragonmen turned to fireflies coming out in the light of the setting sun. She watched it all grow smaller, until she could see them no more.

The sun was dropping around them. The screams faded as they released her, hurried her back to Temple Row. She felt numb and quieted, so much so that the only thing she could hear was a single voice in her head.

Ah, Amoch-Tethr said, *what a pity.*

TWENTY-FOUR

OUR FATHER IS DEAD AND WE ARE ALONE

I remember that my mother liked melon."

Shuro's voice was not soft, Lenk thought.

She had stripped off her outer coat, a sleeveless shirt beneath revealing the angular muscle of her arms. Her eyes were keen and scalpel-thin as she ran a cloth over the blade that lay naked in her lap.

The sword was not a tool. It was she. And its edge was echoed in every part of her body, including her voice.

"Maybe *liked* is the wrong word for it." Shuro held up the sword, studied it. "It'd be more accurate to say that she had a strong hatred for melons. No matter how much I hated them, I had to eat them all. We could eat meat and leave the bone, but she would not abide us to leave the rind of a melon. My father, my brother, and I, we all had to eat the whole thing: flesh, rind, and all. 'It's the best part,' she'd say. But she lied. She simply couldn't abide a melon going unpunished."

She flashed a smile over the campfire. The sort of strained-at-the-edges smile that someone makes when they're doing what they *think* looks pleasant.

"I remember that," Shuro said. "But I don't remember her name at all."

Lenk met her eyes. Even as the firelight painted her skin a pale orange and cast her silver hair bronze, it couldn't color the cold blue of her stare even a little. And he found himself cringing under that blade-sharp stare and looked away, silent.

Just as well. It would have been hard to hear him.

Orange shafts of a setting sun's light pierced the trees, but in the jungle of the Forbidden East, it might as well already have been night.

The canopy seemed to close over their head to provide proper lighting for the symphony that ensued. Insects fought to be heard over the cries of birds, who were in turn rudely interrupted by nocturnal monkeys. Occasionally something bigger and fiercer than the rest would roar and silence them for a moment, only for them to resume.

Whatever that bigger thing was out there, it was the reason their campfire was so small. Gaambols roamed these woods, Shuro had said. Nooseheads lurked in the canopies, packs of yijis stalked the night. If they were lucky, they might run into one of those.

If they were unlucky, there were always shicts out there.

So they sat, they ate dried meat in silence. And Lenk was content with this. He had agreed to stay with Shuro, curious as to what answers she might provide about how she, a young woman with hair and eyes the same unusual colors as his, had come to be here.

And yet he had been around long enough to know that curiosity was just a prettier word for dread, and he felt meat stick in his craw over the fear that she might tell him something he didn't want to know.

"Do you remember your parents?"

Granted, that was a question, but still.

He cleared his throat, swallowed his meat. "Sort of," he said. "I remember they were farmers. We lived in a little farmer village named Steadbrook—burned down, they were killed, bandits or some shit, I don't know. We lived in a little house with my grandfather. He was an adventurer in his day, used to tell me stories. We worked fields. My mother fed hens, my father—"

"What were their names?"

He looked up at her and found her looking intently across the fire at him. Her gaze had softened in an uncomfortable way, her eyes glistening as though she were anticipating a slap across the face as much as an answer.

And when he gave the latter, it hurt like the former. "I don't know."

"Their faces?" she asked. "The color of your mother's hair? The sound your father made when he laughed?"

"I can't remember," he said.

"Did your grandfather have a beard? Did he smell like pipe smoke or whiskey?"

"I don't fucking know, all right?"

He didn't feel the strain in his voice until after he snapped. And he stared at her, surprised at himself, at the way his voice had choked, at the way his eyes suddenly burned. And she stared back, her smile soft and sad.

"Then tell me," she said, "do you remember where you got your sword?"

And he did. He remembered everything about the sword, his grandfather's sword. He remembered watching his grandfather polish it, sharpen it, oil it every day. Every day Lenk had come in from the field, he had seen it hanging on the wall. He could recall the feel of the leather of the grip in his hands as he pulled it out of the ashes of his former home after he had buried all the dead in Steadbrook.

And though he did not tell her, he could see that Shuro knew. Somehow.

"I remember mine." She held up her thin blade, sitting in her hand as if she had been born with it. "My brother was a blacksmith's apprentice. He forged this as proof that he was ready to become a journeyman. I remember every day I watched him hammer on it, sharpen it, smooth out every imperfection. I remember the day he held it, polished to a high sheen, and said it was ready."

She looked at herself sadly in the blade's reflection.

"That was the day he died," she said. "I can remember that. But I don't know what his name was. My father's or my mother's, either. I can't even remember what they looked like when—"

She stared long and hard at the blade. The blade looked back, impassive and unapologetic.

"Family, home, and gods," she whispered to the blade. "All three must be lost before it happens." She lay it back down on her lap. It continued to stare at her. "So that there is nothing left but the blade." She looked back up at him. "And us."

"Us," he repeated. The word tasted heavy. "What do you mean *us*?"

"Farlan," she said, looking at him intently. "Tell me your real name."

Lying had always been Denaos's talent; it took him a little too long to call his story back to mind. "It is my real—"

"You can make a fake name, you can hide your hair, but your eyes want to tell me something." She gestured to her own blue stare. "Mine did the same, not so long ago."

He swallowed hard, looked away.

"Do you want to know what I know?" she whispered.

"No," he said.

"Why not?"

"Because I know it's going to hurt."

"It will," she said. "But you always knew it would."

A moment of silence passed as he chewed his meat and Shuro patiently watched him. When he swallowed the last piece, he wondered if he might start chewing his hand to avoid talking.

"Lenk." The word slipped from his lips. "No surname. Not that I can remember."

"Me either," she said. "Maybe I'm not even Shuro. But it fits." She patted the blade. "Like this fits. A name and a sword were all I had left when it happened to me."

He looked up at her. His breath left him suddenly, as if anticipating the blow that would come after he asked her.

"When what happened?"

She took the breath that had left him, body shuddering as though she had just been struck.

"I guess I would have been maybe fourteen or fifteen," she said. "The night before my brother was to show his work, we celebrated. My father was well-off, did merchant work in Muraska, so we had a feast. I had my first glass of wine. It tasted sweet, so I had too much. I went to bed early.

"I remember more than most of us do," she said. "I remember waking in the night. I remember getting out of my bed. I remember the cold wood on my bare feet as I walked into my brother's room and picked up the blade."

She stared at the weapon in her lap. She picked it up, sheathed it, set it aside.

"And ran him through the heart with it."

Such calmness she spoke with. How many times had she repeated this, Lenk wondered, before she could say it without crying?

"Then I went to my parents' room and killed them, too," she said, methodically and mechanically. "I left out my door and went to my neighbors' house. An elderly couple. I killed them. Then the next house and so on until I had killed thirteen people the first time I ever picked up a sword. I remember that number and little else."

He should have been unnerved by this tale, by the calm way she told it. But the only thing that unsettled him was how calm he felt listening to her. Something about the way she spoke, without boasting or fear, sounded right. Not good, but right. And he needed to hear more.

"Do you still kill?" he asked.

She nodded.

"When you do, how do you feel?"

"Like I did that night." He knew what she was going to say, yet it still made him shudder to hear her say it. "Complete."

"Yeah." He looked away. "Yeah."

"Master Sekhlen calls it the Awakening. We enter the nightmare with our swords bared. Those who survive it wake up with changes. Our hair is the color of an old man's, our eyes are cold, and we..."

"We have a need," she said. "We need violence. It fuels us, makes us strong." She glanced to him. "You had a wound in your side, didn't you? When we first met?"

"How did you—"

"You winced when you stretched," she said. "Does it bother you now?"

He shook his head. Shuro nodded, reaching up to the collar of her shirt and tugging it down. A wound, caked with dried blood, painted a path just shy of her throat.

"Grazed by a *bokka* knife back on the river," she said. "It doesn't hurt anymore. I bet you've taken a dozen such hits: wounds that should have been fatal, injuries that should have left lingering effects. Yet you're still alive, hale and healthy because of what you are. What we are."

"And..." He hesitated, but it was too late. He couldn't stop the question. "What are we?"

"A blade ever honed. A storm ever brewing. A slave to no god, no king, no man. A wind ever moving." She shook her head. "They don't have a name for us, as a people, even as individuals. But we gather together, sometimes, under the only name we have left." She picked up her sword once more. "The Order of the Restless Blades."

At his blank stare, she smiled. "Dramatic, isn't it?"

"I mean, not the *most* dramatic I've ever heard, but...," he began.

"It was our own choosing, the name we gave ourselves, for in the days when we were made, we weren't allowed to carry any of our own." As though it were the most casual thing in the world, she set aside her weapon and asked, "Have you slain demons?"

He reeled at the question; it wasn't something one was asked except by those who already knew the answer.

"I have."

"How many?"

"I lost count."

Shuro raised her eyebrows in appreciation. "And you killed that many without ever asking why you were able to do it?"

"Of course I asked." Feeling quite restless, Lenk rose to his feet, stalked away. "I asked every night, to any god I thought would listen. Why I could kill the demons, why it only got easier to do so..." He let his gaze fall down to the earthen floor. "Why I felt so complete after doing so."

"The question haunted you."

"Doesn't it haunt you?" He whirled on her. "All the deaths. Not just demons, but men, women, anything that gets in your way. Don't you ever feel like you're going to choke on the blood? Don't you ever feel... wrong for feeling so right about killing?"

"I do not," she said flatly. "No more than a sword feels wrong for serving its purpose. For that is why we were made."

"Made." The word didn't have the iron coldness in his mouth that it did in hers.

"As our foes were made," she said. "And no one fights demons as long as you have without knowing what crucible made them."

He looked long into the fire. "They weren't always demons..."

They had once been called Aeons. Servants of gods and men alike, they carried word between the two. Shepherding the mortal creations, speaking on behalf of divine masters, Aeons were outsiders in their own world, denied the euphoria of heaven and the base desires of earth alike.

No one said what had made them lose that position, whether it was anger at their half-formed nature, temptation by the power they were forever denied, or merely resentment of their mortal charges.

Lenk had never asked Mocca.

"But they were made into them, all the same," Shuro said. "And the war between them and mortalkind began. The mortals found themselves outclassed by demons at every turn until they found a new weapon."

"Us," Lenk muttered.

"They say we were made by a dead god," she continued. "A divine being whose essence was distributed among so many mortals to give them the power to do so. Others say we were created by an ancient curse wrought by the first wizards, back when it was wild and primal, before the Venarium and its laws were established."

The latter seemed more likely to Lenk. *Curse* seemed as appropriate as anything to describe it.

"But, personally..." Shuro paused, the words coming with great difficulty. "I think it was the Awakening that made us this way. Demons are shaped by pain and fear, so are we, too, and this is how we fight them. When we have nothing left—no homes, no gods, no...no family—we are creatures like they are. We can kill them, just as we killed those close to us."

The question had been brewing at the back of his mind since she had spoken, since he had met her, since he had walked out of the ashes of Steadbrook. And until now, there had always been more important things to think about: battles to survive, enemies to kill, trials to overcome.

But now he could not think of anything else. And so he asked it, wrenched it free from his lips and threw it cold and flat on the ground.

"Who killed my family?"

And she looked at him, sadly. And she smiled, sweetly.

"Is it not obvious?" she sighed, as though this were a question a child would ask, instead of a man about to shake himself to pieces.

He said nothing. And so she closed her eyes. And she spoke, softly.

"You did."

There were a thousand answers he wanted to offer in return to that. There were dozens of accusations that ran through his head. There were a hundred threats he wanted to make, demanding that she recant. There were a few soft, wordless feelings that he simply wanted to cry out.

But, after a breath, all he could think of was four words.

Why didn't that hurt?

Perhaps he had long numbed himself to the tragedy of his family's violent passing. It had been so long since he'd convinced himself bandits or shicts had burned his village down and slaughtered everyone.

Or perhaps he had always known he'd had a hand in it.

He should have wept. He should have screamed. He should have whispered a prayer.

And it terrified him that he did not.

"Whatever made us," Shuro continued, snapping him from his reverie, "it made us well. We led the charges against the demons, cut them down where they stood, drove back their hordes and spawn and cast them back into hell. And when it was over?

"The lucky of us were cast out. The rest were hunted down and slain. Maybe they thought we had outlived our usefulness, that demons would never return. Or perhaps they viewed us as unnatural, abominations, given how we were made."

"And what do you think?" he asked.

"I think...we are good at what we do. Demons are not kind creatures. They feed on suffering, on despair and on pain. They slaughter the innocent and laud the guilty. They devour, they taint, they destroy, they *kill*. And they cannot be killed but for memory."

Her voice grew cold, hard.

"They remember us."

And as cold and hard as it was, it was the realization that came with it that struck him like a mace to the skull. Suddenly her presence here made a startling amount of sense.

"Mocca," he whispered. No, that was not the name she knew. "Khoth-Kapira." His eyes widened. "You're here to kill Khoth-Kapira."

She frowned, as though she had been hoping to spare him this knowledge. He echoed the sentiment, for he certainly wished he hadn't deduced it.

"The Order exists because it must exist," she said. "We kill demons because no one else can. What mortals know or don't know about us matters little. We must kill the demons because that is what we were made to do."

"You're talking like you're not one of them," Lenk said. "Mortals."

"We aren't. Not *exactly* like them, anyway." She studied him carefully.

"You've been in the city. You've seen the signs: his cultists, his name, the strife that follows. Sekhlen, master of the Order, saw them himself ages ago. He watched carefully, hoping he was wrong, but he was not." She rose to her feet. "Khoth-Kapira is returning.

"When he reigned over the mortals from his seat in Rhuul Khaas, he pronounced all gods dead and instated himself as the lord and savior of his people." She turned her eyes up and to the east. "Among all the Aeons, he was the most envious of the gods' creations, and he sought to remake a world in his image. But where creation came naturally to heaven, he struggled. He strained to create a perfect race, a world where every breath was owed to him.

"The lives he spent making this were…well, even our records strained to convey the number. The Order has watched for the return of many demons, but he has been one of our top priorities. For there was never a doubt to Master Sekhlen that Khoth-Kapira would try to pick up where he left off."

"And they sent you to stop him? One woman? Why not an army? Why not the whole Order?"

"We train specifically to avoid that," she said. "An army would be easily detected. Easily foiled. Khoth-Kapira sees more than you know."

More than one of us knows, certainly.

He opted not to say this. Perhaps it would have been wise to let her know of his conversations with the demon. But when he opened his mouth to, he found his mind drifting back to the city he had seen, of shicts and humans walking together, of the promise that Khoth-Kapira had made.

And maybe he was not ready to dash that dream.

"Why you?" he asked instead.

"Because killing is what we are made to do," she said flatly, "and I was made by the very best."

"Still, how can you be sure—"

"We've seen it." She gestured to the woods around them. "Even now the forest teems with his followers. They come from the cities, the deserts, the mountains: a slow-moving tide sliding inexorably east. They are called to him: the widows, the orphans, the broken. He calls to them, beckons them to his side."

"Is that such a bad thing?" Lenk asked. "Is it so bad that someone out there is looking out for those who have no one to look out for them?"

She cast an impaling glare at Lenk. "Would you trust an asp if it said it only wanted a kiss? Demons are not kind lovers, Lenk. They do not give freely. They do not 'look out' for anyone. There is always a price."

This he knew. From the many demons he had cut down, in Cier'Djaal and the wilds beyond, he knew there was always a price.

Or so he'd thought he knew.

That had been before Mocca, before thoughts of redemption.

Who set the price? The gods? Mortals? Could it not be that a demon could pay it, just as mortals could, with penance? Could it not be that anyone, born or made or cursed, could put their pain and fear behind them?

He stared at his hands. They looked normal to him. Soft flesh, however callused, wrapped around sticky sinew caked upon mortal bone. Like anyone else's. They might have been used to build a barn, drive a plow through a field, hammer a pair of horseshoes on an anvil. They might have rocked a wailing infant in the dead of night, raised the bridal veil on a young woman's face, held her hand years later when she breathed her last and begged him to go on.

But they hadn't done that.

They had found the hilt of a sword, soft throats in the night, the warmth of blood and the splinter of bone. And now all he could see on them was the scars. Scars that looked as though they had always been there.

What had Kataria seen, he wondered, when she looked at his hands? What had she felt when he laid them upon her bare shoulders, when they coaxed breeches off her hips, when they brushed against her lips, wary of the fangs hidden behind?

He wondered whose hands were upon her now.

Through the sweltering heat of the jungle, he felt a chill upon his skin. He looked down and saw slender fingers encircling his bicep. Shuro's skin was cold, cold as the stare she affixed upon him.

"I was found by Master Sekhlen when I was very young," she said. "In that time I have rarely spoken to anyone who wasn't exactly like me." She forced what was either a very awkward smile or a very localized seizure onto her face. "I . . . sometimes forget that not everyone takes the knowledge of what we are so easily. I'm sorry. For . . . for telling you you killed your family." She cleared her throat. "And all that."

"It's . . ." He shook his head. "It's fine."

"It is?"

"Well, no. It's not. But it's not your fault." He smiled at her, tried to make it seem less hollow than it felt. "Can't spend much time thinking on what isn't there, can you?"

She stared at him, through him. "Like your shict?"

His smile faded. He pulled away from her. "She wasn't mine."

"Oh." She winced. "I...sorry about that, too. I guess."

"Not your fault, either. She and I just...we...I don't know."

"I do." Her voice cut him, it was so sharp. "It wasn't just her, you know. It won't end with her."

"What?"

"She'd never understand you. She'd never even know you," Shuro said, earnestness in her voice. "Has she never looked upon you with mistrust? With fear?"

He stared at her, felt something rise in his gullet. "She has."

"And others? Other people?"

"Them, too."

She nodded. "So they do. So they would. All of them. They were made differently than we were, destined for different lives."

He opened his mouth to deny that. When no denial came, he tried to say something, anything beyond acknowledging how much he believed her.

"But you don't have to be alone," she said. And her eyes did not soften so much as glisten, moonlight off the ice of a frozen lake. "You can come back with me. You can come back to the Order."

"Back to killing," he muttered.

"It's what we do," Shuro said, sighing. "But not always. There are times when you don't think of violence, right? There are times when you don't have to carry a sword." Her hand found his, colder now than it had been. "Right?"

He had very much thought so. Once. Now he was not so sure.

"I have seen you fight," she said. "Together we can go to Rhuul Khaas. We can stop Khoth-Kapira. And when it's over, we can go back together. You can be among people who won't fear you, won't hate you for how you were made. You can come with me."

Shuro's voice was no less hard, even when she spoke so enthusiastically. Yet there was a comfort in that iron certainty, an assurance in how simple she made it all sound. As though she merely needed to say it and it would be so.

So much so that he found himself looking down at her hand, wondering if perhaps it was not so cold as he thought. So much so that he found himself whispering back to her.

"I can go with you," he said.

Lenk neglected to say how far he would go. Or even to what end he would go. And he certainly did not tell her that he had been accompanied this far by her quarry.

A decent man would have told her. At the very least, he would have turned her away.

But at that moment, something upon her face that resembled a smile—a real smile, bereft of sorrow or pain or anything beyond the simple enthusiasm of someone looking for a promise of tomorrow—made its way onto his face, too.

He found he could not look away from that enthusiasm, that certainty, that joy.

Not even to see the man in white standing at the other side of the fire, his form as hazy and fleeting as a nightmare. But if Lenk had looked up, he would have seen that Mocca stared at him with eyes black.

And his hands curled into fists at his sides.

TWENTY-FIVE

A Moon Painted Black

They were called scraws. And they had turned a conquest into a war.

From what Gariath had gathered—from human sources and from sources that couldn't afford to be ignorant of human problems—it had begun with the Empire of Karneria. The dark-skinned, fine-boned humans had armed themselves with spear and shield, golem and siege weapon, and a holy mandate to use them all in their conquest to make the world ready for their god, the Conqueror.

With weapons superior and legions innumerable, they had almost done it. Their march north had consumed many nations with names Gariath couldn't be bothered to remember—how important could they be if they had been conquered? From their red-mountained homes, across the plains and forests of the world, the Karnerians were stopped only when they attempted to cross a river called Pike's Ford into the recently unified realm of Saine.

There they had met the pale-skinned, burly Sainites.

And the Sainites had introduced them to the scraws.

They had emerged from their mountain aeries in such numbers as to darken the skies: winged beasts that came shrieking out of the clouds, each one bearing blue-coated soldiers armed with fireflasks and crossbows. They had swept over the legions, who could only stare up agog, and their superior mobility had turned the invincible Karnerian infantry into soft, slow-moving sacks of flesh to be filled with arrows and skewered on lances and incinerated by flame.

The Karnerian march was reversed immediately, and the next decade was spent with the legions retreating south, harried by the scraws, before the Karnerians could figure out how to combat this new menace with bigger bows and new tactics.

But the damage was done. The hitherto undefeated Karnerian legions had met their match. And the scraws had proven themselves a weapon that changed the world and struck fear into the hearts of the Sainites' enemies, be they Karnerian or from the territories previously conquered by Karnerians that now found themselves under Sainite rule.

If one paid attention, the scraws had begun the longest, bloodiest conflict the world had ever seen.

And yet, Gariath thought, *from up here they look like a bunch of stupid pigeons.*

Gariath stared down from the ridge to the convoy below. Stretching miles long, ten humans abreast, until they numbered hundreds, the Sainites trudged across the desert in a line of blue coats and tricorne hats. Their sabers rattled at their hips, their spears were slung across the kits that bent their backs, they sipped from flasks and complained about the heat and the sand and the road.

But Gariath's eyes were on the scraws.

Between each two lines of soldiers, a great wheeled platform drawn by horses stood. On beds of straw, the scraws snoozed as their humans pulled them through the desert.

From so high up, they looked not particularly impressive. Strange, certainly: Their heads were those of sharp-beaked birds, topped with sloping horns, wings sprouted from their backs, their forelegs ended in talons and their hindquarters looked like those of goats.

From here they looked fragile: delicate birds attached to delicate fauns, hollow bones waiting to be broken. Their humans, too, looked weak: frail little men and women wrapped in armor and coats that wouldn't protect them, clutching weapons that wouldn't save them.

And yet there were so many of them. Hundreds, on the march to Cier'Djaal, to add their own disease to that cesspit. And they walked so close to Shaab Sahaar and the tulwar did not even care.

Cowards, Gariath thought. *Huddling in their stinking city, unaware of the human filth that lurks nearby. But then, that is how they live, isn't it?*

He looked over the ridge, to the west, where Cier'Djaal lay. He couldn't see the city, but he could feel it, as he could feel any wound.

And without his even trying, his mind filled with *them*.

And he could see them clearly.

The tall rogue and the short wizard. The pointy-eared one, the one with brown hair.

And Lenk.

The humans. His humans. His *former* humans. There in that city, steeped in its filth, filth that they had chosen and cast him out of.

The tulwar were no different. Weak, cowardly, choosing familiar dirt and death over something brave and uncertain as the wilds. Their blades were empty boasts, hanging uselessly at their waists while humans marched arrogantly through their lands not two miles away.

Cowards.

Weaklings.

All of them. Every one of them.

He held his breath. Caught between the Sainite convoy and Shaab Sahaar as he was, he feared he might choke on the collective stink of fear if he were to draw in a whiff. Yet when he finally allowed his nostrils to be filled, it was with nothing so dramatic as fear.

Merely the reek of pipe smoke.

He glanced over his shoulder and saw company approaching: fat, gray-haired, puffing on his pipe. The old tulwar trudged up to the ridge beside Gariath and cast a look down at the Sainites. He took a long look over the column, saying nothing for a while.

"My father raised gaambols," he said after a time. "My favorite one, a small brown-haired female, died unexpectedly one day. He butchered it, sold the meat to the humans for a pittance, and then bought a map from them. He swore his son would not grow up ignorant of the world and made me pore over the parchment. Every night he would come home from the pens and test me on my knowledge of the map.

"I memorized the nations: Um'Bagwai, Jaharla, Nivoire, Alcumbral…" He chuckled. "I remember thinking, 'Why so many places for humans? Why don't they all just live in one place?' We tulwar are a vast and varied people, we need a lot of different lands for all the different clans. But humans, I thought, only came in just the one color. What did they need all the land for?"

He gestured out to the Sainites, their pale skin and fair hair.

"I had no idea that humans like this existed, back then. I had never seen any human but a Djaalic. I thought there was only just them." He chewed his pipe, puffed out a blot of smoke. "But then, I suppose they thought the same of us."

"No."

The old tulwar looked at Gariath, quirked a bushy eyebrow.

"They don't even think of us." He swept a clawed hand over the Sainite line. "These ones think only of other humans called Karnerians." He narrowed eyes brimming with contempt. "An entire city of warriors hangs over their heads and they give it not a thought."

"I would not say that."

Gariath looked to the old tulwar, followed his finger as he pointed up to the sky overhead. Painted black against the orange of a setting sun, he could see the elegant spirals of a pair of scraws as they sailed lazily through the air.

"Doubtless they have seen Shaab Sahaar," the old tulwar said. "Perhaps they mean to avoid conflict."

"What do they see, then?" Gariath snorted. "A collection of mud huts and rotting wood sprouting through filthy streets like weed. Not warriors. Not people."

The old tulwar loosed a low, thoughtful hum. "The humans saw us that way once. Thus the Uprising. Perhaps you are right."

"You're not an idiot, then. Good. I—"

"Then again, perhaps they are also surveying the city and wondering whether we would be amenable to trade. The humans, also, once saw us as partners."

"Maybe, but—"

"Or are they sizing up our defenses and planning for an attack? Who knows?"

Gariath whirled on the old tulwar with a snarl. "You speak in circles, old man."

"Once you hit a certain age, you're obligated to spew cryptic nonsense from time to time." A yellow-toothed grin formed around the old tulwar's pipe. "How would we convince young fools like you to do anything if we didn't convince them there was some greater meaning to it?"

He held up a gray hand to cut off any protest, leaving Gariath seething.

"But there is a purpose to that, even. We consider all possibilities because the last time we acted in haste, it cost us dearly. It was

Mototaru's passion that drove us to start the Uprising and march to Cier'Djaal, and his hesitancy that sent us fleeing in shameful retreat, carrying our dead on our backs."

"Haste can't kill nearly as swiftly as cowardice does," Gariath snarled, slapping the old tulwar's hand away from his face. "I don't need to know this Mototaru to know he was an idiot weakling. His hesitation to fight was what killed the tulwar, not his decision to attack."

"Possibly." The old tulwar hummed. "But we do not know what he saw that made him turn away. He faced many dragonmen. Bigger than you, even."

"Then he should have fought to the last breath. Died for what he believed in."

"Interesting." The old tulwar scratched the hair around his chin. "So anything worth doing is worth dying for?"

"*Compromise* is a fancy word for *cowardice*."

The old tulwar smiled. No teeth. No mischief. Something whimsical and tender flashed in his eyes, a look he might have offered a grandchild.

"Perhaps, had you been there, the Uprising might have ended differently." He looked out over the ridge. "Perhaps the tulwar would have emerged victorious, won their freedom and their dignity." The smile faded. "Or perhaps you would have led us to kill every human that walked or crawled or cowered in Cier'Djaal.

"Which is why I wonder, dragonman, what you want to see happen in this world." He looked intently at Gariath, eyes hard as rock. "And what would you do to see it."

Gariath looked back over the ridge. In all the time that they had been talking, the line of Sainites hardly seemed to have moved at all. Perhaps they were simply slow. Or perhaps there were just that many of them. So many that, no matter how quickly they moved, there would be no end to them.

"My sons..." He choked on the words. They tasted like dust in his mouth, it had been so long since he had spoken of them. "When they were born, I knew they would live a hard life. We are *Rhega*, we are made strong for that reason." He bit back the dust, forced iron into his throat. "But it wasn't until I went out there, into the world of humans, that I realized there would have been no place for them. And even though they were gone, I didn't..."

"I thought I had found a place," he said. "But I was wrong."

He curled his hands into fists. Felt his claws pierce his palms and make the blood flow between his fingers.

"For them, for us, people like us," he growled, "there will never be a place. Not unless we carve it out."

For a brief moment, his nostrils caught the scent of something. Between wisps of pipe smoke, something hot and fiery and overpowering in its fury filled his nostrils.

But when he turned to see where it had come from, the old tulwar was already walking away, a cloud of smoke haloing his head. And through it his voice cut cold and clear as a blade.

"Then," he said, "I suppose you'd better do exactly that."

He thought to speak, but another scent caught him before he could. The familiar reek of humanity filled his nostrils, but much closer.

He looked down. Among the scrubgrass of the ridge, two miles away from the line, a quartet of Sainites picked their way through with small spears and nets. Foragers, he suspected. Or deserters. Something like that.

And the old tulwar's words rang through his head. What would he do to carve out a place in this world?

His sons were long gone. He had buried them, grieved, tried to join them and failed. But there were many other sons—tulwar sons, tulwar daughters, Daaru and Kudj and Kharga—who would live forever in a shadow, forever displaced, if someone didn't start carving.

He was *Rhega*. He was the strongest. He was the one to fight. He was the one to survive. For so long his place had been to do exactly those things among his humans. But they were gone now. And he had to find a place once again.

Maybe that was why he stepped to the edge of the ridge and leapt off. Or maybe it was because he was angry that he went sliding down toward the Sainites. Or maybe he simply didn't know why he opened his mouth and bellowed.

"KARNERIA! SHAAB SAHAAR FOR KARNERIA!"

But in another breath, it didn't matter.

He was already looking at them as they looked up in alarm, and he wondered which one of them he was going to leave alive to tell the tale.

It might not work.

His breath was labored as he entered Shaab Sahaar. The crowds closed in around him, their stink filled his snout, made it hard to breathe.

They might not take the bait. There was no need to do that. You were a fool. This city can't handle it. It's not going to work. You've killed them all. It might not work. What have you done? What have you done? What have you done?

"Dragonman?"

Out of the noisome crowd, he heard a soft voice and found a small body to match it. He looked down and saw the young tulwar girl, hair still sparse beneath her *chota*, who quickly looked down as embarrassed colors painted her face.

Daaru's daughter. What was her name again?

"Deji," he muttered, softly to match her voice. He knelt down to look at her. "What are you doing here?"

"Mother sent Father, Duja, and Kudj out to buy vegetables. Some Chee Chree refugees came in and they brought things that grow. She says Duja eats too much meat, so she wanted us to buy as many as—" Deji's eyes went wide. She looked up, the color on her face paling. "You're hurt."

"What?"

He looked down at his hands. Blood stained his claws, his hands, all the way to his wrists. How had there been so much? There hadn't seemed this much when—

What have you done?

"It's nothing." He rose to his feet, tried to hide his hands. "I'm fine."

"But you're—" Deji tried to walk toward him.

"Deji!" A loud, boastful cry. Daaru came swaggering up through the crowd, his smile broad and toothy and his arms full of sacks of ripe vegetables. "You wander too much, girl. Your mother worries about your brother too much to be concerned that you might also be *duwun*." He came to a halt, regarded Gariath. "You have returned. Spent much time thinking?"

Gariath said nothing. The only words he could think of were ones he did not want Daaru to hear. He merely nodded stiffly.

"Father, the dragonman—" Deji began to say.

"Ah. Squib see?"

In another moment Gariath was grateful that the lumbering hulk of Kudj—Duja riding upon one shoulder and a giant sack of vegetables on the other—precluded further conversation.

"Squib just need time to think," Kudj rumbled as he emerged from a quickly scattering crowd to join them. "Squibs see question, want answer. Vulgore see question, want food. Take time to taste question, digest, come up with answer. Much better that way."

"So long as you are at peace in the city, I am at peace with you," Daaru sighed. He offered a smile to Gariath. "Though I had to do much to soothe the *Humn* after your...outburst. They are not used to treating with outsiders."

"I am sorry," Gariath said.

It might have been the first time he had uttered those words. But he knew it would not be the last.

"But Father!" Deji tried to speak up. "The dragonman, he—"

"He is still our guest, Deji!" Daaru snapped. "I will hear no more of it. Your mother is already waiting. She will beat us both if I take much longer to...to..."

Daaru looked up, aware of a crowd that had suddenly grown quiet and still around him.

It had happened so slowly that none of them had noticed it. Every tulwar, every man and woman and child thronging Shaab Sahaar's streets, suddenly looked up to the sky, awed. Gariath did not.

For he already knew what they saw.

"Father?" Duja asked from atop Kudj's shoulder. "What is it?"

Daaru had no answer to that. He likely had no idea what to call the great winged beast that hovered in the air over the roofs of Shaab Sahaar, flapping great wings as it surveyed the city below. Nor would any of the tulwar.

None of them had ever seen a scraw before.

"What is it?" one of them muttered. "A giant bird?"

"Chee Chree vegetables," another grunted. "That shit they smoke gets in their food. Makes us see things."

"What's that on its back?" someone else asked, anxious. "Is that a human?"

But Gariath could not hear them over the sound of his thoughts.

It worked. You did it.

What have you done?

Gariath held his breath, unable to bear the scent of their fear as they watched the rider wheel the scraw about. With a shriek the beast took off, flying away from the city. The tulwar's voices rose in its wake, a nervous tranquility breaking their paralyzed panic.

"Vulgore." Daaru's voice was hard as he turned to Kudj. He seized Deji's hand, pulled her toward the giant. "I need you to take my children back to my home. Can you do this for me?"

"Kudj is capable," the vulgore rumbled. "But Kudj not sure if that going to be—"

"More! MORE! THERE'S MORE!"

A cry rose up from the crowd, followed by a hundred more and a hundred fingers to accompany, all of them directed to the sky.

Gariath looked up. He saw the scraws flying toward the city in two perfect rows. Their feathers looked black against the dying light of the sun. The blue coats of their Sainite riders fluttered behind them.

"They're flying so low. What do they want?"

"Go to the center. Tell the *Humn*. Grab your swords."

"Get your children back to your homes. Hurry, damn you!"

What have you done?

He needed to ask the question only once more before it was answered.

In the warbling song of a Sainite bugle from high above. In the shrieks of the scraws as they flew overhead. In the whistle of flasks falling from the sky in their wake like black feathers.

Gariath got his answer.

He had exactly one breath, full of the reek of fear, to appreciate it.

And then the world erupted into flame.

The screams of the crowd were drowned out in the shattering of glass and the roar of waking infernos. The fireflasks burst apart on impact, tar and flame splattering across wooden buildings and dirt roads and bare flesh and chewing ravenously into whatever they touched.

The towering wooden buildings were crowned with flame. Great rows of fire blossomed across the streets, eager gardens that rose up to cut off the fleeing tulwar. The only screams loud enough to be heard over the panic were the death shrieks of those swallowed by the hungry flames.

Just like that. A few dead bodies. That was all it took to send Shaab Sahaar to war.

Or hell.

He felt a grip on his arm. He looked down, saw Daaru's face flooded with color, eyes wide and wild. The tulwar's teeth were bared in a snarl, his mane bristling.

"*Rhega*," he snarled. "To the city center. *Fight* with me."

No questions. No room left for doubt. No breath for fear. All around were the stink of smoke and the shadows of people fleeing, trying to brave the flames as even more scraws flew in, dropping another volley of fireflasks.

This was what Gariath wanted.

This war.

"To the death," he snarled.

And with that they were off.

Leaping through the flames, leaping over bodies, darting through the smoke and tearing through the streets, they ran.

Through the gaps between the wooden spires, Gariath could see them: more scraws descending upon the city from all angles. These seemed overburdened, brimming with some cargo Gariath couldn't see clearly from here. What were they carrying?

Another wailing bugle sounding a charge answered that.

In a flash of blue and silver, Sainites burst from a nearby alleyway not fifty paces ahead. Their lips split with war cries and their swords flashing, cutting down all those who tried to flee past or to protect themselves.

Gariath did not slow down. He felt only the blood pumping in his veins and his legs pumping beneath him as he picked up speed, met their war cries with a howl that drowned their feeble voices, and crashed into them like a ram of flesh and bone.

Sainite blades cut at him wildly. He wasn't sure whom his fists caught as he lashed out: A jaw crunched, an arm snapped, a trio of ribs crumpled. When they finally took stock of their situation enough to back away from him, two of them lay dead at his feet and four more surrounded him.

They didn't flee. They were not afraid. One of them rushed toward him, the Sainite's war cry proud and fearless.

Right up until the arrow took him in the throat.

The rage ebbed from the Sainites' eyes as they saw the hail of arrows falling from above. As they fell, impaled, Gariath looked up and saw lean tulwar in green *chota*s. Their bows were raised in victory, their howls wild across the sky.

"*Chee Chree!*" they cried. "*Chee Chree!*"

The roar carried, on the flight of every arrow as the Chee Chree clansmen and -women drew arrows and fired at the scraws overhead and the Sainites beginning to flood the city below.

The scraws' cargo. They were flying troops into Shaab Sahaar.

This was what he wanted. This was what he had done.

This was he, bleeding from their blades. This was Daaru, at his side once more. This was they, running through the fires falling from heaven and the arrows rising up to meet them as they rushed toward the city center. More joined them, their screams ringing in his ear as they fled with him through the avenues wreathed in flame.

Three dark shapes tore overhead with a screech. The scraws flew over him, to the end of the road, wheeled around. In tight formation they swooped low, sharp lances extended as they flew down the road toward Gariath and the fleeing tulwar.

Gariath skidded to a halt, holding the crowd behind him back as the scraws came shrieking toward them. There was no time to disperse the crowd, and to meet the beasts would be certain death.

Perhaps that was what he deserved.

"*YENGU THUUN!*"

Another war cry came from the roofs overhead, followed shortly by a plummeting form of shrieking fur and muscle.

The gaambols leapt off the roofs, falling like an avalanche upon the scraws. Their muzzles were gaping in simian shrieks, their powerful hands snapping wings, tearing riders from saddles, curling into fists to smash avian skulls. There was no elegance to their attack, no formation or command. The beasts indulged in a brief orgy of violence and meat, heedless of whose it was that they shoveled into their mouths.

Their tulwar riders didn't seem in a hurry to stop them.

"Daaru!" One of them wheeled her gaambol toward them. The one from the streets, days ago. Ululang. "What's happening? We saw these... these things flying on Shaab Sahaar. Why are they attacking?"

"Because they are humans, Ululang!" Daaru roared back. "The city center, does it hold?"

"Tho Thu Bhu clan holds it, along with the *Humn*, but there are soldiers pouring in and these bird-things...Chee Chree arrows can't find them and my gaambols can barely catch them if they fly low enough."

"And Rua Tong?" Daaru asked.

"They are mustering. Most of them were in their homes on the outskirts when the attack happened."

"I must get to them, lead them back to fight." Daaru looked to Gariath. "You must protect the *Humn*. They are our entire people. If you need me to beg, make it quick."

Gariath nodded. "Save your groveling for when I save your monkey ass."

Daaru grinned. "*Un kamaa*, dragonman." He looked to Ululang. "Get him to the city center."

No more than a few brief words were traded before Gariath hauled himself up into the saddle behind her. Daaru took off running down a nearby alley, the crowd he had been leading already scattered. Ululang turned to her clansmen and -women and their feasting mounts and barked an order.

Even with his added weight, the gaambol easily leapt to the roofs of the buildings and took off running, the others close behind. They loped across rooftops, leaping over alleys and swinging from eaves as if they were vines. And from so high up, he could see what he had wrought.

Fire was everywhere. In iron formation the scraws swept over the buildings, dropping more fireflasks, flying in more troops, before taking off again to go pick up fresh squadrons. Chee Chree archers took down a few, but the scraws' vengeance was swift as they swooped down, plucking them off the rooftops and disemboweling them in the air. The gaambols were slightly more effective, leaping from the roofs to tackle the avian creatures out of midair, but just as many were skewered on lances or shot dead by crossbow strafing.

It was war. A real war. This was how war smelled.

All the smoke, all the blood, all the flame and screaming and fear. He thought he might choke on it.

But before he could, he felt his stomach rise into his throat and suddenly drop, hammering itself back into place as his mount leapt from the roofs and onto the street.

He looked up and surveyed their surroundings. The city center sprawled out around them in all its vastness. It looked nothing like the place where he had attended the *Humn Tul Naa* what seemed like so long ago.

Instead of gathering together in orderly clusters, the clans here milled and wallowed in one massive herd, their *chota*s stained black with blood and soot. They moaned and wept, cowering beneath whatever cover they could find. No warriors here; they were children, elders, fathers, and mothers who stayed behind while their spouses fought.

What fighters remained here were Tho Thu Bhu warriors, who huddled at every alley mouth and roadway, huddling behind stout shields to ward off Sainite charges and crossbow bolts. Chee Chree archers lingered on the rooftops, watching the skies.

"Back to the fight for me," Ululang said. "If you're Daaru's guest, I trust you as he does." She leaned back and shoved Gariath off her beast's back. "Don't make me regret that, lizard."

By the time he landed in the dirt, the gaambols were already leaping to the roofs and returning to the fray. Gariath staggered to his feet, suddenly feeling quite sore as all his new wounds and old scars protested at once.

He looked around at the cowering tulwar: their fearful eyes, their lips quivering in nondescript whimpers. Children wailed, parents tried to quiet them, elders simply stared, expressionless, at a sky on fire.

He forced himself to look away. He had made his choices.

This was what he wanted.

Towering over the tulwar as he did, it wasn't hard for him to locate the *Humn*. They squatted near the center of the center, as though they had not moved from that spot since the *Humn Tul Naa*. Their heads were bowed in deliberation, though any of the calm that had been in their voices that night was dead and buried.

"We can negotiate," Gowaa of the Tho Thu Bhu said, breathless. "Offer them trade."

"They came to *kill*, not *trade*, you fat idiot!" Sagar of the Yengu Thuun snarled at him. "We should be out there fighting. Dekuu is leading the Chee Chree. We cannot let them be slaughtered!"

"We can't, no," Dugu of the Rua Tong growled. "But how? These birds. Arrows do not stop them. There are not enough gaambols. We are helpless."

"You are only helpless if you are weak."

They all looked up to Gariath with varying degrees of scorn. He ignored this, as well as the few tulwar who tried to block his way as he waded toward them.

"You sit and talk while your people die," he snarled. "Your warriors are scattered and being slaughtered. Your city is burning. The time has come to strike back. Strike *hard*."

"And what do you think we are doing, reptile?" Dugu growled in response. "Sipping tea? We are not served by sending our warriors out to be killed blindly."

"And yet," Sagar muttered, "they are killed all the same."

"All your clans are here," Gariath roared to be heard above the desperate noise of the center. "All the might of the tulwar is *here*. Rua Tong, Chee Chree, Yengu Thuun, Tho Thu Bhu: Between all of you, you cannot fight *back*?"

"*DO NOT SPEAK TO US OF THIS,*" Dugu roared back, leaping to unsteady feet. Despite his age and size, he bristled with a fury that had not diminished with the ages. "Were it decided by fury and spit alone, the humans would be dead already. As it is, we have no weapons that can kill beasts of that size!"

A moment of silence, choking on smoke, hung in the air between them. When it broke, it was the soft, almost meek voice of Gowaa that did it.

"We have the fishing spears," he offered, sheepish.

"Spears?" Sagar blinked, stunned. "You old fool, we are not fishing."

"Our clan expeditions upriver to hunt sometimes," Gowaa said. "We have spears. Spears heavy and big enough to fight off river bulls."

"River bulls," Dugu repeated.

"But they're too heavy to throw that far," Gowaa said. "You'd never get close to those...those..." He waved his hand to the sky overhead. "Whatevers."

"Are they heavier than me?" Gariath asked.

"The birds? Probably."

"The spears, moron."

"Oh," Gowaa hummed. "Of course not."

"Then they can be carried by the gaambols," Gariath said. "One of them just brought me here." He pointed to the wooden buildings, those still standing. "The scraws fly low to drop their flasks. If you can get warriors up there to throw them, you can use your spears."

The *Humn* exchanged glances, considering. Gowaa looked befuddled at the idea. Sagar shrugged, unable to offer a better idea. Dugu looked up to the dragonman with a scowl.

"But the humans on the ground—"

"Will be met by the Rua Tong," Gariath said. "Before long the scraws will burn everything left. You either do this now or die."

"It will take time to get the spears from our houses," Gowaa muttered.

"Then I will send riders," Sagar said.

They turned away from Gariath as they called warriors over. That was fine, Gariath was content to ignore them, as well. In another moment a small party had departed to go gather the weapons. The plan was set into motion, the defense of Shaab Sahaar assembled.

They would emerge victorious. They would see the humans would attack them, kill them for no reason. They would see he had been right, all along, about everything. And they would march to Cier'Djaal and cleanse that city of filth.

It had worked. They would see.

They would all see.

He looked up to the sky, breathed deep of the plumes of smoke coiling over the eaves of the buildings. The sounds of screams and sobbing had grown more distant, drowned out by scraw shrieks and gaambol screeches as the battle raged over the rooftops.

A flight of scraws swooped overhead and the crowd of tulwar screamed, waiting for fireflasks that never fell.

They aren't attacking, Gariath noted. *They haven't attacked yet. An undefended part of the city, choked with targets, and they haven't so much as dropped a flask here.* He glanced around the square's defenders: sizable, but they wouldn't withstand any direct assault. *What are they waiting for?*

A wordless scream of panic came from the western edge of the city center.

Probably that.

He had scarcely laid eyes on the thicket of tulwar shield bearers at the southern end of the city center before they suddenly went flying. Bodies went tumbling through the air to break upon ground and stone.

The assembled crowds went running, screaming. An avian screech tore through the air like a scythe.

What emerged into the city center could scarcely be called a beast, was perhaps too big even to be called a monster. It was a scraw, but only barely: It stood twice as tall, twice as long, twice as broad as any of the slender creatures sailing overhead. Its hooves were flat and made for stomping, its talons the color of iron, its black fur and feathers painted in blood. Its head was broader and flatter than the others', its beak thicker and sharper, its eyes red and alive with fire beneath a pair of ram's horns sweeping back from its skull.

No rider adorned its back. This beast carried itself too proudly for that. It spread its wings, massive feathered crescents, and reared back. Its shriek shook the roofs and sent the tulwar quaking.

The call was answered in a flood of Sainites, the humans coming in behind the beast with crossbows and blades naked in their hands. The tulwar parted like a tide, struggling to get away even as warriors fought to get to the city center to combat the incursion.

Too much panic in the crowd, too much hesitation in the warriors. Not a chance between them. All would be slaughtered unless—

"RUA TONG!"

Something like that happened.

Gariath looked behind him. From the eastern edge of the center they came: their faces awash with color and their long, curved, killing blades high in their hands. They charged through the center like a tide, pushing the noncombatants behind them as they rushed to meet the Sainites, heedless of the crossbow bolts flying and the blades swinging and the—

Another trembling screech ripped through the air.

The giant scraw strode forward to meet the Rua Tong clan, began swatting them aside with its wings, crushing them in its talons, plucking them up like worms in its beak and bisecting them in one bite. They did not run. They died fearlessly.

And worthlessly.

Bold, he thought. *And so stupid.*

Human, shict, tulwar; it did not matter. Eventually everyone needed him to fix everything.

He gave no roar as he took off at a charge; no one would have heard it through the carnage. But the cacophony of battle melded in his ear-frills, became so muddled and indistinct as to become a sort of silence unto itself.

The sounds of those dying—the Rua Tong bitten in half, the elders trampled underfoot—were silent. He was deaf to the sounds of steel clashing and bolts entering flesh. Even the splatter of blood as the great scraw dashed a limp tulwar body against a wall went unheard. He could hear only himself, only his ragged breaths, only his heart pumping, only his feet on the sandy floor.

And as he drew in a breath of cinders, he heard a single note of silence as he took one great leap.

His body collided with the scraw's face, the blood of its recent kills spattering his skin as it let out a shriek of alarm. It shook its head in an attempt to dislodge him. He gripped it by its horns, swung around to its back, and straddled its neck. The creature's shrieks grew louder, its thrashing more fierce. Gariath held on, tightened his grip, pulled its head back.

Gariath's muscles seared as the creature shook its head wildly. The scraw was strong, no doubt.

But he was strong, too. He was *Rhega*. And he had fought much bigger than this.

He snarled, jerked hard on the horns to pull the beast's head back. He risked letting go of one horn as he leaned forward and brought his claws about in a wicked hook, seeking the beast's face. Something soft exploded beneath his fingers, bathed his hand in warm liquid. The scraw wailed. Gariath grinned.

His time among the humans had not been without merit. They had not been strong, but they knew a few tricks: Never give up too early, never think too hard about a plan.

And always, *always* go for the eyes.

The scraw's anger was fierce, its pain was monstrous. It reared back with such swiftness and force as to cause him to lose his grip, sending him tumbling down its back. He only barely managed to catch hold of its haunches, sinking his claws into its thick flesh.

Its shrieking panic sent it tearing across the city center, galloping haphazardly about the place as it sought escape. Gariath could feel each jolt as it trampled tulwar warrior and Sainite alike, bodies crushed under its hooves and rent beneath its talons. Its wings shook free, spread wide. It leapt.

And Gariath felt the world disappear beneath him.

The scraw carried him high among the columns of smoke twisting into the sky. From here he could hear only the screeches of other scraws as they passed by. Even the sound of his own breath was lost as the beast tore wild spirals through the air.

He snarled. Hand over hand, arms burning as he fought the wind in his face, he slowly made his way up. The thing's hide was thick, it scarcely even bled as he clawed up its back.

He had to get to the head, find a weak spot, bring the beast down. This was the biggest weapon the Sainites had. If it fell, the rest would follow.

If he fell with it...

Well, he supposed he deserved that.

Crossbow bolts whizzed over his head. Sainite riders flew past him, attempting to shoot him off. The wind was too fierce, the great scraw's movement too haphazard.

He had no sooner reached the middle of its back than it dived suddenly, sending him plummeting down its spine. He caromed off its horns, felt the nothingness of empty air beneath it before something sharp pierced his flesh. He felt the scraw's talons sink into his sides, felt its claws tighten around his body, felt the heat of its breath as he looked up into its single red eye and gaping beak, open in a shriek.

He lashed out instinctively, catching the beak with one hand to keep its razor tip away from him. The other shot out in a fist, hammering blow after blow upon the creature's face as it pulled up and shot through the air. But his arm tired swiftly, his hand bled in the thing's beak. The scraw didn't seem to be so much as slowing down from his attacks, and its beak drew ever closer to his head.

Maybe he was getting old.

Or maybe he deserved this, too.

The sound of the wind splitting reached his ear-frills. Another screech tore free of the scraw's mouth, likely aided by the seven-foot length of wood that suddenly protruded from the creature's shoulder.

Gariath stole only a momentary glance, just enough to see them. But a moment was enough.

Upon the towers not yet burned, the gaambols clung to the eaves as their riders drew back tremendous spears and hurled them through the air. Scraws fell, struck dead by the blows, and spiraled limply to the earth.

They had done it. Those cowards, those weaklings, they had somehow made the plan work. Good for them.

He'd have to remember to tell them that, if he lived.

The scraw's iron grip tightened around him. He couldn't hold its beak back any longer. He risked releasing it, smashing his fist against its head with the hope of distracting it long enough to reach out and seize the spear embedded in its shoulder. With a roar he twisted and jerked it free in a gout of warm red.

The scraw's head snapped forward, beak gaping. It stopped with a sudden jerk, a spatter of crimson, as Gariath drove the spear forward and into its collar. Its jagged head bit deeper than any arrow or claw could hope to, plunging into its flesh and past its bones.

If its scream was any indication, the pain must have been unbearable.

He could hardly blame it for dropping him.

He clung to the spear, but it merely tore out of the beast's breast with a spray of gore. He fell, one red drop among many, to the earth. He had no idea how low they had been flying when he was dropped—it certainly *felt* as if it had been very high when he struck the earth and felt his breath explode from him.

And yet he lived.

His wind returned to him in slow, ragged, struggling breaths, but it returned. His wounds ached, burned, and stung from sand and smoke, but no more. His muscles seared, felt as though they had been torn and chopped with a fine blade, but they still carried him back to his feet, after a time.

He looked to the skies, now dark with nightfall. From the fires below, he could just barely see the remaining scraws as they wheeled about and veered back toward the direction of their convoy, chased by spears and arrows.

Only when he was sure they were retreating did he look to the city.

He was not sure how he had expected this to end. Perhaps it had been too much to think there might be cheering for the victory. He did not fault the tulwar warriors for not even loosing roars of fury. But he had not expected such silence from them, such glass-eyed, vacant-faced quiescence turned to a sky they would never trust again.

What buildings had fallen now lay in rubble or smoldered in massive pyres for the dead who had been inside. What buildings stood now groaned precipitously and swayed uneasily as gaambols climbed down. The city was bright with firelight, and the smoke that rose from it was black enough to choke even the night.

They had won. Yet to anyone who might have been watching, Shaab Sahaar was already dead.

TWENTY-SIX

THE WOLVES GATHER

"The first time I ever left my home was the night after my mother died."

These were the first words Kwar had spoken that night.

When Kataria had left Lenk sleeping alongside a fire long since smoldered to whispers, she had gone to the edge of the camp. There, among the dunes and under a pale moon, Kwar had found her.

"I hated my father, the way he wanted to make peace with the humans after what they had done to her. I hated Thua, and how he always cried and begged me to stay. I had nothing left, so in the middle of the night, I sneaked out of my tent and climbed the walls of Shicttown and left into the desert."

They had sat on the edge of a dune together, staring out over the rolling scrubgrass.

"I stayed out there two nights before I ran out of food. My mother had already taught me how to hunt. But I didn't. It wasn't hunger that brought me back to Shicttown that time. Or the next. Or the hundred other times I ran away and came back."

Kwar had looked at Kataria. In the darkness her eyes had looked like nocturnal beasts, alive and hungry.

"I couldn't stand the silence. If I wasn't hunting, I would hear my mother's voice and I couldn't..." Kwar had looked away then. "But when I came back to Shicttown, it was just as bad. Everyone went carrying on, hunting and trading and raising yijis, like Mother hadn't died, like she hadn't even existed. But I couldn't hear her voice, so I stayed. I thought I'd die there."

The smile she gave Kataria then was a lying smile, small and scared.

"But then I met you."

Kataria had pulled her knees to her chest. "You act like that's a solution."

"When I'm around you, I feel...I..." Kwar looked at her hands. "Like I always wanted to feel. We could go, you and I." She made a gesture out over the desert. "Just go. Leave everything."

"What about Thua?"

"I will leave him."

"We'd starve."

"I can hunt."

"We'd die of thirst."

"There are oases."

"We'd be eaten by yijis."

"They don't like the taste of shicts."

"Khoshicts. What about pale shicts?"

"Who would like the taste of a pale shict?" Kwar had nudged Kataria with her shoulder. "You taste like undercooked food."

"Well, why do you even need me if you've got all the fucking answers?" Kataria had laughed a lying laugh. She had stared at the ground. "It's not that simple."

"'Not that simple,'" Kwar had snarled. "My father said the same thing. It's something people say when they're too afraid to act. What's not simple about it? I want to be with you. Do you want to be with me?"

"I do."

"Do you want to be with him?"

Kataria had closed her eyes. "I do."

"How? *How?*" Kwar had leapt to her feet. "He's human. *Kou'ru.* Don't you know what they did to us? What they still do to us?"

"He's not like the others."

"He is."

"I know he's different."

"You've spent too much time around them. You've started thinking like them. You need to—"

"Do not tell me what I need." She had risen to meet Kwar with a snarl. "He *is* different. Different enough to spend two years of my life with. I can't just walk away. I can't just go in the night. I can't kill him like that."

"But you can do that to me?" Kwar had stepped forward, tears in her eyes. "I love you."

"I know." Kataria had pressed her brow against Kwar's. "I know, I know. I can't...I need to..." She had shaken her head. "I can't go." The words had hurt to speak. But they had sounded right. She had let go. She had turned away. "Not yet—"

And Kwar's fist had cracked against her temple.

And the night had gone completely dark.

⊷ ⊶⊱≡⊰ ⊶

Shicts had received few gifts from their maker.

The Dread Goddess Riffid had created strong children and saw no need to coddle them. But the most important gift was the bow and the hands to use it. Shictish hands were fine, made for following tracks and drawing arrows.

Humans claimed to have gods, but it was clear just from looking at their brutish hands that they were simply monkeys who had learned how to grab swords. All their power was in their hairy palms, and their fat fingers struggled with the finer manipulations of more precise weaponry.

Human fingers were clumsy, inept, groping.

Shictish fingers were thin, dexterous, elegant.

And yet, Kataria thought, they all felt the same when they were forced upon her.

"I had heard that touching a human causes hair to sprout out of everywhere." She felt a grip tighten, viselike, around her jaw. "My grandfather always said that's why you never saw shicts with beards." The grip forced her face this way and that, inspecting her. "I don't see any hair coming out of you, though. Is it different for the pale shicts?"

Kataria kept her eyes shut, to hide the impotent anger flashing in her scowl. She bit back her anger, her shame, her helplessness, buried it in an empty mind beneath a layer of darkness. And for a moment she could pretend like the last two days hadn't happened.

But soon enough the Howling reminded her that it had.

His Howling, specifically.

In the darkness of her mind she could hear him: the grinding of sharp teeth twisted in a grin, the excited gibbering whine of a yiji closing in for the kill, the sound of a tongue slurping the marrow from a cracked bone.

And through his Howling, she knew his name.

"Do not act as though you cannot hear me, *kou'loho*."

Yarra.

Her eyes snapped open an instant before he struck her. The blow across her face sent her reeling, but only for a moment. The fire that burned through her veins and bade her lunge at him in response, too, was short-lived.

The rawhide securing her hands behind her back gnawed at already bloody wrists, sapped the fury from her in a twist of sudden agony. Breathless, she slumped against the tent pole she had been secured to, scowling up into the sneer that looked down upon her.

He had a face like a hatchet, all his features coming together in the center in long, hard angles. A hawkish nose and pointed chin split with the twist of his grin, his canines big even for a shict's. His body was too skinny to be a proper warrior's, the muscle beneath his dark khoshict skin flimsy and underdeveloped, unworthy of the bow that he wore strung across his back.

Yarra.

Kataria had learned his name the moment she had laid eyes on him, his Howling intruding into her skull on the grin he wore when she was brought before the *Kho Khun*.

Yarra.

She'd heard his name when she had been marched to the modest tent at the edge of the camp, pressed against the pole and her hands tied. She heard his name with every grin he flashed, every blow he struck, every moment he was within earshot.

Yarra.

She held on to that name, held it in her teeth as she glared up at him. She gnawed on it, chewed it into pulp until the blood of his name filled her mouth. And, with her ears rigid and quivering and her eyes narrowed to thin slits, she reached out with her own Howling, into his skull, and spit his name at him.

He reeled as if struck; for surely he had been, to feel a presence so hostile in his skull, let alone one from a *kou'loho*. And with nothing else to strike with, he raised his hand high above his head and aimed for her jaw. She met him with a snarl, challenging him to bring it down, promising much worse when she got free.

"Yarra."

His hand was stilled by a voice from the tent's entrance. And though it filled Yarra with fear, it filled Kataria with something else. As she looked to the slender shadow filling the entrance, she'd never thought she could hate someone more fiercely than she hated the man before her.

But then, there were so many things about Kwar she hadn't expected.

The khoshict woman pointedly ignored Kataria's scowl as she entered, her attentions focused on Yarra, who gave begrudging attention in return.

"The council is about to convene," she said. "They say they want you on lookout duty tonight."

"Lookout duty?" Yarra cast a sneer at Kataria before looking back to Kwar. He spit his next words. "What of the *kou'loho*?"

Silence for a moment. "They didn't say."

"Fine," Yarra grunted. "If that's what they want."

He offered her a nod of acceptance before moving past her to leave. He had barely taken a step outside the tent when Kwar suddenly spoke up.

"Yarra."

He paused, glanced over his shoulder. "Yeah?"

"You left-handed or right?"

"Right. Why do you—"

The rest of his question was lost in the crack of bone as Kwar smashed her fist against the bridge of his nose. He spun, fell to the ground on his stomach. Kwar slammed one foot between his shoulder blades and seized his right wrist. Swiftly she grabbed his first and second fingers.

"Learn to use your left for a while."

And without a hint of emotion on her face, she bent them back.

And the swift snapping sound paled in comparison to the scream that followed.

"*BITCH! YOU BITCH!*" Yarra shrieked, cradling his fingers as she released his hand. "I'll tell the *Kho Khun*! I'll tell them what you did!"

"I don't give a shit what you say, worm." She reached down and seized him by his hair, pulling him up by the scalp to face her. "But I'll do worse if you don't listen to me." She leaned so close as to spit in his face with each word. "You never touch her again. Not to strike her. Not to tie her. Not even to help her drink. If I ever see you *look* at her wrong, I'll gouge out your left eye and make you watch me eat it with your right. Do you hear me?" she roared, shaking his head. "*Do you hear me?*"

Yarra could but nod weakly and scamper away as she released him. She chased him out with a growl before turning her attentions to her captive.

She met Kataria's eyes for only a moment. Her ears curled themselves over, closing them to anything she might say. Kataria's ears went rigid, attempting to reach out with the Howling, to send something—a snarl, a whimper, anything—to Kwar.

No answers. No pity. Not so much as an awkward look of apology. Kwar had given her nothing but silence since she had been kidnapped. Kataria was not sure why she expected more tonight.

Nor was she sure why she received more.

"He'll heal," Kwar muttered.

"Too bad," Kataria snarled in reply, canines bared.

Kwar turned her eyes away as she stalked behind the tent pole and tended to Kataria's wrists.

"He loves his tribe. He fears for its safety." The khoshict's voice was soft as she began to untie Kataria. "He has never seen a *kou'loho* before."

Kataria winced at that word.

It rang painfully in her ears, now as it had when she had been brought before the *Kho Khun* last night. Now as it had when they had heard Kwar's testimony as to why she had brought another shict as a prisoner. Now as it had when they had branded her with that word.

Kou'loho. One who had been touched by humans. The word was interchangeable with *slave, criminal, unclean*, for the shicts saw no difference.

Kataria had been helpless to deny the accusation. And though she knew the word, she had never thought to call herself it. Not until her own people had.

"The tribes are gathering tonight," Kwar said.

Kataria felt her wrists pull apart suddenly, sticky with blood, as the rawhide bonds snapped free. Tortured skin and aching muscles suddenly screamed out.

"The Seventh is here. The Ninth has been streaming in all day," the khoshict continued as Kataria stepped away from the pole and rubbed her wrists. "The camp stretches out for miles and the edges are patrolled by our hunters. If you try to run…"

Kataria turned. Kwar met her with a pursed mouth and eyes straining to remain hard. If she had a threat brewing behind them, she could not muster the will to speak it.

So, too, were Kwar's hands kept deliberately clear of the knife she wore scabbarded at her hip. When Kataria's eyes lingered upon its hilt, she tried to slide it on her belt to her back.

"You untied me just to tell me that?" Kataria asked with a sneer.

"The *Kho Khun* have called a gathering. Every shict has been called to attend." Kwar's eyes softened as they saw her bloodied wrists. She reached down to take Kataria's hand. "And I untied you because you've been here for a day and a night. What happened to—"

"Don't." Kataria drew her hand away suddenly. She was surprised to feel no heat in her voice, no anger. Rather the words drew out like the cold blade of a knife. "Don't you ever touch me."

Kwar's face flashed, wounded. "I was trying to help you. Yarra, he—"

"You're the same as him," Kataria spit. "*Worse* than him. He didn't betray me."

"I *saved* you." Anger slowly brewed upon Kwar's sharp features. "You couldn't see it, you spent too much time with the human. He was infecting you, making you see things. Some time spent among your own people will make you see that."

"My people?" Kataria held up her bloody wrists. "Anyone who I would call *my* people wouldn't do this to me." She gestured to her weary face. "Or *this*. Or call me a . . . a . . ."

"*Kou'loho*," Kwar snarled. "Do you deny it?"

Kataria remained silent. Kwar grimaced.

"I . . . didn't want that," she said. "I just wanted you to see."

"I see," Kataria muttered. "I see everything."

Now it was Kwar's turn to fall silent. She said nothing, did not look at Kataria as she moved to the tent's flap and held it open. Kataria regarded her for a moment before stalking out into the night wind.

They traveled down the dune, toward the distant sea of campfires and shadowed tents in the valley below. Kwar was never far from her, the sound of feet crunching on the sand the only sound exchanged between them. They spoke not a word.

And in their Howling, there was nothing but silence.

⊷ ⊷⊫⊷ ⊶

Why?

This was the word she had yearned to speak.

There were others she'd had in mind, too, when she had awoken from Kwar's blow. Most of them had been formless snarls of fury. More had been curses. Some had been threats.

But over the hours they had traveled, she had whittled them down to just one word.

Why?

And over the hours, as night became dawn, she had sought to ask it. As she had bobbed and swayed on the slavering yiji beneath her, she had all but screamed it. As she'd struggled against the rope securing her hands behind her back and gnawed on the gag around her mouth, she had been able to come up with but muffled noise.

And Kwar had said nothing.

The khoshict had not even looked back as they rode through the desert. The yijis had romped with a brisk pace, yowling as they took them away from the Lyre. But Kwar had ridden with a head bowed and eyes downcast, leading Kataria's mount by a rope.

She couldn't have been out long. Kwar hadn't hit her *that* hard. But when she had awoken, the familiar dunes that had marked the campsite had been gone. The scrubgrass steadily dissipated. The vast western desert opened up before them.

And any trace of Lenk had vanished.

She should have been more worried for him, Kataria knew. Maybe Kwar had cut his throat. Maybe he was on their trail—though, considering the conversation they'd had, that had seemed less likely.

But as they had ridden on, her thoughts had been for the woman before her.

Why?

Why had she done this? Why had she struck her? Why was she not looking back when Kataria let out muffled cries into her gag? Why was she ignoring her struggles and her protests? Why was she taking her west?

When her muscles had worn out from fighting her bonds, when her voice had gone dry behind her gag, only then had Kataria used the Howling. And when she'd reached out with it, when she'd sought the hidden language of their people, Kwar had met her only with darkness.

Kataria emptied herself into the Howling: a long shrill whine, a snarl of fury, a demanding roar. But each sound was smothered beneath blackness, silenced without an answer. No matter how hard she reached, how loud she cried, Kwar would not answer her.

Only when pale dawn rose, when Kwar looked back just as Kataria looked up, only when their eyes met for one ragged breath...

Only then did she hear Kwar's Howling.

A long, mournful sound filled her. A sorrowful song was cast out into empty air for several breaths.

And then went silent.

⊷ ═◆═ ⊶

Shicts rarely gathered in great numbers.

The Twelve Tribes had each staked out a piece of land and populated it exclusively, warring with the various other occupants of that realm, but they did so only in loose-knit qithbands that wandered wide across those expanses.

The tribes themselves congregated only for mating or for war. The former was a somber affair, the bands usually meeting only for as long as it took to breed and trade before going their separate ways.

But gathering for war was something much more festive. Qithbands from all over would arrive, lured by promises of wealth, carnage, and glory. These gatherings were often marked with celebrations and shows of strength, with young warriors and hunters competing against each other to prove their bravery.

Kataria had seen a few in her day, before she had left the Silesrian to follow Lenk.

But she had never seen anything like what sprawled before her now in the valley below.

Hundreds of tents dotted the valley, rising up around thousands of bonfires. The air was bristling with excitement, war cries and songs of bravery carried on the smoke pouring into the sky upon trails of cinders.

The khoshicts gathered in numbers immense, far greater than she had ever seen. Some gathered in clusters, painting tattoos upon each other's dark flesh, braiding feathers of red and black into their hair, carving shields, sharpening blades, and fletching countless arrows. Many more were up and active, though: leaping over open fires and roaring at each other's bravery, engaging in mock battles with blunted blades, shooting arrows at targets, or simply looking to the sky and letting out loud, enthusiastic shrieks.

This can't all be just for one war, Kataria thought. *Too big to go raiding a village. But still not enough to attack Cier'Djaal.* She looked around the sprawling gathering. *What are they planning?*

Even if she hadn't worn her confusion plain on her face, it was easy enough to mark her as an outsider. Khoshicts looked up curiously at her pale skin and blond hair. Curiosity became scorn as whispers were traded. They turned away, muttering that word under their breath as they did.

"*Kou'loho.*"

More than a few looked as though they wanted to do more. They rose, picked up blades, approached Kataria. Their fury was worn plain on their faces, restrained violence quivering in their muscles.

And each time they did, Kwar would step before her and say nothing. She would simply look at them. They recoiled, eyes wide and white beneath their war paint. Their ears folded against their heads and they slunk back to their tents.

Before she could dwell on this, her attentions were seized by the only other shict who looked as out of place as she did.

In the center of their path, like a rock rising from the sand, stood Thua. Taller and burlier than the other warriors, he wore a severe frown at stark odds with their jubilation. He ignored their offers of fights, *sosha*, and songs as he stalked forward, eyes locked on his sister and ears rigid as hers.

Their ears quivered for a moment, flickering like insect antennae as they communicated in the Howling. But Thua's face twisted in anger and soon the Howling no longer seemed enough.

"What would Father say?" he said suddenly. "What would he say, Kwar, if he saw you now?" His eyes flitted over Kataria. "She's another shict and you...you..." He drew in a deep breath, held it. "I know you're scared. I know you get like this when—"

"Father wouldn't say anything about that," Kwar interrupted harshly. "Father wouldn't say anything. He would crawl back to his tent, puff on his pipe, and wonder how he could appease the humans. He would give them more of our land, more of our lives. The *Kho Khun* is here to actually see something done."

"I know what the *Kho Khun* is here for," Thua snapped. "I know what Shekune is planning. She would take us into a war that would see every shict in this desert dead and rotting in the sun! Everything that Father worked for—"

"Which part, Thua?" Kwar's voice went cold. "Which part of his work? The part where he put us in the humans' ghetto? The part where he had us stop hunting and living like shicts? The part where he let Mother die?" Her eyes narrowed to thin slits. "Or the part where he stole my brother from me?"

There were many ways in which Thua was different from other shicts. He was too tall, too burly to look much like the clever, agile heroes of shictish lore. But when he cringed from Kwar's words, he looked too fragile to be here among the warriors. Or perhaps Kwar simply knew exactly what to say to make tears form at the corners of his eyes.

He wiped them away before anyone but Kwar and Kataria could see.

"I am going back to Shicttown," he said. "Whatever you think of Father, he still holds as much sway as the *Kho Khun*. He will have something to say about this." He looked at Kwar intently, eyes quivering. "Kwar, he would want you to come with me."

Thua's ears rose, quivered. Kwar's ears trembled in response and then slowly lowered, her face following as a frown sunk her features. The quivering of her ears seeped into her entire body as she held back something sharp and painful.

She shut her eyes. She shook her head. Thua's frown echoed her own before he slowly turned around, walked into the shadows cast between bonfires, and disappeared.

In his wake were the echoes of his Howling, sounds he had carelessly left behind for anyone to hear. The throngs of warriors, deep in the excitement of impending carnage, didn't seem to notice them. But Kataria could hear them. And though she didn't understand their meaning, she could hear a singular sound: long, loud, and lonely.

Like what she had heard from Kwar last night.

She turned to her captor, who met her with a look that said, *Don't say anything.*

Whether that was a command or a desperate plea, Kataria did not know. Kataria did not want to know. And so when Kwar gestured with her chin to command her to move, Kataria did, not daring to look back at Kwar's face.

—⋅✦⋅✖⋅✦⋅—

Shekune.

This was the word that had echoed through her head.

When they had arrived at the Gathering in the morning. When

Kataria had been marched in, dizzy from heat and sleeplessness. When she had been thrown to her knees before a pair of sandaled feet and two hundred eyes had looked upon her, bound and gagged and pale.

She had heard the name of their leader.

Shekune.

She who had led a hundred raids against a hundred human villages and killed a hundred humans each time. She who had slain the tulwar of three generations, killing them again each time their Tul sent them back. She who had felled a dragonman in one blow.

Shekune.

Without mercy. Without fear. Without sorrow.

Shekune.

The Spear.

She knew all this, for the khoshicts were telling her. The Howling spoke of all her victories, all her stories, all her kills. All in a single name.

And that name bore Kataria's head low. Breathless behind her gag, she could only kneel and hear the litany of charges against her: abandoning the shictish way, turning her back on her kinsmen...

Being among humans.

She did not so much as raise her head as Kwar listed off every word.

Kwar, whose warmth she could still feel on her skin.

Kwar, whose scent still lingered in her nostrils.

Kwar, whose voice still hung in her ears with those words.

I love you.

She had heard the sentence passed down as an echo. She had not denied the label "*kou'loho.*" She had not resisted when they took her away, nor struggled when they took her to the tent at the edge of camp and bound her to the pole.

She had not done anything but open her ears and listen for Kwar.

And she had heard nothing.

Shekune's name meant "spear," and the leader of the *Kho Khun* stood like one.

She was no longer young, but far from old, and wrinkles weathered her face at the edges of her eyes and the corners of a mouth used to being set in a hard frown. But the harsh angles of her jaw and nose were still strong. Her body was still lean beneath the furs and leathers she wore, the muscles of her arms apparent as she crossed them over her chest. And though gray had begun to streak her raven-black hair, it was all but unnoticeable against the riot of feathers she wore in her braids. Red feathers. Black feathers.

War feathers, Kataria noted as she was marched in to join the assembly. *Red for short war. Black for long war. One for each grudge she carries.* She tried counting, but was discouraged by the sheer number.

Other khoshicts glanced up as she took a seat in the great circle they formed, and indiscreetly scooted away but did not protest. The laws of *Kho Khun* were as old as any tribe could recall and they allowed the presence of every shict, even disgraced ones.

Kataria was less interested in her kinsmen's obvious distaste and more interested in why a *Kho Khun* had been called in the first place.

This was even rarer than a gathering of great numbers; shicts barely ever ceded command of their tribes to others. A *Kho Khun* was precisely that: the formation of a confederacy of tribal leaders with a clear commander. Kataria noted the two ancient-looking shicts sitting behind Shekune: one grandfather, one grandmother. The former wearing a mantle of pale yellow, the latter one of black and white. Day chieftain and night chieftain. These were the elders elected to guide and advise the chieftain.

*Kho Khun*s were never called unless the need was dire. Independent as they were, shicts rarely felt comfortable giving authority to any one person. And with the consent of the elders, the *Kho Khun* had granted Shekune supreme authority.

And she wore it as if she had been born with it.

"Riffid is not a weak goddess," she spoke suddenly. The assembled's ears went upright, intent on every word. "Not like the coddling gods of humans. Not like the Tul, which vomits its people back onto the earth for us to skewer. Riffid gives few gifts." Shekune held up a single finger. "And only one life.

"We live as we must. The land provides and the land takes. So we provide and take, as well. We war when we must, we raid when we must. We are given children sometimes, family sometimes. But then it is over, by age or cold or blade, and we go back to the Dark Forest to join Riffid once more."

She let this sink in. The khoshicts were rapt, leaning forward to listen better.

"Every shict life is precious," Shekune continued. "Because every shict life is earned. It is taken from the hostile land, it is won at the tip of an arrowhead, it is born screaming in the night. Every shict earns their right to stand on this ground. Nothing is given.

"But it is not so for the other races." Venom crept into her voice, acid dripping off the tip of a spear. "The tulwar die and return, thinking nothing of death and having no appreciation for life. And the humans... well, they merely breed. They have so much, taken from our hands, and all they needed to do to receive it?"

She sneered. "They merely fucked."

A rumble of approving anger emerged from the shicts. The Howling went alive, the roar of their unspoken anger so vast it made Kataria's ears curl.

"They fucked," Shekune repeated. "They rolled like rats and they drove us out of our homes through sheer numbers. We ceded land to them, losing it where they had numbers, living with them where they didn't." She looked over the crowd, her eyes settling on Kwar. "I see members of the Eighth Tribe here." She nodded. "Your elder, Sai-Thuwan, is wise. Shicttown is home to many and I will speak no ill of him. But you are here because you know that there is a difference between a home to shicts and a shictish home."

The roar of approval grew, accompanied by blades beaten on shields and bows raised into the air. Shekune raised her hands for quiet.

"Many of you expressed doubt when a *Kho Khun* was called. But you accepted my leadership because you knew what I did." She pointed skyward. "Riffid gives few gifts. But we have received one today."

She held out her hand expectantly. From the crowd a khoshict emerged carrying a spear that seemed less weapon and more monster. Its shaft was thick and notched a hundred times. Its head was jagged and cruelly barbed, designed for dirty deaths and prolonged suffering. She took it in one powerful hand and pointed it west toward Cier'Djaal.

"Over the dunes there lies the human city," Shekune said. "We have heard its strife. The humans' greed tears it apart. They bleed each other in the street like swine and grind each other underfoot like so much meat. Not content with the land they have taken from us, the suffering they have heaped upon *us*, they now turn on each other."

She grinned. Her teeth were broad and sharp. Her eyes and spear glinted as one.

"And I say this is a gift," she said. "Riffid has shown us that the humans are ready to be toppled. Their disease ready to be cured!"

The shicts broke into a resounding roar. Shekune threw her arms out, drinking it in. She no longer called for quiet, but roared to be heard over them.

"We have tested ourselves against the tulwar and found their warriors inept and left their villages burning!" she cried out. The shicts cheered wildly, loosing whoops of approval. "They cower in their shit-stained shacks and tremble at every shadow! This desert shall soon be ours, wiped clean of *them*!"

The roaring grew blood-hungry, drunk on the promise of violence. They wore their rage on their tongues, their victory in their eyes, and the deep hatred of their sorrow in the Howling.

And Kwar's was loudest of all.

"The tulwar shall die!" Shekune roared. "The vulgore shall die! The dragonmen, the couthi and the *humans* shall *DIE*!" The blood-hunger was at its apex now, many shicts standing and shrieking. "Cier'Djaal will burn! This desert will be wiped clean and this land will be earned." She held her spear aloft. "*For the shicts!*"

Their roar was deafening. Their Howling was thunder. The noise was choking, a sea in which any other sound drowned.

"*NO!*"

That being the case, Kataria was surprised anyone heard her at all.

And yet someone had. In the massive crowd, Shekune's eyes, alive with fire, found her. Her ears flattened against the sides of her head, she bared her teeth at the pale interloper. And, one by one, the other khoshicts followed her gaze and fell silent as they scowled at Kataria.

She could feel their stares like a blade bearing down upon her. All their rage, all their despair, was now focused squarely on her. And she found herself choked by it, unable to speak.

"Ah," Shekune said. "The *kou'loho* speaks." She sneered. "I wonder who invited you. But you are not welcome here." She glanced to two nearby aides. "Take our wayward sister back to her tent."

Two young warriors advanced toward Kataria, only to pause at the sound of another voice rising high.

"She has the right!"

Kwar's voice. In her ears, in her head, at her side. The khoshict stood trembling beneath Shekune's gaze, but she did not back down.

"She is not just a *kou'loho*," Kwar said. "She's one of us." She looked around. "She's a shict. She has the right to speak."

Ears quivered as murmurs were exchanged. Shekune narrowed her eyes, but looked behind her, to the day chieftain and the night chieftain. The latter nodded approval first. The former a moment later.

"Speak, then, *kou'loho*," Shekune grunted.

"My name is Kataria," Kataria growled back. "I am from the Sixth Tribe, led by Rokuda."

"I have heard of him."

"And he has heard of you," Kataria replied. "Shekune's bravery is as legendary as her wars against the humans. And this one you want to wage will be legendary, too." She narrowed her eyes. "Because it will kill every shict here."

Shekune's audible scoff was echoed by the growls of the crowd. Kataria gritted her teeth, continued.

"It's true that the humans don't consider us a threat," she said. "Mothers tell their children stories of shicts to make them behave. Old men trade tales in taverns. But to them we are ghosts. Things that might threaten them, but will never kill them." She pointed at Shekune. "If you bring war to them, Shekune, if you kill them, they will know you are real."

"And?" Shekune sneered. "Should they not fear us?"

"They won't fear you, they'll wage *war* on you," Kataria snapped back. "There are only twelve tribes of shicts. How many belong to those of the desert, the Seventh, Eighth, and Ninth?" She looked around. "I've seen the camp. There are many here.

"But there are a hundred human nations, Shekune. And each one contains humans innumerable. They will have weapons, money, trade routes for miles, and *all* of them will come down on your head.

You'll turn the shicts from ghosts into prey, hunted down by the humans."

The shicts crowed in indignation at this. She supposed the fact that they had already been pushed out of their lands eluded them.

"You've been tainted by their presence, *kou'loho*," Shekune chuckled. "You see a few stone cities and think they can do anything. Their houses burn, same as anyone's."

"They burn right now," Kataria said. "Because they fight each other. I've seen how little they respect the lives of their own race. They'd have none for ours."

"*Respect?*" Shekune snarled, sweeping forward. So close, Kataria couldn't help but note how tall the woman was, how easily she towered over her. "We do not want their respect. We want their *blood*. Every shict here has lost something to human incursion." She thrust her spear out to point at a random shict. "You. What have you lost?"

A young male grunted, gesturing to the cloth tied around one eye. "Humans took my eye when I fought to keep them from stealing the yiji I hunted."

"And you." Shekune swept her spear to point at a female. "What have you lost?"

"My father died when the humans tried to burn down Shicttown," the female replied. "I left after that and my mother would not come with me."

"And I?" Shekune looked grimly over the crowd. "I see the empty spaces where more should be. Fathers. Mothers. Warriors and hunters." She turned her glare toward Kataria, the fire growing behind her eyes. "What would you know of it?" She leveled her spear's tip at Kataria. "What have the humans taken from you, *kou'loho*?"

Kataria stared down the weapon's length. Its blade's serrated teeth twisted like a metal grin, awaiting her answer.

She gave it, turning a scowl up at Shekune and slapping the weapon away.

"Given that you won't stop fucking calling me that because of them, I'd say I know a bit about loss. And I told you already, my name is *Kataria*." She stepped forward, trying to ignore how small she felt before the towering chieftain. "Tell us, then, how you plan to kill the humans? Storm their walls with bows and arrows? Break through their stone cities with spears?"

Only this statement quelled their rage. The khoshicts began to exchange murmurs, concern etching itself across their faces as they slowly became aware of just what a daunting task Shekune proposed.

Cier'Djaal was no tulwar village to be burned in a night. It was stone walls and sturdy homes. It would take strategy, cunning, and a prolonged siege to threaten even a weakened city. The realization that the shicts were ill equipped for that had to be humbling, and Kataria took no pride in bringing it.

But at the worry that suddenly flashed across Shekune's face as she realized she was losing the crowd's approval? At that she allowed herself a grin fit for eating shit.

"It is true," Shekune began softly, "that we are few. Even the tulwar outnumber us." She turned and stalked back to the center of the circle. "But is it not also true that they fear us? And why is that?"

The crowd once again turned to her attentively.

"Not because we pound at doors with battering rams, nor because we raise banners and come with war cries and shields. When we come to war, we come from the night. We enter without a word and leave nothing but silence behind us. We are everywhere, in every shadow, in every nightmare, and the blades of our enemies cannot touch us. The land hides us because we are wolves. And how do wolves fight?"

She smiled grimly and reached into a belt pouch. From it she produced a thin vial brimming with a jade-green liquid.

"They go for the throat."

The khoshicts did not cheer at this. They said not a word. Nor did Kataria as she watched, speechless, with creeping dread about what Shekune might hold in her hand.

"In the Twelve Tribes' war against the humans, only three have successfully pushed them out. Only three have reclaimed their lands and added the graves of thousands to them. Our cousins in the jungles of the deep south. The *s'ha shict s'na*."

Everyone drew a breath at that word. And at the next, they held it.

"The greenshicts."

No murmurs of doubt. No roars of approval. Not so much as a word was breathed among the assembled.

A typical reaction to mention of the greenshicts.

Every shict knew of the green-skinned, eight-foot-tall creatures who lurked in the jungles to the south. Just as every shict knew of their legendary distinction of being the only tribes to have driven out human incursion. And every shict knew of the viciousness and savagery that had been committed to do it.

Greenshicts did not fight for land, nor for honor. Their wars were practical. They did not kill their enemies, they exterminated them. They did not reclaim land, they burned it to ash. Their victories came only when every last enemy was dead, down to the last child and elder. And they had spent lifetimes perfecting their crafting of toxins, plagues, and diseases to cleanse the land of their foes.

Kataria was very familiar with their methods.

And her blood ran cold at the thought of what the vial in Shekune's hand might hold.

"The greenshicts are on a mission, brothers and sisters," the chieftain said. "A mission to spread their knowledge as to how to battle the humans. They visited us not so long ago in the lands of the Seventh Tribe and delivered me this." She smiled at the vial as though it were a newborn child, delicate and precious. "The key to saving all of us."

"What does it do?" Kataria asked, straining to be heard over the murmurs that rose once again. "What are you going to do with it?"

"You have a right to speak, *kou'loho*, but not to know."

"And they just *gave* it to you? The greenshicts aren't known for their charity. What did they want in return?"

"What I want," Shekune snarled in reply. "What *all* of us want. A land free from loss, where we can look upon our children and not wonder whether they're going to be killed because their ears are pointed. A land where we can hunt for meat to eat instead of sell. A land for us, the *shicts*, our people. *Your* people."

"But what—"

"No, sister." It was the first time Shekune had called her something other than *kou'loho*, yet the word was not spoken endearingly. "You have asked many questions. Now answer mine." She pointed her spear at Kataria once more. "Do you see a world where humans and shicts live together?"

The question struck her like a blow to the stomach. "What?"

"Knowing what you do of humans, of shicts, do you see a world where we can live side by side, each of us free of fear and suffering?"

She wanted to say yes.

She wanted to say more than that, to speak of how much time it would take, how much suffering it would demand, how after much labor and humility the world *could* be remade. She wanted to tell them of a world that could exist where humans and shicts could look upon each other with something other than fear.

She could hear herself saying such words already, hear the applause they would engender, hear the begrudging agreement from Shekune that would come.

If only she knew those words.

But as the words went from her head to her lips, she felt a familiar pang in her heart. A pain she had felt long ago, when in a forest she met a young man with hair the color of an old man's. One she had felt when that young man said he wanted to stop fighting and live with his own people. A pain she felt now when she thought of his face and his eyes and all the scars he wore.

And a different word came to her mouth.

"No."

No applause. No begrudging approval. Not even a haughty, mocking laughter at her foolishness. The assembly had fallen silent. And Shekune's only response was a grim, knowing nod.

And somehow, that hurt so much worse.

"When I think of the future," she said, "I do not see that world, either, sister. I see one where there are only humans. Or only us. And there are so many that I cannot let down."

The Howling rose inside her head. Every shict heard her words. Every shict saw the same thing. Every shict drew the same conclusion. And their Howling was the long, loud sound of a call to hunt.

"That doesn't mean you can do this!" Kataria said, striding forward. "They'll still fight back! They'll hunt you down! They'll—"

"We have heard enough of the *kou'loho*. What we do now, we do for her as much as for us." Shekune made a dismissive gesture. "Take her away."

A few eager warriors rose from the crowd to obey, but Kwar immediately swept in to stand between them and Kataria.

"She is my..." Kwar stumbled over the word a moment. "My charge." She reached out and seized Kataria by her arm. "I will take the *kou'loho*."

"I already said," Kataria growled, "my name is Kataria. And I already told you..." She lashed out suddenly, one hand grabbing Kwar's belt and the other tearing free from her grip to swing and crack against the khoshict's jaw. "*NEVER TOUCH ME!*"

Kwar recoiled, and the crowd recoiled with her. Kataria stood her ground, hands held closely at her sides, trembling. She watched the shock on Kwar's face turn to hurt and then to coldness as the khoshict swept forward suddenly and smashed her fist against Kataria's stomach.

The air left Kataria in a sudden gasp as she slumped to her knees, then to her face in the sand. She writhed in pain, drawing her knees up to her belly. The pain of the blow was fleeting, though, at least in comparison to the pain that followed.

Many hands—none of them Kwar's—reached down and seized her by the arms. Many hands forced her hands behind her back and forced biting rawhide to gnaw at the wounded skin as they tied her wrists together. Many hands seized her and hauled her away, chased by the hateful roar of the assembly.

Kataria marched without further resistance as her captors returned her to her tent and bound her to the tent pole. She stood there for a long time before she dared to breathe and raise her left leg. She gave it a little shake and smiled at the weight that she felt inside it.

Admittedly, she hadn't planned this. It had just been good timing that Kwar had come close enough for Kataria to covertly lift the khoshict's knife from her belt. And it had just been good luck that none of the others had noticed her slip it into her boot as she had twisted upon the ground.

As for the idea to do it? Well, she suspected she owed Denaos the credit for that. She reminded herself to thank him once she returned to Cier'Djaal.

And she knew she had to. Not for Lenk or the humans, but for the shicts. Branded her though they had, they were still her people. Shekune's plan would only bring down the wrath of all the humans upon them and kill every shict who breathed.

But Kwar's father was respected. Sai-Thuwan would be able to talk to them, to tell them, to save them.

For that she had to return to Cier'Djaal. For that she had to escape. For that she had to hope that the hurt on Kwar's face when Kataria had struck her was genuine.

She had to hope that Kwar still cared for her enough to overlook an empty scabbard.

TWENTY-SEVEN

Two Corpses in One Grave

Forgive me."

These words Dransun said in the dust-laden silence of the temple's attic.

The first words that had been spoken since they had arrived back at Temple Row. The flight from Silktown's gates, hauling the dead and the wounded, had been rife with screams and prayers—not words. The temple below—the pews freshly packed with the wounded—was a formless roil of agony.

And still they were too soft to drown out Dransun's words.

Asper looked up from the cup of coffee she sat with. Dransun had yet to look up from his, even now that it had fallen from his numb fingers and spilled across the floor.

"I should have known," he said, shaking his head. "I should have known it would end like this."

"We both should have," she said softly. "We could have done more."

"I met Mejina once," Dransun said. "At a party. Fashas invited a bunch of us common scum to their houses to pretend they gave a shit about us. I met him. When I raised my hand to salute, he cringed like he thought I was going to hit him. He looked so weak."

Dransun stared at the coffee stain on the wooden floor, face numb with horror.

"I thought he'd fold," he whispered. "I thought he'd make some big talk behind his dragonmen, but I thought he'd fold. But he...he..."

Asper didn't say a word.

She didn't say what she'd seen at the Silktown gates: Mejina's black eyes, Mejina's giant smile. She didn't say that the man standing there had not been Mejina. Words like that would have shattered Dransun.

And she needed him strong tonight.

"I took an oath to serve these people. But now all I can do is watch them die," Dransun said. "Fuck me. That can't be all there is."

"No," she said. "It can't. We can't watch anymore."

At this he finally looked up. At this she finally stood up.

"No more waiting," she said. "Not on rogues, not on wizards, not on gods. We have to take matters into our own hands." She shook her head. "In healing you separate the patient from the source of the disease. This city is sick. If we're going to save its people…"

"We have to leave," Dransun muttered. "After so many years here… how can I?"

"Find a way," she said. "Tell others to find a way, too. As many as you can."

"Where will we go?"

"Away."

"How?"

"Fuck, Dransun, if I think on this too much, I'm going to realize how hopeless it is." She fixed him with a hard stare. "If you can come up with a better idea, then let me know. If not, find as many people as you can who can leave this place. Either way, you've only got a few days."

He opened his mouth to reply, but merely nodded. He rose and departed down the stairs to the temple proper. Aturach would be down there, tending to the wounded. He would need help soon enough.

To treat the large wounds, you have to treat the small.

This is what she told herself when she sat back down and slowly sipped her coffee. This is what she told herself when she felt a shadow loom in the chair where Dransun had just sat.

"You did not pray."

She didn't have to look up to know Mundas's voice. She didn't want to look up to know Mundas's presence.

"Do you think things might have turned out differently had you called out to Talanas?" Mundas asked.

"Talanas was watching, same as I was," she replied. "He saw everything I did. Whatever he chooses to do next is up to him."

And she could feel Mundas nod slowly.

And she could feel him disappear slowly.

And she could feel herself begin to cry slowly.

No sorrow.

No fear.

No anger.

Gariath was sure these things existed, among the coils of smoke and wedged in the shattered timbers of fallen buildings, but he could not smell them. The streets of Shaab Sahaar were rife with cruder smells.

Of smoke.

Of blood.

Of charred meat.

Beneath a starless night and a moon that refused to look away, the tulwar worked. They sifted through rubble, searching for survivors and finding only scraps of people. They placed the dead upon the streets in one line, the wounded in another; a triviality before the latter became the former. The Sainites they merely heaped into two piles: one for their steel, one for their flesh.

The survivors looked scarce different from the dead. Gaunt, haunted, as though they had all been starved of thirty pounds in the few hours the attack had lasted.

Where were their voices? Gariath wondered. Where were their cries for retribution? He would have settled for even curses, even sobbing.

Anything to let him know that there had been a purpose to all this death.

But he made his way through the streets, in silence and in shadow, toward the edge, where the houses turned from wood to clay. This area had fared better, if one was able to appreciate the fine difference between carnage and mere disaster. There were fewer bodies lying lifeless in the streets. The houses were merely scorched instead of incinerated, the worst damage being where a dead scraw had plunged through someone's roof. The Rua Tong warriors who tended to the wounded here wore befuddlement on their faces, unsure how to use bandages instead of swords, unsure how to deal with a problem they could not kill.

Here Gariath at last caught the scent of grief, the ash that remained when anger had burned away. He followed it, the aroma growing more familiar as it drew him to the crossroads of four sandy streets.

There a tulwar knelt.

He knew it was Daaru only after he drew closer. The tulwar kneeling here looked too frail, too broken to be Daaru. His glassy eyes and mouth hung open wordlessly, suggested he was merely one more of the dead. And it was only the shallow breath he drew that showed he was not just another corpse.

But it was Daaru. Gariath knew this only when he saw the body, limp and wrapped in a purple *chota*, cradled in the tulwar's arms.

Deji.

"I forgot my sword." Daaru's voice was numb, words little more than drool tumbling out from between his lips. "She tried to bring it to me. She..." He brushed a hand over the wound gaping in her chest: three lines in a perfect formation. "One of those monsters. I couldn't..."

He bowed his head, unable to say anything more. Every breath he drew in was shuddering and every time he exhaled, there seemed to be less of him.

It was unfair, Gariath thought, when children were gone. They were made of their parents' blood, born of their bodies, nurtured by their breath. When they were taken, all of that was taken with them. But even after they were gone, they seemed to keep taking.

And the parents would keep giving, forever.

Gariath closed his eyes, thought of his sons, of their faces, of their scents, of how they would have gotten along with Deji, of how old they would be right now.

Of how much he had given to them.

Of how much more he had left to give.

"You should go, Gariath," Daaru whispered. "I... Shaab Sahaar will have much to tend to in the coming days."

Gariath grunted in acknowledgment. "Revenge."

"No." He shook his head. "We have homes to rebuild, funerals to arrange..." He looked down to the dead girl in his arms. "Dead to bury."

"Why?"

Daaru looked up for the first time since Gariath had arrived. And for the first time, his eyes betrayed something other than dull glassiness. Outrage, shock, hurt: All were apparent as he looked upon Gariath standing over him, arms folded across his chest, impassive as a mountain.

"What did you say?" Daaru all but snarled.

"Why bother?" The dragonman forced coldness into his voice. "Why not just trust in the Tul to give her back?"

Daaru rose to his feet. His body trembled. Color crept into his face, painted it fresh with rage as he glared up at the dragonman.

"Do not speak to me of Tul, outsider. Do not speak to me of *anything* you do not know. That is not how the Tul works."

Gariath met his rage with coldness, his eyes black and flat as he stared back at Daaru and spoke bluntly.

"Then why are you going to wait for the same thing to happen to your son?"

The rage that painted Daaru's face suddenly snapped then, draining away in an instant and leaving only a cold, naked terror. But what replaced it, what filled his face with reds, yellows, and blues so vivid it was as if they might simply bleed out through his skin, was something strong, something resilient, something unbreakable.

The rage that filled someone's heart where once a loved one had lived. The rage that came from knowing one had nothing left to lose. The rage that flooded Daaru's face, poured into his throat, and came out on a roar that carried across all of Shaab Sahaar.

"RISE UP!"

It shattered the silence of the dead city. People looked up as though they had seen the dead walk. But they approached all the same, for they looked upon the only one of them who yet lived.

"RISE UP!" he roared again. *"SHAAB SAHAAR, RISE UP!"* He swept his gaze around the crowd, let them drink in the colors of his face. *"Against the humans, for our dead, for the Tul! RISE UP!"*

"Rise up?" one of them muttered. "What do you mean, Daaru?"

"They attacked us for no reason," Daaru snarled back. "They killed us simply because they felt like it. We have lived with the dream that we could live apart from them, away from them, but we were wrong." He held up his slain daughter. "We were wrong."

"We have all lost loved ones," an elder chimed in.

"And we have so many more to lose," Daaru roared back. "Who will we wait to take them? Should I wait for the humans to come back and take my son? For the shicts to take my wife? How long must I pretend this world is fair?" He held his daughter high above his head. *"RISE UP!"*

"But the *Humn*—"

"They did nothing while Shaab Sahaar burned!" he howled. "They did nothing while my daughter died! They did nothing while even the *dragonman*, an outsider, fought for us!"

Gariath suddenly felt all their eyes upon him, more keenly than he'd felt any blade or talon. He shifted uncomfortably, as though if they looked long enough, they might know. Everything.

"I was not born *Humn*," Daaru said. "I was not made to lead. I was born *saan*, like so many of you, like my daughter. All my lives have led me to this moment.

"Humans and tulwar cannot live together. Our fathers knew this. We ignored them, content to wait for their rebirth. But what world will they return to? I will go to the human city. I will go to Jalaang, to Cier'Djaal, and beyond. And I will burn every house to the ground before I let them do this again! I will bury my daughter in the ashes of their homes and paint their cities scarlet! I have fire. I have blades. And I have no more words."

He stared out over the crowd, the colors of his face pulsing with his fury.

First silence. A nervous exchange of glances. And then a flash of color.

The answer came in a single glint of steel, stark against the night sky, as a curved blade was held aloft in a hairy hand and a voice roared out in reply.

"Rise up!"

A bow joined it, held up and proud above the crowd, with a voice to accompany it.

"Rise up!"

A spear.

"Rise up!"

A dagger.

"Rise up!"

A single fist, bloodied and trembling.

"Rise up!"

Countless weapons were added, countless voices were joined. From the darkness they marched into the streets of Shaab Sahaar. From the rubble they joined, convening in the city center. From the ruins of their former lives, they were reborn, faces alive with color, voices roaring with fury, screaming with a singular, unbreakable rage.

"RISE UP! RISE UP! RISE UP!"

And from far away, Gariath watched them as they marched.

To war.

Exactly as he'd hoped.

And so it was that he skulked into a nearby alley, his head suddenly swimming. No more blood to clog his nostrils, no more smoke to blind him, nothing to distract from what he had done.

Him. He'd done this. All of it.

What would his humans have said, had they seen this? Would they have cursed him? Or merely applauded how very much like them he had become?

How like them, he wondered, have *I become?*

He looked up, saw the remains of a wooden building, still burning brightly, still spewing smoke into the sky.

He wondered, then, if he could walk into that pyre. He wondered, then, if he could let the flames sear his skin from his sinew, his sinew from his bones, paint his bones black. He wondered, then, if he could burn the human influence out of him.

But then, he wondered, what would be left?

TWENTY-EIGHT

TOMBS OF IVORY AND SILK

There were no gentle ways to win a fortune.

There were tragic ways: from the death of a loved one who had valued gold as much as he valued his inheritors. There were clever ways: at the tips of silver tongues and at the edges of coy smiles.

But the vast majority of wealth was earned the honest way: upon blades wet with red and beneath the marching boots of armies.

Karneria's treasuries burst and withered as territories were conquered and lost. Saine's fortunes rose and fell with each spring that came and heralded a new war. Muraska's wealth lived or died by which of its neighbors it could keep from intruding upon its territory.

There was only so much gold in the world, after all, and that made it worth fighting over. Coin was the blood of cities. As blood was synonymous with wealth, so was wealth synonymous with war. Every city understood this, and Cier'Djaal was no exception.

It just preferred to be more civilized about it.

As insects fed upon blood, so too did thieves come in search of gold. The fashas had long ago given up trying to keep them out and had instead made a proposition: Only the gangs that proved the least disruptive would be allowed to operate within the city.

The fashas had thought this an elegant solution. The Jackals had agreed. And their tentative peace and less tentative fortunes had been won with lots and lots of bloodshed. The Houndmistress had threatened this pact, but the Jackals had found a way to deal with that. And even through the wars with the Khovura, the Jackals had never intruded upon the territory of the fashas.

But Denaos planned to be long gone before anyone could blame him for doing so.

Tonight his concerns were for more immediate things: the thud of guardsmen's boots, the lights cast by streetlamps, the shadows cast by towering manors. He slipped into the latter as soon as he hit the ground, slinking away from the wall he had just climbed over.

The shadows here were not as deep as he'd have liked on a moonlit night such as tonight. The closer a manor was to the commoners in the Souk and surrounding neighborhoods, the less desirable it was. Houses built near Silktown's walls tended to be owned by lesser fashas or greater merchants who could afford only tiny palaces.

The liability of his chosen entry point became clear as soon as he peered around the corner.

It was true that the house guards of Silktown were considered to be mostly a joke, even by the house guards. To their fasha employers, they were just another excuse to flaunt their wealth: handsome men and pretty women they could garb in flashy, useless armor and arm with ridiculous weaponry in the hope of showing off just how much they had spent in the name of a pretense.

Denaos had expected to see a few out, maybe even more than a few. He hadn't expected . . . *this*.

Guards wearing the colors of many different fashas marched up and down the well-lit avenues flanked by perfectly manicured lawns. They stood in front of the grand doors and beneath the stained glass windows. They scanned the streets from atop sweeping rooftops and kept a vigilant gaze upon the clean streets.

They were well armed and well armored. Some of them were even ugly enough to look as if they might actually know a thing or two about fighting.

There had to be fifty within his field of vision alone. And while that was intimidating, it was nothing compared to what strode through their ranks.

The dragonmen, towering high and broad, waded among the house guards' mockeries of military formations. Weapons draped lazily over their shoulders, the horns on their snouts thrust high, they glanced around Silktown with a sort of disdain, knowing that these tiny humans would only impede them if there was a call to action.

Which, on most nights, would be unthinkable: Only a fool came to Silktown. The dragonmen were there largely for prestige and to discourage rabble from entering the district.

But tonight someone was worried enough to have gone through the farce of deploying every guard they had. Someone was worried enough to have at least two dragonmen patrolling the same street, and he could see the hulking shapes of at least three more in the distance. And considering the cost of all this, someone was likely to be several someones.

What could have caused this sudden show of defense? Denaos wondered. He had heard about the massacre at the Silktown gates, where Mejina had commanded the slaughter of dissenting crowds. Did they fear revolt? Revenge? From whom? The commoners weren't enough to challenge them and the Jackals weren't likely to retaliate on behalf of a few dead poor people.

Much more likely they were afraid of Karnerians or Sainites ending the farce of respecting their authority and finally moving into Silktown. But then, the fashas and the foreigners both knew that all the house guards and the dragonmen in the world wouldn't save Silktown from the armies.

Denaos drew in a breath. Fifty or five hundred, it changed nothing. He had come here for one last-ditch effort: Expose the fasha supporting the Khovura and find out what he or she knew. Doubtless that would lead to the lair of the Khovura themselves, and the Jackals could finally turn the tide and take the fight to these deranged cultists. Then they could go about ousting the foreign armies, and Cier'Djaal would slowly mend itself once more.

Funny, he thought. *All sounds so simple when you put it like that. As though fixing a city could be done in one night's time.* He shook his head. *Shut up. You promised Anielle. One more try. One last night. Then you're out. You're not such a swine as to back out from a promise, are you?*

Denaos—and probably Anielle—knew he *was,* in fact, such a swine. But liars as consummate as he had no trouble lying to themselves.

He let his eyes drift across the avenues and plazas, replete with their fountains and statues, toward a prominent house on a small hill.

Even in charred ruins, the house of Ghoukha, burned to a crisp when the Khovura attacked it, loomed large enough to cast shadows over the rest of Silktown. Denaos's eyes were fixed upon a house living in one such shadow.

Big enough to suggest a fasha of at least healthy influence, the manor of Fasha Mejina burned with bright light from within, as though it were struggling desperately to extricate itself from Ghoukha's legacy.

Fitting, Denaos thought. Mejina had been around as long as Ghoukha, but the lackluster silk output of his spiders had earned him a fraction of Ghoukha's success. Rumor had it that he had spent thousands—perhaps even the remains of his fortune—to prove himself the leader Silktown needed in Ghoukha's absence, hiring mercenaries and dragonmen to lock down Silktown and keep the rabble out.

Mejina was desperate to be respected, hungry to be powerful, and willing to throw a lot of money away in pursuit of those goals.

Three factors that made a man look for friends in dark places. Three factors that put Mejina at the top of Denaos's list of suspects.

The sound of hushed murmurs caught his ear as a pair of guards began talking but ten feet away from his hiding spot. He crept back, slinking deeper into the shadows. He pulled a black cloth mask up and over his face, inhaled deeply the scent of washed silks and clean grass that had been scrubbed into the material, just as into the vest he wore over his shirt.

He had expected dragonmen and their keen sense of smell—scent-treated fabrics were used frequently by the Jackals to throw them off. And while he hadn't expected this many house guards, they were still only house guards.

True to form, the house guards barely looked up from admiring their weapons or polishing smudges from their breastplates as he slipped around the alleys near the houses, darting silently through the narrow shafts of light cast by the streetlamps. The ones atop the roofs kept their eyes fixed over Silktown's walls, looking for any sign of an angry mob. No one really bothered to look much at the shadows as Denaos slipped through the back alleys and navigated his way toward Mejina's house.

He half expected he could walk right through them without their noticing and was half tempted to try, if only to satisfy his curiosity, but resisted the urge. Paranoia had virtues Denaos didn't wish to disabuse the fashas of. And so long as their guards had all their eyes on the streets, they wouldn't be looking for people in their houses.

He continued to slide in and out of the shadows, behind backs, beneath gazes, at the corners of wary eyes. Silktown's avenues were long and sprawling, built to accommodate the vast manors that had been erected here when the city got rich, and maneuvering his way toward Mejina's house at the other end of the city had its challenges. But as he probed deeper into the district, he found the patrols thinning out— likely the fashas had them closest to the front to make a greater show of force—and soon he saw his opportunity in an empty street.

Just across the way, smaller merchant houses cropped up, and just beyond their comforting shadowed alleys, Mejina's manse loomed. Denaos paused, drew in a deep breath, closed his eyes, and—

"Do you think it's true?"

Damn it.

"What?"

The voices of house guards came with the rattle of armor and the stomp of boots. He could hear them coming up the street, toward the alley he crouched in. He steadied his breathing, slunk into the shadows, waited for them to pass.

"The mob at the gates," the first guard, a woman, said. "I hear they wounded one of the lizards."

"Yeah?" A second guard, male, chuckled in reply. "I'd have liked to see that. Those smug reptiles are always looking down on us. How'd they do it?"

"Don't you get it?" the woman asked, annoyed. "One of the dragonmen, the only thing keeping the war from Silktown, got *injured*. That's never happened before. And once the *shkainai* hear about it, they'll—"

"They won't," the man said. "The foreigners want this city's wealth. They aren't going to go messing with the money."

"That's what you think. You heard they saw a wizard here in Silktown? Wandering around, muttering to himself, smelling like ashes?"

A wizard? Denaos leaned forward, listening intently.

"Hell. I knew those Venarium fucks were up to no good. Anyone try to stop him?"

"Yeah. I'm sure there's a line of people ready to fight a guy that can shoot fire out his asshole," the woman guard scoffed. "Point is, if you've got wizards running around, what else will come here? Foreigners? Khovura? The Jackals? I hear they're getting desperate. And if the dragonmen aren't invincible, then we are most *righteously* fucked. I got this job because I thought Silktown was safe."

"You got this job because you look good in that uniform," the man said. They were drawing closer to Denaos's hiding place. "But if you want to know if it's true, you could always ask."

They halted, just outside the alley. Denaos didn't have to wait long to find out why. He could feel the reason in the soles of his boots as the cobblestones shuddered with tremendous footsteps. And soon a hulking shadow fell across the alley.

"Hey, lizard," the male guard called up. "Is it true one of you got fucked up in the mob?"

"Huh?" the dragonman boomed back, glancing down as though he hadn't noticed these two tiny humans until they spoke.

"We heard one of you got injured," the female guard said, sounding nervous. "Is it true? I thought you couldn't be harmed."

"As far as you're concerned, we can't," the dragonman replied languidly.

"Oxshit," the man said. "One or two of you went down in the Uprising, my uncle said. You're big and covered in scales, but under that you're as weak as the rest of us."

"Maybe," the dragonman said. He squatted down on his haunches to draw closer to them. The female backed away nervously, the male sneered in reply. "No one ever said *Drokha* don't die. But it's a rare occasion, one that's dependent on a very specific circumstance."

"And what circumstance is—"

The male guard's voice was cut off by the sudden crunch of metal as the dragonman's hand swung out, smashing into the guard's side and sending him flying. He smashed against a lamppost, a crack of bone was heard over the squeal of useless armor bending, and then he tumbled down to lie still on the street.

"Whether or not we can do that," the dragonman replied.

The female screamed and took off at a sprint. The dragonman didn't seem particularly bothered to chase her, nor did he seem particularly bothered by the carcass lying nearby, blood leaking out on the street from where his armor had splintered and pierced his flesh. Rather the dragonman leisurely rose up to his full height, and Denaos held his breath and waited for him to move along.

But the dragonman did not move. Denaos's eyes grew wide as the dragonman's nostrils flared, sniffing the air. And by the time the dragonman looked in his direction and drew in a scent, Denaos had no breath to scream.

No, no, NO! His mind broke into scattered, fleeting thoughts. *How? How could he smell me? I smell right. We planned for this. We—*

And then he eyed the nearby corpse of the male guard. And it hit him: He might smell like silk and grass, but such a scent surely reeked strong and clear amid the stink of blood and death.

And sure enough, the dragonman hefted his tremendous ax and began to stalk toward Denaos's hiding spot.

And so he ran.

He darted around behind a nearby house, felt along the walls for something: a back door, a servants' entrance, a low-hung window, or maybe—

A pipe.

His hands wrapped around the cold iron of a pipe leading up to rooftop gutters—a most detestable vanity, considering how little rain Cier'Djaal saw, but one he was thankful for. He took a keen grip and, using its soldered joints for footholds, shimmied his way up the house's wall and onto its roof.

He peered over the edge and onto the street and saw the dragonman look down the back alley where he had been a breath ago. The monstrous creature sniffed the air, snorted at the darkness, and, clearly not paid well enough to pursue, turned around and stalked back down the street.

Denaos breathed out a sigh as he fell onto his rear. High up here, there was no sound of guards clattering or dragonmen stomping. He could finally hear the sound of his heartbeat and how hard and heavy it came.

Fuck, he thought. *When did it get like this? You used to be able to break into a dozen houses, knife a dozen thugs, light a dozen fires in one night and still be able to think about what you were going to have for breakfast.* He looked down at his hands, callused and broad and rough. *When did it stop being easy? When did you start giving such a shit?*

Another sound pierced the night air: an avian screech that carried over the rooftops. He looked out over there, beyond the walls of Silktown, into the city.

The city, so dark and quiet while Silktown burned and breathed with life. The city, its only lights the fires lit by Sainites as their scraws flew overhead. The city, its only signs of movement Karnerian patrols marching down the streets.

There weren't so many fires burning tonight. Only a few scraws flapped in the darkness. The seemingly endless rivers of Karnerian legions that had thronged the streets seemed like a few scattered blots of inky armor.

Maybe Asper's plan had worked: Maybe the attacks against the foreigners really had weakened them. Or maybe they were just running out of shit to destroy. So many houses stood in ruins, so many stalls had been smashed, so many storefronts hung quiet and empty.

Why should that matter? Denaos asked himself.

Since he had first stepped off the boat and onto Harbor Road, Cier'Djaal had never felt like home. He was always an intruder, a foreigner, a little pale boy in a world where he didn't belong. That had been fine by him; he didn't trust the city any more than it trusted him. There was no regret for the blood he had spilled here.

Ramaniel had never cared about Cier'Djaal.

Why did Denaos?

He looked long to the Souk, the beating heart of Cier'Djaal. The Silken Spire, its three pillars bound together by the silk spun by its spiders, still stood strong, untouched by the foreigners. They still needed that symbol, that idea that they were here to save Cier'Djaal and not destroy it. So long as the Spire stood, they could go on pretending that.

Even if it was all that was left when the rest of the city had burned to the ground.

--- ⪥ ---

Denaos's boots hit the other side of the iron fence surrounding Mejina's estate but half an hour later, after he had made his way through the remaining guards. He darted across the lawn, into the shadows of the manicured trees and elegant hedges of the fasha's estate.

Crouching beneath a low-hanging bough, he glanced up at the windows. All alight, the glow of lamps cast brightness out of every pane. Even the servants' quarters, which should have been dark at this time of night, were bright and cheery.

And yet where were the servants?

He saw no house guards in the bright windows, either. If Mejina had decided to retire for the night, surely the lights would have been doused, wouldn't they?

Perhaps he was out, discussing plans with Khovura allies or Jackal traitors. Or perhaps he was walled up with his servants inside some secret room, terrified of retribution from the Jackals who had caught wise.

A pang of paranoid fear wedged itself between the vertebrae of his neck.

Or maybe someone had told him about Denaos's raid.

What if the traitor had struck again? But who? Not Rezca. Rezca didn't know. And Yerk had gone underground. And that just left...

No, Denaos told himself. *No. That can't happen. Not a single word of this has been breathed to anyone save for Anielle. She's with you. You're going to do this, then run away together. She's—*

He nearly started as a hand was laid upon him. But he steeled himself at the last moment. Two fingers placed on his left shoulder; the sign he and Anielle used to use to let each other know who was behind them when silence was called for.

She crept forward to join him, murmuring through a mask over her face.

"You're late," she whispered.

"If we agreed not to move until we were both here, then I'm not technically late," he replied. "Lot of bodies on the street tonight. How'd you avoid them?"

"Came from the north, through Harbor Road," she said. "Figured you'd do it, too, since it was closer."

"Yeah, well..." He snorted. "How long have you been here?"

"Long enough to see the house is empty. I could have walked in the front door and not been stopped."

"That can't be right," Denaos said. "Mejina had the most guards out on the street. He wouldn't have left his house undefended."

"He would have if he's not who we think he is." She sighed, pulled her mask down. "I was kind of hoping you were late because you weren't going to show up. I hoped you had thought of your idea and seen how little we have to go on. The Khovura are radicals, rebels. Why would they assist a fasha?"

"Why does anyone become a rebel? They want something they don't have. Who better than a fasha to give it to them?"

"I feel compelled to mention that the Khovura are also completely insane. Completely insane and running around with monsters we don't even have *names* for, Ramaniel. Whatever they don't have, they can take, surely."

"If they could, they would have already. There's got to be another angle we're not considering."

"Maybe one you're not considering. You thought Ghoukha was aiding them earlier and we weren't at all ready when they burned his house to the ground and—"

"We weren't *ready* because there was a traitor interfering," Denaos snapped. "And the traitor and the fasha are both helping the Khovura, and the Khovura are just one more thing that's going to kill this city if we don't stop it." He narrowed his eyes upon her. "Why bring this up now instead of, oh, say, any other time we weren't about to break into someone's house?"

"You fucking know why," Anielle shot back. "You've got no evidence and we've got everything to lose. The Jackals are going down, the Khovura are clawing up, and every moment we waste here is a moment we could be spending gathering what we can and getting the fuck out." She winced, voice softening. "Silf hates deals he's left out of, Ramaniel. Best not to offend him further by pulling a dirty job. You know that."

Denaos stared down at his feet. "Yeah, I know that. And you know why I can't go back. Not yet."

"No, I don't know that. I don't know what's driving you. I'd say pride or a sense of righteousness, but I fucking know you don't have room for that inside you among all the stupid. So what is it? Why is this, of all things, important?"

"Because I . . ."

Denaos fell silent. What could he tell her? That there were some acts that could cut even those hearts caked in grime and filth? That some demons couldn't be chased away by drinking so much one's conscience threw up?

Those answers wouldn't satisfy her.

And he couldn't tell her the real story. He couldn't tell her Ramaniel was dead, but not yet buried. He couldn't tell her that Denaos still had a life to lead, one free of past sins like the riots, the Kissing Game, the Khovura. He couldn't tell her that the only way to achieve that life was to shove Ramaniel in a grave and bury him so deep his ghost would never return again.

That would be honest. She hated honesty.

"We made a deal," he settled on saying. "I'll sweeten it for you, even. One hour inside Mejina's house. If I can't find what I'm looking for, we'll leave."

"Leave the house?"

"The house, Silktown, Cier'Djaal, all of it. We'll head right for the gates and head to Gurau and catch the first boat upriver to Muraska." He held up a finger. "If that doesn't sound like enough to you, then you can go now and I'll think no less of you. But if you're coming, I get one hour."

Anielle looked at him carefully, scrutinizing him for another angle, as if she could make this even better for herself. He wasn't surprised when she sighed in resignation.

The sadness that tinged her eyes when she nodded, though? That was unexpected.

"One hour," she agreed, pulling her mask up. "Starting now."

A quick nod, a brush against his belt to check for the comforting presence of his knives, and they were off.

They darted across the lawn, beneath the trees, between hedges, heading for the southeastern corner of the house. Mejina's name was not big, but it was old, and his manor had been erected in the early style of Cier'Djaal, from when the fashas had attempted to belittle each other daily.

The southeastern corner of such a manor was always reserved for the guest quarters. Far out of earshot of servants, these rooms had originally been planned to force visiting nobles to get out of bed and get whatever they needed themselves. Before extravagant displays of wealth became the fashion, "comfort tombs," as they were called, were very popular for spiteful fashas.

Small surprise that they happened to make the ideal point for a break-in.

Denaos swept up beneath the window, five feet above them. He pressed his back against the wall and formed a cradle with his fingers. Anielle acted immediately, placing one foot in his grip and letting herself be boosted up. Denaos glanced up, making sure not to boost her any farther than she needed to see within the quarters.

She glanced down, gave him a nod. All clear. He boosted her up farther, muscles quivering as she made short work of the lock on the window and slipped it open with a squeak.

Her weight left him as she pulled herself inside. He paused, began to count to thirty—it was usually assumed that if a thief reached fifteen without word from his partner, he should go in blade drawn. But he had barely reached eight when he heard a soft whisper from above.

Anielle leaned over the sill of the window, arms draped down for him to catch. He leapt up, they took each other by the wrists. With his feet scrambling against the stone of the walls, they fought to keep silent as she hauled him up and over the sill. They quickly eased the window shut behind them, settled in to have a look around.

By even a merchant's standards, the guest quarters were shabby. By a fasha's they seemed more akin to a prison cell. There was a bed, a low-slung table, and a few pillows for sitting, but nothing else. No artwork to flaunt taste, no bookshelves to flaunt education, even the light was dimmer here, the sole lamp providing little illumination.

Suddenly Mejina's reasons for wanting to prove his worth to Silktown became quite obvious.

Denaos slunk toward the door, peered out, and looked down a long hallway. It ended in the house's *houn*, that reception area where all guests would be greeted. In the light of the lamps, he could just make out a staircase leading to the upper level of the house. Mejina's house might be old-fashioned, but it wasn't so old that he wouldn't keep the important bits—his accountant's office, his study, his records—on the top floor.

But then, fashas also usually stocked servants. From here Denaos saw at least a half dozen doors leading to a half dozen rooms on either side of the hall. Surely there should have been at least one servant attending to at least *one* of them.

"No one here," Anielle muttered quite louder than she should, as if to emphasize that fact.

"Must be upstairs," Denaos replied.

"Or must be no one here," Anielle said. "I don't like the looks of it. We should leave while we can."

"Has it been an hour yet?"

Anielle glared at him. "Asshole."

She made no further protest—or insult—as they swiftly slunk down the hall. The lamps cast too many shadows for Denaos's liking, but to put out the lights would be to give an obvious sign of an intruder. Better to move quickly and hope whoever might see them would do so out the corner of their eye and dismiss it as a trick of the light.

They came to a halt at the end of the hall, peered around the corner into the *houn*. Denaos could see an elegantly furnished room: fairly big, with a high ceiling, plush carpeting, the requisite number of artistic portraits and busts to demonstrate the size of Mejina's fortune. He saw a modest staircase opposite the door, leading up to a landing where two hallways opened up and yawned off somewhere into the darkness.

What he didn't see was a doorman.

No one to wait for visitors, no one to polish busts and dust portraits, no one at all. Even the most frugal fasha kept someone on hand to mind the *houn* and keep it impeccable, lest a rival fasha come and see a house less than pristine and go spread that gossip to the rest of Silktown.

That struck Denaos as odd. It struck Anielle as something a little bolder.

"Well, fuck me." She strode into the *houn*, extending her arms. "How's a fasha that can't even afford a doorman going to support the Khovura, Ramaniel?"

"Keep your voice down," Denaos muttered in reply as he stalked in after her. "And I don't know. Maybe he's helping them to get a payout."

"Really?" She lofted a brow. "How would he be able to pay off a Jackal to turn traitor, then?"

"I don't know, I don't *know*. He's got...some angle, something to offer them, some plan." His own voice rose as he whirled on her. "And I said keep your voice fucking down."

"Why?" She threw her hands out, gesturing to the emptiness of the room. "Who's going to hear me? The fucking statues?" She seized a nearby bust—a stern-looking bald man doubtless intended to be an honored ancestor—and looked earnestly at it. "You're not going to tell anyone, are you?" She wagged the bust back and forth, dropping her voice to lend it dialogue. " 'Not at all, I'm thankful for the company. I've had no one to talk to for a while, because, you see, there's *nobody fucking here.*' "

As if to simply rub that in, Anielle tossed the bust aside, letting it crash against the floor. Denaos winced and reached for his blade. But it was for naught: No guards came crashing through the door, no servants came rushing in to investigate. The echo of the crash lingered in a *houn* empty of everything, anything.

"Ramaniel," Anielle said, sighing. "You've been gone awhile, but some things don't change. If Mejina had anything worth guarding, he'd have guards. But he doesn't. He doesn't have anything because he spent every-thing trying to be Silktown's new head." She gestured around the *houn* and its modest opulence. "He's just one more rich man trying to climb over the heads of other rich men to make himself a little more rich."

Denaos opened his mouth, found no words there. He searched around the *houn*, hoping to find something—an out-of-place object, a missive left carelessly behind, art that looked too expensive for Mejina—but saw nothing. He drummed his fingers on his legs if only so he wouldn't pick up another bust and smash it out of frustration.

This had all seemed so logical when he came up with it. Mejina was the one making waves in Silktown. Surely he had to be getting help from *somewhere*. But the marvelous tapestry of a plot he had surmised unraveled more with every stray thought.

If Mejina truly had a Jackal working with him, he wouldn't be this loud, drawing so much attention to himself. If Mejina truly had the Khovura in his pocket, he would be directing their resources elsewhere, against other fashas, not wasting his time attacking Jackals.

But back in the tunnels, he *had* seen the Khovura emerge from Silk-town. He *had*.

Hadn't he?

He couldn't even recall what that one Khovura, the one with the mutated arm, had said in its whimpering, gurgling babble. Something about going back the way he had come. It had all made so much sense back then: He was going to bloody the noses of the Sainites, he was going to clean up the Khovura, he was going to expose the fashas, and he was going to make up for all the hell he had put this city through.

And his heart sank at that realization.

He had never been searching for a plot. He had never been searching for a traitor in the Jackals or the fashas. He had never been searching for something so tangible, so easy, so firm.

He had been searching for absolution, a way to assure himself that he wasn't the scum he thought he was every night moments before he fell asleep. He had been searching for something that would make the ghost of Imone go away so that he would never look up and see her smiling with her slit throat and bloodied dress.

And everywhere he looked for that absolution, he found nothing but empty rooms and shadows.

Perhaps it was time to admit that. Perhaps it was time to let Ramaniel and Denaos both die, to tuck them into an alley and let them burn with the rest of the city. After all, he had come up with a new life before, he could do it again. It was easy as coming up with a name.

Stonk appealed to him, for some reason.

He was just about to voice this to her when he heard something.

Faint, as though from an act that had been done with great care, but he heard it all the same: the creak of wood and the click of a shutting door from upstairs. He looked up, saw the movement of a shadow as it disappeared down the hall.

"How much longer do I have?" he asked, his eyes on the upstairs.

"Maybe half an hour," Anielle answered, fixing him with a curious glance. "But—"

He was already running, slipping as quickly as he dared, as silently as he could to the staircase and up to the second level. Anielle, in a show of frustration, merely watched him from below with a glare and folded arms. But he saw this only out of the corner of his eye as he leaned against the wall and peered around the corner.

His attentions were for the blue-clad figure making his way down the hall.

Denaos would have called him a noble, were it not for the fact that his fine robes bore holes and frayed edges and the luster of his jewels had faded to dullness. As it was, the man walking down the hall, back turned to Denaos, seemed a little like a vagrant who had looted a very fancy carcass somewhere.

But the man didn't carry himself with the bearing of a vagrant. He strode down the hallway rather than skulking, as though this were his home. Far too shabby to be Mejina, far too well-dressed to be a servant, Denaos could only assume he was an intruder, like himself.

He wasn't holding any valuables, though, so he was clearly no looter. What had he come in search of?

The man stopped suddenly and turned. Denaos slipped back behind the doorway. When no sign of alarm came, he peered back around and saw the man's face: veiled by an indigo swath of silk beneath ochre eyes.

A saccarii, Denaos noted.

A saccarii very interested in Mejina's house. The hall bore many doors on the left wall, with the right dominated by large, sweeping windows. His attentions were focused on one such window, pane shattered and frame splintered. His ochre eyes studied it carefully, never once looking away.

Even as he spoke.

"Exactly what are you hoping you'll see me doing?"

A tense moment passed before Denaos registered that the saccarii was talking to him. And in that time, the veiled man turned and fixed a languid glance upon him.

"If you're here to loot, go right ahead," the saccarii said, voice deep. "Mejina squandered most of his wealth to fund his security efforts, but there remain a few heirlooms you might take." He took in Denaos in another breath. "Though you look a bit overdressed for such low ambitions."

Denaos remained unmoving, hand rigid upon the hilt of his blade. He hadn't been certain what to expect in Mejina's house, but a well-dressed saccarii certainly wasn't it. This was a complication in a situation already crowded with complications.

And yet, he thought, *it's not like anything gets easier with a dead body.*

He slowly released his grip on the dagger. He glanced over his shoulder to the *houn* below. Anielle had wandered off somewhere else—or left entirely, more likely. It galled him to turn away and walk toward the saccarii, but he had no choice.

He had come here for answers and this was the only one he had so far.

Even if it did raise more questions.

"Ah." Recognition tinged the saccarii's voice as he drew closer. "I recall you. I was indisposed at the time, but you came to my home not long ago. You are Lenk's accomplice, no?"

The realization struck him like a lady of good breeding: gently, but firmly. There were only two well-dressed saccarii in Cier'Djaal, and one of them was female.

"Calling him an accomplice makes him sound guilty," Denaos said, "Sheffu."

"Men who are not guilty of something do not flee the city," Sheffu replied. "He sought atonement, regardless of the fact that he did not start this war." He quirked a brow at the tall man. "I suspect you didn't tell him who did."

Denaos leaned back, letting his fingers rest upon the pommel of his knife. He regarded Sheffu evenly, betraying nothing through his pursed lips.

"Don't presume to know Jackal business, fasha."

He hoped that sounded as menacing as he thought it did.

"So you *are* with the Jackals."

"Oh, fuck you, old man."

He was *certain* that sounded far more frustrated than he'd thought it should.

"Fuck it, then," he muttered. "How much do you know?"

"Of Jackals? Not much. But I have been in Cier'Djaal long enough to know which way rats scurry when their holes flood." Though his face was veiled, Sheffu's mirth was all too clear. "You hoped to buy your-selves time to regroup by starting a different war to distract. You did this once, back before the riots, between the Morose Family and Hell's Harlots. But the Khovura required a bigger diversion, so you instigated a war between the Karnerians and Sainites."

He looked out the window, toward distant columns of smoke rising into the night sky.

"How is that working out for you, by the way?"

"Listen, I've been doing this a long time myself," Denaos replied with a sigh. "So maybe, for once, when I meet a mysterious strange old man in an abandoned manor, I could be spared the usual cryptic bullshit and cut to the point?" He tucked a thumb into his belt. "What are you doing here, fasha?"

"The same thing any Jackal would." Sheffu shrugged. "I seek to find the connection between Mejina and the Khovura."

"Then he *was* helping them. I knew it." He slammed his fist into his palm, triumphant. "I *knew* it."

Sheffu eyed him distastefully. "I imagine most rats feel the same rush when they discover a kernel of grain in a pile of offal." He turned away, resumed his stride down the hallway. "Mejina was not helping the Khovura. Not directly. He was a man terrified of losing status. While fear makes excellent pawns, it breeds poor conspirators."

"You can't be serious." Denaos hurried to catch up to the surprisingly swift saccarii. "It all makes sense. Mejina reached out to the Khovura to enhance his own status."

"It is in the fashas' best interests to keep things exactly as they are. Why would they speak to a cult prepared to destroy everything?"

Denaos scoffed. "This is a footwar. We've seen a hundred gangs before the Khovura and the game never changes. The uniforms do, but every thug in the city still wants to rule it."

Sheffu merely fixed him with a look that suggested the previous rat analogy might have been too generous a description for someone of Denaos's intellect.

"All right, fine," Denaos said, "they're considerably more fucked up than your average gang. What would they want with Mejina?"

"Whatever it is, they have already done it. The slaughter at the Silktown gates was out of character for Mejina. He was a small man pretending to be big. Violence is not in his nature."

"How would you know?"

"We had tea often. Among the fashas, Mejina and I were something of kindred anomalies. Pardon the vulgarities, but those broke as shit tend to keep each other company." Sheffu waved a hand. "It is concerning, though. For Mejina to have ordered such savagery, something must have changed. And if the Khovura are behind that change, they are seeking something in the fashas."

"Like what?"

Sheffu halted as the hallway ended, surveyed a tall door that marked its end. "Something they could not achieve through violence, as they did with Ghoukha. It troubles me." He studied the door carefully. "Blades, you will find, are the resort of malicious and desperate men. When they put them away, they are no less malicious, but far more patient."

Denaos met his ochre gaze for a moment. When he spoke, he did so slowly and clearly.

"So," he said, "what did we agree about the cryptic bullshit?"

"I never agreed to that."

Sheffu took the handle of the door and gave it a tug. It held fast. And despite each successive tug he gave, he could not budge it.

"Strange," the saccarii murmured. "It does not feel locked, but..."

"Use both hands," Denaos said.

"That...could prove difficult."

With an exasperated grunt, Denaos nudged the fasha aside. He took the handle and gave it a tug. Sheffu had spoken true: There was not so much as a give, let alone a rattle that would indicate a lock. It was as though the door had been sealed completely into its frame. Undeterred, he took the handle in both hands, put one foot on the wall to add extra pull, and, with a massive heave, jerked it backward.

A slight give. And then an eruption.

The door flew open with a burst of stagnant air, flying off so violently as to hurl Denaos aside and crack against the wall. He staggered back, his marvel at the reaction overwhelmed by the stench that followed.

Stench, actually, might have been the wrong word. The aroma that emerged from the dark room beyond—while certainly unpleasant— was too clean to be called so. It carried with it the scent of packed herbs and stale incense, conspiring to mask some other odor, as though someone had tried to scrub the very air clean.

"No lamps," Sheffu murmured, stepping forward and peering into the darkness beyond the door. "This is the only room without lights."

Denaos followed slowly behind the fasha, into the gloom of the room. Through the fading light behind him, he could just make out the outlines of bookshelves, a desk, cabinets. The windows were shuttered and draped. A study, then; maybe some kind of accountant's office. But before he could dwell on it further, he recognized the scent.

Packed herbs. Stale incense. The things they used to cover the reek of death.

He thought to tell this to Sheffu, thought to draw his knife and leave. But before he could do either, the fasha spoke amid the clatter of things moving upon the desk. A switch was hit. A flame sparked. A wick caught. The study was bathed in a soft orange light.

The better to illuminate the dead body on the floor.

"Ah." There was no sadness in Sheffu's sigh, merely resignation, as though he had always known it would end with this. "Mejina. May you find the peace that money never brought you."

It certainly *looked* as though he had gone peacefully, Denaos thought as he knelt beside the corpse. Mejina was well-dressed in a nice robe, his body unmarred by visible signs of a particularly violent death. No blood, no wounds, no bruises. Even the paint on his middle-aged features seemed undisturbed.

To all appearances the man had simply fallen asleep and not gotten up. Probably quite recently, if the lack of decay was anything to go by: no rot, no pooling of blood, none of the bloating that usually accompanied corpses long dead. He reached down, expecting to find flesh still warm.

And when he plucked up a hand cold as ice, he all but started.

"That... doesn't make sense," Denaos murmured.

"What doesn't?"

"The body is cold," he said. "*Very* cold. There should be *some* kind of sign of rot already setting in, but..." He left that thought hanging, along with Mejina's arm. The limb was stiff, almost immovable. "The body's stiff, but it's too cold for that."

"How would you know?"

Denaos blinked, looked up at the fasha. "Really, is the fact that I know Lenk not evidence enough that I happen to see a lot of corpses?" He shook his head, looked back to Mejina. "Asper showed me a thing or two about decay. Something isn't right here."

"Who is Asper and why—"

"Shit." Denaos drew back the collar of Mejina's robe. Adorning the man's throat was a puncture wound, perfectly circular. "Look at this."

Sheffu leaned down, squinting. "So this is how he died? Stabbed like a dog?"

"Do dogs get stabbed?" Denaos shook his head. "Either way, no. This is too small to be a blade. Barely bigger than a pin. But the wound hasn't closed and it was made too clean, no struggle." He looked up at Sheffu. "Someone stuck him after he was dead."

The saccarii's brows knitted in concentration, his attentions focused on some distant thought.

"The smell," Sheffu muttered. "Like trying to cover up death."

Denaos hesitated to ask how the saccarii had come to that conclusion. But, as he said, he had been in Cier'Djaal a long time.

"There are remedies," Sheffu continued, "toxins and chemicals, crafted by the Bloodwise Brotherhood. The couthi can make things that could preserve a body, prevent decay when injected from within."

He glanced around, drew in a deep breath. "And with the right environment, no light or warmth to advance rot…"

"They preserved his body?" Denaos slowly rose up, staring down at Mejina's cold corpse. "And left it here…for someone to find it."

"That is alarming, yes," Sheffu said. "But not nearly as alarming as the source of the mixture. The couthi are driven solely by money. They do not sell their services cheaply and this…could not have come cheaply."

"A fasha," Denaos said, "that's the only explanation."

"A fasha, yes." Sheffu looked down at the corpse and shook his head. "But not Mejina."

"Then who?"

"One question," Sheffu said. "But one more prominent occurs. If Mejina has been dead for this long, he could not have been the one to order the massacre at the Silktown gates." He began to look up at Denaos. "And that means—"

The saccarii's gaze rose halfway, halting at Denaos's feet. His eyes grew urgently wide and he whispered something profane beneath his veil. Denaos, quirking a brow, followed his gaze down to his own ankles to see what had alarmed the fasha so.

He wasn't quite sure what that thing was coiling about his boot: a thin gray tendril of flesh, shyly slithering around his ankle. He wasn't sure where it had come from or how it had crept upon him. And he certainly wasn't sure what was happening.

Not even as it snapped taut, pulled him hard to the floor, and dragged him screaming into the hall.

He scrambled for purchase, groping at the rugs and clawing at wooden support beams. He tried to fight back, swinging vainly and flailing haphazardly at the tendril wrapped around his leg. But each time, the tendril jerked sharply and slammed him into the wall or against the floor so that eventually he simply tucked his head low behind his arms and hoped that would prevent the worst of it.

But as it snapped around the corner and smashed him against the hall's entryway, that seemed like wishful thinking.

By the time he could feel his body being dragged down the stairs, he was numb to the worst of it. Blood trickled from a gash in his brow, pain reverberated in his bones, but he could scarcely feel the jarring sensation of his limp form being hauled over each step.

His breath left him in a heave as he felt himself lifted off the stairs and dangled upside down in the air. Shadows swam through his vision, rendering the *houn* a dark blur. His ears were filled with noise as the beating of his heart fought against a ringing in his head. His skull felt far too fragile, at that moment, to contain the lead weight that was his brain, and he felt as though it might simply snap the bone and slide out and stain the carpet.

He doubted he would feel it. He was barely sensate enough to see. He could make out dark shapes crowding below him on the *houn*'s floor. They reached up for him with dark hands as his arms dangled lifelessly. They were speaking—he could hear their voices only in swaddled murmurs, their words lost to the sound of his ragged breathing.

Slowly he spun in the tendril's grip like a twitching body in a noose, until he came face-to-face with gray lips trembling in wordless murmur. Before he remembered he was upside down, they looked to be smiling with unpleasant broadness. But as his vision cleared, he could see the entirety of the monstrosity's visage: vast mouth set in a columnar head beneath a pair of eyes that looked as though they had been scribbled black with coal.

A Disciple. A demon. An old man's torso stacked upon the serpentine tail from which he dangled, withered fingers ending in black claws, and daggered tongue hidden behind shriveled lips.

Had he had the sense to do so, Denaos might have screamed, maybe soiled himself for good measure. As it was he could but blink dumbly at the abomination before him.

He supposed he ought to be thankful for that.

"Why do you resist?"

The demon's voice crept past his ears and into his mind as sensation slowly returned to him.

"Millennia have I slumbered at the God-King's request and I awake to a world unchanged," the Disciple rasped in a voice that came from somewhere dark and damp, "as though my meditations were but a blink, my suffering but a breath. I return to find mortalkind still so terrified of knowledge, still quavering in the shadows so that we must lure them out with craven duplicity."

Funny how he couldn't understand the demon any better now.

"Is it any surprise?"

Another voice rose from the floor of the *houn*. Softer, frailer, female. But no less sinister: It raked across Denaos's flesh and set his teeth on edge.

"They wither without guidance," the voice continued, "huddle together beneath silks, mistake the glitter of gold for the splendor of heaven."

His eyes swung low. Even upside down, he could see the splendor of the woman. She stood a glittering jewel amid the black clothing of the Khovura huddled around her. Her dress was an elegant green silk embroidered with gold designs of Ancaa's sigil: hands connected in a circle of fellowship. Her manicured fingers drummed thoughtfully upon her arm. But above the finery of her veil, her eyes burned yellow with contempt.

Familiar contempt.

"Is it any wonder, then," Fasha Teneir hissed, "that they scurry from true light as roaches?"

Denaos's eyes drifted over the Khovura surrounding her. They regarded him with eyes alight with hatred, but he ignored them. His attentions were seized by the one pair of eyes among them that brimmed with fear.

Stood firmly between two of them, her hands tied behind her back, Anielle stared at him from above the gag tied around her mouth. And though she had trained over the years never to feed her captors with panic, it was impossible to keep any sort of defiance up in the presence of a demon.

Denaos would be screaming, himself, had he not been too beaten and bruised to do so.

"Teneir," he spoke at last, tasting blood in his mouth. "You're the one behind it."

Her sneer was plain even beneath her veil. "The familiarity of thugs is something I cannot abide, Jackal, as are whatever delusions you harbor of grasping what is occurring around you."

"You're the one," Denaos repeated, numbly. "You were the one supporting the Khovura. You were the one who killed Mejina?"

At this an amused giggle. "Me? No, Jackal. In no sense of the word did I kill Mejina. How could I when he spent every coin he had on locking down Silktown?"

"Poison," Denaos said, "assassins in the night, I don't know, *somehow.*"

"Ah, I believe you will find that the gossip will speak differently tomorrow," Teneir replied. "Mejina was found dead in his home, cut apart by Jackal blades." She made a gesture toward one of the Khovura, who quickly swept forward and seized Denaos's weapon from his belt. "One of which was carelessly left behind. The fashas will realize that Mejina's paranoia was well founded: Danger lurked around every corner. In their desperation, the Jackals finally snapped and broke their bargains with the fashas."

"Turn them against us," Denaos gasped, "of course."

"Against what? Your paltry gang of thieves is a remnant plagued with traitors, barely even a threat. I merely wish to show the fashas that our only hope lies in uniting."

"Behind you," Denaos said.

"There you are," she replied, voice mockingly sympathetic. "A mule, blind and deaf, will eventually find water."

"The traitor..."

It was an instant. A moment between labored breaths and nothing more.

For just a moment, Teneir had glanced at Anielle.

"Unknown, even to me," the fasha said. "Typical of thieves, no? Good deeds are so foreign to them that they hide from acknowledgment of them."

"Good deeds?" Denaos's voice rose along with his temper. Feeling that had been creeping into his limbs began to surge. "*Good deeds*? You snickering bitch, you *kill people.*"

"So that no more need die," she replied flatly.

"You started a fucking *war!*"

"To end all future wars."

"You're a vicious, conniving, demon-worshipping—"

"And you are a Jackal," she said, simply. As though that were damnation enough. "You and your wretched ilk carved your way to the city's top to sit upon a throne of knives. You encouraged greed and gluttony to reign throughout this city, unchecked. And when Cier'Djaal tried to reject you? When the Houndmistress tried to cast you out?" She stared intently at Denaos, as though she could see right through him and into Ramaniel. "You gave it the riots. You gave it countless dead.

"There is no sin whose hand you can accuse me of kissing that you have not lain with, Jackal. This city is no longer merely ill; its diseases cannot be cured, but must be excised. If Ancaa asks this of me, then I shall be the one to wield the blade."

"Funny you should say that."

Denaos's words were punctuated by the sound of his body hitting the floor as his foot slipped free of his boot and he fell from the Disciple's grip. He anticipated the impact, took the blow with a grunt, and immediately leapt to his feet. The Khovura scrambled to tackle him and found nothing but empty air as he darted through them toward the fasha. The Disciple's tongue lashed out like a whip, catching the leather of his vest and painting a bright line of crimson across his back. He bit that pain back as he pulled a hidden dagger free from his belt, reversed the grip on it, and took a flying leap at Teneir.

Pain he could tolerate. His death he could accept. If he killed Teneir, then he would at least make this city a little less terrible. That would be enough.

All the instincts of a killer coalesced into one breath as he took her in: her dispassionate stare, her soft stance.

Her tender throat.

His blade lashed out.

He gritted his teeth in anticipation of the wash of warm blood.

Teneir leaned back, her head swiveling away from the blow. Far away. Denaos didn't even have time to scream as he watched her neck extend to two feet long, undulating out of the path of his blade. Her eyes narrowed in bemusement as he fell to the ground, dagger dry and eyes wide with horror.

"Alas," Teneir said as her head swiveled forward on serpentine throat, "would that all problems could be solved by violence alone."

"You..." Denaos groped for a word. "Demon. Fucking mon—"

The crack of a fist against his jaw silenced him. The stamp of a foot upon his hand sent his dagger dropping. Then the Khovura simply seized his arms and jerked them harshly behind his back, binding him swiftly. Any further shock he might have had over what stood before him was rendered moot by the gag tied around his mouth.

"The price for honesty is steep, no?" Teneir's head shook. "How long did it take you, human, to admit what you thought of us saccarii?" She gestured to her neck, her hand glistening with scaly patches. "I rose to the ranks of a fasha, a ruler of men and women, and still for this was I looked down upon by the very people I stood above. Does it not strike you as odd that I should own so much, give so much, and still be defined by this deformity?"

"There is a better word for it than that, Teneir."

All eyes went to the top of the stairs. The creature standing there Denaos recognized as Sheffu, but only by virtue of the fact that no one else could possibly be here. For what stood there, naked and pale, was not a fasha, not even a man.

It walked on two legs, but its flesh was covered in scaly patches. Its right arm was fused to its side, its hand dangling limp and useless at its hip. Its lips were drawn in an unintentional serpentine grin, and when it spoke, a long tongue licked out from between its teeth.

"Many more of us call it a curse," Sheffu said as he walked down.

"Sheffu." Teneir struggled for a tone of diplomatic austerity, yet the strain at the edges of her voice was unmistakable. "I did not expect you."

"Nor did I expect you," Sheffu said. "I would never expect another saccarii here." He cast his ochre gaze to the Khovura, apparently not intimidated by their presence. "In the company of *his* servants."

The Khovura reached for their blades, murmuring threats beneath their veils. A hand from Teneir stayed them, though. Even the Disciple merely stared at the intruding saccarii, watching him warily.

"Nor would I expect a saccarii to so adamantly oppose salvation," she said. "Many of us have joined the Khovura."

"Out of insanity."

"Out of *necessity*," Teneir hissed. She took no pains to conceal the rage behind her voice. "Do you not see, Sheffu? Do you not see what we are to them? This city? They mistrust the couthi, they fear the tulwar, they banish the shicts, but the saccarii? They do not even take the time to form an *opinion* of us. We are simply dirt to them, to be trodden over and built upon, and this land was ours before *any* of them set foot on it."

She reached up, removed her veil. The face beneath had once looked human, possibly quite beautiful. But her mouth was stretched at the edges and her lips were scaled. Her nose had receded, becoming nostrils. Her mouth trembled in a quavering whimper.

The sight of such an emotion coming from such a monstrosity made

Denaos queasy, as her face contorted in an attempt to convey the same pain as her voice.

"They don't even *hate* us, Sheffu," she said. "We are not even people to them. Merely one more type of vermin, like any rat or hecatine, to be swatted away and stepped on." She drew in a staggered breath. "And still, there are humans with the Khovura. And still, all are accepted by Ancaa—"

"Do *not* speak that name," Sheffu hissed in reply. "Do *not* pretend you are noble for doing this, Teneir." His lips peeled back, exposing long fangs. "Do you think I have not seen what you have? Do you not think I have heard my name spoken as a joke? To my own face? I know what the humans think of us." He glanced sidelong at Denaos. "Even the best of them view us as tools to their own end."

"Then why do you oppose us?" Teneir said. "Why do you chastise me as though I am some child? Why do you not see the good in what I am doing? I will rebuild this world, into something where no one need be stepped upon."

"Indeed?" Sheffu looked to the Disciple, who stared back at him with scribble-black eyes. "And what price do you intend to pay, Teneir? How much blood will be needed?"

"As much as it takes, Sheffu."

"Then he will take it all. You do not know what forces you are dealing with. He is a lord of lies, a deceiver. The sin of his ambition is made manifest in our flesh." Sheffu gestured to his fused arm. "You have noticed it, no? Every year we creep closer and closer to what we were born from. We are a testament to his hubris, the price we pay for his sins."

"A saccarii life is not a sin."

"No," Sheffu said. "But to do what you're doing... that is a sin. The price you seek to pay, that is too much. We must find another way."

"Ancaa will deliver—"

"Ancaa is a lie."

Teneir reeled. She looked to her Khovura, to the Disciple, to the Jackal prisoners, as if one of them would reassure her. But from them she received only fanatical glares, only a black stare, only terrified eyes. Her face sank, her hands hung limp at her sides. Finding nothing in the eyes surrounding her, she looked down to her robe, to the Ancaa symbols woven into the fabric.

"Why now, Sheffu?" she asked, her voice soft and trembling. "Why now, when it is far too late?"

"It can never be too late," Sheffu said, stepping closer to her. "It can only ever be too long." He extended his one good hand to her. "The killing has gone on too long, Teneir."

"But the humans, they—"

"When you close your eyes, Teneir, and picture the end of this all, after you have slaughtered humans and tulwar and shicts and given them reason to hate us . . . do you see a world safe for the saccarii?"

Denaos's eyes flitted toward Anielle. He saw her body still, her trembles cease as she held her breath behind her gag, waiting to see if Sheffu's words had swayed Teneir, waiting to see if there was a way that they all left here alive.

His own breath came slowly, heavily, labored. His own neck bent beneath the weight of his head, the burden of his own knowledge bearing him down. He could not blame Anielle; she had only ever fought and killed men, she still held on to the hope that these were all they were dealing with. Denaos had faced demons before; he knew better than to hope in their presence.

And yet, as Teneir looked up, her eyes were wet. Her lip trembled. Her body looked as if it might collapse under its own weight and topple right into Sheffu's arm. She took a deep, staggering breath, as though she would burst into tears at any moment.

She continued to look that way.

As she held her hand out to take his.

As her lips parted to expose her fangs.

As her head shot forward on serpentine neck and aimed for his throat.

The surprise on Sheffu's face was hidden beneath a splash of warm life. His shock was choked beneath a wet, gurgling breath. He went limp, supported only by Teneir's fangs lodged in his flesh. And when she withdrew them, he pooled to the floor in a puddle of scales and skin.

"I have seen it, Sheffu," Teneir said, her voice now cold and lips stained red. "I have seen a world where *saccarii* is no longer an insult, nor even a word. I have seen a world where all prosper and thrive beneath Ancaa. And before tonight I saw you with me." Her throat coiled upon her shoulders. She replaced her veil over her face. "Alas. You came to visit Mejina in the night, only to fall prey to the same ambush that the

Jackals had laid for him. I am sorry that it had to end this way, Sheffu." She licked a long tongue across her lips. "Truly."

Sheffu's hand touched the wound in his throat only once. He reached out, fingers wet with his own life, as if he could prove his point if she would listen for just a little longer.

And listen she did. And his last words were choked, crimson sobs that ended as he stared wide-eyed at the ceiling and emptied out upon the carpet.

"Tend to the bodies." Teneir pointed a finger at Denaos. "Use this one's blades. Make it clear that the Jackals were here."

"Evidence is in the flesh," the Disciple intoned. "If the deception is to be complete, let these frail casings be drained and serve as proof."

"No," Teneir said, "they were here when Sheffu was. If they know anything of what he is up to, I wish to know, as well. Take them with us."

Anielle's screaming could be heard through her gag as the Khovura forced her to her knees and slipped a black bag over her head. Even as one slid over his own and his world was plunged into blackness, Denaos could still hear her terrified wailing.

And he wondered if, even without the gag, she could have heard him then.

I should have listened, he whispered inwardly, feeling his heart sink. *Should have listened to you.*

TWENTY-NINE

BURY HER DEEP, BENEATH THE STREET

Dawn.

He blinked.

And then, sunset.

He blinked.

The day was clear and cold and the morning crept over the roofs of empty houses and between chimneys that hadn't sighed smoke since their families had fled.

He blinked.

The sky was red and thick with birds, clouds of crows and long-legged storks that settled like dirty snow on houses and on the street, plucking eyeballs from skulls and strings of meat from limp arms.

He blinked.

The streets were silent and empty in the yawning, vacated way that only roads that had once seen old men pushing carts of dried nuts, craftsmen's apprentices toting heavy loads, harried mothers pulling screaming children could be.

He blinked.

The streets were slick with blood and caked with corpses staring accusingly up at the sky, cursing gods who had not delivered them in their darkest hour and who had sent only crows and storks and gulls to clean up the mess.

He blinked.

His breath came slowly and labored. The scent of brimstone filled his nostrils. Electricity danced in sparks on the back of his neck. Flecks of blood dried on his hands.

He blinked.

And the blood was still on his hands.

The visions changed all the time—it wasn't always crows. Sometimes Cier'Djaal was on fire, consumed in great orange sheets. Sometimes it was empty and every door and window had been boarded up. Sometimes a cloud of midnight hung over it and thin people in gray sheets walked the streets, moaning and weeping.

The only constant was Dreadaeleon.

When it was crows, they squawked in complaint and fluttered out of his way as he walked. When it was flames, he walked among them untouched. When it was emptiness, his footsteps echoed forever. When he walked through the dead, they did not look at him.

Every time he opened his eyes, he felt the haze of broodvine creeping across them and Cier'Djaal changed before him. With every breath he took, the haze dissipated, until he stood once again in a city whole and unstained, however quiet. The Djaalic people still hid and held their breath in anticipation of whatever new hostilities the Karnerians and Sainites would unleash on each other today.

Dreadaeleon had long ceased caring about the people and the soldiers they lived in terror of. He had even ceased being terrified of the visions and how he continued to lose hours, maybe even days, as he wandered through them.

Constants, old man, he cautioned himself. *Keep track of the constants. You're a constant.* He looked at his hands, saw the blood drying upon them. *Scent of fire, sensation of electricity; those are constants. Traces of your power being used. When you're in the visions, magic is being expelled without you knowing or consenting. And people are dying. Someone is controlling you.*

Well, no shit, idiot. We figured that out ages ago. Anything new?

Not yet, you smug son of a bitch. Maybe if you'd shut up and let me think for a—

"Easy!" His voice sounded foreign to his own ears, echoing off the silence of the—momentarily—empty streets. "Easy, old man."

Granted, given the state he was in, it was hard not to go a little mad.

But madness wasn't helpful. He had to think clearly, as hard as it was. Doubtless magic was being used against him.

But how?

The means of controlling a person were few in number and those who might control a wizard were scarcer still. Induced hypnosis was a favorite, but it was unpredictable and required many set triggers or signwords to keep someone from snapping out of it. In a pinch a wizard could seize control of the electrical impulses that ran through a person's body and control them that way, but they would be made painfully and clearly aware of the attempt.

Someone was not simply controlling him, but controlling his reality. Someone was showing him visions: of a hundred futures, a hundred cataclysms, and all the many ways he had caused them.

No man, not even a wizard, could do that. Nothing could.

Short of gods, anyway.

But gods don't exist, do they? They're a barkneck's fantasy to control other barknecks. You've got reason. So use it.

He forced himself to stare straight ahead, ignoring the walls melting away to reveal houses made of bone, ignoring the streets turning to quicksand beneath him.

Your problem is that you're not admitting weakness, old man. You know someone is controlling you. But you don't know how. Obviously they need some sort of connection to you: visual, mental, something like that. Too many places for them to hide in this city. You'll never be able to follow the connection back.

He blinked. The skies rained fire around him and people's lungs erupted with smoke and flame. He ignored them, stepped over them as they fell in ash pillars before him.

But all connections have a limit, don't they? A line can only be drawn so taut before it snaps. You need to get out of the city. And you need to do it now. And you need...

He blinked. An empty street stretched before him, leading to an empty square surrounded by empty storefronts. Over a shut door, he saw a painted sign of a cat curled up, looking up with inviting eyes.

Liaja. You can't leave her behind. They'll use her against you.

He blinked. The sky bled crimson and each drop of blood pooled upon the street to coalesce into a red serpent that slithered around the cobblestones and coiled around his ankles.

She needs you, old man. She needs you to protect her.

He blinked. The skies were stained with smoke. A gargantuan figure of a skeleton wrapped in a skin of shadow, hellish red light pouring from its gaping maw as it shoveled screaming bodies over its teeth and choked on its own laughter, stood over him.

You can fix this.

He blinked. The ground was soft and spongy flesh beneath him and a beating heart the size of a cow hung suspended by chains overhead. He blinked. A chorus of serpents with brass wings flew overhead, their warbling voices causing wood to crack and windows to shatter. He blinked. Dogs with women's faces tore the genitals from screaming humans staked to towering rock.

You're the hero.

He blinked.

He was in the middle of the square.

He looked around and saw the shantytown that had cropped up during his occupation of the bathhouse, now bereft of people. But at a closer look, he saw them: their eyes pinpricks of reflected sunlight from the alleys they crouched within, staring at him with terrified glances. Not so long ago they had viewed him as an incidental savior, a beast whom other predators feared to tread near. Now they looked at him as though they thought he might swallow them whole at any moment.

Possibly because he was covered in blood. Or possibly because they were idle barknecks. He didn't care.

Dreadaeleon stormed across the square toward the bathhouse. He seized the door handle, pushed his way inside. The *houn* stood empty, the house silent, though trails of incense smoke still danced across the air and the steam of freshly drawn baths still gathered in clouds down the hall.

Someone had vacated this place in a hurry. Suspicious.

But again, beyond his concern.

He stalked down the hall. At the peripheries of his attentions, he sensed them: shadows of girls cowering behind their paper doors, frightened whispers and slightly less frightened reassurances from voices trying to stay silent. Try as he might to ignore them, he couldn't help but take offense.

They were afraid of him. *Him.* The man who had saved this bathhouse, time and again, from aggressing armies and spared it the ravages of this war. The man who had graced them with his power and asked for nothing in return, no matter how much he was dutifully owed.

They were afraid of him.

He sniffed, drew in the scent of brimstone.

Perhaps they *should* be, he thought spitefully.

Toward the end of the hall, he waved a hand, and an unseen force drew back the paper door of Liaja's room. He swept in and found her sitting upon the bed, the silk sheets bunched between her fingers as she wrung the material.

"Liaja," he said, suddenly aware of how out of breath he was. "I'm aware what I'm about to say will require both a tremendous amount of faith to believe and a larger amount of tolerance for the cliché, but we have to go now and there's no time to explain."

Liaja did not reply. Liaja did not reply for such a long time that he came very close to reiterating his question, save with more cursing. And so fiercely did his temper boil behind his eyes that he didn't even notice, until the very end of that long time, that Liaja was not looking at him.

And just when he was about to scream, she spoke.

"Go?" She did not sound surprised, or shocked, or confused, or any other emotion that might have been expected. "Where do you want to go"—a pregnant pause—"northern boy?"

"*Away*, you—" He caught himself, tamped his temper beneath a hard breath. "Something is happening. Something I am so close to explaining but can't quite yet. We need to get out of the city."

"We do?" Again her voice was soft. Again she did not sound surprised. Again she did not look up.

"We do," he said, nodding.

"Why do we have to go, northern boy?"

"I just told you. Something is happening. I'm . . . losing time, places. Every breath I take, I'm somewhere else. It's like dreaming while I'm awake and every time I wake up . . . or every time they end, I can feel something happened while I was gone and I find more blood and I—"

"What's my name?"

The question came not as a slap. Rather it was the limp touch of a weak person, a frail defense from someone who should have been defenseless. And still Dreadaeleon recoiled.

"What?" he asked.

"My name," she repeated. "What is my name?"

"Don't be stupid. We don't have time for this."

She looked up at him. There was no coldness in her face. She was dusky glass, something that looked whole and complete and ready to break at any second. And though her hair was neat and her face painted, her eyes reflected a deep weariness.

"What is my name?"

He swallowed hard before answering, the word somehow sounding wrong when he said it this way.

"Liaja."

She shook her head. "That is the name of the lead in *To Wed and Be Bled*. That is not my name."

"I . . . but . . ." He fumbled over his words. "You told me to call you Liaja, the day we met. You never told me your real name."

"And you never asked, Dreadaeleon."

"I would have if I knew how much this—"

"All the times I have listened to you and spoken to you and heard your stories and lectures, you have never asked. All the times you fell asleep in my arms, you have never asked. All the times I stroked your hair and sang to you as you wept and you have never asked."

That much was true. He hadn't asked her anything: her name, about her life, where she had come from, what her mother's favorite tea had been, what poems she liked. But she had always been quiet and coy, hadn't she? She had never *told* him any of this. If only she had just *told* him—

"Liaja." He winced. "Please, I—"

"Northern boy." She rose to her feet. The silk of her robe hung from her body. She found his gaze wherever he tried to look away and held it in her own. "I beg you, let me finish."

He opened his mouth to protest, to explain, to condemn her foolishness. But all he could manage was a stiff nod.

"When you came to me," she said, "that night so long ago, I was content to tend to you, as we are expected to tend to clients here. This is merely what women in my position did, I told myself." She approached him. "And when you wept and told me your troubles, I was content to listen, as I saw what you were: soft, frightened, sweet. And when you killed those men outside the bathhouse—"

"They were going to kill everyone. I had to—"

"I was afraid, yes. But I knew you were not a monster. Wizards...I do not understand them and their powers are not natural. But you..." The ghost of a smile pulled at the corners of her mouth. "You were, beneath it all, my sweet, gentle northern boy. I told myself this. I accepted it."

And then it faded. And the weariness returned. And the fear returned.

"Until three days ago," she said, "when you left."

Three days ago.

The first vision. When he had been speaking to her one moment and the next held a Karnerian's throat in his hands. When he first became aware of their control.

How could he explain that to her?

"And in the days that followed, I have heard so much more," she said. "More Karnerians have died by your hands. Djaalics, too."

That's it, he told himself. *That's what's been happening in these visions. You've been killing. Someone's been using you to do their dirty work. But who? The Venarium?*

"They struck a deal with me, Lia—you—darling," he struggled to explain. "They agreed to let me go if I killed Karnerians. I had to see you again, so I agreed, but they've been controlling me. They're using some kind of magic—"

"You can't ask me to believe that," she said. "You *cannot*. You can ask me to listen to you, you can ask me to love you, but you cannot ask me to die for you, northern boy."

His mouth fell. His heart hurt.

Those words hit him harder than he'd ever thought he could be hit.

"I didn't, though," he said, feebly.

"You came here and just told me of your problems. *Your* deals, *your* days lost, *your* needs, *your* desires, and said that *I* must come with *you*. You do not know my name. You do not know if I'm happy here or if I have plans for tomorrow or two years from now or what I left behind when I came here."

He swallowed hard. "Are you happy?"

The tears formed upon her eyes. They slid down her cheeks and drew clean lines through the paint on her face. She shook her head.

"When you think of us beyond the walls of this city," she said, "am I doing something other than comforting you?"

There were the perfect words to respond to that, somewhere.

In some ancient library that had been sealed up by a devoted scholar when an empire fell, on the lips of a bard drunk into half consciousness in an alley in Muraska, penned in the note of a young man right before he drank poison on the night before the woman he loved married someone else.

Somewhere there were the exact five words he could have said to make everything better, he knew. Somewhere far from here, that he didn't know.

"Please," he said.

And that was not one of them.

"No," she said.

"Please."

But it was the only one he had.

"No."

"Liaja, just—"

"That's not my name!" She all but struck him. He wished she had. "I can't be a prop in your play, Dreadaeleon. I can't attach my life to yours when you don't even see that I have one. I can't...I can't be around when you start killing."

"I won't."

He fell to his knees. The blood had simply left his legs, rushed into his throat, conspired to keep him from saying anything else, and made every word painful.

"I won't, I swear. I won't kill again. I won't hurt anyone. I won't cast another spell, think another thought, speak a single word that isn't totally and utterly devoted to you if you'll only...if..."

He swallowed something sharp. It lodged in his heart.

"Just make me feel strong again. Please."

She trembled, hands in fists at her sides, ready to strangle him, ready to hold him, ready to do anything she was not prepared to do. But she did not do these things. She turned away, hugged herself tightly, and spoke through tears.

"I regret it, northern boy," she sobbed. "I wish you'd never come back. But I knew you would."

"You knew I'd..."

"The rumors of killing were too much, so I sent word. I asked him not to do anything until I said what I had to." She let out a racking moan. "But if you're still here. Please...please don't hurt him. Please let him go."

Dreadaeleon stared at her stupefied.

"Who are you talking to? Liaja, I—"

"Concomitant."

A soft word. One with no power whatsoever. Intended merely to direct his attention to his right.

And there with one hand tucked behind his back, the other outstretched with the palm up, he appeared out of thin air.

Lector Annis.

"I have words for you."

Like a bad thought.

The air rippled before the Lector's palm. The air left the room. In the wake of silence that followed, Dreadaeleon had but enough sense to whisper a curse.

And then everything went to hell.

The spell erupted from Annis's palm in a burst of invisible force, the impact launching out to strike Dreadaeleon in the chest and launch him out of the room, bursting through the paper door and leaving an ugly wound in it before he smashed against the wall of the hallway opposite.

His momentum suspended him against the wood for but a moment and he hung, numb, before he tumbled down and flopped to the floor. The blow had struck the air from his lungs and he gasped desperately, trying to force wind back into his body.

And between his rasping breaths, his thoughts were ablaze.

Betrayed you. She betrayed you. She brought the Venarium down upon you.

No, she didn't know, she couldn't have known, she didn't know.

Later, old man, later. You've got bigger problems.

Bigger problems that appeared as a hand gingerly slid the paper door away. Annis took a single step into the hall, hands folded behind his back, lips pursed, and eyes focused on Dreadaeleon. As though this were not attempted murder, simply a heated argument, and he were merely awaiting a retort.

Dreadaeleon's response came in the scrambling of limbs and the scurrying of feet as he struggled to his footing and tore down the hallway. He flung his hands behind him, felt the invisible force erupt from his palms and propel him further down the hall, away from Annis.

Not that he was afraid. Fear, while reasonable, would be a hugely useless emotion in this situation; he couldn't very well escape Annis now. But he could get away from the bathhouse, prevent Liaja from being hurt, get more room to maneuver and cast.

The air of the square came cold and crisp in his lungs as his magically aided flight ended and he stumbled the last few steps out onto the cobblestones. He whirled about, sliding into a stance and readying for whatever Annis might hurl at him next. If it was fire, he was prepared with frost. If it was frost, he was prepared with fire.

He was hardly prepared for the quick but collected step of the man who came out of the bathhouse, though. Annis emerged with no particular hurry, regarding Dreadaeleon with stark appraisal instead of burning hatred. His voice came with only enough volume to be heard over the ringing in Dreadaeleon's ears.

"Protocol demands that I inform you of the charges leveled against you," he said. "As we've done that several times to no discernible effect, consider this a courtesy. If you surrender peacefully, no further harm will come to you this day."

"*This* day," Dreadaeleon shot back.

Annis lowered his gaze, dark shadows painting his eyes. "I will not tell you that this ends with you alive, Concomitant Arethenes. Your gross misconduct has gone far beyond the scope of our agreement. Your slaughter has been wanton and haphazard. Karnerians, Djaalics, and yet more Venarium agents lie dead. Unforgivable. You are no longer a wizard, nor even a heretic." His lips coiled into a frown. "Merely a rabid beast that needs to be put down."

Annis took a step forward. Dreadaeleon thrust a palm out, summoning the spell to his mind and the energy to his hand. His eyes were bathed in red light, smoke wafted from his fingers as sparks danced across his skin.

But he did not unleash his flame. It would be stupid to make the first move.

"How long did you spend in study to earn your Lectorship?" the boy spit. "Surely a man like you can understand cause and effect. You treated me like a dog and now you're shocked to find I have teeth?"

Annis's eyes shot wide for a moment. But in another breath they had lowered, and his head bowed.

"I am not blameless, no. I let hope overrule reason and enabled the damage to be done. I shall be including that in my report to the Venarium." He looked up, eyes once again narrowed to scalpel-thin focus. "That is an addition to the responsibility, not a negation. Regardless of whose hand wielded the weapon, you are too dangerous to let loose."

"Loose? *Loose?*" Dreadaeleon's laughter pealed out in mad cackles. "How the fuck was I loose? I had barely taken a few steps outside the tower when your control magic started kicking in."

Annis sneered. "You're raving, concomitant."

"Men who fancy themselves smart shouldn't try to play stupid, Lector." Dreadaeleon advanced forward, the fire on his palm stoking itself into a small inferno. "You used magic. Hypnosis. Domination. *Something.* You stole my body, used it to kill for you, and now your deeds are done you're going to toss me aside like nothing."

Annis slid into a stance of his own. "Concomitant, you're clearly unhinged. There is a way to end this without further madness, if you'll simply listen."

"*FUCK YOU!*" Dreadaeleon roared, and his fire roared with him, engulfing his hand in flame. "You call me a threat, a menace. You treat me like a tool, something you can use and break. And you have the gall to wonder why it came to madness?"

"I have no wonders, only expectations. I expected you to uphold your oaths to the Venarium." Annis's voice became a low hiss. "But I see now that it was also a mistake to trust the judgment of a cruel little boy."

No words. Dreadaeleon's retort was a scream, long and loud and swallowed whole by the roar of flames that poured from his hands as he thrust them out at the Lector. The flames raced out in a fiery torrent, cackling as they swept over Annis and smothered him beneath orange sheets. Dreadaeleon howled and emptied himself until the tears boiled on his eyes and the heat curled the tips of his hair to gray.

And the Lector did not so much as blink. He trembled. He grew hazy. He turned insubstantial. And then he simply disappeared.

The flames died down instantly, leaving blackened stone and the stink of char behind. Dreadaeleon stared at the empty space dumbly, breathing in the scent of ash and murmuring befuddlement.

And then something moved at the corner of his eye.

He turned. His feet left the ground. The air rippled around him, flinging him helplessly into the air. Annis stood beside him, a hand up and two fingers extended.

"Ambient light can be gathered and bent in a single location," he said in a soft monotone. "A skilled wizard can sculpt this to his liking, creating an illusionary image. Remember this."

Annis flicked those two fingers. And like dust from his coat, Dreadaeleon went flying. He tumbled shrieking through the air before he collided with a nearby building. He rolled down its wall, onto the cloth canopy of its awning, and split through it. He was scrambling to his feet almost as soon as he hit the stones.

His body was in agony that went deeper than his two impacts. He had expended too much of himself in that last expulsion of fire, he knew, poured too much of himself into the spell. He felt feverish, his body an oven in which the rest of him was cooking.

But he couldn't worry about that now. He couldn't worry about anything but Annis as the Lector came walking, calmly as he pleased, toward Dreadaeleon.

The boy roared once more. He thrust two fingers out. The lightning raced along his arm, gathered at his fingertips in an orb of electricity. Another word and it flew, an azure bolt arcing across the sky and streaking unerringly toward Annis.

And then, suddenly, it veered. It twisted and struck something just above the Lector's head.

Dreadaeleon shrieked in frustration, throwing one more bolt, then another, all to the same effect. When his temper died enough to let him see clearly, he was gasping for air and his knees were trembling. And the Lector kept coming, a single finger raised above his head.

There something dull and metallic shone. A featureless metal cylinder, suspended by magic above the Lector's head. It crackled with latent electricity.

"Lightning is powerful, but obeys certain laws," Annis said, still just as calm as before. "It will always seek out metallic targets unless it is controlled with discipline and practice. Remember this."

Dreadaeleon had no time to retort. He was already running. He couldn't be cornered, couldn't be trapped. He needed room to move.

He found it as he skidded to a stop in the square. He turned to Annis and breathed deeply and called his power to mind. The air in his lungs felt sharp and rasping. The spell was dangerous, interfering with his bodily function, but he didn't care. He couldn't.

He expelled his breath. It turned to a cloud of white frost before him. He reached within it, shaping the shards of ice and stacking them atop each other into several dagger-sized icicles. He thrust his hand into the cloud, sending each shard shrieking out of the cloud and toward Annis.

The Lector met each one with a wave of his hand. Fire blossomed from his palm, roaring to life for just as long as it took to melt each icicle and turn the ensuing water to steam that hung around him in a halo.

"Frost comes from moisture in the breath," he said. "It can be condensed and turned to ice. When it is melted, it does not disappear, merely changes. The energy spent can be energy conserved."

He drew in a breath. The steam rushed into the Lector's mouth. An instant later it emerged as another cloud of frost, bigger than Dreadaeleon's had been. And what formed inside was no dagger, but a large boulder of ice.

"Remember this."

The last words Dreadaeleon remembered before the icy rock flew out of the cloud. The words that still rang in his ears as he struggled to find the power to block it—force to repel it, fire to melt it. The words that echoed in his bones as the ice struck him in the chest and shattered and knocked him to the ground.

He lay there, barely breathing, barely thinking, let alone moving. His shit was reluctant to return to him, it seemed; why would it when he just kept getting it beaten out of him?

He heard the sounds distantly, as though from beneath a great deal of water. Many boots approaching—Venarium agents who had been lying in wait, no doubt. Obviously there so Annis could have the glory.

You stupid ass, he told himself. *Is it not obvious they were afraid of losing more to you? He was protecting them.*

He had the wit to curse himself, at least. So he couldn't be *entirely* dead. Now if only he could move.

But his limbs, frozen and numb, would not respond. And he lay there in place as many shadows fell over him. And he lay unmoving as Annis stood just over his head and looked down, disdainfully.

"Venarie is a limited resource," he said. "It comes from within the body. Discipline is its strength, emotion its anathema. A wizard in the throes of rage is a wizard burning too quickly. Remember this."

"Why?" Dreadaeleon croaked. "Why are you telling me this?"

"Because I wanted to kill you. When Lector Shinka brought word of your atrocities, I wanted to incinerate you and leave nothing left. She talked me down, made me realize that there was still protocol to be followed, still laws that we are beholden to.

"This is how I remind myself of the difference between us, Dreadaeleon. It is law that makes the Venarium strong. It is law that makes a wizard strong. It is law that makes *me* a wizard."

He stared, flatly, into Dreadaeleon's eyes.

"And you merely a little boy who likes watching things burn."

Annis spared a brief glance for the Venarium who had surrounded him. "Return him to Tower Resolute. Prepare him to be Harvested in no more than five days' time. You needn't worry with shackles or Charnel Hounds."

He turned his back to Dreadaeleon. The sound of his boots echoed in the boy's ears as he walked away.

"He is no threat to anyone."

The Grave
of Gods

THIRTY

His Word

The One Thousand and Seventy-Sixth Year
Rhuul Khaas

W*hen I stand upon the highest tower, on a night that is cold and clear, I can just barely see them.*

Torches. At the very edge of my domain, I see them approaching from the west. They almost look like fireflies from here, tiny little things that I could crush between two fingers before wiping their remains off on my robes.

Two weeks ago I could barely see them. They looked less like fireflies and more like the stars one sees after shutting one's eyes.

Two months ago I had only just heard of them. They were the excited babble of a local fool; we locked him away, lest he upset the people.

Five years ago they did not exist.

An army, they call themselves. Not merely an army, but the *army. A union of mortals, under the watchful eyes of heaven, marching from their abodes with the intent to depose those faithful shepherds who watched over them for so many thankless centuries.*

Five years is nothing to beings like us. A mere blink of the eye. Yet in the moment between my eyes' closing and opening, they struck.

I am told that Avictus has fled his citadel, the mortal armies pursuing him north into the mountains. I am told that Vashamond has been cut to pieces in his own courtyard. I am told that Ulbecetonth and all her children have been cast into a dark place to rot for eternity.

And now I am told that they are coming for me.

The House of the Vanquishers, some call them. As though we are fit to be vanquished. As though we are some cruel oppressors, grinding our charges beneath our heels. As though we are slaveholders, tyrants, demons to be cast down to fit whatever grotesque narrative they weave about us.

Do these mortals, I wonder, speak of the sacrifices we have made? Do they speak of all the sleepless years I toiled to cure their diseases? Do they speak of the heartbreak I underwent, watching them suffer so that I might understand them better? Do they speak of the law I have brought, that mortal need no longer view his neighbor as meat to be consumed?

Of course not. The wretches. The swine.

They look upon the diseases I have cured and scream, "Unnatural!" They look upon the knowledge I obtained from dead flesh and scream, "Butcher!" They look upon the law I have brought and scream, "Tyrant!"

All my work. All the blood and suffering. All of it, invalidated, branded as crime, worth nothing. Just with a few words.

I will not lie, it does enrage me. Rage is the burden of the learned, those who demonstrate reason to the primitive and are met with dull stares and slack jaws. And yet, for all this fury, I cannot help but feel pain.

Pain at their betrayal. Pain at their ignorance. Pain at their shallow beliefs.

They claim that the gods have commanded them to rise up against us. They claim that heaven is watching them with interest. They claim that once this is over, they will raise their swords to the skies and be met with a vast and radiant light.

They do not know that they will see only emptiness and silence.

For if the gods were listening, why would I exist? If the gods were kind, why would they have sent me to fix their problems? If the gods cared, why is it I that have spent so long curing their sick, healing their wounded, finding their lost, correcting their mistakes?

All I have done for the mortals . . .

And it is not my name they chant.

Oerboros recommends we flee. Kyrael agrees with him. I have assured them that this will not happen. Mortals are lambs. They may bite, but it is out of fear and not malice. They require guiding hands and strong discipline.

The mortal armies may come. They may knock at my very door. They may scream as many obscenities as they like. But they will learn, just as all have learned. They will learn that the heavens do not open up. They will learn that the gods do not watch.

They will learn that whenever they cry out in the dark, the only one listening is me.

> *From the annals of His Lament*
> *The Sorrow of Khoth-Kapira*
> *He Who Saw the World Crumble*

THIRTY-ONE

The Road of the Dead

Master Sekhlen is the one who trained us. He's the one who found me. He told us our destiny and what we have to..."

Lenk hummed, only half-listening to Shuro as she spoke. His ears were trained on the jungle, his eyes scanning the depths of its foliage.

"...not to say that it's all duty. That's a lot of it, but it's to be expected, right? When you can do something no one else can, you have to do it. But we make time for..."

The Forbidden East had proven entirely deserving of its name in their sojourn through its dense underbrush. Creeping vines, swarming insects, prowling gaambols were all common sights. And while they had yet to encounter one of the pointy-eared fiends, evidence of shictish presence was everywhere.

"...like this one time, Cheloe—one of the newer initiates—actually said to Sekhlen, 'How was I supposed to know the sword was sharp?' I don't think I've ever laughed so..."

Danger lurked behind every tree trunk and within every canopy. And every noise from every shadow could be something ready to kill them. Hence it was simply good planning to do everything in pairs, watching each other's back: sleeping, eating, traveling...

"...I guess this must sound strange, but sometimes the monastery feels more like a family than my actual..."

Even bathing.

It hadn't been Lenk's idea, of course. That is, bathing *had* seemed like a good idea—there were bugs to scrape off, wounds to clean, that sort of thing. And when they happened upon a pool left by one of the Lyre's trickling tributaries, it had seemed almost like a divine command, as though the gods themselves were telling him that he smelled like shit.

He had been happy to stand watch and let Shuro take the first bath.

Or he *would* have been happy, at least. Had Shuro not insisted he get in.

And then followed, herself.

While there were a few reasons this made Lenk terribly uncomfortable, the foremost one was the fact that it was hard to hear what might be out there in the jungle as Shuro continued to go on about the monastery, her fellow initiates, this Sekhlen fellow...

Granted, nothing had come out at them yet. No shicts or gaambols leaping out of the foliage to rip them apart. But Lenk couldn't help but be nervous. Standing as he was in the pool, his clothes in a heap on the rocky edge, he was aware of just how much of him was present to be ripped.

And so he watched the surrounding foliage. He watched the water tumble through the rocks down a slope to gather in the small basin that formed the waist-high pool. He watched every twitching branch and rustling bush and everything but the water. He forgot bathing entirely.

"Hey!"

That is, until he felt someone splash cold water on his bare back.

He whirled without thinking and, at first, saw her smile. He saw lips that could smile so easily, despite the blood that had painted her face in past days, and eyes that looked softer than he knew a person's eyes could be after seeing what she had seen. What they both had seen.

"Are you even listening to me?" she asked.

He was now. He couldn't pay attention to anything but her.

She stood, naked and unafraid, in the pool, hands on hips that he hadn't noticed before. Her hair hung in damp silver strands, draped over her shoulders and down to her breasts. Her body was lean, corded with the muscle that came from a strictly regimented lifestyle and yet possessed of slopes that he only now saw. Her skin was pale, unscarred, and it looked so terribly soft. He hadn't noticed this, either, when she had held her sword.

Once a man or a woman picked up a weapon, they ceased to be. Their hopes and their fears were no longer important, nor even relevant.

All that they were, all that anyone cared about, was in the edge of their blade. People only thought they wielded weapons. But it was they who were wielded. Lenk had never looked past the sword in Shuro's hands.

Somehow he had forgotten she was a woman.

But she never had.

She still stood there, naked and smiling as if there were absolutely nothing wrong with that. As if there weren't things out there that wanted to kill them. She simply stood, unashamed, letting him stare at her.

And he did so. He did until he looked down at his own body. At the wiry mass of muscle tightly packed beneath flesh dotted with scars and healed wounds, reminders of when he had been too slow or too clumsy, reminders of where he had failed the sword he held.

Somehow he had forgotten he was a man.

But she never had.

"Hey." Shuro's hand was on his arm, warm despite the chill of the water, soft despite the calluses on her fingers. "Are you all right?"

"Yeah, I . . ." He muttered something else he couldn't hear. He slowly shuffled in place, turning away. "Sorry, I didn't mean to."

"To what?"

"You know, to stare."

"At what?"

He glanced back at her. "You're naked."

"Yeah. And?" She shrugged. "If your eyes bothered me, I probably wouldn't have taken my clothes off in front of you." Her grin returned. "What's it matter, anyway? We all bathe together where I'm from."

"Not where I'm from," Lenk said.

"Well," she said, "we're not there, are we?"

She said it simply. Yet it hit him all the same.

No, they were not where he was from. Granted, that had always been a nebulous thing; he hadn't had a home since Steadbrook burned down. But he had found a sort of solace in the people he had left behind, one that he had hoped to take with him to Cier'Djaal. Now that city, that solace, those people, they were all gone.

This jungle was not Cier'Djaal.

These beasts were not his people.

This woman was not...

He closed his eyes. The next breath he took was cold. He almost didn't feel it when her hand slid up his arm and onto his shoulder.

"How is it this easy for you?" he asked without looking at her. "How do you just put down your sword like that?"

"I just put it down," Shuro said.

"No, I mean—"

"I know what you mean." She reached up, touched his cheek, and drew his face toward her. "And the answer is still the same. I do my duty, what I was made to do, and then I stop. A blade ever honed. A storm ever brewing. I am a slave to no god, no king, no man." She smiled softly. "And I am Shuro. I am a woman. I like rainy days, I save half the sweet cake I get after dinner for breakfast in the morning, and think pomegranates are a fruit you eat only if you like the taste of tarantula ass."

He couldn't help but chuckle. "And it's just that easy, is it?"

"It's not easy. It just is." She rolled her shoulders. "I'll show you, when we're done."

"When we're done?"

"When Khoth-Kapira is stopped and everything's finished, I'm going back to the monastery." She looked at him earnestly. "I think you should come with me."

The answer came more as a reflex. "Thanks, but I've never been much for staying in one place."

"Well... you've never tried, have you?"

He opened his mouth to retort, but found nothing to say. She was right; the life he'd had before wasn't even a memory anymore. And since he had pulled his grandfather's sword from Steadbrook's ashes, he hadn't stopped wandering, hadn't stopped killing.

Hadn't he set out to stop in the first place?

"If you don't like it, then no one will stop you from leaving," Shuro said. "And if you've got anywhere else to go..."

She let the question linger. Her eyes finished it. Her intent stare was alive with curiosity where there had been only hardness before. The corner of her mouth quavered in a nervous smile.

And Lenk couldn't help but feel a grin of his own at the possibility, a grin that grew broader with each moment his eyes lingered on Shuro's smile.

A monastery might not be Cier'Djaal, but was that such a bad thing? When he departed he had thought only of the good he was giving up: the home he had never found, the wealth that would never be his, the peace he couldn't seem to hold on to. Now, far removed from the city, he could see what else he was leaving behind: streets ruled by violence, people crushed beneath coin, a world where men ate men instead of bread.

A monastery might not have the excitement and the wealth of the city, but he had only ever wanted the wealth so he could leave the excitement behind. What else awaited him there? Quiet, solitude, peace, certainly, but that wasn't what set the grin in his face.

Shuro would be there. And there were more like her. More like *him*. Others who lived with what he did, experienced what he did, suffered the same hardships. The closest thing to a family he could ever hope for.

A monastery. Why not?

He could come to love it, this home that wasn't Cier'Djaal. He could come to trust its inhabitants, these people who weren't hungry for blood and death. And as he saw Shuro's eyes brighten at the sight of his smile, he wondered if he could also come to appreciate a different kind of relationship with her.

This woman who wasn't Kataria.

His smile faded.

The thought came from nowhere, simply falling out of the sky and landing on him with a great weight. He felt suddenly strange for looking at Shuro's naked form, suddenly embarrassed by his own nudity, suddenly possessed of a pain that caught in his throat and grew sharper each time he tried to swallow. He turned away from her, eyes toward his clothes in a heap at the edge of the pool.

"I'll think about it," he said softly.

"Are you all right?" Shuro asked, reaching out to touch him with hands that suddenly felt too warm. "Is it something I—"

"No," Lenk said. "I said I'll think about it." He made a show of looking overhead. "Hour's getting late. We should move."

Shuro said nothing for a moment. He felt her eyes linger on him, then turn away.

"Right," she said. "Of course."

He heard splashing as she moved to gather her own clothes.

You piece of shit, he cursed himself inwardly. *She didn't deserve that.*

He had done well up until now. The constant danger of the jungle had kept him from sleeping deeply enough to dream of green eyes, from letting his mind wander to memories of a tender touch, from thinking about how much it still hurt to remember the empty patch of sand where she had been.

Stupid of him, then, to have thought a quiet bath might be nice. Stupid of him, then, to have thought that he could be a real person without the sword in his hand.

He put that thought out of his mind as soon as he picked up the sword again, resigned himself to the familiar weight of it in his hand. He drew it out of its scabbard, glanced it over for nicks and wear. Satisfied, he jammed it back in its sheath and went about sorting the rest of his clothes.

It was just as he had picked up his shirt that he felt eyes upon him. Not Shuro's. His gaze was drawn inexorably upward, to the edge of the jungle and the white shape standing at the edge of the foliage. From beneath his hood, from a face whose mouth was set into a thin frown, a pair of dark eyes stared at Lenk flatly.

Mocca. Unblinking.

The man in white had been noticeably absent these past days. Lenk would have wondered why he chose now to reappear, if he weren't certain he didn't want to know. Just one more thing to put out of his mind, he thought as he set to drying himself.

With any luck, by the end of the day, he wouldn't have a single thought left.

See, your biggest problem is that you're an optimist, Lenk told himself, two hours later. *You trusted that you'd be able to get by without thinking when you should have just bashed your head in with a rock and not left anything to chance.*

The hours that had passed since they'd departed from the pool had done so in silence. The moment clothes had come back on, whatever semblance of joviality had been between them had faded. And in the quiet that followed, Lenk had plenty of time to think.

Like an asshole.

He couldn't help but continue to marvel at the ease with which Shuro switched between two distinct people. He could barely remember the excited smile and soft eyes of the girl from moments ago. The woman walking beside him now stared out with an iron gaze, face expressionless.

He wondered, absently, if he had caused that. If his response at the pool had been different, would they still be laughing even now? Would this walk into the jungle, over rocky paths and creeping tree roots, be less unbearably awkward?

Knowing his luck, probably not.

Either way, he didn't test his theory. He mirrored her expression even as he mirrored her pace, the two of them delving deeper into the jungle, the only conversation that of the ambient wildlife buzzing around them.

In the silence Lenk had ample time to reflect on the peculiarity of the forest. Namely, the deeper they went, the thinner the trees grew. Many slender saplings cropped up in copses and groves, and a few defiant ancients burst from the ground to stretch tall and cover swaths of land with their canopies. But there was a certain order to their growth, their placement dictated by the ground beneath them.

The earth was smooth, Lenk noted, marred only by the occasional outcropping stone or reaching tree root. Beneath dead foliage and layers of soil, stretches of paved stone emerged like the back of some ancient serpent snaking through an earthen sea. And among the rising trunks of the trees, he could see the ruined frames of houses and the shattered remains of pillars and statues.

Occasionally he caught a glimpse of these latter constructs: a stone body dismembered by time and wear, a robed figure with hands clasped together in benediction and a severed stump where a head should be. Sunken in the earth, a stone face peered up at him.

A familiar face.

He was about to stop and study it further when Shuro spoke up suddenly.

"The path splits here," she said.

He looked up, followed her gaze to the fork in the road. The path was bisected by a tree that had burst out of the ground, low-hanging branches draping the road in a cloak of greenery. Part of it continued as they had been going, while the other veered left in a subtle slope leading downward.

"All right," Lenk said. "Which way?"

Shuro hesitated a moment. "This way." She pointed to the high road. "The high ground is always right."

Lenk glanced toward the low road. "I can hear the river down there. It would have to lead to something."

"The high ground would be the ideal spot to launch an ambush from. The low ground might be dangerous." She stared hard down the high road. "This...this is the best chance."

"You don't sound certain."

"I'm *not*." She whirled on him, lips tightened. "They wouldn't call this the Forbidden East if it had signposts, would they?"

He held up his hands for calm. "I just think we should know. Maybe neither of them lead anywhere."

"Of course they do," she said, tension in her voice. "Khoth-Kapira called himself the God-King. Why would he build an empire in which all roads *didn't* lead to him?" She turned away from him, rubbed her eyes. "We've been heading the right way, I'm sure of it. I just need to... get my bearings."

She glanced up at the tree bisecting the path and doffed her hat.

"I'll climb to a better view. Once we know where we're going, we can set a path." She handed him the garment. "Wait here."

"Right," he said. "I'll go check out the low road."

She looked over her shoulder, eyes hardening. "That's ridiculous. I'll only be a few moments. Just stay here."

He met her glare with confusion. "I'm not going far. If there's anything down there, I'd like to know about it. And we can always use more water."

"We're in the thick of the jungle right now," she said. "It's too dangerous. There could be gaambols or shicts or—"

"We haven't seen a single shict this whole time," he interrupted. "And even *they* don't stalk victims this long. If one of them was going to attack us, they'd have done it by now."

Shuro stared at him for a long moment.

"You would know, I suppose."

Whether she had meant that as an insult or not, her flat tone did not betray. Nor did he have time to take offense before she pushed back the dangling leaves and started down the high road.

"Meet back here in a quarter of an hour," she said.

"Yeah," Lenk replied, voice sour with ire. "Sure."

Her words hung in his head as he started down the low road. Over the sound of his boots on the gradually sloping stone and the buzz of insects in his ear, he could hear her still.

You would know.

They stuck in his neck like a bent nail. What had she meant by *that*?

Even being away from her for a few moments galled him, if only because he knew she was right. The jungle *was* a dangerous place enough without his going wandering through it on his own. But he had to get away from her. He had to be on his own for a moment. Maybe he just needed time to think, maybe he needed room to breathe or maybe...

Maybe being with her, even now, felt like betraying someone else.

The slope of the earth beneath his feet turned to steps, a stairway carved out of stone and set firmly in the dirt. Covered by leaves and disrupted by the occasional rowdy root lurching out between bricks, it was nonetheless impressively well preserved.

Trees rose up on either side around him. On his left they peered between marching pillars in varying states of decay. On his right a sheer cliff wall was overgrown with hanging vines. But beneath that he could see fragments of stone: carved faces peering out with wide eyes, stone children playing between the vines, granite waves frozen in time.

Age had taken its toll—cracks had appeared in the faces, some children were missing, the waves were eroded. And the vines grew too thick for him to see fully what they hid. But even these carvings seemed amazingly well preserved, as though they had been cared for up to the very end.

Whatever that end had been.

Or did it end? Lenk paused, looked around. *Khoth-Kapira was an Aeon before he was a demon. And the mortals overthrew him and cast him down, as they did all the others.* He studied the fresco, squinted. *So why isn't anything destroyed? Where's all the violence?*

Lenk's knowledge of the Aeons was limited, of course. But there were two certain facts to their story: The mortals had cast the demons into hell, and the demons had not gone quietly.

It had taken armies, sieges, years of warfare that had claimed entire races to break the demons' hold over the world. And the wakes of the horrors they'd wrought were like scars upon the world.

Or at least they were supposed to be.

So where were the skeletons? Where were the shattered weapons? Where were the abandoned siege weapons and scars from fire and blood? Where was the *war* that had brought Khoth-Kapira low?

When he came to the bottom of the stairs and rounded the wall of greenery and stonework to his left, he saw no signs of violence. But something else.

And his breath left him at the sight of it.

A harbor. Pristine but for the inevitable age and overgrowth, a harbor sprawled out before him. A stone walkway on either side of the Lyre's course, connected by a small bridge, as the river shot straight through a small chasm dominated on either side by towering cliff walls and shrouded by a bowing canopy overhead. Stone-wrought docks designed for smaller river-going craft jutted out at even intervals along the walkways. Tall bridges reached over the river to connect the two, allowing the Lyre to pass well below as the river continued down the chasm and snaked off into some unseen course.

Bricks had fallen off, here and there. Plant life grew over everything. A bridge had partially collapsed. At the center of the harbor, a stone pedestal rose from the center of the river and sported a pair of granite ankles where a statue had once stood tall and proud.

Age had taken its toll. But violence had not. This place had simply fallen into disrepair, rather than been dismantled, piece by piece. No destruction, no carnage, no bloodshed.

"No war," he whispered to himself.

"Lovely, isn't it?"

Lenk looked up at the voice. The bowing trees overhead cast a shade so deep that he almost didn't see Mocca standing at the end of one of the stone piers, staring out over the harbor. Here among the gray stone, the white of his robes looked less out of place.

"There is something beautiful about age," the man in white mused aloud. "It's the fragility of life, I think. A demonstration of something's vulnerability that makes us covet it." He held his hands out in a helpless gesture over the harbor. "You can only judge beauty by watching the way it crumbles."

Lenk stared at the back of the man's head for a moment before speaking. "Morbid."

"All the great poets are."

"Is that what you are now?"

Mocca cast a look over his shoulder. His lips curled in a smile too soft for the glint in his eyes.

"What I am, the poets are still trying to find a word for."

"I've got a few choice ones for them." Lenk approached the man, coming up beside him and staring out over the harbor. A moment passed between them. "You've been shy in coming around lately."

"I've had things to attend to," Mocca replied.

"Like what?"

"Things."

"What sort of things does a *thing* in my head have to attend to?"

"I exist outside the boundaries of *reality*, let alone your head," Mocca replied with a sneer. "And I'll thank you not to disrespect me by suggesting my machinations are limited to solely one man. The scope granted to me by my unfortunate circumstance bids sights that require my vast attention."

"Oh." Lenk sniffed. "Because I thought it was because you didn't like Shuro."

Mocca offered no response that Lenk could hear. But in the sudden coldness of his face, the swift petrifying silence that hardened his stare, the thoughts of the man in white were impossible to ignore.

"She is quite cross with you," Mocca said simply, after a time.

"I know."

The sidelong look he cast Lenk came so slowly it almost creaked. "Would you like to know why?"

"No." The swiftness of his response surprised even Lenk. "Stay out of her head."

Mocca's face softened with a smile. "I'm insulted that you'd think I'd need to go in there. She's rather pitifully unguarded with her emotions, much like you. That's the first reason she likes you."

"So you were listening, then?" Lenk asked. "Back at the pool?"

"I hope you don't mind."

"I do, a little," Lenk replied, brows furrowing. "I don't know if I'm comfortable with you seeing me naked."

Mocca's smile grew a bit wider, his eyes brightening. "He said to the man living inside his thoughts."

"*You* said that you didn't—"

"I was making a point, nothing more." Mocca turned his gaze back out over the harbor, folded his hands behind his back. "Does the thought appeal to you?"

"Which?"

"Going back with her," Mocca said. "Returning to her monastery, being among others like yourself."

His answer came slower this time, crawling out of his lips on a sigh. "Yeah. It does."

"You sound hesitant."

"Yeah. I do." Lenk let that thought linger for a moment. "I shouldn't, though."

"No?"

"What she's offering is . . . well, it's great, isn't it? She's offering me a place to set my sword down, a place where I can be with people like me, who look like me . . . think like me."

He looked toward Mocca, expecting a response. The man in white did not even look back at him.

"So why shouldn't I?" Lenk continued. "It's everything I ever wanted. And there's nothing"—he paused, choking on something caught in his throat—"nothing left for me here."

Again he looked to Mocca. Again he waited for the man in white to say something. Again his company merely continued staring out over the water.

"So, yeah," Lenk said. "That's what I'm going to do. When this is all over. I'm going back to the monastery with her." He cleared his throat. "It's the only thing I've got left."

A wind carried through the chasm, shaking the trees and emptying dead foliage into the river. The Lyre muttered in complaint, sweeping the leaves away downriver. Somewhere overhead a bird called. The entire forest was speaking.

Except for Mocca.

And Lenk began to feel the time draw out. How long had he been waiting for Mocca to say something? And what was he waiting for? Approval? Scorn? Begging?

"Right."

Lenk's voice sounded coarse and out of place amid the forest. His boots scraped as he turned to go.

"Would you like to know the second reason?"

He turned back around. Mocca was no longer at the edge of the dock. He stood out upon the water itself, a placid rock atop its rushing flow. His eyes were dark and fixed firmly upon Lenk.

"The second reason—"

"Because she sees in you something she desperately craves," Mocca said. "She sees the life she can't remember, the friends she never had, the pain of loss she so desperately wishes she could feel because to do so would mean having known a love outside of her own sword."

"What?"

"When she looks at you," Mocca continued, walking slowly across the water's surface, "she sees a person. A man. Someone whole. That's what she *used* to see when she looked at herself, too. But in your presence, all she can see when she looks at her own naked body is the weapon she was shaped to be."

Mocca's voice came with such invective force that Lenk could but stand there, stunned, as though each word were a fist cracking against his jaw.

"She can't abide this, you know," the man in white said. "She can't stand knowing she's a weapon, possessed of no more purpose than a chunk of steel, as you remind her she is. But nor can she bring herself to leave or hurt you and abandon the possibility you present to her. Hence she wishes to bring you back with her. To the same forge that made her, so that you, too, can be hammered from a man into a weapon."

Lenk's face twisted into anger. He stalked to the edge of the dock, thrust a finger accusingly out over it. "I told you to stay *out* of her head."

"And I told *you* I didn't need to be *in* it," Mocca snapped back. "I merely listened. I have heard the yearning in her voice and I have seen the flashes of hatred across her face. When she suspects you of thinking of the shict, they're there. When she sees your body and all the stories it tells, they're there. She is driven by desperation." He sniffed. "Or love. Same thing, really."

"You're just saying that," Lenk snarled. "You say you've been watching? Listening? Then you've seen her fight. You've heard her talk about stopping you, *killing* you, if need be." He narrowed his eyes. "You're afraid."

"I am." Mocca's voice grew softer. "But not of her." He looked intently at Lenk once more. "You are drawing close now, you know. There's not much time left to decide. What will you do when you and she reach Rhuul Khaas?"

Lenk blinked. Mocca's form quivered at the edges, as did his voice.

"Would you stand with her, Lenk," he whispered, "against me?"

"You're a demon." Lenk forced the words out between his teeth, a rusty blade drawn from a scabbard without oil. "Whatever else you promise, whatever else you say, you were cast down for a reason."

"I..." Mocca let his protest drop. He turned his head away. "The Aeons were never fully divine, you know. Sin was well within our capabilities. I acknowledge that." When he looked up again, his eyes were soft. "But do you not see what she's doing?"

"Her duty."

"Her *function*. She was created for violence, she said so herself. She cannot *exist* without it and she won't be satisfied until you can't, either."

"And what about me, then?" Lenk demanded. "We're the same, she and I. Same hair, same eyes, same story. If she's created to kill, then so am I."

"*NO.*" Mocca's voice thundered through the chasm, bade animals cower in silence and breezes die. "You are *not* like her. Not like them. How much have you sacrificed to get here? To find a way of putting down your sword?"

"And what's it gotten me?" Lenk shook his head. "I haven't fucking *stopped* killing since I came to Cier'Djaal and it's not going to stop now that I'm gone. I've lost blood, I've lost money, I've lost Kataria. But somehow I never, ever lose the fucking sword."

He turned. He began to stalk away, back toward the staircase. He waved a hand fleetingly over his shoulder.

"If I have to hold on to the sword forever," he said, "then it's time I took something in return. With Shuro I at least have someone to talk to. If that's the price I have to pay, so be it."

The sky darkened. The breeze went still. As though all of creation had taken a deep breath and held it.

He was aware, then, of the death of sound: of the wind in the trees, of the birds in the branches, of his own boots scraping against the stone. He was aware, then, of a deep darkness settling into the chasm, an eager nightfall come too early. He was aware, then, of a single source of light.

Coming from right behind him.

"No."

He turned. Mocca's eyes were alive with light, a glow bright and white as any star, pouring from his stare with a terrible glory. The man in white spoke, and his voice sent creation quavering.

"I will not let you."

The light poured out of his eyes, snaking and trembling like a river unto itself. And like a river it flowed: over the water, over the stone, over Lenk. The young man held up a hand to shield himself, shut his eyes and turned his head away, yet it was still not enough. The light seared through his eyelids, made his vision burst with bright-white light.

He shouted out and could not hear his own voice. Only a faint buzzing rang in his ears as he shut his eyes, shook his head, and screamed at Mocca to make it stop.

And stop it did.

The ringing in his ears did fade. And in its wake he could hear the sound of feet scraping on stone, of wooden hulls bumping against docks, of prayers murmured to the flowing river.

And when he opened his eyes, he did not know where he was.

The sun—a sun he did not know—poured light into the chasm through a gap in the trees. The choked vines and dead foliage were gone, having left behind only pristine stonework free of cracks and decay. The Lyre burbled gaily nearby, its flow carrying small rivercraft up and down, beneath the spanning bridges and around the central pedestal that had held a pair of granite ankles only moments ago.

Now it bore a statue of a tall, elegant man. A man whom Lenk had seen before, in all the shattered faces and severed heads of the statues he had come across in the jungle.

Mocca.

His stone gaze, impassive and without pupil or iris, looked over the harbor with unblinking concentration. He watched its boats come and go, its sunlight dance upon the water, its people...

People, Lenk thought. *There are people.*

Humans. Shicts. Tulwar. Vulgores. Of many sizes, many ages, many *peoples*, they gathered. They clothed themselves in white robes, not unlike Mocca's own, and maintained silence but for the prayers they murmured. Boats arrived to deposit more, who would then quietly file up the staircase Lenk had descended and disappear.

They did not look at him. They did not look up at all. Lenk was tempted to reach out and touch one, but it somehow seemed...rude. Offensive, even. As though they were now too pure to accept his dirty hands.

"The Pilgrim's Path."

He turned and saw Mocca. The *real* Mocca—or at least as real as Mocca could be—standing beside him. The man in white stood demurely aside, watching the robed people make their way up the stairs.

"This was originally a small offshoot of the Lyre, filled with rocks and river bulls," Mocca said. "But as it was the only thing remotely close to a landing, people came by the boatload. With all the deaths, only the devout ever managed to make it this far, hence the name. Though we built the dock for them, they kept the name out of respect."

"What did they come for?" Lenk asked.

"One reason," Mocca said, then paused. "Many reasons. Some left behind hardship, some came with the soil of their loved ones' graves upon their hands, some were unsatisfied with what they had. All came for a better life." He smiled an old, weary man's smile. "Through me."

"You?" Lenk asked, not intending to sound as incredulous as he did.

Mocca's smile became a bemused grin. "Me."

"And what did you give them?"

"Many things," Mocca said. "One thing. Some wanted wealth, some wanted freedom, some wanted to be loved. I gave them peace."

"Peace."

"It was in rare supply then. Not quite as rare as now. But shicts still prowled the forests and tulwar still warred with their neighbors. There was still flame and metal and disease, plenty of ways to die, and I couldn't protect them from all of it.

"But the worst of it...the war, the famine, the poverty...that I could spare them. Under my eyes I saw them. I saw all of them. I ensured that they never went hungry. I ensured that they never wanted for purpose. I ensured that they never fought each other, that their races never mattered."

Mocca did not change his tone when he said this. Mocca did not even look at Lenk as he did. But at that moment Lenk knew why Mocca had decided to show him this.

The tulwar, the humans, the shicts. All of them, walking side by side and never once looking at each other with a hostile eye. The sole glances they spared one another were warm, brotherly. Maybe more.

Perhaps this world was not without violence, not without war. There was certainly suffering, as Mocca had said. But among all that suffering, all that hatred, something like this could happen. A place within a violent world where a man and a shict could walk together.

And no one would say a thing about it.

"Sometimes I can't believe it's gone."

Mocca's voice was barely a whisper. Yet it came with such suddenness that Lenk started. When he looked at his company, the man in white's face had fallen. The grin was gone. The lines in his face looked deep, ancient, and full of sorrow.

"It's like..." Mocca held his hands out, as though trying to grasp the scene between his fingers. "I will go back, as far in my memory as I possibly can, to the very beginning, when I first set foot upon the earth. And from there I'll go through every breath I can remember, trying to figure out where everything went wrong and what I could have done differently to have made it better. And then..."

He let his hands fall to his sides, empty.

"And then I still can't believe it's gone."

He's a demon.

Lenk's thoughts spoke of their own volition, they twitched to life as easily as the muscles of his sword arm did.

He's a hallucination.

They told him this as he looked upon the image of Mocca—of Khoth-Kapira, he reminded himself—and watched it grow hazy. His shrouded body trembled at the edges. He took a deep breath and his body grew transparent.

He's in hell for a reason.

And he knew this. And he had thought on it often, spoken of it often. And he had spoken of it with Mocca, even. And he *knew* this.

"May I ask..."

Mocca turned to him. His frown was deep. His eyes were clear. His voice was shaking.

"What you would do differently?"

And his thoughts turned back to green eyes shining over a fire, an empty patch of sand where a body should have been. And Lenk swallowed and sighed. He thought, then, as he had so many times since that night, that there must have been a word.

Or a gesture. Or a look. Or a way he could have wrapped his fingers around hers. There had to have been something, just a single something he could have done that would have fixed everything. That would have made her stay.

And he stared out over the water. And he said the only thing that he was left with at the end of thoughts like those.

"I don't know."

A moment passed. The sunlight overhead grew dimmer, grayer, as though fading behind clouds that did not exist. The murmured prayers of the faithful went silent, even as their lips still twitched.

"Perhaps no one does, when it happens."

Mocca's words were breathless. But his eyes were firm as he stared over the harbor.

"But with enough time, one can learn. With enough time, one can look away from what went wrong and look at the goodness of a work. With enough time, one can see the beauty in a disaster.

"And I..."

Mocca raised his hands, spread them out as though parting a curtain. The sunlight focused into a bright beam of light that swept across the harbor and toward the wall of the chasm, shining upon a gray carving.

"...have had eternity."

Lenk's eyes widened as he saw the fresco—the same fractured, overgrown mess of a wall he had seen before—restored and brought to life beneath the sunlight. He saw its massive scope, how it spanned the entire wall of the chasm, each stroke of the chisel so expertly wrought that he could see the detail in every face upon the fresco.

And they were joyous.

Humans, tulwar, shicts, races he had no name for. Elders and children, men and women, merchants and holy men. They all gathered upon the fresco: praying, trading, frolicking, and dancing upon the waves of a stone river. At the center of it all, looming over them with arms outstretched in benediction, was a smiling man in a simple robe.

Mocca.

Overlooking the scene with a quiet smile. He could see all the people laughing, all the people arguing, all the people embracing. All the people.

And not a single sword.

"It's beautiful," Lenk whispered.

"It is," Mocca said. "It was. It can be again."

"It can?"

"With your help."

"What?"

"All you need to do is stand aside, Lenk."

"I don't understand."

"Lenk."

"What?"

"Lenk."

He blinked.

And opened his eyes to a gray world. The sun was gone, hidden behind trees that shrouded the sky once more. The stone had fractured and fallen and cracked again. The fresco was gone, hidden behind the overgrown vines. There were no people and everything around him was dark once more, but for a shock of blue right in his face.

"Shuro," he said, finally recognizing her and his surroundings. "Sorry, I..." He looked around. "How long has it been?"

"It doesn't matter," she said. She gestured up the staircase with her sword. "Come on. I've found something you should see."

⊷ ⊱⊰ ⊶

After so much searching for the war and the strife that should have been left behind, Lenk finally found the bodies.

Or *some* bodies, at least.

Admittedly, he had been expecting something a little more...skeletal. And perhaps a little less...

Shuro's body shook beside him as she made a gagging sound.

Yeah, that.

While they might not have been ancient as he was expecting, the corpses that littered the jungle floor were far from fresh. They lay in various stages of decay, in such numbers as to make the stink of rot rising from them linger in a cloying, sickly cloud. Some had been chewed on by scavengers—rotted stumps left where entire limbs had been wrenched off by gaambols—and all were swarmed by insects of crawling and flying varieties that scattered in clouds as Lenk approached.

But that wasn't what caught Lenk's attention.

Most of them were human—many of them Djaalics, but a few of them northerners and others. Some more were tulwar. Even a few shicts were here among the dead. And there were many, *many* veil-shrouded, scale-skinned saccarii.

And yet there were no wounds. No weapons. No blood but what had been spilled by the jungle beasts.

So what killed them?

Lenk knelt down, swallowed back the bile that crept into his throat because of the stench that rose up, and investigated a nearby Djaalic. His skin was pale and drawn, his eyes sunken and—curiously—his pants dry. His body hadn't evacuated when he died.

"Thirst," Lenk muttered.

"What?" Shuro called over, having taken several steps back.

"He died of thirst." He rose to his feet, cast a glance over the remaining corpses. "Same with all of them, I'd bet. They probably all were traveling together and ran out of water at the same time. Couldn't find any safe water to drink in time." He scratched his jaw. "But why were they traveling together in the first place?"

"Prisoners, maybe," Shuro replied. "The shicts could have captured them and were ushering them elsewhere."

"Shicts don't take prisoners," Lenk said. "And if they did, they would have killed them long ago." He glanced over the corpses. "Maybe there's something on one of them that will explain it."

He took ten paces among the dead before he noticed his were the only footsteps. He looked expectantly up at Shuro, who still stood well away, staring flatly at him.

"What?" she asked.

"You going to help?" he replied.

"Since arriving here, I have spotted, avoided, and fended off exactly twice as many dangers as you have. I have earned the right not to go searching through smelly carcasses."

"I didn't expect you to be the type to shy away from a few bodies," Lenk said, realizing too late how fucked up it was that he was smiling.

"For one, this is hardly a *few*," Shuro snapped back. "For two, I do not dwell among the dead. When I kill, the enemy ceases to be a threat and I turn my attentions elsewhere." She folded her arms across her chest and frowned. "And for three, you are incredibly disgusting."

He shrugged. "Adventurers get used to it, after a while."

"What? The smell of the dead?"

"Looting is a time-honored tradition among adventurers. We usually get to keep only what we take off what we kill. A trained gag reflex and an eye for coin are about the only perks to this job." He sniffed, began to look among the dead. "I can't count the times we had to search a dead guy for something useful, or go picking the third pocket or—"

"What's the third pocket?"

"Oh. Uh…" He rubbed the back of his neck. "So, this one time, a merchant who hired us tried to knife us when we came to collect. We searched his body for our payment, but we couldn't find it. So Denaos says, 'Maybe he's hiding it between his…'" He coughed. "So, anyway, I lost the bet and—"

His voice trailed off as his eye caught something among the dead. He wasn't sure why he noticed her, a female saccarii, at first; maybe it was just that she had not as many flies on her. But as he drew closer, he saw a familiar veil, scaly patches of flesh he had seen before.

"Chemoi?"

She did not respond to the voice. But as he knelt down, he could see that it was, indeed, the leader of the crew of the Old Man. She had somehow survived the shicts and the tulwar, only to die here.

No, he noted. *She didn't.*

Her body shuddered with the faintest of breaths. He lay a hand on her and felt a body still warm, a pulse still beating, however faint. At his touch her eyelids began to flutter. She drew in a longer breath, ragged with thirst.

"Chemoi?" He leaned down. "Chemoi, can you hear me?"

"What is it?" Shuro called over.

"It's Chemoi," he shouted back. "She's alive. Bring me some water!"

A pause. And then a question fraught with genuine confusion. "What for?"

"What do you mean 'what for'?" Lenk growled back. "She's dry, like the rest of them. She might not last much longer! Bring me some water!"

Shuro's lips puckered, as though she were about to ask the point of that. But the glower he shot her made her think better of it. With a resigned sigh, she pulled a waterskin from her belt and approached as near as she dared before tossing it to Lenk.

He uncorked it with his teeth as he slid one arm beneath Chemoi and gently lifted her. Her body responded to the touch, the limpness of her form straightening out as he brought the waterskin beneath her veil and pressed its spout between thin, scale-flecked lips.

He had to tilt it vertically to let the liquid slide down her throat. But once even a few drops slipped past her lips, her amber eyes shot open. She seized the waterskin and began to drink greedily, guzzling it nearly dry in the span of a few long moments.

"A waste," Shuro said, not bothering to conceal the volume or resentment in her voice.

"She was going to die," Lenk said.

Shuro blinked. "I suppose there must be something about this one that separates her from all the other ones we've watched die."

Lenk cast her one more glare before turning his attentions back to Chemoi. The saccarii gasped as the waterskin went flaccid, coughed as she swallowed the last few drops. She pulled out of Lenk's arms, staggered shakily to her feet, breathing heavily.

"Easy," Lenk said, rising up and moving to help her. "Easy."

Breathing heavily, Chemoi swayed, staggered dizzily to a nearby tree, and leaned against it. She looked out over the jungle with a slightly concussed expression. Only after several rasping breaths did her eyes settle on Lenk.

"You," she gasped.

"Yeah, me." Lenk glanced to Shuro. "Both of us."

"Thought you'd died...," she grunted, taking a step toward Lenk.

"Careful," he cautioned, holding a hand out to steady her. "Don't strain yourself."

"Ain't a strain," she said, shaking his hand off. "Except for figurin' out how you're still alive."

"We have swords," Shuro said. "That accounted for most of it."

Chemoi made a move to continue walking, but staggered back against the tree. "I saw my crew chewed up by river bulls so I could escape. Wish I'd have thought to bring a fuckin' sword."

"We made our way into the jungle from the desert," Lenk said. "How'd you get here?"

"Ran up the coast," Chemoi said. "Got into the jungle, met up with all these..." She looked over the carcasses around her and shook her head. "Huh. Fuck. Guess I didn't dream that they all died."

"They've been dead for a day or two, at least."

"Yeah, we ran out of water. None of the pools 'round here were safe to drink. I gave them all I had, told them we should go back and get more, but they wouldn't. They were looking for something."

At this, Shuro swept forward. "What?"

"I dunno. They called it the Promise. Rool Coss or something?"

"Rhuul Khaas." Shuro scowled over the corpses. "These were cultists. Worshippers of Khoth-Kapira." Her scowl sharpened itself to a deadly stare she leveled at Chemoi. "And you were with them."

The saccarii held up her hands. "Don't look at me like that, pink. It was either go with them or get eaten by gaambols. I thought I could travel with them long enough to find a way out of the jungle."

"And so you went further into the jungle?" Shuro made no effort to hide her hand as it drifted near her sword's hilt.

"It...it wasn't like that!" Chemoi protested, backing up as far as the tree would allow. "They were crazy. They kept babbling about promises and gods and lies and shit like that. If I tried to leave, they would've killed me!"

"They have no weapons," Shuro said, curt as her fingers wrapped around her sword's grip.

"They didn't need them! The look in their eyes...they were mad. They would have strangled me, bashed my fucking head in with a rock or something!" The panic in Chemoi's voice crept into her eyes as she looked wildly to Lenk. "And even if they hadn't, where would I have gone? Into the jungle to be killed by gaambols or shicts? I couldn't go anywhere!"

Lenk's own eyes offered nothing in return but a cold scrutiny as he studied her. The fear in her eyes seemed genuine enough—but then, it was easy to see why someone would be afraid of Shuro—and she was drawn tense against the tree. To the outside eye, she looked exactly as she said she was: terrified, weak, and helpless.

But he hadn't lived this long in *this* profession by trusting appearances. Especially in instances with as many corpses involved as these.

How had the cultists come this far without being torn apart by beasts? How had they known which way to go through the forest's passages? And as pertinent as these questions all felt, there was only one that really bit at the back of Lenk's neck like a bug.

What had they seen in Chemoi to take her with them?

That same question seemed to have occurred to Shuro, as well. And judging by the steel hiss as she began to draw her sword, she seemed to have found an answer to it. Chemoi let out a whisper, shrill and faint and pleading.

"Wait," Lenk said suddenly.

Chemoi's eyes all but melted with relief. Shuro shot Lenk a challenging scowl as the young man interposed himself between the two women. He met the saccarii's stare, lips pursed. He thrust the waterskin into her hands. At her confused stare, he pointed back down the way they had arrived.

"The road goes all the way to the forest's edge," he said. "It gets obscured in some places, but if you stay out of sight and follow it, you can make it back and follow the coast to a settlement somewhere. There's clean water around here, if you can find it."

She canted her head to the side, searching for an answer to offer him. He did not wait for it before glancing at Shuro and gesturing with his chin farther up the road.

"Let's go," he said.

Shuro's eyes did not soften, but her blade slid back into its sheath, however hesitantly.

While she might have protested his desire to leave Chemoi alive, she at least agreed with leaving her behind. Lenk hadn't done that to appease her, though; the way ahead would be hard enough without all the questions that Chemoi's presence would bring. And considering the company they had found the saccarii with, any one of those questions' answers could be a knife in the neck.

In truth, there was an unnerving amount of logic in killing the saccarii.

But, as he set off down the path and stepped gingerly over the corpses, he realized that the unnervingness was what prevented him from doing it. The vision Mocca had shown him—the pristine light cast over pilgrims upon flawless stonework—clung to him like an itch he couldn't scratch. But Mocca's words were more akin to a wound that would not heal.

What would you do differently?

He had asked himself that a hundred times since leaving the harbor. He had thought of a hundred answers. But the only one that felt as if it offered any sort of balm to that wound was the one he had just made.

He would stop killing. And he would start by sparing Chemoi. It might not have made sense, but it at least felt right to him.

And yet, as he cast a glance to his companion, who in turn kept her eyes on the road ahead, he couldn't help but wonder why coldly practical Shuro had agreed with him.

But that was another question he had no answer for. For the moment he allowed himself to at least have *one* problem solved neatly.

"HEY!"

Or at least it was *supposed* to be.

"Get back here, you fuckers!" Chemoi shouted after them. "You can't just leave me here!"

"We certainly are physically capable of doing so," Shuro called back. "What you mean to say is, 'You shouldn't just leave me here.' And considering we disagree there, we will not be coming back." She sniffed. "Fucker."

"But I won't last a night out here!" Chemoi's voice became more plaintive, desperate. "Come on! I...I can help you! I can carry your equipment or...or..."

"You have nothing to offer us," Shuro said. "And if you keep screaming, you'll dry out your throat. So save your water and—"

"I know a shortcut!"

This time it was Shuro who held up a hand to stay Lenk's progress. The young woman turned to look back at Chemoi, who stood petulantly among the dead, trembling. She said nothing else, merely folding her arms and turning her blue stare expectantly at the saccarii.

"At least...I think I do," Chemoi said. "The cultists here..." She kicked the nearest one. "They were talking 'bout some kind of way into the Promise. A way that no one else knew. They said it was close. *Real* close."

"So tell us where it is," Shuro said.

"So you fucks can leave me and find it yourselves?" Chemoi shook her head. "You take me with you. When you've done whatever the fuck you're doing, you take me back. Promise me that and *then* I'll show you."

Shuro shot Lenk a questioning glance. Doubtless she was wondering the same thing he was. Even the most detailed maps of the Forbidden East were vague, and Rhuul Khaas's location could be a total mystery. If anyone knew the location of the city of Khoth-Kapira, it would be his cultists.

Or Mocca, Lenk thought. *But if you asked him, you'd have to explain to Shuro why you were talking to a man only you can see... who also lives in your head... and is also a centuries-old demon, yeah, maybe just take the saccarii with you.*

He nodded toward Shuro. She sighed, looked back to Chemoi.

"Fine," she said. "I promise."

Lenk was impressed. From her tone she almost sounded sincere.

One would have to be as close to her as he was at that moment to see the look in her eyes. Only then would one realize that to her a promise was just a couple of words. And only then would one realize that to her the saccarii was just another body.

Like all the others lying motionless around their feet.

—— ❖ ——

It took a few more moments for them to get on their way. Chemoi had scavenged as much as she could off the bodies of the cultists, finding a satchel's worth of supplies: a few pieces of dried meat, hard bread, things that had not saved them.

Suspicion and resourcefulness were qualities that Lenk couldn't help but admire. But the saccarii's true merit showed in the hour of travel that followed.

True to her word, she led them off the beaten path. She took them off the ruined road and up a sloping path that led to a higher plateau in the jungle. Initially Shuro expressed wariness, eyes never far from their guide and hand never far from her sword. But soon the trees began to thin out and the road returned beneath their feet. The plateau's paving seemed much better preserved, and the statues and pillars that marched the road were not quite so dilapidated. Shuro gradually eased.

Lenk, however, did not.

The presence of cultists in the jungle could not have been mere chance; they had to have been called, as so many others had been called to Khoth-Kapira. That made sense, Lenk thought, as the God-King still craved freedom above all else.

Freedom that Shuro was intent on denying him.

Lenk cast a glance to the woman, as he had so often done. And as he had so often done, he couldn't help but feel a pang of envious marvel at her: the surety of her stride, the unwavering resolve of her stare, the way she walked with her sword as though it were weightless, just one more part of her body. She was a woman who had been trained all her life to do this, had no questions about it, and couldn't think of herself doing anything else.

No doubts. No fears. No wondering whether or not she was doing good by stopping Khoth-Kapira.

Lenk suspected she might not be the best person to confide his own reluctance in.

Truthfully, he was slightly ashamed to admit it himself. Khoth-Kapira was a demon. Khoth-Kapira had visited so much untold suffering upon this land. He had denied none of this, embraced it even. He wasn't being duplicitous, making excuses or offering reasoning.

He was merely asking for forgiveness.

"*Merely,*" Lenk scolded himself. *As though anything with demons could ever be "mere." Don't fool yourself. He's out for conquest. He wants to reshape the world into one where he is king, where he controls everything, where...*

A shict and a human could walk together and no one would say a fucking thing.

An unbidden thought. A scratch that never stopped bleeding. An image he could never get out of his mind. And with it came only more questions, questions that gouged deeper wounds in him.

And they all ended with that one.

Would you do it? For her?

"You all right?"

Shuro's voice made him jump. He looked over to her with more wariness than he'd intended to show, perhaps fearing that she had somehow heard his thoughts. At times her eyes looked sharp enough to do that.

But this time she looked at him as she had back at the pool: She was soft, concerned, like a normal woman.

"Yeah," he said. "Just . . . you know. We're getting close."

"I know," she said. "But don't worry. It'll be fine."

"You think so? We don't know what awaits us."

"If you're scared," she said, shooting him a wink, "I'll protect you."

Lenk rolled his eyes and privately wished that had been the first—or even the fifth—time a woman had said that to him.

They continued in silence, but it lasted not much longer. As the road continued to slope up, as the trees continued to thin, there was a sound that grew increasingly louder. It began as a distant rumble, then grew to a faint growl, and by the time the road had run out, it was a proud, endless roar.

"Sweet Khetashe," he whispered, staring up. And up. And up.

In four colossal columns, water fell from the sky. Pure blue ribboned by white froth, the columns fell from a shroud of mist that congealed overhead, concealing their origin. A great chasm yawned open before him, separating him from the waterfalls by the length of ten men. And on the other side of it loomed a sheer cliff face rising directly up into that mist-shrouded heaven.

"Incredible." The word had even greater meaning coming from someone like Shuro. She stared up at the four falls with a child's gaping wonder. "Where's it all coming from?"

"Gods, maybe." Chemoi walked ahead, apparently unimpressed. "Could be the source of the Lyre, even." She stalked to the edge of the chasm, peered down. Mist rose from beneath just as surely as it fell from above. "This is the place, though."

"What place?" Lenk asked.

"Those cultists kept talking about this place." Chemoi veered to the right and started following the chasm's edge. "Their leader wouldn't shut up about it. Told them stories every night about how they'd ascend out of darkness and into heaven to be at Khoth-Kapira's side."

"They're cultists," Shuro said as she and Lenk followed. "That's probably just metaphor."

"Not the way he said it, it ain't."

They followed the edge until they came to a long stone bridge reaching out across the chasm. Peculiarly, it didn't seem to reach the other side. And it didn't lead to anything but another sheer stone face that rose up into nowhere.

Yet Chemoi went rushing down its length. Lenk and Shuro hurried to catch up, following her to the very end of the bridge.

There, fixed to the left side of its edge, stood a peculiar contraption. A frame of bronzed metal stood, tarnished by age but untouched by rust, anchored to the stone. It bent beneath the tension of several thick strands of what appeared to be translucent silk, unfrayed and glistening as droplets of mist coursed down it. Lenk would have called it a harp, if not for the fact that adorning one edge of the frame was some manner of device: a long plate that lay several metal rods across the silken strings.

"This is it." Chemoi spoke loudly to be heard over the roar of the waterfalls. "They said some shit about a harp that called the angels."

"What does it do?" Shuro asked, peering at the device.

"How the fuck should I know?" Chemoi shrugged. "Those guys were fucking crazy."

Shuro stared at her flatly. "Well, thank goodness we brought you along, otherwise we might miss out on these little nuggets of wisdom."

"You want nuggets, you can wait until I've eaten and *then* we'll—"

"Shut up for a moment." Lenk pushed his way between them, investigating the device. "Look at this thing here." He tapped the metal plate adorning the edge, and the rods quivered in response. "There's some kind of thing on the plate here."

"What kind of thing?" Shuro asked.

"I don't know...looks almost like a key. If I can just—"

He could just.

And he did.

It took nothing more than a quick twist. The machine quivered, as though come to life. Lenk sprang backward, nearly drew his sword. But he and the two women remained still as the machine let out a sharp clicking sound.

The rods stiffened suddenly and drew backward, drawn by some manner of mechanism hidden within the frame. Tiny hooks at the tip of each rod caught each strand and plucked it. The strands quivered, sending flecks of water off them as five notes hummed out in harmony.

"The fuck did that do?" Chemoi muttered.

Something moved in the air before them: a shimmering of light as more droplets were flicked off something.

More strands, he saw. Each strand of the strange device ran from the top of its frame across the chasm to the sheer stone wall. And as each reverberating note reached the wall, he saw more shimmering. He walked to the edge of the bridge, peered out as far as he dared, and squinted, trying to see. Some sort of translucent material covered the stone face, running down it like a tapestry. It quivered with life as the sound ran down it, sending it glistening as though it were made of silk.

He hadn't seen anything like that since—

"Cier'Djaal," he whispered. His eyes shot wide in recognition. "The Silken Spire." He stepped away from the edge. "Son of a bitch, that's a fucking spider's web."

"What?" Shuro's question was joined by the sound of her sword hissing out of its sheath. "What the hell did this thing just do, then?"

No need to ask.

They found out in another moment.

From the darkness of the chasm, it came. First as a distant groan of something very old waking from a very deep slumber. Then as a scraping sound as something dragged a large weight across the stone. And finally as a long green leg, thick and hairy and ending in a sharp spike.

Lenk's sword came out as the beast emerged from the shadows in all its horror. From so high above, it certainly *looked* like a spider: a bulbous body, a small head, eight long legs. But this one was positively gigantic, bigger even than the things in Cier'Djaal. It moved slowly and ponderously as it clambered its way up the web-coated wall.

This creature lacked the predatory swiftness of its smaller brethren. Really, it seemed in no particular hurry as it came up the wall, looking as though it had been more inconvenienced than anything else. Its eyes—only two, Lenk noted—did not have the soulless gaze of a hungry beast, but rather a sort of ancient weariness that somehow struck him as familiar.

It wasn't until the creature came even closer that Lenk realized why that was. The whole thing was coated in a thick, rubbery mass of vines that entwined all over its body. Several dozen fungal caps, bright red, grew from its bulbous posterior. And each leg was tipped not with a spike, as he had thought, but with a root.

The damn thing was a plant.

"Like the Old Man," he whispered.

But no one noticed. Not as the spider came crawling up the wall, past the bridge, and came to a halt above their heads.

From its spinnerets dangled a cord of silk thick as a man's thigh, and it descended to some manner of cradle or gondola wrought of the same metal as the harp-like device. Without even swaying, the cradle came to a halt perfectly level with the bridge.

Not a bridge, Lenk realized. *A dock. A loading dock. It wants us to get on.*

" 'Ascend to heaven,' eh?" Shuro stared up at the beast suspiciously. "I suppose that's what they meant."

"See?" Chemoi said. "I told ya."

"You didn't tell me there was going to be a fucking spider."

"It ain't a spider, can't ya see? It's a—"

"It wants us to get on," Lenk said. And as if to prove that, he took a step forward, stopping only when Shuro put a hand on his shoulder.

"What if it's a trap?" she asked.

"It might be," Lenk said. "It might not be. But this is where the jungle ends. If Rhuul Khaas is anywhere"—he pointed up—"it's up there."

Shuro frowned, looking disappointed less with his answer and more because she couldn't think of a better one. She sheathed her sword, took the lead, and stepped tentatively onto the cradle.

Almost immediately it shifted. Sensing weight, the spider began to stir on its perch. Lenk and Chemoi banished any fear they might have had as they rushed forward and leapt onto the cradle just as the beast began to move again, dragging the cradle up and into the mist-shrouded sky.

Lenk swallowed a sour breath. Though it swayed slightly, the cradle felt firm and its silken support cord looked sturdy. The thought of falling did not worry him quite so much as the thought of ascending higher.

As they cleared the mist, he could see great carvings in the stone walls. Four massive heads of serpents, the water emptying from their ever-gaping jaws, stared ahead with unblinking eyes.

He stared up as the bright-blue sky began to seep in through the mist. Looming overhead he could see the shadows of statues rising out of the stone, all depicting the same thing.

The smiling face of Mocca, arms open in benediction, welcoming him to Rhuul Khaas as though he had been expecting him this whole time.

THIRTY-TWO

A BURDEN OF STEEL

For the *Rhega*, fighting was nothing special.

Males and females came together once every few years, exchanged blows and bites and claws before mating—which involved a fair bit of violence itself. Fists were exchanged to see who would raise the resulting children, before the mates parted. Elders schooled their pups by ending each lesson with a headbutt. Young *Rhega* became fully grown the day they could beat their parents into submission. Old *Rhega*, sensing their time was near, wandered out to find a fight they couldn't possibly win.

For the *Rhega*, fighting was just something that was done.

Like eating, like shitting, like any other part of life.

For tulwar?

"A fucking mess," Gariath growled as loud as he possibly could.

He wasn't sure why. It wasn't as if they would hear him on the front line.

That there *was* a front line was just one more irritation in a slew of irritations that had cropped up since they had arrived at Jalaang. They had marched all night to reach the city. Their charge had broken with the dawn, faces alive with colorful fury and mouths gaping with war cries.

It had all seemed so simple.

Rush the city. Open the gates. Get inside. Kill the humans.

Easy.

But as the sound of dying tulwar reached him, he was beginning to have his doubts.

From high upon the dune, he scowled down at the battlefield. In great hordes the tulwar gathered at the walls of Jalaang.

Tho Thu Bhu warriors crowded the front, holding the line behind their stout wooden shields. Chee Chree archers hung at the back, sending arrows and war cries alike up at the battlements. Between the two clans, Rua Tong warriors seethed and roiled, waiting for their chance to spill blood.

All told, there must have been close to a thousand and a half tulwar on the field.

And they were being held back by...

Gariath squinted. He couldn't see how many humans were on the battlements, but it was a much less substantial number.

Clad in the flimsy armor of the Jhouche guardsmen, the human defenders of Jalaang retaliated with crossbow fire. Those Chee Chree arrows that could fly high enough clattered off the battlements.

The mounted warriors of the Yengu Thuun clan milled at the rear of the battle, a few gaambols short. The bold beasts that had led the charge now hung impaled on spikes jutting from the battlements.

"Well, what the fuck do you expect?"

A voice from behind him: Ululang of the Yengu Thuun. Her growl was met with noises of disapproval, but she bellowed louder.

"You sent us in without scouting," she snarled. "Did we not even *think* to look for spikes?"

Gariath turned. At the top of the dune, what passed for leadership among the tulwar stood squabbling among themselves. Daaru stood, arms folded, scowling at Ululang as the tulwar woman gesticulated wildly out over the field. Dekuu, the elder 'the *Humn Tul Naa* had elected to lead the others into battle, merely rubbed his eyes in weary frustration.

"We had no choice," the Chee Chree *Humn* said. "Jalaang is the only clean water source between here and Cier'Djaal. When we marched during the Uprising, it was just another oasis."

"That was years ago. It has become Jalaang." Ululang pointed out to the city. "A fortress designed *specifically* to repel an attack from Shaab Sahaar, *including* gaambols."

"We can't afford a siege," Daaru said, looking intently to Dekuu. "Cier'Djaal will send reinforcements. If we aren't entrenched in Jalaang by then..." He let the threat hang, sighing. "Yengu Thuun was our best hope. If they can just get over the walls, they can open the gates for us."

"Why not just break it down?" Dekuu suggested. "What the fuck did we bring the vulgore for?"

"About that..."

A bellowing roar rose up from the field.

Kudj's lumbering shape rose from the crowd of tulwar like a mountain, and his voice drowned out their war cries as thunder drowned the sound of rain. But for all his size and strength, he could do little more.

And the reason for that became apparent as a chorus of screams pierced Gariath's ear-frills.

A mere thirty paces from Jalaang's gate, a heavy battering ram lay in the dust. The tulwar who had been carrying it lay skewered by two immense spear-long bolts that pinned them to the earth. Atop the gate a small team of humans set about reloading the massive ballistae they had fixed there.

"The vulgore could shatter the gates quicker than a ram, but those giant bows would kill him even faster." Daaru growled. "We need a new idea, Dekuu Humn Chee Chree."

"There are two gates to the city," Dekuu said. "We could go around, try the western—"

"The humans could get their troops to the other gate in half the time it took us to round it," Ululang snapped. "And that gate faces Cier'Djaal. Any reinforcements from the city could cut off a retreat."

"There can be no retreat."

Gariath's voice cut through the argument like a hatchet as he stalked forward. His eyes were dark in the sunlight, his teeth white as his lip curled back in a growl.

"If you run now, they'll come after you," the dragonman said. "You can run across the desert, they'll chase you. You can cower behind your city, they'll burn it down. You can die and hope your Tul brings you back and they'll kill you again and again and again."

He narrowed his eyes, spoke through clenched teeth.

"You fight here," he snarled, "you die clean. You run, you die slow."

Ululang stared at him as if he were crazy. Dekuu scowled at him as if he dearly wished he had a way to refute that. Daaru nodded at him, as though he had been thinking the same thing.

As well they should. Gariath had practiced that speech a hundred times before he could say it without hating himself.

"We get nowhere if we can't get the gates open," Dekuu muttered, turning toward Ululang. "Can you get the beasts to charge again?"

"Eventually," she replied, shrugging. "The gaambols follow the head of their troop. Ours got spooked by the charge and now the others won't go until he does." She rubbed the back of her neck. "We can try to nerve him up a little, but..."

"How long will it take?"

"As long as he needs."

"What? Can't you encourage him?"

"It's an eight-hundred-pound monkey, you shit. I can't exactly give him a speech about the magic of believing in himself."

"Unbelievable." Daaru stared out over the field. "So many warriors, each of them worth three humans in a fight, and a big piece of wood keeps them from this city." He narrowed his eyes, color flooding into his face. "From what they deserve."

Gariath breathed in the scent of Daaru's anger. It hung in a thick, heavy cloak around him, along with the acrid reek of his fear, his pain, his sorrow. He was a creature of stretched seams and loose nails, ready to break apart but for the cords of anger he wrapped around himself.

Gariath didn't need to know his scent to know this. He had felt that way before, had felt that way since he held his sons' still bodies in his arms. Gariath knew this by simply looking at Daaru.

Just as Gariath knew that these humans of Jalaang were not responsible for his daughter's death. Just as Gariath knew that Daaru could kill these humans, the Sainites, the Karnerians, every last human in the world, and the pain would never go away.

Just as Gariath knew he couldn't tell Daaru that. Not now.

Now he needed anger. Now he needed fury. Now he needed war.

He needed all this death to mean something.

"Well, whatever the hell you're hoping on giving them, you won't today," Ululang grunted. "We're out of time, out of ideas, and out of options."

"Forgive me for ruining the drama of the moment..."

Their attentions all turned down the dune as a lone figure approached. Gariath's nostrils were suddenly flooded with the scents of distrust, scorn, hatred. But above even all of those wafted the familiar scent of pipe smoke.

The old tulwar.

Leaning heavily on a walking stick, sweat drenching his brow, breathing heavily, he trudged up the dune. He flashed a soft, gentle smile at the assembled tulwar.

"But you still have one option left."

"*You*…" Dekuu uttered the word as he might utter a particularly blasphemous profanity. His face screwed up in search of an emotion to match the tone of his voice. "How did you come here?"

"With immense difficulty," the old tulwar replied. "Your army set an amazing pace, General. I was hard-pressed to keep up."

"I am not a general," Dekuu snarled. "This is not an army. You are not welcome here."

"No? You are commanding what appears to be a military siege of a fortified city. If you have different words for that, I am happy to use them."

"Heed the last part," Daaru growled. "You are not welcome here."

The scent of tender, old hatred roiled off the others in waves. But the old tulwar betrayed nothing. His smile was serene as he puffed his pipe.

"I will be gone shortly," the old tulwar said. "Will you not permit a *Humn* to lend his expertise?"

Gariath lofted a scaly brow. It was only a minor surprise to him. After all, as far as he could tell, the qualifying traits of a *Humn* were, in order: fat, smelly, old, tulwar.

Like this fat, smelly, old tulwar.

"Expertise," Dekuu spit. "As though you—"

"He's a *Humn*," Ululang interrupted. She looked meaningfully at Dekuu. "Still."

Dekuu sneered at this, but did not protest further. He looked to the old tulwar and grunted. This the old tulwar met with a bow.

"You are, in my humble opinion, failing to live up to the humans' expectations." The old tulwar clenched a fist. "When the Uprising came, they shut themselves in their homes for fear of the savages knocking at their doors."

"We are not savages," Daaru growled. "We are not what they think we are."

"No. You are fighting a war on their terms. You are agreeing to play by their rules and this is how the humans win the game."

"Then what do you suggest?" Dekuu asked.

"He who sets the new rules"—he turned, gestured down to the sandy plain from which he had trudged—"must first break the old ones."

All eyes went down to the plain. All eyes fell upon the shapes meandering toward the dune.

Tulwar. A clan Gariath had not seen. They rode gaambols the color of coal, their own fur likewise stained black and their faces painted with white. Knives made of twisted metal hung from straps upon their saddles. They carried twisted-looking spears, cruelly edged swords, weapons Gariath couldn't even guess the purpose of, let alone the names.

Tulwar. Barely numbering seventy. Just tulwar.

"Oh, fuck me," Ululang whispered.

Or perhaps not just tulwar.

The scent of scorn and resentment hit Gariath's nostrils once more, but carried with it a reek of fear that bordered on animal in its intensity. The tulwar on the dune tensed collectively as the tulwar leading the troop of riders below spurred a mount on. The gaambol let out a hoot of excitement as it came loping up the dune.

The woman—or at least Gariath *thought* it was a woman—riding the beast's shoulders stared down at the assembled through a broad grin.

Her teeth were yellowed and her gums were black. Her eyes were red-rimmed and she looked as though she had not slept in days. The sword she carried on her back looked too big for a man twice her size, let alone her. Her *chota* was tattered, poorly stitched, and cut where massive scars had healed in twisted knots beneath her fur.

If scents could scream, hers certainly would. And it would rave, rant, and howl to be heard over the reek of gaambol shit.

Not that she seemed to notice this. Or the resentful scowls cast her way.

"*Kalaa maa*, my friends," she said, her voice raspy and dark. "What fortune that we happened to spy your march. No one seems to have mentioned to us that you were going to a fight." She wagged a finger at them. "If I were a less trusting woman, I might think you didn't want us to come."

"Chakaa." There was awe in Dekuu's voice as he uttered the name. Not the pleasant awe that came from witnessing a miracle, more like the terrified awe that preceded empty trousers' becoming full. "Chakaa Humn Mak Lak Kai."

"Dekuu Humn Chee Chree," the woman named Chakaa said. She inclined her head in an unreturned bow. "I am surprised to only see you out of Shaab Sahaar now. I would have thought you'd be out fighting shicts with us." She let out an unpleasant, barking laugh. "Considering how many Chee Chree corpses I saw the pointy-eared things using as fertilizer."

Gariath would have called that an insult, yet there was no malice in the woman's voice nor on her stench. By the broadness of her smile, she seemed to genuinely think that was hilarious.

Which *might* have explained why the remaining tulwar merely stared at her in stunned silence.

"Well!" Chakaa chirped, glancing at Gariath. "What is *this*? You are no clan that I have seen. No tulwar at all." She leaned over, squinted. "Are you?"

"No," Gariath growled.

"No? Then what are you doing here?" She stared at Gariath, unblinking, before her eyes widened in recognition. "Ah, of course. He is a *daanaja*. Why else would he be here?" She laughed again. "Well, it is fortunate that we came, no? You would not want anyone else by your side for the glorious slaughter that awaits—"

"*NO!*" Dekuu held up a hand, made the sign of the Tul from right to left. "You are not needed here, Chakaa Humn Mak Lak Kai, and neither is your clan. We shall handle this our own way."

"If I was not needed here, I would not have been asked to come," Chakaa replied simply.

Dekuu glared at the old tulwar. "*You.*"

"Do not blame him," Chakaa said. "Since I am here, I was clearly meant to be here. And as I am meant to be here, I will take care of your battle." She gestured to the city. "Since I missed the last Uprising, it is the least I can do. Do not worry, Dekuu Humn Chee Chree. Chakaa will take care of you."

She spurred her gaambol around, barked an order to her clan. She took off down the dune and the rest followed her toward the front line.

Whether from relief from her stench or relief from something else, the tulwar all exhaled when she left. Whatever calm blossomed in

Chakaa's wake, though, quickly withered as everyone whirled upon the old tulwar with murder in their eyes.

"How *dare* you," Dekuu snarled, "how *dare* you bring them here!"

"I merely traveled with them," the old tulwar said. "They came all on their own. And now they are here and willing to help. The humans will not expect them. They never fought in the Uprising."

"No," Ululang said. "Not a chance in hell would we fight alongside the Mak Lak Kai."

"Why not?" Gariath asked. "They're crazy, stupid, and smell like shit. Why would you let all that go to waste?"

Daaru grimaced. "They are *malaa*. Outside the Tul." At Gariath's confusion he sighed and made the sign of the Tul from left to right. "When Rua Tong or Chee Chree dies, they go back to the Tul. They return elsewhere as Yengu Thuun or Dei Hun Jaan or Kalak Ka. The Mak Lak Kai never return to the Tul. They never leave." He reversed the sign of the Tul. "If the Tul will not take them, they are not meant to be in our company."

Of course. It would have to be something that stupid.

Fighting was supposed to be simple, easy, like any other part of life. Humans sullied it by hiding behind walls and refusing to die. Tulwar complicated it by bringing all manner of ridiculous superstition into it.

Like any other part of life, only the *Rhega* knew how to do it right.

Gariath stalked off down the dune, saying not another word. He ignored the confused calls of the tulwar as they shouted after him. He ignored the sounds of carnage rising from the field. He ignored everything.

"And where are you going?"

Except a question carried on a voice thick with pipe smoke.

He turned and glared at the old tulwar, snorted.

"Speak plainly, speak honestly," the dragonman said, "or I'll smash your skull and no one will blink an eye. Did you bring the Mak Lak Kai?"

The old tulwar's face hardened. "I did."

"Then you lied to the others?"

"That, too."

Gariath nodded. "You are good at lying, elder. Do it one more time."

He pointed to the field. "Go to the vulgore. Tell him to be ready to charge when I give the signal."

"And what do you intend to do?"

Gariath turned, stalked away toward the line of Mak Lak Kai mustering down upon the field.

"Everything. As usual."

—•—⊫—•—

"Aha!" Chakaa looked down from her mount, grinning broadly. "The *daanaja* comes to grace me with his presence! I can take it that I am blessed this day, no?"

Gariath fixed her with a curious glare for a moment, half tempted to ask, half taken by her stench, before he remembered that he had come here with a mission.

"What is your plan?" he asked.

Chakaa looked taken aback. "Plan?"

"You want to attack the city, right? What are you going to do?"

"I am not sure I understand the question." She pointed over the heads of the tulwar invaders to Jalaang's distant walls. "I have a big sword. I am going to use it to kill a lot of humans. Then we will see how I feel. Maybe lunch."

"Yes," Gariath growled, "but how are you going to do it?"

Chakaa blinked, then shrugged. "Chakaa does not ponder 'how' a thing is done. Chakaa intends to do it, so it gets done."

Gariath blinked. Slowly.

She smells like shit. She's got shit for brains. She says shit like this.

He let out a long breath.

This is a good idea you had here.

"We need to get over the walls," Gariath said. "Once we break their stupid toys, the others can break down the walls. Can your gaambol jump?"

"A Mak Lak Kai's gaambol jumps higher than any other's." Chakaa gasped, smiling with delight. "And just like that, Chakaa knows what to do. You see, *daanaja*? It simply works out."

"Can your beast carry me?" Gariath asked, with some reservation. Not that it seemed a *particularly* intelligent idea to get so close to the woman, but he needed to make sure this worked.

Chakaa, in reply, scooted forward on her mount and patted the beast's back. "He is the troop leader, strongest of them all. He could carry twelve *daanaja*."

Gariath nodded, then glanced to the field. The tulwar still held in a thick wave at the wall.

"I'll go tell the warriors to make way for us," Gariath said, "then we can—"

"No need," Chakaa said. "They will move for us."

"You're sure?"

She smiled, a little less crazed, a little more sad. "I am *malaa*."

At this Gariath felt the need to ask, if only to sate his curiosity before he died.

"They hate you," he said. "But you want to help them. Why?"

Chakaa stared out over the field, at the roiling waves of tulwar. At the dying warriors, screaming as arrows put them down. At the impotent archers, flinging arrows at a wall that could not be moved. At the stoic shield bearers, their line wavering beneath the hail falling from the walls.

"The Tul does not make mistakes," she said softly. "If it has cast us out, it has done so for a reason. If that reason is that we may do what they, with their wailing children and their weeping spouses, may not, then I am happy to see it done."

She looked down to Gariath and grinned broadly.

"But come, *daanaja*," she laughed, extending a hand to Gariath, "you are ruining this with your serious talk. This is a slaughter. We should be celebrating!"

He had doubts. But no time for them.

All that he had sacrificed to get to this point, all the blood spilled and bodies fallen, they could not be in vain. He reached out and took her hand. Chakaa paused as her fingers wrapped around his, looking reflectively at him for a moment.

As though wondering which of their hands was dirtier.

She helped haul him up and behind her. He settled upon the gaambol's back, felt the muscles of the beast reverberate between his legs as it let out a low growl of irritation at this new rider. But any thoughts it might have had of rebellion seemed to dissipate the moment Chakaa opened her mouth and let out a roar.

It was a language Gariath could not understand, a language of a single sound. And whatever it was, it commanded the attention of her clan and their beasts. The Mak Lak Kai warriors immediately fell in behind her, forming a thick spearhead formation. Steel hissed as they drew their bizarre weapons. Their gaambols hooted in excitement.

There was no order given. No command spoken. They did this, Gariath knew, out of instinct. They did this because they knew nothing other than this.

War.

Blood.

Fury.

And as they spurred their gaambols forward and broke into a trot, they moved with a self-assured, unquestioning resolve. Like horses going to water for a drink, so went they to war.

Chakaa's roar flowed from her mouth, coursing from tulwar to tulwar, each of them taking up the war cry whose sound tore above the sounds of carnage on the field. Like a disease it spread to the gaambols, the great beasts loosing bestial shrieks in agreement of their riders' fury. Their howls became a storm that rose from the Mak Lak Kai as they spurred their mounts forward, the gaambols' feet thunder beneath them.

The other clans—the Rua Tong, the Chee Chree—looked up at the sound. And, as Chakaa had said, parted like a wave. Their eyes were filled with dread, turning away as the Mak Lak Kai riders tore through them. But the Mak Lak Kai had eyes only for what lay ahead, only for the woman riding at their front, only for the massive blade she hefted over her head.

"*The Tul won't take us back!*" she roared, her voice splitting the battlefield. "*There is nothing for us but this moment! This battle!*" She thrust her blade forward, spurred her beast to a charge. "*MAK LAK KAI!*"

"*MAK LAK KAI!*"

The roar was taken up by each warrior, it burst from their mouths like blood from an artery, uncontrollable and unstoppable. The sound of battle ceased to be so noisome, the sound of death ceased to be so impressive. With the howl of their fury and the thunder of their mounts, the only sound was Mak Lak Kai.

The walls of Jalaang loomed large. Gariath could see the humans reorganizing their troops, deploying them to the section of wall where

Chakaa's charge was heading. Arrows flew from the battlements in mosquito clouds, falling to gnaw at flesh and drink of blood. Gariath could hear gaambols shriek behind him as their hides caught arrows. He heard bodies fall, struck from their saddles. He felt Chakaa's body shudder before him as she was struck once, twice, two arrows quivering from her flesh.

And not once did she stop screaming.

"MAK LAK KAI!"

Another shriek, another spur, and they were aloft. Gariath felt the great beast beneath him tense and leap, hurling itself at Jalaang's wall. The human defenders fell back, scattering in a shriek as the creature scrabbled at the battlements with its paws. Gariath clung to its harness, struggling to keep hold of it. Chakaa merely laughed.

"Knock knock!" she roared, swinging her sword at the humans as the gaambol found its footing and clawed its way up onto the battlements.

More followed. The wall shook as more gaambols hit it—some impaled themselves on the spikes, others crawled over the carcasses of their brethren. Neither the Mak Lak Kai nor their mounts seemed to notice their many wounds, wading into battle with flailing claws and swinging weapons.

The humans struggled to find their nerve. Gruff-looking sergeants pulled weapons free, barked orders at their soldiers to draw steel. Some fled, more stayed, wading into the fray with swords drawn and hacking at their massive foes. Many fell beneath the Mak Lak Kai's wild swings, many more were plucked up and crushed between powerful gaambol claws.

But there were more. There were always more. In the distance a bell tolled. In the city below, Gariath could see more soldiers flooding out of their barracks, armed with crossbows and swords to reinforce the lines. There were many. Too many for even the crazed Mak Lak Kai to fight.

He leapt from Chakaa's mount, tumbled to the stone walkway of the battlements. He shot to his feet, darting beneath a leaping gaambol that crawled its way onto the battlements, leaping over a tulwar corpse as it fell, arrow-riddled, to the stone.

He ran, bowling over humans who tried to flee, smashing aside those who tried to stand, ignoring the nicks and cuts of those who scored glancing blows against him as he tore across the battlements toward his goal.

The gates of Jalaang.

And the ballistae that hung over them.

He picked up speed as the great weapons came into view. Their crews—two men to each weapon—turned to see him coming, too late. They struggled to pull free their short swords. But by the time steel had cleared sheath, Gariath was already charging.

Leaping.

Falling.

His fist came smashing down upon the helm of the man in the lead. He staggered backward, flailing blindly as he backed into a ballista. His companion lunged at Gariath, his feeble blow batted away as Gariath seized the man's sword arm and twisted. A sharp snapping sound followed, but the ensuing scream of pain was cut short as Gariath seized the man by his throat and hoisted him off his feet. He pressed forward against his last two foes, letting the man in his hands take their swords as he continued to shove forward, his bulk driving them backward until they reached the edge of the battlements.

And fell.

They disappeared beneath the mass of tulwar below, who spared only a glance for them before looking back up to the dragonman standing tall atop the battlements. Gariath unfurled his wings, outstretched his claws, and let out a roar over the tulwar. A roar that was soon answered.

And none answered louder than Kudj.

The vulgore came charging forward, lumbering on his hands and feet like a great ape. He hit the gates of Jalaang, sending the wood cracking, the doors shuddering. He bellowed, pounding on it with great fists until the doors finally swung open.

And the tulwar poured in.

Just as Gariath had hoped.

Their war cries were renewed, their weapons flashing as they fought to get through the gates and meet their foes in the city streets. The humans fought to get into formation against this new threat, clashing with them. The world below was a riot of color, the facial colorations of the tulwar and the armor of the guards splashing red with each other's life.

And yet Gariath hardly had time to appreciate it. For his attentions were drawn across the city, to the far side of the wall and the other gate. The one facing Cier'Djaal.

From which reinforcements were supposed to come.

A great cloud of dust was rising some distance away. He couldn't see what it was from here. He rushed to the edge of the battlements where a lookout tower stood. He quickly scaled his way to the top over a crude wooden ladder, took a moment to dislodge the two archers at the top and throw them into the melee below.

From so high up, he could see it. A massive cloud of sand was rising, kicked up in the hustling trail of a team of sixteen oxen. The great beasts bellowed in protest, whipped along by human drivers as they hauled an incredibly oversize carriage.

More troops? No. The carriage was built too oddly for that. Its wheels were oversize and reinforced, meant for carrying a heavy weight. But the carriage was built too small for a lot of men. It seemed as if it had been constructed for a few very large individuals.

And then Gariath's heart fell.

For he knew what was coming.

The beasts arrived within only a few more breaths. The team of drivers immediately hopped off the carriage and ran to its side. There they seized a great chain and pulled it down.

The metal wall of the carriage came crashing down, forming a great ramp. And it shook upon its wheels as a great gray shape rose up and emerged into the daylight.

Ten feet tall. Broad as a rock. Hefting an ax the size of a man over his shoulder as he lifted a horn-topped snout to the sky and inhaled deeply.

Gariath didn't need to smell him to recognize Kharga. Just as he didn't need to see the other two dragonmen emerging to know he had to act.

※ ＊ ※

"Come on! Hurry!"

Over fallen human soldiers.

"Keep going! Bring whoever you can bring!"

Past knots of fighting.

"How many? More. We need *more*!"

Through the streets of Jalaang.

Gariath ran with a dozen tulwar warriors at his back. Those he could tear away from the fighting and who respected—or feared—him enough had come with him. But a dozen was not enough, and there was no time to explain why.

The main street of Jalaang was a clear shot from one gate to the other. The sundered gate that Kudj had broken through stood open, with tulwar warriors still flooding in. It was the one that loomed before them, still barred and blocked, that Gariath was concerned with.

The battle behind him was going well. The sound of tulwar battle cries grew louder and louder, drowning the sounds of humans barking orders to each other. Their fury could not be stopped and, in a short time, they would have this city.

If Gariath could just keep that gate shut.

But the scent came with each breath he took: the scent of an old hate, a familial anger, one that felt tender inside his chest as it filled his lungs. And it grew stronger by the moment.

"Now! *NOW*!" he roared. "Up against the gate!"

Gariath slammed his body against the door. He felt every shudder of the wood as a dozen tulwar added their weight to his. He drew in a breath and held it and hoped that it would be enough.

And as his ear-frills filled with the sound of the earth shuddering beneath the thunder of heavy feet charging, he knew it wouldn't.

A heavy roar split the air. A heavy weight struck the door. Wood exploded. The sky spun. The earth left him.

And amid a shower of splinters, Gariath flew.

His breath exploded out of him as he struck the earth and tumbled across the sand. He could feel the impact of other bodies as the tulwar landed around him. Some clambered back to their feet with agonized groans. Some did not move at all. Gariath tried to find his vision in a swimming head, tried to find his breath in his lungs.

He did. And with them came a familiar stink.

"No shit!" a booming voice bellowed.

He smelled her before he had sight to see her. A *Drokha*. Female. Reeking with angry excitement. When he opened his eyes, the vision matched.

Ten feet at least. A slab of muscle and bone and sinew wrapped in a thick coat of gray scales and walking on two thick legs. The single horn topping her snout had been polished to a high gleam above a savage, toothy grin.

"They've got a *Rhega*." The female's grin grew broader as two heavy hands tightened around the grip of an even heavier hammer. "And here I thought this was going to be boring."

The reek of her joy was overpowering. Not quite as much as the sight of her, of course—no dragonman ever felt all right around a female of the breed—but Gariath's knees felt shaky as he clambered to his feet. He held out his arms in challenge, calling her to him, if only to catch his breath.

She seemed all too happy to oblige, stomping forward to meet him.

"RUA TONG!"

A war cry hit him a moment before the tulwar passed him. Youths, reeking with fury and their faces and weapons painted with blood. Six of them, howling a challenge, rushed past Gariath to meet the female. She hefted her hammer. They leapt at her. She swung.

And three limp bodies went flying, smashed out of the sky like errant flies. The remaining three tumbled to the earth as they all but bounced off her hide. Two let out choked screams punctuated by snapping sounds as she brought her foot down upon them. The third rose, tried to flee.

And failed.

She plucked him up in one hand. Her grin broadened savagely as she began to squeeze. There was a short shriek, a wet pop. And her teeth were painted red.

Gariath had no prayers for gods, no sacred words to utter, no deity or creature or heavenly body that had given him vocabulary adequate for what he had just seen. And so he said the closest thing he had.

"Shit."

Didn't quite cut it.

"Come on, you old men!" the female called out over her shoulder, making a beckoning gesture. "You're going to miss all the fun!"

"Yeah, yeah," another voice replied. "If you kill them all, I still get paid."

"SHIT."

The second time, either.

Two more of them came lumbering past the door, both male. One of them had the wear of age to his scales, and he clutched a sword the size of a human. The other came in with a tremendous ax, glancing around the fallen bodies with disdain before his eyes settled on Gariath and flashed with recognition.

"*Rhega,*" he growled.

Kharga, Gariath thought.

The third time he did not even bother to swear. He was already running, the thunder of their pursuit rattling his body.

Why had he not prepared for this? he asked himself. When they had said "reinforcements," why had he thought that only a few humans might show up? Had he been so blind in his need to drive the tulwar here? What else had he not thought of?

A horn's blaring call to retreat went up. The human forces of Jalaang were already fleeing, ignoring Gariath as he charged through them toward the knot of tulwar flooding through the broken gates. There were many human bodies left behind, as well as a few tulwar. But with weapons bared and bloodied and aloft in victory, far more were alive.

And not nearly enough.

"Quit celebrating, morons!" he roared to be heard above their jubilation as he rejoined them. "The fight's not over."

"What?" Daaru, standing atop some crates he had been directing the battle from, looked at him with concern. "What do you—"

"Ha! Here they are!" The female's voice boomed with laughter as she came thundering into view. She hefted her hammer, the two males at her back, and lumbered toward them. "First one to a hundred wins!"

The stink of fear rose up among the tulwar in a sudden, overpowering cloud. Their cries of jubilation turned to panic. They seemed to fall back in a single wave at the sight of the three great behemoths advancing toward them. And for a moment it seemed as though all of them, every last warrior, would break and run.

And Gariath could not blame them. They had been reared on tales of the Uprising, of how the most glorious moment of their race had been quashed beneath the massive feet of these dragonmen. And now they gazed upon the brutes, their scales smeared with the blood of their fellows and their strides easy, almost bored, as they came forward.

Gariath would not blame them for running.

He would blame only himself. He would blame himself for driving them here. He would blame himself for starting this whole thing. He would blame himself for all the lives lost and blood spilled to get them to this point. He would watch them run and leave Jalaang and vengeance and everything behind and be left with no one but himself.

And he could not do that.

The *Rhega* were not a people of words. No prayers for gods. No speeches from leaders. No verse from poets. They had but one word that was uniquely theirs.

And as he stood before the tulwar, the only thing between them and the dragonmen, he planted his feet, he spread his wings, he opened his mouth and spoke it.

A challenge. A rally. A threat. All these things and more in a single, resonating roar that cut through the air cleaner than any blade and was met by the crowd.

"RUA TONG!"

A roar taken up.

"THO THU BHU!"

A roar multiplied.

"CHEE CHREE!"

From warrior to warrior.

"YENGU THUUN!"

And mouth to foot.

In a wave they rushed forward. With weapons aloft they rushed forward. Their war cries naked and bare as the colors of rage painting their faces, they rushed forward. Gariath in their number, they rushed forward.

And were met.

The female's voice rang with laughter as she swept her hammer out to send them flying in twos and threes of boneless bodies. The older male grunted with annoyance as their blades and arrows bounced off his hide, before skewering them upon his sword. And Kharga grimly strode over carcasses he hacked apart as he waded into the fray.

At least fifty were dead in the span of as many breaths.

Bodies flew. Red painted the sky. War cries met laughter and the tulwar did not recoil. To the last they would fight. Gariath knew this.

At the very least, he had to make sure they didn't go alone.

He rushed toward the nearest foe. The older male caught a glimpse of him as he approached, swung his sword instinctively. Flecks of blood fell from the blade, spattered Gariath's skin as the *Rhega* ducked beneath the blow. The male grunted, impressed.

"A *Rhega*," he said. "I thought you all were dead."

"Not yet," Gariath snarled back.

"Right." The dragonman drew back his titanic blade. "Not yet."

Whatever blow was intended to come never did, as a great shape came barreling out of the fray to bowl headlong into the older male. He grunted with the blow, staggered away from it. When he looked up, a meaty red fist collided with his jaw.

"*KUDJ!*" the vulgore howled, hammering blows down upon the older male.

The male shoved him off, a glare in his eyes suggesting he had found a worthy opponent. Their feet like thunder, the two giants began to wrestle with each other through the flow of the battle.

Gariath could not afford to see who was the victor, let alone help. His nostrils quivered with scent. His ear-frills trembled with noise. A familiar shadow loomed over him.

"There you are!" The female kicked a body out of her way as she came crashing toward Gariath. "Tricky little *Rhega*, thought you could hide from me!"

Her hammer came down in a spray of sand as he narrowly darted out of the way. He scrambled inside her reach as she tried to pull back her massive weapon. He gripped the belt of her kilt; with any luck he could scramble up her body and get to her eyes. With any luck—

"Hey!"

She caught him in a massive hand, plucked him up and brought him before a giant grin. Heedless of the arrows flung at her, she smiled as her hand tightened around him, creaking his bones inside his flesh.

"*MAK LAK KAI!*"

A shadow descended upon the female. From high above, a black gaambol came crashing down upon her head. Chakaa howled with laughter as her mount shrieked with fury. It clawed at the female's eyes even as Chakaa hacked at her scales.

She snarled, dropping Gariath and her hammer both. She grabbed the gaambol in two massive hands, lifting it high above her head and dashing it to the ground. Chakaa's body bounced off the sand and Gariath went scrambling to her side as the female dragonman raised a foot high and brought it down on the shrieking gaambol's skull.

"You're not dead," Gariath observed.

He hadn't intended to sound *quite* that surprised, but now that he could see Chakaa up close, he was a little amazed. The woman was scored with cuts and gouges, a few extra arrows jutting from her hide. She swung sleepily to her feet, body like jelly from the impact she had just taken. She looked at Gariath, grinned stupidly.

"What did I tell you, *daanaja*? I am *malaa*."

Her eyes snapped open with a sudden, crazed life.

"The Tul won't take me back."

Gariath glanced up at the female, struggling to get her weapon back as Tho Thu Bhu shield bearers harried her with spears. His eyes drifted up to the battlements.

"Can you distract her?" he asked, pointing to the female.

"If I have a few more bones for her to break, sure." She shrugged. "But, since you asked so nicely..."

Once more she leapt at the female. Gariath did not stop to see if she succeeded or even if she survived. He rushed toward the battlements, leaping over human corpses as he climbed the stairs leading to the top of the gates.

Weapons were a mystery to him—he had never needed more than his own body. But he had seen the pointy-eared human use bows all the time. It didn't look too difficult.

How hard could using a ballista be?

He hefted one of the spear-sized bolts, loaded it into the machine. The crank to pull it back was enough to require two men, but he managed it in a few breaths. With a growl he struggled to turn it around—the thing hadn't been meant to face into the city. But eventually it came to point at the female, flailing to pry Chakaa off her face.

He narrowed his eyes, growled, kicked a lever.

A string snapped. The bolt flew. A great red spurt painted the air. The female blinked, too stunned to even look at the bolt jutting out of her neck before she fell to the earth beneath the hacking blades of the tulwar.

He grinned. Admittedly, he hadn't expected that to work. Now all he had to do was—

A scream pierced the air. He looked up to see a tulwar body flying out of the crowd and directly toward him. The body struck him, the tulwar scrambled to hold on to him, and both of them went plummeting to the ground. Gariath fought to get free of the tangle of limbs, but could not find his feet before another foot found him.

Kharga snarled, kicking the *Rhega* aside and sending him rolling across the dirt. Gariath felt something inside him creak in protest, threaten to break from the blow. His breath came in short gasps, but even that was enough for him to smell the overpowering reek of Kharga's hatred.

He looked up, saw the behemoth charging toward him. Blood painted his scales and his ax. His feet were caked with gore. Not a single scratch lay upon his body, except...

There. His knee. A black mark. Some kind of wound, maybe. Maybe nothing more than a bit of soot.

But Gariath had no other options. He seized a nearby fallen sword from the grasp of a dead warrior, rushed to his feet, and charged. No breath to drive him far or fast, no life to carry him any farther than he needed, no wit to do anything more than duck beneath a heavy ax's blow, leap forward, and jam his blade at Kharga's knee.

The flesh gave way like something soft and dead, squishing as the blade entered. Kharga howled in agony, dropped his weapon, fell to one knee, and tried to claw the blade out.

The chance did not go unseized. The tulwar were upon him in an instant, screaming as they swarmed over him and hauled him low to the ground.

Gariath could but watch as Kharga disappeared under them, as their blades rose up and down, growing redder and redder, as their war cries ceased to hold anything resembling fury, courage, passion.

He watched as they stabbed and cut and hacked and reveled in the spattering gore.

How long he watched, he did not know. When they had gathered around him, he could not say. What they were chanting when he finally looked up, he barely knew.

"Rhega!"

Him.

"Rhega!"

His people.

"Rhega!"

They raised their fists and blades to him. Their howls turned to cheers and cries of victory. Their gaambols shrieked and pounded the earth in triumph.

They had won.

And Gariath stood at the center of it, staring out over the sea of gore that stained the streets and the mounds of hewn flesh that piled high, and gazed upon their victory.

His victory.

As they chanted his honors.

Over. And over. And over.

THIRTY-THREE

WHITE WINGS SPREAD WIDE

Across all twelve of the tribes, the story was always the same.

Other races had gentle gods who listened to their fears and coddled them with rainfall and sunshine.

Not so the shicts. Riffid was not weak. She had cast them out of the Dark Forest and into the daylight, given them the Howling and the bow, and told her children never to return.

No one knew what sin the shicts had committed to offend their goddess so. But every shict knew she was not to be denied. And when a shict died and returned to the Dark Forest to be forever hunted by Riffid, he was spoken of not fondly as a grandfather, but in soft whispers, lest Riffid hear those who spoke of him and come too close herself.

This was the tale that all shicts were told when they were old enough to hold a bow, to hunt, to kill. And it carried an important lesson.

And Kataria could remember, too, the lesson she had been taught that night she first heard the tale.

"When you must shoot, shoot true. When you must hunt, hunt tirelessly. When you must fight, fight to kill. For should you fail, there will be no gentle god to await you on the other side."

She kept these words firm in her mind, as she had done all day. For there was no doubt in her mind that the shicts holding her prisoner would have the same words in theirs.

She opened her eyes and felt the twinge of pains that were becoming familiar now: the gnawing of rawhide on her wrists, the ache in her joints as she knelt down on the sand before the tent pole she had been tied to, the sweltering heat of the desert. But this latter pain grew dimmer with each breath, and through the holes in the tent, she could see the day turn from orange to purple.

Evening settled.

She drew in a deep breath.

She let her ears rise up to rigid, quivering points.

And she listened.

Ever since she had arrived, the Howling had filled her head with the sounds of snarling, roaring savagery that heralded a tribe's going to war. But now these sounds were fading, leaving only cries echoing off a vast nothingness.

The camp was emptying.

Shekune's army was on the move.

She drew herself up to an awkward knee, trying to angle her boot up behind her so that her bound hands could grip it. After some blind groping, she found its hard leather heel and pulled. The dull sound of steel striking the sand behind her as the knife tumbled out of her boot was a relief to hear.

The shriek of agony as raw, bloodied skin was exposed to air, she decided would be slightly less so, and she bit it back.

The blade had been digging into her ankle for ages now, cutting her freshly every time she was released from her bonds to eat or relieve herself. But she had bitten back every twinge of pain that it had brought, walked swiftly to avoid drawing attention to the blood filling her boot.

She couldn't afford to let them search her. More lives than just hers relied on her escaping.

The sounds of that night—of the rage and the sorrow of the khoshicts' Howling—still beat around in her skull, a beast trying to claw its way out. They seeped into her thoughts and dreams, so that she couldn't close her eyes without hearing their fury.

She could not blame them for wanting revenge, for believing Shekune could give it to them.

But they had only fought humans, never lived with them, never known them. To them humans were still half myths themselves: weird, wild creatures who made a formless face upon which all their troubles were blamed. They couldn't know just how many humans were out there, how much fiercer their weapons were, how very eager they were to use them.

They couldn't know that this war would end with them all dead.

That thought conspired with her desperation, made her fingers shake as they groped blindly for the knife behind her. She found the blade first, cut her fingers on it, bit back the urge to cry out.

No, she scolded herself. *No time for crying. Get out. Get to Shicttown. Warn them. Save everyone. You can cry after that.* She inhaled sharply. *Okay?*

Okay.

She gritted her teeth, found the hilt of the knife, and began to work it awkwardly at her bonds. She jabbed herself with its tip more than once, but she could feel the bonds give way with each clumsy pass. They snapped free, drawing from her a sharp gasp of agony as her bloodied skin finally had the room to ache properly.

She held her hands before her. Her wrists were raw, her fingers were cut, her palms were red with blood both dried and fresh. She drew a breath, stared at her fingers as she moved them, one by one.

They stung, they ached, they made her wince with every twitch. But they could move. And if they could move, they could fire a bow.

Good enough.

She took the knife in hand, crept to the edge of the tent, leaned to its flap, and listened with ears rigid. No sounds of breathing, nor words, nor footfalls reached her. Her guard had likely gone off somewhere else—maybe to see off Shekune's army. Or maybe just to piss.

She couldn't afford to wait and find out which, though. She slipped out of the tent flap and beheld an empty dune before her. Only a few tents dotted the ridge that overlooked the camp, no guards or lookouts between them, by sight or sound. The few campfires up here illuminated no bodies. She was alone.

Or mostly, anyway.

She moved carefully to the dune's edge and looked down over the valley. As she'd suspected, there were drastically fewer fires burning. Amid them, a much less sizable force went about the business of cooking, making weapons, and tending to yiji packs. These would be the crafters, the herders, the elders: those who were not fit for battle and would stay behind to make ready for the return of the warriors.

The warriors who had followed Shekune out into the desert.

Kataria closed her eyes, listened for the sound of their march, to see how far out they had gone. Nothing but silence greeted her, as she had feared. Spectacle and savagery had their allure, but only well before they marched.

To shicts, war was the same as hunting: something that demanded swiftness and silence.

But swift as they might be, they were still thousands and she was but one. She could make it to Cier'Djaal well before they could. She could warn Sai-Thuwan, ask him to intervene. He was the leader of the Eighth Tribe, easily Shekune's equal. He could speak out against her, force her into discussion, make them find another way.

Assuming Kataria reached him in time.

She crept along the ridge as she scanned the camp below, searching for a yiji corral left unattended. If she could steal one of the beasts, she could ride it toward Cier'Djaal. Of course she would need to steal enough food and water for both her and it to—

"Who's there?"

She froze in place at the sound of a voice. Her head turned slowly to look behind her, she was ready to bolt at the sign of a guard. She saw nothing, though, but sand and shadows around her.

"Has someone finally come to kill me?"

The voice came again. And upon hearing it, she knew it was no shictish voice. It was too raspy, too withered, a stale wind forced through a hole choked with sand.

"Well, don't be shy," it rasped again from a nearby tent, its voice broken by errant clicking noises. "Let's not make it any more awkward, shall we?"

It wasn't until the voice laughed—a hideous, chittering sound—that she recognized it. She swept to the tent, shoved back the flap, and saw her suspicions confirmed in a single glance.

The night had left precious little light to see by inside the tent, but there was no darkness thick enough to hide the peculiarity of the prisoner inside.

A tall, muscular figure knelt at the center of the tent. Flashes of moonlight through slits in the tent betrayed glimpses of pale flesh drawn tight with scars and painted with bruises and cuts. Two powerful arms were drawn over his head, stretched out and bound to two stakes flanking him. A pair of finer, more delicate hands emerging from just beneath those were bound before him. The creature looked to have been taken harshly: The reek of blood was all around him and his body trembled in agony.

Yet for all this, there was just enough moonlight for her to see the scars of his face twist as his mouth curled into a smile.

Or what Kataria assumed was a smile.

It was hard to tell with couthi, what with their giant fucking mandibles.

"Ah, so it's you." Man-Khoo Yun's voice was dry, his laughter even more so, like the cracking of baked earth.

"You don't sound surprised," Kataria replied.

"I'm not," the couthi said. "It would seem logical that they'd grant you the honor of finally killing me after so many days of torture. I am, after all, the one who exposed your conspiracy."

"Conspiracy," she repeated flatly.

"If one can call it that," Man-Khoo Yun said. "Let the humans be buried beneath the knowledge that I warned them about you and your whole misbegotten race."

"Yeah." Kataria sneered. She held up her bloodied wrists. "You uncovered my plot to get myself tied to a tent stake and left half-starved for days. Fucking brilliant work there, insect." She spit at the earth. "Whatever happened, I wasn't a part of it."

"Ah, yes." Venom crept into Man-Khoo Yun's voice. His ropes creaked as he tried to lean his battered body forward. "One tribe kills a man's wife, and when he has a grievance, the other tribes tell him they are not responsible. Then when they kill his son, the first tribe tells him that *they* are not responsible. So a man has two bodies and, somehow, no one is responsible." He grinned morbidly. "When Bir-Nal Than fell, we called it 'the shictish miracle.'"

Her ears shivered at those words.

Bir-Nal Than. She had heard the name of the former couthi capital before, spoken frequently in the tribal fires. It was the great victory of the shictish tribes over the expanding couthi empire. One did not speak of Bir-Nal Than without speaking of the fires that had been lit in its burrows, the tribesmen who had sliced the faces of the defenders, the dead forest whose branches they had hung the couthi dead in. One did not speak of Bir-Nal Than without breathless admiration for the old war.

Man-Khoo Yun, though, spoke of it with a voice choked and black eyes glimmering.

"Countless dead," the couthi said. "Countless murdered. While the armies were out hunting your warriors, you circled back and attacked the city. All our young, all our maidens, all cut to pieces and fed to your beasts. And then you simply scattered back into the forests, vermin fleeing a corpse picked clean."

"That was..." Kataria swallowed hard. "My tribe was a part of that, but not my qithband. I wasn't there, neither were my parents."

"Tribes, qithbands, parents...," Man-Khoo Yun all but roared. "For the couthi, family is something worth fighting for, worth dying for. For shicts, family is a collection of bodies you point to and say, 'No, *they're* responsible.'" He snapped forward in his bonds, the ropes snarling as they bit into his flesh. "*My* family is dead. *My* face was carved by their knives. What did *I* do to deserve that?"

When the bonds would not give, when the fire in his voice begat only a hacking cough, he fell back and hung from his ropes. But though his breath was ragged, his black eyes continued to burn with a fire too immense for the battered mess of his body.

"What did your humans do to deserve their fate?"

His words did not bite at her like a knife. He had not the strength to hurl them so far, so hard. Rather his words dribbled out of his mouth on rasping breath and pooled on the sandy floor in an ugly puddle of hatred and scorn and truth.

And she couldn't deny it. Not a single ugly word.

She knew nothing of Bir-Nal Than but stories. The numberless couthi dead left behind were all the same: words lost in campfire stories.

Shicts, too, were the same, she supposed: stories, tales, legends of long-eared ghouls that haunted the night, told by worried human mothers to naughty human children.

When Man-Khoo Yun looked upon her, he didn't see Kataria. That word had no meaning. When the khoshicts looked upon humans, words like *Lenk, Asper*, and *Denaos* had no meaning, either.

They saw only stone houses built on their lands. Only forges that churned out blades that killed their people. Only beasts that would one day hunt their children.

Maybe that was just the way of things, then.

There were no people, only stories. It was easier to kill a story than a person, to think only of the villainies recounted in the tales than to think of bodies hanging from dead trees and screams eaten in the cackle of flames.

Maybe.

And maybe she was about to make a huge mistake as she approached Man-Khoo Yun with the knife in her hand.

It was stupid, of course. Stupid to think that she could spare a world steeped in war another corpse, that the world would even notice a dry spot among all the blood staining it, that things might end without bloodshed for once.

But she had the feeling that there'd be enough violence in the days to come that she could afford to skip it this once.

And so she reached up with her blade. And so she sawed at the ropes securing his larger arms to the tent poles. And so she stepped away as he collapsed, weary, to the sand.

"You can try to kill me if you want," she said, regarding him coolly even as he glowered murderously at her. "But if you want my advice?" She pointed the blade at his broken body. "You got it worse than I did. You could attack me, maybe even kill me." She sniffed, flipped the blade in her hand. "If you really wanted it. But by the time it's over, you'll be in no shape to escape. So you can fight or you can run."

She stepped back farther, until she was out in the cool of the desert night. She spread her hands out wide.

"Up to you."

For a long time he stared at her, his eyes inky voids that drank what insignificant light there was inside the tent. When he finally did move, it was shakily. He rose to his towering height and stalked out of the tent. Towering over her, mandibles glistening in the moonlight, he still looked as if he would have a good chance of strangling her with those giant arms before she could stab him to death. But it'd be a wager. And neither of them had that kind of ferocity left to gamble.

Maybe that was why he turned from her and why he stalked away. And maybe it was foolish to think that he might go back to his people, that he might have the one story that existed in the world about a shict and a couthi who did not kill each other one fateful night.

Maybe.

Or maybe he'd just make a useful distraction as her pursuers had to choose between chasing him and chasing her.

No fucking point in waiting to find out, she thought.

And she turned and began hurrying down the dune.

——— ✦ ———

Should go back.

Too many thoughts.

Should go back and get a yiji. You can't make it on foot.

Too much air.

No time. Can't go back and risk getting captured again. Have to keep moving.

Free from the confines of the camp, her head clear of the fury of their Howling, Kataria found her thoughts coming swiftly.

Too swiftly.

They tumbled about in her skull, clashing off each other with resonating bangs that sent her temples throbbing. She felt suffocated by the open space around her as she put the camp behind her. Now that she was free of the immediacy of escaping her prison, the enormity of her task did not so much lie before her as bear down on her like a wolf whose jaws were tightening on her neck with every step she took.

It had all seemed so simple when—

No, not simple, she corrected herself, necessary. It had been necessity that had given her the will to escape. She had to stop it—Shekune's war, the inevitable human retaliation, the doom of all shicts—and she had to do it quickly.

Only now, beneath a pitiless moon on an unforgivingly clear night, did she stop and stare and realize that her plans were as empty as the desert that sprawled out before her.

No landmarks. No trails. Nothing but dunes upon dunes to guide her. How could she find her way back to Cier'Djaal through this? How could she hope to beat Shekune and her army, who had lived in this desert for generations, there? How could she get to Sai-Thuwan in time?

And who was to say he would listen? That Shekune would listen? She had heard the Howling of the khoshicts; their hunger for war had rung so loudly in her ears that it had knocked the wind from her lungs.

They might ignore her. They might go ahead with their plan. And the humans might not stop with the khoshicts but go on to eradicate the Twelve Tribes entirely.

And what if she was captured again and forced to witness it? What if Lenk was out there and they found him? What if Kwar realized her dagger was missing? What if . . .

What if I can't do it?

It was that thought that spoke the clearest, loudest, and it would not stop repeating itself in her head. She felt the thundering of her heart in her throat, the taste of something sour on the back of her tongue, the scent of salt in her nose.

She asked herself this, again and again. And when she could no more, she asked the desert.

"What then?"

And the desert offered no answer.

Not so much as a breeze to stir a single grain of sand in response to her. She opened her ears and heard nothing. No sounds of the Howling. No lonely cry of wind. She could hear nothing.

Nothing, at least, but the creak of a bowstring being drawn.

She whirled about, flipping the dagger in her hand and drawing it back, ready to throw. She tensed, expecting to find a stalking hunter behind her or a yiji-mounted rider bearing down on her.

What she did not expect to find was a child.

No, not a child, she recognized. A man. But not by much.

It took her a moment to recognize him as Yarra, the youth who had been charged with watching her. All the arrogance and scorn he had shown her when she was bound had vanished, chased away by eyes wide with fear and lips that struggled to force a command out.

"D-don't move!" he cried out.

The command might have carried more weight if the bow he held weren't shaking. The shaft of the arrow rattled against the bow, his stance was weak and ungainly, his fingers—bandaged from when Kwar had broken them—awkwardly gripped the arrow's shaft.

Kataria had seen this before—trembling hands, darting eyes, heavy breathing—in every young shict.

He had faced only targets of wood and straw, she knew. He had never put arrows in something that bled. She would bet he'd never turned his bow on anything that walked, let alone another shict.

Gone was the boastful warrior who had gloated over his captive. Left behind was just a scared, trembling boy.

"You...you have to come back to camp with me," Yarra said, licking his lips. "Or I'll shoot."

"No, you won't," she said, the firmness of her voice strangling the quaver of his.

"I will!" he insisted. "They told me to...to shoot you if you tried to escape."

"But you didn't," she replied. "You could have shot me from thirty paces. But you came close enough for me to use this." She gestured with her chin to the blade she held drawn back. "You don't want to kill me, Yarra." She let her voice slip lower, into a softer tone. "You don't want to kill another shict."

Shame flashed across his callow face for a moment, quickly swallowed by his fear, but it was clear enough for her to take a bold step closer. He retreated a step in response and held his bow up higher.

"Stay back!" he said.

"I don't want to, either, Yarra," she said, ignoring the command. "I don't want to see any shicts die. That's why I've got to go to Cier'Djaal. Shekune will kill us all with her war. The humans will retaliate and leave not a single shict alive."

"Shekune said..." Yarra swallowed hard. "She's going to bring us revenge. She's going to show them that we're to be taken seriously!"

"Who's going to die for it, Yarra?" she asked. "How many humans are you going to have to kill for that to happen? How many shicts are they going to kill in return?"

"I...I don't know. Look, just come back and—"

"You *do* know," she snapped. "You know as well as I do and every fucking shict in that camp knows that there's no way to win this without so many fucking dead that it won't even matter who won." She bit back her anger. "I can't let that happen, Yarra. Not without trying to stop it."

His lips quivered, trying to form a reply. The fear in his eyes spread to all parts of him, choking his voice in his throat and making his tongue swell. His hands continued to shake. His arms would be getting tired, Kataria knew; bows were meant to be drawn and fired quickly, by instinct, not held for so long.

He would tire soon. The fear in him would sap his strength. Then she could get close enough to knock him out and escape.

"Yarra, listen to me," she said, "I don't want to hurt you. I don't want to hurt *any* shict. Put down the bow."

"I...I can't. Shekune, she trusted me with this. She said—"

"She said what, Yarra? That shicts should kill shicts?"

"No, she said—"

"I don't fucking *care* what she said." She bared her teeth in a snarl, tensed. "She's *wrong* and she's going to get us all fucking killed if we don't stop her."

She took another step forward.

"Yarra, just—"

"NO!"

Instinct.

That's all it was. Instinct.

Instinct from a hundred battles fought that made her dart to the side as the bowstring snapped. Instinct he didn't have from a hundred battles he'd never see that made his arrow go wide. Instinct she had fought for, worked for, bled for that made her arm snap forward and send the dagger flying toward him as he awkwardly twisted.

It was just rotten luck that made it find his ribs.

She cursed—at him for firing, at herself for throwing. He cried out—a name she did not recognize. But neither of them spoke loud enough to drown out the sound of the blade finding its mark. And as she heard the meaty smack of steel biting past muscle, she knew that the throw had been pitilessly perfect.

He went rigid, arm tucking into his side in response to the pain. He collapsed, his cry came out thick and burbling. She ran to his side, found the blade lodged to the hilt in his flank. It had found its way between his ribs, punctured a lung.

"Yarra!" she cried out, falling to her knees beside him. "Yarra, I..." She gritted her teeth, balled her hands into fists, and snarled, "You asshole. You stupid piece of shit, *didn't you fucking hear me*? Didn't I say to put the bow down? *Didn't I?*"

His response was a bubbling red froth that poured from his lips as something inside him ruptured and spilled out of his mouth. His response was a futile clutching at her arm with a hand gone rigid with desperation. His response was the fear in his eyes fast fading, giving way to an empty lightlessness.

"Yarra," she said. "Yarra, listen to me. I'm…I can…"

Her mouth hung open, wordless. What could she say? What could she do?

It would not change anything.

It would not make the light stay in his eyes. It would not make his hand not go limp. It would not make his last words be anything but a few choked, gurgling sounds.

And when he went still, and lay staring up endlessly at a night as dark as his eyes, she said nothing.

What would it change?

This question hung over her head. She looked over the desert.

And the desert offered no answer.

◦—◦

It was getting colder.

The night gnawed at her bare flesh as she trekked across the dunes. The wind traveled west, as did she, and bit at her back. It was almost unfair, she thought, that something so sweltering by day should be freezing at night. She would do well, she knew, to find shelter and wait out the night on the leeward side of a dune, much like the one she was trudging down.

But she did not.

She forced herself to feel the cold, its bitter chill and gnawing wind. She forced herself to feel the soreness of her wounds and the ache in her feet. She forced herself to feel the weight of Yarra's bow and quiver upon her back, as keenly as if she were carrying his corpse.

For this weapon was his corpse. All that was left of Yarra, everything he'd meant to the tribe, was on her back now. He had died because of her. Many more would if she did not keep moving.

She could not afford to forget that.

Not that there was much chance that she would.

She could still hear him, the last sounds he had ever made. And though they had been gurgling, choking sounds that had escaped his lips in runny froth, she knew the word he had spoken.

Why?

If she had just held her dagger for just a moment, if she had just run, if he had just believed her . . .

But he hadn't. He trusted Shekune more, as all of them did. And now he was dead.

The quest to save countless shict lives had begun with one dead by her own hand.

And the rest? she asked herself in the spaces between her footsteps. *When the rest of them trust Shekune? What are you going to do to them? Are you going to kill them as—*

"No!"

She shook her head, hard enough that she might fling the thoughts from her skull. She bit down, gritted her teeth so that she heard the muscles of her jaw creak.

No more time for thought, for fear, or for doubt. Yarra was dead, killed by her hand. The rest of them would be, too, if she didn't put every part of herself into moving.

"West," she whispered to herself as she looked up toward the distant dunes. "Keep west and eventually you'll find—"

Her voice died on the breeze. She froze in her tracks as the moonlight shone down upon the crest of a dune looming before her.

There, painted black against the night, she saw a bestial, four-legged shape. It was hard to make out in the darkness, but she could see the glint of fang, the flash of steel.

A rider.

There was a sign of movement, and the rider's mount spurred it forward. A yiji's baying cackle carried over the dunes, heralding its approach as it came down the slope toward Kataria.

The sound was enough to set her skin crawling, but not enough to frighten her.

That honor belonged to the sound unspoken, a formless snarl that reached across the night sky and into Kataria's ears.

A mournful wail. A tender sound meant only for her. One she had heard before, on a warmer night and in closer company.

"Kwar."

The word came with the rattle of bow, the creak of string, as Kataria drew an arrow back and took aim.

The yiji came loping down the dune—quickly, but far from frenziedly. In the span of five breaths, it was close enough that Kataria could see its rider clearly. Her face was set in a hard blade of a frown, her braids whipping about her face as she spurred her mount forward. But even as dire as her expression looked, the khoshict's eyes were as wild as ever and Kataria could see their burning darks clearly down the shaft of her drawn arrow.

The breeze quieted. She held her breath, stilled her heartbeat. She watched those wild eyes grow larger with every step the yiji took as it came loping toward her.

The perfect shot.

"Shit."

A curse.

"Shit."

An arrow falling to the earth.

"Shit, shit, *shit*."

Footsteps crunching on sand.

She was running, breathing heavily as she spit curses at herself for not taking that shot. Yet within moments she could not curse loudly enough to be heard over the sound of the yiji's eerie giggle.

Kwar came rushing up beside her, past her, circling her mount around to block Kataria's path. The paler shict came to a halt, drawing another arrow from her quiver.

The bow trembled as she raised it and drew the arrow back awkwardly. Her heart thundered in her ears, her mouth went dry. The arrowhead shook as she aimed it at Kwar, then past Kwar's ear, hoping that a grazing shot would scare her off.

Maybe Yarra hoped the same thing.

She tried not to listen to that, either.

Kwar swung her legs over the yiji's humped back, landed hard on the sand. She took a moment, fixed her dark eyes upon Kataria before she stared at the arrowhead pointing at her. For a long moment, she stood there, as if waiting for Kataria to fire.

And when she finally walked toward Kataria, she did so slowly, without attempting to dodge or weave. Her eyes locked on Kataria's, dark and steady while Kataria felt her own quivering in their sockets. She came to a stop an arm's length away from Kataria, the tip of the arrow grazing the fabric of her shirt.

She stood there, staring, and whispered.

"Do it."

No threat in Kwar's voice. No command. No challenge. The words left her mouth on a quaver. Her eyes watered. Her hands were clenched into fists.

"Do it," she said again.

It was those eyes that made Kataria slowly lower her bow.

"If I can't live with you, then I don't want—"

And it was those words that made her raise it again.

"*Don't*," she snarled. "Don't you fucking finish that sentence."

"I was just—"

"You kidnapped me," Kataria said. "You didn't even wait for me to make up my damn mind. You paraded me around my people like I was a trophy. They *looked* at me like I was one."

"I know. I'm sorry, I—"

"I don't want to hear that word," she said. "I don't want you to pretend that this is something you can make up for."

Her eyes watered, but she did not weep. Her body shook, but she did not break. The muscles of Kwar's jaw tensed.

"What do you want, then?" she asked.

I want you to turn around, go back to wherever you came from, and never think of me again.

I want to go back to the time I met you and walk away.

I want... I want to just stop until everything is over.

These she did not say.

"I want," she spoke in hard words, "to save my people."

"Your people..." Kwar paused. "*Our* people want war."

"They won't get it. Shekune will lead them to their deaths."

"Shekune is strong. The second-strongest shict I have ever seen. She has power. She has weapons. She has—"

"And the humans have numbers, power, land," Kataria said. "The humans have *everything*."

Kwar's gaze dropped to the earth. "I know," she whispered. "I know they have everything. I wanted to take it from them. Like they took everything from me." Her voice dropped low. "My mother, my father, my brother..." She looked only halfway up at Kataria. "You."

"They didn't. *He* didn't."

"I didn't know that! Some part of me did, but not the part that was speaking the loudest. I was afraid that you would leave, that I would have nothing, that I would be like them." She gestured back toward the direction of the shict camp. "Like the rest of our people. Their land, their families...everything was taken from them by the humans. They have nothing left to lose."

Kataria stared at her, eyes so hard they might cut Kwar if she didn't blink.

"There is *always* something left to lose," she said.

Kwar met her gaze.

"I know," she whispered. "I knew that when you looked at me the way you did two nights ago."

"I told you, don't—"

"Please, just..." Kwar winced, holding her hands up. "I need you to know this. I never meant to hurt you. I was just..." Her hands fell, empty. "My mother once told me I should have been born a yiji, that I would be more comfortable if I had many littermates and slept in a pile." She smiled weakly. "I remember being so mad, thinking she was saying I was some dirty beast. I never understood how right she was.

"Until she was gone." Kwar closed her eyes. "My mother is dead. My father is a coward. My brother won't speak to me. I am surrounded by my people, but I am alone." She looked intently at Kataria. "I stand two feet from you and I am still alone."

Kataria felt heavy. Her arms hung at her sides, the bow suddenly unbearably hard to hold. Her head slumped forward, eyes to the earth.

"You don't get to do that," she said. "You don't get to make me feel like this, like you have a good reason."

"It's not good," Kwar said, "but I did it."

"So, what, you want me to forgive you?"

"No. I want to ask you something." Kwar looked at her intently. "Who are you doing this for? For us?" Her jaw tightened. "Or for the humans?"

"Fuck, I don't know." Kataria rolled her shoulders, helpless. "Is it so hard to believe I don't want *anyone* to die? I know what the humans do to the shicts, but I know that Shekune can't solve it."

"Then what can?"

Kataria stared at her. "I don't know. But neither she nor I can solve it if everyone's dead."

Kwar said nothing for a time. She looked long over the dunes. A cold breeze blew her braids across her face.

"Shekune's army is large, but they're still shicts," she said. "They know the desert well and have covered a lot of distance already." She looked at Kataria. "We can beat them to Cier'Djaal, if we ride hard and sleep little."

"We," Kataria repeated.

"We." Kwar whistled sharply. Her yiji, which had been busying itself chasing some nearby scent, came loping over. She mounted it in short order, straddling the large crest of its back. "You and I."

Kataria regarded her warily. "You expect me to trust you?"

"I expect you to not have much of a chance of getting across this desert unless you do."

"You kidnapped me."

Kwar sniffed, shrugged. "You stole my knife."

"Yeah, to free myself because *you kidnapped me.*"

"So you agree we've both made mistakes."

"What? I—"

"Do you want to stop Shekune or not?"

"I do." Kataria glared at her. "But just a moment ago, you said you wanted to take everything from the humans."

"I still do."

"Then what are you doing this for?"

The faintest of smiles. Not her usual predatory grin, nor her haughty smirk, nor anything Kataria had seen before. Kwar's lips curled up into something soft and weak that befitted the sound that played through her head.

"For you," she said.

THIRTY-FOUR

A Coffin for
a Thousand Men

Do you feel that?"

Lenk stirred out of his slumber at the sound of Shuro's voice, his senses returning as she shook him gently.

It was dark, long past the late-afternoon sun they had set out beneath. He must have dozed off at some point during the trip. He wasn't sure how long they had spent climbing the mountain.

Admittedly, he wasn't sure how long climbing a mountain via the silk cradle of some hideous plant-monster-spider-thing was supposed to take, either. But that was the question Shuro had been about to answer, for in another moment, he felt it.

They were slowing down.

He looked up. The curious creature still clung to the webs upon the mountain's face, but its multi-limbed gait became more ponderous and thoughtful.

As they continued to ascend the mountain, Lenk became aware of metal rods inserted into the rock, one on each side and spanning about the length of the creature's width from leg-tip to leg-tip. Holes had been drilled into the metal to provide some manner of grip for the creature.

A landing structure, Lenk realized. They were arriving.

Shuro, too, realized it. For her hand was once again on his shoulder. When he looked at her, she held her blade up meaningfully. He nodded and drew his own. Not that either of them had any idea what awaited them up there.

But really, he thought, *if you have to ride one of these monsters to get to a place, what are the chances that there's anything pleasant waiting for you?*

"This cradle is probably more defensible than anything we'll find up there," Shuro muttered as the spider creature continued its ascent. "If there're attackers waiting for us, we stay here. Make them come to us." She glanced over her shoulder at Chemoi. "And you stay behind us."

Both Lenk and Chemoi nodded at that, the saccarii with considerably more enthusiasm.

The metal structure in the mountain's face grew suddenly more elaborate, rising up over a ledge above and creating two long arches that stretched up and over the lip of the rock. The creature followed these arches, its movement going from vertical to horizontal and ushering the cradle into a small gap that served as a loading dock.

Lenk tensed, unsure of what to expect.

After all, what *did* one expect to find in a forgotten city once ruled by a demon? More demons was a likely guess. Some manner of ancient defense system, maybe. Living statues or acid-spitting goats or babies that *looked* like babies but were actually evil squid-babies.

Lenk hadn't thought too hard about it.

But what he had not expected to find was exactly what he found when the spider came to a halt and the cradle bumped gently against a stone dock.

Nothing.

A vast amount of nothing stretched out on all sides of him. Through the darkness he could scarcely see around him but for some key details.

To either side he could see the mountain's face had been carved to a fine, flat edge that gave way to a vast flat space, as though someone had simply shorn off the top of the mountain to build something on the flat spot that remained. Embedded in the edge were other metallic loading structures, other docks, presumably for other creatures like the one that had brought them here.

The remains of small stone buildings and various forms of cargo long rotted stood nearby. This had been a busy place, Lenk guessed, some kind of loading bay from which goods and people had been transported to and from the jungle below. The air was thin and cold up here, far from the sweltering oppression of the jungle's humidity.

A kingdom in the clouds. Perhaps the closest thing to heaven mortals could know.

Beyond the loading bay, Lenk could see the shapes of buildings: towers and houses and domed structures. But they stood darkened and quiet, shadows against the starry sky.

No enemies. No defenses. No danger.

Nothing.

"Peculiar," Shuro said. She stepped off the cradle and onto the dock, glancing around.

Lenk looked at her for a moment. "Well, I mean...*yeah*. We just rode a giant spider to a dead city. Seems a little late to start calling—"

"I mean there should be something," Shuro said. "Some kind of enemy...a guardian or something. Khoth-Kapira was, our information tells us, paranoid and suspicious. He wouldn't have left nothing for whoever came to his final resting place."

"Thing about final resting places," Chemoi said, following them off the cradle and onto the dock, "is that they're *final*. Once yer dead, ya ain't get a say what happens to ya or yer city."

"Demons don't die," Shuro replied without looking back. "Not in the way we understand. The fact that there's nothing here means that there's nothing we can see." She hissed out a soft breath. "Which means that there's something out there we can't see."

"An ambush?" Lenk asked.

"Possibly," Shuro said. "Or whatever's here isn't aware of us yet." She sheathed her sword, tucked her hair beneath her black hat. "I'll go on ahead and survey the surroundings." She glanced back at Lenk. "Half an hour. If I'm not back, come looking for me, but do so with the assumption that it's not safe."

"What?" Chemoi asked, shrill. "Ya can't leave me here!"

"Lenk will stay with you," Shuro replied.

"Why do I gotta stay with *him*?"

"What's wrong with me?" Lenk asked.

"Well, no offense intended, pink, but I been spendin' enough time around the two of ya to know which one of you's got the balls here."

Lenk blinked, looked at Shuro. "Yeah, feel free to take her with you."

"I can move more quickly alone," Shuro said. "And I can't afford to be slow here. Half an hour. No later. Don't kill her until I get back."

Lenk blinked. "I . . . uh, wasn't planning on killing her."

"Oh. Uh, yeah, I know. I was . . . joking."

"Oh. Right. It's hard to tell what with the . . ." Lenk made a vague gesture about his face. "You know, face."

Shuro's brows knitted in a glare. "Right."

Mercifully, she left, disappearing between two of the ruined buildings and into the night. Chemoi skulked off to go huddle behind some ancient cargo, taking shelter from the wind. Not desiring to be in the company of either of them, Lenk merely sighed and walked to the edge of the dock, staring down over the precipice.

The mountain was a sheer drop down a vertical stone face. The jungle below stretched out like a particularly unruly rug and Lenk could just barely make out the scrublands where the forest gave way to the desert. Far up here he found it easy to believe that Rhuul Khaas could stay forgotten for so long. Who would think to look all the way up here for a city?

For that matter, who would *build* a city up here?

Mocca would, he thought. *No, not Mocca. Khoth-Kapira.*

But they weren't different people, he had to remind himself. Mocca was merely one name worn by a demon with many.

And Khoth-Kapira *was* a demon.

Still, Rhuul Khaas, remote as it was, hardly fit the image of a demonic fortress. There were no charnel pits, no perpetual flames, no writhing bodies impaled upon spikes. In fact, there was a rather shameful lack of spikes altogether, considering.

The air was thin and clean up here. The roar of waterfalls down below was a quiet mumble, fighting with the moaning wind to be heard. It was peaceful up here. Quiet. Serene.

"Hello?"

His hand went to his sword as he whirled about. His eyes swept the darkness, seeing nothing but the same ancient black shapes amid the pervasive gloom. The hairs on the back of his neck stood up on end.

Someone had spoken to him. He had heard their voice right next to his ear, a whisper from the darkness. It had been elegant, soft, almost melodic.

He glanced behind him. Even if the saccarii *hadn't* had a voice like a kitten being strangled, she was still huddled down behind the cargo, shivering thirty paces away from him. He opened his mouth to ask her if she had heard it.

But he heard it again first.

"Is someone there?"

Again, right beside his ear. Again, he whirled around. His sword was out and in his hand, though he wasn't quite sure why. There was damn near nothing that could have sneaked up behind him with his back to a plummeting sheer drop.

"Somethin' wrong?" Chemoi asked, eyes fixed on his steel.

"No," Lenk replied, though the hesitation in his voice suggested otherwise. "No, I thought I just heard something is all."

"Ah, there you are."

Lenk swallowed hard, resisted the urge to whirl around again. His body tensed as the voice from nowhere chimed into his ear.

"Has someone at last come to grant a reprieve from my long vigil?" It did not speak. *"Or are you merely a reprieve from boredom?"* It chimed. *"I will not turn either away, mind."*

It was not so much a voice as a sound. It was not so much words as it was music. He could understand it, discern its meaning, and yet it sounded like nothing he had ever heard: a song not meant for mortal ears, a quavering harmony that drilled into his head, the resonant echo of a very old brass bell struck with a very old oak stick.

Not the sort of thing one goes seeking out.

Yet not the sort of thing one could really afford to leave be, either.

Sword in hand, Lenk edged his way toward the nearby decrepit buildings, scanning the gloom for the source of the sound.

"Hey! *Hey!*" Chemoi piped up from her spot. "Where ya goin'? Ya can't just leave me!"

"I'm not," Lenk replied. "I'll be back soon. Stay here and stay quiet."

"But Shuro said—"

"If she should return first, fondle her balls until I come back."

Chemoi muttered a few choice curses at his back, but he did not turn around. His eyes were fixed on the darkness, searching for any sign of movement as he crept past the shattered buildings. Beyond their stone frames, the land opened up. Massive distant shapes loomed, but he could see nothing in his immediate vicinity.

All around him, he could see nothing but blackness.

And one spot of light.

Mocca stood like a ghost lost in gloom, wandering down a darkened street that yawned out into the black. He didn't seem to register Lenk at all, his attentions focused on what appeared to be a long, thin lamppost long dead, one of hundreds marching up the street.

The man in white paused, hesitation playing on his face as he studied the lamppost. Warily he reached out a hand as if to touch it. But before his fingers had even brushed it, he winced as if burned and drew them back.

"Something the matter?" Lenk asked.

Mocca did not look at the young man as he approached. His eyes were fixed on the lamppost, his words a breathless whisper.

"I remember this," he said.

"This street?"

"This lamp," Mocca said. "And this street. And every brick upon it and every building here. I was there for every construction, every project, every artifice wrought. I remember *all* of it." He stared at his own hands. "And if I touch them...and my hands go right through them, I fear that I will realize this isn't real."

Lenk glanced at the lamppost, reached out and wrapped fingers around it. The chill of metal greeted him.

"Feels real enough to me," he said.

"Time has a way of twisting memory," Mocca muttered in reply. He gazed out over the darkened city. "Far below, in the darkness to which I was cast down, I could think of nothing but Rhuul Khaas. The city I had built and the people I had left behind. Down there I could but dream. And in my dreams, all I saw were its edifices and statues, its lights and sounds. And as the decades dragged on and things around me got darker, the city only became brighter and grander in my dreams until I feared to wake and see only blackness."

He held his hands up high, inviting the entire city to rise up and embrace him. And when all that came to meet him was the moaning wind, he looked almost disappointed.

"And I return to my city," he said, "and I see only blackness."

"It has been a while," Lenk said.

"Too long," Mocca said. "Maybe so long that the Rhuul Khaas I thought of existed only in my dreams."

"How would you know?" Lenk looked around. "It's pitch-black out here. You can't see a damn thing."

"For the moment."

"What?"

"No, never mind, it's…" Mocca paused, stared thoughtfully at Lenk for a moment. "Actually, you might think it a little interesting."

"Look, I know you're used to talking in cryptic gibberish, but this is a bit much even for—"

Mocca shut his eyes, smiled softly, and disappeared into thin air.

"—you."

Lenk looked around for the man in white, but saw nothing.

And then he saw light.

The lamppost beside him suddenly flickered, a soft orange light rising up from inside a translucent globe seated at the top. A small vial within bubbled with a liquid that radiated a light that steadily grew brighter.

And soon it was joined.

One by one, on either side of the street, many more lampposts marching the avenue awoke. Their light was faint at first, but grew steadily, and each one lit up faster than the one before it. Soon they were springing to life everywhere, upon every street and every corner, until the entire city was bright as day.

And Lenk saw Rhuul Khaas for the second time.

Buildings of obsidian and marble stood silently, their walls reflecting the light of the lamps and making the city seem even brighter. Aqueducts ran a spider's web over the sky. Domed buildings squatted next to towering obelisks. Temples and homes and gardens and streets sprawled everywhere. Fountains depicting stone children playing, statues depicting learned men and women, pillars adorned with words written in a language painful and beautiful to see…

He had seen it before.

Mocca had shown him, in visions, but to see it here, to know it really existed.

He had no words.

"What… but… *how*?"

Or at least no intelligent words.

"My blood."

He turned. Mocca stood beside him again, staring up at the same lamppost. He gestured to it, the tiny vial ensconced within the globe.

"A single drop was all it took," he said. "It burns brightly at my will. I was afraid it wouldn't work, but apparently I can still do it."

"How did you do all *this*?" Lenk gestured over the cityscape.

"Same answer," Mocca replied. "Blood, sweat, labor, and love. I was not alone in it, of course. Others brought the stone up, tilled the fields on the countryside below, mixed the mortar, and laid the foundations. But the designs were all mine." He smiled sadly. "I was hesitant to awaken them again."

"Why? This is...incredible."

More than incredible, Lenk reminded himself. This was *it*. This was what he had come here for. The Forbidden East, Rhuul Khaas: All of it had been leading to this moment.

Somewhere out there was the Library of the Learned. All he had to do was find it, find what lay inside, and he could have his new life.

He paused. He blinked. He found he couldn't remember the name he'd been promised.

"It is incredible." Mocca suddenly sighed. "After so much time. Even if the gardens are overgrown and the stones are cracked, it is as beautiful as I remember. And yet..."

"What? What's wrong?"

He replied in a choked voice.

"They're gone."

Lenk was about to ask who when it struck him. In the absence of darkness, the silence was all the more profound. Where there should have been people laughing and merchants yelling and lovers sighing contentedly on benches, there was only the mutter of a bitter wind.

In his visions he had seen people of all kinds—tulwar walking with humans, humans walking with shicts. Yet the twisting streets of Rhuul Khaas were empty, devoid of life and death alike. There were no bodies in the street, no bloodstains, no signs that anyone had died here, let alone lived here. It was as though they had simply left, one by one, until the final person here simply went through and extinguished all the lights until it existed as it did now.

"Where did they go?" Lenk asked.

"Elsewhere, I suspect," Mocca said. "This city ran on my will, my body. The lamps fed on my blood, the law was based on my wisdom, the food was delivered by my creations. When I was cast down, what would be left for them?"

He drew in a breath and the city seemed to inhale with him. The lights flickered, then stilled. The wind ceased its wail. All of creation waited for his next words, including Lenk.

"But think of it," Mocca continued, "think of what I could do. Think of what the world would be like, to be surrounded by this." He spread his hands out wide and spun in a circle, his laughter childish and whimsical. "Proof, *living* proof that there *is* a power out there that loves them and wants them to be safe, to be happy. No more children sobbing in the dark, wondering who is listening to them. No more armies marching under the orders of a god who never spoke to them. No more people tortured for a ritual that has no meaning.

"With all that I knew, and all that I've learned, I could do it. I could make Rhuul Khaas beautiful once more. Or even the entire Vhehanna Desert, from Rhuul Khaas's highest tower to Cier'Djaal's lowest slum." He turned to Lenk, his smile broad and free. "Imagine it, Lenk. I could watch over everyone, hear their every prayer, their every sorrow. The hungry man who needs bread? I can get it to him. The woman whose husband beats her? I can save her. The lovers whose families forbid them from being together? I can make them happy."

He swept up to Lenk, reached out as if to seize his hands, but stopped just short. He trembled, the lights shuddering in unison with him, going soft as he whispered.

"Can you imagine it?"

And Lenk could.

Because he had seen it. He had seen the streets filled with people, heard their prayers and laughter, smelled the scent of their sweat and labor. He knew it had existed, because Mocca had shown him. He could imagine it, he could need it, and he would have said so, loudly, if not for the voice that chuckled just behind his ear in a quavering brass note.

And spoke.

"You're not really believing this, are you?"

"Lenk!"

He blinked.

Mocca was gone. His head spun, as though the visions that had so filled his mind were leaving him empty and weightless as they flooded out of his head and left him with stark reality. The lamps still burned quietly and Shuro's form was like a black spot upon their brightness as she came running toward him.

"Where the hell have you been?" she asked, breathless from running.

"I was..." Lenk shook his head. "I thought I heard something. I went to go investigate."

"Chemoi's gone," Shuro said. "Taken by something."

"What? Are you sure?"

"I *would* be, if you had done what I told you to," she growled. "Lights just came on. Something changed in the city now that we're here. What else could it be?"

"I...I don't know." He shook his head. "Maybe she wandered off or got scared and hid somewhere?"

Shuro glared at him for a moment before snorting. "Maybe. I don't know. We'll keep an eye out for her, but she's not our priority. Something is stirring in this city. Khoth-Kapira might be waking up and he's somewhere here. We'll have to find him quickly."

"We?"

"It's too dangerous to split up now." She pointed out across the city. "We'll start on the outer streets and work our way in. Once we find signs of demonic taint, it should be easier to find him."

Taint.

Demons.

That's right, Mocca was a demon. A demon who had been cast down into hell. A demon who spoke of soothing children's tears and saving weeping women. A demon who had built a city out of nothing and made it a haven so people could live in peace.

Mocca was a demon...

Whatever that word meant now.

"Hey!"

He blinked. Without his noticing, Shuro had already started down the street. She looked at him expectantly.

"Well?"

"Sorry," he called after, and started running toward her. "Sorry."

They went off at a light jog, hurried but ready. They exchanged not a word—Lenk said nothing of Mocca, of Khoth-Kapira, of the things he had seen. How could he? Could he say anything that would change her mind? Would she simply slay him outright for even speaking of him?

Eventually she would learn. Eventually he would have to make a decision. Eventually the word *demon* would become something hard and real to him.

For now, though, silence was fine by him.

"Come to me, my fleshy friend. Come and keep me company."

If not by everyone else.

THIRTY-FIVE

WHEN BLOOD HITS THE WIND

Voices in the dark.

Fervent whispers pleading to names never spoken aloud.

Her voice, screaming his name, growing fainter until it disappeared.

Denaos could hear them, in dreams tinged red at the edges, in piece-meal choruses, in memories of echoes. They flew around his skull as it lolled on his neck, and slithered into his ears as they rang until he could hear no more.

Shadows of heads bowed and hands clasped.

Shafts of firelight painting walls red.

Blood on the sandy floor, sliding from his brow and down his face.

Denaos could see them, in eyes that swam in their sockets and in visions darkening. And even as he looked at them, they blurred as though being submerged beneath rising tides, until they were plunged into blackness.

Hands on his arms.

On his legs.

Lifting him.

Cold stone on his back. Cold iron around his wrists. Cold air on his blood as it wept from a dozen cuts and bled down his body.

Denaos could feel this as he lay on the altar, but only for a moment. Just as he could see, just as he could hear, but only for a moment. There was only enough of a human left in Denaos to experience one sense at a time. Everything else went to the pain.

A cold hand on his naked chest, gliding down. Slender fingers drummed upon tortured flesh, timid to touch the sticky rawness. He winced. Nails slid over his stomach, prodded curiously at the bruises left there from blows by knotted ropes. He groaned. A single digit found a single cut, parted the flesh like a curtain, and wedged itself inside the sticky, spongy sinew beneath.

And then he screamed.

Half-lidded eyes snapped open. Ragged breaths scratched raw at his throat. The scent of his own life, caked and stuck on his naked body, filled his nostrils. The sound of his shriek dying, smothered in the tiny room, hurt his ears.

Pain brought him back to life. Pain reminded him he was alive. Pain would not let him rest, would not let him drift into the warm blackness that reached out for him, stopping just teasingly short of embracing him.

He was alive because he had not felt enough pain.

The woman had made sure of it.

Teneir.

He recalled her name, if nothing else. He could not remember where they had taken him when they dragged him out of Mejina's house—someplace beneath the earth and dark and filled with shadows. He could not tell how long they had tortured him—days . . . or perhaps just hours, maybe. He could not remember where they had taken Anielle, what they had said to him before they drew their blades, what name he had screamed out when they cut his flesh . . .

But he recalled Teneir.

Her soft, rasping voice. Her yellow eyes. Her single finger held before his face.

"Look at this."

But that blood on her finger. That was his.

"You bleed red," she said, "the same as I do. Your flesh is soft and yielding, as is mine. If I were to take this"—Metal scraped across stone. She held up a jagged blade, wet with his life—"and plunge it here"—she held the tip over his chest—"and then here"—she moved it to her breast—"we would both be dead. As far as the knife is concerned, we are the same. And it is the knife who decides who lives and who dies. When you and I are both dead, it will not mourn for one of us any more than it does for the other."

Yellow eyes bloomed into life before him, bright suns at the center of the darkness clouding his vision. Teneir's head hovered over him, her veil hanging around a long, serpentine neck. He could only take her in in glimpses: malformed nostrils, lipless mouth, fangs glistening as she spoke.

"A knife does not care. To a knife one life is as good as the other. How odd it is, then, that a knife should be kinder than a human."

The blade traced a small path down the center of his chest, pausing to kiss fondly at the red lines it had previously carved in his flesh. He cried out, but she took no notice.

"Or a shict. Or a tulwar. Or even a saccarii," she said. "Cier'Djaal is a city of many sins. There is not a race whose life spans long enough to find the original." She let out a long sigh. "Sheffu tried. Perhaps he even came close." Her gaze drifted off to a nearby shadow and lingered there. "I wish there had been another way."

Her serpentine neck twisted about as she looked back at Denaos. If the slackness of his jaw and the glassiness of his vision caused her any alarm, she did not show it.

"Did you know him?" The groan he offered did not seem to perturb her, either. "He was a good man. A *yenthu*. One of the very last." A smile meant to be something other than unnerving split her face. "When I was young, when my father did not have a house so nice as the one I live in, I remember being visited by a *yenthu*. He told me so many stories of the saccarii, where we came from, how we survived all these years. He made me realize that I could not end up like the other saccarii, dying in the Sumps somewhere. He made me realize I had to be worthy of those stories.

"Do you know how to kill people, Jackal? Not a person, but an entire people?"

She was talking to him. Her eyes were fixated on his. They held him, those eyes, kept him from slipping away into darkness. Some animal part of him knew that to close his eyes when hers were upon him would be to invite death.

"Many have tried to kill the saccarii. Long before the Jackals ever heard the name *Khovura*. The shicts pushed us out of the forests. The tulwar pushed us out of the desert. The humans pushed us into the sea. First they killed our hunters, then they killed our soldiers, then they killed our mothers. But the saccarii did not *truly* start to die until they killed our storytellers.

"Without stories, people do not know where they came from or what they are supposed to be doing in this world. They begin to believe that they came from nowhere, go to nothing. That they are simply born, that they simply die, that they leave nothing but a rotting body. Without their own stories to tell, they begin to believe the stories *other* people tell about them."

Teneir sighed, walked to the side of the altar, and stared intently into Denaos's eyes. Her hands slowly went to the clasps of her robe and, one by one, began to undo them. The silk fell from her body, pooled around her feet, so that she stood as naked as Denaos.

But what lay beneath her clothing was not the soft flesh of a human.

What lay beneath her clothing, Denaos wouldn't have had words for even if he'd had sense to speak them.

Her skin was covered in scaly gray patches, glistening with moisture. Her limbs snaked out, fluid and jointless, like ribbons in the wind. Her breasts had withered away, disappearing back into her body. Whatever had seemed human about her before was now hidden behind a patchwork quilt of scales and stretched flesh.

"What do you see when you look upon me?" she asked, her eyes never leaving him.

He choked out a word, something he couldn't hear over the ringing in his ears. She frowned, the tips of her fangs protruding from her lips.

"The shicts looked upon us and saw beasts to be hunted. The tulwar looked upon us and saw monsters to be shunned. The humans look upon us and cannot tell the difference between a saccarii begging in the street and a pile of refuse. And without our stories to say otherwise, so many saccarii begin to believe that they are beasts, monsters, refuse...

"Sheffu knew this. The human fashas said the same things of him that they did of me. Had he not been so closed-minded, we would have been fast allies. We could have found a world without the need for the Khovura. But he spent his time chasing demons and cures. He looked upon us and saw a curse.

"Whereas I...I see strength."

She stared down at her hands, flexed each finger. They did not curl like normal fingers, but coiled into tight spirals.

"Because of this, the saccarii stand outside all races. And because of this, we can see what is happening around us. We see the rich people eat each other and throw their bones to the poor, who kill each other for scraps. We see the shicts kill the tulwar kill the humans kill the shicts. We see people bow to gods, but worship the fashas, who in turn bow to criminals like you.

"Only the saccarii can see it. Only the Khovura can stop it. Only I can end it." She closed her eyes. Her breath came out in a low hiss. "Ancaa has given me this gift to keep me on the outside, to keep me observant, to show me what I must do. And more importantly, she has shown me what I *can* do."

Teneir's eyes went wide, staring up through the stone ceiling, to some distant vision Denaos had no hope of seeing. Her voice became soft and reverent, every word sacred.

"I have seen it," she said. "No more killing each other in the name of gold or god. No more prices attached to people. No more fashas to rule us, no more thieves to steal from us, no more Cier'Djaal. What will rise up in its place will be something glorious and beautiful and Ancaa will watch over it. And all of us in it."

Her head swiveled on its serpentine neck. Her eyes narrowed to thin slits upon him, a pair of ochre blades that cut through keenly as the steel in her hands.

"You look scared, Jackal," she said. "Do you fear my appearance?"

Her neck extended, her head sliding over him. He felt the chill of her breath upon the warmth of his wounds. He felt the very small space between his naked flesh and her fangs as she leered over him.

"Or do you fear my words?" Her tongue flicked against his flesh with every word. "Do you fear the truth in them, Jackal? To know that this city bleeds and yours was the hand that twisted the knife in its back?" Her head drew back, face emblazoned with a disdainful sneer. "Or are you so vulgar as to merely fear for your life?"

Had he the breath or the sense to speak, he might have denied that.

He could not deny that it was fear that coursed inside him. The pain that wracked his body from his bruised and bleeding flesh fed that fear, made it grow fat inside him until it was something thick and wriggling inside his chest, desperate to slither up his throat. And so much of it was for himself, his broken body and his many wounds.

But more of it was for someone else.

The last word he had heard Anielle speak—or scream, rather—was his name. Over and over, an echo disappearing down a dark hole. He had been sick with pain, too much so to tell where they had taken her. But there, in the back of his head, between bursts of agony, he still heard her.

And more than afraid, he felt sick. From his fears. From the fact that Teneir was right. From not having left this all behind when he'd had the chance.

"For the saccarii, death lost its power long ago," Teneir said. "We live with the threat of it since the day we are born. The only fear I feel is for saving this city. The only fear I feel is that there are more of your kind out there." A coy smile—or a macabre mockery of one—played across her face. "But not for long."

Somehow, through the haze of agony, he knew what she was speaking of.

"I had long wondered what price the Jackals had sold their souls for," she said. "I was surprised when one of your own tried to buy it back. Surprised...and gratified. It was encouraging to see one of your kind try to atone for their sins."

"Traitor," Denaos gasped out, barely aware of the words leaving his mouth. "Rat."

"Would you call a soldier who laid down his sword when ordered to kill children a traitor?" Teneir asked. "I would not. I would call him a good person. As I call your 'rat' a good person. They saw what you were doing to this city, saw it bled dry by your crimes, saw the gold and food stolen from the hands and mouths of its hungry and poor, saw the despots you kept in power when you could have removed them.

"How long can you be surrounded by filth before the stench is unbearable, Jackal?" She leaned over him, close to his face. "And when your hands are the ones caked in filth? How long can you bear the knowledge that it spreads to everything you touch?"

"Who?" Denaos gasped. "Who?"

She smiled, sadly. "You know who."

Anielle.

Her name, a needle in his neck. The way she had tried to convince him not to go to Silktown. The look she had exchanged with Teneir. Little looks, little words, little lies said by a woman who was an expert in them. With each one he recalled, the needle dug farther into his neck, and he heard her name over and over.

Anielle. Anielle. Anielle.

No.

"Forgiveness is in the soul of Ancaa's hymns," Teneir said. "Ancaa tells us that the things we condemn a man for—his poverty, his violence— are things thrust upon him. So, too, are the crimes he commits. So, too, are the lives he takes. The Jackal came to us, repentant. And we, devout of Ancaa, forgave."

The words hit him, sank into him, drifted into his body and settled in his back like congealing blood. And he simply listened, numb.

"And such good works were done," she continued. "We stopped your crimes from extracting coin and blood from innocents. We burned the unrepentant from their dens. We...killed them." Over these last words, she hesitated briefly. "But I knew that would be necessary. A healthy body must have its tumors cut out, from time to time. If it will mean that Cier'Djaal will be great and just again, if a few must die—"

"How many?" The words tumbled out of numb lips, dribbled down his chin.

"Hm?" Teneir glanced at him. "We slew perhaps...a dozen of your criminal ilk in one den, then a dozen more in—"

"How many will you kill?"

"As many as it takes...at first. Cier'Djaal's illnesses are many. But there will come a time when the world is bloodless and there will be no need to—"

And he laughed.

It was not the right time to laugh, he knew. And judging by the scowl etched across Teneir's face, she knew this, as well. And truthfully, he could not say why he did.

Perhaps his body had simply been broken to the point where his mind followed. Perhaps, with everything in him being spent on feeling pain, this was all that was left. But in those fleeting glimpses where his sight was not quite so hazy and his breath not quite so ragged, he liked to think it was because of the great absurdity.

"No wonder you got one of us to join you," he said. "We've done this dance so many times, our feet just go before the music starts."

"You speak riddles."

"No. Silf help me, but no. You finally make sense to me now. You're just like us. You and Ancaa."

"Blasphemy."

"We did the same gods-damned thing when we made it. We were going to change things, be the *last* gang Cier'Djaal would ever need, make this city fucking work."

"You will *not* speak of Ancaa in that way."

"How the fuck do you think we got big?"

"Silence."

"You think we took a consensus? Went door to door? We cut kids' fingers off. We hung men by their necks from bridges. We cut them up and salted them and sold them by the fucking pound."

"I said *silence.*"

"And every time, *every* fucking time, we said, 'This is what we have to do, this is how we make shit work, this is it.' But it never ended. We killed people to make it big, we killed people to stay big." His laughter was hysterical shrieking smothered by the confines of the cell. "And you think you're different."

"Curb your blasphemies, you *vile* little—"

"You'll have priests instead of fashas, ushers instead of thieves, but you'll cut people apart all the same, otherwise people will start asking questions. You'll be doing just as much killing, burning, raping as we did, but you don't have the fucking balls to call it what it really—"

Laughing.

Then screaming.

Cold stone.

Then burning warmth.

Her coiling fingers were on his chest, her fingernails hooked into his skin. They raked down, carving eight deep furrows in his flesh and leaving eight red lines to blossom across his pale-pink skin. He thrashed in his bonds, screamed into the ceiling.

"You think that's it? You think the world is just that way because you say it?" Teneir tore her nails out of his chest with a spurt of blood. She shrieked to be heard over him. "You and the fashas only think that because you've always been the ones to make the rules and your rule was always blood because *you* could always spill it."

She swept to the head of the altar. She seized his hand in one bloodied grip, her knife in the other.

"But you're not the only ones who can do that. Not anymore. I will tear your world apart, piece by piece. Do you see?"

He felt the knife come down. And then he felt...nothing. An absence. A coldness of air hitting his blood.

And then blazing agony. He wiggled his big finger and felt nothing there. Nothing but sticky warmth painting his palm.

"Do you see?" she demanded.

Slower this time. The knife moving back and forth, sawing instead of slicing. A thick popping sound. Another chill, another blaze of pain, another emptiness where a finger should be.

"Do you see?"

Jabbing. A thin point working its way between two flat joints. Wedging, levering, twisting. Cold. Hot. Screaming, endlessly, each scream ripped free from his throat.

Never loud enough.

Never loud enough to not hear her.

"*Do you see, gods damn you?*" she screamed. "*Do you see?*"

Darkness.

Alive?

Breathing. Cold. Pain.

Alive.

His eyes fluttered open, after several tries. They were afraid to see where he was. When they did, he was still where he had been. It had not been a dream. It had not been hell. The altar beneath his naked body was warm now, warmed by his own flesh. The manacles around his wrists still cold. And his head burned, a fever of self-defense, his brain trying to burn out the pain.

He tried moving his right hand. Pain. And nothingness.

She had taken them.

All four of them.

Down to the first knuckle.

He wanted to cry, but no tears left. He wanted to die, but too much pain. He wanted to go back into the blackness he had just crawled out of...but no. It would not come for him now.

He lay there. And he breathed. And he choked on his words. And he listened.

Screaming.

Always screaming.

Someone was screaming down the hall. It was getting louder. Angrier. Bodies hitting the floor. Fires crackling, roaring, laughing at their screaming. He could not put the sounds together, could not make sense of them.

Not until the door burst open.

"Son of a bitch, there he is." Deep voice. Familiar. Resonant. "Don't just stand there. Get the shackles off him. There's the key, over there. Hurry, we don't know how many are left."

"Whft fbfft thg rfht?"

"I don't fucking care. Move."

Rattling of iron. Chains coming off. Someone moved his hand. He felt the emptiness again.

Someone looking down over him, white eyes in a black face, hidden by a hood. No concern visible, no face visible, but the red tip of his cigarillo still burned.

Yerk.

"Ramaniel," he said. "Are you dead?"

"No," he said. Truth.

"What did they do to you?"

"Don't know," he said. Lie.

"Rezca had you followed, thought you were up to some shit," he said. "But we didn't track you down until just now. We're in Silktown, somewhere underneath it. We didn't even know about these tunnels, Ramaniel, or we'd have been—"

"Anielle."

"What?"

"Anielle."

"What about her?"

"Where is she?" Denaos asked. "Did you find her?"

"She's . . . not here. Should she be?"

"Find her. Somewhere here . . ."

"'There is no other place, Ramaniel. There is this cell, a hallway, a storage room . . . she is not here."

Lie?

Truth.

He knew it was a truth. He had bled for it. He had screamed for it. He had nothing left to deny it with.

Anielle was the traitor.

This was all he had left to feel. All the weight of that truth, settling down on him, as Yerk pulled him off the altar, swept him over his shoulder, and carried him out.

Denaos stared down at his hand. Four red smears stared back. He wiggled them.

Funny, he thought. He could still feel them. Somewhere cold, somewhere dark, he could still feel them as he wiggled them.

Funny?

Lie.

THIRTY-SIX

THE SERPENT'S LAST MEAL

They had been a large family.

Or perhaps a family that had just had company over that night.

Or perhaps a widower who had laid his table out each night for children who had left and a wife who would never return.

Lenk didn't know. But he couldn't help wondering as he looked back
up from his journal to take in the scene before pressing charcoal to page
to continue his drawing of it.

A stone table. Not the roughhewn slabs that would make up a fortress's walls or a street's bricks, but a smooth slate polished to what had
once been a high sheen, seated upon four elegantly carved, slender legs.
Arranged upon it: seven plates, seven knives, five objects of cutlery he
did not know the purpose of, four wooden cups long rotted, one large
platter with its last meal forever remembered as a dusty stain. Around it,
seven chairs arranged neatly but for one that had been left sticking out
at an angle. That one was a small chair with high legs. Made for a child.

Lenk paused, looking at his work.

Absently he began to flip back through the other drawings he had
made that day.

A bed left unmade, a single dusty cushion upon the floor.

A shrine with prayer mats left out and mercifully spared from rot.

A fountain depicting a woman pouring water into a basin, jugs left
overturned on it.

Then he flipped the pages forward to the dining room. Then back
again. Then forward once more. Over and over.

As though he expected there to be people there the next time he
turned the page. As though he had simply forgotten to draw them.

He couldn't say why the drawings, the images of lives abruptly over, unnerved him so. He had, after all, seen an awful lot of dead bodies. But they were not scenes. They were stories. The swords fallen from their limp hands and the fragments of their shattered shields told dead men's last stories. He knew death well. He could explain a dead body.

And, morbid as it was to admit it, he would have found the city of Rhuul Khaas a thousand times more bearable had its streets been littered with skeletons and its walls painted with blood.

At least then he could have had *some* idea of what had happened. At least then he could have explained it to himself.

A bed for two people, unmade? A jug overturned at a dry fountain? A child's seat, left slightly askew at a set dinner table?

He had no idea how to explain that. Without a carcass, they were just...sentences. Fragments of a story that had happened long ago and would never be told again.

And he needed to know how it ended.

Everything Mocca had shown him—pristine streets, buildings rising to heaven, works of art on every corner—had been shown in good faith, and everywhere he went, he could see the city that he had seen in his visions.

But there were no people. No tulwar discussing philosophy with humans, no shicts haggling with tulwar.

No humans walking hand in hand with shicts.

Had they all died? Had they ever even existed?

The scenes he had drawn would not tell the tale. Mocca would not show up to confirm or deny, one way or the other. And the scarce company he had up here...

"Are you lost?"

...was proving no help at all.

"Or have you simply found something more interesting than me?"

Lenk was an adventurer. This meant that he tended to find the sort of shit that those in respectable professions—like mercenaries or mass murderers—tended to avoid. This being the case, a voice in his head—or at least very close to his ear—did not entirely shock him.

"Oh, no, I completely understand. Why seek out the speaker of an ageless voice in a long-dead city forsaken by gods and man alike when you could admire some graffiti in an alley? On the east side, there's a lovingly rendered depiction of a cock that you might find interesting."

Fuck if it wasn't annoying, though.

He resolved not to listen to it. Or to try his best. Rhuul Khaas might have seemed a city badly in need of occupancy but for the knowledge that Sheffu, Shuro, and even Mocca had confirmed. It had once housed people. Now it did not.

This city was a tomb. And Lenk knew enough to know that when something in a tomb talks, a wise man does not answer.

"*This* is what you've been doing?"

But then, wise men were rarely in tombs to begin with.

Lenk looked up. Shuro stood in the doorway, the afternoon light stark against her and painting her as a shadow. Yet her eyes burned cold as they scowled down at him.

"*Drawing?*" She swept toward him, seized his journal from his hands. "You missed our meeting time! I sent you out to find Khoth-Kapira! I thought you had been killed! And instead of either of those, I find you *drawing?*"

"I thought it might—"

He didn't finish that thought. He was already diving to catch his journal as she hurled it to the ground. When he cradled it to his chest, she was snarling at him.

"Do you not grasp what we're doing here?" she demanded, striding up to him. "Do you not understand the importance?"

Her face was a hairbreadth from his. Her breath was hot and angry upon his cheeks.

"Khoth-Kapira was the scourge of the ancient world."

Something twitched behind Lenk's ears. The sound of a wooden stick gliding along the rim of a bell. And he heard it.

"*Lie.*"

"He held thrall over *thousands*, slavishly devoted to him!" Shuro continued.

And the voice answered.

"*Lie.*"

"He was—no, *is*—the most dangerous creature in *two* worlds."

A pause.

"*True.*"

"We are here to stop him. We *cannot* fail at this."

A laugh. "*Lie.*"

"You and I, we are the only ones who can."

"*Possible.*"

"So I need you to answer me." She looked at him, intensity flaring in her eyes. "Are you with me, Lenk?"

It was only after several breaths had passed that Lenk realized he was waiting for the other voice. But it wasn't coming. Dumbly he nodded. She relaxed, though not by much, and nodded back to him. Turning sharply, hand on her sword, she swept to the door, pausing there. After a moment she spoke, without looking over her shoulder.

"You're very good at that," she said. "Drawing, I mean."

And she was gone.

And though there were a number of things askew in what had just happened, Lenk had only enough sense for one of them. And, from the faint chuckling just behind his ear, he knew which one.

"*I sense as though I've caught your attention, my honored guest.*" A low, reverberating hum. "*I can hear your pulse quicken, your breath grow shorter. Expected. Though I quite wonder why you didn't show such reaction earlier.*"

Lenk swallowed hard, quickly replaced his journal in his pack, and hurried to catch up with Shuro. She was walking down one of Rhuul Khaas's streets—not at all different from dozens of others they had searched through the night and the morning in the hunt for Khoth-Kapira.

Undeterred, she was already explaining her plan for expanding her search.

Or so he assumed.

It wasn't as if he could hear her at that moment.

"*Or should I wonder at all? You are here, after all, the grave of the God-King. No one finds this place who does not already know where it is. If you are here, you are a man used to poor decisions and frequent laments. Am I right?*"

He didn't answer. The voice chuckled regardless.

"*A stop in pulse. Your heart's beat slowed by a fraction. Typical behavior of those who keep secrets. Do not worry, my friend. Even if I were in a position to stop you, I would not.*"

Shuro paused at the center of a great square. Lenk found his gaze drawn inexorably down a darkened alley between two looming buildings.

"Unless," the voice said, *"you've not come to slay Khoth-Kapira?"*

Pulse quickened. As did breath. As did heart. He did not need the voice to tell him that.

"She is quite correct," it continued. *"He was brilliant, of course. Brilliant, beautiful, and tragic. But above all else, he was dangerous. Yet if you've come here with nothing but steel to kill him, you'll fail."*

He looked to Shuro. She was pointing to various locations, deciding where to go next. She looked at him for approval, he nodded without understanding. She smiled.

"Do you wish to fail?"

His pulse answered.

"Seek me out."

He looked to Shuro. She looked back. There was something sad and warm on her face, a smile that was alien to eyes such as she had—such as they both had. She placed a hand on his shoulder, nodded at him, and turned and departed.

And something in him dearly wished he had listened when she'd spoken.

But that something was drowned out by the sound of beating heart and quickening pulse, of desperate breath and trickling sweat. And the voice. Always the voice.

"Seek me out."

He did.

Shuro had doubtless told him to spread out and search and meet up elsewhere. And when he didn't show up, she would doubtless come and find him. He was not worried about seeing her again. Lenk and dangerous women had a habit of finding one another inadvertently.

People in his profession had to spend their worries carefully; there were, after all, an awful lot of things out there deserving of it. And as Lenk went down the street opposite the direction in which Shuro had left, his worries were reserved for something more subtle.

Such as the inexorable feeling looming over him: an unseen hand reaching out from the dark shadows of an alley and seizing him by the collar of his shirt.

He did not resist, turning and following it into the alley. He did not resist as it continued to tug on him—weightless, insubstantial, impossible—and he continued to follow it. But as he turned down streets, up stairs, through alleys, and over bridges spanning dried creeks, the sensation turned from that of a draw to that of a pursuit.

Less and less he felt fingers around his shirt, the tug of a desperate grip. More and more he felt weight upon his shoulders, a cold breath down his neck. And as he walked, that breath grew. It became eyes upon him, teeth around his neck, a hand reaching out to touch his shoulder.

In the space between the moments when compulsion turned to dread, he knew he should turn back. But by that point turning back meant turning around. And turning around meant seeing what was at his back.

And that was impossible.

That sensation chased him through the city of Rhuul Khaas and all its silent ghosts until it brought him to a building.

A library, perhaps. Maybe a temple. While no building in Rhuul Khaas was specifically lavish, a few, like this one, rose up on small hills that had been carved into stone steps. Some, like this one, had pillars that marched to the left and right of their entrances. And each of a select few had a spiraling tower that rose high into the sky, just like this one.

But while Lenk had not explored the entirety of Rhuul Khaas, he had not yet seen a building with blood smeared across the door.

It was tall. It was metal. It wore a large red cross that stretched over its face and onto the bricks of the building's doorframe.

Lenk stared at it, considered turning around. And in answer to his thoughts, he felt that unseen presence bearing down on him, as if nudging him forward. He drew a breath, reached out, took the door by its handle.

"Ah."

He paused. The voice spoke in his ear.

"Gently, please. The door is rarely opened and makes a dreadful racket."

If there were a sign he should not open the door, that was it.

And if he had not heeded any of the thousands of other signs he should not be here, he saw little argument for heeding this one.

No matter how gently he pulled, the door did not so much groan as scream. The hinges wailed, the metal shed rusted flakes, and the whole thing felt as though it might simply fall off and crush him beneath it.

He had to use both hands, he had to dig in his feet and grit his teeth, but the door opened.

And the echo of its scream was swallowed in the blackness that sprawled before him.

He stood for a moment, staring into it. And it spoke.

"Do come in."

It spoke from within the darkness. Not next to his ear. Its voice quavered and reverberated like a tolling bell, echoing from within.

"You're letting in a draft."

And from very close.

He entered the room. His footsteps echoed in a vast space. There were no windows. There were no other doors. There was no light. Even the sunlight from the door behind him seemed hesitant to follow him in. He could see nothing to either side or dead ahead of him.

Save one thing.

There, maybe two hundred paces ahead of him, was something stark in the darkness. Brightly polished copper gleamed, even without light to reflect. At two hundred paces he thought it was a door. At one hundred he thought it was a mirror. But at twenty he could see it was a face.

And it saw him.

Its expression was neutral, its features beautiful. It possessed high cheekbones, thin lips, an elegant nose and sculpted brows. But its eyes were black and empty, like a mask's, and they stared down at Lenk from high off the ground.

"Ah." So close, he felt its voice in his bones. Yet this close, it sounded distinctly male. "I am not sure what I was expecting. But I am not surprised that you are one of them."

"One of what?" Lenk was suddenly aware how very soft his own voice sounded in the reverberation of this creature's.

"There are no true names for you," he said. "No god would deign to give you one." Though its metal face was unchanging, Lenk had the distinct feeling that it was smiling at him. "We knew your kind only by your blades and your eyes. In those latter days, that was all we saw of you before everything went dark."

Lenk felt his breath go cold at that. He opted not to ask the creature to elaborate.

"And what do I call you?" he asked instead.

"Oh, where to start?" The creature gave a deep, weary sigh that sounded like porcelain cracking. "It seems the longer you live, the more names you get. The worshipful call you one thing, the defiant call you another, sooner or later you forget what they called you before you came down to the mud." He looked up, past the ceiling and into heaven. "When I was up there, I seemed to have no need for one."

Lenk blinked as the realization hit him. "Aeon. You're an Aeon."

"That's not what we called ourselves, certainly," he said. "But it will serve. I was one of two cast down—" He paused, considering. "Pardon me, *sent* down. We were summoned and bade to attend to the needs of our master." His black eyes gazed thoughtfully at Lenk. "The one you have come to slay."

"Khoth-Kapira."

"We called him something else."

"What was that?"

"It was…not important." The Aeon shook his head. "Not at first, anyway. Names only started to matter once he wanted everyone to know what he had done. In the beginning, building was what was most important.

"He began with the fields, teaching them how to farm. He moved on to their homes, teaching them how to build. He learned of their bodies, taught them how to clean their needles and repair themselves. He was obsessed with creation and viewed every invention as something to be infinitely proud of."

"I can't blame him," Lenk said. "I've seen Rhuul Khaas. It's incredible."

"Rhuul Khaas was important to him, yes. But Rhuul Khaas was just a name. In those early days, he was driven simply by the urge to create. And we watched him do it, Kyrael and I."

"Kyrael." Lenk tasted the name, found it sharp and unpleasant in his mouth. "So you did have names."

"After a time. We were offered them. Rewards for our faith in him." There was a lengthy pause, the slow breath of an old man before he slides into darkness. "I remember the day he gave me mine. I remember the honor that came with it. How I loved it." The Aeon spoke, softer. "As much as I loved him."

Lenk stared at the mask. "What did he call you?"

It happened softly, as softly as his voice. Within the voids of his eyes, two pinpricks of white blossomed.

"My name . . . the old tongue . . ."

And grew.

"My name was Oerboros."

Until it was bright as the sun.

"And I was *light*."

Lenk shielded his eyes with his arm, turned away from it. It was no mortal light that burst from Oerboros's eyes, no merciful sun or shy moon. This was a judging light, a light made for seeking black sins and iron truths. It burned, never enough to be truly painful, but enough for Lenk to know that it went past the skin and saw something deeper within him. When he lowered his arms, he was not sure what he was expecting.

But there it was.

Wings. Bright and glittering emerald scales that shimmered beneath Oerboros's light. Ivory feathers that wafted gently in a breeze that wasn't there. Neither reptilian nor avian, they were . . . something Lenk had never seen before. They filled the whole room, each one several times the size of Oerboros's body, stretching wide to cover the vast walls, forming a shell of green and white that twitched and shuddered at this new light. Majestic. Brilliant. Lenk had no words to describe them.

Nor did he have words to describe the body they were attached to.

It had once been beautiful, Lenk could tell: shapely muscle beneath stretched skin the color of polished copper, not quite masculine, not quite feminine, not even androgynous, but something completely its own.

The ruin of his body was a stark contrast to the glory of his wings. His skin was dull and tarnished with age. His muscles had withered and sagged beneath flaccid flesh. He hung, emaciated and weak, from the wall. Six long spears jutted from his chest, his arms, his legs, his neck, pinning him to the stone.

"You are staring, mortal."

Lenk blinked, looked up. "Well, yeah . . . I mean, you're kind of fucked up."

He stared at the ragged breaths the creature took, at the wounds that still bled glistening blood, at the skin that could not close around the spear hafts impaling him.

"I suppose that is my fault," the Aeon said. "Forgive me. I could not control myself. It has been so long since I have spoken my own name." His voice turned dark for a moment. "Or his."

"What...what happened?"

"To me?" Oerboros's chuckle was a harsh thing to hear. "To Kyrael? To *him*? To Rhuul Khaas?" He shook his head. "They are the same tale. If you are here, perhaps you've heard part of it already. We Aeons, shepherds of mortals, were sent to witness, to protect, to guide..."

"And you grew greedy," Lenk said, "corrupt, envious of gods and mortals alike. You exploited us, enslaved us, persecuted us..."

"And you struck back," Oerboros said. "While I may argue what led to it, the final sentence in that story is that the mortal armies came and overthrew us, cast us down into the darkness below. Most of us, anyway. Some of us they merely left to rot."

"But that doesn't make sense," Lenk said. "If there were armies, there should have been a battle, shouldn't there? But I've not seen a body here, not so much as a bloodstain until I found you. You expect me to believe they came, did *this* to you, and nothing else?"

"Ah, mortals. So obsessed with flesh. You don't believe anything exists until you destroy it. I am certain there would have been more bodies, had Kyrael not intervened. Her love for our master was as deep and devoted as my own. As was that of all his subjects, those citizens of Rhuul Khaas whom she saved.

"When they had cast down Ulbecetonth, Goraccus, and the others, the mortal armies came for Rhuul Khaas. Our master retreated to his study, to contemplate his defenses. He had expended so much of himself in his creations, his buildings, his legacies, that he would kill thousands before he let a single one of them come to harm.

"It was that love for his people," Oerboros said, sadness in his voice, "that desperation to preserve them, that drove Kyrael to do what she did. Acting in his interests, she opened our defenses to the mortal armies, permitted them to evacuate the city. She thought that the sparing of his citizens would earn his affection."

Oerboros paused. When he spoke again, his voice shook.

"Of my many regrets, of all my failures, I wish above all else I could have helped her."

"Then what happened?" Lenk asked. "The mortal armies came and it simply . . . ended? Without a fight?"

"It was not a fight. No. The master was furious. By the time he had visited punishment upon Kyrael, he had no time but to command me to guard this, his most precious chamber, before he retired to his study with his most trusted Disciples."

The demons, Lenk realized. *Those snake-things in Cier'Djaal.*

"It was your breed that led them. Your eyes sparkled in the night as they marched upon his study. He could not resist them. His Disciples were killed and packed in salt, thrown into darkness with him. They found me a little later, while they searched for heretical doctrines to burn. They destroyed much of this city, but I held firm to my promise." He laughed, blackly. "Even when their spears pierced my flesh, I held firm. I did not let them past me. I did exactly as he asked me, and my love for him has given me centuries of unending agony."

"Then why tell me this?" Lenk asked.

Oerboros looked at him. The light from within his eyes dimmed slightly.

"Love is a curse, mortal," he said. "It serves no mortal function, aids in no survival. It is the last word of a black joke told by an ill-humored creator. Time is the only truth. And with time I have seen the folly of my love, felt it with every breath I've taken.

"My master was brilliant. But above all else he was obsessed. Try as he might to create, he could not do the work of the heavens. And it drove him mad. So mad that he would throw away everything, we who loved him and treasured him, in the name of preserving his legacy. He knew he would return someday, but he spoke only of finishing his work, of completing his worlds. Not once did he care what happened to Kyrael and me."

"So you're telling me this . . . out of spite?" Lenk asked.

"Partially. And partially because I know he has been speaking to you. I have heard his voice, heard the tales he's told you. He was always fond of storytelling. And like all good storytellers . . ."

Oerboros's wings quivered. And slowly they began to retract.

"He never tells you the best part."

With a long, breathless groan, Oerboros drew back his wings. Dust fell from his feathers. His scales creaked like metal. And as they folded up against the Aeon's body, Lenk could see what he had been guarding.

Books. Vast shelves of them. Stacks on the floor, towering so high as to be monuments. Empty inkwells and ravaged quills. These had all been penned by the same hand, the same mind.

"The Library of the Learned," Lenk whispered.

Funny, he had been expecting something more ominous: black tomes in cages, profane verse scrawled on the walls. This looked more like the study of a frazzled mind. And nowhere was it more obvious than on the walls.

Parchments. Paintings. Prints, drawings, essays. From floor to ceiling, the walls of the chamber were filthy with paper. Sketches of anatomies of creatures known and unknown, lengthy studies written in a language long dead, designs for devices whose engineering Lenk could not even begin to fathom; there was not a spot of bare stone to be seen among all the papers pinned to the wall.

Most of it Lenk did not recognize. But some of it...

"I've seen this before." He peered at a detailed drawing of a creature: a titanic body upon four trunk-like legs, its head thick and heavy with two black eyes and several sprawling tendrils that hung down to its feet. "The Old Man. This is the creature we rode to the Forbidden East. And this!"

He pointed to another drawing nearby, depicting a spiderlike creature with thick, vine-like growths covering it. It was the thing that had carried Shuro, Chemoi, and him up the mountain's face. The creature, its cradle, and its landing apparatus were all drawn in meticulous detail.

"We rode this thing up the mountain," Lenk said.

"Creatures of his design," Oerboros interrupted. "My master's subjects were vast and his location isolated. He required immense muscle to move people and supplies to Rhuul Khaas. While beasts of burden might fail, plants could sustain themselves."

"So the Old Man *was* a plant. The spider, too?"

"Indeed. An elegant design, really. The plant was the product of careful breeding, a vine that would aggressively grow around the skeleton of a long-dead beast and form the foundation of its body. From then it could be controlled with simple commands, set on routine paths that would allow it to cart things from the desert into the mountains."

"Incredible."

"No. *Incredible* would have been an adequate description after his third creation. By the time he created his plants, words ceased to be sufficient to describe his brilliance."

"Nothing about this makes sense." Lenk shook his head. "He's a demon, a creature who only understands pain and sorrow. I've fought them, killed them, know they're vicious." He looked up to the pinned Aeon. "But this isn't the work of a demon." He threw his arms wide. "Rhuul Khaas is not the work of a demon. It's the work of a genius."

"Genius is a measure of mind, not of heart," Oerboros replied. "And my master was but one mind. Many bodies were required to build his artifices, many pounds of flesh were weighed to further his knowledge."

"But his subjects stayed, didn't they? Whatever he did to them, they didn't leave."

"They didn't know they could. Nor did Kyrael. Nor did I."

"But you're a—"

"I am Oerboros. And Oerboros did not once think to leave. Not even when the first spear pierced my flesh."

"I don't understand." Lenk rubbed his eyes. "You speak with two mouths. Sometimes you talk about him as though you couldn't live without him, sometimes you talk about him like you could kill him. Which is it? Is he a monster or a miracle?"

"There is no exclusivity between the two words. What you see here is the extent of his mortal knowledge. These were both the utmost and the barest of his designs. He had accomplished so much . . . yet it was not enough. When machines and drawings could no longer satisfy him, he turned his attentions toward creation. *True* creation.

"That was when he ceased to be the master I knew, the master I loved."

There was another groan as Oerboros raised his withered legs. Bones popped and creaked beneath the sagging flesh. But behind them another door loomed.

"But perhaps you should see for yourself."

Lenk spared a queer look for the wrought iron of the door, and a queerer look for the impaled being above it. But just as soon as he started to feel doubt, he felt something stronger. That sensation of something bearing down on him, of a presence looming behind him, returned, and the decision was no longer his.

He hurried to the door, forced it open with a grunt and a groan. A small circular chamber opened up before him, with a spiraling staircase leading both up and down. Likely, he suspected, the upper staircase led to the tower he had seen rising out of this building. But below…

"Your answers dwell," Oerboros said, "in the darkness."

"Of course," Lenk muttered.

The stone of the staircase was clean, sturdy, remarkably untouched by age. Great care had gone into its creation, it seemed. It was certainly not the construction that gave him a creeping sense of unease.

That he attributed to the stench.

It began faintly, a small shudder of foulness in the otherwise tranquil air. But with each step it grew stronger. The air stagnated, growing foul and acrid, at once the wallowing reek of rotted filth untouched for years and the seething stink of acid gnawing on bones.

By the time Lenk had discovered the chamber, it was almost enough to drive him to his knees.

He covered his mouth and walked into a vast space, as large as the chamber above had been. But here there was scarcely any light, the sole source of illumination being a flickering globe fixed to the ceiling, not unlike those of the lamps he had seen on the streets above. This one's light sputtered and dimmed, offering only the barest hints of a glow.

And by it he could only barely see the pit.

Ten paces farther and he would have fallen in. A well-carved, perfectly square pit dominated the room, reaching from wall to wall, with a path that was little more than a ledge big enough for one person adorning the wall Lenk had just emerged from. But spanning the pit was a stone walkway, sturdily built and free of decay.

Lenk approached it, trying to ignore the steadily growing stench. He walked across it, biting back vomit. And after a long moment of trying to find the courage to do so, he looked over the edge.

At first he saw nothing but glimmers of reflected light across a liquid surface. Water? No, it smelled far too terrible for that. It moved sluggishly, thickly, like a stew.

Of all the things Lenk could have been feeling, he wouldn't have thought he'd feel disappointment. Yet being sent into a dank chamber by a forever-dying creature from heaven just to look at a hole full of smelly fluid seemed somehow . . . anticlimactic.

And Lenk would have walked away feeling just that.

Had the fluid not suddenly looked back at him.

Two eyes flashed in the darkness, ochre tinged with red. A face leered out of the fluid, a coarse mockery of a man's. There were two thin slits where a nose should have been, a face covered in thick patches of scales, bereft of hair or eyebrows. And when it opened its mouth, its jaw gaped wide to reveal long fangs as it looked to Lenk.

And screamed.

Soon it was joined. Dozens more eyes blooming in the darkness. Dozens more mouths opening in agonized wailing. Arms emerged, glistening with fluid and reaching clawed hands toward him. Serpentine coils twisted in the water, cresting backs and tails flicking out. They crawled over each other, these abominations, in a desperate attempt to reach out for Lenk.

And through his horror he realized that no two of them were alike. Some had one arm, some had none, some had four. Some three eyes. Others had mouths that stretched impossibly wide. Many had legs that ended in coiling tendrils. Some had tufts of hair growing out of them. Some had scales, some had glistening flesh.

The only thing that united them was the pain, the terror, the desperation to be heard that was etched across their faces and written in the stagnant air by their screams.

And at the sight of them and all their twisting, writhing, shrieking, all Lenk could do was scream back.

"*Gods.*" He fell to his rear end, screamed as one hand slipped and dangled over the edge. The barest tip of a scaly appendage reached out and brushed his fingers. He pulled it back, crawling to the center of the walkway and huddling into a fetal position. "Fuck, fuck, fuck, *fuck.* They're fucking—"

"Saccarii."

A voice. A white shape in the darkness. A dark face with a dark frown. Mocca.

"Or what I had hoped would be saccarii." The man in white's voice was a wistful sigh. He stood at the edge of the walkway, staring down at the abominations writhing below. "Sadly, I never got them quite right."

"What the fuck do you mean 'quite right'?" Lenk stared at Mocca, mouth agog. "You *made* those things?"

"I tried," Mocca replied. "Gods know I tried. Years I spent designing them, drawing them, perfecting them. I ran through every formula, every calculation, every variable. In my mind they were perfect. But when I actually tried to give them life…"

He held his hands out helplessly over the pit. The misbegotten creatures below reached back and wailed.

"What the fuck are they?" Lenk asked. "Those aren't saccarii."

"Not as you know them, no. Those saccarii you see in Cier'Djaal today were the closest I had come to perfection. When the mortal armies came, they escaped and found their way down to the wild, where they spread. Peculiarly enough, they were one of my more simple designs." He stared down into the pit and sighed at the writhing, gnashing accord below. "The rest of them, the…flawed ones, were left here to rot. They never could, of course. My blood kept them alive."

"That's your *blood* down there?"

"It was the agent that permitted them to change. Even my Disciples carry it." His gaze grew deep as he looked at the creatures below. "Their minds were never fully developed. But even then they could recognize concepts of closeness, of tenderness. I visited them often. When I was cast down, I could still hear them, trapped in their pit, crying out for their creator. I heard those cries become maddened as they wallowed and their minds turned to dust. They always were such delicate creatures."

He glanced at Lenk. "Though I'm sure you've noticed that spending so much time away from me has caused most of them to start reverting."

Memories flashed through Lenk's mind: images of the saccarii and their scaly flesh, of Sheffu's arm fused to his side, of their ochre eyes and the long hisses of their language.

"Reverting to *what*?"

"Originally they began as serpents. I found the form elegant in its simplicity, something basic upon which I could build. From there I could expand their function."

"To *what*?"

Mocca cast a smile at him, something soft and sad. "It was going to be perfect. The craft that went into them allowed for expert malleability. I could shape their form to whatever was needed: extra arms and increased strength for physical labor, additional eyes for surveillance, enhanced intellect, whatever was needed."

"You were making a slave race."

"No. *No*." Mocca's eyes flashed in the darkness. He whirled on Lenk, anger etched on his face. "You don't understand. You're *just* like them. They never understood that I could do it better, that I could *perfect* them and..."

As the horror on Lenk's face deepened, Mocca trailed off. He let out a short breath and regained his composure, though his ire remained plain.

"Rhuul Khaas could not subsist on goodwill alone. It needed labor, law, guardianship. That had to come from somewhere."

"Oerboros said it came from your people. He said you sacrificed them to further your knowledge."

Mocca looked away. "Oerboros was always gifted with a rather frustratingly apt perception."

"Then it's true. It's fucking *true*." Lenk staggered to his feet, though he found his legs shaky beneath him. "All that you showed me, all those people, all those wonders—"

"They exist," Mocca interrupted, waving a hand. "You've seen them for yourself. I was not lying. I merely find myself reluctant to dwell on the cost that they commanded. I did not wish those who adored me to bear the pain of progress. The saccarii were intended to be a way to offset that. Not a race of slaves, but of martyrs, the noble chosen who could bear the burden of civilization more efficiently than any human, shict, or tulwar. But no one else could see the *purpose*, let alone what it took to create—"

The man in white's hands trembled. He shut his eyes, clenched his jaw. Slowly he exhaled.

"My penance began long before I was cast down, Lenk. I saw a world of mud and ashes, people rutting in filth and gnawing on bones, and I sought to solve it. In my haste, my pride, my...my *need* to do it better, I..." He rubbed at his eyes. "I made mistakes, Lenk. Mistakes I have had lifetimes to contemplate.

"But just as the saccarii have begun to collapse without me, so has the world." Mocca swept an arm out in a vague direction. "You've seen it yourself. You've seen the wars, the strife, the great famines of kindness that mortalkind insists on inflicting upon itself. I sacrificed much to learn, to build, to create, yes. But they sacrifice more and build nothing but bigger graveyards. I can fix them, Lenk. I can *fix* this."

"I...how?" Lenk shook his head. "How is it progress if it needs people to die all the damn time? How the fuck does that fix anything?" He looked to Mocca, alarm in his eyes. "If you came back, who would you kill?"

"I would try not to."

"You don't 'try' not to kill people. You either do it or you don't."

"No, Lenk. I am not vengeful."

Above the screaming from the pit, above the bile rising in his throat, above the soft words of Mocca, Lenk could hear it. The tinkling of a bell. A solitary giggle right behind his ear.

"*Don't tell me you believe him,*" Oerboros whispered from somewhere else.

"I...I don't know."

"Oerboros," Mocca hissed, clearly having heard it. "Don't listen to him, Lenk. His mind is as twisted as theirs. In his long years as—"

"*A race of martyrs. Ha. He created the saccarii merely because he couldn't stand the idea of something being beyond him.*"

"Silence," Mocca snarled.

"*Of course they came out as abominations. Creation cannot simply occur from formula and design. Even his blood couldn't sustain them. All his powers of fleshcrafting and they still crumble without him.*"

"Oerboros, I *command* you to—"

"*Oh, do be quiet, old man,*" Oerboros whispered. "*Mortal, you seem inquisitive. Perhaps you should ask him what happened to Kyrael.*"

"Kyrael..." Lenk looked at Mocca. "There were two of them. Oerboros and—"

"Kyrael betrayed me," Mocca said. "I was grief-stricken. I was angered. I did things I—"

"*He doesn't seem keen to answer you. Pity. Perhaps you should see for yourself?*"

"Lenk, do *not* listen to him."

"*Top of the tower. Look east, to the reservoir.*"

Lenk looked long at Mocca. Mocca looked back at Lenk, helpless. And Lenk was running.

"Lenk, *wait*!"

He did not wait. He did not listen. He ran from the room, back up the spiral staircase, past the chamber where he had found Oerboros, and up until he could smell clean air again. He burst from a hole into a small observatory at the top of the tower, and there he looked long to the east.

Before he even saw it, he felt it. That desperate, eerie presence. That breathing down his neck, that anger and hatred that reached out and seized him and forced him to look.

There in the distance, at the edge of the city, was a massive pool of water. A reservoir surrounded by a great pillar at every cardinal direction. From their peaks extended long chains that all met in a central point above the center of the water. And from them dangled...

"Khetashe," Lenk gasped as he saw it.

An Aeon. Like Oerboros. Nearly genderless, naked and withered and hanging from her ankles. Long blue wings drooped low. But even from this great distance, Lenk could see their brilliant luster, as he could see the silver mask that was her face. And stark against her faded perfection, an ugly red gash.

Her throat was open, blood flowing freely from a severed jugular. Yet she was still alive. Lenk could feel it, feel her breath, feel her pain, feel her choked, agonized pleas. She was alive. She was bleeding.

As she had been for centuries.

"Kyrael," Lenk whispered.

"We do not die, mortal. We feel pain, but never do we collapse from it. Kyrael's blood has filled this reservoir for centuries, tainting the water that flows beneath the city, out the mountain and into the river. You yourself have likely tasted her, at some point."

"Mocca... Khoth-Kapira did this?"

"All because she tried to help. All because she loved him, as we did. He could not bear to be helped. He could not bear to have someone presume to act outside his wishes."

"But he said—"

"Didn't he just? He said those words back then, too. And we believed him. Look at us now, Lenk. Or if you don't wish to... look to your friend."

He glanced down to the city and he immediately saw her.

Shuro's dark form was rushing down a street, her blade flashing and bloodied. Behind her followed several more shapes. Great, misshapen creatures with bulging limbs, lolling heads, gaping jaws. Their howls carried through the air, he could hear their hunger for her blood from here.

And once again he was running.

THIRTY-SEVEN

WOODEN SMILE, HOLLOW EYES

"Do you have yijis in the Silesrian?" the rider asked.

She gave no answer.

"No, I guess you wouldn't. They probably don't like the cold. Do you ride anything out there?"

She gave no answer.

"I guess that's also a silly question. I've never been there, but I've heard the trees grow so close together that only squirrels and shicts can get through them. I guess you can't use a squirrel as a mount, huh?"

There was a nervous laugh. But not from her.

"My mother saw its borders once. She went there to meet the tribes of the north. She told me about the trees. Did yours ever tell you any stories of our desert?"

She gave no answer.

"My mother taught me many things. She taught me how to ride a yiji. They have a weird gait to them, see? Their backs are crested, like a wave, so each step they take makes them snap like one. They're like to throw you right off if you don't have something to hold on to."

A long moment of silence passed.

"The backs make them hard to find saddles for, too."

Another long moment.

"Would you just hold on to me already?"

And finally she gave an answer.

"Do you remember what I said?"

"When?"

"Nights ago. At the *Kho Khun*. Do you remember what I said?"

"... Yes. I do."

"What did I say?"

"You told me not to touch you."

"Do you think I didn't mean it?"

And now the rider gave no answer.

━━◆━━

Kataria did not dream often, of late.

Her body was always too weary from riding day and night. Her mind was always too taxed with desperation to reach Cier'Djaal in time.

When she did dream, she dreamed only in noises, in wordless howls and formless snarls. She did not dream of freedom, or of home, or of her mother. Or even of Lenk.

She dreamed of *her*.

Which, she reasoned as her eyelids began to flutter open, was likely why she continually woke up angry.

Then again, that might also just be the pain.

Her mind awoke before her body did, recognizing the orange glow of sunset through half-lidded eyes. Once she opened them just a hair wider, her muscles began to protest. She was aching and sore from too much riding and not enough food, and every sunset was heralded first by heat and next by agony. Her wounds had yet to heal properly and her ankle and wrists were still raw.

It was not healthy, she knew. She could not afford to ride like this much longer. But she could afford even less to wait to recover.

Shekune could have already covered half the desert by now. She had to keep going. In her mind she knew this.

In her body, though?

She tried to rise. Her muscles groaned at first. Then screamed outright when it was clear she was not going to be deterred. She pushed herself all the way up to her rear before giving up and collapsing down onto her back. Breathing heavily, she shut her eyes.

Traveling through the desert by day was not as efficient as doing so by night. It was only just now sunset. Surely, they would not start riding until later. Surely, she could spend just a *little* more time lying here.

This all seemed like a fine idea until she felt something prickle across her skin.

Something soft, fleeting, and sensual crept across her belly, like fingers sliding up her stomach and toward her chest.

Instantly pain was replaced by anger. Instantly her teeth were clenched in a snarl.

"What the *fuck* did I tell you?"

Her hand shot down to seize the offending fingers. Instead of dark skin, though, she found something hairy and writhing in her grip. She sat up, squinted through the sun's glare at the hairy tarantula that wriggled about in her hand.

"Ah," she said. "Sorry about that." She glanced around the small clearing where they had made camp until she found a small, bulging pouch right where she had left it. "Sorry about this, too."

She loosened the pouch's drawstrings. Within, the dozen or so other tarantulas made a futile break for freedom before she tossed this newest one in and cinched it tight again. She had felt bad about it, at first—but the damn things got everywhere. And if they didn't want to end up in a pouch, they shouldn't keep crawling over her.

This seemed a reasonable penance to her.

Despite her protesting body, she rose to her feet and looked around. Nestled between two dunes that provided adequate shade, the little oasis—scarcely more than a stubborn tree and some scrubgrass surrounding a resilient pond—provided some semblance of solitude. All that remained here besides her and her few supplies was the pack of six yijis lounging by the waterside.

As she stirred they looked up at her, but quickly lost interest and returned to lapping at the water.

They were what she had been told were referred to as "*tama'shi*" or "painted." Only half-domesticated, these yijis were turned loose in the desert to roam in packs. While they hadn't lost their instinct to hunt and wander, the khoshicts had trained them to accept riders who approached them correctly. In this way the *tama'shi*—so named for the painted bands around their forelegs—could serve as mounts that simply wandered the desert and waited for riders, usually congregating at oases like this.

The humans of the Vhehanna, she had been told, spoke in hushed whispers of khoshict hunters who could pursue their prey day and night without their mounts ever tiring. In truth they simply changed mounts frequently, just as she had done to cross the desert so swiftly.

There was much, she admitted, to be admired about the khoshicts.

"Hey!"

And much more to be loathed.

She looked up the southern dune and saw Kwar there, standing atop the ledge. She was painted dark against the setting sun, so the intensity in her eyes was all the more apparent. Kataria's ears twitched, hearing the faintest sounds of her Howling and the urgency it carried.

"We've got trouble," Kwar said.

"Shekune?"

The khoshict shook her head.

"Round-eared trouble."

⚊ ✦ ⚊

Silence.

For a long time, silence. So deep that it hurt when words were spoken.

"I'm sorry."

Words like those—not true words, not strong words.

"I'm sorry."

Those were weak words. Words that needed breath and tongue and lips to speak. Words that had been uttered so many times in so many days.

"I'm sorry."

She had not responded to those.

She had tired of hearing them.

Why she had responded to these, she didn't know.

"I know."

The words had felt weak, flimsy in her mouth.

"If you know, then why won't you talk to me?"

"Because you don't get that."

"Get what?"

"You think *sorry* is an arrow. You think you can shoot it and then it lands and that's that. But it's just a word."

"I came with you, didn't I? I took you through the desert. I'm going against Shekune, my own people, for you."

"Our people. Do it for them, not me."

"What do you want from me?"

"Nothing. I don't want anything."

"But I—"

"Except silence."

And for a time, it had seemed as if she might get it.

But time was something she never had enough of.

"I was scared."

She had made no reply.

"I was scared that you would leave me. I was scared that I would be alone."

"I don't care that—"

"I'm not saying this for you. Not all for you, anyway. I just...I need someone to know. I didn't want to be alone. I didn't want you to go off with him. I didn't...I'm sorry."

A longer silence.

"Do you expect me to forgive you?"

"No."

A colder silence.

⊷ ⸎ ⊷

"Funny," Kwar muttered, "from up here, they look kind of like us, don't they?" She cast a sidelong look at Kataria, eyes drifting over her pale flesh. "Well, like me, anyway."

Kataria spared a glare for that before glancing down the slope of the dune to the road below. Night had fallen quickly, and by the time they had arrived at the well-worn road that wended its way to Cier'Djaal, it was too dark to see except by the torches below.

From here, Kataria thought, they did not look much like shicts. Their skin might have been dark, they might have walked on two legs, but that was where the similarities ended. They walked too stiffly, their movements uneasy and rehearsed, and they stumbled over any terrain that hadn't been worn flat by all the feet that had come before theirs.

Humans did not remind her much of shicts.

And Karnerians did not remind her much of humans.

Clad in black armor, their dark skin glistening by the light of the tall torches they'd staked into the ground, they looked less like humans and more like suits of armor that had spontaneously begun to move. They clenched spears and shields tightly. They patrolled up and down the road in precisely timed movements. They swept their eyes over the horizon, searching for enemies.

What they expected to see, Kataria did not know. But she could guess.

A long train of wagons made its way along the road, drawn by oxen and mules. Though for now it had ground to a halt and soldiers tended to the beasts and cargo. She saw crates of supplies: weapons, oil, food, and other matériel. Every fourth wagon was a wheeled platform carrying an enormous barrel from which the soldiers drew water from a spigot.

Reinforcements. Headed for Cier'Djaal. By the rate at which the soldiers were drinking from their mobile reservoirs, she suspected that they had been marching all day, keen to get to the city. Perhaps their war with the Sainites was not going well. Or perhaps they were on the verge of crushing them.

Either scenario did not bode well for the shicts. Shekune would meet far more resistance than she was anticipating, no matter what her plan was. All the more reason to hasten to Cier'Djaal.

"We should move before they see us," Kataria said, voice low. "They'll eventually come up here."

"Can't," Kwar replied. "They're blocking our route."

"What do you mean?" She pointed down. "That road leads to Cier'Djaal, doesn't it? We can just follow it to the city."

"If we were humans, sure," Kwar replied. "And if we wanted to arrive too late to do anything. This road winds its way through the dunes. Good for merchants who have heavy things to carry. Yijis don't care about dunes. Good for shicts who want merchants' heavy things."

Kwar pointed over the road, toward a distant dune.

"There's another oasis beyond the road, just an hour by foot through the sands. We keep another pack of *tama'shi* there. They know the way to Cier'Djaal quicker than any road could take them. We want to reach the city in time, we need to go through, not around."

Kataria sighed, staring down at the Karnerian convoy below.

Those soldiers not patrolling were unfurling bedrolls, stripping off only what armor they needed to divest to be comfortable and bedding down right beside the enormous wheels of their wagons. No tents pitched, no latrines dug. Clearly they intended to be moving again before too long.

But before too long was still too long. Kwar's father, Sai-Thuwan, would need time to make his case. Which meant they needed to get there quickly.

"All right," Kataria whispered. "See that one, there?"

Kwar followed her finger to one of the Karnerians. This one stood more armored than the others, but with his helmet off that they might see his face. He didn't carry spears and shields like them, but a large, ornate sword at his hip. The soldiers offered salutes as he passed, and he paused every so often to say something to them.

"The leader," Kwar said.

"The others are all focused on him," Kataria said. "Put an arrow in him, the others will all move to defend him and give us an opportunity to pass. It'll be close, but it can be done if we hurry."

"That won't work," the khoshict replied. "There's not enough cover down there. They'll see you."

"It'll be dark."

"Close enough to hit him, they'll see you."

"I don't have to hit him. I just need to make sure that they see some-one *try* to hit him. We'll have a few moments while they try to protect him, then they'll start searching. Be ready to run."

Kwar shook her head. "No. I don't like this."

Kataria looked flatly at Kwar. "Look into my quiver."

Kwar glanced down at her hip. "Ten arrows."

"Did you happen to see any fucks I could give for what you think?" Kataria rose to her feet. "Follow me, twenty paces behind. Be ready to—"

A hand shot out, caught her by the wrist. Anger surged up inside her. She whirled on Kwar, shoving her off, face screwed up in fury. She barely remembered not to scream.

Barely.

"What did I tell you?" she snarled. "What did I *fucking* tell you about touching—"

Kwar was not looking at her. The khoshict's eyes were on the convoy below. She held up a finger for silence—which Kataria quietly praised herself for not biting off. Her ears rose in quivering attentiveness.

"Do you hear that?" she whispered.

In another moment Kataria would not be able to hear anything over the curses she would be spitting. But for *that* particular moment, she paused and listened.

Wind.

Yijis growling.

Soldiers muttering.

"What, the soldiers?" she asked. "I can't hear what they're—"

"Not that." Kwar gestured to her trembling ears. "*That.*"

Kataria closed her eyes, let her ears rise up. Nothing. Nothing but wind and ghosts and the sound of her anger and . . .

No. Not anger.

Not *her* anger.

A distant cry, restrained and muffled, but unable to silence itself. It was not spoken to her, so she heard it only faintly. But she heard it, she recognized it. The Howling.

"There's a shict nearby," she whispered.

"Three of them," Kwar said. She gestured with her chin. "Down there."

Kataria strained her ears, following the sound down to the road. Her eyes settled upon a Karnerian walking past some wagons. He paused near some other soldiers, saluted, began to make small talk. He looked like any other Karnerian: rigid, ungainly, clenched.

She would never have guessed he was a shict if she couldn't hear his Howling from here.

Fuck, she thought. *I guess they* do *look like us.*

He was tall for a shict, only slightly less burly than the Karnerians. With his ears and face mostly hidden beneath the helmet he wore, he wouldn't look like anything more than a slender soldier. And the other Karnerians seemed content to treat him as one.

She searched the camp, located the others in short order: another one patrolling on the opposite end of the convoy, a third one making a show of checking over supplies. No other Karnerian seemed to look twice at them, or even once in most cases.

"Did you know about this?" Kataria asked, looking to Kwar.

Even if Kwar *had* had a sense of subtlety stronger than a wolf in heat, there would have been no mistaking the shock on her face.

"No," Kwar whispered. "I . . . I had no idea. What are they doing down there?"

"It changes nothing," Kataria growled. "We still need to get across. One arrow, just a few moments to run." She drew an arrow, nocked it. "You ready?"

Kwar looked to her pale companion, opened her mouth to speak. The nod she offered, while shaky, was stronger than any words she could have offered.

Kataria returned the nod as Kwar rose to her feet. Together they began to stalk down the dune's slope.

"It's more than just Shekune, you know."

She had been listening for some time, but did not reply.

"A lot have answered her call. Hunters from the Eighth Tribe, assassins from the Ninth, and her Seventh has the fiercest warriors in the desert. Thousands of them. She didn't threaten them. They came willingly. All shicts love war."

"Not all shicts," she had said, finally.

"Enough do."

"Enough for what?"

"Enough to wonder what you're going to do after."

"After I stop her?"

"If you can. What happens next? What happens when they want war again?"

"I don't know."

"What happens when the humans attack us?"

"I don't know."

A long silence. And then soft words.

"Are you going to leave?"

"I don't know."

"To find him? The human?"

"Is that what this is about?"

"No." Hesitation. "Yes." Desperation. "What am *I* supposed to do?"

"Find another shict to be with."

"It's not that easy. The tribes all want me to breed when my time comes. But I don't...you know, with males..."

"That's not my problem."

"You can't do that."

"Do what?"

"What do you think? That you can come in, save the shicts, have a say in how we do things, then walk away? We're people, not bones you can gnaw on and toss aside. If you leave—"

"If I leave, that's my decision."

"And if you make it, what right do you have to decide for anyone else?"

A long silence. And then hard words.

"I don't know."

--- ⚔ ---

The elders said the shicts discovered fire long before the humans did. They lit it long enough to cook their food and then wisely put it out.

The humans, having figured it out much later, promptly cheered and whooped and danced around the fires they left lit all night. And the next morning, all of them lay dead with arrows in their throats from the shicts who had followed their lights in the darkness.

Kataria had listened to only a few of the elders' stories. They tended to be repetitive, always ending with dead humans. But she had listened long enough to learn the value of that particular one.

Fire had a way of making people comfortable. They put too much trust in it, huddling too close to it to ward off the night. Their eyes adjusted to the light, so much that they had a hard time seeing anything beyond it.

And even though the Karnerians had many torches staked into the earth, and even though their eyes *looked* vigilant enough as they stared out over the darkened desert, Kataria did not fear being spotted. She moved slowly through the scrub and rocks that littered the road's edge, body low to the earth like a cat's and every step just as deliberate.

Thirty paces away from the edge of the torches' rings of light. Any closer and she might be spotted—but that was quite a big *might*.

With every wary glance she cast toward the convoy, she grew more convinced that their vigilance was a product of rehearsal. Though they tried their best to look alert, they couldn't help but stifle yawns and shift restlessly. A few particularly bold ones muttered curses about watch duty and their hard-assed commander.

Whether or not the commander had a hard ass, Kataria could not say. From here it was hard to tell through all the armor he wore.

Tall and standing authoritatively, he stood near one wagon, a ledger in his hand and three soldiers wearing plumed helmets—subcommanders, Kataria guessed—standing attentively nearby. She caught a few words as she crept closer, something about deadlines and arriving in Cier'Djaal in time to relieve the speaker there.

Had she had any room left in her skull for it, she might have been worried about that. But at that moment all she had left was a bow in one hand, an arrow in the other, and two eyes on her target.

She crept a little closer. Her ears were open, listening for any sound of an alarm, a sign that she or Kwar had been spotted. But she knew none would come; Kwar, twenty paces back, was even stealthier than she was. She drew as close as she dared, nocked her arrow, and squinted through the darkness at the Karnerian commander.

There. Her eyes rested on a spot on the wagon he stood beside, just two finger's lengths from his ear. *Shoot there. Just close enough that it looks like a near miss. The others will crowd around him to protect him and you can make a break for it.*

She drew a breath.

Or they'll immediately fan out, find you, and gut you. But maybe you should have thought of that sooner, hm?

No time to think of a better plan. Every moment wasted could be another dead shict.

She narrowed her eyes.

She raised her bow.

She drew back the string.

An arrow flew, its shriek heard for just a fraction of a breath before it ended in a crunch of metal and a messy splattering sound. The sub-commander twitched, at first, neither body nor brain aware of what had just hit it. And by the time he crumpled to the ground, an arrow jutting from the side of his head, it seemed his fellow Karnerians weren't quite sure, either.

Hell of a shot.

Made her wish she had been the one to make it.

Or the seven others that came shrieking out of the darkness.

"AMBUSH! TO ARMS!"

"PROTECT THE SPEAKER!"

"GET UP, HEATHENS! GET UP!"

Each word they screamed into the night was followed by the wail of arrows flying. Each rattle of armor as sleeping soldiers roused themselves and seized their shields was followed by the crunch of metal and splintering of wood. Each cry of alarm was followed by a cry of pain and a body hitting the sand.

That's how it sounded, anyway.

Kataria couldn't see. She was belly-down in the dirt, hands over her head, stock-still as the arrows flew over her head. They did not scream, as arrows shot haphazardly did. They sang, each one a single note of a black dirge that lilted on the whistle of feathers and the moan of metal heads.

That's how she knew there were shicts out there.

How had she not seen them? How had she not *heard* them? Was she deaf to their Howling? Was she blind to their movements? Was Kwar?

Kwar.

Her chest tightened at the name, a surge of panic rising up inside her from a dark place. Had she seen the arrows in time? Had she escaped? Had she—

"*Wall formation!*" A deep voice bellowed a command. "*Shields up, you fools, shields up!*"

Kataria dared to peer up from the sand. She saw the dead first, the Karnerians who had been too slow to move, too quick to rise. They lay, arrows jutting from their heads, their chests, their necks. She saw the living next, standing tall with their shields in hand, forming a wall of metal to face the hills. There were no wounded. Or at least, no Karnerians who had been hit less than fatally considered themselves wounded. Those with shafts in their legs and arms stood side by side with their fellows, facing the hills.

Their shields clanged together as they pressed shoulder to shoulder. Their spears rattled as they leveled them warily out into the night. They stood tall, heedless of the dead beneath their feet. Two hundred armored Karnerians, black armor glistening in the firelight, formed an onyx wall against the night.

So much for getting past them now, Kataria thought.

Their commander, plumed helmet atop his head, strode behind them. His sword was raised, his voice carried over the night.

"*Stand tall, you sons of Daeon! The Conqueror is watching.*" His bellowing commands struck a hymn-like cadence. "*Whatever cowardice lurks within the shadow pales before the might of the Empire! Let them come! Karneria Eternal!*"

"*KARNERIA ETERNAL!*" The soldiers took up his roar, shouting into the night.

But the night did not shout back.

And whoever was out there, they did not come.

No challenging taunts. No rallying war cry. No wail of arrows. The attack, it seemed, had finished just as suddenly as it had begun.

And Kataria had just about begun to believe that when the first Karnerian fell.

No arrow. No wound. He was perfectly living one moment, perfectly dead the next. His shield clattered as he slumped forward, his helmet slipped from his head and rolled across the sand. He lay so still and so silent, one might have thought he was simply sleeping.

One might, that is, until his body spasmed with a sudden, bloody vomiting.

"Daeon's will...," the commander began to gasp, but he had not the words to express what he saw at the dead soldier.

Or the next one.

Or the next one.

One by one they began to fall. Some screamed out before they did. Others had just enough breath to let out a single panicked gasp. They fell, they spasmed, they spilled themselves out of their mouths, and they lay still.

And when no fewer than sixty were dead, only then did the commander seem to find the words for it.

"Fuck," he gasped. "*Fuck!*"

She couldn't fault him for that response, Kataria thought. But she had already figured it out. She wished she hadn't. She wished she could have had a few more moments of unthinking horror, but it had all come together.

Shekune's weapon from the greenshicts: the vial of green liquid in her hands.

The shicts disguised as Karnerians.

The big water barrels on the wagons.

She poisoned them, she thought. *She's going to poison all of them. That's how she's going to fight the humans.*

"Close ranks! *CLOSE RANKS!*"

The commander bellowed, the soldiers obeyed. They rattled in their armor as they came together, the still-living Karnerians. But now that their dead outnumbered them, their wall no longer looked quite so perfect, their armor no longer quite so glossy. They were not going to survive this night.

And they were not the only ones to know it.

Softly at first, they came wailing. Their war song carried over the hills, hundreds of voices raised in whooping cries joined by the shrieking howls of beasts. Starkly then, they appeared. Dark shadows against the night sky, cresting over the hills atop four-legged mounts. Swiftly at last, they came. Their faces were wooden, their grins were carved, their eyes were hollow.

And their blades were sharp.

Khoshicts. Hatchets flashing. Short blades gleaming. Spears smiling.

Their yijis came charging down the hill, cackling with anticipation. War cries tore from the grins carved into their faces. They came. Swiftly, surely, unstoppable, charging toward the Karnerians.

And Kataria ran.

No thought for the Karnerians and their spears and their formations. She had no thoughts left. Only the need to move, the need to run, the need to get away. She was on her feet, rushing toward the convoy.

"Shicts! They're fucking shicts!"

"Son of a bitch, how?"

"Take their fucking ears! DAEON IS—"

If Daeon heard that soldier, he never answered.

The khoshicts burst from the gloom, a roar upon their lips that was shared by their yijis. They tore into the Karnerians with the screech of metal and the howl of beast and laughter at the impending slaughter.

Shields splintered as spears punched through them. Blood spattered upon the sands. Soldiers screamed, stuck on blades. Soldiers dragged to ground by yiji jaws never got the chance to scream. The khoshicts and their mounts toasted their impending victory with a wordless, shapeless howl.

That's what it sounded like, anyway.

Kataria certainly wasn't about to stop and look. She ran past the slaughter, past the wagons, into the darkness beyond.

A shadow moved at her side. A heavy shape caught her in a rush, knocked her to the ground.

"Filthy pagan scum." The commander's voice. "You *dare* attack a convoy of the Empire?"

She whirled onto her back, saw the commander looming large over her. His sword was high above his head. His face was etched with the agonized madness of a man who had seen his company collapse in the span of a few breaths.

His blade came down quickly. But Kataria was quicker. Fear gave her speed, sent her rolling to the side. Instinct gave her reflex, sent her rising to her feet. As for what made her reach for the pouch at her belt . . .

Well, maybe that was just luck.

But she tore free the sack, hurled it at the commander. The bag struck him square in the face, the laces came undone, its flap flew open. And the dozens of tarantulas within celebrated their newfound freedom by crawling and biting every morsel of Karnerian flesh they could find.

Her panic became his. He dropped his blade, took off running, screaming, pawing at his face as he tried to dislodge the spiders.

Would that she had time or thought to appreciate that sight.

But like everything else tonight, that moment ended in a bloody mess.

The commander, twenty paces away, came to a sudden, jerking halt. He grunted as something burst from his back. A spear's head, jagged and hooked and smiling a red, bloody smile. Kataria recognized it before anything else. Before the commander's corpse fell to the ground. Before she saw the khoshict standing over his lifeless body.

Shekune.

She wore a mask with slanted eyes and a mouth full of sharpened teeth, like a demon's. And stretched over the wood: the dried flesh of a human face, gaping in its last scream.

Her spear, its red smile and its steel teeth, spoke for her. In the groan of metal and the ripping of flesh as she tore it free from the commander's corpse. In the spattering of blood and the whistle of metal as she held her arms out wide. In the crunch of sand and the distant sound of men dying as she began to walk toward Kataria.

Slowly.

Arms outstretched.

As if to say, softly: *Try.*

And Kataria did.

She nocked, she drew, she loosed. She missed. Arrow after arrow, shot after shot. And whether it was fear that shook her hands or exhaustion that blinded her, her arrows did not scream, nor sing. They muttered, they cursed, they flew wide: over Shekune's shoulder, past Shekune's ear, in the dirt by Shekune's feet.

She shot until she reached for her quiver and found empty space.

And Shekune's arms dropped.

As if to say, softly: *Oh, well.*

She took up her spear in both hands, leveled it at Kataria, tensed and made ready to charge. Kataria held up her bow, a flimsy defense she knew would do nothing. But she had nothing left.

Nothing but an empty quiver and the shadows around her.

One of which suddenly moved.

A shape came screaming out of the darkness. Screaming, not crying in war or in pain, but in rage and need and desperation. It leapt, it caught Shekune about the waist and bore her to the ground. A fist came up, then down. There was the crack of wood. When it rose again, splinters were embedded in its knuckles. When it came down again, the crack was of bone on flesh.

"Come on."

The shape was up on its feet. A bloodied hand reached out for Kataria's. Wild eyes met her own.

"Kwar," she whispered, breathless.

"She won't stay down," Kwar snarled. "They won't stay still. We run for the hills. *Now.*"

No thought for refusal, for resistance, for Kwar's hand around her wrist. No thought for her feet moving beneath her, for the sound of crunching sand growing louder as the sound of carnage and bloodshed grew fainter. No thought...

But one.

For a look cast over her shoulder. For the sight of Shekune standing. For the mask that hung, shattered, off the khoshict chieftain's face. For the bloody grin of her spear, the silent wail of her mask and the victorious shadows of her warriors and the slow raising of her hand.

As if to say, softly: *Next time.*

THIRTY-EIGHT

An Ethical Knife in the Back

The official reason for the Venarium's creation was, verbatim: "To assure safety, discipline, and control to those individuals gifted with Venarie and, through them, to provide the same to the world."

That more or less covered the unofficial reason, as well, which was that wizards had been right on track to blowing the shit out of the world for a while there.

As the histories went, wizards were more or less content to live in harmony until the emperors, kings, and lords of the lands realized that men and women who could spit ice and shit fire would be pretty handy in a fight.

Loyalties were invoked, conscriptions signed, bribes offered, and every fashionable army suddenly had a wizard to throw at its enemies. They would rain lightning on enemy formations, grab catapult-tossed boulders out of the sky, and freeze entire harvests to starve out villages.

When one wizard decimated an army, that army would get its own wizard. And as wizards tended to burn out rather quickly when they weren't budgeting their powers, they were in high demand and would often fight to avoid being conscripted. Armies were killing wizards, wizards were killing armies, and, of course, the civilians got quite thoroughly fucked.

Even for a time when war was quite messy, things were remarkably chaotic.

The Venarium was formed with the assistance of several nations—some still around, some long since departed—to put an end to this. Instantly wizards were forced to give up their nationalities, families, and prior loyalties and swear obedience to a system that would ensure their cooperation. The Venarium was granted sovereign lands in other nations and access to their resources in exchange for keeping the wizard threat under control.

And while many armies were reluctant to give up their pet wizards, few argued with the establishment of the Venarium. For they could think of absolutely no other way to stop a man who could kill with a thought and a flick of his wrist.

Of course, Dreadaeleon knew, there were ways to stop such a man.

And naturally, the Venarium knew them, as they were keen to remind him once he was in their custody once again.

Gestures, stance, and posture were important to channeling and connecting the flow of Venarie in a wizard—sitting him in a thick wooden chair and shackling his wrists and ankles to the armrests and legs, respectively, dealt with that. For the words of power that called on the Venarie and made it manifest, there was a delightful device known as a *Seen-and-Not-Heard*: a viselike muzzle that forcibly held shut the jaws of a wizard.

But even a bound and gagged wizard could be a threat if he could concentrate. That was why his cell had one source of light: a globe overhead that flickered on and off erratically. And just in case that wasn't enough, one male and one female Librarian—elite members of the Venarium—stood guard not ten paces away, flanking the only door leading out of his cell and their eyes constantly locked on him.

They unlocked him long enough for him to eat, drink, and expel bodily excretions—all of which he was permitted half an hour for—after which he was promptly locked back up and their long vigil resumed.

But it wasn't all bad, he thought. He had to endure it for only a few more days before they finalized their report to the Venarium command and received permission to summarily execute him and Harvest his entrails.

And hey, he thought, *at least Admirable Tibbles is here.*

The Charnel Hound sat on its haunches, a mere two paces away. And though it looked at ease, it could strike and snap his neck in an instant. Not that it seemed inclined to at the moment. If the Charnel Hound held any enmity over his previous escape, it didn't show it.

Though, he asked himself, *how* would *a thing made out of severed cocks show enmity? I suspect it'd be pretty obvious.*

He stared forward, dumbly.

You have to be able to laugh about these things, old man.

He had no energy for laughter, even if he hadn't been wearing a muzzle.

The animal panic that had come from waking up in chains had long since ebbed away from days without sleep, hours of flickering light, not so much as a moment when fewer than three people—or creatures— had eyes on him and were ready to kill him.

He supposed he deserved it. The chaos he had caused was enough to warrant a stern reprimand, but he had killed far more than he had been permitted. Another member of the Venarium was dead because of him, as far as he knew. Possibly a fasha, too; the Venarium investigators were still piecing out his crimes. But they knew a wizard and a nobleman were both dead and, from what he had gathered, they seemed perfectly willing to blame him for it.

Not that he could really dispute that, even if they were to take the muzzle off long enough for him to speak clearly. He had spent most of those days in a broodvine-induced haze, wading through rivers of gore and clouds of carrion birds alternately. He couldn't explain where he had been during that whole time or *whom* he had killed.

He found himself itching at the thought of it. Even now the haze of broodvine hadn't wholly left him. He felt cloudy without being numb, drowsy without being able to sleep, the memory that he had once felt so amazing rubbing against the reality that he now felt pitifully mortal.

It drove him mad. Or would have, had he been allowed room and thought to go mad. As it was, he did what he had done every time he started to feel the need to go mad.

At least Liaja is safe, he told himself.

And, as he did every time he told himself this, he quickly added:

She betrayed you.

And he countered:

She thought she was helping.

She's the reason you're here.

She didn't know. She's not to blame.

She should pay. They all should.
Well, no matter. You're going to die anyway.
That's true.
And he sighed inwardly.
At least Liaja is safe.
And that was enough to carry him through the next few moments, at least.

But before he could launch down that avenue of thought for the six thousandth time that hour, he noticed something. Or rather, he *didn't* notice something that his guards did. He saw in the sudden tension of their necks, the hardening of their eyes, that they sensed something he didn't.

Magic. Someone was approaching.

The two Librarians slid into a stance, eyes glowing with Venarie, ready to attack the next thing that walked through the door. But as it creaked open, the next thing that *did* walk through it instead set them at ease, firing off crisp nods of acknowledgment.

"Lector Shinka," the female Librarian said. "Is there an emergency? We did not receive word that you'd be arriving."

"That depends on your definition of *emergency*," the Lector, her robes immaculate and her smile pristine, replied. "Personally, I consider it rather mundane. But if you were to ask the clerk, your failure to fill out a daily observation report is tantamount to the entire city going up in flames."

"You didn't fill out your report?" the male Librarian asked, looking to his colleague.

"No." She sighed, rubbed her eyes. "I didn't think it was important. Or not as important as watching the prisoner, at least."

"Personally, I find your priorities well in order," Shinka said. "But Lector Annis is quite intent on having things done *exactly* according to protocol."

"Imagine that," the male Librarian muttered.

"Indeed, not quite out of character for him." Shinka cast a sidelong eye toward Dreadaeleon. "Though I imagine it's because he wants absolutely no document conflicting with his demand that the heretic be eliminated with prejudice."

Dreadaeleon couldn't muster much more than a thought for that.

Bad luck, old man.

"Regardless," Shinka continued, "at the insistence of the Lector and the Archives, I must ask you to head upstairs and fill out the forms. Shouldn't take more than an hour if you're swift."

"But…" The female Librarian looked over her shoulder at Dreadaeleon. "I have orders. The heretic is dangerous."

"The Charnel Hound and your colleague will be adequate for guarding a bound prisoner," Shinka replied. "And, not to suggest you're inattentive or anything, but I *am* a Lector, you know."

"Of course, Lector. My apologies." She glanced to her companion. "One hour. I'll be back."

"He's not going anywhere," the male Librarian replied.

"Right, just…be careful, okay? He killed Kazimir."

"Kazimir died for what he believed in."

"Yeah."

A brief nod to her companion, a deeper one to the Lector, and the female Librarian exited the cell and shut the door behind her. For a very long moment, Shinka and the Librarian merely stared at each other.

Oh no, Dreadaeleon thought. *If they start kissing now, I think I might scream.*

"That's forty breaths," Shinka said. "Enough time for her to have reached the stairs?"

"I'd say so," the Librarian said. "She's very punctual. Always gets to her duties in time."

"Marvelous. Watch the door for me. Let me know when you hear someone coming."

"Of course, Lector." He glanced toward Admiral Tibbles. "What about the Hound?"

"The damn thing can't understand speech or repeat what it's heard. No need to worry." She gestured to the door. "Leave. This won't take long."

"As you say."

The male Librarian departed. Dreadaeleon watched as Shinka retrieved from the corner a stool occasionally used by the Librarians to rest their feet. He tensed up as she took a seat in front of him.

"You're a smart boy, concomitant," Shinka said, suddenly seizing his attention. "I trust you know this already, but just for formality's sake,

I'd like to make it clear that if you do anything other than speak—and speak with all the respect a Lector is owed—when I remove this contraption, I will not hesitate to crush your skull with a thought." She looked at him intently, tapped her fingers upon his muzzle. "We are understood?"

Admittedly, he was confused. That might be the sleepless hours or the broodvine withdrawal or maybe she really *had* said something that insane. Regardless, he nodded his head weakly and she nodded back.

"Let's be clear about one thing, concomitant." Shinka reached around his head, undoing the straps and buckles around his muzzle. "Your life, at this moment, is not your own. I can end it right now, if you wish, quickly and cleanly. I can sit back and watch Annis rip you to pieces in a few days' time. Or, if you're feeling particularly bold, I can save it."

The Seen-and-Not-Heard fell from his face. He stared blankly at Shinka for a moment. She furrowed her brow, expectant.

"Not feeling bold, then? Shall we discuss the first option?"

"No, it's not that," Dreadaeleon spoke through a dry mouth. "I'm just aware that we've had this conversation before." He wriggled his fingers, the sole movement that his shackles would allow. "I seem to recall it ending poorly for me."

"Ah. I suppose I owe you an explanation for that…and an apology."

"I suspect they go hand in hand, Lector."

"It was not an accident that your priest friend came to appeal on your behalf," Shinka said. "Nor was it an accident that I agreed with her idea. I had made up my mind to do so long before she arrived, when an agent of mine stationed in her temple reported her plans to me."

"You have agents?"

"That can't surprise you."

"It does when you could just as easily use scrying magic to find out what's going on in the city."

"Magic can be traced. Not a single syllable of Venarie is uttered within Tower Resolute without Annis knowing about it. Gold, I suspect, could also be traced if anyone bothered to do so. Fortunately, you and the Primary Lector have similar mind-sets. He never once suspected that I employed outside influences."

Dreadaeleon's mouth hung open, struggling for the words to convey the questions brewing inside his skull.

"But then, like you, the Primary Lector didn't suspect a lot of things, hm?" Shinka smiled softly. "He didn't suspect that he would be swayed to agreeing to releasing you, he didn't suspect that you would kill a wizard *and* a fasha." Her smile grew decidedly darker. "And he didn't suspect that I'd be behind either of them."

Dreadaeleon narrowed his eyes. He was nowhere near sleepless or withdrawn enough for this to make sense. But as he thought on it, a realization struck him.

"The hallucinations," he whispered. "The broodvine. I kept seeing visions, images of death. I thought they were simply out of control, but—" His eyes widened. "*You.*"

"Honestly, that was the part of the plan I wasn't certain of. 'Surely,' I told myself, 'he'll realize that broodvine hallucinations can be controlled by another wizard. He did that to Palanis, after all.' But you didn't. Tell me, concomitant, do I attribute that to luck or skill?"

"That's how you convinced Annis to let me go, too," Dreadaeleon whispered. "You used some kind of mind magic on him to control him."

Her laughter was loud, unrestrained, and just the *slightest* bit condescending.

"'Mind magic'? Listen to yourself, concomitant. You can't be that dense."

"Then how?"

"Annis is a man completely convinced of his own power and infallibility who will never be second-guessed by someone he perceives as inferior," Shinka said. "Wizardry allowed me to control you, but I've been controlling arrogant men all my life."

"So you made me your murderer, your killer."

"In a way," Shinka replied. "I knew your power was too unrestrained and wild to create the kind of controlled chaos that Lector Annis had agreed to. I was anticipating simply waiting for him to rein you in and do away with you and using the aftermath to my advantage. But I realized I could use you to a greater purpose.

"Fasha Mejina was proving to be a difficulty. He was rallying the fashas behind him and asserting control over Silktown. Relentlessly paranoid, there was no way we could get a normal assassin in to kill him. But through some careful alterations of your visions, I tapped into powers you didn't even know you had. It was easy enough to have *you* kill the fasha and allow us to put a pawn in his place."

"Who . . . is 'we'?"

"You haven't figured that out, either, then?" Shinka smirked. "I suppose I can forgive you that. Who would suspect the Venarium of being involved with the Khovura?"

"Who, indeed," Dreadaeleon growled, "would suspect wizards of dealing with fanatics? And for what purpose? To eliminate Annis?"

"Of course. His decision to release you was one step toward undermining his authority."

"Which you intended to use to *assume* his authority."

"Naturally."

"Typical. Does this come down to the old cliché of you pursuing some nebulous definition of power?"

At this, Shinka's mirth faded from her face. "No."

"Then what are you—"

"Fourteen hours."

"What?"

"Fourteen hours," she repeated. "I've done the calculations in my head, over and over. Fourteen hours, maximum, is the amount of time it would have taken us to secure Cier'Djaal."

"I don't follow."

"The bulk of it would be the scrying. Ten hours for scrying and divination, being generous, to find the Khovura's lairs. We could send out rats and dominate other beasts to this end, if needed. But it wouldn't take much longer than that. Give maybe half an hour to send our best Librarians to these locations and the rest of the time would be spent kicking in doors and roasting, freezing, or electrocuting the Khovura cultists, leaving Cier'Djaal free of violence."

"But that—"

"Or do you want to know how long it would have taken us to drive the Karnerians and Sainites out of the city? Six days, twelve hours. How about how long it would take us to cast down the fashas and set up a new government? Ten months, three weeks, five days, three hours. Or would you like to know how easily we could have stopped the riots? Three hours. Or how about how long it would have taken to destroy the Jackals? Five days."

She settled back on the stool, her back perfectly rigid, hands placed on her knees, and stared thoughtfully at Dreadaeleon.

"During all of these activities, the most objectively powerful force in the entire desert was sitting in its tower, reading books, while the world burned down around its ears." She breathed out a cold breath. "The Venarium has the power to do more good for this world than any army, any king, any cult. We have the power to bring down greedy fashas, to burn thieves in their dens, to cast out corrupt priests, to save any life we so choose to, and we do *nothing*."

"The Sovereignty Pact is a pillar of the Venarium way," Dreadaeleon said, though he imagined that sounded a bit weak coming from a heretic.

"The Sovereignty Pact is an outdated *relic* of a time long gone," Shinka said. "We feared wizards would burn down the world, but the petty lords and kings thought that might rob them of the fun of doing it themselves. I was watching Cier'Djaal *long* before the Khovura showed up. This city, this *world*, is diseased. We are the only ones with the power and the means of burning that disease out."

"So you allied with the Khovura to do it? In your plea for sanity, you trust the gibbering sermons of fanatical thugs?"

"I do not. Fasha Teneir approached me with the intent of keeping the Venarium out of what she considers her impending take-over of Cier'Djaal. It is my intent to permit her long enough to rid the city of the Jackals and then promptly inform her that her services are not needed. I have enough loyalists, such as one half of your guard detail, to form a suitable interim government."

"Teneir," Dreadaeleon said with a sneer. "And a classic backstab. Denaos would deride this as hackneyed."

"Who?"

"Unimportant. I take it you are closing in on the reason you're telling me this."

"I *did* mention I could save your life, didn't I?" Shinka's smile returned, soft and gentle. "And if the Venarium can fix an entire world, they can certainly smooth things over with your female companion, can they not?"

Dreadaeleon's voice was a hoarse whisper.

"You," he said, "stay *away* from Liaja."

"I have no intentions of harming her or doing anything you don't wish me to, concomitant. But it would be no particularly great effort to explain to her how you were forced into this role against your will, hm? That the crimes you committed were not of your doing? She would understand, surely."

"No," Dreadaeleon said. "What you're offering is—"

"Is not complete. Go with her, kill her, talk to her, do whatever you want. Once I am in control of the Venarium, I can have your entire record expunged, your entire existence erased. You will go down in history as neither a heretic nor a valued member of the Venarium. You will not be hunted, not be contacted, not be so much as thought of. You will be *free*. Even without the girl, that thought must appeal."

It did.

Gods, how it did.

To be free, to answer to no one and fear nothing, was something that would appeal to him even if he *weren't* facing death. No more people treating him like a tool to be used, like a criminal whose law simply hadn't been invented yet. No more Annis, no more Asper, no more...

Liaja? Could it be true? Could she really be persuaded to see him as he was? A hapless pawn in all this?

He wanted to believe that.

So much so that the next words he spoke felt as if they might cut his mouth.

"What do you want me to do?"

"I was anticipating that Annis would kill you," Shinka said. "In the aftermath I could decry his decision to release you and you wouldn't be around to contradict me. Though I'm surprised at his decision to spare you."

"Why?"

"Is it not obvious? He fears you. He saw what you did to Palanis. He knows that your time spent adventuring has left you in a better position to fight him. He thinks you might pose a threat to him. On your own, you might not..."

"But with you..."

"Now you understand." Shinka rose to her feet. "I will have my loyalists placed on your guard detail. They will permit you regular sleep and meals, that you may be ready for when I require you to strike. After that... you need only kill Annis and you will have your freedom."

She turned to depart, sparing a glance for Admiral Tibbles. The

Charnel Hound stared eyelessly forward, heedless of the conspiracy that had just been born. She walked to the door, placed a hand on its knob, before he called out.

"What if I fail?"

She paused.

"What if I can't kill Annis?" Dreadaeleon asked. "What if your plot doesn't work?"

"Then," she said softly, "I will watch you die. I will claim that you overwhelmed me and forced me to do as you commanded. Annis will believe every word and I will think of something else."

"You are confident."

"I am."

"You are clever."

"I am not," she replied, opening the door. "I am simply surrounded by men who mistake magic for power."

THIRTY-NINE

PILGRIMS ON A RED ROAD

We were unlucky."

Low words from a voice like an oak tree falling. Gariath had no interest in answering them. He dipped a cupped hand into a bucket of water on the floor before him. He withdrew a palmful of liquid, poured it over his head.

But even without looking up, he knew his company had not left. He sighed deeply in answer.

"Oh?"

"Mm. Our warriors swept the city and found only enough supplies to last us a few more days. The siege took too long and many merchants escaped down the river with food and material we needed."

Gariath grunted.

To him that was a perfectly acceptable answer. Unfortunately, his company did not agree.

"There is better news. The victory gave many doubters in Shaab Sahaar pause. More warriors are coming to Jalaang from the city. They will bring food, weapons, cloth. But it will take time. Even if they are not harassed by shicts, it could be a week before all of them arrive here."

"Uh-huh."

"That's more weapons and more warriors to wield them. As word spreads, even more will come from the outlying villages. But that is no assurance. This city is defensible, but even with twice our warriors, a decisive attack from Cier'Djaal could dislodge us."

Gariath drew in a breath. With every word the stench of pipe smoke grew stronger. He looked up, glared across the room.

"You've got a reason for telling me this," Gariath growled.

The small, single-room house he had claimed for his own had little in the way of furniture besides a table, a bucket, and two stools. The occupation of a single tulwar—seated in the corner, his hefty form painted a dull orange by light seeping through shuttered windows—should not have made things seem quite so cramped.

But then, that hefty form was currently cloaked in a cloud of pipe smoke that grew steadily larger with each breath.

"I had merely assumed the general would want a report as to the status of his troops," the old tulwar replied, chuckling.

"Tell them not to call me that," Gariath said.

"They don't. They call you *daanaja*."

"Whatever. Tell them to stop it. You can tell them I don't care about numbers or reports or whatever the hell they do, either."

"Interesting strategy." The old tulwar stroked his chin. "Tell me, General, how do you expect that to work out when the army of Cier'Djaal—whichever one it is now—decides to march on our position with more warriors, more weapons, and a strategy that *isn't* stupid as shit?"

"There's no need," Gariath growled. "We'll march on Cier'Djaal, burn it to the ground. The city is weak, gnawing at its own throat. They won't be able to face us."

"Cier'Djaal is *always* gnawing at its own throat. The fashas are forever strangling one another, yet they still managed to work together long enough to turn back the first Uprising. Them and their dragonmen."

Gariath paused, stared down into the bucket of water. His quivering reflection stared back. As distorted as his face was, though, the cuts and bruises upon it were still clear.

"The prisoners?" Gariath said.

The old tulwar did not answer for a moment. When he did his voice was tired.

"They are secure and unharmed," he said. "No more than they were when the city fell. The third one we could not save."

"Right."

"The warriors were not happy. Wounds inflicted in the first Uprising still sting. It's a mark of their respect for you that they agreed not to kill the prisoners."

"I don't care."

"You need to."

Gariath looked up, glowered. The old tulwar's eyes pierced through the pipe smoke, fixed on Gariath like a blade.

"Whatever you may think this is, however you see it ending, understand this truth." His voice grew hard and dark. "This is a war. We may have struck the first blow, but the humans *will* strike back. We have taken one city from them. They won't let that stand. There needs to be a plan of defense."

"Ask someone else, then. Daaru or the others—"

"Daaru is a warrior, but also a grieving father. Left to him, we would run into Cier'Djaal and be hacked to pieces. Dekuu is a *Humn*, good for leading in times of peace, but not war. Ululang cannot conceive of a plan that does not involve her monkeys, and Chakaa is... well, Chakaa. Warriors, yes. Leaders, no. I could make a warrior *into* a leader, but they do not speak to me."

"And why not?" Gariath snarled, rose to his feet. "Or rather, why is that my problem?"

The old tulwar settled back on his stool, regarded the dragonman coolly, and spoke softly.

"Because, *daanaja*, it was you that dragged us into this."

Though he spoke calmly, the accusation in his tone was unmistakable. But it went no further than a tone, an implication. His eyes betrayed no fear, no threat. His body remained relaxed and fat. And of his scent, there was nothing but the reek of pipe smoke.

Even as Gariath stalked forward, loomed over him, bared teeth in a snarl, the old tulwar did not so much as blink.

"Who are you, elder?" Gariath growled. "*What* are you?"

"Someone with secrets, like you," the old tulwar replied, calmly. "And like you, someone who wishes to see Cier'Djaal burn. And if you would just *listen*—"

A knock at the door. It creaked open before anyone had bidden entry. Light flooded the dark confines of the room. And standing there in silhouette, Daaru fixed Gariath with a dire gaze.

"Gariath," he said. "Humans. Maybe two thousand of them, marching on our position."

The dragonman merely narrowed his eyes. Even before Daaru had finished his sentence, the desperate scent about him told Gariath everything.

"And," Daaru whispered, "a northerner is leading them."

Almost everything, anyway.

—⊷≡⊶—

"What's that? What are those things on the walls? Those aren't Djaalics!"

"Mama? What's happening? I can't see. Pick me up!"

"Tulwar. They're tulwar! Fucking oids! What are they doing in Jalaang?"

"Ancaa preserve us, we should have stayed in the city."

"The northerner led us here. Why'd we trust that woman? I told you we shouldn't have!"

Asper could only barely hear them: the murmurs, the gasps, the occasional cry of fear from the crowd of thousands behind her. She offered them nothing: no assurances, no apologies, not so much as a breath.

She had no words for what lay before her.

When she had called for the exodus of refugees from Cier'Djaal, the long, silent march to the city of Jalaang had given her plenty of time for fear.

She had worried she would arrive, with thousands of refugees—families, elders, widows—and find the gates shut. She had worried she would arrive, with those hungry and wounded, and find no food or shelter to give them. She had worried she would arrive, with a force so big that no god could look down on earth and not see them, and find heaven silent.

And surely all these fears had come to pass.

But not in all the nights she'd lain awake or all the days she had marched numbly had she worried she would find this.

Great plumes of smoke rose from behind the walls, stretching into the sky like black worms. The stiff carcasses of men in battered armor hung from the walls by their necks, or their ankles if they had no heads. And from atop the battlements, several hundred paces away, hundreds of faces awash with colors of red, yellow, and blue snarled at her.

Tulwar. Hundreds of them. Long limbs clutching long blades. Hairy bodies stained with red wounds. Teeth bared, eyes narrowed, manes wild. Tulwar. Firmly in control of Jalaang.

She had no words for it.

What could she possibly say?

"Well, we're fucked now, aren't we?"

Admittedly, that was both accurate and concise. But Dransun had said it first.

"How?" Aturach's words were slightly less concise. "How could this have happened?"

They stood on either side of her, Dransun to her left and Aturach to her right. At the head of the great column of refugees that sprawled out behind them, the three stared out over Jalaang. Aturach looked on the verge of tears, while Dransun's weary frown seemed to suggest he'd known something like this was going to happen.

Asper, at that moment, was still not sure which expression fit her best.

"They built Jalaang so that this wouldn't happen," Aturach said, voice quavering. "After the Uprising, they said . . . they said . . ."

"They lied," Dransun growled. "The fashas have always been full of shit. Jalaang's been more trading post than garrison for ages. Every year we saw less and less Jhouche go out there."

"And you didn't say anything earlier?" Aturach demanded. "You couldn't have fucking *mentioned* this?"

"I didn't know, boy. How could I have? The tulwar have been crawling into Cier'Djaal, looking for work, for years now. We thought their backs had been broken."

"Well, they fucking *weren't*. We led these people out of Cier'Djaal, we told them they'd be safer out here, away from the foreigners. We *promised* them—"

"We didn't promise them *shit*. They came because they wanted to, not because—"

"They came because they had no other choice! And now they have no choice at all, save exactly *which* painful death they want to choose and—"

"Don't think I don't know what they're going through, you sanctimonious little—"

"Fucking worthless piece of—"

So many words.

So many curses and prayers and cries.

They rose up from Dransun, from Aturach, from the refugees, and fell upon Asper like rain from an iron-colored cloud. She couldn't feel them. She couldn't hear them. They simply swirled about her, passed her by, and drifted off into a sky where no one was waiting to hear them.

She could muster but one word to add to them. And she did not speak it.

How?

How could it have gone so wrong?

How, after all her plans, all her dealings, had it come to this? After courting Jackals and dealing with wizards, she had still lost Cier'Djaal. After she had beseeched fashas and begged gods, so many people had died. After giving up everything to cross the desert with the weak and wounded, she had found only carcasses and smoke.

What god would allow this?

What sin had she committed that her punishment would be so severe? What had she done? What *could* she have done that she hadn't? What was she going to do?

What was she going to tell them? All of them? Any of them?

Her lips felt numb, unable to form even a single word. Her tongue felt swollen, as if she would choke on it at any moment. She swallowed something hard that settled in her belly like a stone.

And she knew she had to find the words.

But the word she found was nothing that they needed to hear. The word she found was harsh and full of black fire.

And she found it on the battlements, red-skinned, horned, and towering over the tulwar who clustered around him reverently.

"Gariath."

"What?" Aturach asked.

"*Gariath,*" she repeated.

"Who the hell is—" Dransun began.

"*GARIATH!*"

She hurled the word, screamed it over the desert.

"*GARIATH!*"

She spit it, a stain on the sky, as she stormed across the sands and held her fist up at the battlements.

"*GARIATH!*" she roared. "*GET DOWN HERE AND FACE ME, YOU LIZARD PIECE OF SHIT!*"

This close, only two hundred paces or so away from the gates, she could see him clearly. She could see the disdain on his face, the anger in his eyes, the contempt in his arms folded across his chest. She could also see the dozen or so bows drawn on her from the tulwar above.

She didn't see Dransun or Aturach until they were right beside her, grabbing her arms and pulling her back.

"Asper, are you insane?" Aturach demanded. "Get back to the refugees!"

"They're fucking savages, priestess," Dransun said. "We'll die if we don't—"

"No, we'll die if *I* don't, Dransun." She pulled herself free from their grips, stalked forward again. "*GARIATH! COME DOWN HERE AND ANSWER ME!*"

To their credit, neither Aturach nor Dransun tried to grab her again. Out of their stupidity, neither Aturach nor Dransun tried to run. Through the sole luck she had been afforded, no arrows fell from the battlements to impale her then and there.

Instead the tulwar archers looked to Gariath. But his eyes were fixed on her for a good long moment. And when it was done, he turned away and disappeared from the battlements.

Asper drew a breath. And held it until a few moments later, when the gates of Jalaang came creaking open.

It had been weeks since she had seen Gariath, but he wasn't the sort of creature a woman forgot easily. She remembered the slow, purposeful stalking of his gait. She remembered the way his hands were always curled into fists. She remembered his ear-frills and his wings and his tail.

But fuck me, she thought, *I don't remember him being* that *big.*

He came striding out of the gates, shadowed by the pyres burning behind him so that all she saw was a black shape topped with horns and wings and claws. No longer the companion she had traveled with. Now he was a nightmare walking out of a bad dream.

Two tulwar walked with him: one a tall young man with a warrior's poise and a blade to match, the other a shorter, older, and fatter one who puffed a pipe leisurely as they walked forward. As though he were simply out for a stroll and not walking to see whatever was about to happen.

Asper wished she had some idea herself. And though she didn't know what was going to occur between her and Gariath, she knew it'd be ugly.

That much was evident in the glare he cast down at her as he came to a halt, looming over her from five paces away.

"You're not dead," he observed.

"Surprised?" she asked, not bothering to hide the anger in her voice.

"No," he said. "You never could do anything right." He looked over her head, toward the column of refugees behind her. "But I guess no human can if there are this many of you left."

"They're refugees, Gariath," Asper said. "People fleeing the city. Many are sick, wounded, young. They need food and water and shelter."

Gariath looked down his snout at her. He blinked once.

"You should go find them some, then."

She had, of course, expected him to say something that would make her want to hit him.

She hadn't expected him to say something that would make her left arm burn and a little voice in the back of her head hiss.

Kill him.

"There aren't any other settlements," Asper said. "The villages outside the city couldn't hold so many people."

"And Jalaang can't hold so many humans and so many tulwar," Gariath replied. "So look elsewhere."

"Jalaang is *their* city!"

"Was."

The heat in her arm burned brighter. The voice of Amoch-Tethr grew louder, punctuated by a shrill giggle.

Oh my. I can feel your anger, my dear. We are going to kill him, aren't we?

"Gariath, *please*," she whispered through clenched teeth. "Listen to me. These people are victims. They've done nothing wrong."

"They have," the dragonman replied bluntly. "They fled the city now, when their lives were threatened. But they stayed when the city ate its people like meat. They stayed when their own people died so they could get more coin. They stayed when tulwar were ground under their feet, doing their dirty work so they could pretend they didn't smell like shit." His lips peeled back in a snarl. "They stayed for greed. They left for greed. The stink of that city is all over them."

"And for that, you'd condemn them to death?" Asper asked.

Gariath looked at her carefully for a moment, then looked over her head to the refugees, considering an answer to that question.

"Take them elsewhere," he said.

"Where? I can't take them back to Cier'Djaal."

"No," he said. "You can't. It won't be there by this time next month." He leaned toward her, his breath hot on her face. "Its stink is on you, too. You spent too much time in its walls, ate the same diseased meat as the rest of them. But I'll fix it. Like I fix every other mistake you've made."

She narrowed her eyes, refused to turn away. "What do you think you're going to do?"

"I will burn it to the ground. I will melt down every coin every hand of every human has ever touched. I will bury your rich men and your guards and your silk-eating swine so deep in the earth that you'll hear them screaming when you put your ear to the ground. I will *save* these humans. I will *cure* them."

Asper stared back at him, eyes wide and mouth open, struck dumb by the sheer hatred dripping off his voice. She had no words to reply.

"You are out of your fucking mind."

Or at least she'd *thought* she had none.

"Burn a city? How many people do you think you'd kill for that?" she asked.

"Many," he replied.

"And how many tulwar do you even *have*?"

A pause. "Many," he repeated.

"And for what? All because we wanted to stay and protect the city? Because we *did* stay and protect the city while you ran away and hid in the desert?"

It wasn't anger that flashed across Gariath's features. That would have been too tame a word for it. It was fury that painted his face, that coursed down his entire body and sent his fists quaking and poured out of his mouth in hot words.

"You're a human," he said. "I would tell you this isn't about you, but you'd never believe it." He turned away from her. "Go back. Find somewhere else to hide. When the city is burned down, you can build in the ashes."

His tulwar accompaniment spared a glance for her before turning away themselves. She was left struggling, again, to find the words to hurl at him. Not that she didn't have ideas. They were forced into her head from the fiery giggles boiling up in her arm.

Kill him, Amoch-Tethr whispered. *Right there. At the base of his skull. Just one touch. Just two breaths. I can end him, eat him, consume him. The others will flee without him. I can feel their fear from here. They need him. They need his strength.*

His strength.

"Fight me!" she roared.

At this, the tulwar stopped and looked at her. At this, Dransun's and Aturach's eyes nearly popped out of their skulls. At this, Gariath paused and looked halfway over his shoulder.

"I challenge you," Asper said. "If you win, we'll leave, fine. If I win, you give us food."

He did not reply for a long moment, then waved a hand, dismissive, and continued stalking back toward Jalaang.

And she found the words she needed.

"*COWARD!*" she roared.

Gariath stopped.

"You're nothing but a coward!"

Gariath turned to face her.

"You hide behind your walls and your monkeys and your big, insane speeches because you know the reason you want to destroy Cier'Djaal is that you're *afraid.*" She spit on the ground. "Afraid that we won't need *you* anymore."

And Gariath roared.

A deep, bellowing sound that carried across the desert and sent the tulwar cringing behind the battlements and the refugees recoiling in horror. Asper winced at the sound, felt it echo in her entire being, save for one spot.

Dear me, Amoch-Tethr giggled. *He is mad, isn't he?*

"Dransun," she said, turning to the captain. "Give me your sword. Shield, too."

"Uh...yeah." The impact of what was happening suddenly struck Dransun like a weight. He quickly doffed his sword and the buckler he wore on his back. "Give me a moment, I'll give you my armor, too."

"No," Asper said. "I've seen him rip plate off one man and force-feed it to another man. It'd only slow me down. I need to be light and fast."

"And you want to fight something that can do *that*?" Aturach looked nervously over his shoulder. "Asper, what are you even going to do?"

"I'm going to beat him," she said. "I'm going to make the tulwar lose faith in him. If we can do that, maybe we can force them out."

"With refugees? No. We don't have any fighters in—"

"Aturach." She drew Dransun's shield over her forearm, cast an iron look over its rim at him. "I can't run. Not one more time."

And he returned a cotton look: weak, helpless, soft. "Asper, you've got us this far. You're holding us all together. If you lose this…"

He let that possibility hang. And she looked to her left arm and felt the heat rising beneath the flesh.

"I won't lose," she said.

She could tell by the look on his face that he had more to say, more reasons for her not to go through with this. And if she had given him half a moment, the vast majority of those reasons would probably have sounded pretty sensible.

But she couldn't afford even half a moment of doubt. She was on her feet, shield in one hand and sword in the other, off at a trot toward Gariath, who stalked forward to meet her.

Right now this was all she had to fight with: a chunk of wood, a chunk of metal, and a vain hope that they might work. And they might. Killing Gariath *might* send the tulwar running. Or at least make them reconsider holding out on her. But then, it might just make them angry.

A lot of things might happen. But as she closed the distance with Gariath, she realized that there was one lesson he had taught her.

Sometimes one just had to start killing shit and hope for the best.

She was tense as she drew toward him, a tight coil that sprang with each step. But as he stalked toward her, his stride was easy, slow, as though he had already won this fight. It was not arrogance on his part, merely a statement of fact.

One he intended to prove as he drew back his arm and swung.

His outstretched claws sailed over her head, rending the air as she ducked low. She drew back her blade, ready to thrust out and catch him in the torso. But instead she was forced to raise her shield as his foot shot out in a vicious kick.

His leather sole struck it, sent a shock that rattled through her arm and into her ribs. She had to clamp her teeth shut just to stop them from shaking. She had been hit by Gariath before, but never like this. Before it had always been a chastising cuff or a teasing flick. Nothing like that blow.

He meant to kill her this time.

She lashed out of her defensive crouch with a snarl, swinging her sword out as she lowered her shield. He took a long step back, darting out of the way, sparing a contemptuous snort before swinging another arm out at her. She slipped back, brought her shield up, felt his knuckles graze the wood.

Easy, she thought through the shock. *Deep breaths. Concentrate.* She pulled the shield closer. *You've seen him bleed. He's not invincible. He's like every other monster you've faced. Take him down, body part by body part.* She tightened her grip on her sword. *He's not a dragonman, he's a—*

Anything she might have told herself after that, she'd never have believed.

Even if she could have heard it over the sound of wood splintering.

Gariath's fist came smashing through the shield, splinters lodged in his red flesh and spattering his own warm life across her face. She had barely enough time to recognize his hand before he suddenly jerked it back, taking the shield and the woman still attached to it with him.

Asper cried out as she was hauled from her feet and swung in a broad circle. She heard leather straps snap. She felt herself flying. She struck the sand and skidded across it before she slid to a halt. She groaned, trying to clamber to her feet.

Gariath took a glance at the shield hanging off his wrist like some macabre bracelet before he grabbed its rim and jerked it free. He tossed it, punctured and useless, to the side and fixed his sights on her.

"Turn away now," he growled as he advanced upon her. "Run back to your humans. Lead them somewhere else. I don't care and I won't follow."

"I can't do that," she said. Her body protested as she rose to her feet, legs aching and arms sore. "These people are counting on me."

"To die?"

"To fight."

She held up the sword in both hands, holding it out before her in a stance she had seen Lenk use before. Her bones felt as if they'd snap, her skin felt as if it'd break, but she forced her stare to be as hard as the steel she looked down.

"And I will."

She advanced a step.

"For them," she snarled. "For all of them. I will."

A step became a charge. A snarl became a roar.

"And I'll never *stop*!"

She leapt, swung. The blade came down.

A brush of flesh.

A tiny blossom of blood.

That's all her sword managed to claim before Gariath caught her by the wrist. She squirmed in his grip, kicked out at him, beat at him with her free hand. But against his scarred flesh, her blows were breezes and her blade was barely more than that.

"*Humans,*" he growled as he drew her closer with one hand. "You always act so desperate, as though everything in the world rested on your shoulders alone." His free hand drew back. "But your bodies are too small to take that kind of burden."

His fist slammed into her belly, knocked the wind from her, sent shock waves coursing through her.

"They will *break*."

She never even saw the next blow.

She barely even felt the fist smash against her jaw.

It was a blow that knocked everything out of her: sight, sound, sense. Something inside her came loose.

When she hit the ground, she still didn't know what had happened.

Vision darkened. Through glimpses she could see blood—hers—pooling on the sand, her teeth lying in it like porcelain fragments of a shattered doll. She could see him looking down at her with pity and with contempt and with hatred and trying to decide which of those to listen to. She could see him turning and walking away.

And slowly she could see the darkness closing in. Her head rang with a distant whining sound. Her blood dribbled down her mouth. But that was fine. She couldn't feel it. She couldn't feel anything.

Get up.

Except that.

Get up, my dear.
Burning. Fever. Bright.
Get up and finish your work.
Laughing. Squealing. Starving.
Get up and kill him.
She somehow found her way to her hands and knees. She somehow found the sight to look back. The refugees were there, watching, in horror and in shock and in fear.

And in anger.

Some of them, men and women, younger and older, armed with blades and rakes and sticks and whatever they had, were stepping up. They were pushing their way to the front. In their hands were weapons. In their voices were anger. And in their eyes.

Iron.

"Hey!"

She cried out before she knew she had. She stood without remembering getting to her feet. She held her sword despite not remembering finding it.

And when Gariath turned, he beheld a red, broken smile aimed at him down the length of a blade.

"That all you got, you scaly shit?"

It wasn't anger that was on his face. Not even fury. Rather it was an absence that cast his face into a hard, dark scowl. A void where the last vestiges of mercy fled him as he lowered his head.

And charged.

Steady.

Amoch-Tethr purred inside her head.

Gariath's feet thundered across the sands.

Let him come to you.

Amoch-Tethr giggled excitedly.

Gariath's teeth parted, soundlessly.

Together, my dear. Together.

The skin of her arm burned. A bright-red light blossomed beneath. Bones were painted black by a hellish glow.

Gariath's claws were out and the sound of his breath was in her ears.

NOW.

She swung her left arm out, reached for his throat. Bright-red flash, sin-black bones, fingers brushed against his flesh and tiny coils of steam whispered.

And did no more.

Her reach halted. She looked to her left, saw Gariath's claws wrap around her elbow. Her eyes widened, saw Gariath's claws sink into her flesh. She had a single moment for a single thought.

No.

And then he twisted.

A loud snap.

A louder scream. From her. From Amoch-Tethr. Their agonies tore through her skull, through her body, out her mouth. Tears welled in her eyes. Her left arm flopped uselessly to her side.

Maddened by pain, she swung her sword out, shrieking. She drove him back a step, another and another.

"You monster," she roared. "*You fucking monster.*"

"I gave you a chance," he snarled back.

"*You coward!*" She swung her blade again. "You turned! You left us! You left *everything* behind!"

Her blade struck flesh. Blood wept down its fuller. She saw his hand tightened around the blade. She saw him tear it out of her grip and throw it aside.

"Leave you? Leave *you*? To *what*?"

His bloodied hand reached out, seized her by the throat, and tore her off the ground.

"To the city you wanted? To the city you turned your back on? To Lenk and the other humans you abandon now that you've got new ones?"

He seized her by the ankle, raised her high over his head.

"After all the bones I broke for you, after all the enemies I killed, I never left you." A roar tore from his throat. "*YOU LEFT ME.*"

She was hurled to the ground, bounced off it, rolled across the earth to lie limp in the sands. No breath. No pain. No sense left for anything like that. Barely enough vision to look up, to see him looming over her, to see him raise his foot and position it over her head.

It felt as if it took an eternity to come down.

There was a soft sound, the smack of flesh.

And when an eternity passed and it still hadn't, she looked at his eyes.

They bulged from their sockets. His entire body was trembling, but unmoving, paralyzed. Her head lolled to the side, looked behind him.

There, insignificant against his bulk, stood the tulwar. The old one. The fat one. His pipe was in his mouth. His feet were firm on the ground. And his fist was firmly planted between Gariath's shoulder blades.

And Gariath did not move. Gariath barely breathed.

A flurry of movement. The old tulwar's fists flew, striking several more points upon Gariath's body. The dragonman's foot lowered, limp. The rest of him followed, collapsing to the earth beside her.

Not dead. Still breathing. Just barely. She could see that. The old tulwar had paralyzed him somehow, struck him in such a way as to render him like her.

Fallen. Useless. Numb.

Things grew dark. She could barely see the other tulwar rush out to help the old one grab Gariath and drag him away. She could barely feel the hands of Aturach and Dransun seize her and spirit her back to the refugees. She could barely hear the cries of concern as others rushed to her aid, brought blankets and water.

Darkness reached out for her, as before.

And when she listened for a voice inside her, all she heard was Amoch-Tethr.

Screaming.

＊＊＊

"Why?"

Feeling had returned to Gariath's limbs just a few moments after he had been dragged back into the gates of Jalaang. And while he stood under his own power again, he felt it wise to make certain that feeling had returned completely to him.

"Why?"

And he did so by smashing his fist against the old tulwar's jaw.

"WHY?"

The old tulwar sprawled out on the floor of the house, staggering to a sitting position. Under different circumstances Gariath might have been impressed that one so old had taken such a beating from him and remained conscious. But as it was, the fact that the old tulwar looked up at him and sneered through a bloodied mouth was merely aggravating.

"You know," he said, "a more worldly person might be more interested in the how. The Way of the Wooden Fist is not a maneuver seen by many, let alone felt."

"Answer me," Gariath growled.

"The Muusa Gon were keepers of ways like this," the old tulwar replied as he unsteadily rose to his feet. "Healers, originally, they learned the functions of the body, the weak spots on a creature that can make his muscles seize and nerves go cold."

"You're insulting me."

"I'm telling you about our people," the old tulwar said. He wiped blood from his lips and smiled. "Do you not find it interesting?"

Gariath swept across the floor, seized the old tulwar by his robe, and pulled him off his feet. His teeth were a hairbreadth from the tulwar's face, his nostrils drank in the perpetual stink of pipe smoke. Even here, even this close, the tulwar's scent betrayed nothing.

"You ended it," Gariath snarled. "I would have killed her, if not for you. I would have *won*."

"I did," the old tulwar replied simply. "And you would." He stared flatly into Gariath's black eyes. "Because you didn't know whom you were killing."

"A human. My *enemy*."

"I saw more than that." The old tulwar's voice grew harder, older, all the years inside him rising into his throat. "I saw a human, yes. I saw an enemy, yes. But I saw a girl, weak and no match for you. I saw a wounded woman, barely able to stand and challenge you. I saw *you* turn to attack a foe you had bested, because she called you some *names*." He sneered. "At that point I could watch no longer."

"So you betrayed me?" Gariath demanded, shaking him.

"No," he replied calmly. "I stopped *you* from betraying *us*."

"What?"

The old tulwar's hand rose. Two fingers extended, found Gariath's wrist and pinched lightly. A sudden surge of pain shot through his arm, bade him drop the tulwar. He landed lightly upon his feet, turned, and calmly walked to collect his pipe from the floor.

"You never saw, *daanaja*, because you never *looked*," he said. "If you had, you would have seen them, the humans in that rabble behind her."

"Weaklings," Gariath snarled, rubbing at his wrist. "Farmers, wailing pups, and bent old men."

"Humans," the old tulwar snapped back. "Humans who looked to her as our warriors looked to you when we seized this city. Had you killed her, they would have rushed forward with their frail weapons and attacked to defend her."

"And we would have killed them. Every last human, we would have—"

"NO."

The old tulwar's roar was impressive.

But it wasn't his voice that rendered Gariath speechless.

Anger. It burst from the old tulwar like a wound whose stitches had just been torn free. It peeled off him in an overwhelming reek, a sudden burst of emotion that had been growing ever since he had decided to bury it so many years ago. An anger so raw, so old, so deep that it flooded Gariath's senses: sound, scent, and sight alike.

"They would have killed them, yes," the old tulwar bellowed, rushing toward Gariath. "They would have killed them, those soldiers, those farmers, those mothers and daughters and old men and children and every last human until their swords stuck to their hands with blood.

"I will not let you do that, *daanaja*," he said, color rising into his face as he bared yellow teeth. "Killing those humans would have made them monsters, made them *everything* the humans say we are. We are *not* monsters." He slammed a fist against his chest. "We are *tulwar*. We are warriors. We are hunters. We protect our families and we do what we must and we try to survive. We are not monsters."

He shook his head.

"And we are not your weapons, either."

Gariath's eyes widened. The old tulwar fixed him with a penetrating stare and, for all the effort with which Gariath had tried to sense the elder's emotions, he wondered what the old tulwar had been seeing in him this entire time.

"Shaab Sahaar would have broken eventually," the old tulwar said. "Clans would have fought, ties would have dissolved. The wounds of the Uprising were too deep to heal there. We needed to finish what we started. And so, when you led them to Jalaang, I said nothing. I knew you could take us there.

"But I will not let you use them. I will not let you view them as weaklings, like you view the humans. I will not let you watch them die for whatever petty grudge you hold against the humans.

"Daaru, Chakaa, the other young tulwar...they look up to you. They see someone strong, someone mighty. They don't know what I do." He sighed deeply, all the anger seeming to seep from him in one great breath. "If you would lead them, lead them. Know them. Protect them. But if you would use them...". He fixed Gariath with a glare. "Then one of us had better kill the other, because I have no intention of watching that happen."

The dragonman said nothing for a long time. The old tulwar's anger slowly ebbed away, the scent of his fury dissipating. But what was left behind was no mere reek, but embers of a flame that had not died, merely quieted, and that waited to be stoked once more.

"Your name," Gariath said. "You said it wasn't important."

"And you believed me."

"I don't anymore."

The old tulwar nodded. "In another life I was he who would save his people and did not. I was he who led them into the jaws of Cier'Djaal. I was he who rose first and fell first." He straightened up to the proud tulwar he once had been. "Mototaru Humn Muusa Gon."

"You began the Uprising," Gariath whispered.

"And I will see it finished," Mototaru replied, calm. "Will you?"

Gariath said nothing. He looked down at the floor. He continued to do so, in silence, until there was a knock at the door.

When it opened, it was Chakaa's leering face that looked in. She glanced from him to Mototaru, then back to the dragonman.

"I had thought you'd have killed him by now, *daanaja*," she said. "Do you perhaps wish me to?"

Gariath glanced back to Mototaru, then shook his head. "No."

"Are you certain?" She patted the hilt of the immense blade strapped to her back. "Such a betrayal as the one he visited upon you must be avenged."

"There was no betrayal," Gariath said. He paused, sniffed. "The blade the human used was poisoned."

"Poisoned?" Chakaa's eyebrows rose.

"This one"—he gestured to Mototaru—"saw that and intervened. He saved my life."

Chakaa's face twitched as skepticism and disinterest battled before the latter ultimately won out. "As you say, *daanaja*. Poison, huh? Interesting trick. Well, they will not like to hear it, but I shall go tell the others, then."

"Do that," Gariath said. "And tell them to make ready."

"For?"

"More warriors are arriving from the desert. We will gather as many as we can, arm them as best we can." He stared at her. "And then we march on Cier'Djaal."

At this her eyes lit up. Her grin grew broad and feral.

"That," she said, "they will like to hear. I will tell them, *daanaja*."

She left. Gariath looked at the empty space where she had stood. From the streets of Jalaang outside, the scent of burning pyres rose and the howls of warriors drifted in.

"*Daanaja*," Gariath muttered. "She started calling me that. Now they all do. What does it mean?"

Mototaru did not look up as he packed his pipe with tobacco, lit it, and took several long puffs.

"Demon," he said, simply.

"Ah."

Darkness.

Only darkness. All around her. She had expected this. Welcomed it. Welcomed being spared the sights and sounds and blood and screams and tears and death. Welcomed cold. Welcomed numbness. Welcomed silence.

Found none of it.

Only darkness. Only heat. Only pain.

And a voice.

Well, that was disappointing.

"What happened?" she groaned.

Hm? Oh. Well, we lost.

"I'm sorry."

Well, it's not entirely your fault, I suppose. I could have done more, advised you better. We put too much faith in my abilities.

A brief, dark pause.

I tasted him. The barest lick of his flesh. To be denied a mouthful was . . . words fail to describe the cruelty. Had I consumed him, I could have—

"Please," she gasped. "He was my friend." She winced. "Once."

No longer.

"Does he know about us? About you?"

I don't think so. He was simply too strong, like his forebears. Pity. I doubt I'll ever get to taste something like that ever again. Everything else will simply taste like dust in comparison. Sad, isn't it?

"It hurts."

I suspect it might.

"Am I going to live?"

For now.

"Am I going to be okay?"

No.

Laughter. Sad. Short. A sigh.

But none of us are.

And all was silent, just for a moment.

Light came back to her swiftly and unmercifully, stinging her as she opened her eyes. Or eye, rather; the right one was swollen shut. She suspected that was the smart one of the two. Somehow she suspected that she wasn't meant to have awakened, that she should have stayed down in the darkness.

But when had life ever been that kind to her?

"She's awake!"

She recognized Aturach's voice before she recognized his face as he loomed over her. And she recognized his face before she recognized her surroundings. The orange light of a setting sun seeped through the canvas walls of a low-slung tent, painted her sweat-slick bedding and body.

She lay clad in her short-cropped undershirt and breeches, her robes folded neatly nearby. She rose to get them, found she couldn't. Not with one arm, anyway. Her left had been fitted with a sling and splint. Her ribs were tightly wrapped with bandages. Her body felt numb.

Not numb enough to make it forget the beating she had received, though. Agony welled up inside her at the slightest movement and she found herself propped up by hands that felt more powerful than they looked.

"Easy," Aturach said. "Easy. I tried to use a hecatine to numb you, but I don't think it worked all the way. And it certainly won't save you if you overstrain yourself."

"Overstrain myself," Asper repeated. "I feel like I'm going to snap in half if someone tells a good joke."

"That's . . . probably not too far off."

"How bad?"

Aturach winced. She glared at him through her good eye.

"How bad?" she repeated.

"Your arm's broken. Ribs are cracked. Your jaw's saved, but not by much. And your pendant . . ."

He glanced to her folded clothes. There, atop them, lay her pendant. The Phoenix of Talanas had been placed carefully upon a white cloth. Its left wing had been broken off and lay beside it, red with blood.

Her blood.

"We pulled it out of your chest," Aturach said. "I can't tell what's going on inside you, but I don't think it's good."

Worse than he knew. Just by breathing she could tell something important inside her had been fractured, ruptured, whatever. But through the agony, she couldn't tell which or where. Not yet.

"Why'd you do it?"

To look at Aturach, one would think he was the one in agony. It couldn't have been more than a few hours, yet he looked as though he had lost six weeks of sleep. His eyes were red and puffy, the trails where tears had made their way through the dust on his face still fresh.

"Why'd you fight him?" he asked. "That thing was a monster. He was going to kill you."

"There wasn't any other choice."

"Bullshit."

"Yeah?" She snorted. "Maybe you could have said something *before* I got my ass kicked, then." She pushed him off as fiercely as she dared to lean back onto the bedding. "What happened?"

"After that thing went down, we grabbed you and ran away. The refugees fell back to a nearby valley and made camp here. The tulwar didn't pursue, thank Talanas."

She would have scoffed at that if she hadn't been sure it would rupture something inside her.

"Should have left me," she said. "I fucked this up. I fucked all of it up."

"You did, yeah," Aturach said. "But not for the reason you think, or did you not fucking hear me earlier?" He leaned down beside her. "You're the reason we got as many as we did out of Cier'Djaal. You're the reason we got this far." He growled, spoke through a clenched jaw. "I don't know what made you fight that monster or what made you think you could win, but yeah, you fucked up by doing it. And that's because I don't know how you fucking missed that you're not alone."

"If you're going to give me some bullshit speech on friendship—"

"Not friendship. Responsibility. You led these people out of Cier'Djaal. You led them through the desert. You held us together. You have men, women, children, elders, all relying on you. You *cannot* be so fucking selfish as to think you can die now."

His words didn't hurt *quite* as much as her broken bones.

But they came close.

They weighed on her, bore her down, made her drape her good arm over her eyes and take a deep, staggering breath.

"You're wrong," she said. "We are alone. I led only a handful out of Cier'Djaal, left more to die in the city. And where did I take them? To the gates of a city controlled by tulwar about to march on Cier'Djaal."

"I hardly see how that—"

"Tell me Talanas is looking out for us," she interrupted. "Tell me Talanas is up there, watching us. Tell me we're all not just deluding ourselves."

Aturach told her nothing.

He knelt beside her, folded his hands in his lap, and stared at them.

"If you're going to ask me to tell you something that will make you believe again, I'm not going to," he said softly. "Somewhere between fleeing my city and trying to keep you from dying, I couldn't find the time to pen a speech to restore your shattered faith.

"But if you want me to tell you the facts…" He looked at her, eyes quivering. "If you want me to tell you that you nearly died to save these people and they are keen to return the favor, then I can probably find that time."

Voices rose from outside the tent, carried on the silence of the sunset. Aturach looked past the flap to the outside.

"Or you could just listen for yourself."

Asper paused, listened. She could make out forceful words, inflamed voices, and found herself unable to subsist on those scraps alone. Slowly, with an immense amount of pain and help, she edged her way to the tent's flap and looked outside.

The refugees had gathered around a large central bonfire, their eyes lit as they stared upon it. Or rather, upon the figure standing before it.

"Karnerians! Sainites! Khovura!" Dransun stood tall before the flames, fist held high and voice roaring to be heard over their crackle. "And now tulwar. Now a fucking monster! She stood against it, she fought it to a standstill, she was beaten and battered and still it could not kill her. You saw the beast yourself!" He thrust a finger out over the crowd. "Will it kill *you*, Djaalics?"

"*No!*"

"*Fuck no!*"

"*Death to the tulwar!*"

They cried out. Men. Women. With many voices.

"They took Jalaang," Dransun continued. "They killed your brothers and sisters there. They burned its houses to the ground. These savage animals now look to Cier'Djaal to do the same. Will you let them, Djaalics?"

"*Never!*"

"*For Cier'Djaal!*"

They rose up. The old. The young. They raised their fists to Dransun.

"The northerner stood against the foreigners. The northerner stood against the tulwar. The northerner did us a service. We owe her a debt." Dransun threw his arms out wide. "Will you repay it, Djaalics?"

No words this time. Nothing but one loud roar as they raised hands above their heads and filled the evening sky with steel. With rusted weapons and heirloom blades, with dented rakes and gnarled sticks, with everything they could find.

They stood tall.

"So they're willing to fight now," Asper muttered.

"They see what they stand against," he said. "They know what's waiting for them if they try to run or hide."

Asper rubbed out a kink in her neck. "Gariath says they have many tulwar behind the walls. I believe him. A handful of Djaalics aren't enough to challenge them."

"You'd need an army," Aturach said.

"I'll need two," she replied.

Aturach canted his head. "What are you saying?"

"I don't know," Asper said. "Nothing that makes sense just yet." She sniffed. "But since I'm not talking sense, I might as well say I've got to go back to Cier'Djaal."

"Last we heard, the Karnerians and Sainites were still fighting."

"Have they killed each other?"

"Not yet."

"Good," she said. "Let's hope they left enough to kill the tulwar."

"There's talking nonsense and then there's outright fucking insanity," Aturach said. "What makes you think you can turn them against the tulwar?"

"I'll have a word with them."

"Why do you think they'll listen?"

She looked down at her arm in the sling. Beneath the cloth, beneath the flesh, beneath the sinew, she could feel the bone. She could feel the break, the agony welling up from it. It was enough to make her wince just looking at it, enough to make her grit her teeth in agony, enough to drown out the sounds of the roaring crowds outside.

But not enough to numb her to the heat, not enough to make her numb to something moving within her arm, not enough to silence the sound of Amoch-Tethr giggling faintly.

"Because," she said softly, "I'm done talking."

FORTY

NEVER LET GO

Horses were swift and gaambols were maneuverable, but in the desert no mount rivaled a yiji.

They were hardy, storing fat and water in their crested backs so that they might wander the deserts for days. They were able to run swifter than the wind if they had blood in their noses. And while it was hard to verify, many shicts said that their eerie, gibbering laughter was evidence that they had great senses of humor—though they tended to prefer jokes whose punch lines involved someone being torn apart.

But what *really* made a yiji invaluable was its adaptability. On the desert plains or in the forests that edged them, as eager to ford rivers as they were to caper across fields, yijis were at home in just about any environment.

"Come *on*."

Which made the current disobedience of Kataria's mount doubly puzzling and thrice as frustrating.

"Move, you dumb thing!"

Kataria growled, kicked at the yiji's flanks, tugged on its mane. The beast did little more than whine and whimper, taking a few steps here and a few steps there before circling around and refusing to go farther.

It had been acting like this since they had emerged into the Green Belt, creeping over the dune walls of the valley and into the plains and paddies that made up Cier'Djaal's outskirts. And while it had managed to slink through the various farms and villages that dotted these fertile lands undetected by the human farmers and their beasts, the closer they got to the city, the more irritable the yiji had become.

"Don't do that." Kataria looked up and saw Kwar guiding her own beast over. She made a gesture at Kataria. "You're fussing with it, nudging and tugging. Be forceful with it." She made a fist. "Show the yiji you *deserve* to ride it."

"It's not *my* problem," Kataria snapped back. "The last ones we rode were just fine. This one is...I don't know, sick or something."

"Yijis don't get sick."

"Don't you tell *me* that. I've *seen* what these things eat."

Kwar snorted, spurred her beast about in a circle. She pointed long to the horizon. Against the setting sun, the Silken Spire burned like a torch, its glimmering silk bright against the shadowy spires and walls of Cier'Djaal.

"The city is *right* there," she said. "The hunters will just be returning now. If we can hurry, everyone will be there to hear what you have to say."

"Well, that sounds pretty great." Kataria gestured to the beast between her legs. "If you'd kindly translate that into whatever smell this thing needs to understand, we can be on our way."

Kwar looked down at Kataria's mount, sniffed. "She's frightened."

"Of what?"

"How should I know?" Kwar eased forward on her mount. "But she wants to return to her pack. Just hop on to mine and we'll ride the rest of the way together."

"No."

"No?"

Kataria's ears flattened against her head, she bared her teeth. "Nothing's changed, Kwar. I told you never to touch me again. I meant it."

It was hard to say what, exactly, Kwar was.

Selfish, of course. Obnoxious and childish, as well. Hot-tempered, feral, and downright pigheaded when she wanted to be were also accurate descriptors.

But there were tenderer sides to her. Sides Kataria remembered, at night, when unexpected chills crept over her and no one was there to draw warmth from. Memories of mischievous smiles and wild eyes. Memories of fingers sliding down her arm to intertwine with her own. Memories of someone who wore her fears plain on her face and gave her laughter freely and seized by the shoulders and kissed without thinking.

These were also Kwar.

But when Kataria spoke to the woman before her as she just had, when the fire in the khoshict's eyes dimmed and her ears drooped and she looked to the earth, it was hard to say what that woman was.

But she wasn't Kwar.

"I told you I'm sorry," she said.

"And I told you that you don't get to apologize for that."

"Even after I've come all this way?" Kwar held up her hand, the wounds on her knuckles scabbing over. "Even after *this*? I punched Shekune, the greatest chieftain who ever lived, for you. And it *hurt*. And I'd do it again and break my hand, my arm, my whole body for you."

Kataria met her with pursed lips and short words.

"Do this for our people," she spoke softly, so as not to betray the quaver in her voice, "not for me."

Kwar looked as though she might break down crying. She looked as though she might leap off her yiji and strangle Kataria right there. She looked as though she might turn her beast around, start walking, and never stop.

For a moment she seemed to do just that. She spurred her yiji past Kataria and began to head back.

But then, Kwar *was* pigheaded, when she wanted to be.

"For our people," Kwar said.

And then she let out a scream.

Kataria hadn't heard anything like the noise that tore itself out of Kwar's mouth, not until her yiji echoed it, anyway. The beast rushed forward, jaws gnashing and nipping and biting at the ankles of Kataria's mount. Her yiji yelped back, darting away from Kwar's mount, trying to get around it. But everywhere it turned, Kwar's yiji was there, jaws clamping and laughter gibbering.

Kwar spurred it forward, made it bite and gnash at its sister until Kataria's mount finally turned and took off running.

Directly toward Cier'Djaal.

Clever, Kataria was forced to admit.

She might even be forced to admit it to Kwar, if she didn't break her neck. The yiji's frantic lope beneath her left her clinging to its mane to avoid being flung from its back.

The beasts tore off, baying and loping through the fertile fields of Cier'Djaal's farmlands. Shepherds guiding their flocks in from the day's grazing went screaming in one direction, their goats in another. Small yokes of oxen huddled together, lowing as the yijis went rushing past. The beasts themselves ignored these easy meals, driven as they were.

The city walls loomed larger with every stride the yijis took until they towered over Kataria.

Good, she managed to think through her iron grip on the beast's mane. *We'll be there in no time. And once we are, we can make our way into Shicttown, find Sai-Thuwan, and—*

That last thought went flying as her beast skidded to a sudden halt.

She was tossed unkindly from its back, sent shrieking over its head to tumble across the sand. The few abrasions she earned were not enough to deter her from scrambling to her feet even as a curse scrambled to her lips.

"Hairy, lazy, disobedient, four-legged, motherfucking piece of—"

Whatever the end of that curse might have been—and Kataria was certain it would have been among her best—she never got to speak it. As soon as she found her feet, she found Kwar hurtling toward her. They collided with a shriek, falling to the earth.

The shicts fervently untangled themselves in time to see their yijis turning and bolting away from the city walls and fleeing into the hills.

"Ha!" Kataria whirled on Kwar, triumphant. "I *told* you it wasn't me!"

"*Sh'ne! Sh'ne kaia!*" Kwar chased the beasts a few steps, shouting commands in shictish after them, before giving up with a snarl. "Fucking weird," she muttered, brushing sand from her skin and clothes as she walked back. "They've never done that before. Something scared them."

Kataria was tempted to ask—after all, it was just good business knowing what sort of thing could frighten a beast that looked like the misbegotten offspring of a drunk hyena and a sober camel—but she resisted. The walls of Cier'Djaal rose up behind her, swallowing the dying light of the day. No time to worry about the sensitivities of beasts.

Kwar apparently had the same idea. She soundlessly followed as Kataria took off, walking south along the wall.

Heading through Cier'Djaal's main gates would be madness. Even if they hadn't been guarded, even if the streets *hadn't* been a battleground for the Karnerian and Sainite armies, they were still a winding, twisting labyrinth of houses and storefronts that would take hours to navigate.

However brief her time in Shicttown had been, though, Kataria had learned the khoshicts had a few ways of getting in and out of the city without going through the main thoroughfares.

And as they stalked south, they found that the walls of the city grew lower and more dilapidated. Eventually the towering, well-wrought walls of Cier'Djaal proper gave way to the splintering palisades of the outer city: an old, decaying memory of what Cier'Djaal had been in its infancy, back when this had been an actual city and not just a ghetto in which to cast the shicts.

Columns of smoke rose over the walls; the fires were likely burning for the evening's cooking. Though the noises from inside were somewhat quieter than Kataria would have expected for this time of day.

"Should be around here somewhere," Kwar muttered as she pushed ahead of Kataria. She walked the palisade, running fingers along the timbers until she found it. Tucked between two of them, she pulled out a hidden rope tied to the top. "Here." She glanced at Kataria, snorted. "You should probably go first. Wouldn't want you having to touch something I already did."

The venom in her voice went without response. Kataria cast a glare at her as she seized the rope. One moment to tug on it, one more to make sure her bow and quiver were secure, and she was climbing.

"Wouldn't want you having to touch something I already did," Kataria thought back to herself in what sounded like a very good mimicry of Kwar in her head. *Like it's my fault.* She winced as she hauled herself up the wall. *Suck it up. Make it quick. Talk to Sai-Thuwan, tell him about Shekune, then you never have to see her again. Then you can go.*

The thought that followed struck her like a fist.

But...go where?

Back to Lenk? Even if he wasn't dead, even if she could find him, what could she say to him?

But she couldn't stay with the khoshicts, could she? Even if they *didn't* cut her down for speaking out against Shekune, what hope could she have of finding a place with them after killing their greatest chance to strike back at the humans?

She couldn't be with them. She couldn't be with Lenk. Where could she go?

It felt as if she used to know.

But, she thought, perhaps she could figure that out later. She reached the top of the wall, swung a leg over. Whatever happened later, that was later. Whatever happened now, that was everything.

She took a breath and dropped down.

She landed beside a figure. She looked up and saw a dark-skinned face and wide, startled eyes. She had expected that.

What she hadn't expected was for them to belong to a human.

From beneath his helmet's visor, the Karnerian soldier's face was agog at the sight of a shict fallen from the sky. However slow his eyes might have been to understand, though, his hands were faster. Certainly faster than Kataria.

By the time she had her bow up, the soldier's sword was already in his hand. By the time she remembered she had spent all her arrows, the soldier's feet had left the earth as he leapt at her.

There was a scream.

There was steel.

None of it was hers. Or his.

Kwar fell from the sky, landed hard on the Karnerian's back, and bore him to the ground. She didn't appear to hear the snap that followed when his belly struck the earth—or perhaps she simply wasn't satisfied by it. Her dagger was in her hand, her teeth were bared, her ears were erect.

And she was stabbing.

Once, twice, six times. Messy business, in the neck and the cheek and any bare flesh that she could find. When it was done, the Karnerian lay oozing onto the sand. The woman who rose up wore eyes that burned bright through the spattered mask of gore across her face. And Kataria found herself tense, unable to look away.

Here. This creature. *This* was Kwar.

"No."

That voice, that soft whimper of fear that escaped her lips, that was Kwar, too.

And as Kataria looked up, it was she, as well. For as her eyes went wide, they were stung with smoke. And as she opened her mouth to scream, someone else did for her.

Shicttown once had been a ghetto.

Shicttown once had been a village.

Shicttown now was a funeral pyre.

Its tents were ablaze, erupting as Karnerians ringed them and tossed torches into them. Its yijis were butchered meat, dead on the ground as pups whimpered and nudged the carcasses. And its people…

Its people were everywhere.

Some fled, screams cut short as Karnerian spears pierced their backs. Some fought, swinging hatchets and blades before being brought down by Karnerian swords. Some begged, finding no mercy beneath the black visors of the helmets that scowled down on them one last time before their blades came down.

Everywhere they lay bleeding. Everywhere they lay burning. Everywhere they lay still.

"Father."

A voice.

"Father!"

Kwar's.

"Kwar!"

Kataria cried out, reached out, but neither availed her. Kwar was off, running, ears aloft and full of the Howling. Kataria tried to follow that sound. But she heard nothing but a twisting, shrieking cacophony; hundreds of voices screaming out for each other.

She shut her ears. She pressed them against the sides of her head and gritted her teeth as she took off after Kwar.

Over corpses, behind burning tents, around soldier formations. The Karnerians didn't look like people, didn't even look like humans. They were shadows at the edges of her vision, faceless suits of black armor that stalked among the fires, cutting down anything not wearing their colors. No rapine howls of pleasure, no savage looting, no barbarity.

Simple killing. Crude slaughter. Just another day for them, like all the others they had trained for.

Kataria did not look at them. She did not stop. She kept her eyes on Kwar, just as Kwar kept her eyes ahead, chasing an unspoken sound with no heed for the slaughter surrounding her. Luck had kept the soldiers from noticing her. But it would not last.

So Kataria ran faster.

Just as Kwar turned into the gap between two tents, Kataria leapt and tackled her to the ground. She was met with snarls and beating fists as Kwar attempted to writhe out of her grip.

"Let me go!" she growled. "Let me go, my father needs me!"

"They'll see you and kill you, too!" Kataria replied, tightening her grip. "We need to think this out. We need to—"

"*STOP!*"

The voice was one Kataria knew. The plaintive cry of a voice used to speaking with authority suddenly realizing its own impotence.

Sai-Thuwan.

Beyond the two tents, out in a large sandy space littered with bodies, the elder of the Eighth Tribe stood. His hands were extended in pleading, his eyes were wide with horror, his lips were struggling to find words with enough power to make the slaughter end.

"Please!" he cried out. "You must stop this!"

But the ears that his voice reached did not seem moved.

Karnerian soldiers surrounded him in a ring, spears drawn on him and shields raised. They held themselves, though, at the raised gauntlet of a towering Karnerian, every hairbreadth of him wrapped in armor but his shaven head. A severe face scowled down the length of a sword at Sai-Thuwan, and Kataria remembered it.

Speaker Careus. Leader of the Karnerians.

"You had the power to stop this," Careus said. "Had your people not attacked our convoy, had you been content to sit in your deserts and gnaw bones, we would not be here, savage."

"There's been a mistake!" Sai-Thuwan said, voice strained with desperation. "We did nothing, human, I swear to you! We're the Eighth Tribe. It's the Seventh that lives in the deserts. They likely—"

"Likely what, *oid*?" Careus spit the word. "Likely attacked because of a mistake? Likely slaughtered my men by *accident*? Those few that returned to us spoke of abominations: poisons that tore them apart from the inside, survivors flayed and hung from trees, cowardly ambushes in the dark."

"I...I don't know!" Sai-Thuwan said. "Maybe they...they felt threatened, I don't know! But we didn't—"

"Threatened? *Threatened?*" Careus's iron visage began to crack. "Is that what I should tell their families? Shall I tell their widows that they *threatened* a bunch of oids? Shall I tell their children that they'd still have fathers if only they hadn't *threatened*?"

"We can work this out." It wasn't clear whether Sai-Thuwan was trying to reassure Careus or himself. "We can work this out! We can make payments. We have hides, *sosha*. We can—"

"No, savage. The life of a Karnerian is not bought. It is forged in Daeon's arsenal, sent to earth to be shattered in his name. We are the Sons of the Conqueror, destined to bring order to this world."

Careus's hand went to his sword. The hiss of its steel as it left its sheath spoke louder than even the screams surrounding them.

"And we do not treat with animals."

"FATHER!"

Two voices rose. One was Kwar's, the other was not.

Thua, large and brawny, erupted from a nearby spot. His hatchet was in his hand, swinging a broad arc that took a Karnerian in the neck from behind. He tore it free in a gout of blood, swung into the next one before he could react, splitting his helmet and sending him to the ground.

"Father, *run!*" he screamed. He turned eyes, wide and wild as Kwar's, to Sai-Thuwan and gestured. *"RUN!"*

Sai-Thuwan screamed an unheard reply. Kwar shrieked unheard curses as she tried to free herself from Kataria. Karnerians breathed unheard prayers.

Thua's Howling screamed louder than the dying and the living.

His hatchet whirled, swinging wide and splitting spears and shattering shields. Gutting necks and cleaving into chests and splitting arms down to the bone.

The Karnerians thrust, scored glancing nicks and cuts here and there. And each one was met with an edge whetted with red as Thua howled, hacking limbs and splitting collarbones.

"Let me go! *LET ME GO!*" Kwar was screaming, writhing, shrieking, pounding, hitting, clawing. "I have to help my brother! I have to help Thua!"

Kataria snarled, clung, bled. And she did not let go. She accepted her bruises and her cuts and all the pain. She knew she could not let Kwar in there.

Because she knew how this would end.

With a roar of challenge, Careus swept forward, bringing his sword down in a savage hack. Thua whirled, brought his hatchet up to block it. The blow brought Thua to his knees. Careus's boot lashed out, caught him in the chest, and knocked him back.

He staggered, rushed to his feet, hurled himself at the Karnerian. He swung his hatchet in savage arcs, painting the sky with the gore that dripped from its edge. But where savagery had brought the other Karnerians low, it could not catch Careus. He moved, parried, saw each wild strike before Thua had even made it. His furious roars seemed impotent, his wild thrashing seemed pointless.

And yet he did not stop. He continued pressing forward, screaming, howling, slicing.

Until he swung too wide.

Too much energy spent. Slow on the backswing. His blow went wide. He brought up his arm to protect his chest.

And Careus's sword sheared right through it. It passed through his forearm, sank into his chest. Thua jerked on his blade, as though he had just been slapped instead of impaled. His eyes were full of disbelief, even as his life leaked out from between his lips.

"THUA!"

Kwar reached out for him, screamed for him, struck at Kataria's face to be released. Kataria accepted this. She accepted the pain.

Realization set into Thua's face as he slumped to his knees. As he looked, slowly, for a father who had disappeared, something dawned inside his eyes. A sort of peace, a wisdom that looked odd on a man so young.

In those last moments, before his head left his shoulders, Thua looked very much like his father.

Careus's sword hung steady in the air. As the headless body fell to the ground beside him, he did not even deign to look at it. He merely flicked gore from his blade and began ordering his troops to collect their dead.

And Kwar said nothing.

She did not scream. She did not speak. She did not move.

The khoshict went limp in Kataria's grasp, as though it were she who had just been killed instead of her brother. She stared forward, eyes wide and unable to comprehend what they had just seen.

But she did. Kataria knew this because, no matter how tightly she pressed her ears shut, she could not block out the sound of Kwar's Howling.

Long. Loud. Louder than the dying, Kwar's voice reached inside Kataria's head, into her skin, into her heart. It sat there and let out a long, sobbing scream.

It hurt to Kataria to move. Every time she did, Kwar's Howling plunged deeper.

But she did move. She rose to her feet. She hauled the khoshict to hers. She aimed herself toward the wall of Shicttown and started for the last exit she could remember.

She drew Kwar close. She held her tight.

And she did not let go.

FORTY-ONE

THE HAND THAT HOLDS THE KNIFE

He could still feel them.

Isn't that funny?

Days later, after the gutter-priests had done what they could, after the wounds had been cleaned and cauterized and bandaged and treated, he could still feel his fingers as if they were there.

Where do you suppose they are, anyway? Denaos asked himself. *Still down there in that dark hole, maybe. Do you suppose that woman cast them into some ritual fire for sacrifice? Or maybe just a regular fire to get rid of them. Oh, say, what if a rat got them? Yeah, you could turn the corner right now and see a big fat rat with your pinky in its mouth and chase it all over town trying to get it back. Wouldn't that be funny?*

He stared at his maimed hand.

Laugh. It's funny.

His mouth hung open, but no sound came out. Breath came instead, sickly and sour-tasting. It didn't taste like his breath. Not the way he remembered. He wondered then, if he were to close his mouth and will himself to simply stop breathing, would he die? Or would he just pass out and get the only sleep he'd had since they had pulled him out of that hole? Either one seemed as if it would be rather nice.

Easy there, fellow. This is all becoming a tad morbid.

And these didn't sound like his thoughts. These sounded like the thoughts of someone else. Or someone he once was or might have been.

Shit, what happened *down there?*

That thought, admittedly, could have been his.

Because, as much as he tried to think on it, he still wasn't quite sure. Whenever he closed his eyes—and he did that very briefly lately—he saw only flashes: scales coiling, ochre eyes flashing, the silver flicker of steel, and then pain.

Pain he recalled clearly. The blade chopping through one digit, sawing through the next. The feeling of cold wind on hot blood. The shrill screams that had torn themselves from his mouth and how they just did nothing. No matter how hard he screamed, there was no end to the pain.

Even now.

The gutter-priests had given him a flask of whiskey to drink from whenever the pain acted up. He had gone through it quickly. He had nothing left now when his fingers began to ache.

No, he corrected himself, they were stumps. The stumps where his fingers should have been ached. Yet he could *feel* them still. Or rather, he felt the absence of them.

When he twitched the stumps of his fingers, he felt them not moving. When he pressed his hand up against the cold stone of Cier'Djaal's wall, he didn't feel the chill of it. And when his whole hand ran along those stumps, searching for the fingers that had first held a girl's cheek, that had wrapped around blades and bottles with equal skill, that had plucked pockets and locks and skirts and belts alike...

They weren't there.

And that hurt in a way he could not explain.

He had been carved by a demon's claws, gnawed on by monsters, choked out by men—and at least three women—twice his size. He had been beaten, burned, hurled, bludgeoned, and broken before and had always walked away. Sometimes with a limp and sometimes by crawling a little to begin with, but he had always emerged and been ready to take it again.

Four fingers. That's all they had been. Four chunks of meat attached to bigger chunks of meat. No matter what he might have thought of them, they had just been meat. Losing them wasn't the worst thing that could happen to him. Nor even the worst thing that *had* happened to him.

So why does it hurt so much?

A shriek. Ten feet away from his head. He looked to his left. The seagull looked back at him, just a touch offended that he had so rudely lowered the tone of its home.

Denaos blinked, looked around. The scent of salt. The muttering of waves. The dim burning of those few streetlamps that someone had bothered to light, bravely standing up against the cold night creeping in from the sea.

Harbor Road.

Years ago a pale boy from the north had stepped onto these docks and Ramaniel had been born. Years later Ramaniel had died and it was Denaos who had stepped onto the boat that took him away. And just a few weeks ago, Denaos had come back.

No matter how many times he died and came back, Harbor Road never seemed to care. It was always the same press of flesh that sought to be the first to take money from those coming ashore and the last to send silk off with those heading to sea. Live or die, Harbor Road never changed.

Until tonight, anyway.

Battles between the Khovura and Jackals hadn't been enough to drive merchants away; after all, street violence was Cier'Djaal's second-biggest commodity. Only when the foreigners' war intensified, when fireflasks fell like rain, had the regular merchants pulled up anchor.

And with the carcasses gone, the vultures had fled. The sailors who had brought the wares left with their ships. The prostitutes who sold them comfort and the taverns that sold them courage had retreated back to the shadows. Warehouses had been locked up and given cursory guard that was always ready to flee should the foreigners decide to take their fight there.

All that remained on the streets was a few unlucky sailors who had been left behind and the few unlucky bars that had booze to sell. All that remained in the water at the docks was a few fasha pleasure barges that had either too many guards or not enough goods to attract thieves.

And seagulls, of course. There were dozens of the feathery little fuckers lording over their new kingdom.

But overall, Harbor Road looked quite a bit like an open-air tomb with plenty of room.

Which, he supposed, explained why he was there.

He couldn't remember how he'd gotten here. Nor even where he had been before setting out. He had finished his whiskey, found the pain still present, wandered out to find more, and simply never seen the point of stopping.

And somehow he had ended up here, in the stale salt air and among the sleeping drunks and seagulls picking at offal in the alleys.

And it still hurt.

"Ramaniel!"

He cringed. Voices seemed to do that to him lately. He didn't bother to turn around at the one that came from behind him, nor at the footsteps that followed it. The hand that was laid on his shoulder felt abrasive, like a palm bristling with needles.

"What are you doing out here?" The voice sounded strange in his ears. "I've been looking everywhere for you."

It wasn't until Anielle was in front of him, her needle-hands on his face and forcing him to look up into her dark eyes, that he recognized her. And that lasted for only a moment. Whatever she saw in his face, it twisted hers into that of someone he didn't know.

If he had ever known her at all.

"Fuck, Ramaniel." Her eyes drifted to his maimed hand. She winced. "Rezca told me what happened. Silf alive, I didn't want—"

"Rezca?" Denaos muttered.

"The gutter-priests told him. He was the first one I found when I came looking for you. I escaped that place, wherever it was Teneir took us, and I went to find you, but I . . ."

She paused, glanced around.

"It isn't safe out here," she said, voice dropping. "No place is safe."

That much made sense to him, at least.

She took his whole hand in her own, wrapped her fingers tightly around the ones he still had. And it still hurt. Somehow it still did.

"Come on," she whispered.

And he did. His legs felt numb under him, simply following along as she pulled him down the streets and past the drunks and empty bars and quiet whorehouses.

She was saying something to him, but he couldn't hear her. He couldn't hear anything in that open-air tomb but the sound of her footsteps and the heavy gulps of sick breath he took. And they echoed forever.

It was the pain. His ears were full of it. Her hands were made of knives. His skin was made of paper. Every time she pulled, he felt like bleeding. Every time she squeezed, he felt like weeping. And every time she reached back with her other hand, as though assuring herself that he was still there, he felt like screaming. But it would do no good, he knew. He wouldn't even hear it. He couldn't hear anything.

She did it.

But that. Those three words.

She did it.

A nail in his ear. His thoughts a hammer. Coming down, over and over. *She did it.*

His thoughts. Or someone else's. Ramaniel's or Denaos's or some other dead man's. He didn't know. And he couldn't shut them out.

All the ways she had tried to convince him to leave with her. All the ways she had tried to keep him away. All the looks she had spared, the words she had said. She hadn't been there when Yerk came to save him. She was gone. And now she was here.

Escaped, she said. How could she have escaped while he was left to bleed out in the dark?

A slurry of fears and pains ran through his head until they formed scaly lips, Teneir's mouth puckered in a smile as she hissed.

You know who.

Her name, a needle in his neck.

"I'm sorry."

He heard her voice. He started, looking down at her. They had stopped moving, in an alley somewhere, amid refuse and castoff from the sailors. No sounds here, no echoes. He could hear her.

"I'm so sorry," she whispered. She looked up at him, eyes brimming with tears. "I shouldn't have run. But they left my shackles loose and I heard the screaming and I ... I just ..."

Escaped.

Unscathed.

From a den below the earth, filled with Khovura and whatever monsters Teneir commanded.

How?

"Ramaniel," she said, gently cupping his face. "Ramaniel, I should have done more. I should have convinced you. I should have drugged you and taken us to a ship and left when ..."

But she hadn't.

And they hadn't.

She had wanted to leave, but she hadn't left him behind. She'd had something left to do with the Jackals. She had wanted so badly to leave, but she hadn't just left on her own.

How?

"No. I won't give you excuses." She shook her head. "I won't do that. We're together now. We've escaped. We've…we can get out of here, Ramaniel. Finally. Please, let's just go. Let's just leave this behind."

He couldn't.

No matter where they might run to, whatever they might leave behind, he would still hurt.

"Ramaniel." She drew his face closer to hers. "Please." Her breath, warm and healthy, upon his lips. "Forgive me."

She drew his lips to hers, closed her eyes. Panic surged through him at her touch, at this closeness, at how easy it was for her to do it. But slowly it faded. And slowly pain followed. Almost.

"Forgive me," she whispered as she parted from him. "Forgive me." She took his maimed hand in both of hers. "Forgive me."

She drew it up to her lips, hesitated a moment. Then, gently, pressed her lips to the bandage and closed her eyes.

And then, in the span of the echo of a seagull's cry, he knew why it hurt.

Because of her.

Because she had done it to him. Because she had escaped and he had not. Because he had bled and she had not. Because he hadn't listened to her. Because it didn't make sense. Because it made perfect sense. Because she was the rat. Because he was the fool. Because she had betrayed him, betrayed the Jackals, betrayed the city. Because he hadn't been able to save them, the people, his friends, his fingers, any person or any thing. Because the blade was in his hand. Because—

The blade was in his hand.

He didn't remember how it had gotten there.

His forearm was on her throat.

He didn't remember doing that.

But there it was. The blade at her throat. Her eyes wide with fear. Her mouth, open and quivering. Her screams choked behind his arm as he pressed her against the wall of the alley.

His stumps aching, on fire. His blade trembling, a tear falling from her eye as a wordless plea fell from her mouth, both of them hitting the steel. He pricked it beneath her jaw, watched the blood blossom. His thoughts, a hammer in his ears, over and over.

She did it.

Left you to die.

Escaped. How? She did it. She did it. She did it. She did—

Steel flashing.

Falling.

Clattering.

His voice, raw and painful in his ears.

"Go."

Her voice, sharp and full of needles.

"Ramaniel, don't—"

"GO."

He didn't remember what she said before she left. He didn't remember what she begged of him or what she denied. He didn't remember when she disappeared or when he staggered back and pressed his hands, whole and maimed alike, to his face, and collapsed.

And he didn't remember who it was—Ramaniel, Denaos, or another dead man—who emerged from the alley and staggered off into the night.

— ❧ —

Still night.

It felt as if hours had passed. More than enough to let the day come. Not that it mattered, of course. He had some vague notion that things would be clearer in daylight; must have heard Asper say that somewhere or something. But clarity wasn't what he needed. What he had done was all too clear. What he needed now was something dark and quiet to smother it beneath.

And the night was inadequate for that.

So, like most vermin, he slunk away, and crawled under a bridge and stared down at the water.

Silktown had been built across the streams where the sea ended and the Lyre River began to wend its way out into the desert. The fashas liked the natural barrier to separate themselves, and the architects they had commissioned had crafted arches that spanned the waters.

The sons and daughters of fashas, young lovers with unnecessary dreams, often stood on those same arches at night. Drunk off the promise of their easy futures and carefree presents, they would kiss coins and toss them into the water to make wishes that had already been granted. Enterprising urchins, such as he had been, found it profitable to lurk under bridges and go diving for these little tokens of adoration.

A rich man's kiss could buy an awful lot, back in those days.

He stared down at the river, swift and black and rushing as it ever had been. Back then the promise of coins at the bottom of it had made it seem less daunting. But tonight it looked like some gaping maw that swallowed everything.

He stared at it, into it, as though if he stared long enough, Anielle might emerge from it as she had so long ago and hold aloft a golden coin and say, "Throw away those rags, pale boy, I'm buying you something pretty."

In hindsight, a happy ending had never been possible. Not for people like him. Those were for people like Asper, women who did good work and found good men and had hard and happy lives. People like him led easy, dirty lives whose happiest ending usually involved doing what those good, hard folk couldn't.

For a long time, he had been fine with that. He had been fine being the man who did what the others couldn't, the man who got his hands dirty, the man who knew the dark secrets and the dark trades. Asper could heal the sick and inspire the hopeless. He could just stick a knife where it needed to be stuck.

Turned out he wasn't even very good at that.

The rat had been one of the Jackal heads. That's how they'd known about all the Jackal operations and sabotaged them. The rat had been working with a fasha. That made sense, too. Anielle had wanted out, had had money to get out, had wanted him to go with her. Teneir had even said so. And then Anielle had escaped while he had been left behind.

It all made sense. Bloody, ugly, dark sense. And when it came down to it, he hadn't been able to do what had to be done.

Maybe that was why everything still hurt.

Footsteps scraped on stone to his right: deliberate, to let him know someone was coming. He looked up, caught a glimpse of starlight reflecting off Rezca's spectacles before he came beneath the bridge. He settled beside Denaos without a word, stared down at the river alongside him.

Two northerners. Last heads of the Jackals, save Yerk. Ironic, Fenshi might have called it. But then, Fenshi never really understood irony.

"You are bloodied," Rezca noted.

"Yeah," Denaos said.

"Anielle is dead, then."

A pause, longer than he intended. A lie, harder than it used to be.

"Yeah." Denaos looked at him. "You figured it out?"

"Shortly after she came to me to find you. I got the impression she was trying to avoid me. But I saw what happened to..." He made a gesture to Denaos's hand. "And then her, without a scratch. I put it together. Too late, sadly."

"You should have been the one to do it."

"I should have."

"You're supposed to be in charge."

"I am."

"You failed."

"I did."

There was remorse in his voice, but not a lot. Rezca didn't work that way. He allowed himself to feel as much as he needed to, but that wasn't much. Head of a gang like the Jackals, he had to be hard.

"What now?" Denaos asked.

"Regroup," Rezca replied. "Consolidate. Assess our priorities and act on them, same as we did after the riots."

"Teneir's the fasha behind the Khovura," Denaos said. "Should go after her."

"I am aware of that, yes." Rezca's face lowered. Slowly he removed his spectacles and rubbed his eyes. His body shook with an involuntary chuckle that he couldn't contain. "Silf, but isn't this a fucking mess?"

Denaos didn't disagree.

"Ever since I came off the boat and into this city, I can't remember a single time when the fashas actually ran things." He looked to Denaos. Beneath the glare of his spectacles, his eyes seemed clear and calm. "It's always been down to the thieves, hasn't it? Fashas squabble, thieves sort it out. Merchants dispute, thieves get things moving. Richest city in the fucking world and it'd all come crashing down if its vermin stopped working for a day."

"Shit's always been bad," Denaos said. "Not as bad as it is now."

"No, not as it is now." Rezca sighed. "Did you want to be a thief, Ramaniel?"

Denaos stared at the river. "No one wants to. It just happens."

"Yeah. It just happens. Same as any shit." Rezca rubbed his neck. "When we were kids, we told ourselves it was just to get by. When we were young, we told ourselves it was just to get big. Then suddenly we're on top and doing the same shit every other thug before us did."

"Just happens," Denaos repeated.

"Yeah. Just happens." Rezca chuckled, replaced his spectacles. "I had this idea that I was going to be the one to change things, you know? Stop lurking in the dens and taverns and actually step up. Unite the fashas, bring the Jackals out, form an army, turn this city into a nation instead of a pack of dogs gnawing at each other. We already ran the city. Wouldn't have been too hard to bring it out in the open."

"You ever heard of a thief going out in the open?" Denaos asked.

Rezca paused. "No."

"Me neither."

"Still...that's how it's always gone, hasn't it? We keep doing things the same way because that's the way they've always been. More killing, more burning, more stealing. And this city never goes anywhere because of it."

"Where's it supposed to go?"

"Someplace where foreigners can't kill thousands over shit from a spider's anus. Someplace where no one has to sell themselves for food. Someplace where we can earn lives without having to buy them."

"An idealist criminal," Denaos said. "Fenshi would have applauded."

"Fenshi's gone. Anielle's gone. Yerk vanished in the night. You and I are all that's left, Ramaniel. You, me, and whatever ideals I can scrape together."

"And you want to build a city on them, huh?"

"More than a city. A nation. The world envies Cier'Djaal's fortunes. It's time we showed them an entire system they can envy. I can make that happen."

He rose to his feet, brushed his leggings off.

"But I can't do it alone, Ramaniel."

Denaos drew in a breath full of the scent of water. He looked up at Rezca. He saw those calm, clear eyes through the glass of his spectacles. He saw the smile that men as hard as Rezca weren't supposed to have. He saw Rezca's open hand, extended to him.

Just half a breath before he felt Rezca's knife enter his back.

No pain. Not this time. Just cold steel parting flesh and sinew and scraping against bone. Just warm life seeping out of him and staining his clothes. Not even a thought to spare as it plunged into his back three more times.

"Teneir has resources I don't," Rezca said between strokes of the blade. "Her ideals are ridiculous, of course, but this city won't run without me, no matter how hard she prays. It really was the better deal, Ramaniel."

Denaos froze, twitching, body unable to understand what had just happened. His mouth craned open in an agonized shriek that wouldn't come. He rolled onto his back, eyes welded shut, limbs locked in mid-spasm. He felt Rezca loom over him, lay a hand gently upon his shoulder.

"Anielle would forgive you," he said. "But not me. I hope you'll tell her, though..." His voice shuddered, broke. "For what it's worth, I am sorry."

Steel in his chest. Stone beneath him. Blood blossoming in bright trails as he was pushed gently over the edge and plunged into the water below.

And sank. And sank. Until it no longer hurt.

FORTY-TWO

THE BLADE, FALLEN

It had once been a man.

Or a saccarii. Maybe a tulwar or a shict. A warrior, a merchant, or a beggar. Maybe a father or a grandfather or just some orphan who wandered into the wrong place and said the wrong words.

Doesn't matter much now, I guess, Lenk thought as he peered out from the doorway. *Whatever it is, it's an ugly son of a bitch.*

And yet as he dared to edge closer to the door and look out onto the street, lit by the unnatural light of the globe-lamps, *ugly* seemed too weak a word and *son of a bitch* too generous.

It loomed seven and a half feet tall, its upper body a mass of bulging, bloated muscle that its skinny, all-too-human legs seemed ill equipped to handle. Its left arm was just as thin, while its right was an almost hilariously disproportionate pillar of muscle ending in a massive clawed hand. Its chest was a barrel-shaped mess of scales and leathery skin. The remnants of its face, which once had been a man's, were contorted in a gaping-mouthed, unblinking vision of agony.

And somehow, for all its misshapen horror, that still wasn't the weirdest thing about it.

From each of the abomination's shoulders sprouted a long, glistening serpent. And where the formerly human face was a witless, unseeing patch of flesh, these serpents swung their spade-shaped heads around on writhing coils. Their eyes were bright with attention, tongues flicking in and out as they searched the empty street.

A moment. They swung their heads over to Lenk's hiding place in a nearby door. He held his breath and slid slowly behind the frame.

They can't see you, he told himself to keep himself calm. *They can't see you. Stay calm. They can't see you.*

Their twin gazes rested on his hiding spot for a tense, breathless eternity. Then, slowly, swung away and turned their attentions back down the street. The tiny legs of the abomination quivered as they began to haul the bulky mess of muscle atop it down the street, seeking prey elsewhere.

Lenk waited until the feeling of wanting to vomit passed. That, he supposed, was as good an indication as he was ever going to get.

"It's gone," he muttered, turning to the darkness of the house. "Are you all right?"

Shuro didn't take her eyes off the bandage she was wrapping around her arm. She looked more annoyed than in pain, which Lenk couldn't help but feel impressed by—he had seen the gash that thing had made in her arm.

"I was careless," she spoke through clenched teeth. "Let my guard down. Won't do that again."

"You could be forgiven." Lenk eyed her sword lying beside her, its blade slick with red. "You killed about six of them first."

"And there were twenty more." She leveled an icy glare at him. "There will always be more. The fact that they're here means we are out of time. Khoth-Kapira has called his chosen. He is ready to rise."

Lenk wanted to counter that, or at the very least ask her how she was so certain. And he just might have, had his eyes not been drawn by a flash of movement within the empty house.

There, white against the darkness, Mocca stood at the back of the house. His eyes were affixed to Lenk with a hard look. His lips were pursed in unwavering silence.

A day and a night had passed since Lenk had discovered his secrets: Oerboros, his breeding pits, his plans. A day and a night of finding Shuro, fighting their way through the twisted, hulking forms of the Khovura. A day and a night of fleeing, searching, surviving.

In all that time, Mocca had never once disappeared from his sight. And in all that time, Mocca had never once said a word.

His face was unreadable, his expression inexplicable. Lenk was tempted more than once to just start screaming, demanding what he wanted. And he might have, had Shuro not been by his side this entire time.

"So what do we do?" Lenk asked.

"We stop them," Shuro said. Her sword all but leapt to her hand as she rose. She inspected it, drew a cloth from her belt, and wiped it clean. "There are a number of ways a demon might be called back from hell and our order is not clear on how these are done. But we know that they all require outside intervention."

"That's what the Khovura are here for. Hell, they must have crossed miles of desert," Lenk said. "So we stop them and..." His eyes drifted up. Mocca stared back, silent. "And we stop Khoth-Kapira from returning."

"The Khovura would be here to protect whatever they're using to call to him," Shuro said. "A ritual, maybe. Or a sacrifice. Whatever it is, it'll be done in a single location."

"Find that, find the Khovura, stop them," Lenk said. "Easy enough."

"Easy." Shuro made a sound that was either a chuckle or a grunt. "Sure."

"You're sure you can handle it?" Lenk eyed her arm. "With your wound and all..."

"Whether I'm sure or not is irrelevant." Whatever mirth was in her vanished, replaced by cold words and cold eyes. "I have a duty to do, so I will do it."

Lenk nodded. "What about Chemoi?"

"Not a priority. If she's not dead, we'll find her after we're finished."

He had expected that, spared nothing more than another nod for it. He returned to the door of the house, leaned out, and glanced up and down the street. Beneath the artificial orange light of the marching lamps, he saw nothing.

"All clear," he said. "What do you—"

He turned and found her standing not a hairbreadth from him, eyes locked on him. Her stare was as deep and blue and intense as ever, but the severity he usually saw inside her eyes was softened, somehow, resolution replaced with a quiet desperation.

"I need to tell you," she said, her voice frightfully soft, "that I hope we both survive."

Lenk blinked dumbly. "Is there a reason for—"

"Because we might not," she interrupted. "And this whole time I've been talking of duty, I forgot you never swore the same oaths I did. You could go now, if you wanted." She glanced to the floor. "I wouldn't stop you."

And there she was again: the Shuro he had seen so rarely that he wondered, at times, if he had simply dreamed her. A girl with a carefree laugh and shy eyes who got nervous around him. It was as though there were two women, and Lenk wondered which was the real one: the swordswoman with a hidden laughter or the girl who buried herself under oath and duty.

Maybe he could find that out, he thought. Maybe, after all this was done.

After all. . . a cold feeling welled up inside him, an iron knife stuck in his belly that cut its way up to his throat. *What else do you have to go back to?*

"I'm here," he said. "You're here. We're not leaving without each other."

She looked at him for a moment. She did not so much move toward him as fall into him, stumbling awkwardly to him and pressing up against him. She wrapped her arms around his body, held him tightly, as though this were her very first hug and possibly her very last.

"Thank you," Shuro said.

She pulled away from him. And just like that, the girl was gone. Her eyes were hard as the hand clenching her sword. She spared him one more look before pushing past him and stalking out into the street.

She glanced down to one end of the street, made a motion for him to follow. He did so, blade in hand as he counted ten paces behind her: enough to move and enough to be close should they be ambushed. They kept close to the walls of the buildings lining the streets, walking beneath the shadows of the looming houses and temples as they followed the street west.

In the open air, their footsteps made not a sound. The guttural roars and hisses of the Khovura abominations were silent. Even the wind no longer moaned, leaving the city in a state of absolute silence.

"She loves you."

Naturally, Lenk supposed, Mocca *would* choose this moment to start talking.

"Or at least the idea of you." The man in white appeared at the periphery of his vision. "One can hardly blame her. Surrounded as she was by acolytes and hearing of nothing but duty, you must seem rather exotic."

Lenk ignored Mocca—or tried. He kept moving, kept his eyes forward, left Mocca behind. Though it didn't help. No matter where he walked or looked, the man in white was always there, at the edge of his vision.

"Not to imply that you lack virtues," Mocca continued. "Well traveled, courageous, having seen places and met people she could but dream of...well, who could fault her being attracted to the idea of that?"

Eyes forward, he told himself. *Eyes forward, sword ready, ears closed.*

"I imagine the idea of her has allure, too, doesn't it?" Mocca's voice was flat, incisive, a scalpel blade given sound. "Once this is all done, you could go back to the monastery with her. Of course, they've trained all their lives to kill, so your desire to put down your sword will sadly go unfulfilled. But then, that hasn't been working out, has it?" No mockery. No sneering. That was a cold, bleak truth. "And who knows? They've been training all their lives to kill *me*. And once I'm gone, perhaps they'll dedicate themselves to something else?"

He chuckled. "After all, it's not as though this world will be any less awful for my absence."

Lenk had known a few demons. He had killed each and every one of them. And each and every one of them had died screaming, cursing, savagely wailing in the agony of their last moments. Demons were plucked from hell and given a brief taste of a cleaner world before he sent them back to the darkness. It made sense that they would resist going back with everything they had.

To hear one of them speak so casually, so calmly of his own demise, left Lenk slightly unnerved.

It's a trick, he reminded himself. *Remember what you saw down there. Remember what he's done.*

He kept his eyes on Shuro as she led the way, creeping toward an intersection where the street emptied out into a square.

"Perhaps you weren't meant to put down your blade after all," Mocca said, his voice trailing behind Lenk's ear. "There were thousands of opportunities to do so, after all. But you're still here, aren't you? At the very least, were you to go back to her monastery, you wouldn't be alone. You could share time, share a bed, perhaps more."

Shuro swept to the corner of a nearby building, crouched down, and peered out over the square. Lenk began to rush to join her.

"Of course," Mocca said softly, "she's not the one you love."

And Lenk froze in his tracks. Mocca's voice was a slow poison spreading through his veins, making his blood run cold and his guts clench into knots. Whatever warmth had lingered from Shuro's embrace was gone. What remained was a cold truth, ugly and heavy as a beaten anvil.

Shuro had many sides to her, it was true. But whether she was the girl who had been given a sword too young or the warrior with flashes of laughter and shyness, it didn't matter.

She was not Kataria.

But then, that didn't matter, either, did it? Kataria was gone, fled with another woman, of her own kind. Wherever she was, if she was even still alive, she was happier. And even if she wasn't, she was not here.

Shuro was here.

His blade was here.

And so, so many things he needed to stick it in were here.

Up ahead, Shuro waved him over with an urgent expression on her face. He hurried over, crouched down behind her by the building's corner. The giant square, a nexus of four streets, was dominated by a towering statue at the center. Mocca's robed body rose from a stone pedestal and atop his shoulders, one head with four of his smiling faces looked down each street.

But it was what lurked beyond the statue that drew Lenk's attention.

Hulking and withered, slithering and shambling, hauling flaccid limbs and sprouting serpents, their faces contorted in witless agony, the mutated remains of the Khovura dragged themselves across the street on the far side of the statue. More emerged from other streets, joining them in a slow-moving river of malformed flesh, all of them flowing into the street leading north with a singular purpose.

Both Lenk and Shuro breathed shallowly, did not move. The multitudes of heads present in that macabre parade did not turn their way yet, but the slightest movement might draw their attention. Stillness was imperative, silence was absolute.

"Have you forgotten?"

Almost absolute.

"You began this journey for a new life and the shict, and now you have neither." Mocca leaned over him, speaking bold words that no one else could hear. "No matter whether I live or die, you'll have nothing left but the very sword you've tried so hard to put down."

Shut up, Lenk thought, as though he could simply will Mocca's silence by thinking hard enough. *Shut up*.

"And all of it, all the promise I hold and all the good I could do, you're willing to throw away for what?" Mocca hissed. "The words of a spited lover? The mistakes you saw in the pit? They were but the cost of creation, sins I paid to bring progress and perfection to a people sorely in need, sins I have paid for over thousands of years. Am I not entitled to redemption? Am I not permitted to atone for those sins by improving this wretched world?"

Lenk wanted sorely to scream, if only to shut up the man in white and drown him out with sheer noise. But he didn't dare speak now and reveal his secret to Shuro. Now was not the time.

"So that's it?" Mocca muttered, sounding almost petulant. "Wars I could end, diseases I could cure, lives I could save . . . you don't care at all for them? The misery of this world does not move you? So be it."

A pause. Long and filled with dreadful anticipation. When Mocca spoke next, it was a whisper right next to Lenk's ear and it carried with it the venomous chill that he had felt.

"But what of Kataria's misery?"

Every muscle beneath Lenk's clothes clenched. His blade shook in his hand. Only by the sheerest will did he not whirl and strike at Mocca for even speaking her name, for all the good that would have done.

"Forgive me," Mocca whispered. "I know it was your desire that I stay away from her and out of her head, and perhaps that I sought her out will be but one more sin for which I'll atone. But I did. I reached across the desert and found her." He hesitated. "She . . . did not leave you by choice, Lenk."

"*What?*" he demanded, narrowly avoiding shouting out.

"Silence," Shuro hissed, remaining still.

"She was taken in the night," Mocca continued. "And now she stands at the center of a war that will soak this world to its core in blood. I have

seen it, all of it. The shicts are on the move, ready to slaughter. The tulwar march to Cier'Djaal to burn it to the ground and the humans stand
poised to tear each other's throats out before all they know becomes
bone and ash. A hundred tides of battle and they will all converge upon
her."

It's a trick. Lenk repeated to himself, over and over. *It's a trick, it's a
trick.*

A pause. A singular, momentary absence of thought. And then...

But if it isn't...

"Lenk, listen to me," Mocca said, "I have made countless mistakes,
maybe some so severe that I cannot fix them, but failing to stop this war
cannot be the last one I make. I can save this world. I can save everyone.
If you cannot put down your sword, let it be used to save a thousandfold
more lives than it's claimed. And if none of that moves you..."

Mocca spoke softly.

"Then let me save *her,* Lenk."

Lenk looked at him, at this man, this figment, this demon. And in his
eyes and in his face, it was easy to forget what he was. Within his eyes
danced urgency, desperation, impotence: common maladies of common tyrants whose grasps had proven slipperier than they'd thought.

But looming large over these vulgar emotions, the slate upon which
they were chiseled and the cracks at the edges, was a more peculiar emotion. One that Lenk had seen before in the eyes of men and women who
knew the value of life shortly before it was taken.

Fear.

Honest, breathless, common fear. Such as any mortal would feel.

"Let me do this, Lenk," he whispered. "Let me help her."

"They're gone."

Mocca vanished. Lenk's attentions jerked back to Shuro. She was up,
creeping out into the square. The shuffling, groaning press of flesh continued toward the street leading to the north two hundred paces ahead,
none of them bothering to look behind them.

"They're all heading to the same place," Shuro whispered. "That's
where it's happening."

They crept down the street after the Khovura procession, sticking
close to the buildings. The city grew like a forest around them. The
humble low-roofed domiciles rose with each city block, becoming

towering spires that reached high into the night sky. The glowing lamps thinned out, plunging the city into a deeper darkness.

And as one light died, another was born. In the distance, through the oppressive press of spires and towers, a red light blossomed, a drop of blood pricked from a black finger. It grew with each step, a bold and hellish crimson that seemed to brighten and dim with every breath Lenk took.

A heartbeat.

And with it a voice.

"Kapira . . . Kapira . . . Kapira . . ."

Growing in cadence, in fervor.

"Kapira . . . Kapira . . . Kapira . . ."

And in volume.

"Over here."

Shuro seized him by the shoulder, pulled him into the darkness of a nearby building. A pack of abominations came slithering past a moment later, heading north toward the light.

Just how many *were* there? Lenk wondered. How many had they already seen?

"Stairs over here," Shuro whispered.

The interior of the building seemed to be a library of sorts, its scrolls and tomes long rotted away and its shelves well on the way to joining them. And though it was difficult to see within, Lenk made out a dim shaft of light at the rear of the room illuminating a spiraling staircase leading up. He followed Shuro as she followed it, scaling up to another level, then another, until they emerged onto the roof and into the chill wind of the night.

The buildings here pressed close together, and it was easy enough to pick their way across the rooftops and toward the red light that reached up into the night sky with darkly luminous claws.

While it had been merely unsettling when viewed from the ground, from this high up it seemed less like a light and more like blood painted across the sky. It pulsed and quivered with a life that it should not have. Just looking at it made Lenk want to turn and run until he reached the cliff and then hurl himself off.

Yet Shuro did not turn back, so neither did he. They moved carefully across the roofs until they came to the very last edge of the very last building. And there he saw it.

Carnage.

Perhaps he had been naïve to believe that Rhuul Khaas had fallen bloodlessly, or perhaps simply hopeful at the dearth of evidence of violence around the city. Whether it had been foolishness or hope, he didn't bother asking. As he gazed upon the vast circular plaza that opened up before him, he realized that the savagery that came with casting down Khoth-Kapira hadn't been absent.

Merely contained.

Here was the destruction, in the char and soot and dried ichor that painted the faces of the buildings black. Here was the devastation, the benevolent faces of the statues that had watched over the plaza smashed and scarred. Here were the dead...

And there were many.

They stood, rather than lay, their flesh rent from their bodies and their bones scorched black. Some held rusted weapons aloft, some hid behind shattered shields, some were caught in mid-stride, fleeing from a horror they'd never escaped. They, mortal men and women who had had the tragic honor of witnessing the fall of a god, forever frozen in their final, fleshless moments.

And all of it was illuminated by the light, red as blood, weeping from a wound at the very center of the carnage.

A great rift, as though someone had taken a rusty knife and carved a jagged scar in creation, sprawled across the plaza. From within, the hellish red light emanated, illuminating crumbling stone and painting shadows deeper than the night.

"Kapira...Kapira...Kapira..."

Among all the horror, the misshapen and malformed bodies of the Khovura were almost unremarkable. They huddled around the rift, their chant sounding more like a collective pleading whimper. Upon each of their twisted faces, illuminated by the red light, was etched the unmistakable desperate need of people who had nowhere left to turn but here.

"Look there," Shuro said, pointing down. "Is that..."

She didn't finish the question. Nor did she need to.

There, at the edge of the rift, given a respectful space by the Khovura, stood Chemoi. Her attentions were turned to a black book in her hands, its pages wrought with twisted sigils that became black words from her mouth, carrying loud and clear to wrench themselves in Lenk's ear.

He knew the speech, if not the words. He had heard them before, on the tongues of demons he had sent back to hell.

"The Tome of the Undergates," he muttered. "How the fuck did she get it?"

"Irrelevant," Shuro snarled. "We were idiots to leave her alive, but that's also irrelevant." She hefted her blade, rose to her feet. "We move quickly. Once your boots hit stone, I want you to rush Chemoi. Stop her at all costs."

"What?" Lenk blinked. "And what will you be doing?"

"I will handle the Khovura."

"But there are at least twenty down there!"

She seized his hand in hers, his stare in hers. "This is what we were made to do, Lenk. Everything relies on us doing it."

What we were made to do.

Made. Not born.

"Are you with me?" she asked.

He swallowed hard, nodded. She returned his nod, released his hand.

A breath held. A blade quivering. A grip tightened.

And then they were running.

They swept across the edge of the rooftop, toward the crumbling ruin of a statue looming high over its eaves. They leapt as one onto its shoulders, slid down the length of its stone robe, hit the floor of the plaza.

And they were striking.

No war cries, no oaths, no curses; not for weapons like them. They were silent, no noise but their feet upon the stones. They were swift, no hesitation in their blades flashing in the darkness. They were fearless, charging even as the Khovura took notice and turned to rush toward them.

And they were killing.

Lenk saw the battle in fragments, a glass portrait of slaughter shattered into a dozen pieces.

A hulking brute lunged at him with monstrous claws outstretched and found his blade thrust deep into its chest. No sooner had he kicked its carcass away than a writhing serpent appendage swooped toward him, fangs bared and hissing. His sword was up, carving a perfect arc and cleaving it just behind the neck. The coils of its body writhed wildly, spraying gore from its stump even as Lenk's sword found the abomination it was attached to and struck it to the earth in a messy, violent chop.

They came in a shrieking charge: a mass of twisted flesh and many mouths, rushing toward him.

And he hacked. And he cut. And he carved, tearing limbs from sockets, wrenching blades in ribs, smashing heads with pommels.

And still, somehow, his carnage paled in comparison to Shuro's.

Where he was brutal, she was refined. Her body was a shadow, insubstantial wherever the Khovura tried to strike. Her blade was lightning, striking wherever she set her eyes. And her voice was silent, but for a single word.

"*Go,*" she told him.

As more Khovura came wailing from the shadows, Lenk saw his chance. A path was clear to Chemoi, who cast him a glance before returning to speaking from the dread book in her hands, her voice urgent and wild. As Shuro swept forward to intercept the Khovura, he rushed toward Chemoi, leapt at her, and caught her in a tackle.

They skidded across the stones, dangerously close to the edge of the rift. And from here Lenk could see down into its depths and saw nothing. A blackness so deep and so hungry that it reached out for him with unseen hands, begged him to come down and keep it company.

He looked away, lest he find himself seized. And in the moment his attention was distracted, Chemoi's knife flashed. She cut him across the collarbone, drawing a spurt of red. He cried out, clutching at the wound and giving her enough room to wriggle out from under him and get to her feet.

He leapt to his own footing, held his sword out before her as he moved to keep her from the rift. Without her veil, her face was twisted in a scaly, reptilian snarl and her yellow eyes were wild.

"The dead cultists we found you with back in the jungle," Lenk said, "you weren't following them. You were *leading* them."

"That was the plan," Chemoi said.

"From the beginning?"

"The very beginning. Ain't no accident you wound up with my crew on the Old Man."

"Should I ask why?"

"You shouldn't," Chemoi growled. "Because you should already know. I scrape and bow and serve humans for the scraps they deign to throw me. I watched my friends and family starve in the Sumps. I grew up in a world that treated its *bugs* better than it treated me. And when Khoth-Kapira told me he'd make it better?" She spit. "Why *wouldn't* I do it?"

"That doesn't mean you can do this."

"Try and stop me."

She shrieked, hurled herself at him. He swung his sword high over her head as she ducked low and angled her blade at his belly. He caught her by the wrist, twisted it, tore another scream from her mouth that he silenced by smashing the crosspiece of his sword against her face.

She fell to the ground, groaning. He reversed his grip on his sword, brought it up to plunge into her chest. She looked up with a sneer full of blood.

"Do it," she said. "Ain't like anything's left for me here."

Lenk's hand twitched. His blade trembled. He began to move.

"Do you see, Lenk?"

A voice, calm and clear amid the chaos. There, at the periphery of his vision, he saw the man in white. Mocca, hands folded behind his back, walked forward.

"People who would rather die than live in this world? People for whom there is nothing left? I can save them.

"I can save all of them." Another voice. Mocca was behind him, looking over his shoulder. "I can fix all of this. You know I can, Lenk. You've seen my works, my sins, my potential. You know what I can do. I can save them.

"And you can kill them." Another voice. Another Mocca. Standing over Chemoi, looking down at her with pity. "Those who live tomorrow will envy those who die today. I have seen it, Lenk. A great war, one that will span this desert and this entire world and drown it. You have seen it, too. In the wars and hatreds and fears that shape these people. It will birth a monster. And it will consume everything you hold dear and everyone you love.

"But you know that." The fourth Mocca. Slowly they all turned to him. Slowly they advanced upon him. "Kill her, Lenk. You will kill forever. You will kill everyone. You will be the very sword you sought to put down and you will be the blade that bleeds the world dry.

"...a war to end all wars..."

"...rivers of blood, mountains of corpses..."

"...I could save them, all of them..."

"...without me, this world will..."

They kept talking, all four of them, one after the other until their words were a whirlwind in his ears. He shut his eyes, clenched his teeth.

"Lenk."

He opened them. Only one Mocca stood before him. Honest fear in his eyes, hands held out in benediction.

"If you love Kataria," he said softly, "then help me save her."

In his eyes Lenk saw it. The dread truth, the realization that for all his treacheries and sins, Khoth-Kapira spoke one truth.

He loved Kataria.

He had to save her.

And he knew the words that would be spoken next before they left Mocca's lips.

"Stand aside."

Lenk lowered his sword. Lenk backed away.

Mocca closed his eyes, smiled, and disappeared.

What confusion Chemoi felt was short-lived. Instantly she was up. The dread book was in her hand, unfurled. She was at the edge of the rift, her chant resumed.

And Lenk stood aside.

And watched.

"LENK!"

Only for a moment.

When he turned he saw Shuro standing at the center of a massacre. Well-carved Khovura corpses littered the ground around her, contorted in their final spasms of agony and bleeding from the cuts she had left them.

Her face fell as she took in the scene before her. And she was once again that little girl: small and afraid, with eyes struggling to find the words to ask why.

Why he had betrayed her.

"Shuro," he said, "I'm sorry. I had to—"

"No."

A cold voice. A cold stare. A cold blade.

The girl was gone. Shuro was gone. The woman standing before him was somewhere in between. Tears fell from her eyes. Her face was twisted with fury and pain. She took her sword in both hands.

"It doesn't matter now."

And she rushed toward him.

If she was fast before, she was inhumanly fast now, sweeping up to him in the span of two breaths. Her blade was flashing, striking him at all angles, all openings. His own sword fought to keep up, groaning where hers sang, stumbling where hers danced. And with each blow he blocked, he felt the shock of it run down his arm and into his ribs.

She struck with fury. She struck with sorrow. She struck with pain.

And he felt it. His guard slowed, his feet tripped. Her blade scored him and opened up his arms, his legs, his shoulders. He felt as though he wept from a hundred cuts, so that when her foot shot out and caught him in the belly, it was but an afterthought, just one more pain among many.

He staggered to a knee. His blade came up, blocked hers as it came down. But she pressed with such anger that she pushed his sword nearer. And over their locked steel, he could see in her tearstained eyes that she would extend him these last few breaths as a courtesy.

He breathed in.

Her sword came lower.

He breathed out.

Her steel grazed his cheek.

He shut his eyes.

"Lenk," she whispered, "I should never have—"

He didn't hear what she said next.

He didn't hear anything.

Not over the sound of a single word. A wrong word spoken for the right reason. The last letter of the last word in a speech never meant for mortal ears.

And though he could not understand it, he knew simply from the way it left Chemoi's lips, writhing in the wind like a living thing, what it was.

The chant was over.

The world was saved.

For a long moment, nothing happened. Lenk, Shuro, and Chemoi held themselves tense, looking around. The pulsing of the red light stopped. The wind ceased to howl. The night descended swiftly to smother any noise.

For a long moment, creation held its breath.

And then screamed.

Clouds swirled overhead. Wind whipped around them in a howling torrent. The blackened bones of the mortal armies crumbled into heaps. But it was the earth that spoke the loudest, an agonized groan escaping it as the city shook to its very foundation.

From deep within the rift, something screamed. From deep within the rift, something stirred. From deep within the rift, something emerged.

"Yes," Chemoi shrieked. "*YES!*"

A tremendous black hand, wide and long as a man, rose from the rift, came smashing down upon the plaza. Another joined it, reaching out to seize the lip of the rift. The earth groaned, the rift widened, the red light dissipated and was swallowed back beneath the earth. The plaza was plunged into darkness as something hauled itself out and up.

And up.

And up.

The three mortals were stunned, speechless at what they saw looming over them. Two titanic, muscular arms swept out from a colossal torso. Writhing, serpentine coils danced around a mass of a head in a wild halo of snakes. It was a man, but too great to be one. A monster, but too perfect to be one. A demon, but too...too...

From a body swathed in darkness, two great white eyes stared down at the three mortals, each one struck speechless, unable to find any word for this.

Save one.

"Khoth-Kapira," Lenk whispered.

"The God-King," Shuro said. She fell to her knees, her battle forgotten. "I...I have failed..."

"*No, child.*" A black voice bloomed in the darkness, spoken from somewhere far away and unbearably close. "*You have been blessed.*"

The great black head slowly surveyed the darkness around it, its white eyes taking in the ruin of its surroundings. Every breath he took seemed to drink in the air and sound around him.

"*The wind,*" he whispered, his voice harsh and quiet. "*I can feel it. I can feel...*" He slid his colossal hands across the stone. "*It is real.*" He looked down at the mortals. "*You are real. I can see you, hear you.*" His eyes narrowed upon Shuro. "*Touch you...*"

Slowly the great shape reached down. Black fingers extended, as though to seize Shuro, who stared, numbly, at the ground.

"*No!*"

Lenk's voice seemed so tiny, so frail, so utterly insignificant in the face of the great darkness that loomed over him. And yet it listened. And yet it stopped.

"Please," Lenk said, "let her go."

The two great white eyes fixed upon Lenk. The black voice whispered to him.

"*She would kill you,*" he said. "*She does not understand.*"

"I know," Lenk said. "Please."

They stared at him a little while longer, those eyes. And there was nothing in them. No fear. No understanding. Nothing that indicated that they had even heard him.

And yet...

"*A boon,*" Khoth-Kapira said. "*The first of many.*" He rescinded his great arm. "*Go, child. Tell your masters that this world will thrive, despite their efforts.*"

Fear returned to Shuro, long enough to take her to her feet and send her running. But even as she ran, she looked over her shoulder. And even as the darkness grew deeper, Lenk saw her eyes.

And he felt a cold pain in his chest.

"*Do not fear.*"

A voice. Not Mocca's.

"*Her life will be one of many saved.*"

Khoth-Kapira's. Cold. Dark. Near.

"*And even as she curses your name, it will be thanks to you that she has life to do it.*"

Lenk turned. Lenk looked up. Khoth-Kapira looked back to him.

"*I will save this world, Lenk,*" the God-King said. "*I will make it clean again.*"

And slowly the great demon inclined his head low in reverence. The serpents writhing about his head did likewise. And Lenk felt Khoth-Kapira's voice touch a dark place within him.

"*And it is all thanks to you.*"

SALVATION

A_{h."}

Mundas opened his eyes. He looked up. Something had changed.

"He has returned."

"He?"

It took him a moment to recall where he was. A meal of spiced mutton, grilled potatoes, and rice sat before him, untouched. A goblet of wine was beside it, likewise ignored in favor of a simple cup of water. All of this was upon a fine dining table in a fine room, bedecked in tapestries depicting symbols of many hands interlinked in a circle.

"Pardon," Mundas said as he looked across the table. "She."

Teneir's eyes lit up with joy above her veil. Her claws drew deep furrows in the wood of the table. But to her credit, she did little else.

"I knew it," she said. "I knew my faith would be rewarded."

"Indeed," Mundas said, inclining his head to her. "Your cooperation is much appreciated, though the cost of life it came for is regrettable."

"The cost was necessary," the fasha said from her side of the table. "I am willing to pay any price for Ancaa's return."

"Your enthusiasm is noted," Mundas replied. "Though it is our immense hope that her return will prevent the need for any further bloodshed. To preserve life is the entire cause for the Renouncers lending their aid to you."

"And *that* is noted, as well." Teneir raised a goblet to him. "Your insight and planning were essential to this. And finally, all the pieces are coming together."

"Your negotiations were fruitful, then, I take it."

"Indeed. Ghoukha is long dead. Mejina, likewise, is gone. The remaining fashas will look for a leader. They will find it in me."

"And the Venarium?"

"Shinka has pledged to stay out of our way. Whether she intends to honor it or not will not matter once Ancaa returns." Teneir ran a finger around the rim of her goblet. "Likewise, my contact within the Jackals has just assured me that all the remains of his gang are loyal to him and him to me."

Mundas frowned. "I trust in your discretion, though I lament the need to associate with murderers. I mistrust that one."

"As do I. He will doubtless try to betray me. But treason is only good as long as it's hidden. I will tame him."

Mundas nodded, but said nothing. Teneir's eyes narrowed.

"You're concerned about something," she said. "I don't like that look."

"The priestess of Talanas is a subject of discussion," Mundas replied. "We are concerned that more may flock to her banner and divide the faithful."

"*Her,*" Teneir hissed in displeasure. "Worry not. Once I expel the Sainites and Karnerians, faith in her will falter."

"As you say." Mundas rose from his chair, inclined his head. "I shall leave."

"So soon? But you did not even touch your food."

"I am not hungry at the moment. Thank you for the water, fasha."

"Priestess," Teneir corrected him.

"Pardon?"

"Ancaa is coming. I wish to welcome her properly by the title of priestess."

Mundas nodded, but said nothing. He left without another word.

He made his way through the decadent halls of Teneir's manor at a swift pace. When a servant emerged from a nearby room and began walking alongside him, he didn't even look up.

"She seemed happy," the servant said, chuckling.

"Fanatics are easy to placate," Mundas said. "I will not begrudge her indulgence so long as she can unite Cier'Djaal for the coming of the God-King."

"And you think she can?"

"If I did not, I would not have aided her as I have," Mundas said.

"The Talanite concerns me, but not overmuch. I believe the people will see the wisdom in uniting once the God-King makes himself known."

The servant hummed an agreement. There was the sound of skin stretching. When Mundas looked over, the servant was gone and the late fasha Mejina walked alongside him.

"I have received word," the creature known as Azhu-Mahl said.

"Troubling word, I assume."

"Our plans have apparently caught the attention of other Renouncers."

"This was not unforeseen. Who?"

"Qulon."

"Of course."

"You don't seem concerned."

"The pact we swore is still in effect. Though Qulon may oppose our ideals, I trust she will not interfere with us directly. What mischief she can cause won't be enough to stop what we've put into motion. We were fortunate to have avoided her notice until now."

Skin stretched again. Azhu-Mahl's shape changed once more into that of a tall, grandfatherly man in the white robes of a Talanite priest.

"I wish I shared your optimism," he said.

"I am not optimistic. I am certain. For too long has this world suffered under the yoke of deaf gods who hide away from their faithful. A living god, a god-king, will provide the guidance that mortalkind needs."

"So you say. Though you're aware he *is* a demon, no?"

"A meaningless title. I would think that you, who shed shapes like clothing, would understand the fleetingness of such things."

"Mm. Funny thing, what I do. If shapes were so meaningless, I wouldn't be able to see the hope in a man's eyes when I appear as his long-dead wife. I wouldn't be able to convince three dragonmen to slaughter a mob. And I certainly wouldn't have been of much use to you."

They emptied into the *houn* lobby of Teneir's manor, halted before the door. Mundas glanced to Azhu-Mahl.

"Your point?"

"Titles are meaningless to you," he said. "Much is meaningless to the Renouncers. We are . . . detached from mortality. Let us not forget that when we presume to save them."

Azhu-Mahl smiled, opened the door, and disappeared in the night. Mundas turned, looked around the *houn*. The circular linked arms of

Ancaa were emblazoned on every tapestry and sat in sculpture on every pedestal.

He wondered if their impending guest would find this symbol flattering when he arrived.

But then, perhaps that, too, was meaningless.

He closed his eyes. He took a breath.

And he was gone.

extras

orbit

meet the author

Photo Credit: Libbi Rich

SAM SYKES is the author of the acclaimed *Tome of the Undergates*, a vast and sprawling story of adventure, demons, madness, and carnage. He lives in Arizona. He once punched an ostrich. What a great guy.

introducing

If you enjoyed
THE MORTAL TALLY
look out for

GOD'S LAST BREATH

Bring Down Heaven: Book 3

by Sam Sykes

Lenk had no idea what to call them. He could barely stand to look at them, let alone name them. Their own names they had given up long ago to become what they were today, and any word he might have had for them seemed somehow insufficient to describe them.

Except the one leading him.

He had decided to call this one Jef.

It just seemed polite.

"Wait," Lenk said as he looked up at suddenly unfamiliar buildings. "This isn't the way to his quarters."

"Not quarters," Jef hissed. "Not today. The master is in the square. He has something you must see. He has something he must show. We must watch. We must know. We must..."

The creature's voice trailed off into a witless burble that Lenk strove to shut out. He hated listening to these fiends, hated looking at them, hated being reminded what they were.

And what he had done to aid them.

Their path wound them through the city streets, up a long staircase and into the city's upper levels. A stone walkway circled a great plaza. And what lay within it, surrounded by great statues of benevolent robed men, Lenk could not ignore so easily.

A wound in creation, a scar that could never heal, a hole that stretched below the streets of Rhuul Khaas, beneath the earth itself, and into someplace much darker. It stretched across the plaza in a jagged scar, a gaping black hole around which the dawn hesitated to tread and left the statues and their smiling faces bathed in shadows.

Lenk could not look at it.

And Lenk could not look away from it.

Every time he looked upon it, his mind slipped away from him, back through the days to the fateful night he had stood before it. Back to the night when it had bled a red light and stained the black sky. Back to the night when he had looked into a woman's eyes, as blue and deep and full of fear as his own, and made his choice.

His choice that had made her try to kill him.

His choice that had summoned these abominations here.

His choice that had freed the thing that had lurked in that dark scar.

He turned away, hurried to catch up with Jef as the creature shambled across the walkway and between nearby buildings. But he could not outrun his thoughts.

Often, he wondered if Shuro had escaped, if she had made it out of Rhuul Khaas unharmed. Only rarely did he wonder if she sharpened her sword for him, if she hated him for his choice.

He suspected he already knew the answer to that.

But he could not think on this for long. For it wasn't long before he couldn't think over the noise.

A distant burble. A formless wail. A verbal poison that seeped past his clothing and into his skin, echoing in the deep sinew.

Noises. Hundreds of them. Straight ahead.

"Come," Jef gurgled, shambling forward. "Come with me. He wants you. He needs you to be here... he needs you to see..."

Lenk glanced over his shoulder, as if wondering if he could flee from this. But he knew he could not. This city was not his home. And one did not reject an invitation from its master.

And so, keenly aware of the sword on his back, he followed Jef into the crowd.

He lost his guide within moments, the misshapen creature disappearing into the hundreds of other misshapen creatures as their fleshy throngs closed in around him. Yet for all the glistening flesh and molten deformities pressing in on him, there were deeper horrors.

"—master, please, master, help me—"

They groaned.

"—it hurts! Oh gods, what have I done, it hurts so—"

They wailed.

"—told me I was foolish, I was insane, they never listen, they NEVER—"

They screamed.

Their words clawed at his ears, at his flesh, burrowed into his sinew. Their every letter was wracked with agony, with fear, with desperation. It hurt to listen to, hurt to be around, like their every word poisoned the air around him and made each breath like agony.

And in the space between each word, he could hear his thoughts.

You did this.

Between his ragged breaths, he knew.

You brought them here.

And when he shut his eyes, he heard it.

You let him *out.*

"Children."

A single word, spoken softly. Yet it rang out over the square as clear as a note from a glass bell. And the reverent and their wailing fell silent at it.

"Stand aside."

And in a shuffling, awkward mass, they did. A great curtain of flesh parted, leaving a long wake of stone that stretched between Lenk and the center of the square where a dais rose.

Lenk wasted no time in hurrying down it, keeping his ears shut and his eyes down at the street. He only knew he had reached it when he saw the shadow stretching out upon the stones before him.

The shape of a stately robed man.

"You're late."

Whose beard writhed.

"Did my child find you all right?"

Lenk looked up and the first thing he noticed was Mocca's smile.

Set beneath gentle eyes and framed in a face with elegant, dark-skinned features, it was a warm, grandfatherly smile. The kind that perfectly complemented the soft white robe that Mocca was garbed in and matched his thin arms outstretched in benediction. Still, Lenk thought it odd that he should notice that first.

As opposed to the beard of serpents coiling out of Mocca's jaw.

"It's not your child," Lenk replied.

At this, the serpents hissed, perhaps offended on behalf of their host. Mocca merely smiled and shook his head.

"Do they offend you, my friend?" he asked.

Lenk stepped up onto the dais beside Mocca and turned and gazed over the assembly. And they, with their thousand terrified eyes, stared back. It wasn't long before Lenk cringed and turned away.

"They're monsters," he said.

And they're here because of you, he added.

"You lack respect."

An ancient, rasping voice reached Lenk's ears. A darker shadow loomed over him.

He looked up into eyes that were black, as though someone had scribbled over them with coal. An old man's face, skin gray and fraught with wrinkles, scowled down at him from its position in an elongated head. Withered limbs ending in black claws stretched out as its old man's body, flabby and emaciated all at once, leaned forward. In lieu of legs, a great serpent's coil brought the demon closer to Lenk.

"It is the burden of the layperson," the Disciple hissed, a long purple tongue flicking out of its withered mouth. "Come, let us show you what we have sacrificed."

"Enough."

Mocca raised a hand. The demon froze, inclined its massive head, and settled back upon its coils. Lenk shuddered—it hadn't been so long ago that he was killing demons like these, wiping their stain from the earth. Now he stood alongside them.

And their king.

"I suppose they are hideous to you, as they are to me," Mocca said, looking over the crowd. "But then, I suppose you only see the flesh: the twisted muscle and jagged bone."

"Do you *not*?" Lenk asked. "Can't you hear them? They're in pain."

"They were in pain long before my Disciples changed them," Mocca said, gesturing to the demon. "The ugliness I see here is the fear and desperation that drove them to this. The ugliness is the city that cared not a bit for the mother whose children were killed in a thieves' war, it's the people that would not loan a man a shovel that he might bury his father." Mocca's expression grew cold. "It's the world, Lenk. It's the fear and hatred and terror they were given that drove them here, to me."

He spread his arms out wide over the crowd. And they raised a hooting, gibbering, wordless screech at his gesture.

"And it is I who shall cleanse it."

Admittedly, Lenk didn't intend to snort.

Because, admittedly, it wasn't the brightest idea to backsass a man with snakes growing out of his face.

Yet it wasn't rage that painted Mocca's face when he turned to look at Lenk. Rather, it was a decidedly unamused frown.

"I've had centuries to rehearse this, Lenk," Mocca said. "Don't rob me of the drama."

"You just make it sound so simple," Lenk replied, shaking his head.

"Is it not?"

Lenk stared at him flatly for a moment. "Not a week ago, you crawled out of a hole to hell. I'm standing in the middle of a city that shouldn't exist, surrounded by ungodly monsters who look at you like a god, hanging around a demon and, if that wasn't fucked up enough, you've got snakes growing out of your face. There is no part of this that is fucking simple, Mocca."

"Khoth-Kapira," Mocca corrected him. "And do not forget why you are standing here, why you helped me out of that pit. You know as well as I do that this world is ill. Its plagues are wars and violence. You have seen them up close."

Lenk could only nod weakly. So many weeks later, so many miles away, he could still remember it all: the battles between the Karnerians and Sainites that had driven him here, the brutality of the shicts and the tulwar in the tribelands that had harried him. Just thinking about them made the sword on his back feel heavier.

As if to remind him that this was not a world where it could be dropped so easily.

"Mortality is defined by its brevity, Lenk," Mocca continued, folding his hands behind his back as he looked over the crowd. "By its very nature, it is in a headlong rush to end itself as quickly as possible. The wars you have seen, the wars that will yet come, are but a symptom of a base plague that wracks this world."

"You sound so certain," Lenk said.

Mocca hesitated. "Should I not be? When I speak of a war of wars, a time of strife and of suffering so great and so vast as to boggle the minds of gods, do you truly believe such a thing could never come to pass?"

Lenk closed his eyes. His scars ached. His shoulders sagged with the weight of his sword and all the weight of the blood it had spilled.

"The lives I will save here, Lenk, are nothing compared to the lives I will save by preventing this cataclysm. So many will owe their lives to you, Lenk." Mocca paused, glanced over his shoulder and regarded Lenk out of the corner of his eye. "Or perhaps you would be satisfied with just one?"

All other pains in his body fled at the sudden chill that swept through Lenk's body. Mocca's words sank into him deeper than the abominations' ever could. And as they settled in Lenk's flesh, he knew what Mocca spoke of.

Kataria.

She was still out there, somewhere. Somewhere in that wasteland, filled with its violence and its hatreds and its countless people and their countless bloodthirsts. Wherever she had disappeared to, Lenk did not know. But he knew she needed his help, as he needed her.

And he needed her to stay alive.

And that was the reason, he told himself. That was why he had freed Mocca. That was why the abominations were here. That was why he shared the company of demons. That was why this was all worth it.

He told himself this.

He shifted his feet. The weight settled on his back.

The sword didn't believe him.

Something touched his shoulder. Mocca squeezed his arm gently. With a hiss, his beard of serpents slid away, retreating back into his flesh. What was left was just a man with dark eyes and a gentle smile.

"We will save her, Lenk," Mocca said. "Her and so many others. I have the power to help them, to prevent so much bloodshed. But I cannot do it without you."

"Me?"

"Does that surprise you?"

"Sort of. I mean, didn't they call you a god-king once?"

"Gods are nothing without faith," Mocca said, shaking his head. "And I am nothing if you do not believe in me." He fixed his eyes intently on Lenk's. "Do you?"

Dark eyes. A gentle smile. A neatly trimmed goatee and perfectly manicured fingernails.

Funny, Lenk thought. *Look at him in the right light, he looks just like a man.*

And in the golden rising dawn, Lenk could almost believe it. He could almost forget that there had just been a beard of vipers a moment ago where flesh was now. He could almost pretend he hadn't seen this man crawl out of a pit so dark that light feared to tread there.

Almost.

But this was not a man. And this was not Mocca. This was Khoth-Kapira, the God-King, cast down from heaven to earth and from earth to hell for sins ancient and countless. This was a demon. Foe of man. Enemy of the Gods.

And yet...

Man was intent on killing himself and everything around him. And the gods did not answer their prayers.

And when gods were silent, demons spoke.

Lenk placed a hand on Mocca's. He felt flesh. Warm and alive.

"I do," Lenk said.

Mocca smiled, nodded. "Then let me show you."

"Show me what?"

Mocca released him, turned back to the crowd. "How I will fix this." He leveled a finger at the crowd. "You. Child. Step forward."

Somehow, they knew to whom he spoke. The crowd of abominations shuffled aside with a murmur, revealing a misshapen creature. No more horrifying than the others, Lenk thought; this one had thin, spindly legs, a long flaccid arm that dragged behind it, a mouth rimmed with fangs, and a single unblinking eye focused on Mocca as it shuffled forward.

A man? A woman? Lenk couldn't tell. Not even when it approached the dais and sank to its knees before Mocca.

Mocca sighed, laid a hand upon the molten scars of its brows. He stroked its head, pity playing upon his features. The creature leaned into his touch, a pet deprived of attention.

"You poor soul," Mocca whispered. He shut his eyes, breathed deeply. "I see them. Your family. I feel your hatred." He shook his head. "But you mustn't hate them, child. Their cruelty was driven by their fear. The same fear that drove you to the embrace of my Disciples." He ran his fingers down to the creature's gaping jaws. "Alas, they are but pupils. Their methods are...inelegant."

The abomination loosed a sound halfway between a groan and a whimper. A formless plea lurked between them, the piteous cry of a terrified animal. Mocca simply smiled and took its face in both his hands.

"In such a short life, you have felt so much pain. I can ease it." Mocca tilted his face toward the sky. "If only you accept...just a little more."

A single breath. His eyes snapped open. And the light of the dawn paled before the golden light that burst from Mocca's stares.

That same light poured out of his fingertips and into the creature. It let out a squeal, struggled to escape Mocca's grasp. But his fingers sank deeper into its flesh, white smoke sizzling off his knuckles as the golden light seeped out of his digits and into the creature's flesh. A dark voice from a deep pit tore free from Mocca's mouth.

"A little more," he said. *"Witness my miracle."*

The creature's shriek was lost, as was its form, bathed in a light so bright that Lenk had to shield his eyes from it. And when that was insufficient, he shut them tight and looked away, trying to ignore the terrified wails of the crowd.

Only when they stopped did he dare to open his eyes. The light was gone. The screams had quieted. And in their wake, Lenk's curse seemed woefully insufficient for what he saw.

"Gods..." he whispered.

"No," Mocca said. "Me."

The creature was gone. No, not gone. Changed. It no longer stooped, but stood tall and proud. Its molten flesh had tightened across the broad muscle of a body, hale and whole. Its flesh was dark and warm, its hair was black and lustrous, its face was square and handsome and terribly human.

It was...

He was a man.

No, more than a man.

Lenk saw it in the length of his fingers, the strength of his naked body, the height and the hair and the bright yellow eyes. His face was angular and beautiful, too much for any normal human. This was...he was something else. Something more. Something powerful.

He looked down at himself, at his long fingers and his thick legs and his nakedness. His face brightened with a childish disbelief as he took himself in. And when he finally found breath to do so, he screamed. Not the terrified, agonized scream of the damned, but the joyous, bright wail of the living.

"Master!" he screamed, falling to his knees before Mocca and coiling around his feet. "Master, you have saved me!"

"I have, child," Mocca said, nodding. "And I have so much more work to do." He stepped over the man, toward the crowd, and extended his arms. "And who among you shall also witness?"

They let out a feral, animalistic screech. In one surge of glistening flesh, they rushed forward: monstrous limbs outstretched and mouths gaping in wails.

And once more, Lenk had to cover his ears. But it did no good.

"—master, save me! Save me! I have been faithful! You promised—"

They screamed.

"—it hurts so much, master! Make it stop! Make it stop, please, I beg—"

They wailed.

"—let it end! LET IT END! OH, MASTER, I WANT SO BADLY—"

Their every word was wracked with such agony that it was poison that seeped into Lenk's skin. He could stand it no longer. He turned, fought his way through the throng of monstrosities, who ignored him in their rush to approach the dais.

And when he was finally clear of them, he turned and cast one final look to the center of the square.

And there he saw Mocca, his arms outstretched, his beard of vipers writhing, a hundred misshapen hands reaching out toward him.

And a look of ecstasy scarred across his face.

introducing

CHAPTER 1

It was all going so nicely, right up until the massacre.

Sir Hjortt's cavalry of two hundred spears fanned out through the small village, taking up positions between half-timbered houses in the uneven lanes that only the most charitable of surveyors would refer to as "roads." The warhorses slowed and then stopped in a decent approximation of unison, their riders sitting as stiff and straight in their saddles as the lances they braced against their stirrups. It was an unseasonably warm afternoon in the autumn, and after their long approach up the steep valley, soldier and steed alike dripped sweat, yet not a one of them removed their brass skullcap. Weapons, armor, and tack glowing in the fierce alpine sunlight, the faded crimson of their cloaks covering up the inevitable stains, the cavalry appeared to have ridden straight out of a tale, or galloped down off one of the tapestries in the mayor's house.

So they must have seemed to the villagers who peeked through their shutters, anyway. To their colonel, Sir Hjortt, they looked like hired killers on horseback barely possessed of sense to do as they were told most of the time. Had the knight been able to train wardogs to ride he should have preferred them to the Fifteenth Cavalry, given the amount of faith he placed in this lot. Not much, in other words, not very much at all.

He didn't care for dogs, either, but a dog you could trust, even if it was only to lick his balls.

The hamlet sprawled across the last stretch of grassy meadow before the collision of two steep, bald-peaked mountains. Murky forest edged in on all sides, like a snare the wilderness had set for the unwary traveler. A typical mountain town here in the Kutumban range, then, with only a low reinforced stone wall to keep out the wolves and what piddling avalanches the encircling slopes must bowl down at the settlement when the snows melted.

Sir Hjortt had led his troops straight through the open gate in

the wall and up the main track to the largest house in the village…
which wasn't saying a whole lot for the building. Fenced in by shedding rosebushes and standing a scant two and a half stories tall, its
windowless redbrick face was broken into a grid by the black timbers
that supported it. The mossy thatched roof rose up into a witch's hat,
and set squarely in the center like a mouth were a great pair of doors
tall and wide enough for two riders to pass through abreast without
removing their helmets. As he reached the break in the hedge at the
front of the house, Sir Hjortt saw that one of these oaken doors was
ajar, but just as he noticed this detail the door eased shut.

Sir Hjortt smiled to himself, and, reining his horse in front of
the rosebushes, called out in his deepest baritone, "I am Sir Efrain
Hjortt of Azgaroth, Fifteenth Colonel of the Crimson Empire,
come to counsel with the mayor's wife. I have met your lord mayor
upon the road, and while he reposes at my camp—"

Someone behind him snickered at that, but when Sir Hjortt turned
in his saddle he could not locate which of his troops was the culprit. It
might have even come from one of his two personal Chainite guards,
who had stopped their horses at the border of the thorny hedge. He
gave both his guards and the riders nearest them the sort of withering
scowl his father was overly fond of doling out. This was no laughing
matter, as should have been perfectly obvious from the way Sir Hjortt
had dealt with the hillbilly mayor of this shitburg.

"Ahem." Sir Hjortt turned back to the building and tried again.
"Whilst your lord mayor reposes at my camp, I bring tidings of
great import. I must speak with the mayor's wife at once."

Anything? Nothing. The whole town was silently, fearfully
watching him from hiding, he could feel it in his aching thighs,
but not a one braved the daylight either to confront or assist him.
Peasants—what a sorry lot they were.

"I say again!" Sir Hjortt called, goading his stallion into the
mayor's yard and advancing on the double doors. "As a colonel of
the Crimson Empire and a knight of Azgaroth, I shall be welcomed
by the family of your mayor, or—"

Both sets of doors burst open, and a wave of hulking, shaggy beasts flooded out into the sunlight—they were on top of the Azgarothian before he could wheel away or draw his sword. He heard muted bells, obviously to signal that the ambush was under way, and the hungry grunting of the pack, and—

The cattle milled about him, snuffling his horse with their broad, slimy noses, but now that they had escaped the confines of the building they betrayed no intention toward further excitement.

"Very sorry, sir," came a hillfolk-accented voice from somewhere nearby, and then a small, pale hand appeared amid the cattle, rising from between the bovine waves like the last, desperate attempt of a drowning man to catch a piece of driftwood. Then the hand seized a black coat and a blond boy of perhaps ten or twelve vaulted himself nimbly into sight, landing on the wide back of a mountain cow and twisting the creature around to face Sir Hjortt as effortlessly as the Azgarothian controlled his warhorse. Despite this manifest skill and agility at play before him, the knight remained unimpressed.

"The mayor's wife," said Sir Hjortt. "I am to meet with her. Now. Is she in?"

"I expect so," said the boy, glancing over his shoulder—checking the position of the sun against the lee of the mountains towering over the village, no doubt. "Sorry again 'bout my cows. They're feisty, sir; had to bring 'em down early on account of a horned wolf being seen a few vales over. And I, uh, didn't have the barn door locked as I should have."

"Spying on us, eh?" said Sir Hjortt. The boy grinned. "Perhaps I'll let it slide this once, if you go and fetch your mistress from inside."

"Mayoress is probably up in her house, sir, but I'm not allowed 'round there anymore, on account of my wretched behavior," said the boy with obvious pride.

"This isn't her home?" Hjortt eyed the building warily.

"No, sir. This is the barn."

Another chuckle from one of his faithless troops, but Sir Hjortt didn't give whoever it was the satisfaction of turning in his saddle a second time. He'd find the culprit after the day's business was done, and then they'd see what came of having a laugh at their commander's expense. Like the rest of the Fifteenth Regiment, the cavalry apparently thought their new colonel was green because he wasn't yet twenty, but he would soon show them that being young and being green weren't the same thing at all.

Now that their cowherd champion had engaged the invaders, gaily painted doors began to open and the braver citizenry slunk out onto their stoops, clearly awestruck at the Imperial soldiers in their midst. Sir Hjortt grunted in satisfaction—it had been so quiet in the hamlet that he had begun to wonder if the villagers had somehow been tipped off to his approach and scampered away into the mountains.

"Where's the mayor's house, then?" he said, reins squeaking in his gauntlets as he glared at the boy.

"See the trail there?" said the boy, pointing to the east. Following the lad's finger down a lane beside a longhouse, Sir Hjortt saw a small gate set in the village wall, and beyond that a faint trail leading up the grassy foot of the steepest peak in the valley.

"My glass, Portolés," said Sir Hjortt, and his bodyguard walked her horse over beside his. Sir Hjortt knew that if he carried the priceless item in his own saddlebag one of his thuggish soldiers would likely find a way of stealing it, but not a one of them would dare try that shit with the burly war nun. She handed it over and Sir Hjortt withdrew the heavy brass hawkglass from its sheath; it was the only gift his father had ever given him that wasn't a weapon of some sort, and he relished any excuse to use it. Finding the magnified trail through the instrument, he tracked it up the meadow to where the path entered the surrounding forest. A copse of yellowing aspen interrupted the pines and fir, and, scanning the hawkglass upward, he saw that this vein of gold continued up the otherwise evergreen-covered mountain.

"See it?" the cowherd said. "They live back up in there. Not far."

———

Sir Hjortt gained a false summit and leaned against one of the trees. The thin trunk bowed under his weight, its copper leaves hissing at his touch, its white bark leaving dust on his cape. The series of switchbacks carved into the increasingly sheer mountainside had become too treacherous for the horses, and so Sir Hjortt and his two guards, Brother Iqbal and Sister Portolés, had proceeded up the scarps of exposed granite on foot. The possibility of a trap had not left the knight, but nothing more hostile than a hummingbird had showed itself on the hike, and now that his eyes had adjusted to the strangely diffuse light of this latest grove, he saw a modest, freshly whitewashed house perched on the lip of the next rock shelf.

Several hundred feet above them. Brother Iqbal laughed and Sister Portolés cursed, yet her outburst carried more humor in it than his. Through the trees they went, and then made the final ascent.

"Why..." puffed Iqbal, the repurposed grain satchel slung over one meaty shoulder retarding his already sluggish pace, "in all the...devils of Emeritus...would a mayor...live...so far...from his town?"

"I can think of a reason or three," said Portolés, setting the head of her weighty maul in the path and resting against its long shaft. "Take a look behind us."

Sir Hjortt paused, amenable to a break himself—even with only his comparatively light riding armor on, it was a real asshole of a hike. Turning, he let out an appreciative whistle. They had climbed quickly, and spread out below them was the painting-perfect hamlet nestled at the base of the mountains. Beyond the thin line of its walls, the lush valley fell away into the distance, a meandering brook dividing east ridge from west. Sir Hjortt was hardly a single-minded, bloodthirsty brute, and he could certainly appreciate the allure of living high above one's vassals, surrounded by the breathtaking beauty of creation. Perhaps when this unfortunate errand was over he would convert the mayor's house into a hunting lodge, wiling away his summers with sport and relaxation in the clean highland air.

"Best vantage in the valley," said Portolés. "Gives the headperson plenty of time to decide how to greet any guests."

"Do you think she's put on a kettle for us?" said Iqbal hopefully. "I could do with a spot of hunter's tea."

"About this mission, Colonel…" Portolés was looking at Sir Hjortt but not meeting his eyes. She'd been poorly covering up her discomfort with phony bravado ever since he'd informed her what needed to be done here, and the knight could well imagine what would come next. "I wonder if the order—"

"And I wonder if your church superiors gave me the use of you two anathemas so that you might hem and haw and question me at every pass, instead of respecting my command as an Imperial colonel," said Sir Hjortt, which brought bruise-hued blushes to the big woman's cheeks. "Azgaroth has been a proud and faithful servant of the Kings and Queens of Samoth for near on a century, whereas your popes seem to revolt every other feast day, so remind me again, what use have I for your counsel?"

Portolés muttered an apology, and Iqbal fidgeted with the damp sack he carried.

"Do you think I relish what we have to do? Do you think I would put my soldiers through it, if I had a choice? Why would I give such a command, if it was at all avoidable? Why—" Sir Hjortt was just warming to his lecture when a fissure of pain opened up his skull. Intense and unpleasant as the sensation was, it fled in moments, leaving him to nervously consider the witchborn pair. Had one of them somehow brought on the headache with their devilish ways? Probably not; he'd had a touch of a headache for much of the ride up, come to think of it, and he hadn't even mentioned the plan to them then.

"Come on," he said, deciding it would be best to drop the matter without further pontification. Even if his bodyguards did have reservations, this mission would prove an object lesson that it is always better to rush through any necessary unpleasantness, rather than drag your feet and overanalyze every ugly detail. "Let's be done with this. I want to be down the valley by dark, bad as that road is."

They edged around a hairpin bend in the steep trail, and then the track's crudely hewn stair delivered them to another plateau, and the mayor's house. It was similar in design to those in the hamlet, but with a porch overhanging the edge of the mild cliff and a low white fence. Pleasant enough, thought Sir Hjortt, except that the fence was made of bone, with each outwardly bowed moose-rib picket topped with the skull of a different animal. Owlbat skulls sat between those of marmot and hill fox, and above the door of the cabin rested an enormous one that had to be a horned wolf; when the cowherd had mentioned such a beast being spied in the area, Sir Hjortt had assumed the boy full of what his cows deposited, but maybe a few still prowled these lonely mountains. What a thrill it would be, to mount a hunting party for such rare game! Then the door beneath the skull creaked, and a figure stood framed in the doorway.

"Well met, friends, you've come a long way," the woman greeted them. She was brawny, though not so big as Portolés, with features as hard as the trek up to her house. She might have been fit enough once, in a country sort of way, when her long, silvery hair was blond or black or red and tied back in pigtails the way Hjortt liked... but now she was just an old woman, same as any other, fifty winters young at a minimum. Judging from the tangled bone fetishes hanging from the limbs of the sole tree that grew inside the fence's perimeter—a tall, black-barked aspen with leaves as hoary as her locks—she might be a sorceress, to boot.

Iqbal returned her welcome, calling, "Well met, Mum, well met indeed. I present to you Sir Hjortt of Azgaroth, Fifteenth Colonel of the Crimson Empire." The anathema glanced to his superior, but when Sir Hjortt didn't fall all over himself to charge ahead and meet a potential witch, Iqbal murmured, "She's just an old bird, sir, nothing to fret about."

"Old bird or fledgling, I wouldn't blindly stick my hand in an owlbat's nest," Portolés said, stepping past Sir Hjortt and Iqbal to address the old woman in the Crimson tongue. "In the names of the Pontiff of the West and the Queen of the Rest, I order you out here into the light, woman."

"Queen of the Rest?" The woman obliged Portolés, stepping down the creaking steps of her porch and approaching the fence. For a mayor's wife, her checked dirndl was as plain as any village girl's. "And Pontiff of the West, is it? Last peddler we had through here brought tidings that Pope Shanatu's war wasn't going so well, but I gather much has changed. Is this sovereign of the Rest, blessed whoever she be, still Queen Indsorith? And does this mean peace has once again been brokered?"

"This bird hears a lot from her tree," muttered Sir Hjortt, then asked the woman, "Are you indeed the mayor's wife?"

"I am Mayoress Vivi, wife of Leib," said she. "And I ask again, respectfully, to whom shall I direct my prayers when next I—"

"The righteous reign of Queen Indsorith continues, blessed be her name," said Sir Hjortt. "Pope Shanatu, blessed be *his* name, received word from on high that his time as Shepherd of Samoth has come to an end, and so the war is over. His niece Jirella, blessed be *her* name, has ascended to her rightful place behind the Onyx Pulpit, and taken on the title of Pope Y'Homa III, Mother of Midnight, Shepherdess of the Lost."

"I see," said the mayoress. "And in addition to accepting a rebel pope's resignation and the promotion of his kin to the same lofty post, our beloved Indsorith, long may her glory persist, has also swapped out her noble title? 'Queen of Samoth, Heart of the Star, Jewel of Diadem, Keeper of the Crimson Empire' for, ah, 'Queen of the Rest'?" The woman's faintly lined face wrinkled further as she smiled, and Portolés slyly returned it.

"Do not mistake my subordinate's peculiar sense of humor for a shift in policy—the queen's honorifics remain unchanged," said Sir Hjortt, thinking of how best to discipline Portolés. If she thought that sort of thing flew with her commanding colonel just because there were no higher-ranked clerical witnesses to her dishonorable talk, the witchborn freak had another thing coming. He almost wished she would refuse to carry out his command, so he'd have an excuse to get rid of her altogether. In High Azgarothian, he said, "Portolés, return to the village and give the order. In the time it will take you to make it down I'll have made myself clear enough."

Portolés stiffened and gave Sir Hjortt a pathetic frown that told him she'd been holding out hope that he would change his mind.

Not bloody likely. Also in Azgarothian, the war nun said, "I'm...
I'm just going to have a look inside before I do. Make sure it's safe,
Colonel Hjortt."

"By all means, Sister Portolés, welcome, welcome," said the older
woman, also in that ancient and honorable tongue of Sir Hjortt's
ancestors. Unexpected, that, but then the Star had been a different
place when this biddy was in her prime, and perhaps she had seen
more of it than just her remote mountain. Now that she was closer
he saw that her cheeks were more scarred than wrinkled, a rather
gnarly one on her chin, and for the first time since their arrival, a
shadow of worry played across the weathered landscape of her face.
Good. "I have an old hound sleeping in the kitchen whom I should
prefer you left to his dreams, but am otherwise alone. But, good
Colonel, Leib was to have been at the crossroads this morning..."

Sir Hjortt ignored the mayor's wife, following Portolés through
the gate onto the walkway of flat, colorful stones that crossed
the yard. They were artlessly arranged; the first order of business
would be to hire the mason who had done the bathrooms at his
family estate in Cockspar, or maybe the woman's apprentice, if the
hoity-toity artisan wasn't willing to journey a hundred leagues into
the wilds to retile a walk. A mosaic of miniature animals would be
nice, or maybe indigo shingles could be used to make it resemble
a creek. But then they had forded a rill on their way up from the
village, so why not have somebody trace it to its source and divert it
this way, have an actual stream flow through the yard? It couldn't
be that hard to have it come down through the trees there and then
run over the cliff beside the deck, creating a miniature waterfall
that—

"Empty," said Portolés, coming back outside. Sir Hjortt had lost
track of himself—it had been a steep march up, and a long ride
before that. Portolés silently moved behind the older woman, who
stood on the walk between Sir Hjortt and her house. The matron
looked nervous now, all right.

"My husband Leib, Colonel Hjortt. Did you meet him at the
crossroads?" Her voice was weaker now, barely louder than the

quaking aspens. That must be something to hear as one lay in bed after a hard day's hunt, the rustling of those golden leaves just outside your window.

"New plan," said Sir Hjortt, not bothering with the more formal Azgarothian, since she spoke it anyway. "Well, it's the same as the original, mostly, but instead of riding down before dark we'll bivouac here for the night." Smiling at the old woman, he said, "Do not fret, Missus Mayor, do not fret, I won't be garrisoning my soldiers in your town, I assure you. Camp them outside the wall, when they're done. We'll ride out at first"—the thought of sleeping in on a proper bed occurred to him—"noon. We ride at noon tomorrow. Report back to me when it's done."

"Whatever you're planning, sir, let us parley before you commit yourself," said the old woman, seeming to awaken from the anxious spell their presence had cast upon her. She had a stern bearing he wasn't at all sure he liked. "Your officer can surely tarry a few minutes before delivering your orders, especially if we are to have you as our guests for the night. Let us speak, you and I, and no matter what orders you may have, no matter how pressing your need, I shall make it worth your while to have listened."

Portolés's puppy-dog eyes from over the woman's shoulder turned Sir Hjortt's stomach. At least Iqbal had the decency to keep his smug gaze on the old woman.

"Whether or not she is capable of doing so, Sister Portolés will *not* wait," said Sir Hjortt shortly. "You and I are talking, and directly, make no mistake, but I see no reason to delay my subordinate."

The old woman looked back past Portolés, frowning at the open door of her cabin, and then shrugged. As if she had any say at all in how this would transpire. Flashing a patently false smile at Sir Hjortt, she said, "As you will, fine sir. I merely thought you might have use for the sister as we spoke, for we may be talking for some time."

Fallen Mother have mercy, did every single person have a better idea of how Sir Hjortt should conduct himself than he did? This would not stand.

"My good woman," he said, "it seems that we have even more to parley than I previously suspected. Sister Portolés's business is pressing, however, and so she must away before we embark on this long conversation you so desire. Fear not, however, for the terms of supplication your husband laid out to us at the crossroads shall be honored, reasonable as they undeniably are. Off with you, Portolés."

Portolés offered him one of her sardonic salutes from over the older woman's shoulder, and then stalked out of the yard, looking as petulant as he'd ever seen her. Iqbal whispered something to her as he moved out of her way by the gate, and wasn't fast enough in his retreat when she lashed out at him. The war nun flicked the malformed ear that emerged from Iqbal's pale tonsure like the outermost leaf of an overripe cabbage, rage rendering her face even less appealing, if such a thing was possible. Iqbal swung his heavy satchel at her in response, and although Portolés dodged the blow, the dark bottom of the sackcloth misted her with red droplets as it whizzed past her face. If the sister noticed the blood on her face, she didn't seem to care, dragging her feet down the precarious trail, her maul slung over one hunched shoulder.

"My husband," the matron whispered, and, turning back to her, Sir Hjortt saw that her wide eyes were fixed on Iqbal's dripping sack.

"Best if we talk inside," said Sir Hjortt, winking at Iqbal and ushering the woman toward her door. "Come, come, I have an absolutely brilliant idea about how you and your people might help with the war effort, and I'd rather discuss it over tea."

"You said the war was over," the woman said numbly, still staring at the satchel.

"So it is, so it is," said Sir Hjortt. "But the *effort* needs to be made to ensure it doesn't start up again, what? Now, what do you have to slake the thirst of servants of the Empire, home from the front?"

She balked, but there was nowhere to go, and so she led Sir Hjortt and Brother Iqbal inside. It was quiet in the yard, save for the trees and the clacking of the bone fetishes when the wind ran its palm down the mountain's stubbly cheek. The screaming didn't start until after Sister Portolés had returned to the village, and down there they were doing enough of their own to miss the echoes resonating from the mayor's house.